THE DEATH OF MY BROTHER ABEL

Gregor von Rezzori was born in the Bukovina in 1914. He studied at the University of Vienna and for a time lived in Bucharest.
In Germany, after World War II, he became active as a writer
and in radio broadcasting and filmmaking.

Mr. Rezzori's first books included *Maghrebinische Geschichten*
(1953) and *Oedipus siegt bei Stalingrad* (1954). Another novel, *Ein
Hermelin in Tschernopol*, which appeared in the United States
under the title *The Hussar* in 1960, won the author the Theodore
Fontane Prize in 1959. American readers first discovered Mr.
Rezzori as a writer in English with the appearance in *The New
Yorker* in 1969 of a story entitled "Memoirs of an Anti-Semite,"
which subsequently appeared as a section of the novel of the
same name, published in 1981. *The Death of My Brother Abel* was
first published in Germany in 1976.

Mr. Rezzori lives with his wife, Beatrice Monti, in Tuscany.

Jack O'Connell
Seattle
26. Februar 1988

GREGOR
VON REZZORI

THE DEATH
OF MY
BROTHER
ABEL

TRANSLATED BY JOACHIM NEUGROSCHEL

ELISABETH SIFTON BOOKS

PENGUIN BOOKS

ELISABETH SIFTON BOOKS • PENGUIN BOOKS
Viking Penguin Inc., 40 West 23rd Street,
New York, New York 10010, U.S.A.
Penguin Books Ltd, Harmondsworth, Middlesex, England
Penguin Books Australia Ltd, Ringwood, Victoria, Australia
Penguin Books Canada Limited, 2801 John Street,
Markham, Ontario, Canada L3R 1B4
Penguin Books (N.Z.) Ltd, 182–190 Wairau Road,
Auckland 10, New Zealand

Originally published in German under the title *Der Tod Meines Bruders Abel*
by C. Bertelsmann/Mosaik Verlag
This translation first published in the United States of America by
Viking Penguin Inc. 1985
Published in Penguin Books 1986

LIBRARY OF CONGRESS CATALOGING IN PUBLICATION DATA
Rezzori, Gregor von.
The death of my brother Abel.
Translation of: Der Tod meines Bruders Abel.
"Elisabeth Sifton books."
I. Title.
[PT2635.E98T613 1986] 833'.912 86-91463
ISBN 0 14 00.9690 6 (pbk.)

Grateful acknowledgment is made to the following for permission to reprint copyrighted material:

Basil Blackwell, Oxford: An excerpt from *Ludwig Wittgenstein, Notebooks, 1914–1916,* translated by
G. H. von Wright and G. G. M. Anscombe.
Pantheon Books, a Division of Random House, Inc.: An excerpt from *Madness and Civilization,* by Michel
Foucault, translated by Richard Howard. Copyright © 1965 by Random House, Inc.
Princeton University Press: An excerpt from *Fear and Trembling,* by Soren Kierkegaard, translated by
W. Lourie.
University of Michigan Press: An excerpt from *Manifestos of Surrealism,* by André Breton, translated
by Richard Seaver and Helen R. Lane. Copyright © 1969 by The University of Michigan.

Printed in the United States of America by
R. R. Donnelley & Sons Company, Harrisonburg, Virginia
Set in Janson and News Gothic

For whom else but you!

THE DEATH OF
MY BROTHER ABEL

□   □   □

I RAN AFTER HIM. I caught up with him at the stairs. He turned to me and saw my face as I asked him, "You're coming back for sure? You promise?"

He kissed me very tenderly on the forehead and on the eyes and on the mouth and took my hands and kissed one and then the other, saying, "I swear to you, my darling, of course I'm coming back."

"Why don't you take me along right now?" I asked. "I can come with you right now."

"Like that—naked as a worm?" he asked and kissed my breast. (I only had a towel wrapped around me.) I said, "I'll run and get dressed." I wanted him to come back to the room with me.

"I'll wait for you here," he said. He was very sweet with me. He took my face in both his hands and pulled it close to his—and then tapped his finger on my nose. "Hurry up, then." I ran back to the room to get quickly dressed.

When he had first tried to pick me up, I wanted to turn my back on him. A type like him means trouble. Well into his forties and suspiciously elegant, with no real money behind him, if you know what I mean. But I'd had a bad day: two johns in the morning and then no one else until five. It was a foggy day; you could scarcely see your hand before your eyes. I noticed right off he'd been drinking. He staggered a bit when he came toward me and said, "You're very beautiful, my pet; we're going to have a good time. But would you mind waiting for one minute? I want to get an Alka-Seltzer at the drugstore. I've drunk quite a bit and I haven't eaten all day." I thought to myself, Whatever you get at the drugstore, you can go fuck your mother with it, and your little sister too. But I only walked a couple of steps away from him, up to the streetlamp and no farther, and I was too lazy to signal to Ginette, who probably was only half a block away in the fog. (She'd been standing out there all day long too.) Five minutes later, he was back, Alka-Seltzer in hand. (Whatever you really ate in the drugstore, you can shove it up your ass, I thought.) "Shall we go?" he said. "Or do you have another engagement?"

Any other day, I wouldn't have taken him on. But the fog was getting on my nerves, I was tired of standing around, my feet hurt. I wanted to stretch out for fifteen minutes, even with a guy on my stomach. Besides, something in his face made me feel I could deal with him easily if he tried any funny business: there was something soft and dreamy about him, and he seemed preoccupied. Like Ginette's brother, who paints and bums around and always wants to kill himself. (All the same, you can really have a good laugh with him.) So I only said, "Do you have a hundred francs?"

And he said, "I thought children and soldiers paid half price. Why do I have to pay double?"

I said, "Then take your tube of Alka-Seltzer and shove it up your mother. It's probably just the right size for her."

But he laughed and said, "You're mistaken. My mother was very beautiful and knew some better sizes. She lived from it, you know—as you do."

I thought to myself, You can tell me a lot of crap. Everyone makes up stories for us, and so do we, especially when someone asks what's a nice girl like you doing in this racket anyway. I've got six different versions in stock, all of them very believable. Anyhow, it doesn't matter much if a guy is bullshitting you or not when he tells you stuff, whether he wants you to believe he's a baker or a Rothschild. In fact, it doesn't matter at all. So long as he screws like a baker (fast and honest) and pays like a Rothschild, then everything's okay. But usually it's the other way around: they fuck you for hours and then they won't even treat you to a tisane over and above the fifty francs.

He tried another trick. He pushed two hundred francs into my hand—and now I was on the alert. 'Cause if a guy starts out like that, there's a catch somewhere. Then they've got some special kink—they want to spank you, or want you to spank them. But he wasn't English; he had a very slight Russian accent. Probably some Jew from Hungary or Rumania—we'll see, I thought. Anyway, he took my arm like a fiancé, and I tried to shake him off, and he didn't say, "Ohlala! Are you ever touchy!" but instead held on and said, "Don't be afraid. I don't want anything from you that will humiliate you and make you feel ashamed. The first hundred is for bed and the other one for friendliness, that's all."

I've heard that line too: "That's all." But no john ever thought of saying, "I don't want anything from you that will humiliate you and make you feel ashamed." I had to think about how that fitted in with him. Anyway, I let him take my arm, and we walked to the hotel like a married couple going home from a movie, warm and close together and in step.

When he paid Gaston for the room (without hiding the fact he had money in his pocket but without showing off about it either), he said, "And please leave us undisturbed for a good hour." I tried to give Gaston a look meaning I wasn't planning to waste the whole evening. But the bastard glanced away and said, "Certainly, sir. You've paid for twenty-four hours." So I thought Gaston knew him, and the fellow was a cop. But then I realized it was only his tone of voice (and the tip, too, of course). That prick Gaston simply caught on that this was one of those johns who are at home in hotels (and much better ones than this). They instantly had that goddamn secret understanding, like all bloody bourgeois types: bicycle nature, if you get what I mean; they bow upward and tread downward, and they'll all get strung up when the Red Internationale finally wins. Anyway, I couldn't count on Gaston, and when we were up in the room, the usual stuff began. He wanted me to take off everything including my panties ("Your feet will warm up faster without stockings," and all that shit), and when we were both finally lying in bed stark naked, he took me in his arms and lay back and said, "Let's smoke a cigarette."

I wanted to explain that he'd better not think he could play a joke on me for two hundred francs, and he ought to tell me what the hell he wanted or leave me be and go home. But when he lay there with his head on the pillow, staring up at the ceiling, I thought to myself, He's just impotent, or he's got problems getting it up—after all, he's not young anymore. I'm gonna have a lot of trouble with him; I'll probably have to suck it. Anyway, let's smoke a cigarette first, for Christ's sake. Maybe he'll doze off, and I can leave without him noticing.

So we watched the smoke going up to the ceiling and we didn't say a word, like a married couple after a movie. Skin to skin under the blanket and head to head on the pillow. Except once, he asked, "Don't you recognize me? I was at the Madeleine once with a friend who had a quickie with you. Pretty much in broad daylight. A German. He couldn't speak a word of French. Of course, that was a while back, more than three years ago." And I shook my head—who cares about his friends.

He didn't say anything else; he kept smoking. And once, he turned his face to me and kissed me on the temple. Strangely enough, he seemed like a kid when he did that, all dreamy. Then he carefully put out his cigarette in the ashtray and mine too and he uncovered my breasts and stroked and kissed them and said, "You're beautiful." And I thought to myself, If it's gonna be difficult, then let's get the show on the road. So I grabbed his dick to get it into shape, but he was stiff and it was okay. He started caressing me too, and so he wouldn't get me really excited I pretended I was; I put on a good act, like I couldn't wait for him to get into me. But he held me close and he only kissed me—not on the mouth, of course (I wouldn't want chancres on my lips), but everywhere else on my face, in a gentle rain of small tender kisses. Finally, I got so impatient I couldn't think of anything better to say than "You forgot to take your Alka-Seltzer." Naturally, he only laughed and said, "I don't even know where it is. In some pocket or other. No, wait: I think I left it downstairs on the clerk's desk." And when I quickly said, "I'll get it for you," he kissed me on the forehead again and said, "That's all right, my love. I don't need it now. I'm not drunk anymore."

It was like we'd been married for ten years, and I decided to really bullshit, and I said emphatically, "Come to me now, but first you got to put on a rubber." But even that didn't faze him, though usually johns give me the longest arguments. He was as patient as a Franciscan and he smiled down at me (he was resting his head on his arm and looking into my face kindly, as if he was my aunt), and finally he said, "Don't be difficult, dear. I'm not sick. If you like, you can examine me." So that's the way it was. Okay!

I looked him over and milked him and squeezed him so hard that I figured blood would come out. In any case, he was no Jew. And finally, he pulled me back on the pillow and said, "That's enough, isn't it?" And he was already inside me; I don't even know how, but as skillful as a monkey and real deep right away. And he stayed like that for a while and just slowly moved around in me.

It wasn't the way it sometimes happens to a woman—a fellow comes along and gets into you, and suddenly you come, even though there's nothing special about him and you don't especially dig him—it's simply that you're compatible in some way you can't explain. That wasn't it. I just started liking it. His tenderness, too. He wasn't excited the way men usually are. He could have gone outside on the street with the same expression on his face. Except that he looked happy. He closed his eyes whenever he gave me one of his soft, tender kisses.

I thought to myself, So that's what he's trying to pull, the bastard. He likes to blow your mind. When I acted like I couldn't wait anymore and wanted him to give it to me now, and began wiggling my ass and breathing heavily and rolling my eyes, he held me tight and said, "Shhh!" The way you shush a child. So finally I asked him, "Why don't you come? Do you have problems?" And he said with the quietest voice in the world, "I like to have a little fun doing this. Don't you?"

I told him he couldn't expect that from me. First I said, "I only come with my husband. You can understand. He's the only one who gets that from me." And I was about to invent a fellow I lived with, who protected me and who I came with (even though that never happened with my Jules and was anyway very rare— once with Ginette, and with a man yes, but only once, a long, long time ago). But he must have smelled a rat. He said (still smiling and in his quiet voice), "Don't tell me fairy tales. You're just lazy, that's all. I can understand that you can't come with every man if you don't want to ruin yourself. But I'll give you another hundred francs, so you can take the rest of the night off."

If a woman doesn't want to come, then a guy can screw his cock to shreds, and with a fellow in his forties it takes a while any-how—and who wants to put up with that? If I hadn't been so tired and bored with standing around in the fog, I would have thought up something to get rid of him. Instead, I said to myself, Let him go on, he'll get horny enough to come before it gets tedious. So I shut my eyes and let him poke around in me. But soon it got weird: it was just too pleasant. He was incredibly skillful and lay on me without crushing me, and he was well built and he had no flab and he had a smooth skin and he was nicely washed. I thought to myself, Christine, my girl, if you get soft now, you might really come, and then you'll stay with him for a couple of hours and sleep till the day after tomorrow, and you may even fall in love with him, for Christ's sake, and then you'll be up to your ass in trouble. Pull yourself together, kid, and try to get rid of the guy as fast as possible, and go out into the fog and earn an honest living.

And at that same instant, he said to me (still in the same voice, as though we were sitting on a bench in the Jardin des Plantes), "Listen, my dear. You're very sweet. Let me make a suggestion. For a couple of days you try to get used to me and to living with me. I earn enough to spoil you a little. If it doesn't work out, we'll go our own ways as the best of friends, and I'll see to it that you won't have lost too much income. And if it works, we'll stay to-gether as long as it works. I'm anything but rich, but I write screenplays, and that pays off nicely. If a woman with a good head on her shoulders takes care of it, one can live comfortably."

It wasn't my first offer of this kind, and what pissed me off most was the way he used the screenplay stuff as bait. You can fool some dime-store clerk that's still wetting her pants, but not a working girl like me. And besides, I thought, who does this bastard think you are anyway? Does he think that because he's got his dick inside you, you can't think clearly? Why doesn't he just take a violin and fiddle a tango in your ear! And because I was mad, I did something dumb, and I thought to myself, If you tell me stories, buddy, then I'll tell you a couple too, and I said, "You're sweet, baby, and that's why I won't be nasty and lie to you. You see, I can't live with a man. I can't come with men—I don't know if I am a lesbian, but in any case, I can't stand having a man around for more than half an hour."

Even while I was saying it, I realized how stupid it was to tell him that. Though it *is* true, sort of. The one time I've come in the last couple of years was with Ginette when a john took both of us up (which, naturally, doesn't mean I'm really a lesbian). And you're always a sucker when you tell the truth. I was only hoping that if he thought about me and Ginette, he'd finally get going and I could get him off my belly. He instantly said, "If that's the only problem, darling, then we can take as many girls to bed as you can manage."

And I didn't even have time to think, Of course, you pig! when he already had his hand on me, and I could barely say, "Take your hand away!" when he started to shove into me very hard, and maybe I accidentally thought of Ginette and the way she comes when some guy fucks her and I play around with her—anyway, I didn't push his hand off—and all at once, I felt I had to come, and I screamed, "What the hell are you doing to me!" and I felt him coming at the same time, and I came too and I didn't know what was going on, only that he had his mouth on mine and was kissing me wildly, and I didn't care that a stranger was kissing me on the mouth, because it was good and just like making love.

The worst part was that I dozed off right away. (I'm like a man in that respect.) But I couldn't have been sleeping for long, maybe fifteen minutes. And when I awoke, it was like being lifted up by a wave when you're swimming in the ocean—and he was there and he caught me in his arms.

But that was only a dream. Actually, I awoke because he was caressing me. He had uncovered me totally and was kneeling over me and stroking my body, my shoulders, my arms, my breasts, my hips—and as though something exquisite remained in his hands, a fragrance or shimmer, some rare feeling of warm fullness, he kissed his palms and kept kissing his palms the way an

Arab or Hindu prays. It was very sweet, and I pretended I was still asleep so I could enjoy it, dope that I was. He wrapped me in his goddamn tenderness—I got so mad I nearly started to cry. "You lousy bastard," I said, "you pig, you sonofabitch!" I hit him, and he laughed, and so we scuffled around, almost tumbling out of bed, and then he was in me again with his monkey skill, and this time he didn't need any help from his fingers, and I didn't think about Ginette, or anything else, I just came like in some porno book, where they always come like it was as natural as pissing.

Afterward I was cheerful, like when I sometimes take the evening off and drink a little, and me and Ginette's brother go to the booths behind the Place Blanche and I try my luck in the shooting galleries. Christ, was I hungry! And for half an hour we tried to figure out what we wanted to eat and where, and he said he didn't know any of the bistros I knew and he had to get to know them. But then he said, "We're so close to Prunier, why don't we go there?"

And I said to him, "I don't want to make trouble for you. They all know me here in the neighborhood and they won't let us in."

And he said, "But, darling, they'll have to get used to seeing you in my bad company." And so we fooled around until we finally telephoned down to Gaston to send something up.

I said, "Now we'll see how you can spoil me. I want champagne and caviar and oysters and lobster and a filet mignon. You're lucky the shops are closed now, otherwise I'd have taken you on a spending spree."

And he said, "A couple of diamonds at Cartier, and Yves Saint Laurent's spring collection, is that it? I'm going to give you a good spanking and stick you in the kitchen and make you cook for both of us and spend no more than ten francs a day. You can go to the movies once a week and that's all."

And here a kiss and there a pinch and a thump, so that we nearly started screwing all over again. But luckily, room service came up with the food, and boy was that ever a bullshit deal! I let the waiter know as much too. "Lemme see the bill!" I said to my companion. "They're ripping you off like there's no tomorrow," I said, and that was a stupid thing, which cost me dearly, I later realized. If I hadn't been kind of dizzy, I would have understood on the spot by the way the waiter looked at me.

But I was all crazy, I really didn't know why. We ate, and he fed me like a little girl and didn't want to have anything himself. He just watched me, and while he watched he became very sad. He looked so sad it nearly broke my heart. I think he'd been drinking all day and now he was having some more, and the depression was breaking out. To get him to eat, I put pieces of food in my teeth and held out my mouth so that he'd kiss me and at least take a piece of bread. And to keep him from drinking too much, I drank the wine out of his mouth. And when he wanted to send for another bottle, I said, "You've had enough now and you're going beddy-bye. I'm so tired I can't keep my eyes open."

Once again, we lay side by side like a married couple, him on his back and me half across him with my head on his shoulder. But neither of us could sleep, and finally I asked him, "Why aren't you sleeping?"

"Why aren't you?" he asked.

"I keep thinking," I said.

"What about?" he asked.

"About me and about you. About both of us."

"Me too," he said. Then I thought he had really gone to sleep and I wanted to give him a good-night kiss, and he gently hugged me. He wasn't asleep.

I was very happy and I said to him, "Do it again. Think about yourself, not me. I'm too tired to come again. But I wanna feel you in me and feel that you're happy." He must have understood it was a present. He simply rolled me over and put his cheek on my breast, and then he got into me. It was a quiet, enjoyable fuck, like between a couple that's had a lot of practice fucking together, and it was nice the way he came: with a moan of surrender. I couldn't see him in the dark (we'd put the light out so we could sleep), but I know how they come—they look so wild, as if they wanted to bite God in heaven, and yet it's their only human moment.

We fell asleep, and it was still dark when he woke me up. I sensed that he was dressed and I was scared to death and I said, "You're not leaving me!" And he fondled me and kissed me and calmed me. He was only going away for a couple of hours, until I'd slept enough, then he'd come and pick me up, he said. He only had to put his things in order. "*Il faut que j'arrange ma maison,*" he said. And I believed him and I kissed him and said, "Hurry up. I won't be able to sleep a wink till you come back."

But then, when he closed the door behind him, I got scared, and I jumped out of bed and grabbed a towel and wrapped it around me and ran after him into the corridor and only caught up with him at the stairway. And when he said, "I'll wait for you here; be quick, then," I ran back into the room and just pulled on my shoes and skirt and sweater and coat. I stuffed the stockings and the garter belt and the bra into my handbag. I really hurried. But he was gone.

☐   ☐   ☐

IT IS NIGHT. In a shabby hotel on the Place des Ternes, in a small room with flowery wallpaper, he sits at a dressing table with a covered mirror.

The room does not face the street, it faces an air shaft. It is now the only room in which a lamp is lit. He writes, *Il arrange sa maison.*

He has four folders in front of him. They are marked "Pneuma" and "A," "B," and "C." Two suitcases and several cartons of papers surround him on the floor. He occasionally rummages in one of them, takes out a sheet, and inserts it into one of the folders; then he busily continues writing.

The first folder is open. It says:

PNEUMA

> The most extreme language of madness is reason, but sheathed in the enchantment of the image, restricted to the phenomenal space that it defines—whereby both of them create, outside the totality of images and the universality of speech, a peculiar abusable organization, whose obstinate specificity constitutes madness.
>
> MICHEL FOUCAULT, *Madness and Society*

□   1   □

AS IF HE HAD BEEN CAST AWAY among the lotus eaters, he seemed to have forgotten his fatherland. He knew he was a stranger. The tired ocean-wind told him so, tossed it into his face—the wind that blew, day in, day out, sweeping across bleak marshland and weed-choked rubble fields and straying into the gaps and ruins of meandering streets. The heavy sky told him so, day in, day out, the dove-breast clouds, scraped by the broken rafters of gabled roofs; their shadows scoured the houses red and sore, water dripped from their feathers, till they whitishly dissolved; sometimes they perished from the arrows of a chary and distant sun, arrows that pierced them and fell brittlely on the twisted loading cranes in the bombed-out harbor, where their splinters scattered over the wet stone jetties, palely brass-bright, cradled in the cold water, until new flocks of doves flew over, breast to breast, and quickly pecked them up.

The nights hushed it toward him, step-queens, no moon drifted through his blood, no dream-drunken bird measured the stillness of a black-and-silvery landscape with its warbling. Masses of cottony darkness pressed heaven and earth together, smothered the sparsely beaded streetlights and the tatty illuminations of scrip-shabby department stores into pale fog-aureolas and let their oily shimmer ooze into the black canals.

The pale air carried it to him, in gull shrieks expelled wildly into nothingness, weaving the emptiness of eternity on gull wings—a nightmare carnival: Pierrots shooting clownishly to

and fro and up and down, crossing, chasing one another, reeling,
plunging, now surrounded by powdery whirls of snowflakes, now
streaked obliquely with strands of rain. He could hear it in the
city's din, which surged restlessly like the straying wind, now and
again punctuated by the walrus bellow of a ship's siren. He heard
it in the constricted voices, the faded intonations, the crumbling
speech of the people whom he passed during his constant, futile
walks: pale, blond men and women who looked at him with eyes
of faded blue in which blank uncomprehending amazement
froze into the enigmatic gaze of mermaids. Strangeness was be-
tween him and them, and they were not linked by the strangeness
to which both he and they were condemned.

□   □   □

YES SIR. That's how it ought to start. Orphically. The evocatively
murmuring past tense. Rubble Age in Hamburg-on-the Elbe,
Germany, 1945–48. Enigmatic gaze of mermaids (read: Hanseatic
boredom). Cast away among the lotus eaters (read: displaced
person). Sheer poetry, that's how I set it down. With a throbbing
heart full of sacred hope: *As if he had been cast away among the*
lotus eaters, he seemed to have forgotten his fatherland—period.
With a dying fall . . .
    The first sentence has to ring like bell metal:

> Solidly immur'd in earth
> Stands the mold of hard-bak'd clay . . .

Schiller, Mr. Brodny, in case your memory's failed you. You
probably call him Skyler now. Well, we still call him Shillah.
Lives with Lolita in Alaska. We are proud of him. Singing and
ringing cherub's voice. Singing and ringing for a child's heart.
Daddy, tell me a story. *Sissignore, subito!* The communication of
fatefulness arouses our consciousness (or is it our conscience?
consensuality?). Okay then, tell me a story, if possible in three
short sentences. Of course this would require form. (Schwab
would have said, *"Ni plus, ni moins."*)

:: 14 ::

That's not our strength, alas; I mean, us Germans. For the French, yes. Infrastructural formalists each and every one of them—despite Vichy and Oradour, Algeria and Monsieur le général de Gaulle. Despite the inundation of their intellectual world by Spaniards, Balkans, Russian Jews. A culturally homogeneous national style, you know. (That's what Scherping says, too, our mutual friend and missing link, big-time publisher, mass-culture maker, so he ought to know—perhaps not without a touch of nationalist envy, but no matter, the fellow is a masochist.) Arouses our consensuality. In any case: the Frenchman's gift of form has always been obvious in his literature. First-rate, damn it! Not a superfluous syllable. Every *chef d'oeuvre* its own table of contents, so to speak. Never a word too many. Exemplary. Well, and their wines? You agree with our friend Schwab, right? And the women—let's not get into that. And the French cuisine— mmm, mmm. And the Impressionists, too, logically; and of course Paris! Paris, man! The music, needless to say, comes from us. Offenbach (a Jew, but musically pure German). Wagner (first a scandal, but then acceptance). The only native a fellow who sounds like what French girls wash their pussies in: Bizet (highly esteemed by Nietzsche, to be sure).

As for my part, sir, I'll sing about Paris in any style you'd expect—for instance Art Nouveau-ish waltz-wave-welling: *And if it weren't for Paree, then I'd dream about you and mehehee* (whirl and hop) . . . or else brisk, with marching brass blaring: *Oh come to the drum to Paree, old bum!!!* (thundering drums and clashing cymbals) . . . Life is a swallow's flight, damn it. For the French, of course. For us, it's not so smoothly skyhigh. We're known for being musical, but verbally we're rather cloudy, amorphous, nebulous. No wonder, what with all that hard-to-communicate fatefulness of ours. The conflict-ridden soul, you know. The forehead circled by too many, too vast, too stormy thoughts. The everlasting struggle between pure philosophy and great art. *"J'comprends jamais c'qu'tu veux dire, mon ours"*—Gaia's constant complaint. *Ours des Carpathes*, mind you, not a German bear.

In fact, I'm no more German than you, brother Brodny, are American. Of course, you live overseas, clear-seeing from one continent to the other. Who else but a pure Anglo-Saxon could chatter as pragmatically as you do about formal strength, formal problems, form-forming talents in the European nations? One man's meat is another man's poison, as they say—or do you prefer the equivalent in Yiddish? I can be of assistance either way, a polyglot *homme à tout faire*. Always at your service, sir! . . .

But then, what difference does it make who is what? We are not simply and resolutely one thing or the other. Not in this dynamic time. Sometimes, a man is both and yet neither, a blend of nothing and everything. People like us, for instance—writers, among others, literary agents coping with different realities. A refugee's fate. An émigré's destiny. We lost our true fatherlands and then forgot them among the lotus eaters. Or elsewhere, while passing through, you see, passing through history, through our personal neuroses. . . .

What, by the way, was your fatherland, dear Mr. Jacob G. Brodny? Geographically, in any event, *Europe centrale*? Am I right? Just like mine, accidentally. One of those countries that were born with the peace treaties of Brest Litovsk and Trianon. About the same time as I was born. Back then, as you will kindly remember, in the drab horror after the first blood-and-filth-and-iron chaos known as a world war—Doubleyou Doubleyou One, in this case. After the soil was plowed with shells and fertilized with blood, our continent was as fecund in giving birth to new fatherlands as darkest Africa is today. Incidentally, both of them enjoying American midwifery in their difficult hour. Granted to them out of the noblest principles, of course: the American notion of freedom and similar human rights tolerates no empires, hence no colonies either, whether black or white and no matter what continent. Understandably so. If we are to believe Nagel (and why shouldn't we? He's a writer of international renown, a bestselling author, the sincerest bard of German probity, Scherping's house-star, the nail in Schwab's coffin, and presumably the supplier of some of your fattest commissions)—I say: if we share his opinion, arms should be given only to sovereign states. Got the message?

Well, in adjusting the demand to this supply, I have stumbled into an *embarras du choix* (pretty in German: *die Qual der Wahl*). There are too many fatherlands for me to opt for any single one. Lack of character, I know. Like my stance in the war as a sort of draft-dodger, not honorably mutilated, like Nagel. But mind you, I thought it gave me my only chance to achieve the dignity of a Nobel Prize (in literature, of course). For doesn't this anointment of individuals with a knack for writing—systematically selected one by one among all of today's fatherlands, from Iceland to Ghana—doesn't it constitute a clear testimonial that each of the chosen nations had attained the cultural level that permitted it to fly national colors in full self-assurance and have an army equipped with automatic weapons to defend its cultural identity? A few of them have even got the prize several times— according to higher cultural levels and therefore greater need of armaments. One suspects that after everybody has had his turn, the Nobel committee wouldn't know where to turn next. Yet never has the Nobel Prize been awarded to a stateless writer. I thought it was about time. I was wrong, of course. And as regards myself, there is a particular difficulty; the prize is never awarded for books that have not been written. Too bad. In certain cases it would come into more deserving hands. But let us say no more. Nagel will get the prize. *Hail to him with victor's laurel!* Had Schwab not been cremated, he would turn over in his casket like Saint Lawrence on the grill.

Incidentally, this brings me to something I should have thought of earlier. Schwab, as Scherping's editor for so many years, must have crossed your path; after all, you're the great— what am I saying?—the greatest, anyway the shrewdest of international literary agents. I'd give a lot to know what your meeting was like. As abortive as ours? Odd that he never mentioned it to me (but then, he was so tight-lipped, my dear dead friend). In contrast, I couldn't wait to write down the absurd story of our encounter. With the aim, naturally, of telling the whole world about it (in the book for which I would be awarded the Nobel Prize, of course).

Che buffonata! You had the impression (to my keen regret, I assure you) that I was trying to make fun of you. I suppose you made the common mistake of misconstruing my ironic tone. Allow me to set matters straight: irony is not aggressive; it is the natural expression of a sad cur, not a biting cur. Especially when confronted with overweening self-assurance, if you get what I mean. Granted, my reactions are neurasthenic. But I live among Frenchmen, I am overwrought. To be fair, let me confess I probably didn't get that way here alone. A decade and a half on German soil—that's no bed of roses, either. But the French gave me the *coup de grâce*. Be patient with me, Mr. Brodny. *Abbia pazienza!*

□   2   □

NOW, WHAT DO YOU HAVE TO SAY, Jacob G. Brodny, full-fledged citizen of the U.S.A., with military and other honors in the European Theater of Operations, superman of the literary business in the finest neon-haloed American way—what do you have to say about this challengingly arrogant self-assurance of the French? Sclerotic? Fossilized? Granted. Nevertheless: isn't it a thorn in your world-ruler flesh? Being French, as we are continually told here in Paris, is not simply having a nationality. Oh no: it is a divine right, a higher form of existence, growing from a more valuable chthonic origin and precipitated from the mother liquid of a nobler national spirit. And this in your, in the American, century, Jaykob Jee!—when any other form of existence than the American form is scarcely possible in the western part of the world! A phenomenal evolutionary obstinacy, don't you agree?

In the past, we were used to this sort of thing. The unpigmented, rabbit-toothed arrogance of the British, for example. The furious national consciousness of the Balkanese—say, the Serbs (just think of Sarajevo!). Germans, too, could afford to be blatantly German. That was simply normal in the waltz-wave-welling concert of nations, and it was part of the European panorama. A crazyquilt of ethnic groups, and each individual a proud something: a Briton, Bulgarian, Bosnian, Dutchman, Helvetian, Italian. Particularly Serbs, when they thought of themselves as

Serbs, regarded themselves as something far more important than when they simply thought, I, Miloš, or I, Yanko. Miloš the Serb was virtually a Miloš squared, an intensified Miloš, raised to a higher state of identity. The individual is not lost in the collective; on the contrary, he is transubstantiated into a clearer form and a higher specific gravity. Nagel writes, "To belong to a nation in body and mind, to represent a nation·in language, in appearance, and in character, is a kind of nobility!" A fortune-cookie truism that we ought to bear in mind. Schwab, a true German, found it a little fishy—understandably. As a German, one gains one's best form by strictly disavowing Germanism (à la Goethe or Hölderlin). But that does not reduce the universal validity of Nagel's statement. Certainly not for the French.

And isn't it astounding in a time when a people, a nation, can no longer even constitute a collective in and of itself? When it can no longer be a mold for national characteristics or develop a specific style? Show me the stylistic difference between a Spanish and a Swedish gas pump. The scenic difference between a stretch of highway or an airport near Hamburg, Germany, or Rome, Italy, and Dallas, Texas. Today, all we have is a supranational style, and this style is American. A bit of highway near Pearris, Freanss, is already pretty American and thus no different from one near Tokyo, Jippan. Likewise the airports and gas pumps both here and there. Yet the French keep getting Frencher and Frencher. The Spaniards, the Swedes, the Germans, the Italians, the Dutch, the Japanese are visibly turning into gum-chewing, computer-pious Americans. The French, however, have never been so intensely French as nowadays.

You will probably ask why this is weighing on my mind? Well, sir, it concerns a bizarre hobby (in the past, it would have been called *spleen*). I am seeking the other half of my life. Like Aristophanes' lovers, I am seeking a lost part of my own self, the other half of an original dual. It went astray at some point or other—I suspect on an icy-clear day in Vienna, March 1938. I was barely nineteen innocent years old. Those years were amputated from my existence like Nagel's right arm. Since then, I have been on the trail of their feelings. For, like Nagel, who claims he can still feel the fingers of his missing hand move, I too can feel my then self in an abstract way.

Well, I am looking for that other part of my life wherever I might find it: in countries, landscapes, clouds, towns—yes indeed, especially cities, which, with their lights, fragrances, noises, colors, forms, moods, sometimes resurrect in me the totality of moods, forms, colors, noises, fragrances, light effects of an entire era (abruptly, with painful bliss and, alas, only for a fleeting microsecond; for, mind you, the cities of today are no longer the same as those of yesteryear). In short, I am seeking the other half of my life in the vestiges—or rather in the echo—of its time. A time that is growing more and more discernible as a style. Fashionably specified by art historians: the era that developed Art Déco from Art Nouveau. The time of Europe's flirtation with America (I, with my past amputated from my existence, could attend the wedding only as an onlooker). I am seeking a Europe that might still be European. Funny, isn't it? . . .

Actually, you ought to sympathize with this, Mr. Jacob G. Brodny. First, as a nostalgic Jew. Like every good American province, Europe today is fairly *judenrein*. But things were different once, weren't they? If not a promised land, then at least Europe was a long-experienced and beloved land, a land in which you Jews fulfilled many of your boldest promises but, above all, found your most ruthless murderers. That makes for an unusually strong tie, doesn't it? . . . Aside from that: as an ex-European—Eastern European, to be sure—you too presumably had half of your life sliced off. You may have no reason to mourn it, but be that as it may, you've gone with the times. Whether bravely or cheerfully, you jettisoned anything about yourself that was a vestige and echo of a past form of life and vigorously settled into a new life-style—everybody's new life-style—and you became an American. In the great collective of the United States of our Western World, your halved self was transubstantiated into a new, bursting fullness. Your Americanness simply booms in one's face.

I, for my part, have made myself delinquent by dragging the past into presence. I cannot wholly renounce something that is somehow still alive within me, albeit in an abstract, ghostly way, like Nagel's shot-off arm. Thus, nothing new has come of me. And of course I most certainly have not remained what I was. So kindly understand what I find so fascinating about the French. Not only have they remained what they were, they have even become more intensely what they had been. Schwab was filled with excited sympathy for this phenomenon. As for myself, I can't disguise my envy.

Cast to and fro by the capricious fate that attends a moviemaker (I'm a screenwriter, as you know), I commute through the various mini-metropolises of Europe: Vienna, Madrid, Rome, Munich, Copenhagen, Milan, West Berlin. A Europe that is woefully shriveled, likewise mutilated by one half, ridiculously provincial, suburban, desolate. But for several years now (ever since a crazy romance with an American fashion model named Dawn, at least since Schwab's death), it's been safest to contact me here in Paris. No household of my own, of course. After my dismal experiences in an abortive marriage in Hamburg (with Christa), I tried to settle down here (with Gaia—chocolate-brown giantess, half Afro-American, half Rumanian blood, Princess Jahovary— sounds like a freak show and looked like one, too). My attempt at domesticity failed, but you'll hear about that later. Now, what so utterly frustrated me here is the unbelievable, downright incredible hard surface of the French. Cartesians clear as crystal, these fellows, and coalesced into a geode. It makes for a world that's not so easy to get into. At any rate, I haven't managed, even though I sense—good Lord! even though I *know* that it's my world.

Yes sir, it is my world in almost every way, and I (or at least the I of the lost half of my life) am contained in it integrally. Here, nearly everything of the lost half of my life has been preserved: forms, colors, tones, fragrances galore, an entire language-world, any amount of Art Nouveau and Art Déco. And yet here I lose not only my sense of having once belonged to a world like this but any solid foothold in time, above all in the present.

The world is an event in which I do not participate, have never participated, and will never participate. The world is a French event, and I am not French. I am not even a *boche*, like Schwab—a potential killer of Frenchmen (I repeat: an intimate kinship, almost an identification). Nor am I American, which would be a different form of potential killer of French essence. I am nothing. Not only stateless by citizenship but rootless by blood, *déraciné par excellence:* truly without a fatherland or a father, a fellow who doesn't know who his procreator is, and whose mother deserted and betrayed her nation, a fellow who is neither here nor there, unbaptized, with no religion, suspiciously polyglot, devoid of any tie to any tribe, to any flag. . . . But of course in quest of all those things.

The exceedingly lovely, the wondrously beautiful city of Paris, *la ville lumière,* gives me not the least bit of help in my quest. On the contrary. The devastating presentness of its history excludes me as much as its historical presence does. In the uninterrupted continuity from Charlemagne to Charles de Gaulle there is not the tiniest gap for me to squeeze into. And yet the half of the life that I and my kind lost in that March of 1938 belongs far more here than anywhere else. I mean to say: the European Europe from which that half was born, in which it grew up, and whose colors, forms, sounds, fragrances, moods constituted its pattern, is far more present here than anywhere else. Where else might I seek it, if not here? Here, I am incessantly on the track of my self—sometimes, for auspicious, breathtaking micro-moments, I am even on my heels. But I will never reach my self.

How can I make this clear to you, my esteemed Jaykob Jee? As a man who has traveled the world over, you must, of course, know Sneek, the Dutch Venice? There, you can punt along in a heavy boat, infinitely slowly, through leaden canals. To the left and the right, the banks drag by with such sluggish drowsiness that one expects the houses to topple forward like the heads of exhausted people, their eyelids shutting. Well, in a movie script I once wrote, which like so many others will remain unrealized wishful thinking (none of my producer-piglets will ever want to film it), I describe a chase in Sneek. A man has to catch up with another man at any cost, and the other is several boats ahead of him and flees . . . very slowly flees . . . infinitely slowly and always just beyond reach . . . and that other man is, of course, himself.

I ASSUME that you too, sir, are not unfamiliar with such existential conditions, slipping off into the dream dimension of slow motion (with a resulting personality split). After all, this is a phenomenon of the times; I mean to say, a special perception or awareness of time that is inherent in our era (and also, by the way, the first step for hashish-eaters, opium-smokers, et al., in their psychedelic wonderlands).

I would not be amazed to experience this in Vienna. That is where I lost the first half of my life, and for consistency's sake I ought to look for it there—and never find it again. You will, I hope, understand me when I say that I lost it *precisely because that half is present there*. Not really, though. Like Vienna as a whole, that half is present as a dream. A dream preserved in a museum. Vienna and I, we are both timeless, a dead man's dream in a dead city's dream. On March 12 of the year 1938 Vienna died before my eyes and, with it, my then living and lived self. But we still keep on dreaming our selves. Vienna and I belong together for all time—but no longer to me.

Please understand my difficulty in explaining myself, dear Mr. Jaykob Jee: what I am seeking in the lost half of my life is not my *then* self but rather that within it that might connect in some way to my present self. Connect in such a way as to make me believe that it really was I and not just a dream, a legend, a literary invention, a fiction within me. A hopeless enterprise, you will adn .t: I am seeking *myself* in the European cities where I am cast away by my flimsy profession, as if they were not the cities and sites of my past but the cities and sites of my present. And there, there is no place for me. I seek my self in the airports, the highways, gas stations, Hilton hotels, supermarkets, movie studios, office high-rises of Madrid, Rome, Munich, Copenhagen, Milan, West Berlin, Paris. In seeking my self I seek a European continuity (Schwab would have said, "*Ni plus, ni moins*"). This European continuity is to be found neither in the well-preserved remnants of the past in today's European cities nor in their modern aspects. They are as disconnected from their past as I am from mine. Only, as I said, in an occasional split second of recognition do I find myself or a city as I knew it in the past. And these split seconds make my search the more intense, and the more futile. To put it in a nutshell, my esteemed Mr. Brodny, I am seeking my identity, as you would call it. A genuinely American, a so to speak banally American, phenomenon. As a hopelessly dyed-in-the-wool European, I have cause to doubt my reality.

I am capable of illustrating this condition with several documents. Permit me to lay two of them before you. Together, they should make the situation clear. The first is a sheet of paper (it seems to me our existence is entirely on paper), and unfortunately I can no longer say for sure whether it was part of a draft of a letter, in which I tried a while back (roughly three years ago) gently to tease my late friend Schwab from a distance (Paris-Hamburg), or whether it was one of the endless monologues that I delivered to him for the same reason when he came from Hamburg to visit me here in Paris, soliloquies intended to provoke a reaction from his dulled and yet at times doubly fine alcoholic's mind. I used to put them down the moment I got home—for particular purposes, as you will soon comprehend. But ultimately it makes no difference whether it's the one or the other. Let me give you the excerpt:

. . .You remember that passage in Nietzsche where he announces a coming artistic era? Well, that era has arrived. Today, everyone must *realize his potential*—to wit, by producing art. Be creative! Produce! Give shape! Form! When distinct talents are lacking, make literature! One has the impression that for people like us, puberty drags on until a climacteric—and indeed beyond it. It is obvious that teenagers live with a sense of unreality and are looking for the meaning of life (and thereby their identities). But middle-aged bank directors, too, collapse before me in sobs and confess, with their heads in my lap, that they would give all their wealth for my gift of literary self-expression. Every jackass feels the urge to realize his potential artistically. Statesmen like Winston Churchill and Amintore Fanfani find their true selves in painting. In Parisian society (which in my uncle Ferdinand's day was not afflicted by self-doubt, no, sir; it was a homogeneous conglomerate of

Guermantes, Verdurins, and Rastaquères) every beautiful lady at least does interior decorating if she doesn't have her hands full being an archaeologist or running a gallery. And other arts and artistic crafts are flourishing, too. You'd be amazed at what you can get into a film (and then into a bed) with a nod and a bit of celluloid. And if you expect a nineteen-year-old of today not to discover the true meaning of life in throwing ceramics (such as I, throwing caution to the winds, dared to propose to my son), then you have only yourself to blame.

Certainly, this is an encouraging sign of a general ennoblement in mankind. An upward development toward the spiritual realm, which one ought to applaud. To use the terms of my uncle Helmuth, an electrical engineer and spiritist, we are already living in a different vibrational state, already more dematerialized and spiritualized than ever before. We have ascended one level closer to God. But I don't feel quite right about it. I fear that we have once again reckoned without God's less spiritual other half—namely, without Mother Nature.

This powerful lady is always on the lookout to catch the flies that have all too ardently swarmed onto the honey of the mind because they have the delusion that this is the *true* reality. No, sir: the true reality is not in the illusions of the mind. It is in Ma Nature herself and nowhere else. She will grab anybody by the scruff of the neck if he finds her rules too brutal, too monotonous, too idiotic and would rather ignore them. Anyone who prefers to follow laws other than those of the everlasting stupid cycle of procreation and annihilation is already playing on his own, and at his own risk. He should not be surprised if she raps him on the knuckles.

Yes, indeed, I too bow respectfully to the beautiful courage of the human race, which keeps creating new fictions in order that it may confront the perpetual threat of cruelly productive-and-destructive nature and claim undaunted that existence must have some other purpose than merely eating and being eaten. I admire the insanely courageous way mankind tarries in the as-if, its insistence that we may have other aims than to breed and to kill. But not everyone is up to staying awake during such sleepwalking. Art is opium for today's people. Only a happy few consider it their damnation.

Ask Nagel, he writes so nicely about it: "If any of the acrobats under the Big Top knows there is no net under him, he can still dare to try his stunt. But woe, woe unto him if he realizes it only when he is already on the tightrope. . . ." Here, I once again agree completely with our friend

Nagel. A dangerously large number of dilettantes step out on the high wire, nowadays. More and more of them, bolder and bolder. Everyone wants to get up there. This cannot end well. Certain experiences in Vienna make me feel that in the long run Mother Nature will not be content to look on at this collective somnambulism. I would not like to be called to account with the others when she intercedes and begins to set things right.

My friend! I admire your courageous "Nevertheless!" I take my hat off to Nagel whenever another of his books appears on the market (as a best-seller). I bow respectfully to you, Schwab, for obviously still planning to write your book despite heartrending, soul-churning doubts whether any more books should be written in this book-flooded time. But I, for my modest little part, no longer indulge in the lovely illusion that I might thereby succeed (like Münchhausen by his own pigtail) in pulling myself out of the realization of the total absurdity of existence. No, no. I shall not step out on the tightrope. I shall remain pious. (Please tell this to dear Scherping, too, for he might still live in the lovely illusion of getting my manuscript one of these days!) I shall remain an obedient servant of Mother Nature. Living against one's time—such has always been the attitude of the dandy. In this area of artists and self-realizers, I take the liberty of being a dandy in the purely biological form of existence. I run no risk. I perform my biological duties, nothing more—and you know how seriously I take this activity. I realize my potential not in artistic creations like everyone else but rather in acts of destruction. Murder, alas, is something I can do only in dreams, but, for example, I systematically wipe out everything I have written during the past few years. No more kidding around with art. Eat and be eaten. I did my best, recently, with quite an amount of expensive food—come and join in. You can still eat well here in Paris. And of course, in between, I set my sights on even the tiniest possibility of a quick, pleasant copulation. On the off chance of procreating if my partner has not taken the right precautions. For this too was Mother Nature's intention when she created me.

So much for the first document. The second might be dated a few months later. I found it among the papers for my book where it had slipped in, by goodness knows what accident. A similar accident played it into my hands a few days ago. *Le voilà.*

Paris in the blossoming of May. *Printemps* posters behind brightly greening plane trees. The first summer frocks. All the airy kitsch of Dufy.

S. has arrived unexpectedly. During the day, we sit outdoors in front of the Flore, the Deux Magots, feast at Lapérouse or Chez Anne, shuffle through museums. At night we play Russian roulette. It doesn't take much psychological flair (as in Professor Hertzog's school) to guess why he sticks to my heels like that. He simply doesn't believe in my calm. He thinks my mental state phenomenal. Something uncanny. He thinks I'm dazed, in a kind of trance (like one of the mediums in my late uncle Helmuth's spiritist circle in Vienna: outside myself and somewhere in space, only loosely attached to my body by an astral umbilical cord, while the emptied shell of my body is open to any spirit that wishes to sojourn in it—in my case, needless to say, the demon of despair).

He regards me as a character in a novel. Hence, I have to act like one. In a novel, it would be impossible to make you believe in a man who, after the end of a love affair in which he has carried on like a lunatic for three years, gets down to business with a smile—as if he had not personally experienced all the magic of insanity and happiness and misery and anxiety and senseless hope and foolish perseverance but had read about it in some pulp paperback, which he has only just put aside, or seen it in a movie. Such a character is convincing only if, behind his feigned imperturbability, he nurtures the intention of killing himself. And that is what S. expects me to do. *Ni plus, ni moins.*

After all, he ardently envied me for my madly loving a crazy wench like that American. His rhetorical question: "Who's capable of such folly nowadays!" (I see his face before me as he exclaimed it. It was raised heavenward, as during a hymn. Cousin Wolfgang up in the church choir: *"Queeheeheeheen of heaheaheaheaven, rejoice, Maahaa-haa-rie-ha! . . ."*)

Who can still perform this at the age of forty-five? In 1964, the second half of the twentieth century, if you please—who can still afford such feelings? Fall in love like a schoolboy? At best, a menopausal department-store executive in a movie. But people like us—inhabitants of a crater landscape, an emotional world that has been analyzed to atoms—if anything is still stirring then it's allergies. . . .

So if someone like us kicks up such a splendid fuss, then there must be something exquisite behind it, don't you think? The intention to transvaluate that experience artistically into something exemplary. If you don't do that, you're cheating and you'll have to pay for it. You can't just escape it by producing psychosomatic sugar in your urine. Nowadays, neuroses are children's ailments. Any self-respecting person thus frustrated has to kill himself. *Ni plus, ni moins.*

Actually, S. has come to Paris because *he* has reached the end of his rope. Scherping finally went through with it and fired him from his editorial position in his publishing house. Fired him as well as his secretary Fräulein Schmidschelm, which S. considers particularly insidious. But of course he has to admit that Schelmy is quite happy about it: now she's free of the burdensome job of rescuing the boss from the claws of Gisela or lovely Hely in the whorehouse or tracking him down during a boozing tour with his terrific *aunt.* Schelmy has settled down on her regular stool at Lücke's Bar, clearing off only when the place is closed (all together six hours out of twenty-four).

He, meanwhile, has panicked. Not because he's worried about his further material existence (although in such cases, a thoroughbred burgher albeit an intellectual probably can't stop the involuntary tightening of his sphincter). Of course, Scherping gave him—had to give him—a handsome amount of severance pay. Obviously he was forced to do so by a murderous contract (probably still fuming at the thought, grinding his teeth in woe and weal). For now, our friend S. is rolling in money. But fear is bubbling out of every pore. The "hour of truth" has come. *He has no more excuses not to write his book.*

First he came here. Hopelessly behind the times: still dreaming the dreams of Futurists, Constructivists. Sees their dreams as having come true here—in Paris of all places! Divine city of Reason on earth. This is where the human being first becomes human. Temple of the World. Ziggurat: hieratic tower connecting heaven and earth. Pure and simple: the City of Man: ANTHROPOLIS.

As a matter of fact, he's taken refuge with me. As usual, he wants to crib something from me. He's looking for my secret motor, my special driving force—something he thinks I've got over him. Some perfidious secret of existence. Some crafty, not quite permissible, ethically and aesthetically not quite unobjectionable, but incredibly practical, exceedingly effective trick for living. Something that makes me appear livelier, more present, downright realer in his eyes than the phonies all around (including Nagel, delusively spawning best-sellers). Livelier than he himself, *en tout cas*. Yet he knows my eyes are as open as his own. It's a miracle.

He confesses this to me with a moan of beautiful, admiring envy. He calls it the thing that's "hale and hearty" about me. A "vitality that is not yet wholly disintegrated." An "existence that has not yet become wholly abstract"—with the chance to perform like a department-store executive with December stirrings and fall in love with the most banal of all love objects, a photographer's model!

Yet at times he regards my vacant-eyed and ingenious concordance with life as sheer flimflam. So much the worse! For then, you see, he becomes intrigued by the fact that my flimflam works. This too requires qualities and abilities whose nature and origin are puzzling to him. He looks for them in my life story. Even though he all but knows it by heart, he listens to me more attentively, investigates more conscientiously, more methodically than ever. I supply him generously. (A Russian proverb says that you can choke a guest with cottage cheese.) He takes secret notes. Thinks I don't realize. (I take my own notes about him afterward, at home.) But biographical data are not enough for him. He rummages about in my present circumstances. Paris, he feels, is a trump in my game. He combs the city for the secret nutritive powers with which it presumably nourishes me. He has come as a scientific Hercules, who, before the fight, begins by taking a tiny sample for chemical analysis from the soil from which Antaeus draws his rejuvenating strength. Of course, he also wants to be cradled a bit: *Fais dodo, Colin, mon petit frère, Fais dodo, t'auras du lolo. . . .*

My brother Schwab. My brother Abel.

Needless to say, I promptly told him about the grotesque circumstances under which I broke off with Dawn. I didn't spare the details that might excite him (*"Il n'y a pas de détail,"* says Valéry). Everything very literary, to be sure. Just as he expects of me. First (in a gentle manly, cultivated, discreet, tastefully allusive way, of course), I gave him a glimpse of my desperate financial situation: more debts than a village dog has fleas. Christa, my divorced spouse, now morally supported by Witte, has found a lawyer who would squeeze alimony for her and our son from my tombstone. Plus trouble galore with the producer-piglets: my recent screenplays are not being taken. So I ought to have cut down to the bare bones in everything. Yet I live the life of Riley. I reside sumptuously at the George V. I still keep an apartment for my eccentric beloved, even though it has been empty for months now, awaiting her. (I used to go there daily to put fresh flowers in the vases and change the milk, the steaks, the salubrious vegetables, the eggs in the icebox; she eats everything raw; at the Marché Buci, they are ardently sympathetic and treat me like a worried father: "*Mademoiselle est votre fille, n'est-ce pas?*" Certainly. Humbert Humbert's the name. And *mademoiselle* is out of town? *Evidemment.* And Papa's apartment-sitting for her while she's gone. Yes, that's what young people are like nowadays. They want to live independently but they can't really manage on their own.)

Mademoiselle was out of town a lot during the past few months, goddamn it! I couldn't get anything else done because I spent my days combing Paris for the bitch! Do you know how many lousy little hotels there are here where a silly American model can hide out? Just like the stars in the sky: God alone has counted them. I'd like to have His problems. He didn't comb through each and every one of them for a lunatic girl who might have sneaked in to spend an entire weekend in a darkened room, consuming nothing but raw eggs from a plastic box, instant coffee from little packets, chain-smoking, pill-popping, afflicted by unnamable terrors, shaken by ineffable fears, in danger of falling asleep with the cigarette in her pretty kisser and burning up in bed. He didn't hang on the telephone for nights on end, waiting to get through because the night clerk had deserted his post and was screwing *madame la patronne* two flights up. . . .

Be that as it may. In that very spot, the sleazy, sordid hotel on the Place des Ternes—which our friend S. knew well enough, didn't he?— she had found refuge with the handsome Pole and the breathtaking French madame. In the same room where the scene with the Indian doll had taken place two years earlier (S. blushes even now at the mere mention of it). Our first love nest. The setting for an unspeakably arduous, unspeakably joyless deflowering (at the mere thought of it, *I* blush). I don't understand why it didn't occur to me right away to look for her there (probably because of that gloomy association; our erotic conquests; the proud moments of our lives—oh shit!).

In the end, I found her. With great delight, I can report (relishing S.'s round-eyed interest) on how I had to construct a whole set of fictions, a real house of cards, to lure her out of her hole: the past was snuffed out as if our relationship had never existed—that is to say, never reached a higher degree of intimacy than that of casual acquaintance. ("Oh, how nice to see you!") I called to ask if she would go out with me. (Her *date* for tonight.) Needless to say, I brought flowers, two dozen white roses. With scrupulous narrative precision I described to S. how she had once again kept me waiting for hours before she descended the stairs in a black Pola Negri gown, parodying herself with symptoms of daffy insanity: prancing toward me with the marionette gait of a mindless model; her hands, in black elbow-length widow's gloves, dangling affectedly from bent arms; her head sporting a gigantic black mushroom-shaped stump of a hat, which cast its shadow over soup-plate-sized dark glasses sparkling with green and violet reflections, so that all one could see underneath was the mouth and chin and throat—very red, very white, perfectly beautiful: the tragic lips of Garbo, the tender and resolute chin of Ava Gardner, the stem-like throat of Audrey Hepburn, all the clichés of standardized female beauty in a halved head, as in a *Vogue* fashion photo.

My friend listens breathlessly as I describe with cruel precision the way she came along, sashaying and hip-wiggling, how she affected incredibly phony theatrical nonchalance as she called out "Hi!" in the guttural tone of her sophomore Americanese, with the jaw-gaping cheerleader-smile that revealed all her immaculate glowing toothpaste-commercial teeth back to the molars. The way she didn't even bother holding out her cheek for a kiss (after all, I am her *date* tonight, am I not?) as she zoomed past, wantonly purposeful as a bumblebee in flight, and headed toward the handsome Pole's desk and instantly got on the telephone. The way I waited for her, holding my bridal bouquet of roses stiff in my lap, clumsy as a provincial beau at his first gallant rendezvous. The way I was forced to listen to her talking on the phone with somebody I didn't know, of whose existence I had had no inkling whatsoever until that moment. The way she said with desperate woe, "No, no! You can't leave me like that! You know I love you!" And the way I felt nothing, absolutely nothing, not the feeblest sting of jealousy, not even curiosity about whom she was saying it to (for at last it was not tormenting conjecture but certainty, *reality*).

The way she then finally came to me, wordlessly taking the roses and following me out to the car—all this with the robotic motion and lifeless visage of a hypnotized woman. (I couldn't see her eyes behind the monstrous glasses under the brim of that blasted stump, but I knew every feature of hers so well that I would have read the grief in the tip of her nose. Incidentally, her mouth was the mouth of a tired child made up for carnival: the festival had not been the expected happy delirium but, rather, wild and noisy and chaotic, full of crudeness, gloating malevolence; now, it's over, the dream is dreamed out.)

She did not reply when I asked whether I should take her to dinner, to the movies, or elsewhere. To a dance café perhaps? Home? Where was that? In our—in her apartment in the rue Jacob? Whom was I talking to? Whom was I thinking of? Did she want to go to bed perhaps? A tasteful idea. . . . Finally, since I knew she enjoyed riding in an open car, I drove her to the Bois de Boulogne.

Ah, splendid! A starry sky over the rustling backdrop of black foliage, silhouettes that looked cut out of tin. In the daytime, it probably greens brightly during this season. Nature. Calms the nerves. Relax, my love.

Naturally the cars coming our way blinked their headlights at us. One even did a U-turn behind us, caught up, and cut us off, so that I had to slam on the brakes. Two guys got out, leaving their girls inside. But I knew what they wanted, so I waved them off and drove around them and on until we were off the main road. (One of the men, incidentally, had let out an appreciative whistle when he saw what was visible of Dawn under the black mushroom.)

In the side road where we finally halted, another car approached us. The driver stuck his head out the window and suggested group sex somewhere in Neuilly.

"Non merci, mon vieux, nous avons des problèmes, tu vois."

"Oh là là! . . ."

Dawn remained wordless and motionless throughout. (Don't act so puritanical, I thought, you with that unknown guy you love so much you don't want him to leave you, you bitch!) But the night was soft, and naturally I couldn't help myself, I had to talk. Had to tell her what I felt for her. What I had suffered because of her. Suffered mainly because I had been forced to torment her (to my son: when Daddy spanks you, it hurts him more than you). That I had been forced to torment her because I loved her tremendously (just as Daddy loves his little boy). That she had never understood this to the full extent of the causal nexus (just like Daddy's little boy). How regrettable that was, what a waste of good living time if one thought about it, wasn't it? Ye how beautiful how wonderful it could be if . . .

Around us, the lovely city of Paris hummed and seethed (some umpteen million inhabitants including the suburbs: first-class nuclear target). And there I was, talking once again—to my shame! Once again spewing out the contents of my soul. *Vomitatio animae*. The emotional essence of my fermented inner life ("a speciality of the bloody fucking middle classes," as John and Stella called it).

Thus did I talk, spitting forth a lover's verbal gruel. Nonstop and in detail. Soliloquizing. Talking out my *Weltschmerz* to her. The ordeal of human life. God's heartlessness. Needless to say, I did not make it sentimental (people like us avoid sentimentality like the plague). I said, "I'm sorry, my darling, I know it's not agreeable to be loved, but . . ." I spiced my verbal gruel with piquant little jests she would surely not enjoy. ("What does Torquato Tasso say? Two souls, alas, are dwelling in my breast. . . . That's not quite the case with me. Two breasts, alas, are dwelling in my soul, and they're yours!") In short, I did everything to make myself disagreeable.

Overhead, in the dark backdrop of branches, the stars were twinkling. Many, many. God alone has counted them. It must have taken HIM HIS sweet time. Galactorrhea in the firmament. And it's big. If you imagined the sun (its diameter one hundred and nine times the size of the earth's) as the head of a pin in Berlin, then the next fixed star would be like a soccer ball in Hamburg. And here I was sitting and talking. Pouring out verbal gruel. About my love.

Embarrassing. But—oh my goodness! What man hasn't been guilty of this sort of thing? And I of all people—how often, how many shameful times, had I not done this! Talked away at some then beloved female, tormented, pigheaded, persistent. Sputtering verbal trash: aphorisms, sublimated from my spiritual ordeal. Sentences fraught with confession. Metaphysical knowledge. Existentialist philosophy. Blurted out to the beloved female body, to the sweet female flesh, to the soft skin, the fine, frail limbs, the tender curves, the airy, fragrant hair—oh misery! To eyes in whose depths I found the answer to myself. To a face that briefly epitomized the sweetness of life—a mother, a sister—the fulfillment of the dream of being One, of blissfully entering, dissolving into, another human being. (How did Scherping put it? "If only they couldn't speak. If they just barked or meowed, then we would not expect them to react humanly like you and me. . . .")

Oh well. In this case, this now beloved pair of eyes was concealed by the soup-plate-sized black glasses under the brim of the gigantic black hat-stump. I could just barely make out the tip of my present adorata's nose, and under it the mouth: the beautiful lips over the poignantly tender (and solid) chin over the stem-like girlish throat over the narrow shoulders and the beloved little breasts: two touchingly young, tender, bud-like handfuls of girlish breast (thoroughly Art Nouveau, but now covered by the black satin of the Art Déco gown—so let's stick to the lips).

The lips hovered, graven blood-red in the dull white of the cheeks, chin, and throat, in the compact blacknesses of the hat and gown and car-seat leather and nocturnal foliage under the starry sky. It was a strangely isolated pair of lips, a detached yet delicate piece of anatomy with a mysterious life of its own. A mute mouth. A mouth without a face. And without an explicable expression, not cheerful and not dismal, not proud, not humble, not yearning, and not scornful, not smart, not stupid: just mouth. Beautifully human (albeit human in a zoologically universalized manner: the mouth of mankind, of the species of man; and at the same time, something animal-like in and of itself: a mouth-animal, shaped like a blossom for mimicry . . .). Where the lips swelled there was a wan, slightly greasy glow: reflection of starlight, sparkling too in the black glasses above and in the curve of the windshield in front and on the nickel fittings of the car door at the side.

And all this was embedded in white roses. For she had untied my bridegroom's bouquet and strewn the flowers in and around her lap. She sat in white roses, like a black swan. Her black torso loomed out of white rose blossoms into the black night. Above hovered the mouth.

I, however, sat next to her, talking. Talking my heart and soul out of my throat. And while I was talking and talking, about my tremendous love, about my misery and wretchedness, about my lofty goals and wishes—for both of us, to be sure, for both of us!—this mouth suddenly laughed. The red lips gaped, revealing two lines of white teeth, well formed and regular, two glistening rows. And while this mouth laughed, soundlessly and without the shaking of vulgar hilarity, her hand in the black widow-glove reached into the roses, drew out one of the blossoms, and put it to the lips, passing it over them as if to cool them. . . . And suddenly, from between the bars of teeth, the tongue shot out and seized the blossom and yanked it into the teeth, which snapped shut and shredded it.

A fascinating spectacle. I depict it vividly to Schwab. I let him take part in it, and he follows it spellbound, suffering with me as the red mouth devours the white rose. The mouth kept laughing, soundlessly; small, white tatters of shredded petals stuck to the red lips. By the time the trimming and the stem were all that was left, I had stopped talking, switched on the engine, and was driving Dawn back to the hotel.

I had always captivated her with finely polished chivalry. ("We're not used to such nice manners anymore, you know.") And so this time too I did not hold back. I got out, walked around the vehicle, and held open the door, handing her out of the car. A ludicrous gesture of farewell, I admit (a movie script would have said here, on the left, "Musical leitmotiv begins softly"). She took two or three steps toward the hotel entrance, then wheeled around, came over to me, pressed her breasts, abdomen, and thighs snugly against me, and whispered in a passionate, husky tone, "Darling, do you think you could spare another thousand francs? I need it to pay the bill here and some other things."

Her mouth laughed again when she put away the money and left. The white roses were scattered from the car seat across the sidewalk all the way over to the hotel entrance, like a strip of moonlight on a dark lake, with a black swan floating through.

And because of that, S. expects my heart to burst in my chest!? . . . I peer into the round, gaping eyes behind the inch-thick glasses of the book worm. (Aunt Hertha rattling on the shithouse door, behind which Cousin Wolfgang has locked himself in to read undisturbed: "You'll go blind someday!")

Well, what world-shaking event had occurred? I had lost Dawn. This time for good. Irrevocably. No, this time she wouldn't come back. Okay then—what's so exciting about that? To be sure, she wasn't just an extraordinarily beautiful but also an extraordinarily interesting girl, mad as a hatter, no doubt, but only sometimes, periodically. In between, she could be as smart, as merry, as full of wild joie de vivre as any thoughtless young thing. . . .

A completely intimidated person, you see, the creature of a civilization of money, of sheer collective madness, bewildered by the myth of success, scared by the menace of failure, a child still, barely twenty years old—I should really have borne a paternal responsibility, but the role doesn't seem to be mine; I failed shamefully even with my son (probably by trying too hard, she would have said). And of course, the age gap was rather large for the glorious lover, I assume, even though there had been moments of incredible intimacy, we had plunged into one another with exuberant tenderness—a sudden profound union of souls and senses, of the kind that has been rather infrequent since the fashionable obsolescence of D'Annunzio's emotional world. Ah! Her gigantic gray feline eyes close to mine (without the black glasses, of course), her lips laughing happily (not scornfully), her beloved beautiful happy mouth . . .

And I had lost her. And the man reeling under the impact of this blow is not I: he is my friend S., named by me Johannes Schwab. As though I had not personally experienced this whole foolish love story, which any sensible person would only shake his head at; as though I had experienced it vicariously for him, Schwab— What am I saying? For our generation, allegedly incapable of achieving much of a festive inner state, as though it were suffering from a kind of emotional scurvy. It was an act of salvation, in a word. From now on, people could point at me if anyone started in about the death of emotional life and the shift of feeling to collective experiences like soccer matches and politics. I was the witness to the contrary. I was the model exception, if you please. My emotional life was of prewar quality. I maintained the link with the emotional possibilities of our fathers. I was living proof that continuity had not been broken, at least in this respect—the "specifically European conception of love and capacity for love," as Schwab puts it. That is to say, "love as a revolutionary act, as the revolt of the individual against the barriers of society." Phew! Only I was capable of such a thing; not as an adolescent, mind you, no, as a mature, reflective, much-tried adult. This, too, a way of dragging the past into presence—but an active way, mind you, not the passive one of nostalgic re-evocation. . . .

And now what? Now that I had reached the head of the class and now that—as foreseen—the entire emotion business lay in pieces, I refused to take the next logical step! I was not desperate, I did not shoot a bullet into my head, I did not join the Foreign Legion in order to vanish forever into the unknown! No. I was, I am, as cheerful and serene as ever.

It doesn't help to tell S. that I am only sort of partially involved, insofar as it is not my entire self that lost Dawn. Only one of my two souls is concerned. Only one half of my self can be blamed. Her loss, I say, is entirely the fault of those traits and qualities of mine that were stamped in me by my formative years in Vienna, yet are more characteristic of today's spirit than of the past's—philistine characteristics, petty bourgeois obsessions. For instance, the disgusting eagerness to take possession, to know better and help out, to educate and alter. As though it were one of the tasks of love to develop the other person toward so-called normality at any cost. (For instance: my persistent concern about Dawn's health, both physical and mental, my pampering and caring, my making sure that nothing happened to her, that she didn't do anything to herself. The picayune morality, the anxious conformism behind all that, and of course the cannibalism, the eating of human flesh in mental and physical ownership. In short, everything that made John and Stella so violently hate the "bloody fucking middle classes and their shitty morality" and that had been, alas, planted in me during twelve Viennese years with Uncle Helmuth, Aunt Hertha, Aunt Selma, and Cousin Wolfgang.)

In contrast, however, I tell my friend, there is an entirely different side to me, belonging to the *Zeitgeist* of another past, the side with which I won Dawn in beautiful freedom: overlooking any craziness of hers, fulfilling every foolish wish, never correcting or criticizing her, agreeing with all her mad ideas, even feeding her pills instead of *foie gras*, buying her mushroom-like hat-stumps instead of fancy hats, suffering with a smile when she dressed like a scarecrow . . . In other words, my really artistic side, not the petty-artistic petty bourgeois but the artist within me who knows there is no net under him. The man with an understanding for alienation, the admirer of generosity, distance, elegant neutrality in handling human relationships—traits I had managed to copy from such outstanding personages as Uncle Ferdinand. The cautious live-and-let-live attitude of Uncle Agop Garabetian's extraordinary amiability. The imaginativeness, the delicious playfulness of a Bully Olivera, whose acquaintanceship had been one of the most fruitful gifts of my unbourgeois childhood before Vienna. . . . Had any of the three of them, for instance, learned that someone wanted to kill himself, he unhesitatingly would have given that person the opportunity. . . .

And this side of mine, I tell friend S., did not lose Dawn, can never lose Dawn. And most certainly not if the shitty middle-class morality of the other half of my soul was what made her leave me. "You understand what I mean," I say to him. "The very thing stated by Romano Guardini, whom you so highly esteem: 'The first step to the other one is the movement that *takes away the hands* and clears the space in which the self-concerned quality of the person can come into action. This motion constitutes the first effect of *justice* and is the basis of all *love*.' "

He turns crimson. He thinks I'm trying to make fun of him. He regards my quoting (especially from Guardini!), my attack against the middle classes, and my ironical eulogy of the plutocrats Uncle Ferdinand, Sir Agop Garabetian, Bully Olivera, as a venomous personal jibe. "Don't act more cynical than you are," he says.

I say, "You misunderstand me. I'm quite serious. I'm talking about something that's very much on my mind: a sociology of the emotions, which I have been planning to work on for some time now. I maintain that the relative emotional frigidity of the uppermost (and lowermost) strata in any society is paired with a keener sense of reality than that of the ones between. With the realism of a more thorough knowledge of life. Soul (I mean an especially passionate mental tension designed for suffering) seems to be a prerogative of the middle strata. The sentimental romanticism of the bloody fucking middle classes, as John and Stella have always said. The bourgeois invents emotions that he can no longer draw from immediate contact with life. Ask Scherping, he knows a thing or two about it. He also knows what thrives especially well in these inner miasmas: a proclivity for the fictive, for the as-if, plus, of course, any amount of artistic art, especially literary art. Which you might consider an advantage. But interhuman relations are thereby unbearably complicated. I wish I had listened to Dawn's warnings in time. You know, she used to say, 'Most people fail because they try too hard.' It's really just like writing books, isn't it? If only we were more lighthearted, we'd be like Nagel and produce novels as if there were no tomorrow. Dawn could be very shrewd sometimes."

Once again, I'm the one who's talking. But he doesn't laugh and he doesn't eat a rose. His upper lip (a bit long and sensitive as a feeler, yet resolute above the severely retracted lower lip: the mouth of Paul Klee) trembles, as it usually does when he's very nervous. A couple of fine little drops of sweat hang above it. (Lately, he's been drinking oceans of rum and Coca-Cola, and he's always quite proud when he expertly orders, *"Un autre Cuba libre, s'il vous plaît!"*) His eyes are lucid and dull, like the eyes of a boiled fish.

And I am talking. Spouting confused verbal gruel. I say, "Why, on the other hand, were there so few neuropaths in Uncle Ferdinand's circle of friends, in the 'Middle Kingdom' of his playmates at the polo grounds and baccarat tables of Deauville and Monte Carlo? After all, their monstrous wealth and constant idleness ought to have created all kinds of neuroses and psychoses. But not a trace. On the contrary: the serenest rapport with life. Not a hint of communication problems or the like. Model sociability: Uncle Agop's parties were epoch-making. Bully Olivera had more friends the world over than Dr. Schweitzer. Plus the smoothest, most graceful love affairs with dozens of women. I remember what Uncle Ferdinand said to me about his relationship with my mother when I visited him for the last time, in Bessarabia, during the winter of 1939–40: 'She was an ideal mistress in the truest sense of the word—not only a great beauty but a great teacher of life. She used to say, "The entire secret of a harmonious mind lies in the ability to recognize imminent convulsions and to prevent them in time. If you desire something that you can't get—then a cramp will form. You have to relax it before it distorts everything else. *Vous comprenez, mon ami? . . .*" I did understand her,' Uncle Ferdinand went on. 'She taught me that the encounter of two people is like the collision of two billiard balls: only *one* point of one touches *one* point of the other. We must never expect to know the other one entirely, nor ourselves to be known entirely by the other—that is to say, comprehended. Therefore we must never judge the entire relationship. For only a moment later, some other point of mine meets another point of yours, changing the relationship entirely. The number of possibilities is infinite. Every instant is new and without precondition—that is to say, with no rights deriving from a previous moment. Hence, every instant of rapport is a gift. Every possible next instant of estrangement is due to a change of reciprocal position that must be respected.' That," I say to S., "is what I call realism. There's something really artistic about it. I wish our politicians had it, not to speak of us writers . . ."

Schwab merely squirms. As if I'd hit him in the groin. He hears scorn and malice in every word. He believes I am out to torture him. His hand trembles so badly that his Cuba libre sloshes out of the glass before he brings it to his lips. His sensitivity provokes me to bait him. I needn't think up anything. Whatever I say elicits something from him.

I say, "I don't quite know whether I should be flattered or insulted by your suspicion that my equanimity about losing Dawn may not be genuine. That it is only feigned to camouflage dramatically different feelings." (I intentionally use the word "camouflage," which is bound to provoke him.) "How little you know me! I mean, how poorly you appreciate my literary *déformation professionelle*! Don't you notice? I'm so fascinated by myself *as a case* that I haven't got a scrap of attention left for my personal feelings. I observe myself with scientific interest—I am so trivial to myself that I can afford to do this. I must ask for indulgence: regrettably, I cannot suffer, as you wish, after the loss of my beloved, because for the time being I am much too interested in what actually went on here. Anyway, it was something that didn't simply happen to me. It was something that, as you witnessed, I undertook of my own free will and with open eyes. After all, I dashed into this madness consciously and deliberately: I needed the experience. An experience, though, that was the very opposite of what you think. And yet: possessed by my foolish love for a will-o'-the-wisp, an apparition of a human being, a sheer fiction of a woman, a fata morgana of a love object, I no doubt went through something exemplary—I mean, something beautifully consistent with the *Zeitgeist*. Once again rummaging for the lost half of my life (its better half: its paster past), I was doing something in its style. Thus, not only did I repeat something, individually, but something repeated *it*self through me: the *it*, the *id* in me, part of the collective of my race, my civilization, my culture, and my time. It did what is due to be done in this time. Even in my extravagance, I was once again merely a leaf in the wind of the *Zeitgeist*—isn't that a breathtaking thought? Everything that occurred, exactly as it occurred, is typical of the time. For instance, the abstractness, the echoishness of the relationship between Dawn and myself, the experience detached from ourselves and all surrounding reality, not to mention the high symbolism of her farewell gesture, first eat the white rose and then make the sluttish request for money—simply glorious!! But you must understand," I say to friend Schwab, "that I now yearn for a less anemic reality. After so much abstraction, so much fiction, such a toying as-if, I would like to feed on raw flesh and warm blood. . . ."

I do so every evening at a honky-tonk on the Place Blanche where a troupe of delicious black women are making a guest appearance. They too perform in the Folies Bergères style of the Mistinguette and Josephine Baker era (ergo, they too revive the past), with pistachio, violet, and flamingo-colored ostrich feathers foaming on their heads and from their tailbones, with sequined corsets, and span-long stiletto heels under their sinewy feet. They hurl their wonderfully limber legs at the rotating colored lamps under the ceiling, as if they were trying to yank them out of their hip joints. They bend their pelvises forward and backward and around with such sharp, grotesque contortions that one involuntarily bends with them, vibrates with them in the reflexes of an erotic shadowboxing. Their solid, fine-tipped breasts jiggle like rubber, and the lianas of their arms intertwine and unravel to the intertwining and unraveling saxophone voices of the Dixie band accompanying them. In short, they are worthy of admiration. I tell S., "Worthy of ad-miration. You have to come and see them, ab-solutely!"

He doesn't need to be asked, he latches on to me anyway, he never leaves me unguarded for even an instant. This suits me fine: I've already left a small fortune with the black beauties anyway; I've borrowed the money from the clerk at the George V. God's and the movie piglets' providence will see to it that he gets the money back. In any case, for now, S. has the honor of paying the bills.

He does so with blatant pleasure. After all, something's being given to him. The spectacle offers scenes that you won't catch anywhere else. For example, on the very first evening, the third from the right in the chorus line, a particularly sinewy and well-proportioned chorine, was irritated by her left-hand neighbor (softer, taller, more voluptuous), presumably because of the attention I paid the latter—an incessant torrent of flowers, a gigantic, sky-blue teddy bear, champagne between the numbers, whereby, needless to say, I drew the general attention of the audience to her. Finally, at the end of the performance, it was time for the star parade and the artistes were presented by name, each one stepping forward and curtseying to our applause. The sinewy girl calmly waited for my favorite to bow and me to unleash universal jubilation (the pimps and beatniks and tourists attending the spectacle were amused by my clowning). Then, upon being called, the irritated chorine stepped forward very prettily, curtseyed, and then sprang back with the agility of a monkey—planting the stiletto heel of her strapped shoe on the naked toes of her voluptuous colleague. The victim folded up in pain like a penknife.

Needless to say, the aggressor was the one I took home that evening (to the apartment in the rue Jacob that I had been keeping for months to welcome Dawn at her rueful return). I did not comfort the victim until the next evening. And needless to say, S., in his old rattletrap VW with double-H (Hanseatic Hamburg) license plates, tagged along both times. He pursued us straight across Paris to the Rive Gauche, even though I finally got sick of it and had fun steering my Ferrari very fast along the boulevards with lots of side streets, from which another car might legally shoot out at any moment. But S. behaved courageously, downright heroically. He would not give in until he'd seen my Ferrari parked in the rue Jacob.

There was a third and fourth nocturnal drive (after all, the troupe had sixteen beautiful, coffee-brown girls), and we didn't have an accident until the fifth time. I had just barely squeaked through a traffic light when it changed from yellow to red. S., not far behind me, lost his nerve and slammed his heavy Teutonic foot on the brakes. He failed to notice that some guy in an old 204 was practically tailgating him—an atavistic hunting instinct, as we know, aroused by an apparently fleeing object. The yokel smashed right into S.'s rear.

I halted and backed up. Nothing much had happened, thank goodness. Just a lot of noise and banged-up metal. No one was hurt. S. complained about a whirring in his head, but then the old boy had been boozing rather heavily. It was a miracle he had been able to drive at all. The cars were wrecked, of course. The engine in S.'s Beetle had been shoved into the back seat, the hood of the old 204 was arched up. But it was three A.M. and no one cared about precise details. So the matter was settled on the spot and without the police. The two drivers exchanged insurance numbers and encouraging pats on the back while I interpreted. Then I loaded S. into the (rather narrow) back seat of the Ferrari.

That evening, for variety, I had made my choice from the audience rather than the troupe: something unusually exotic, also coffee-brown but pure French (whereas the troupe came from Jamaica), extraordinarily elegant and expensively perfumed, luxuriously hung with real jewelry (discernible by the nasty flashing of the pure-water diamonds), yet quick, witty, obviously of above-average intelligence, yet also over-lifesized, with mammoth thighs and the gigantic face of a merry-go-round moor—and she called herself Princess Jahovary! I found her fascinating. "Isn't she fas-cinating?" I said to S. after picking her up (she was with some suspiciously chic cocktail-party types, but I quickly maneuvered her away from them and to the bar). She obviously enjoyed me too. She said she was an agent for popular music, a record manufacturer. Not a kept woman, as the diamonds had led me to think. We drank two or three whiskeys at the bar. Then it was time to go. I took her by the arm and waved good-bye to S. (as on the previous nights). And as on all previous nights, he hurriedly paid the check and plunged after us into the Russian roulette of side-street traffic. The fact that he was shot down from behind was (as John would say) tough luck.

The one who really took it amiss, however, was the chocolate-coated

Princess Jahovary. She wanted to get out when I wedged my dazed friend S. past her fullness into the back seat. She asked me to see her to the nearest taxi. When I told her we were only a few minutes from the rue Jacob, she acted as if this were the first she'd heard that I intended to bring her there, and she staunchly demanded that I drive her to the sixteenth arrondissement, where (typically) she resided. Nor would she hear of my first dropping S. at his hotel. So I drove her to the sixteenth arrondissement. Slowly and carefully, at her express wish. She was not just vexed, she was downright furious. *"Un bel caratteraccio!"* I mumbled to myself. She asked me where I had learned Italian. I said that knowing several languages was not always a sign of a good education but often merely the leftover of a checkered career. And did she, as Princess Jahovary, speak Rumanian? No, she said, her mother had never spoken it to her. And her father? "He was American." Aha. No further comment.

But her anger had obviously cooled and she was cheery again. An Aries, no doubt? She blithely admitted it. S. had fallen asleep in the back. He had probably drunk a lot more than I realized. He was snoring and we laughed.

When we arrived at her building (a ponderous Second Empire façade, the thick leaded-glass panes of the entrance door safeguarded by numerous iron-rod flourishes crowned with brass buttons), she became affectionate but refused to ask me up. Nevertheless, we had something of an erotic scrimmage, and since S. appeared to be fast asleep in the back, we were not exactly cautious. I complimented her on her beautiful lips and said I'd love to give her a white rose to munch on—and she must have misunderstood, for she took me at my word, even though the bud was really cyclamen-colored.

I don't know what came over me. In any case, I felt a particular pleasure with this mountain of chocolate-brown flesh in jingly jewelry and a Balenciaga *tailleur* and sporting the ridiculously arrogated name of a Rumanian princess. Perhaps it was something utterly subliminal, the perverse notion that I was morally ravishing something abstruse, a sideshow curiosity like the Trunk Lady or Sheila the Elephant Girl. But whatever, I behaved quite uncontrolledly, moaning loudly and grinding my teeth. Finally, unable to hold back any longer, I bit her mahogany neck so that she too emitted a series of tiny, lustfully painful cries. Then, very confused, she fled into her mammoth burgher palace, and I drove S. to his hotel.

Wher, we arrived, he was sitting bolt upright in the back seat, to my astonishment, and his eyes were open. He didn't say anything. Nor did I. Finally, not without effort, he crept out of the car, trudged around it, stuck his head in at my window, took my hand in his two hands, squeezed it ardently, and said emotionally, "Thank you! Oh thank you!" Shaking my hand, he kept repeating, "Thank you! Oh thank you!" Then he vanished in the hotel entrance. I drove through the dead streets to the George V. It was four A.M. and the dawn was budding. At eleven, he rang me. He had made up his mind to fly back to Hamburg.

I drove him to the airport. He showed no sign of remembering anything. I even had to give him a blow-by-blow description of his accident, although he did understand that his car was wrecked and he had done what was necessary to have it towed away. We drank a farewell whiskey at the bar. When his flight was announced, the tears gushed into his eyes. He could barely speak. He held my hand again and stammered, "Thank you! Thank you for everything!" Shortly before going through the gate, he turned back to me once more, reached into his pockets, and hauled out fistfuls of bank notes, which he pressed into my hand: "Adieu! And thank you! Farewell! Adieu!"

That's how *reality* presents itself to me.

□   4   □

SO THAT WAS my friend S.'s last visit to Paris—in fact the last time I ever saw him. He flew back to Hamburg, where by means of a devious combination of alcohol with every kind of upper and downer he inveigled Mother Nature into sparing him the embarrassing circumstance of a suicide. Within a few months he succeeded. By the end of December of that same year (1964) he was dead.

You, Mr. Brodny, will probably fail to respect him because of this. Please bear in mind what a delicate case he was. Even when I first met him in Hamburg in 1948, he couldn't get over how unpredictable mankind was and how confused the world. A Gottfried Benn fan, you see. A Benn reader believes in the power of the mind. Of course, he knew about the mind's vulnerability. I wonder how he would have endured the present (and with it the ever more clearly looming future). How would my image have changed in his eyes? I am not speaking about the curious fact that the chocolate-brown giantess was to be Dawn's successor in my heart and my ardent mistress for two years before she too passed away. By the way, her mother really was a Rumanian princess and called Jahovary. But more about that later.

As for the confusion of the world: even the documentary value of jottings like those presented above is questionable. I have in my possession certain papers (along with many more, which were meant to serve literary purposes) concerning Schwab's visit to Paris a year before the visit just described. At that time, I made a point of opening his eyes a little to the childish expectations he came here with whenever he fled Hamburg and its philistinism (then his regularly plunging into a spiritual low when he went home, an abyss with an alcohol pond waiting for him at the bottom). In short, I took care of him.

This was not a completely pleasurable business. It really upset me, I can tell you. He was already rather groggy when he came from Hamburg came after me: his chubby German hand reaching out for Mama's apron string. I picked him up at Orly. If a first glance was not enough to tell what a state he was in, then he would have betrayed it on the ride to his hotel in the rue de l'Université. (Besides, I was trying to drive at a snail's pace, as much as the curses and shaking fists from the vehicles around me permitted: Parisians prefer fluidity in traffic, as you know.)

Schwab's baggage had gone astray; it had been flown somewhere else—I believe to Caracas. Running around after it, waiting for hours and filling out loss forms and insurance questionnaires, had reduced him to hysteria. I had to bombard him with nonstop gin-and-tonics to prevent an outburst. He was wearing a heavy turtleneck sweater (not a Hanseatic outfit but, with corduroy slacks and a beret, the guild costume of German intellectuals in the fifties, which costume he carried on into the sixties—typical of people who live in the past but consider themselves avant-garde!). He was wet with sweat like a beaver just out of the water; it was October, but as warm as summer. During the drive (his fingers clutching the edge of the dashboard, his nose pasted flat against the windshield, beads of sweat on his upper lip), he told me he had had a row with Scherping. About me, but originally about Nagel—an unspeakably ridiculous business:

He had had a few weeks of intense, highly stimulating work while on the wagon (had even seriously thought of finally beginning his own book) when Nagel came along with something that caused him profound embarrassment. Nagel entrusted him with the one hundred and fifty opening pages of a new novel (the seventeenth in sixteen years) for a first reading, with an urgent request for absolute secrecy, especially in regard to Scherping. He, Nagel, was fed up with the renowned (Hemingway-like) directness of his narrative art and had tried a stylistic experiment that he wanted to present to Scherping only when he was sure it worked. *Magari!* In reading these pages, Schwab plunged into abysmal melancholy and hence into a battery of Saint-Émilion 1957, which I had once brought to him in Hamburg—two dozen bottles. It was a smooth, mannish wine, not all too heavy and yet full of strength, a true friend and comforter. Nevertheless, during the first dozen bottles, he did not dare venture out of the house, because he feared (correctly, no doubt) that Nagel was lying in wait to hear his verdict. He was living on old rolls and liverwurst and a tiny remnant of cheese, and he wouldn't answer the phone when it rang. Schelmy, his secretary, had been told to spread the news that he had gone to Bückeburg. (Why Bückeburg of all places is still unclear.)

By the time he came to the second case of wine, he was no longer able to leave the house. He lay on the sofa under a pile of rustling manuscript pages and had no intention of ever standing up again. But he had got enough nerve to act—albeit not enough to look Nagel in the eye or even call him and tell him man to man what he thought of the form and content of his work in progress. (Even now, at my side, telling me the story, his goggle eyes widening in fear of what he thought was dangerous driving, he expressed himself rather evasively.) He did not want to write to Nagel; a letter would be too formal, too callously depersonalized, and also too blatant an admission of his cowardice (*déformation professionelle*: the written word reduced to a sheer defense barricade and we withdraw behind it). So, in order to show that he was a warmhearted friend, a sympathetic human being, and even in need of sympathy himself, and also to demonstrate his fine detachment from the message itself, he selected the up-to-date device of the tape recorder—a flight into abstraction for which he would pay dearly.

Ingenious man! With the timbre, the brio, the tremolo of his abstracted voice (a voice at anyone's disposal, so to speak), he hoped to express all the things that would excuse his lack of enthusiasm. Not the words but the voice alone was supposed to document his sincere interest, the honesty of his involvement, his conscientious perusal of the manuscript, the ordeal of reaching a verdict given the complex situation; likewise his admiration of the risk Nagel had taken, his hope that a second, carefully composed attempt might lead to eventual success. . . . In words, this sounds quite discouraging, you know; but the voice ought to quiver in paschal promise, expressing everything that the meager word distorts; and yet, forty-eight hours of isolation and the thirteenth bottle of wine gummed up his speech faculties, including the use of his vocal cords, rather badly. The first tape, he now surmised, must have sounded faltering. It probably consisted mostly of pauses, heavy breathing, tortuously begun and hastily concluded verbal digressions, frequent harrumphs, coughs, sudden spluttering assurances of sympathy—in short, everything that would make Nagel impatient and annoy him in the extreme when he heard it—all this interspersed with the annoyingly undefinable noises of a smoker, matches being struck and cigarettes being put out too energetically in an ashtray, new cigarette packs furiously ripped open (his fingers already trembling violently; this increased the softness, anxiety, femininity, sensitivity of his hands, which, by the way, were very beautiful), and of course the clinking of glasses and bottles, gurgling, splashing, swallowing. (And Nagel had been abstinent for years now, never even touched a woman anymore, in order to devote himself entirely to his art— like that little Algerian painter, late at night at the bistro counter behind the Place Pigalle: "*Je donne tout cela à mon art!*")

For all that, the first tape was a highly interesting acoustic document. I proposed that he get it back from Nagel and send it as an experiment in avant-garde music to the Donaueschingen Festival.

But my suggestion did not have the liberating effect that one hopes for from humor. Schwab remained afflicted, bewildered. He was brooding about the sequel.

He moaned. It must have been at around the fifteenth or six-teenth bottle (the fortieth minute on tape) that he finally got down to the nitty-gritty—namely, the difficulty, nay, virtual im-possibility, of writing today. Writing in general and novels in par-ticular. The insane presumptuousness of writing novels after Joyce. And certainly niting wrovels, hmm, excuse me, of, clink clink clink, blubblubblubblub clink swallow-swallow-swallow, heavy breathing, of writhing navels thorough-attack-of-whoop-ing-cough clink clink in a totally sanforized pardon me standard-ized society. And at this point, he felt he had to come to Nagel's request. But now he feared he might have already pronounced a scathing condemnation of Nagel's experiment. (Indeed, Schelmy later claimed that it did sound like one.) And so he quickly began to flog his theme, but then he lost the thread of the argument as well as his temper, becoming very offensive, even insulting—but that, thank goodness, was articulated only to the extent that the seventeenth and eighteenth bottles permitted. Besides, he had al-ready been in the dream dimension of slow motion for a long time. Still, he had enough strength left to call up Schelmy and, in a slurred voice, to tell her to pick up the tape and deliver it to Nagel promptly, and not to listen to a word of it or breathe a syl-lable about it to Scherping. After that, he was unconscious for forty-eight hours—he was a strong man.

Fortunately, I do not have to introduce Nagel or Scherping to you, honored Herr Doktor J. G. Brodny. (Doctorate from the University of Czernowitz? German faculty? Improbable; more likely Berlin, late twenties, non-racist intellectuals' paradise of the "doomed system-era," as the Nazis would later call it; degenerate art; Art Déco. Fluorescence of the already rotten *Geist. Roman-isches Café.* But that would require a whole biography, with the migration story, so let's omit the "Herr Doktor.") In any case, you are familiar with both Nagel's irascibility and Scherping's vacillating hysteria. (After all, I had a carefully considered reason for imagining you as being partly clued in and familiar with the milieu—whereby it occurs to me that you may know about the incident I'm describing. But that wouldn't matter much.) Thus, I can save myself the trouble of depicting what happened to Nagel when he played the tape. . . . In our early period, during the Hamburg ice years right after 1945, when Nagel and I were still friends, and he still drank our home-brewed beet schnapps in manly nonchalance, he once, as impetuous as ever (a Sagittarian), almost swallowed an Alka-Seltzer tablet (black-market item, back then) without water. I picture his reaction to Schwab's tape as rather similar. The foaming Nagel instantly hopped into the car (button gear for amputees) and fetched up at Scherping's home, brakes screeching. Together with the chief bookkeeper, the head of production, and the sales manager—three solid German men with correct haircuts—and with Schelmy as a witness, they listened to Schwab's tape. Needless to say, Scherping swore on a stack of Bibles that he would finally can this editor, an increasingly uncontrollable drunkard; he would dismiss him on the spot without notice or severance pay; he would drive him in disgrace from the publishing house. (Nagel allegedly demanded this, and indeed it occurred six months later.)

However, what occurred the next day was something that S , in turn, did not have to depict for me—*conosco i miei polli.* When Schwab showed up at the publishing firm, he was *not* bewildered, crestfallen, intimidated—as now, here, at my side, in the Paris lunchtime rush hour (he did not know the meaning of fear, only fantastic anxieties, such as the anxiety of my killing him in my car). Oh no, in Hamburg he behaved quite differently. Towering upright and gazing straight ahead into space, disdainfully slamming doors with his barbed, accentuated "Good morning!" he popped up in Scherping's office, still half plastered and irritated by an acid stomach, angrily craving beer, his rumbling belly filled with leonine courage that recently (just when?) had spurred him to some daring deed he simply couldn't recollect no matter how hard he tried (a tape? but what had he done with it? he hadn't sung on it, had he?). At first, Scherping was speechless. Completely.

Completely and with dark bliss, I assume. For that was exactly the situation he had been hoping for, had been imagining all along, the bloody masochist. ("If you only knew to what farfetched and insidious lengths we go to get our pleasure," he once confessed to me.) Finding himself powerless before an underling whom he intended to push around, being tormented, humiliated, treated like a little pile of shit by him—that was a night of love. And Schwab was the very man whom Scherping dreamed of for the part. Far, oh ineffably far, far more sly, stealthy, secretive than even the most severe woman: he was the Father in his heavy demonic nature, the Dostoevskian *starost* in his dark power. (Just imagine Schwab when the Slavic strain—his mother's maiden name was Mietschke—began to predominate in his bespectacled Luther-head. "A mountain with a stormy peak," Schelmy once said, frightened but poetic.)

And if I knew my duck, he must have gone along with the part that was offered him, the old slut. . . . In any case, he said it never came to an argument between him and Scherping about the Nagel affair. Before the subject could come up, he declared rather brusquely that he could no longer work for Scherping if he was not granted an appreciable sum to encourage the projects of certain authors. Scherping, who smelled a rat, asked, "Which authors?" pleasurably lying in wait. Schwab named not Nagel, as expected, but *me.* Scherping screeched out his fury into Hamburg's anemic autumn air. (It was the time of the asters, and Schelmy had opened the window on Rothenbaumchaussee to let in a bit of afternoon sun.) Now, his fury was vented against me. For fourteen years, raged the suffering, pain-loving publisher, he had been waiting for my manuscript. The multiple advances were reaching astronomical heights. Meanwhile, he raged on, I had absolutely no intention of writing even one more line of the novel, I was still prostituting myself disgracefully with movies. If he, Scherping, took the bait and forked over a new advance, the recurrent and promising beginnings I kept sending in would cease altogether.

Well, and so forth. An old and—alas!—all too true litany, after which a completely unleashed Scherping vanished for special treatment with Gisela, in Hooker Alley. S., however, hopped the next plane to Paris.

And now here he was. In shock treatment because of my drag-race-driving (yet I can swear I drove no faster than normal, even

if S. maintained that the curses and shaken fists had been provoked by my inconsiderately cutting, dangerously passing, and
illegally squeezing into gaps in the lines of cars). He clutched the
dashboard, longed for his baggage, and perspired.

I had to stop at the Deux Magots—one hundred and fifty yards
from his hotel—because he needed another gin-and-tonic to
moisten his glands. Before I could catch him again, he dashed
across the boulevard to the nearest drugstore. Meanwhile I got
entangled in an exceedingly unpleasant argument with a motorized policeman sporting an insect-head helmet (Death's mes-
senger in Cocteau's *Orpheus*) who was trying to flush me out of
my parking space. Then S. came back with a bulky armload of
big and little boxes; generously littering the street with wrappers
and bits of cardboard (and ignoring the now acute risk of becoming a traffic casualty), he pulled out vials, phials, and tubes and
stowed them away in his baggy trouser pockets.

In the hotel in the rue de l'Université, after demanding the
room in which Oscar Wilde had died (it was a different one each
time), he gobbled up pills from his bare palm the way insane
Nebuchadnezzar devoured grass. Even before we went for breakfast in the Rose de France on the Île de la Cité (he loved the little
square that opens up to the monument of Henry IV on the
bridge), he quickly had to down yet another gin-and-tonic. Now
he was staggering along in wavy lines, which he occasionally interrupted with a surprising sidestep. We ordered some *rosé
d'oignon* for our meal, and he used it first to wash down another
handful of very tiny, nasty-looking tablets. Then, as he told me
with a sigh of relief and a bitterly twisted mouth, he was sufficiently fortified to let Paris collapse upon him.

This was my moment. This was what I had been waiting for. I
affected a bored mien. I said indolently, almost casually, "It's
grand that you're here—to welcome you in posh Hamburg par-
lance. After all, stopping cold-turkey could lead to withdrawal
symptoms, mightn't it, psychological disturbances due to a sudden change of environment. Anyway, grand that you're here, as I
said. But don't expect too much from the therapeutic effects of a
sojourn in Paris. What you see before you here—this sun-dappled,
life-teeming Paris, this energetic, challenging city with its tre-

mendous traffic and busy crowds, a city of noble tradition, of course, a French reality beyond any doubt, this shiny world that allows you only to be a marveling, admiring spectator—is nothing but a myth you have brought with you. Imported from Hamburg-on-the-Elbe. Sheer deception. Another attempt to drag the past into presence. The actual truth looks slightly different.

"When they're making a movie, and they want to give a modern cityscape a period character, they sometimes take small cardboard cutouts painted naturalistically—walls, merlons, gingerbread eaves, gables, oriels—and attach them to the camera lens, replacing or concealing whatever is missing in reality or destroys the illusion. That is, whatever does not fit in with the desired representation. Photographed together, the real city and the cutouts yield the intended image perfectly.

"I am expressing myself graphically enough, aren't I? I mean, it would be wrong if you had the idea that this is a solid, closed world, a world of Frenchmen, to which you find no entrée because you yourself, as a German true to his cliché, are too formless, too weightless, too nebulous. On the contrary, you have to realize that here, beyond the cutout of Paris that you carry before your eyes, evolution has taken a step into another state. This different state of things doesn't allow you to communicate, because it's you—yes sir, you, yourself—who has too clear a form, is made of too solid material, flesh, bone, a turtleneck sweater, corduroy pants. In short, it's *you* who are too much alive. An act of dematerialization has taken place here, in Paris, to which we have not yet attained. A rarefaction of matter, as when water is transformed into steam. The molecules have moved apart, making contact and communication impossible—not really for psychological reasons but purely for physical reasons.

"I grant you, it's not easy to accept this. The city of Paris is constructed of hard stone. The French are a hard people. Their roots vein the rock beneath their soil, a fine soil, a rich earth that brings forth wheat and wine grapes in abundance, and, one would think, an earth whose children are cheery, sociable, bighearted. But no, they have stony faces, their souls are frozen in the glacial coldness of a national culture that produces instant classics, that emits each classic with a helmet, a shield, and a spear, like Pallas

Athena springing full blown from the brow of Zeus. They still have the gift of form, these French. They think and speak nothing but beautiful petrifacts. When they laugh it sounds like pebbles clattering. . . . And if one is not made of stone as they are (and is a pederast in the bargain, for along with a few exotics, a couple of Balkanese, and some Russian Jewesses, pederasts are the ones who make the stone circus here dance to their tune), if someone does not belong to their stony world, he is simply ground down into sand. Soon he no longer exists, no longer finds himself present, finds only rubbish left over from himself, *materia prima* of which he once was made, now pulverized, scattered. He is no more than a humming in his own skull. Well, that is true, and yet it's just another illusion again. Reality is paradoxically the reverse. The stones are of a lighter matter than even what remains of you. For all this is utterly abstract. It takes place in the concrete, but so implausibly, so absurdly, so unconnected with nature, that only lunatics can accept it as reality.

"Granted, you have problems with the language. This leads to even greater deceptions and misconceptions. Despite eight years of school French, eight years of studying this beautiful language that institutions of humanistic learning count among the living languages, and that is as alive as the grillwork on a Gothic church window—despite eight years of French, you, a highly educated man, can manage in this language only to claim proudly that you are the state, and not much more. And there's little one can do with that nowadays, the state being the most controversial institution in the modern world. Here, you are restricted to the purely optical; that is, so to speak, to the zoological.

"Here in Paris, you see mainly Frenchmen. Well, for all his national characteristics, a Frenchman looks as universally human as any other exemplar of the White Race. All in all, the French are an important, probably the most important, nation in Europe. If one is mute with the French, it is not just for reasons of linguistic ignorance—if you will forgive that expression—but out of admiration. Unfortunately, this obtains most of all for the French themselves. In spite of all their chattering, they are mute with admiration for themselves, I swear to you: you could be as eloquent as Cyrano de Bergerac, but your chatter would never succeed in snapping the French out of this admiration. You could never wake them up. They live in a kind of trance—not merely a different state of consciousness but a different state of biological existence.

"You have come to Paris in vain, dear friend. Encounters such as you may have envisaged (Goethe runs into Lavater: 'You?'— 'Me') do not occur here, not even as a hostile collision. And it is no advantage to you that a Frenchman can identify you as a *boche* a kilometer away; forgive me for saying so. It does not even bring you hatred, which, after all, would be a relationship of some kind, even if in the negative, so to say.

"Not even the aggression normally and subconsciously released by the collective mind against old archenemies (I mean the aggression that once acted as Keeper of the Seal for such tensions in old Europe, so that one could call it the 'Sinfonia of Nations'), not even this ancient human feature emerges here. This cannot be good in the long run, my friend. I worry about our dear old continent. You feel like a stranger here, all right. As if you had been cast ashore on a different star, a different world, which makes the lotus eaters seem your nearest kin. Do you believe you are the only person who feels like this?

"No, no, I tell you: the sense of being fundamentally alien here, of finding oneself on a different planet, among Martians, is not restricted to us non-Frenchmen, us foreigners, us transients in Paris. Some fifteen million native Parisians and purebred Frenchmen share that feeling with us. Just about everyone here lives on a different star. Simply through the abstraction of this French world, which immunizes the individual against immediate humanity. Believe me, friend, it won't help you to truck through the streets in your still-earthly constitution, with good German fat on your belly and beer-thickened blood in your veins. One doesn't inveigle one's way into life here by being conspicuous. Take me, for instance: I am certainly anything but a run-of-the-mill type in these surroundings—true, I'm not exactly striking, but at least I can't be easily classified, readily placed in an ethnic category. I'm rather shapeless, amorphous. An ethnic jellyfish, as it were. A non-Frenchman with no pronounced racial characteristics or identifiable accent (since I don't give my diction the broadness of padded American shoulders, as certain other people can). Fitting in with no ethnological cliché and yet easily made to fit any at all, I can pass as a European, anyway. Whenever I find it too difficult to explain why I am not the child of any fatherland, too difficult to cite my confused background and the requisite facts about the ethnic, geographic, and historical conditions of Central Europe, then, I can get away with calling myself a White Russian, Dutchman, Swiss, North Italian, or Irishman. But not a Frenchman, for God's sake. So one cannot deny there is something blatantly different about me.

"Now, one might think I could easily get lost in the crowd here, on the much-celebrated Paris boulevards, which, as we all know, sport the dregs of the melting pot and carry the scum of mankind as if it were the head on a glass of pilsner beer, though I don't stand out in any way, either in clothing or in conduct, though I am not visibly stunted or crippled, not spastic or mongoloid, and though I don't have an obvious nervous tic—an angular jerking of the head out of the shirt collar, or even a sneering sidelong twist of the mouth, tightening the nostrils and giving them a deathly pallor; in short, though I am conspicuous by being inconspicuous, as it were, yet anyone coming toward me stares at me in order to tell me that I am a stranger. Mind you, not physically a stranger. Forget that. Yet I am essentially, substantially, and fundamentally foreign. I am nevertheless no more foreign than anyone else. I'm a stranger because this is a world of strangers. In short, a tench world.

"The stares of the people coming toward me are neither curious nor disapproving nor even hostile, but certainly not pleasant or friendly. All they express is complete indifference. But they want me to feel this indifference. As if I were supposed to realize that I am not worth so much as a shrug, even as an alien. Just like any fellow Frenchman. *On se fout de nous, monsieur,* because it's intrinsic in the French national character. *On se fout de nous comme on se fout de tout le monde.* They don't give a fuck about us *parce qu'ils se foutent d'eux-mêmes.* And they want us to know it.

"Let's face it, friend. We are devoid of a physiognomy, so far as they are concerned. We could run around without a face, as if painted by Magritte: a patch of blue sky with a cumulus cloudlet between hat and coat collar. But the French seem eager to make us aware of the abstract manner in which we exist here without existing for them, the abstract manner in which they too exist here without existing for one another: optically experienced not as human faces but as physiognomic splotches in the continuously and nervously altered, shifted, changing mosaic of the city; flesh-colored swabs in the torrent of hundreds of thousands of nonexistent coexisters on the streets, avenues, boulevards, and promenades; the flotsam of detached anatomical parts—a pair of eyes, an ear, a nose, a tuft of hair (lots of hair recently, long smooth curly kinky bushy shaggy matted hair), a bald pate, an extremely beautiful wart, the amazing craquelure of veins in a drunkard's cheeks, the scrotum-like bags under a rich dowager's St. Bernard eyes, the ludicrous drama in an intellectual's knitted brow ... drifting rubbish, as I said, lamentable testimonies to earlier human presence in a flooded area. The inundating element in which all these things float is the French national awareness. And now I ask you: is this a suitable price to pay for an all too weighty heritage of form? ...

"Have you ever figured out how I really live here? Enviably naturalized, right? A true-blue Parisian. Chives in my soup. Greeted like a long-familiar person by the hotel clerk, by the concierge in the rue Jacob, by the waiters at the Flore and the Deux Magots, by the newsdealer at the corner stand, by the greengrocers in the Marché Buci. Granted, a long-familiar person with whom, for ten years now, they have never exchanged more than sporadic sentences about the weather and the lousy political situation. Of course, I also know a few Parisians who belong to a less accessible category. All kinds of movie people, not only the aloof creative ones but also the solid business kind: distributors, theater owners. I also know a lawyer, a banker, why, even pillars of culture, for instance an art dealer, a publisher, a museum director. We call each other 'cher ami,' we invite each other out for lunch or dinner, with wives, if you please. My captivating way with the ladies even gets me invited to people's homes. I send flowers, exchange hugs, we drink aperitifs, I shine, I fondle the kids, the maid, I praise the food, admire the family porcelain, the wine, the elegant furnishings, I piss into the family bathroom sink, dry my hands on Monsieur's towel, brush my hair with Madame's brush—why, greater intimacy cannot be imagined, except of course the ultimate one. But that too has occurred, yes indeed. One has exchanged lewd tendernesses with the wives, *même dans le lit matrimonial.* The husbands were away. But even then, one parted with the feeling of having rid oneself of a burdensome obligation. At least with a sense of relief that one wouldn't have to go through the same thing again for another six months.

"I go out of town a lot, unfortunately. Still, I come back regularly, and then I may possibly have folkloristic experiences that make it seem as if some forgotten corners of existence still had the exciting vividness that, before losing the first half of my life, I once assumed was naturally present and profuse everywhere. For instance, my aforementioned concierge in the rue Jacob evidently couldn't stand watching me suffer over Dawn, so she invited me to her niece's wedding in some almost rustic *banlieue* out near Le Bourget. And there I could sniff the warm, wine-soured, garlic-sharpened breath of the common people. Since then, I say hello to every street cleaner I see because I imagine he might have been one of my fellow celebrators from that festivity. We ate and drank gargantuanly. We whirled in waltzes, swinging tubs of sweaty female flesh laced up to an ironclad roundness. We avowed our mutual friendship and banged each other so hard on the back that our tonsils slid out through our teeth. Here too, of course, it came to lewd business with one of the bridesmaids, a girl in her thirties and hence short of breath during the inspection of erogenous zones. We made a date to get to the bottom of the matter, but naturally I didn't show up. I'm sorry now, although one must be cautious in such matters. The *animal triste post coitum*, you know, is especially dangerous here in Paris; one gets the craziest ideas.

"I remember a girl sitting at the next table in the Flore. I had been ogling her for a while, not only because her profile was vaguely reminiscent of Stella's (an Algerian Jew, presumably) but because everything about her—looks, eyes, mien—simply shrieked out her loneliness. She sat there, crushed beneath the terrifying ordeal of being human, the curse that dooms us to live in an eternally irreconcilable dichotomy: on the one hand, we are herd creatures who can't get along without one another and who are unhappy alone; and on the other hand, we hate the crowd, hate the others with all our soul; yet we suffer from being imprisoned in the cage of the self, unable to escape, unable to reach the other, unable to find salvation from ourselves. . . .

"This was so tremendously eloquent in the girl's wan face that I had to keep peeking at her. She couldn't ignore this in the long run, and when I stared very hard, she turned to me and our eyes met. At first, it was very beautiful—or would it be better to say very pure in a bleak way. We knew what we wanted from each other and what we could best expect. We were agreed without having to pretend we had come even a millimeter closer together. I motioned to the waiter and paid for my Pernod and her coffee. We exchanged the first word out on the street, to decide where we were going.

"I could have taken her around the corner to the rue Jacob. The apartment was available. Dawn had taken flight again and I had temporarily given up looking for her. But she might return at any moment. So we went to the girl's place. It was far away, near the Boulevard Extérieur.

"I don't have to describe what happened at this pad, which was unfit for human habitation. It was stereotypical, starting with the horror in her (and probably also my) eyes when we set about doing the dreadfully intimate initial manipulations of sexual intercourse, then, horridly enough (registered in full consciousness), the mutual raging, which did occur after all, and finally, the heartrending silence, which neither of us dared break, since a wrong syllable, a false tone, might have led to murder.

"Because she lived on a dead-end street and in an absurd one-way traffic tangle to boot, I had parked my car out in the boulevard. It was shortly before evening. The stores and offices had already closed, and even a nearby gas station was shut. Oddly enough, I can't remember the season. I know I didn't have a coat—but I seldom wear one, even in winter. You go from heated buildings to heated cars and than back again into heated buildings. So you don't really need a coat. But I believe it was the evening of a long summer's day. The precarious hour before darkness, when the Paris sky displays a full, an absolutely inexhaustible gamut of oppressive, heart-stopping stages of decay. The lava of cars flowed in two opposite torrents, roaring and glistening metallically along the boulevard. And there were swarms of pedestrians: the street teemed and crawled as with termites, pouring from all sides toward a black whirlpool, a vortex which, like a funnel, sucked in the thronging vermin, gulping it down in masses. The entrance to a Métro station, of course. Evening rush hour.

"This was fascinating to observe in my vulnerable spiritual state, removed from my everyday run of the mill. I stood in one spot for almost twenty minutes, watching the sidewalk shaft with its Art Nouveau frame as it sucked in humans swarming like insects. Gradually, the trickle thinned out, grew sparse, while the sky slowly receded, duller and duller, more and more spacious, backing away from the earth as though having nothing to do with it, until at last the final stragglers were sucked from the street.

"As mysteriously direct as the first star that suddenly shines in the heavens, the streetlights went on, pallidly dotting the pigeon-blue, which darkened as it flowed out into the evening. And soon the torrent of cars on the boulevard streamed out too. All at once the city was utterly silent. I stood alone in an empty world.

"Believe it or not, I found this so beautiful that tears came to my eyes. I felt like the Prodigal Son who has found his way home. I understood how very much we really are the children of this world, this world of termites; children of the artificial rocky wastes, of twilight before nightfall. . . . Oh God! the stifling courage of the wan streetlamps . . .

"I went to my car. The street was completely lifeless. One good housewife had slipped out of a building to walk her dog. She had her back to me while the dog pulled her along, the leash taut as iron, and the dog's nose sniffed and scrubbed along the piss-black edge of the sidewalk. When she heard my footfall behind her, she was so startled that she jumped and let out a noise like a valve cap being sucked shut. A man on the street at this time of night could only be her murderer.

"Now let me ask you, Johannes Schwab, whether this isn't our real home. I mean, what are you actually looking for when you come fleeing here from Hamburg-on-the-Elbe? After all, you've got enough folklore there—at least in the philistines around you, those dangerous provincials who seem to be designed by Wilhelm Raabe or Wilhelm Busch or even Wilhelm II, and who adapt themselves so well to the new termite state of mankind. You don't mean to tell me that out of sheer German *Wanderlust,* you've come from a world of *Gemütlichkeit* in order to be uplifted by a Paris that, with the pure notes of the sky, the river, and the beauty of the city, greets your mind as splendidly as the beginning of the *Eroica* and intensifies as soulfully and is as spiritually inflaming. No, no, my friend. The Paris of the Eiffel Tower and the Louvre, of the *bâteaux mouches* and alluring luxury garments in the shop windows along the Faubourg Saint-Honoré; the *bouquinistes* on the banks of the Seine, whose stalls, as we know, can be combed for bibliophilic *trouvailles* (for instance, a copy of Nagel's first novel, no?); the *ville lumière* of first-class hookers and the charming folksy eateries in Montparnasse and around Les Halles, where one can feast on delicate, garlic-dripping snails out of cans and all kinds of radioactive oysters—all this is not for our kind, it's for Americans: a super-dimensional Disneyland. People like us are looking here for something completely different: namely, THE CITY, the metropolis with all its perverse charms and exquisite terrors, above all the unreal and the surreal. The abstract and the fictitious. The as-if of the humane in the inhumane. We are intoxicated by the loss of reality here, under the bombardment of tattered impressions, the drumfire of the fragmented, the disjointed. Wasn't it Uncle Vladimir who said that 'reality' is a word that should never be used without brackets? Nowhere can we become so urgently self-aware as here in the frazzling stream of the crowd. Nowhere is our 'I' so fully shaped as in encapsulated anonymity. Only when the world dissolves into disconnected entities drifting by like flotsam in a flood—an ear, a wheel, an umbrella, a dog turd, a shop sign, a gaze—only then do we realize how grand we are. Only here can we understand that we carry the entire cosmos within ourselves, that we must become artists so as to express our inner wealth—and are even more majestic when we renounce the temptation to communicate our inner wealth. . . . Here, in the torrent of the anonymous crowd that overflows all shores, everyman is sovereign.

"Each plows his hard bow through the torrent, a figurehead of his loneliness, and gazes with stony eyes at whatever drifts past: that was you, that was what I was for you, a smashed bureau with gaping drawers between a hat and a collar, half a roof and perched on it a cat that fled up the chimney between a shock of hair and an ascot, a mouth flitting past like a weary butterfly, unhappy, angry, obstinate, earnest, dreamy, disappointed, passionate, sensitive, whining, closed upon the soundless shriek for self-realization. . . . And these, too, as you see, are merely reminiscences of art history.

"Let them pass, we are not attached to them, we are not sentimental—at least not in the long run. This too dissolves, everything dissolves into swatches, color strips, structures, patterns. It eventually turns monochrome: gray, the color of madness. . . . And don't tell me it doesn't make you feel as snug as a bug in a rug.

"But, of course, this is no vacation at a health spa to buoy up your soul so that you can go home to Hamburg fortified and endure life there for another six months. On the contrary: this place visibly sucks the marrow from your bones. It puts you into a different state, as though you were still yourself but vaporized, as it were. Instead of being made of skin and fat and flesh and bones all welded into your Jockey shorts, you are just a tiny cloud, the astral phenomenon Schwab. . . . But that is an intensification, believe me! The transubstantiation of ourselves into the abstract is an intensification. And how proud we should be that we are capable of it—this abstraction of ourselves—*without the aid of writing, without committing ourselves to paper*! The others who write, and whom we so greatly admire—what are they if they do not realize themselves on paper? For example, your friend Nagel, *our* friend Nagel, if you insist. He's a delightful fellow, after all, and a great one, isn't he? But he's important only on paper. Tolstoy was a creep, Proust a fop, Joyce a stigmatized petit bourgeois—if you take off his glasses and comb his hair to the side, he looks like Hitler. But on paper, oh my! What demigods they are!

Do you follow me? Or am I too muddled—this wine has more of a kick than one thinks. Also, I'm alone so much here that I'm not used to talking, especially in German. If you think my words are swarming like flies on the dung heap of my thoughts, then please tell me so, I'll shut up. . . . No? You're much too kind! Well, as I was saying—an abstruse notion, you will think: the crystalline hardness of the French, their quality of being formed, their capacity for form . . . all this must be due simply to this abstraction and transubstantiation into a different state of density. . . . Perhaps a human being first truly realizes his potential in pure abstraction. After all, the most forceful human image is, no doubt, that of the man at Hiroshima whose silhouette was burned to stone by the atomic flash. . . .

"So, keep a stiff upper lip! Walk on with your senses alert in a tench France, wander with your senses open to nothingness through this beautiful bright world that is Paris, or rather this beautifully abstract overworld. . . . You know, the thing that has always made photography (the invention most expressive of the *Zeitgeist*) dear to me is the dialectics of positive and negative—don't you agree?—whereby particularly the latter is informative. For instance, I heard a little story here that articulates the terror of a certain German past in the negative, so to speak. The story was told to me by a tiny homosexual Jew who managed to escape from Berlin in 1939 just before the war broke out. He was sixteen years old at the time. Well, just before he fled, he went into a pissoir in Charlottenburg with a big Jewish star on his jacket, which he tried to conceal, as best he could, beneath his lapel. A moment of twofold relief—gratefully enjoyed—but then a tremendous shadow suddenly fell on him. He looked up: next to him, a gigantic SS-man in uniform was unbuttoning his fly. The SS-man looked down at him and said: 'You're a Jew, aren't you?' Our little homosexual could only nod. The SS-man: 'Well, then, c'mon, gimme a kiss!' . . . But I forget why I wanted to tell you the story—ah yes, of course: because you presumably wish to write about Paris; you have to make literary use of your Paris experience. Could you do so, *fairly and honestly,* knowing about such events and realities, as if the things you saw around you here were still real? . . ."

I AM GOING into such detail about these not exactly edifying incidents because, as I have said, I am in possession of some notes about them. These notes were penned by S., whom you encounter in these pages as Schwab. This is not the place to explain how I obtained them, nor do I wish to go into the matter of which varying or even contradictory descriptions of particulars are closer to the truth. Likewise, I need not expatiate on my intentions in contrasting the two notes.

Paris, October 1964. Thanks to alcohol and H.'s new pills, rather blurry impressions. We walk past the Madeleine. No longer on speaking terms. A day of agonizing tensions. I arrived by plane from Hamburg this morning. He didn't pick me up (even though Schelmy wired the arrival time). Supposedly the telegram reached his hotel too late. I'd like to believe him (but I don't). Trying to explain my embitterment to myself. Childish reason: I'd been looking forward to riding in his new car. Also, I lost my baggage. Tiresome, humiliating language difficulties (yet his fluent assistance would have embittered me even more).

The flight was very hard on me. Right at takeoff, heart problems, which kept on and then worsened unnervingly when the plane landed. Throughout the flight, the roaring P.A. system right by my left ear: "Ladies an' zhentlemen, Capitaine Malfichu and his crew welcome you aboar' our Caravelle Seine-et-Oise." P.R. vulgarity. The donkey's language drill: "At your left an' below you, ladies an' zhentlemen, you may look now on ze town of Fulda" (pronounced Faldeh). And the icy seething of the turbine, which presses toward the bull's-eye, over the backs of the herding cloud lambs as one wing rises ominously. . . . Fear, malaise, claustrophobia. I want to get up, and drop back in the seat, fettered: I forgot to unfasten the safety belt. All very ridiculous, very embarrassing. I couldn't get rid of the seething in my ears. It remained there all day long. (Dr. Hertzog is probably right; I take too many barbiturates and smoke too much; two and a half packs of Lucky Strikes yesterday—the half I had begun was empty by the time we landed. Didn't sleep at night, of course; tried to dope myself around three A.M. with a bottle of rotgut Algerian wine—no use, just a gush of stomach acid, so I doubled the dose. Only to hover among dreamy states of *Angst* and hallucinate along the brittle ridges of nightmares. Woke up around seven: pervitin. Hertzog promised me new prescriptions, but he'll give them to me only if I come back to the clinic for two weeks.)

At Orly, my suitcase was nowhere to be found. After long, torturous fumbling in French, I understood: it had flown to Tangier. Since it had been pretty cool in Hamburg, I was wearing a thick turtleneck under my jacket. Paris welcomed me, stunningly summery. I sweated like a polar bear. I couldn't eat breakfast on the plane (the Montessori kindergarten spoons and the stewardesses' robust solicitude were too reminiscent of the psychiatric ward). So I had my first coffee at the Deux Magots. Then, parching thirst. The only way I can cope with it lately is a gin-and-tonic with lots and lots of ice (it doesn't agree with me, but the immediate effect is beneficial). At my second drink, he stands before me. His eyes only graze the glass, but he's too alert not to notice that I caught his lids narrowing. He therefore says casually, "Hey, that's a great idea, I'll have one too."

Elephant-taming methods. I sense that I'll have to armor myself with great patience just to endure twenty-four hours in this place. He tries to calm me down about my suitcase. "Are you invited to a reception at the Élysée? Well, then. It makes no difference at all what you run around in. I masquerade as a luxury gigolo just so that nobody will notice how broke I am. You can buy soap cheaply here, and I can lend you a razor. If it's absolutely necessary, we can stroll over to the Boulevard Saint-Michel and spend fifty francs on three shirts and six pairs of catamite briefs."

I was irritated by his bogus linguistic nonchalance; the cheap freshness, preciosity decorated with the affectedly correct pronunciation of "Boulevard Saint-Michel" (although I'm grateful to him for not saying "Boul' Mich' "). Also, I left two manuscripts in the plane, things I'm supposed to read. He doesn't find this so awful either: Schelmy must have copies she can send me. It makes me furious: Schelmy has no copies; I took the manuscripts precisely in order to spare her such measures of solicitude; now they're lost for good (this will lead to unbelievably obnoxious arguments with Scherping).

"Maiden efforts by promising young talents?" he asks, reaching for my cigarettes. "Or even one of yours?"

For an instant, I'm alert, eager, almost delighted. What is he after? Treating me with numb-fingered caution, the way you treat a paranoiac: you clear anything out of his way that you think might anger him. A moment later, he trips me up from behind. Yet inside, he is so nervous that he trembles. I catch myself thinking, irritatedly, So he's concerned with me. I make him uneasy. Why does he put up with me? He needs me. I'm necessary to him because I work for Scherping and I can turn the faucet on and off for his advances. His writhing helplessness is poignant. His confused life grinds him down. One has to protect him.

I compliment him on his suit. I mean it honestly, but it sounds a bit venomous. (My exact words are "Once again you are almost disreputably elegant.") He smiles sneakily. It amuses me to see him wondering what he can get me with. (I anxiously await the outcome.)

We drink another gin-and-tonic (my third). Paris begins to collapse upon me. I've been here for three hours already and I still have the plane turbines seething in my ears. If I went to my hotel now, I'd tumble into bed and sleep the rest of the day away. So I drink another coffee (and take another pervitin on the sly). He ignores it. Occasionally (as if he realizes that I don't want him watching), he wraps himself up in a newspaper. I know that he scarcely ever reads the papers, nothing interests him in them. So he is only pretending to read; he puts down the paper the instant I swallow the pill. In a chatty tone he asks me about Hamburg. But I interrupt and ask how he found me. A piece of cake: he asked for me in the hotel and was told that I went out right away; the most obvious thing was to check here.

This riles me. I'm annoyed that I'm so predictable. An unimaginative provincial who arrives in Paris and can't think of anything better to do than sit on the terrace of the Deux Magots. He actually says as much quite brazenly: "Nice sitting out here, isn't it? Especially on such a lovely day. One learns quickly that you can't have it better here in Paris. Nothing is quite what it is. But everything's bursting with clues. You're being taught the as if. That guy over there, squinting so obstinately, is not Sartre, but he could be. And the gay black is not Baldwin, but he could be, and why shouldn't one take him for Baldwin? After all, the wild strawberries at Maxim's were grown in a hothouse, but that doesn't ruin the *tarte aux fraises.* On the contrary, it's what guarantees perfection. The mixture of types here is very skillfully prescribed by a public-relations firm working for the Ministry of the Interior: not inauthentic—that wouldn't seem Parisian—but simply artificial. Imagine how gladly you'd have stayed in Hamburg if there, too, the thugs and loiterers on the hooker alleys of the Reeperbahn were on fixed salaries, paid by Hamburg's Cultural Affairs Department."

These are attempts at needling me—but they are too uncandid to penetrate my skin. I feel much more lucid now: the pervitin is taking effect. But I can't stand it here anymore. I suggest a walk. The Place Furstenberg is a few yards away. ("Almost quite genuinely Parisian, especially if you bear in mind that a church tower designed by Bernard Buffet casts its shadow upon it. . . ." He's bending over backward now and frazzling my nerves.)

I have to get outdoors. I want to gaze along the Seine. We wander over to the Pont Neuf. The day is delicious; the morning fog has dissipated radiantly. But I'm sweating hard in my heavy clothes. I have to take off my jacket; I'm so badly soaked that I'm shivering. I get in a desperate temper about my body. I tell him more about my ailments and Hertzog's therapeutic method than I care to have revealed. I instantly regret it and ask him, more aggressively than I intended, why he's smiling. He asks me please to excuse him. He says that our being on the Pont Neuf reminds him of a passage in Proust: Swann, deathly ill, goes out into society once more, knowing it's the last time. He runs into Guermantes and wistfully tells him that they probably won't see each other again. Guermantes, about to move on to another reception, and only listening with half an ear, booms cheerily, *"Vous! Vous nous survivrez tous! Vous êtes fort comme le Pont Neuf!"*

I don't quite know how I'm supposed to take this anecdote, as pointed malice or as sovereign tactlessness. While I think about it, he himself realizes the ambivalence and turns it to his own advantage: he smiles insolently, as if he had deliberately led me up the garden path.

I sense that none of this is quite right, but I feel like an oaf. His unimpeachability humiliates me. He is healthy, alert, elegant. He speaks about Guermantes and Swann as if they were part of his daily circle of friends here. He reads his Proust in French. I snort in my bearskins and remember that only two hours ago at the airport, I was humiliated to see how poor my French is.

My eyes swim as I gaze up the Seine. (I still have my reading glasses on, I couldn't find the other pair in my pockets, it's probably flown to Tangier with the suitcase.) His eyes are imperturbable. For him it's an everyday scene. But, as if to show me that he feels what it means for me to be here, he makes an ironically melancholy remark and then launches into his love story—with an aloofness that is sheer stratagem: he underplays it, reduces his chaotic existence to a microscopic slide. It sounds written. The effects are precisely worked out. He arouses my curiosity. I want to find out what the truth is. I offer to go with him to the hotel where he speculates the girl is hiding.

We walk halfway across Paris (but I can't think of any other way to tire him out). At the Madeleine, we wander into the stalking-grounds of hookers who roam the area in daylight. A redhead with provocative breasts sizes us up at a glance. She spots the john in me. It doesn't elude him. He jokes: "One can smell your solidity, and my disreputableness. I'm too smug for a big spender and not authentic enough for a good pimp."

This too makes me feel clumsy and awkward. I am moving crudely and ponderously through a light world. The air here is light; the people walk more lightly, speak more vivaciously; the colors shine effortlessly and lie upon things more lightly. I love this lightness, which I do not possess. (The remedy that Hertzog gave me, without letting on what it was, put me into this lightness. I have to get H. at least to give me a hint about the pharmacological, or rather toxological, makeup: I am systematically poisoning myself.)

But the thought of it makes me light now too. My mood lightens. I feel hungry. He knows a restaurant not far from the hotel we are heading toward. A year ago, an extremely embarrassing scene with an Indian doll took place in this hotel. Incidentally, I think I remember the restaurant too: its name is Laget.

In half an hour, we are there. The food is marvelous though much too heavy. The wine is heavy too. I feel numb after the first glass. But I can still see well enough to observe how embarrassing it is that I slip off my jacket but refuse to let the hatcheck girl take it. He says a few words to her that I don't understand, but she leaves with a smile. I have the impression it was a joke at my expense. He now quite bluntly makes fun of me; he quips his way through a distasteful tirade about his religious upbringing, full of allusions that again I don't understand. (Apparently he thinks I want to propose that he write his book about theodicy, even assumes I intend to write something similar myself.) Again, I drink more than I can take. And I have to pay the bill too. It's dismayingly high, and I have trouble concealing my shock. (I do so by announcing that I want to dine here every day; I'm in a very good mood as it is; I order more wine and two *framboises* with my coffee.)

As we get up, an irritating mishap occurs. I want to say, jokingly, *"Allons, enfants de la patrie!"* (one of the few French phrases I recall from school), but I bellow out the words. I'm so startled that I almost knock the table over. The wine bottle tumbles from its basket, the remaining wine spills across the tablecloth. We walk to the hotel. He shows me the room where he lived and wrote while waiting for the girl (in a different room, one flight up) to ask for him: three o'clock at night or seven in the morning, depending on her whim or mood. If he went out, he gave the porter the most detailed information for her on where she could reach him, when he planned to return, and when he'd be at her disposal again. (With a smile, he says, "Discreetly at your service any hour of the day or night, the perfect nurse," as if he wants to recommend himself to me.)

He offers to drive me back to the Left Bank. His car is parked in a garage a few steps away on the Place des Ternes. I beg off. I'm at the end of my tether. I want to be alone. But I tell him, "If you'd like to come with me, I'm going back on foot."

He cheerfully agrees. "I'd love to." And gently takes my arm because I am about to run down a baby carriage. All along the Avenue des Ternes, he chats away at me (with constant gentle grabs at my arm to steer me past hindrances). But eventually he lapses into silence. He only asks once (when I stumble), "Shouldn't we really take a cab?" I retort that as a good German infantryman I marched all the way from the Ukraine to Mount Athos, but I get the words out only in fits and starts.

The redhead is still standing by the Madeleine. I shake him off. "Excuse me, but I think I'm going to go off with this girl."

He says, "I'll wait for you in the café over there." I feel a momentary urge to punch him in the nose. His eyes are as imperturbable as when he gazed along the Seine. But he gives the girl a small, encouraging smile. She makes a face at him: *"Salaud!"* Then she takes me by the arm.

Half an hour later I am standing on the street again, alone, slightly plundered, humiliated. I am thirsty, and, heedless of screeching brakes and invectives, I veer across the square to the café. He is waiting for me at one of the outside tables. I join him wordlessly. He doesn't speak either. I order a cognac (saying, with venomous pride in my French, *"Une fine de la maison"*). He has a drink too. The jets booming in my ears are unendurable. I see his bright, alert eyes. "Ready?" says he. I stand up (not bumping the table this time, but the chair behind me topples over and he catches it). I say, "The perfect nurse." He does not answer. He picks up the bank note I threw on the table and presses it into my hand. It is the last one the girl left me.

He heaves me into a cab. I say, "I want to be alone!" He tells the driver the address and gets in next to me. "You will sleep marvelously. Call me up whenever you like. You know, I'm waiting."

I hear myself say, "But not for my call."

He says, "For your call."

I bow and kiss his hand.

□   **6**   □

ET VOUS VOUS EN FOUTEZ, monsieur. Lei se ne frega. You couldn't give a bloody fucking shit.

And of course you're perfectly right. You're in the business. It's your century. It's your world. And I feel lost in it, that's my problem.

Only, I would like to trouble you a bit with this problem, dear Mr. Brodny. Look: as a stranger by calling, predestination, and vocation, I am accustomed to running through the world in one abstracted way or another. The pretty curtain-raiser to my unfortunately still uncompleted book surely showed that.

But now, I am speaking about Paris, dear friend—a city still at the heart of Western Civilization, one would think, and not at its extreme periphery. Yes, it may even be considered its throbbing heart; still the center of its cultural life, the spiritual termite queen of Europe. Yurop, sir. How do you spell it? Why You-Are-Oh-Pee-period. Yurop—a remote American province, as we now all know, as everyone knows, down to the last sneering oil sheikh, but nevertheless a province that is said to have been the cradle of this renowned Western Civilization, the homeland of our fathers, mothers, all our blindly self-assured, dynamic, expansive forebears. Of course you and your fellow bearers of stars and stripes know it in another way. For you it became an integrating component of the world only recently, as the theater of WW II—a vile abbreviation for a collective suicide, by the way. The *European Theater,* as it is rather characteristically known in the trade. Enter at your own risk—albeit with a guarantee of an honorable funeral even if your body parts are scattered and far flung during the spectacle. Swarm on so-called V-Days (Vee for Victory, *mon cul*) and after, as a tourist, to the *Ville lumière*. Believe me, buddy, it does make a difference whether you think of a continent as a homeland or as an operational terrain where the air is sometimes unhealthily filled with iron. For you, sons of the New World, masters of one half of the globe in your youthful freshness—for you, the charm of this strange continent named Yurop probably consisted in the liberating dynamics of the landscape of catastrophe: the panorama in which fields and forests, marshes and meadows wasted by storms of fire, battered by hailstones of iron, and shacks and castles, churches and privies are likewise smashed to rubble, and in whose yellow rivers dead cattle and household goods drift—half a roof and perched on it a cat that fled up the chimney, for instance; and so it makes no difference whatsoever where you shit cook screw play with an orphaned puppy for a short while puke up your booze or kick the bucket.

But for us, if you please, this was once the sweet core of the world, a sturdy world, a world whose morbid charm and kitschy beauty you and your kind could scarcely have come to know in their juicy freshness after the steel tempest of WW II. Despite the efforts of people who try to awaken your understanding of the values of the past by constantly evoking it, like Schwab and your humble servant, you could at best assimilate those values in Disneyland. Indeed, it was a wonderworld of many-towered cities, teeming with colorful people in colorful costumes (burghers placidly strutting about among them, the biggest one a man with a skew nose, clipped mustache, polka-dot bow tie, dachshund, and Nobel Prize, master and dog tried and tested in disorder and early sorrow). Our souls lived in that old world of the faraway times, when Nuremberg was renowned for its *Lebkuchen* and its toy boxes, not for its trials and the subsequent gallows. The times when in such ghastly places as Cologne or Coventry the gingerbread houses crowded in intricate confusion around the cute dignity of the stepped town-hall gables, shadowed by the heavenward soaring of cathedrals. When the inti-

macy of town and country would be enjoyed in an Easter promenade along the city walls (with many-voiced bells ringing for
Beethoven's deaf ears and the seductive devil playing around as
Schopenhauer's black poodle). When the vast countryside was
lovely with its silent lakes and ponds reflecting the cloud castles
of the minnesingers and the poetic Wittelsbachs on the mountains. The lead-glistening light of storm-brewing, grain-ripening
summer afternoons long ago reflecting the heaviness of our hearts;
the murmuring of brooks under alders and hazelnut bushes, from
which beautiful Melusina peers out, palely glimmering in the evening, when the birdsongs go silent and the wan sky over the forest has kindled the first star. Melusina, mind you, and not the
radioactive refuse of the nearest chemical factory . . . and Alpine
peaks, whose glaciers shine over King Laurin's rose garden and
not over the Munich–Venice highway, which even South Tirolian separatists approve of. The fragrance of firs over Fontane's
sandy marches and Stifter's timber forest of spruces, amidst the
mourning torches of cypresses at Duino and on D'Annunzio's
Versiglia shores. And Mozart, Bach, and Handel, and crisp
golden-brown Viennese *Backhendl* with fresh green salad. . . .

Right, Mr. Brodny, old pal? That was Europe for us. Or rather,
that was *we* ourselves. *We* were Europe. We carried it within us,
in our thoughts and feelings, in the self-assurance of everything
we did, the way the French carry France and the hard city of
Paris within themselves, though with the slight difference that
we, at that time, were alive, were made of flesh and blood. Europe—that was the native soil of our *style*, continuously producing new forms, our always definite, specific essence, the
this-and-no-other way of our existence.

And the many-domed, many-towered city of Paris in the glistening dragon-scale of her roof slates under the capricious sky:
she was one of the constellations by which the course of that
world was fixed. More than any other city, she was the spirit of
our spirit. She came directly from our blood as almost no other
city did. Yes, indeed, you heard correctly. I say: *we, us, our—our*
spirit, *our* blood. For I include myself, despite all the snide hardness of the French today. I consider the city of Paris not only as a
city of theirs. It still belongs to me as well. I'm conceited enough

to consider myself a child of Western civilization, albeit a found-ling, if you like, or a stepchild, since the lost half of my life mainly belongs to the half of Europe that did not pass into American hands; still, women in Kishinev did not wear veils—Pushkin hated the place, but he occasionally visited it to see classics like Racine, Molière, and Scribe. It even had an electric trolley line (not in Pushkin's time, of course, but during my childhood). I may be wrong, though: the droshkies had the same foot bells as the streetcars elsewhere, and perhaps I'm even confusing this with my memory of Jassy or Czernowitz. You can certainly cor-rect me here, Mr. Brodny.... You see, I left Bessarabia at a tender age; I was brought up in Vienna—after a fashion, admit-tedly, but still in European traditions, intellectual attitudes, emo-tional norms (intellectual errors and emotional failings, if you prefer). We never managed to establish with any certainty in which church of the Christian communities, and indeed even whether, I was baptized. But anyway I'm not circumcised. In-deed, my Viennese relatives were out-and-out anti-Semites. If my cousin Wolfgang had not died a hero's death very early in WW II, he would most certainly have occupied a high office in the SA and, after denazification, in West Germany's judiciary.... With a probability verging on certainty, I can claim to be pure Aryan, albeit not raised in the cult of Wotan. I was urged to fear God and love his sweet son—with a beard on the cross, and without a beard as dear baby Jesus. I speak four of the main European lan-guages quite fluently, plus a few less important ones (for in-stance, Rumanian and Yiddish) rather glibly. Not to mention my infamous talent for imitating any dialect in a highly entertaining fashion. I can sing songs from Hungarian, Rumanian, and Greek operettas. My Balkan culture, which I sometimes even exploited professionally, was the true substance that I gave to my formative years in Vienna. Still and all, I have read around in seven litera-tures, I eat with a knife and fork, shave daily, suffer from the same tooth decay as Tintoretto, Blaise Pascal, and Oscar Wilde. I can't simply be dismissed without further ado as a Levantine stranded in the West, some member of an auxiliary nation, like a Volhyn-ian German resettled in the Reich, a type having as great a right to asylum here as a Tartar abandoned by Barnum's international

Show of Shows. I presume to be as much at home on this side of the Elbe as on the other. By no means—I don't need to emphasize it—am I an American. I was, alas, not so consistent as you, Yankev Brodny. I did not become what our sort logically had to become after losing our other half.

And yet it happens that I have to run around in Paris as a stranger, and, on the other hand, converse with you, J.G. the American, as if you were my brother Cain! . . . I consider myself just as obstinate, just as anachronistic, as the French. And yet, dwelling among them here, I feel as if I'd been cast away among the lotus eaters. Here, Jaykob Jee, here in Paris, here in the brightest jewel in the diadem of cities that once crowned Europe, here in the one true metropolis left in Yurop, here I remain a stranger, and I become more and more of one, the more I recognize it as spirit of my spirit, form of my blood, the more intimately I find it within me, the more ingrown every pissed-on cornerstone and little pile of garbage is in me. Homeland—its scent of exhaust fumes and empty vegetable baskets, its dove-blue and lemon-yellow light, the pale salamander bellies of its scrubby plane trees, its murderous car races in the streets, its witty sky above the dragon scales of roofs along the Seine. . . . Under this sky, sir, in whose moods and whims I am greeted again by all the promise of my childhood, all the delights I expected of the world, all the yearning of my adolescence, all the urgent eroticism of my youth—under the sky of my life's other half, which I refuse to give up for lost—under this sky, I, and everything around me, including myself, become more and more abstract, more and more unreal, lose more and more density. As though the world were stretching out, spreading its material thin, flying apart in something like a universal molecular expansion. The things that were solid are starting to flow and the things that flowed are volatilizing in the ether. The Boulevard Haussmann—a white stream, shoreless like the Rio de la Plata. The Place de la Concorde—a Turner bay in which an obelisk is melting.

Do you still consider this Paris, monsieur? Do you still believe this is Pearris, Freanss, a place in the core and heart of Yurop, our old quondam Europe? Geographically at least still on this continent, built on terra firma, and not an island floating in the unfathomable depths and distances of no-man's-sea? . . . I, for my part, am no longer certain. I do not gain a foothold here. I'm lost here just as mindlessly as the German drunkard Schwab. His plight is my plight. I have nothing over him. True, I have lost half of my life, it was amputated. But I am lying when I say I have forgotten it among the lotus eaters. It is a lovely phrase that is meant to be touching, the opening phrase of a book that has never been completed. In fact, I have forgotten nothing of the blood-warm reality of the world of yesterday. I still carry my Europe within me. But a decade slips in between its image then and its image today—ten years that I likewise cannot forget, that afflict me in nightmares and daytime visions, all kinds of brutalities amid fantastic light effects, all kinds of incomprehensible events, spooky goings on, which—alas! alas!—also belonged to the all too warm-blooded living reality of the world of the past. For instance:

Salzburg, November 1938. Sheets of rain.

We have come to town from our cuckoo-clock cottage on the Mondsee. Stella is preparing to return to Rumania. John, entrusted with mysterious diplomatic missions, has left us to our own devices all summer. We have weathered the Sudeten crisis and the spectacular Munich Pact with complete tranquillity. We learned of them from illustrated gazettes in which the grocer wrapped the cheese and from the mailman's political comments. ("You see? When they saw they can't pull one over on our Führer, they dropped the Czechs, those bastards, those lousy sonsabitches. . . .")

World events reach us here in tardy echoes, thinned by the mountain air and soothed by the indolent ringing of cowbells and the humming of flies in the summer heat above the lakeside meadows. World history hangs over us as remote as the thunderstorms that arise daily between the glacier peaks, rumble a bit, and are then dissolved by a dazzling sun back into the sheer laundry-blue of the Alpine sky.

But were that history to take place over us, with us, we would pay as little heed. We do not exist in the world of others but only for each other. We have no eyes for what is happening around us, we see only each other. We have no wants, no wishes except for each other. . . .

Nevertheless, Stella is wise enough to tell herself (and me) that our refuge from a reality that is patently becoming ominous is due to John, and that it is advisable to follow John's directions.

These directions are very precise. In a letter from Warsaw (where he was transferred from Prague), John writes that it would be advantageous if Stella came to Bucharest. There it could be proved through my elective and nominal uncle Ferdinand (who had vanished from my life for twelve years) that I am a Rumanian citizen. John feels it would not be advisable to come to Bucharest myself and take the matter in hand, for I would most likely be drafted on the spot. It would be better if I dealt in some other way with this irksome business—which can most likely be deferred but will be unavoidable in the long run. I should approach it in such a manner as to leave myself elbow room later on. Uncle Ferdinand (who, incidentally, is delighted to hear from me), says John, will know how to settle this satisfactorily through his connections. In any case, given the circumstances, I would not be safer anywhere than as a friendly foreigner in Hitler's Greater Germany, so I am to stay where I am: on an Austrian lake that now is part of Greater Germany. However, says John, Stella's presence in Bucharest is indispensable.

This means separating from Stella for a certain time, probably an unendurable period for both of us. But for me it means definitively cutting my umbilical cord from my Viennese relatives. (Uncle Helmuth—his dander up because of my relationship with a Jewess and, through her, naturally, with all sorts of foreign plutocrats—has already cited his rights and duties as a guardian several times.) Meanwhile, we have packed our bags.

It is raining in Salzburg. We park the car at the Österreichischer Hof, where we plan to spend the night. There are almost no people about. I have trouble finding a porter at the hotel to carry our bags from the car. No one cares to show his face—and if he does so, then grouchily. Something is in the air.

Stella asks for a newspaper. We learn about the murder of the German official vom Rath in Paris and about the spontaneous reaction of the German people, who have avenged themselves on Jewish stores, homes, and synagogues.

On our way through town, we occasionally step on fragments of glass. The huge panes of a dress-shop window have been smashed. In the devastated display, a mannequin has been stood on its head, naked. Some wag has thrust a chicken-feather duster between the legs. An SA man, with a grim chin strap around his extortionist face, is guarding the artwork. His eyes follow us like those of a distrustful watchdog as we pass by so closely that we almost graze him. He gapes at the small blue-yellow-and-red Rumanian flags in the buttonholes of our raincoats.

We are expected for dinner at the home of Stella's cousin, who has been living here for many years, married to an official in the provincial government. No one (least of all he) has any illusions that he will keep his job with a Jewish wife. She does not, incidentally, look at all Jewish. She has nothing of Stella's thoroughbred looks; she is blond and rather plain. What makes her attractive is a fine touch of sorrow, mildly overlit by diligent kindness and friendliness ("an incredibly dear dumb goose," says Stella).

The husband is the prototype of the former Austro-Hungarian civil servant, the son of a privy councilor, the grandson of a head of department, a man of jittery, almost servile *politesse,* behind which he absentmindedly thinks of something completely different. He is dry and yet no doubt profoundly sentimental, much more intelligent, much quicker, and also wittier than he cares to seem, likewise much more reserved and arrogant. (Stella says, "At first glance a spineless creature, but at second glance he's full of surprises.")

They both adore Stella and treat her like a princess who occasionally deigns to step down to them from her grand world. They emphasize their modest provincialism with an insistence that is not without a certain irony, especially since their allegation so sharply contradicts the discreet refinement of their household, the exquisite food, which is limited to the most traditional dishes of the Viennese cuisine, the collection of choice and lovely peasant furniture and other folk art in their home, and their extraordinary musicality and literary culture.

They have cooked up an explanation for my constantly being with Stella, and they whisper the explanation to anyone who might be surprised at my hanging around her. They say that I am probably John's son; in any case, he was more than just close to my late mother. Of course, they do not hide the truth from themselves about the nature of my relationship with Stella and about the circumstance that John could not have been the only candidate for my beautiful mother's favor and thus for the possibility of fathering me—indeed, he would have to share the candidacy with a good dozen other gentlemen of his age group and financial position (including, last but not least, "Uncle" Ferdinand). However, Stella's kinfolk merely require an alibi to be as kind, as amiable, and as overpolite to me as to anyone whom convention does not force them to reject.

The maid opening the door for us, a middle-aged rustic innocent who has served them for a long time, is visibly abashed and embarrassed. When Stella asks after her health, she is taciturn, though she normally melts under Stella's sumptuous gratuities. To our astonishment, we find the parlor filled with people. A slightly awkward circle has formed; from its center, at our entrance, a count towers up. The bearer of a grand name closely identified with the most glorious defeats of the Austro-Hungarian army, he is the host's childhood friend and classmate from the Theresianum. He too admires Stella and has known John for ages. His handshake is warm. He is wonderfully elegant in his folk-costume suit, gigantic in his corpulence. An antediluvian breed of man.

We are introduced to the others. To judge by their names, noses, and accents, they are all undeniably Jewish. Berlin Jews, rich ones, who fled to Salzburg before the *Anschluss* and are now trapped here. An exception is an extremely dapper, crisply stylish man in his mid-forties who must have come to Austria from Lemberg or Kecskemet. The host and hostess let on that these are not expected guests; the events of the previous night have brought together people who are more or less strangers, a sort of catacomb community.

The events are discussed in great detail, and the count is of the opinion that such outrageous vandalism would not have occurred without the annexation of Austria's much fiercer anti-Semitism to that of Germany. When contradicted, he heatedly insists upon his view, as though defending a privilege that may be taken away from Austria, which has already been shamefully pruned and now even incorporated in a despised Germany. But soon, intimidated and visibly disgruntled, he lapses into silence. The Berliners inundate him with a torrent of horrifying examples of pure-German cruelty, launching into a sort of contest as to who can come up with the most fearful atrocities. The elegant room, decorated with Alpine art products, fills up with dreadful tableaux of gorilla-like SA men putting out their cigarettes on naked female breasts ("and such lousy brands too!" quips the Kecskemet dandy, who can't hide his eagerness to join in). They forget about His Lordship and Austria's share in anti-Semitic barbarism. This is private shop talk. We three Gentiles—the count, the host, and I—are soon excluded from the animated conversation about hair-raising cruelties. To be sure, it is not so easy to picture them in their full terrifying measure: the people who are narrating them (and who are also identifying with the victims) are physically intact, indeed obviously mindful of their bodily well-being; they are well groomed, luxuriously nourished, expensively dressed. It would take a very active imagination to visualize them as cowering under riding-crop lashes in latrine ditches or kicked into bloody mush under boot heels. The host (quite reserved anyhow) occasionally ventures to ask, "Did this happen to you personally?" Or, "Did you witness it?" And each time, he is put in his place by an indignant retort in Berlinese: "Hell no! But these are the facts, baby. Back home, every kid knows about them!"

Altogether, there is too much putting-in-place and impatient one-upmanship in this Berlin speech, with its delicate undertone of Semitic singsong. These trapped émigrés are cultivating it with some verve, and eventually it becomes unbearable for Austrian ears. The increasingly irritated silence of the Aryans would have long since warned more highly strung city slickers that a regrettable and perilous tradeoff is in the making: a virtually physical repugnance toward anything Prussian is creating an alibi for a perhaps suppressed but no less inveterate hatred of anything Jewish. Stella is the only one who appears to sense this. She remains sovereignly neutral; and wherever she can, she mellows the fervor, which lets justified indignation degenerate into tongue-lashing. She has skillful objections and intelligent arguments ready, but she makes no headway against the passionately concentrated Berlin snottiness and certainly not against the obnoxious wittiness of the élégant from Lemberg or Kecskemet.

He is a lawyer, he claims, and sees things as a professional who has given up wasting even *one iota* of his intellect on the perversions of justice committed by a horde of savages (he calls them "Hitler's brownies"). "So what d'you want, anyway?" he yiddles spiritedly. "When dey let the goyim go after us poor Jews, it's alvays de same thing, I tell you. Whether it's de Inqvisition in de fourteent' century—"

"The thirteenth," the count corrects him.

"I'm talking about the Spanish Inqvisition, but t'ank you anyway," the snappy dresser from Kecskemet parries. "Didn't it go on from around 1230 till 1834? A good six hundred years, if you please—even if it wasn't always against us Jews—de killers also went at each other's troats. And in our enlightened twentieth century, it's exactly the very same thing. De goyim are relishing de blood. So should we cudgel our brains whether things are a little bit less just here or a little crueler there than for de past two thousand years? I ask you."

He, by the way, is the only one here who is personally acquainted with the Nazi authorities' rigorous methods. He was arrested right after the *Anschluss* and held in custody until recently. His experiences have left him—to the general amusement—with a wealth of anecdotes, which he tells very wittily, leaving open the question of whether one should be enraged at the stupidity and inventive cruelty of the examining judges, guards, and attendants or emulate him in taking the whole thing stoically and ironically, as an absurd nightmare.

"Yet still and all, you *were* examined by judges?" the host throws in ambiguously.

But the breezy lawyer crows proudly, amid universal jubilation, "What can I tell you, already? I'm a criminal and not a political prisoner!"

One of the women from Berlin leaps up and kisses him spontaneously: "Oh baby! You I love!"

This is the signal for the count to rise (his head almost bangs against the ceiling) and to beg the hostess (who is suddenly very embarrassed) please to excuse him: he must, alas, go on to a late meeting.

"But we are expecting you to stay for dinner," she pleads helplessly, looking at her husband. But she gets no support from him, instead is tersely informed, "I suppose Max must have misunderstood. In any case, his meeting is more important."

The host reaps a thankful glance from the count, who now bows over Stella's hand tremendously and corpulently. With an emphatic amiability that excludes her from the others, he says, "I am inconsolable, my dear. I was so looking forward to seeing you. Please give my very best to dear John. And let's get together very, very soon!"

Pirouetting with elephantine grace, he spirals up from the hand kiss, managing as he twists to bid good night to the others with a gesture of apology, as though to indicate that his size prevents him, in this constricted space, from making an individual farewell to each person without greatly inconveniencing everyone else. Now, having turned his back to them, he leaves, throwing his tremendous arm around the narrow shoulders of the host, who sees him out of the room. We hear their muffled speech behind the door and their occasional bitter mirth.

The hostess desperately tries to catch Stella's eye, but Stella is gazing absently into space. The Berliners too have lapsed into dull silence, and not even the breezy lawyer from Kecskemet has a quip at hand to dissipate the general abashment. This embarrassing tension is further heightened when the returning host, instead of rejoining the group, peers rather ostentatiously at his watch and then goes into the next room to switch on the radio for the eight-o'clock news.

But this exposes a pugnacious streak in the hostess. With an openness that almost makes her pretty, she declares that she was expecting only a few guests, namely the count, Stella, and me, for supper. But if the others would be satisfied with potluck, then they'd all be welcome. However, she says, she has to ask them to pitch in and help because her maid gave notice this morning—she does not have to explain why.

Her suggestion is accepted with enthusiasm all around. Everyone goes into the kitchen, where the Lemberger or Kecskemeter and the Berlin woman who declared her love for him prove to be proficient and inventive amateur chefs, making us all work amidst great hilarity. The atmosphere becomes downright boisterous, especially since the host, an old-time Austrian, is incapable of rudeness under any circumstances. Making the best of a bad situation, he serves an excellent Valtellina wine—but he turns away in disgust when one of the belatedly invited guests calls it "swell booze."

In the dining room, the table is quickly set for twelve instead of five, and naturally we do without being placed—everyone sits where he likes. The meal has the relaxed mood of one eaten in an Alpine hut, which leads some of the Berliners to shed the coarse Salzburg loden jackets, to which they are obviously unaccustomed. The wine connoisseur talks away at the host, who is seated rather far down the table; he assures him that there are two things he finds charming about Austrians, whom he does not otherwise exactly hold in high esteem: the Viennese *Heurige* and the informal, natural ways of Alpine inhabitants, especially the Salzburgers and Tirolians; he can't quite get along with Styrians and Carinthians. The host listens wth the expression of a man suffering from a toothache. He also winces each time his Berlin neighbors bang a piece of cold meat or a dollop of potato salad on his plate, telling him he's too skinny.

The meal drags on, more wine is brought. The Kecskemeter picks his teeth as his eyes pass assessively over the Baroque treasures of the dining room. And needless to say, the general conversation soon swings back to current events. The focus is no longer the persecution of Jews but rather the figure of the archvillain and enemy of mankind: Adolf Hitler. One of the Berliners, dispossessed of his huge department store on the west side of Berlin ("I managed to scram in the nick of time—and now they've caught up with me here"), draws a disastrous picture of the German economy, a catastrophic situation that he blames solely on the stupid, obstinate, amateurish interference of the Führer (he calls him "Gröfaz," an abbreviation, sounding typically Jewish, of *"Grösster Führer aller Zeiten"*): "Don't let's kid ourselves: German thrift, German industry, German organization would make the economy work even with this top-heavy rearmament, if that swollen-headed Austrian peasant didn't stick his nose into everything. . . ." Then comes example upon example. Similarly, the foreign-policy problems of the Third Reich are harshly criticized. These people have no illusions whatsoever that the peace just saved by the Munich Pact is only delaying the moment when the "Gröfaz" will feel like starting his war. And finally, they get down to the personal and the private. They quote psychological data about the character of Adolf Hitler, speculate about his relationship to his parents and about his abnormal sex life. The woman who kissed the Kecskemeter claims that the Führer is a sado-masochist: he gets his satisfaction by finding some pure, blond female, scantily clad in velvety deerskin, and forcing her to confess that she wants to sleep with him; he then insults her in the most disgusting way and drives her out.

The hostess cannot refrain from saying, with an uneasy sigh, "What a dreadful man!" Oddly enough, it is this rather tame comment that makes the host burst into an unbridled roar. Beside himself, trembling and foaming as if in an epileptic fit, banging his fists on the table, making the glasses and plates jump, he screams in a hoarse, breaking voice, "I won't tolerate this any longer! I won't allow such remarks made about this man in my home! This man is loved and honored by millions of people! He has restored human dignity to millions of people!" He shakes his fist at his wife. "This man is a saint for me, do you finally understand? A saint! . . ."

Bessarabia, winter 1940.

This is an early winter of the Ice Age, which began one day in March 1938 and will last in two phases for the next ten years to come, until summer 1948.

The world is still full of beauty, albeit frozen. A blue-white-and-gold world. The deep-blue Rumanian sky is as spotless as the snowland beneath. There must be a powerfully shining sun, but I cannot place it in my memory. Its light is everywhere, dazzling from the great white waves of the swaying fields and from the twist in the river valley, from the furry hoar on twigs and boughs and on the crooked snowed-in fences of the village, where the house walls of old, weathered wood glow like gray silk under the snowy burden of the roofs—a light like molten brass and so cold as to be brittle and seem fragile.

I am a soldier: I am *serving my country with a weapon in my fist*, as the national rhetoric puts it. We have ridden out to a drill after stuffing newspapers under our greatcoats and into our boots, and still we writhe in the biting cold. Nevertheless, our spirits are almost recklessly high. We are serving our nation rather comfortably. We play at being soldiers, whilst elsewhere the war has long since become deadly serious. We too are armed to the teeth and have live ammunition in our pouches, but we are not yet confronted with an enemy to measure ourselves against. We know that our Fatherland is theatened on many sides—and most directly here in Bessarabia. But this is gobbledygook, just as our willingness *to defend the Homeland with weapons in our fists* is still nothing but claptrap and gestures.

We enjoy the sublimity of this claptrap, the nimbus of heroism it decorates us with. But even more, we enjoy our rough youth and, unconsciously, our blessed anonymity in a collective. In our uniforms we are Lieutenant Jonescu or Volunteer Popescu or Private First Class Petrescu only for the sake of functional differentiation. In reality, we are all young men doing military service with no responsibilities except toward certain phrases. Serving in this way, however, we are *sons of the people.*

They creep from their huts, our people, swarming toward us to greet us, bringing *tzuika*—mild, oily plum brandy—and delicately rancid cakes: a people smelling rancid in their sheepskins, with deeply notched peasant faces, children peeping timidly from behind their mothers' aprons, silver-haired old men, trembling, dribbling, with broken voices, and here and there the cherry-dark eyes of a girl, the double humps of firm breasts under an embroidered blouse. . . . We have dismounted and are chatting with the people who have their hands in the sleeves of their sheepskins and are stamping from one foot to the other in this awful cold. War? Yes, soon there will be war here too. Those fellows over there, across the Dnieper, don't want us to keep this good land. But we shall show them that it's our land, our Rumanian earth. We, the sons of the people, will defend this soil with weapons in our fists. . . . The phrases come trippingly over my lips, well drilled. I am so proud, so moved, so delighted to be a son of a people—whose language I hardly ever speak, whom I hardly know, whom I have hardly ever seen or experienced except in such a folkloristic genre picture as this: costumed farm laborers with backs crooked from bending over furrows and before all kinds of masters, servile people with friendly grins, people who have grown out of their soil, with hair like grass, with skin like bark, with hands like tree roots—and young girls plump as cherries.

And we among them in our uniforms and helmets, warriors hung with sabers, lances, and carbines, with our hoary, steam-breathing horses—it all looks like an opera set.

The music is supplied by the dogs. There must be hundreds, to judge by the din. They are barking their lungs out. They are yanking so hard at their chains that they turn over in midair. They snap blindly, furiously, into the blue winter sky, drooling, foaming, until someone finally notices that this raging is aimed not only at us and our horses. The dogs are pulling in another direction . . .

whence a boy comes running and screams, *"Lupu! Lupu!"* He claims he's spotted a wolf.

This causes the genre picture to break into dramatic motion. All the men dash toward the end of the village where the boy came from. All the women scatter like chickens and chase their children to yank them into the huts. All these people are screaming as if impaled.

It being our duty to defend the Homeland against all enemies, with weapons in our fists, we have, needless to say, raced ahead of everyone else. Right behind the last of the handful of huts, we sight the wolf.

It could also be a very run-down dog—after all, it is quite improbable that a wolf would show up so close to a settlement in broad daylight. But there is no time for such reflections now. We have already torn our carbines from our backs; rifle shots are already lashing the air, swirling up tiny fountains of snow around the "wolf"—I catch myself firing bullet after bullet without really aiming, much less hitting the mark.

Our yelling and surging at the end of the village has sent the "wolf" into swift flight. Then—presumably frightened by the shots all around him and perhaps even grazed or struck by one—he doubles back, and to his misfortune we have him as he flees broadside past us instead of sharply away from us. He is hit by a few bullets or bullet fragments. He bends to a bow, snapping at the bullet wounds, but an enormously powerful will to live pulls him forward. Only now he flees more slowly, more heavily, sits down crookedly on his hind legs when he is hit again. We naturally redouble our banging, and every time the wolf marks a new hit, the united peasantry around us howl triumphantly until their yowling is exceeded by a louder, more energetic one: the roaring of our officers, who command us to stop our senseless shooting on the spot.

It is as if we had suddenly awoken from a fit of possession. The possession is still on our faces; I see it in my buddies' wild eyes and uncontrolled mouths. It must be in mine too, no doubt. The possession yields to the foolish insight that something inexplicable has happened to us, simple as it may be to explain. We lost our heads. The live ammunition in our pouches had to explode sooner or later.

We're in for it now. But who could have thought of doing something wrong by shooting when the entire village was shouting and pointing to its archenemy. . . .

The wolf—or stray dog—keeps twitching and then collapsing. The bullets are in his flesh, he has fire in his bowels, he turns around in circles, biting his flanks, one can see him spraying blood. A few courageous peasants set out to club him to death with cudgels. But, incredibly tenacious, he gets to his feet and drags off. It is a triumph of the will to live, to survive at any price. It paralyzes our hands. My head whirls, I've probably drunk too much *tzuika* too fast. I feel sick. I have to throw up.

Berlin, 1941. Nighttime, total darkness.

I come out of the Jockey. I've been feasting. I've devoured Baltic lobster, Hamburg *Stubenküken, omelette surprise;* I've boozed on gallons of Chablis, Mouton Rothschild 1935, port and Courvoisier and Heidsieck, danced the rumba and the samba, and whetted my genital in my trousers on the pokey pubic bone of an East Prussian girl while dancing to the German version of the Jewish song "Oh Joseph, Joseph, won't you make your mind up." "She wants no flowers, she wants no chocolate, she wants just me and only little me." And now it's time, now the thing's working on its own, "check, please," and out—and in. . . .

We're on the street now. It's pitch-dark. Berlin is blacked out because of air raids, so you can't see your hand before your face. A cab with narrow slits of light on the blackened headlights drives up (they know where to find the fares vital to the war effort), and I step into the meager glow, raise my hand—I have no right to use a taxi, since I'm neither an armaments specialist nor in the Reich Food Agency nor in the Reich Security Service nor a doctor nor a diplomat nor an expectant mother, but my pockets are full of cash and cigarettes (there's a war on, you understand, we'll be honest again after the Final Victory). So I open the cab door and start pushing the girl in—when a figure leaps out of the dense blackness, shoves the girl and me away, and squeezes into the car. I reach in to haul the fellow out—after all, *I* stopped the taxi, it's *mine*, first come, first served—but then I feel the leather of a uniform coat under my fingers. I get scared. I'm a foreigner, all I've got is a highly suspicious document that describes me as being "On a Special Mission" —obviously a draft-dodger, probably even a deserter. It's not advisable. I'm about to let go, to murmur an apology. But the man shrieks, "What! Grabbing an officer of the German *Luftwaffe!*" A fist smashes into my face. I'm scared. I've got to do something. I punch back blindly, strike too low, and bruise my knuckles on his collar. Something is dangling there, something with hard sharp edges: a Knight's Cross.

I am terrified. I am scuffling in the darkness with an officer wearing a Knight's Cross. This is *lèse majesté*, a desecration of the Third Reich, no mercy can be shown for this. . . . Another car comes along, the narrow glow from the headlight combs the street. The Knight's Cross is lying on the asphalt—and the fellow is punching out wildly. But I've got him by the collar, I press him down, shove my knee between his legs, smash my fist into his kisser. The other car has driven past without stopping. I get a punch in the stomach—not very hard, he's no athlete. But I have to finish him off before he draws his pistol or his aviator's dagger and simply rubs me out. He can do it, he has to, he's a uniformed member of the armed forces, he's duty-bound. . . . I smash my fist once more into his Adam's apple, he chokes noisily. He's young and rather thin, a kid, barely twenty-one, no doubt—like me. Only I'm bigger and stronger. But if a patrol car comes, I'm done for. He's an officer of the most daring German service branch, highly decorated; he risks his life, whereas I . . . well, here I risk my life, too. They'll make short shrift of me, shoot me down on the spot like a mad dog. I bang his head against my raised knee; I hold the collar of his leather coat in my left hand and hit him with my right, knocking the edge of the collar out of my fingers. Somewhere, a flashlight beam starts to flit through the blackness. The air-raid warden from the next building, probably. I kick the leather sack, punch a mash of hair, blood, and flesh, he sinks to his knees, his head knocks against the fender of the taxi, I push the girl in, jump in after her. "Get going!" And the cabby hasn't stirred all this time, he probably hasn't even looked around. But then there's nothing to see, I can barely make out his silhouette before me in the darkness, in any case it's solid, no neck, he's probably well on in years. Thank God, all this was none of his business, the results were too uncertain, he doesn't get mixed up in things like this. . . . And the flashlight beam dances closer. The cabby shifts the car into gear, the taxi starts off—slowly—much too slowly—the flashlight beam moves through the car window—I duck, pull the girl down next to me—now the cabby shifts into second and then to third—and I suck the blood from my smashed knuckles ("Watch out, boy, my dress!") and peer through the back window: I see the parabolic section of the flashlight beam whooshing across the asphalt and fishing, out of the blackness, the crumpled figure in the blue-gray leather coat, casting a flat atomizing shadow. Then, the flour-white beam swings up and after us—but its light atomizes too, before reaching us. I see only the round, white-yellow core of the flashlight. . . .

We arrive at my place, a highly respectable family boardinghouse in the Wielandstrasse. In front of the house a black Mercedes is parked, and behind it a military jeep. I am sick with fear: they've already come for me. My first impulse is to shout at the cabby to keep driving. But then I tell myself it won't do any good. I calm the girl. I'll need her to testify that I was attacked and responded in self-defense.

The SS officer waiting for me in the parlor is extremely correct. After checking my papers, he returns them to me with a click of his heels, apologizes, saying he has to see the girl's papers too, reads a well-known name, bows with military terseness. "Excuse me for disturbing you."

He turns to me. "I was ordered to search your room. Could you please make sure that nothing is missing?" In my room, three men are rummaging through my closets and valises. One of them reports, "Nothing, *Sturmführer!*"

The SS officer waves them off. "In order, so far." He says to me, "Would you please come to this office tomorrow morning at eleven." He hands me an address: Elsternplatz, in Grunewald. He gives me the Nazi salute and withdraws with his men.

For a while, I am breathless with terror, unable to grasp what all this means. Then it hits me, to my consternation: Stella. She's tried to get to me again and they've caught her.

Near Stargard, Pomerania, 1942.
In a manor house, evening, after a hunt.

The hostess: ". . . Well, the groom slipped right through her fingers just three weeks after the wedding . . . and then the business with the boy—why, it's horrible: during the Polish campaign, right in the first few days . . . it's hard to keep all your marbles after that . . . and then this all the time [drink gesture with the thumb sticking out of the fist], but otherwise a marvelous woman, manages on her own terrifically. . . ."

The hostess lived in Argentina before the war. ". . . Argentina? What do they eat there?" "Well, in the Pampas, they mainly eat asado." "What?!" ". . . Asado. You simply have to try it sometime, Schnipps. It's fantastic." "I just can't imagine it." ". . . fantastic, I tell you. A whole sheep roasted on an open fire . . ." "No! Outdoors, of course?" "Like Joan of Arc, the virgin." "I thought she was the last in her line." "No, well, joking aside, it's really fantastic. And then when the gauchos take their knives—" "But why knives? Vaseline does the job just fine!" ". . . our Henning's still the same old swine!" "But what do we need gauchos for, gang? We can make our own asado. . . ." "You're not going to wake up everyone on the estate just for that!" "Why, it's almost midnight." "Is anyone still hungry?" "When I tell Stolze—Stolze, I say—third year of the war or not, it's all the same to me—Stolze, I tell you, will do it straightaway." "And outdoors, you say?" "Naturally. It's in the Pampas. Where are you going to find a shelter there?"

"Now listen, Stolze, we've got some foreign guests, and we want to show them that even in the third year of the war—by the way, would you like a schnapps? Well, let me introduce you. Overseer Stolze." "Why, you direct this estate, Stolze, eh? Don't be so modest!" "Stolze's fantastic. Nothing's impossible for him." ". . . Well, we shall try and catch one that's not too old. We'll do it before you can say Jack Robinson." "We can all pitch in to help with the fire. It's better if there aren't too many witnesses." "A little nocturnal exercise is good for you—right, Jutta?" "Why don't you ask your old lady?" "But wear rubber boots, people." "Christ, is it ever cold!" "Someone bring the bottle—I mean, one for each of us, of course." "Naturally, if the wood isn't dry . . ." "Do you know she can do it—still and all, it's the third year of the war." "Why, Schnipps is out of his mind! Listen, cow pats are not peat." "What do you need a glass for?" "You're pouring the booze all over my dress, damn it." "Just pull your fur a little tighter around your modest charms." "Stolze is just fantastic." "He's absolutely reliable. He'll just report that the sheep died." "Hey, I'm going to slap your hands!" "Listen, that smoke is abominable! No, no, no! No Pampas for me . . ." "Obviously the wood is wet." "Stick in a good-sized piece." "I see what you mean by that—" "Henning, you old swine!" "My feet are soaked already." "Now, listen, a party pooper—" "Hey, look: the head's turning brown!" "It's more natural in the rear." "If I catch cold and pass it on to the kids . . ." "You'll pour your workers a round, won't you, Stolze?" "Hey, that's enough wood now. The whole house'll go up in flames soon." "Actually, the dripping fat ought to be—" "Christ, I can't see a thing because of this lousy smoke!" "Don't stand in the wind!" "You mean before you and not behind you?" "Well, even with that fire it's getting a bit nippy out here." "Stolze can tell us when it's ready." "Let the men—" "You can get drunk indoors too. . . ."

"You look like a chimney sweep." "Stolze said at least another half hour. . . ." "You know, life in the Pampas isn't my cup of tea. . . ." "My stockings are all screwed up in the rubber boots. . . ." "Someone put another record on." "You smell so nice—where do you live?" "Come on, I just scorched my hand. I've got to cool it off somewhere. . . ." "In his old age, Schnipps is having the best time of his life." "Of course, if the younger men are at the front—" "Who needs all that light for dancing?" "I hope you don't find this frivolous. . . ."

"And the fire out there—it's just terrifyingly beautiful!" "Can you get any more liquid into you?"

"Let's see that stuff—the lasso or chimborasso or whatever it's called. . . ." "Goodness, is that edible?" "I feel like a cannibal." "Didn't I tell you? Charred on the outside and raw on the inside." "But we can't just throw it away—what a waste!" "Just imagine, a whole sheep. I could trade one for a crate of French—" "The wood is probably drier in the Pampas." "That filet steak with goose liver at Horcher's—well, you can just keep all your Pampas and your old gauchos. . . ." "Yes, but what are we going to do with the stuff now?" "Why don't you give it to the Russians?"

"Have you lost a lot of them too?" "If you want to split hairs, it's really not quite proper—after all, they're POWs." "Just another crazy idea. They're much too weak for farm labor." "Two thirds of them kicked the bucket the very first day." "The poor guys are so starved they eat grass like cattle!" "And you want to give them a whole sheep?" "They'll all croak on you." "That's what Udo said. If someone's starving, then don't give him too much to eat too suddenly. . . ." "Well, none of our people are going to touch this. I know my Pomeranians all too well." "What the peasant don't know, he don't eat." "Stolze'll figure out something. He's fantastic." "Just dump it in the carp pond." "That's why the eels get so fat in the Baltic, quite a lot of drowned—" "When I picture the thing oven-roasted, golden-brown, and with nice green beans . . ." "Anyway, put out the fire, Stolze. No enemy pilot has ever wandered this way—but you never can tell." "Goddamn it, Henning, if you don't keep your hands to yourself . . ."

1943, summer evening
in the valley of the Unstrut, Thuringia.

We are drinking punch under a gigantic, night-black copper beech. Tiny fireflies are dancing over the cobalt-blue lawn around the black shade of the bushes. The host: in his late forties, corpulent, rosy, his sparse hair almost totally white (you can't see much of him: except, when he crosses his legs, you sometimes catch a dim reflection of his old patent-leather pumps, one of which is strangely inanimate, like the shoe on a wax figure). The hostess (on the narrow side of a white iron table, more speculative than visible): delicate, nimble, with huge, dreamy, hazel-brown eyes shimmering wet in the matte oval of her face. The son (first lieutenant in the parachute troops): his uniform occasionally glitters with its German Cross in Gold, Iron Cross I and II, Close Combat Pin (he calls them his "Christmas-tree decorations"); now on furlough from Münsterlager, where he is a drill instructor.

"You can imagine what a load off our minds that was; *pourvu que cela dure,* of course."

". . . Possibly they'll grant me one more little outing to the front lines. . . ."

"You see, he wants the Knight's Cross *à tout prix*—because of the property."

"After all, it didn't help Horst any that he volunteered right off and went through the entire Polish campaign and lost a leg. Afterward, they fired him anyway. . . ."

"And when Ottfried died in action . . ."

"And if you get killed, my boy, then the property won't be of much use to you. . . ."

"Is that sheet lightning or a real thunderstorm—or what?"

"Nope, the *Leuna Werke.*"

"Can you imagine: they asked us seriously to plant rubber trees! Once the *Leuna* is gone . . ."

"It's a miracle anything's left of it. Now they're attacking twice a day—"

"That jasmine's delightful."

"We've got all the time in the world to take care of the garden. We can't go out anyway."

"Otherwise he's a very decent sort. He's the brother of the brother-in-law of our manager. He says, 'All I can do for you is simply have you stay inside your own four walls. If you leave the area of the house—that is to say, the park, you know—you have to wear the star. I would avoid doing that if I were you.' "

"No, the kids are not really quarter Jews. Herbert and I are each half. According to the prevailing algebra, that equals more than half Aryan blood—enough for fighting, anyway. But not enough for more—I mean, morally."

"It makes things a bit difficult with the help, of course. They hanged our old chambermaid because she had something with a Pole here from the camp—"

"We almost got mixed up in it ourselves—"

"But ever since Jürgen got the German Cross in Gold—"

"It does help, after all. . . ."

The new chambermaid emerges from the thick darkness around the jasmine bushes. "Dinner is served, if you please."

The son gets to his feet. "Well, let's do something about our slender figures."

"Please go ahead. We're not allowed to sit at the same table with you people—we're not Aryan enough. . . ."

1944, Berlin.

Air-raid-shelter group. Ashen faces. The women dressed as if they were about to go sledding in the park: fur coats over coffee-brown sweat-pants; small plaid scarves wound around their curlers like something between a turban and a Phrygian cap. Whining kids groggy with sleep. The few men—aged, their faces notched with hunger creases. The long-drawn-out howling of the all-clear signal releases some of the tension like a valve in a high-pressure boiler. Sighs of relief. People gather up the belongings they have dragged down here. Crawl out between damp walls and support beams. They're familiar with the whole hulla-balloo. These nighttime interruptions are part of daily life with its obnoxious routines. But still, it's a bother every time. Shouts from outside. A couple of people running along the street. When the basement door is opened, a smell of burning wafts in.

I find myself in a motley group who are viewed here with wry displeasure. It is a small party, given by a young councilor in the War Economy Agency. The scent of our cigarettes has drawn notice, but the real provocation is the cloud of good French perfume around the girls, plus the very hard accent of the little Brazilian attaché. . . . Luckily, a few aerial mines exploding nearby diverted attention from us. There was pandemonium here for a good half hour. Only now do we feel our nerves quivering.

And the present mood is all the more euphoric. Not cheery, however, but coldly passionate, almost malevolent. We don't give a good god-damn now about the angry glares of the mothers, herding along their exhausted flocks of kids. We dash up the stairs, three or four steps at a time, to our host's apartment. Soon champagne corks are popping.

And there are rolls with the finest Pomeranian sausage, and fantastic rumba records brought by the Brazilians. One of the girls is already dancing on the table, her skirt pulled up to her crotch. But she doesn't dance for long. Suddenly, she stops dead, gapes straight ahead, and cries, "My baby!" It has just struck her that she left her child with her parents in the Motzstrasse. Where the thick parachute mines came down. She won't be held back. She doesn't even pull on her coat. She simply runs out into the night in her dress. Since I've got my eye on her and don't want her to vanish in the night, I run after her.

We don't get far. At the second corner, where a building is on fire, we are thrust into a bucket chain. An irate air-raid warden, obviously of high authority, waves a pistol in the air. He sticks it under the nose of a man who declares that he is a doctor and could probably be employed more usefully elsewhere rather than here, in this senseless attempt to pour bucketfuls of water on a blaze that no brigade can bring under control. "You will do your duty like everyone else!" screams the air-raid chief. "You know I have the right to shoot you if you resist my orders."

We take the opportunity to short-circuit the bucket chain. We sheer out, passing a full bucket to the man in front and an empty bucket to the man in back. Our success with this awkwardly simple trick puts us in a good mood. We hold hands as we run through the smoking streets. But it's a long way to the Motzstrasse, and we probably won't get through anyhow. Flames are lighting up the sky over the ruins in the next few blocks.

The girl (she's so young you wouldn't guess she had a child; a minor accident, no doubt)—the girl gets tired. Tired and cranky, like the kids in the air-raid shelter. She launches into the same pouty Berlin jargon: "Hey, man, how'll we ever get to Motzstrasse if everything's cookin'? I'm wreckin' my shoes—just look!" She has an insight of stoic grandeur: "Either they managed to get out alive and everything's fine and dandy or they're dead. Either way, I can't do anything."

We briefly reflect whether we should go back to the party. No, we can scarcely expect it to get any better. My apartment—in another highly respectable family rooming house, different from the one three years ago—is rather far away.

"Well, then, let's go to my place. It's right around the next corner." We hold hands again. You can say what you like, but it's good to survive.

1945, near Buchholz, on the Lüneburg Heath.

The dawn begins over the black saw-teeth of the pines. The sky turns cold and smooth like polished stone. A hundred yards ahead, the freight cars that have toppled from the embankment are blazing. The air smells of burning rubber—or something of the kind; the smoky flames inundate the potato field with an eerie brownish red. In the ditch a few patches of March snow are melting rosily. A handful of men are working on the tracks—six or seven, guarded by three others. The workers are convicts from Altona who wear prison uniforms with round, rimless, visorless caps. The guards are elderly policemen. In the cattle cars of the train, which is standing by the pines, mainly women are peering out—but in their condition it is hard to tell their sex; they could just as easily be half-starved men. For three days now, I'm told, such trains have been rolling through here nonstop, supposedly to a big camp near Belsen. The strafers have set a couple of trains on fire. Perhaps some of the people have managed to sneak into the bushes, but it doesn't matter—they won't get far. They're too feeble to survive outdoors, and no one will take them in and hide them—it's too risky. They're guarded by a single man here, an old geezer with a gigantic rifle—he looks like a World War I Homeguardsman. He carries the rifle on a strap across his back and he props his arm on the barrel like a huntsman. He only casually notices the few figures who have jumped out of the train to take a shit.

There is something macabre yet idyllic about this dotted line along the dark stretch of the waiting train: from this perspective, a long alignment of crouchers facing in different directions with dropped pants or hitched-up skirts revealing naked, lamentably bony behinds. Completely emaciated arses, so sharp they could shit into bottle necks. . . . And one of the men embraces his thin thighs under the knees and peeps back over his shoulder—like a faithful dog that has to shit but doesn't want to lose sight of its master. And he hops away from his pile, hops like a frog, glancing around with bulging eyes—does he have worms? In his nutritional state, he can't possibly be constipated—or is he embarrassed? . . . At any rate, he destroys the alignment, breaks out, disrupts the parallel—he is already close to the buffers between two cars, where he probably wants to hide—aha!—where he tries to creep through and vanish in the underwood of the pines on the other side. . . . He has turned his skull ahead and peeps under the buffers and is about to take his final leap. . . .

But the Homeguardsman has noticed something. There's something wrong. The alignment of shitters is untidily interrupted. . . . The Homeguardsman slowly removes his left arm from the rifle barrel; his right arm reaches for the strap; he pulls the rifle from under his armpit, takes careful aim——he's probably taking fine sight, the target's not more than perhaps forty paces off——and the shot sings and lashes onto the train and then across and beyond to the jagged black wall of pines, which catches it and hurls it back, making it echo, across the potato field . . . and the shitting frog simply keels over on his nose; not even his arms let go, embracing his thighs as if they were his most precious possession on earth . . . he merely keels forward, and his naked white backside is turned toward the heavens like a moon howitzer; it suddenly seems tremendous, seems to swell, a gigantic, shiny egg, as in a Bosch painting; it lacks only a huge funnel stuck in it or a crane flying up from it. . . .

1946, in a train compartment
between Frankfurt and Würzburg.

I have a travel order from the British military government, and thus I have the right to take Allied trains. In scheduled German trains——that is, the ones hung with human clusters like bacchanale festoons——I may use the cars and compartments reserved for members of the occupation forces. In the British zone, such compartments are nearly always empty. In the American zone, they are moving brothels for GIs riding alone or in tiny groups. Between the main stations on a given stretch, a relay service of *Fräuleins* has been set up. They climb in with a john at one station, screw all the way to the next station, and then pick up another client for the return trip. Commuter sex, paid for with PX commodities: cigarettes, chocolate, nylons, canned meat, coffee.

I have come from Bad Hersfeld (from John) and am going to Nuremberg to appear there as a witness. I have had to transfer several times: from a local to an express, from an Allied to a German train. The trip drags on and on. It is my first one after the war; I am seeing a wealth of medieval images: ruins, lunar landscapes, scattered beaten people. The Germans wear rags on their feet and coffee cozies on their heads. When they come to a railroad depot, they start out from far away, from their caves in the rubble fields. They swarm along like lines of ants, over trodden footpaths that wind through remnants of houses, right through the traces of former kitchens and parlors with nettles luxuriating in the corners.

I see many genre pictures: the bare breasts of nursing mothers, grandfathers carried piggyback, silent gaping faces, trembling hands spooning out bread soups, sleepers piled up like logs, waiting rooms in which people cook and launder . . . the Germans are as human as in their fairy tales: a round-eyed, wonder-eyed, flabbergasted humanity, as if they had looked into the face of God.

The trip has been going on for days. I witness raids of people swarming on incoming trains, human surf breaking against the sides of railway cars, foaming up over the roofs and sticking there. Every train is crusted over with people like an old ship's hull with mussels. When the train chugs out of each station, it drags along human seaweed, human sludge. . . .

Over all this, there are yellow sunups and red sundowns, pale days, lulled by the rising and falling of telegraph wires. Fluffy, feathery skies. Landscapes screwing into and twisting out of the square of the train window. Furrows in the fields, breaking open with a hum, fanning open. Gliding mountain chains, approaching hills. Embankments that hurl the scent of hay in my face and then are torn away. Black nights with racing clouds through which the sickle moon slits its way. Corpses of cities in the silver milk of starlight.

I begin to acclimatize myself to my trip as to a destiny; I learn to adjust, to orient myself, to seize my advantage: I have to find food, occasionally wash and shave, the toilets are stuffed with people, the station kiosks are looted bare, there are fistfights over a rationed herring sandwich. But I am alone in my Allied compartment—until Frankfurt. Then the German railroad service shoves an Eastern European in on me: a Ukrainian, a displaced person en route to Munich (that much is intelligible). We get along on the handful of Russian fragments I picked up in Bessarabia. Our communication remains rudimentary, and besides, he is not very sociable. He gazes out the window and sings, sings tender, nostalgic songs in smoky vowels and melting labials: *mnyeshmyets khroshtshuy svolyeshtschik,* or whatever. Songs about his little pony or his mother, in any case about deep homesickness and a long road.

Meanwhile, the train lumbers off again, pulling out of the human ooze, out of the desperate tumult, away from the shouts, gliding out of the floury lamplight under the shot-up station roof, heading into the abstractly alive blackness of the switch yard: bars, twisted and torn, the skeletons of charred railroad coaches, engine wrecks in magical presentness. The down-slanting shine of the illuminated train windows wanders on, a gliding chain of yellow rectangles: they tremble over black crushed stone. The first window leaps up a sooty wall and drops back, the others follow. Rectangle upon rectangle they repeat the leap and drop back, stretch, undulate, expand, shoot out into the darkness, contract, throw themselves like folded carpets over a ramp, lose a half in a pit and pull it out again. This becomes a dance, a grotesque geometrical dance of submission, a constructivist parody of assiduity. Rectangles squeeze into squares, squares distort into trapezoids, constrict diagonally into isosceles triangles, straddle their legs and do splits, rip apart into hyperbolas and pour into the endless night. And the wheels grind in the tracks, rattling harder and harder, more and more noisily, crackling through switch clusters, shaking and jerking through the cars, wrenching them into the predetermined track . . . a saurian leaps out of the darkness and attacks the train; he is smashed back; the mammoth proboscis of a water pump makes a grab for me, black and huge, run down by the pack of train-window lights; in back of it, red and green eyes flare up, move along, and are driven away, torn into, sucked up by the general falling, receding.

And the Ukrainian sings. Sings mournfully with a rocking head. His pony surges by the crib, his mother waits for him, he is very homesick, and the road is long . . . *svysh yaaa schtschlik kasyateee*, or whatever. . . . His song has seven times seventy-seven stanzas, it is as endless as his journey, as endless as the night into which the beat of the wheels carries us, faster and faster, banging more and more breathlessly. . . . I stand up, put out the light, and wrap myself in my coat. I want to sleep, lulled by the Ukrainian's singsong. . . .

But the compartment door is yanked open, a cold gust of air smashes in, a black hand switches on the light. A giant Moor in an olive-green uniform coat is standing there, a woolen cap on his woolly skull.

"Get outta here, you fuckin' kraut!"

"Kraut yourself!"

"I said, get outta here!"

"I won't. I've got a travel order."

"Shove it up your ass!"

"All right. I'll call the MP."

"But I got a girl."

"Who cares?"

"I wanna screw her."

"Go ahead!"

He vanishes into the dark corridor. I pull the door shut, turn off the light. He yanks the door open again and pushes the girl inside. She sits down, a ruffled black bird, her claws holding her handbag in her lap, her face a doughy splotch with two gigantic, dark, sunken eye sockets. . . .

The Negro hangs his coat over the window to the corridor—the curtains were cut away in 1944, perhaps they were made into a child's dress, the child is probably moldering under ruins somewhere, perhaps a corpse was wrapped in them. . . .

"Get to the other side!"

"You might say please."

He grins whitely from unspeakably pure, tender-rosy gums. A strip of light from outside sweeps across his black face, he holds out a pack of cigarettes to me. I change from my window corner to the corridor corner of the other seat, wrap myself in my coat, pull up my legs, and push the Ukrainian snugly into his corner.

The Ukrainian keeps singing, unmoved, drawing the notes from his pumped-up chest, squeezing them through his larynx, mashing them into the ooze of the labials: *shtcholoy vyzian beshnyevo-o-o-*, or something like that. . . . His pony can kick the bucket, his mother can go fuck it, Bessarabia is far away, and homesickness fills him with dismay, like the joy under the frock, and the song is as soft as the cock. . . .

The Negro tilts the girl up on the now empty seat. I pull my coat up over my head. I don't want to see what's happening, I can picture it: his black paw between her legs, burrowing through the panties (if she's wearing any), burrowing into the black fur, the middle finger groping for the wet slit, the other black paw kneading her breast. . . . I pull my coat tight over my face. There's a buttonhole through which I can peep: *monsieur le voyeur, le triste sire . . .*

In the window, the dim reflection of the compartment door through gliding nightland, with telegraph poles whirring past; black agglutinations of bosky hills under the drama of the romantic German sky;

shredding clouds, racing patches of mist; and pale and plump the girl's white thigh, rising, crooking at the knee, the stocking sliding down, the leg dangling, searching for a foothold, helpless, and behind it, in between, over it, under it, the dark mass of the Negro, his back slowly moving up and down, indolently palpitating, the olive-green torso with a black ass cut off by the white stripe of the lowered shorts, the girl's hand on the back of his neck, as if they were dancing. . . .

Now and then, light flashes overhead: a lineman's house with a lamp whooshes by, the lanterns of an overpass. . . . And the Ukrainian, with dangling head and, no doubt, watery gaze, seeks the moon in the apocalyptic clouds and finishes his song, swallows, begins a new one, even more mournful, more nostalgic. The road is long, the vowels draw the wanderer's weary feet from the ooze of mashed consonants: *vshotchokhoy kakda tsmyelyshnuyaaaa wayakhoy shtshaluuuy vshoshoooo.* . . .

The air in the compartment thickens, I sweat in my corner, powerless, grim, *monsieur le vivisecteur.* . . . In his buttonhole, the dandy wears the orchid of a white female thigh with a Negro back wedged in. . . .

1946, Nuremberg.

A therapy to harden the soul. Pastor Kneipp's method. A ruthless alternating cure of impressions. Boiling baths and icy showers.

I take part (as a *mess-allié,* so to speak) in the glory of the victors, accusers, and judges. I am distinguished, I belong to the supermen. I eat with the Allies in the cafeteria of the Fürth courthouse. In the lascivious lard of shimmering canteen grub, six courses, splotched on a punched aluminum tray. In line. Queuing up with prison guards, tabloid reporters, file rummagers, gonorrheal secretaries—your turn, buddy. The ladle shits: brown cutlets—move on—a puke of piercing green canned peas—move on—a pile of pus-yellow corn—move on—the lymph of mashed potatoes—move on—a canned pineapple slice, canned condensed milk, coffee, Coca-Cola, a chocolate bar—move on—cookies, white bread, canned grapefruit juice, canned beer, cigarettes galore. . . .

Outside, the people are starving, selling their little sister or the dead son's Knight's Cross for a carton of Lucky Strikes. In here, we are showered with music from the loudspeaker can: "Blue Moon"—

"Stormy Weather"—"Moonlight Serenade"—"Temptation"—"Stardust" . . .

Stella. She's the reason I'm here. Here, justice is being done before World History. Make sure you get a seat next to the black-haired girl with the pale cheeks and dark eyes. She survived the uprising in the Warsaw Ghetto. You just wouldn't believe how much knowledge goes into a pair of eyes, big and dark as they may be—she probably screws like an angel. . . . And while we feed our faces here and work on the choreography of mating, somewhere off at an angle, upstairs, in one of the thousand honeycomb cells of the Fürth courthouse, the main defendants are being tried. When you've swallowed your canteen vittles, drunk the coffee and the rest of the canned beer, burped, put out the cigarette, wiped your kisser with the paper napkin, you can go upstairs and watch them being driven through a caged corridor like lions in a circus. The biggies of the crumbled Third Reich: Göring, Hess, Ribbentrop, Keitel, Kaltenbrunner, Frank—twenty-two men in all, accused of crimes against humanity, all kinds of war crimes, crimes against peace, conspiracy. . . . Inside, they fill two rows of benches—twenty-two men of the white race, as pale as intestinal worms (they've been living by artificial light for nine months) but washed, clean-shaven, with clean hands and brushed suits. Göring in a kind of martial silvery gray: double-breasted flannel jacket, marshal's piping on the breeches, Krakoviak boots on his short, fat legs. He's alert and lively, very interested in everything going on about him, slides around on the bench and peers everywhere. Next to him, Hess's saurian skull looks as if it had just clambered out of a diluvial ocean, sending a first bewildered glance into the prehistoric world from beneath the overhanging bushy eyebrows—when you encounter that gaze, you are peering down two gun barrels. Ribbentrop's bank-officer mug: empty, tight-lipped, arranged in dourly dignified wrinkles. Keitel's maître d' skull. Kaltenbrunner's dripping Aztec profile. Frank's man-in-the-street mien puffed up with a convert's remorse. The homosexual scrotum in Funk's cheeks. Schacht's Punch-and-Judy head. . . .

outside, in the impoverished vending stalls of the bombed-out city, you can purchase them (with Hitler, Himmler, and Goebbels in the bargain) for a handful of marks: carved as ornamental corks for liquor bottles—bottles for liquor that can't be had anyway, that can be found only by Americans, Englishmen, Frenchmen, in the Arabian Nights bazaar of the PXs.

And here, on the witness stand, a man from whom secrets are being wormed out—grave worms: "So you admit that you actively participated in the mass shootings of thirty thousand Polish citizens, most of them of the Mosaic faith? Fine—now who gave the orders for this action? . . ."

the grave worms creep through the tremendous Fürth courthouse, crawl through the labyrinth of its corridors, through the chasms of its stairwells, crawl in and out of its thousands of honeycomb cells, creep up the waxed lace-boots and into the machine-gun muzzles and under the grim chin straps and into the nostrils of the massive GIs standing guard at every corridor corner, outside every door behind which something important might happen: "Our boys—we're so proud of them. American boys are not like others—only American boys have mothers—that's why they kicked the shit out of the goddamn Nazis. . . ."

and that's why the *Fräuleins* suck their cocks dry. When darkness comes, the streetwalkers ripple out from Fürth to Nuremberg, throng about the railroad station (which still reeks of fire and decay and wet rust), hurry around the old city wall, the garbage-filled moat. No poor light bulb glows on the shredded ivy of the tumbledown stone wall. There's smooching and hootchy-kootching in the dark. Sometimes a match flares up and a Rembrandt-like blackamoor's skull burgeons from the night with a Camel in his kisser. Then someone whispers in the dark: "Sir, sir, listen, sir. My sister—sixteen years old . . ."

But we scoot past in windy jeeps, whoosh through the figures, our headlights hurling them into the background of the witch-hunt. The driver's silhouette is like cast iron, a black, helmet-crowned wedge pushing them apart. He steers the light beams with one finger, his right arm embracing the seat at his side, his left foot propped on the clapped-down windshield, his right foot pressing on the gas. . . .

we streak with the gale toward sparkling lights, a Christmas wonder candle: in a flood of neon, the Grand Hotel Excelsior rises from the German rubble-night like a mescaline vision. In the light-bulb Alhambra of the entrance, the doorman, the big fat uncle of little-father tsar, in a sky-blue admiral's uniform, woven into the spaghetti tangle of his silver fourragères, assisted by iron men with machine guns, planted bayonets. . . . They check the guests' passes; he pushes them through the revolving door, bowing and scraping. "Good evening, sir! How are you tonight, sir? . . ."

Inside, fashionable thronging and jostling at the bar. Athletic backs in olive-brown uniform jackets, rugby-player legs in officer's pinks, bare female shoulders, Chanel No. 5 from the PX in their armpits, Kleenex-cleansed necks under the touched-up hairlines: "I want you to promise me a job in Subsequent Procedures, darling—or where else should I go when this mess is over and they're all hanged? . . ."

Britons interspersed: a Labour MP with a pimp's pompadour over the low furrowed forehead of a morning-gazette reader, surrounded by His Majesty's Own Hampstead Archers: Kitchener mustaches under Semitic noses, ringdove voices, Mayfair accents with a touch of Budapest, Honvéd elegance in khaki: shoulder straps waxed to a mirror shine, discreet little stars on the epaulets. A Foreign Office man: pinstriped suit, striped shirt, striped tie, ascetic scholar's head, boyish hair, boyish naïveté, shy boyish smile.

and Frenchmen: smoothly turned, with rattails under their noses, swift mouse eyes.

and Russians: in military tunics with board-like shoulder straps, shorn skulls, muzhik backs, muzhik movements. . . .

a Texas parrot shriek: "Aahhuuuho! so you're a colonel—don't tell meee!"

And whiskey, bourbon, vodka, dry martinis, Bloody Marys, bloody chips, and fucking salted almonds. "Come on, have one more on me!" and a fanfare from beneath: the floor show is surging, the rumba booming. "And now, ladies and gentlemen, our greatest hit, Miss Rachel Shefczuk of the Frankfurt Stork Club in her dance of the seven veils!" Tipped breasts brought into form by uplifted arms, Grete Wiesenthal leaps ending in a split, the white crotch cracks on the dance floor, a *Stars and Stripes* reporter snaps flashbulb shots . . . a look around: journalist mugs in officer's uniforms, Jewish court stenographers, female interpreters, the black-haired girl from the ghetto doesn't seem to be here. Wonder if anything else is happening—but first something to eat. . . .

the snack bar is on the first floor, the big windows look out on the sidewalk, the room is filled with barrels of lemur food, just serve yourself. Hamburgers, cheeseburgers, fuckburgers with mustard, with horseradish, with catsup, with Tabasco sauce. Beer, tannic Chianti, Coca-Cola, orange juice, grapefruit juice, tomato juice. White bread, black bread, gray bread, milk for teetotalers, apples, pears, oranges, bananas, Japanese dwarf mandarins (canned), Chinese lichee nuts (canned). . . . Gray blobs in the blackness of the windowpanes:

Nurembergers standing outside, staring in, hollow-cheeked, round-eyed, wide-mouthed, gaping at this fairy-tale abundance. This can't be real, there's no such thing, this is *verre eglomisé*. They stare without expression, without greed, without envy. This is so opulent that it's beyond their grasp. Movie splendor. *The Indian Tomb, The Treasure of the Silver Lake, Ali Baba and the Forty Thieves*. You can look at it and not even dream about it, there's no such thing, you can't believe that so much food can lie around freely, all you have to do is dive in and stuff your mouth, as if in Neverneverland—it's humbug, a daydream. . . .

and every half hour, one of our boys comes, oh aren't they wonderful, with a helmet and chin strap and chewing gum between his molars, he sticks his machine-gun muzzle into their backs and pushes them away—wiping the blackboard of the windows like a big, wet sponge.

The street is empty. Beyond it, the shredded ivy hangs on the tumbledown city walls. Where do they go when they are shooed away from here? Not over there? Not in there, behind that wall? . . . I've been there, I've ventured fifty or sixty feet into the necropolis of a smashed Nuremberg—and have fled back as though from a plunge into the deep, found refuge for my salvation in the sparkling neon lighting of the Grand Hotel Excelsior, with whiskey, bourbon, floor shows, and Texas parrot shrieks. . . .

Never, not even in my most frightening dreams, have I experienced such solitude, such an abyss of desolation. This is no ruin of a city, this is the negative of the very notion of a city. The existential void per se. No, they can't possibly live there, no rat can live there, it would become moonstruck, it would be frightened of ghosts, it would have to see a psychiatrist. . . .

In the daytime, it's still bearable (although only just). A rubble field, yes indeed, but what a rubble field. Just let someone try to move freely through such a filthy anachronism: a medieval town of gingerbread houses shattered by sophisticated bombs and razed to the very foundation walls. It's almost like a murder in a nursery. Incomprehensible, repulsively brutal. A child's hair and bloody brain-mush sticking to a smashed rocking horse . . . and crickets are chirping from the steppe grass that has grown out of the crib. . . .

you can spend hours here strolling through the brick dust without hearing any other sound than this ghostly summer chirping of crickets, without seeing anything stir. Aside from the ghostly chirping, everything is deathly silent here in the old part of Nuremberg. You tower head and shoulders above the fragments of old houses and churches. Beyond the rubble cone that gently slopes up into a hill, the castle still hovers as though placed there from a box of toys. And at its foot (better: at its roots), a few narrow-chested frame walls remain upright, a quarter of a weary old gable roof hangs askew from a chimney pillar, and timberwork torn from the walls is still supporting half of a doll's room. It is as though in that terrible night when fire and explosives came pouring from the heavens, the tiny Gothic houses of this town tried to flee to the old stronghold to crowd, panicked, under its protection—and the destruction caught up with them before they could get even halfway there. And the ineffable, inconceivable horror ripped them apart, halving them, quartering them, mutilating them, and spellbinding them to the spot. . . . Now they stand in shreds, as though hexed and cursed. . . .

I sat down on the defense wall of the castle, letting my legs dangle, and gazing—gazing. It was a splendid day, a day in early autumn, full of misty light, and the demolished town of Nuremberg lay at my feet, flattened into its ground plan. The picturesque, medievally narrow world of nooks and crannies was vast and empty, topograpically marked off, abstractly drawn in two dimensions, like a blueprint. Only at the root of the castle trunk were those three or four ghosts of gingerbread houses still looming, having been spellbound in their flight. . . .

and they gave me food for thought: I had already seen them somewhere, once. I knew their contours, sharp as if etched in silverpoint, and this faded coloring, the watercolor in the dusty wall-yellows and old brick-reds of the rubble . . . I had once absorbed all this painfully—but when? where? . . .

When it came to me, it struck me so hard that I almost fell from my airy wall-seat. They were the same contours, drawn with a hard pencil and sophomorically accurate, the same faded watercolors as the studies that Private First Class Adolf Hitler (at the time, more artistically than politically committed) had doodled into his sketchbook in France during World War I: shot-up farms in September light. . . .

But this cannot be talked about here. Not even with the pretty survivor of the Warsaw Ghetto. This is not the time or place for cultivated salon chitchat. This is a setting for important events. History has caught up with itself and is now taking place in the present, is even taking a step into the future. Here, a milestone is being placed in world history, casting a warning shadow into times to come.

Everybody says this to himself three times a day (at lunch in the cafeteria, at cocktails in the bar of the Grand Hotel Excelsior, at the slow waltz shortly after the floor show in the Excelsior *souterrain*). Here, too, we live more intensely under the magic of claptrap. We live in the nimbus of specialness. We are witnessing an historic expansion of international law. The Hague Convention of 1926 managed only to condemn war as a crime; it offered no legal sanctions against the perpetrators (much less defined the crime of conspiracy). Here they are now, the conspirators responsible for the last war, sitting as defendants in two fenced-in rows of benches, and we already know how this will end. The milestone in world history will once again be a gallows. . . .

They seem to know this themselves, the twenty-two defendants. They act stoic, sharply watched as they are by helmeted GIs, who, as a token of the solemnity of this historic moment, are wearing white cotton gloves on their dangling butcher paws. And across from them, raised up on a platform, throning at a long table, as in da Vinci's *Last Supper*, sit the judges.

In the middle, Our Lord Justice Sir Geoffrey Lawrence looms from the elbows to the head as an isosceles triangle (the acme pointing to God). Christian England, the bulwark of Western Civilization, invented by Dickens in his finest hour: graying in the dust of files to abstract, patriarchal justice; learnedly sucking a pencil, discreet harrumphs purging the throat, mind, and conscience; and in the sea-blue eyes under the periwig (here doffed) the eternal boyishness of Britain. . . .

and to his right and left, the apostles. (Not a zodiac describing twelve but one more than half, namely seven, the number of perfection and performance; the judges are arranged not dramatically in four trios, as seasonal constellations, but in the four-times-two-makes-eight of eternity.) At the left of Our Lord's British colleague, two Frenchmen (their artistic tailor is Daumier, the name of one of them Henri Donnedieu de Vabres) in bat cloaks, vain neck-bands, puffy lawyer-caps: the black brethren of the white cook and the red Communard, gazing with astute Cartesian eyes from behind their thriftily iron-framed glasses, and paper-flower bouquets of *éloquence* proliferating from their narrow lips. . . .

and to the right, two Americans, Midwestern senator busts: square-shouldered, square-headed, square-faced, square-minded, crafty in philistine droning, bull-like aggression from all pettifoggery of Civil Law, world potentates in cast-iron self-righteousness. . . .

finally, farther to the right, two Russians in bombastic People-owned generals' uniforms (albeit without the full pomp of medals—Nikichenko doesn't want to boast): over blood-red epaulets the size of meat platters, their stubble heads are as immovable as rocks on which the fuss and claptrap of the Capitalist Imperialists shatter and become null and void . . . one of them sheds an occasional Mongolian grin over a piece of paper, on which he doodles motionless. He is drawing caricatures of the people called to the witness stand, and whenever a drawing is especially successful, he feels a childlike joy. . . .

and there, on the witness stand, a man moved by the revival of memory tells about a mass shooting somewhere in Volhynia. His nerves can't take it, he weeps, although without tears: the sobbing shakes him dry, his shoulders heave, he can barely squeeze out the words. He goes into agonizing detail about another man who was to be shot in a group. The mass grave was already dug, twenty yards by ten, several rows of corpses were already lying in it. And this man had a child at his side, his son, eight years old, a bright little boy—dry sobs, quaking shoulders. . . . Our Lord Justice soothingly taps a sucked pencil. Would the witness kindly pull himself together and speak more succinctly, the Court's time is limited, this carrion-smelling nightmare is only supposed to take nine months, long enough to give birth to a legal changeling. . . . So the witness pulls himself together and tells about how this child did not quite understand what was going on, he spoke confidently to his father, but noticed by the father's—how shall I put it?—absent, abstracted expression that something unusual, something ominous was afoot . . . the child suddenly became frightened and began to ask what was happening, why so many corpses were lying in the ditch. And the father caressed his head and spoke calming words to the boy: It's not half so bad, my child, there is almost something good about dying young— And then the rattle of the machine guns or the automatic pistols or whatever they used— The witness can't speak, and Our Lord Justice clears his throat. This is a private digression, as it were; the witness should confine his testimony to the fact of the shooting alone (if possible with precise data on the number of marksmen and victims)—harrumph, yes. The issue here is some thing more general, that is to say, human rights in the legal sense, i.e., we must accurately establish crimes of such magnitudinous planning and perpetration as to involve international law. . . .

and meanwhile: the voices of the simultaneous interpreters chirp away in four languages like twittering parakeets from the glass cage on the witness stand, secretaries for both prosecution and defense are walking up and down with copies of documents and affidavits for tomorrow and the day after and handing them from one table to another where the testy, frustrated lawyers sit. The court reporters, bored, bang away at their steno machines in a slow-motion estrangement from typing. Defense attorneys scribble away at objections for the day after tomorrow. Prominent guests with earphones in the spectators' section are deeply moved; they enjoy the dramatic events, enjoy their witnessing an act of World History. . . .

I too cannot escape from the magical events in the tiny courtroom. I have to come. These events are too interesting. I must not miss them. Now that I'm here anyway, I at least want to watch some of it. . . . I've been listed as a witness, true. But I have every reason to doubt that I'll ever be called: I have only *one* murder to testify about, whereas here the issue is hecatombs. Stella's death is a private digression, so to speak, nothing for me to flaunt here: you probably won't be questioned here for fewer than ten thousand corpses. (John knew this, must have known it, but it was presumably his last good deed for me: to get me out of the German starvation world and shelter me among the grave worms.) The great moment will most likely not come: I on the witness stand eye to eye with Göring (after all, he's the one, the bastard)—I, an extra in World History. . . .

nevertheless, I am to keep ready, I have to get my hair trimmed every week. After all, you can't enter World Events looking sloppy, with a gigolo's mane. Besides, the dark-haired girl from the Warsaw Ghetto said that long, neglected hair reminds her too much of old times—wouldn't shaven heads be an even stronger reminder? Anyway, it's fun going to the barber. Way over there, in the farthest wing of the courthouse, I know a barber shop for guards—our boys so prim and proper, aren't they an example for everybody? Jungle life demands such knowledge. At the Excelsior, I would have to spend good vouchers on a haircut, whereas here, for a couple of cigarettes, I can get shorn, shaved, powdered, massaged, and Brylcreemed. With the money I save I can buy the most wonderful things at the PX: nylons, for instance, for which certain girls will do certain things, or else quite simply cans: of corned beef, meat and vegetables, pork and beans: the last seven years have pretty much emaciated everybody, you're not always up to snuff with the *Fräuleins*. . . .

besides, the barber shop isn't far from the corridor where the black-haired girl is working on the statistical survey of the victims in the Ghetto uprising. You might fragrantly stick your freshly Brylcreemed head in the door and casually ask how things are going (she's shown me the number tattooed on her arm, a barely legible blue spot in the very smooth skin with tender-blue veins; still and all, it's a sign of intimacy, an earnest of a burgeoning human relationship). Perhaps you can offer her the happiness of falling in love with her: *Love bade me welcome*, and the dead soul lived again. . . .

Perhaps she'll sing you something in Polish, a yearning that wells up out of mashed labials. Maybe even something in Yiddish (while my Brylcreem-smooth skull lies in her lap), tender Yiddish songs as in Bessarabia long ago. *Di bist sheyn in maine oign, sheyner fin der velt—ikh hob on dir nisht kain khazuren, alles mir gefelt. Mcyg zain tserrisn dus neyzale, meygst hubn seykhele vi an eyzele; Di bist sheyn in maine oign, sheyner fin der velt*. . . . That would be beautiful, that would snuff out a lot, that would be balm for my heart, the old shard. . . .

you see, it's under great stress here, my heart. Pastor Kneipp's alternating baths make it pound in my tonsils a good dozen times a day. In the barber shop, for instance, they have a shoeshine boy and clown (as a back-court fool, so to speak, a caricature of all the postwar German lemur traits), a little boy they picked up somewhere: a wild, lice-ridden tatterdemalion, an unspeakably repulsive blob of slime, pesky as a blowfly, leechy as a crab louse, a microbe apprentice, pederastically fingered, pickled in gonococci like an eel in green— You have to have seen with what democratic openness this basement rat throws himself at the victors—you have to have watched it. This is how it goes:

The door opens, but not far enough for a chief of the Praetorian Guard. He does not merely enter, he towers his way in. Everyone in the barber shop is flabbergasted (especially I: I've been subpoenaed as a witness for the prosecution, but still and all, that's just a gnat's eyelash away from being a defendant—and here I am, frivolously having my hair pomaded). The Praetorian bulks in the room. His skull is wedged in a helmet polished like plexiglass. A helmet of the avenging angels, it almost bangs against the ceiling. The barbers' razors tremble at the throats of the hygiene-needy, who, choked by their white towels, ogle up at the avenging angel. . . .

and he, the avenging angel, stomps closer in waxed lace-boots with thick rubber soles. Under his Grail-castle helmet, his kisser floats on the chin strap: T-bone-steak-fed American, sprouting from violent Lithuanian seed in Iowa, Irish madness in the brain, Dutch narrow-mindedness in the blood, Puritanical witch-burning fanaticism in the eyes, chewing-gum between the crushing nutcracker jaws. He snorts from his nostrils above them like a bull of Colchis. His thorax, squeezed upward by a ten-inch-wide motorcyclist belt, is swollen like a barrage balloon over whose tip a truck is accidentally driving. A rubber club dangles from his wrist over the sausage-stuffed white cotton glove. . . .

Yet, the basement rat is not intimidated. It scurries out of its corner and leaps at him, hurls itself at one of his leg columns and embraces it in a perfect tackle—straight out of Yale. Such a center-tackle throw will shake Congress, will be discussed for decades at the White House. . . .

but the avenging angel isn't in the mood today (maybe his *Fräulein* gave him a dose of the clap, or a superior chewed him out for having a hint of five-o'clock shadow or not having the dewy scent of Mennen). He merely swings out his leg ("Fuck off, you bastard!")—and the rat flies through space with a whine, landing in its corner, crumpling in pain, wrapped up, burrowed up in its rags, and its face peeps up, that blob of slime, and it is the dismayed, deeply frightened face, marked by utter sorrow and utter injustice, of an abused child with huge injured eyes, which grasp nothing and accuse the ungraspable—

and this child says, tonelessly, hopelessly, desperately, in a small, soft, childlike voice, "But you were the one who taught me to be a smart boy. . . ."

1948, autumn, Munich-Geiselgasteig.

To get the feeling that I live in a dream world, I wouldn't need the plunder and false magic of this movie world: palaces consisting only of façades, rooms with only two walls, singers interrupted in their singing, dropping their arms in the middle of the most theatrical gesture, closing the mouths that had just been snapping at the air as though hunting an invisible fly—while their voices keep right on singing dulcetly in playback until the sound engineer interrupts and spools them back in a whistling monkey jibber for replay. . . . I wouldn't need the destruction of logic in time: the film stories narrated back and forth, higgledy-piggledy, the end coming first and the beginning at the end. Or the lack of division between fiction and reality: Robinson Crusoe, Madame Dubarry, and Professor Dr. Sigmund Freud all joining me for lunch at my table in the canteen, each of them totally immersed in his part, whereas, in front of the camera, they are embarrassingly the disguised actors Meyer, Müller, and Lembke. Everyday life outside, beyond this world of shadow and folly, is no less a surrealistic dream.

The city of Munich is still lying in its mortar dust under the intact Bavarian postcard sky, with buildings broken out of the streets like teeth from a carious mouth. But the gaps now exert a magical lure. The rubble fields are gilded, they once again have a tangible realty value. New buildings are sure to proliferate shortly: business fortresses, office palaces, tenement barracks, twice, thrice, ten times bigger than the houses and buildings that used to stand here and have sunken into debris, ten times more space-efficient in honeycomb subdivision, yielding ten times more rent, so that new capital is quickly created to tear down whatever still survives to the left and the right, and to replace it with buildings that grow high, ten times, twenty times bigger, roomier. . . .

All at once, we see department stores bursting with all kinds of wares, snazzy places. I can go in and buy an alligator handbag for Christa, or else a plush doe by Frau Käthe Kruse or the war regalia of a Sioux chief for our little son. I thus woefully redeem my bad conscience for earning money sumptuously and spending it frivolously, indeed irresponsibly and heedlessly, for not husbanding, and certainly not saving, not gathering, but rather acting as if it were still the worthless old money, the trashy Reichsmark, instead of the sound and weighty Deutschmark with which we must shape our future, with which Germany, Europe, Western Civilization must rebuild from a rubble pile into a new efflorescence, with which we must create a new and this time permanent and definitive economic miracle.

But that's just it. It's all too miraculous for me. I truly believe this is a fairy tale. Whatever money I earn runs through my fingers like water; for me it's movie money, dream currency from a dream reality. The very way I earn it is dream-like and incredible. There's no fathoming what prompts Stoffel and Associates (my "movie piglets," as Christa calls them) to grab up every other, often maliciously ironic brainwave of mine in order to *create a simply great project.* The projects will most likely never be filmed. But thanks to some bank and tax manipulations beyond my ken, one project will enable the producers to *create* a different, even greater, even more profitable *project,* and thus to acquire the capital for newer, bigger studios and even newer, technically even more perfect cameras (the basis for even bigger *projects,* in which there'll be some pickings for me). . . .

I watch this brouhaha and I imagine that things will keep on like this for me too, bigger and faster and more and more lavish. I place my naïve confidence in a mysterious auto-functioning and parthenogenetic self-growth of prosperity. After all, that's what's happening all around me. The grocery stores are bursting with stuff to feed your face with. The hams, the sausages, the pâtés, meat salads, *ragouts fins,* the cheeses, the primeurs, the fruits are doubling, tripling, decupling overnight. The shoe-store displays are collapsing under a plethora of shoes; never have there been so many shoes since people stopped going on foot—for hardly anyone walks now; people take cars; you can buy them again; they stand, shinily painted in venomously synthetic candy colors, behind mirror-glass panes at the dealers' showrooms, bigger and bigger, faster and faster, more and more cars. . . .

The miracle took place overnight. It was a new era, altering "reality" no less than that day in 1938 that cut off the first half of my life and launched the ten-year Ice Age. This time too, like that Twelfth of March back in '38, a solstice day, if I remember correctly: a bright day on which the sun stood still in the clear heavens. Yesterday, the world was still a gray, wretched world, a world of timid hope. Today, at one fell swoop, it was all there, everything that might be hoped for—except hope; hope had become superfluous. Yesterday, people were skulking through the streets, gray-faced, dourly suffering, but occasionally envisioning Utopias—futures that would be different from everything that had previously enslaved us and made us wicked, a human society in which at last, at last, the dichotomy between the individual and the herd animal in us would be harmonized. A fantastic expectation? But why not? All possibilities were open. That was one good thing about the last gray phase of the Ice Age: the total demolition, the annihilation of everything, of all cities, all so-called values, and most thoroughly the state, the social fictions, the image of mankind. . . . Yesterday, we were still allowed to dream that we could reinvent everything. . . .

that's what it was like yesterday. And then, overnight, everything essentially became what it had been before the Ice and Rubble Age, the same corrupt world, the same world of money—only in a cunningly new, brightly promising, insidiously abstract way.

The same people who were starving yesterday but willing to share a piece of bread were stuffing their guts today and gobbling up their neighbors' food. The same people who were thoughtful yesterday, willing to have certain embarrassing insights, critical more of themselves than of others, forgot all about yesterday—except for the things that gave them an advantage over the others. The same people who were full of ideas and plans yesterday, who sought new forms, new ways of living, wanting to set up *kolkhozy* for soil-tilling intellectual workers, wanting to exemplify a rediscovered human dignity—those same people now had no trouble resigning themselves to the perfidiously substituted possibility, were thoroughly imbued with its presentness, offered no resistance to it, were buoyed and borne by it, soon regarded it as a fresh element in which they could swim like trout in mountain water. . . .

For it was an anciently promised world in a new promise, a different Thousand-Year Reich, a different Millennium—only this time from overseas. This time, not primordially and mythically rooted in the dark precincts of a barbaric past but modern, bright, rationalistic, and yet blessed with God's approval. You made a fool of yourself if you tried to warn against it apocalyptically in an amateur preacher's tone. It was a "reality" stuffed with all the values of Western Civilization. It had every kind of freedom and thus every possibility of human dignity. It was merely a question of choice, of the ability to go without. It resounded with lovely rhetoric about democracy, progress, humanized technology that would serve man and not vice versa, fine phrases about racial equality, ecology, protection of animals. . . . People could go right ahead and build cities again. Why, they were building the one grand City of Mankind: Anthropolis, the New Jerusalem, which the pioneers had sighted in the Golden West. The Star-Spangled Banner waved over it. . . .

but alas the construction of this new promised world from the ruins of the old one came about too swiftly for us, too surprisingly, too much like a magic trick: you couldn't help suspecting some conjuring. You see, it really did occur in the twinkling of an eye, overnight: yesterday, people had been starving or profiteering, their only survival chances in the black market; today, everyone, without exception or distinction, held forty Deutschmarks in his hand and could buy anything he liked and anything he could afford or whatever his common sense bade or forbade. Forty Deutschmarks. *Ni plus, ni moins.* If you were capable of making forty Deutschmarks be fruitful and multiply, you could gorge yourself, fatten your body, buy new clothes, furnish your home, rebuild your house, found a business or an entire industry, drink as much champagne, whiskey, beer, wine, Coca-Cola as you liked or could stand; you no longer had to feel like a pariah, a subhuman, gleaning the cigarette butts of Allied occupation soldiers from the asphalt and picking through their garbage cans for no-longer-edibles; you now faced those soldiers on the same brow level, as it were, or at least on the same esophagus level. And all this was extremely implausible, though factually documented "reality"—though implausible, yet not to be denied.

Schwab had come to Munich on behalf of the North West German Radio Network (in cooperation with the Bavarian State Radio Network). As one of Scherping's editors, an important figure in the resurrection of German cultural life, he was supposed to put together a nighttime program about the situation of writers in Germany during the first three years after the end of the war. Needless to say, these literati included people writing for the newly emerging film industry—hence, in Schwab's opinion, myself. We taped my contribution. Then came the day of the currency reform. On the morrow, I went to the cashier's office at the radio network to pick up my fee, which had been agreed upon in Reichsmarks but was given to me in Deutschmarks, five hundred Deutschmarks. Every other inhabitant of the three Western occupation zones had forty marks at his disposal. I was the richest man in the country.

Needless to say, we headed straight for Humpelmeyer's Restaurant. We couldn't get over the menu. We ordered brook trout, saddle of venison in cream with lingonberries, *omelette surprise.* We washed it down with two excellent Franconian wines and a bottle of Châteauneuf du Pape. At the next table, a man who had eaten his way deep into a roast goose followed our mordant commentary: "It may interest you to know that I am looking for someone to bring charges against parties unknown for mass manslaughter and damage to health," he said fervently. "All this stuff"—he pointed his knife and fork at the filled dishes all around—"didn't tumble out of the clear blue sky yesterday.

It must have been somewhere; people were hoarding it. For what reason, I ask you, for what purposes? Just go into any drugstore: you'll have no trouble whatsoever finding medicine that you couldn't get for love or money the day before yesterday. Where does it all come from? Something's wrong here. There's some vile swindle involved. Somebody must be doing a gigantic business. But tens of thousands had to starve to death. Mothers had to watch their children die because you couldn't get black-market penicillin for even thousands of marks, and today you can get it at any drugstore for a couple of pennies. We've got to get to the bottom of this."

We agreed with him and asked why he didn't bring charges himself. He said, "If I did, it would be interpreted politically. I was Gauleiter of Linz for a while."

It took only a few weeks to dispel any quandaries about the new "reality." Now it is overwhelmingly present. Like that Twelfth of March, 1938, in Vienna, which separated the first half of my life from me, this new reality projects all previous experiences into the realm of dreams. But in this way, detached from the past and having, epiphany-like, virtually turned into its own realized future, this reality is itself becoming unreal.

Supreme Movie Piglet Stoffel shows me his patronage by, *inter alia*, entrusting me with all sorts of missions that he thinks are sensitive and that have nothing to do with my capacity as idea man and screenwriter-to-be (he calls them "friendly favors" he "would not like to ask of anyone else"). And now he's "approached" me with a "request": a girl describing herself as an actress (she's taking lessons with some fluttery mime whose political past has damaged him) is on the cast list of the big new project of Astra Films (*A Woman Cheats*—a story of mine). Sure, it's a small part, but you've got to start somewhere, says Stoffel. ("The company has to make sure there'll be future stars. Otherwise, five or six years from now, we'll be screwed, with our stars sludging through their menopause.") Actually, the child (just nineteen) is a younger, wilder Astrid von Bürger: a dark-curled Brunhilde beauty, yet slender and firm. (I suspect that Stoffel sees not just a cinematic future with her.) But, unfortunately, she's "strange," as Stoffel puts it. "Take the kid in hand. I'd like to know what's with her. She's not off her rocker, but she's very weird. You'll notice it right away."

After a dinner in Boettner's Oyster Rooms (three dozen Limfjord Colossal, with Chablis, black bread and cheddar cheese, then a two-inch-thick filet steak, a carafe of Chambertin, melon sherbet; six weeks ago, they served rationed herring paste and cabbage stew here), she reveals her secret. Her real name is Ernestine (Ernie) Rosenzweig (stage name: Gudrun Karst). Her father, pure Aryan despite the suspicious name, was a traveling salesman in the lovely land of Franconia, the Romantic Road. He was killed by some drunken rowdies (SA) owing to a misunderstanding caused by the unfortunate name. Fearing lest her daughter fall victim to the same misunderstanding (the family lived in Dinkelsbühl), the mother put little Ernie into a Nazi nursery at the age of three. At fifteen she had a general's rank as leader in the Bund of German Maidens. At sixteen (1945) she was commanding a Bund of German Maidens camp in Allgäu, five thousand feet above sea level, three hundred and sixteen fourteen- to eighteen-year-olds who were being trained in close combat and the use of bazookas. She says she would have been willing to fight with a razor. Had anyone dared to tell her to her face that the war could not be won, the Russians were in Berlin, the English and the Americans outside Frankfurt and Hanover, she would have scratched out his eyes and bitten out his tonsils. But no one dared. Next there was a regiment of spahis who, man for man, screwed their way through every last girl in the Maiden Bund.

Then Ernie became a lieutenant's booty. He was friendly to her and promised her a career as a nightclub dancer once the nonfraternization rules loosened up a bit. She can't remember how she lost him (or he her). At any rate, she got to Munich, using some food from the *ravitaillement* of the French occupation to find shelter in a family rooming house run by an old-time screen star, Erna Morena. The identical Christian name won the lady's maternal sympathy. Through her, she gained entry into the movie world. "But you can understand," she says, "that I usually feel as if I were in an aquarium, where things, people, and events swim every which way, like tenches."

She is the right partner for me. (Christa obstinately refused to leave Hamburg; and after our son's birth, she bluntly declared that she found conjugal duties more repulsive than pleasurable. But that shouldn't serve as a pretext for me; I have promptly filled the gap in the mosaic of my sensual life.) In Gudrun Karst, I have found my spiritual complement. Together we swim through the aquarium of tenches.

I make sure that the underwater fauna surrounding her is tropically varied. I've rented a place for her with a countess to whom I had access by way of Christa's relatives. There, Gudrun is meeting all of Bavarian nobility and the (likewise Catholic) Upper Silesian nobility who have fled here. She already shrugs scornfully at the mention of names from the odd years of the Gotha Index of German Nobility.

I am wheeling and dealing to have her elected this year's Mardi Gras princess (it promises to be smashing). At the Astra Films ball, which will greatly overshadow that of Gloria Films, she cannot as yet play the starring role. This part is automatically awarded to Astrid von Bürger as a former star and Stoffel's spouse. But Gudrun Karst will lead the Pleiades, the group of seven up-and-coming starlets to be introduced to the public and the press. Bele Bachem is already designing the costumes with Bessie Becker.

The press (which is having a tremendous upswing in the new "reality") is starting to get seriously interested in Gudrun Karst. To give her the status of a working student, I have registered her at the university (as a psychology and sociology major). Every morning when she is not shooting, I send her to school in a horse-drawn carriage (the last hackney cab in Munich). We have lunch at the Vier Jahreszeiten, which is also the seat of the Montgolfier Club, an association of hot-air balloonists that Gudrun wishes to bring to life. In the evening, she plays Anouilh and Claudel.

At night, in the Rococo bed of the merely half-bombed-out home of the countess (I told her I have unfortunately drifted away from Christa—all too Protestant, alas—because of religious problems), I give Gudrun's mind the finishing touches. I explain the eschatological character of the time we are living through: the messianic promise of Americanism, the Paradise of smart boys on earth, coming before doomsday. I tell her about the effect of atomic bombs and how the dollar got its name from the *Thaler*, which in turn got its name from Joachimsthal, where uranium was first discovered in pitchblende. We chat about the German women who, like Scarlett O'Hara (like Christa), swore they would never go hungry again, and about the hazardous childhood of their sons, who, in the midst of bombings, gleaned pieces of fallen coal on railroad embankments from under passing freight trains; and about the later offspring, who are children today and whose every wish we fulfill (like me with my little boy) before they so much as sense the wish themselves.

Even our erotic relationship is spiritualized. When her senses gain the upper hand, I have her reexperience the spahis, man for man. She now quite regularly confesses to me when and under what special circumstances and conditions she felt pleasure against her will. Then, released and sobbing, she drifts off in my arms.

And all this for the sake of Astra Films Art and their reality. Verily, I say unto you: the future lies in abstraction.

□   7   □

SUCH AND SIMILAR THINGS, my dear Mr. Brodny, stand between me and the image of the old Yurop, in which the other half of my life is lost, and are the reason I can't tell you the plot of my book in three sentences. The story proliferates with no help from me, quite on its own, in parthenogenetic self-propagation under my hands. Whatever I narrate breeds more narrative. Every tale hatches ten others: a hybrid cell growth that cannot be controlled by any form. It's the disease of our time. Cancer everywhere. Ask Dr. Leblanc.

This and little else was the gist of my endless conversations with Schwab. Paris, city of dreams, offered us any number of topics. Everything steered us to that cancerous proliferation. For instance (in connection with the definitive, I might almost say incorrigible, form of the French): the curious fact that in our hemisphere we could obviously now create any number of fatherlands (along with Uganda and similar exotic ones elsewhere; in the German-speaking area there are now two, and with Austria and German-speaking Switzerland it would make four), but no new people, no new nation; while at the same time, you have the identity loss of most European nations and the sclerosis of the French.

A development of form as an evolutionary stage that has been outgrown, as Professor Leblanc maintains— But it would be too much trouble now formally to introduce the great physician and researcher; let's save that for later. Anyway, his views are not in-

teresting per se but solely in regard to the situation in which he
developed them—namely, at Gaia's deathbed, two years ago,
during one of our hectic and boisterous chats, when my brave beloved, the chocolate-brown Princess Jahovary, laughing once
again—

(laughing with dreadful exaggeration, intoxicated in her more
and more extravagant decay: all thirty-two horse-healthy mulatto
teeth seemed to leap from her mouth, the lips could barely re-
strain them, the violet hue they had assumed in the past few
weeks turned pale under the tension, like overly taut rubber-
bands—oh Lord! how often, how ardently, how voluptuously and
pleasurably, had I kissed them when they were still oxblood-red,
those sucking soaking stamp-pad lips melting creamy-mild under
mine! How tenderly I had marveled at them with my worshipful
dwarf-gaze, the midgets of my fingertips lusting for exploration,
the hopping troll of my tongue running over the beeswax-warm
mahogany of the cheek hills and slipping into the rococo pits of
the corners of the mouth. There, with her fleshiness, voluptuously notched like a fruit bursting in sweet overripeness, the
thread-fine bright line—the blemish of mixed blood—sprang
forth; as at the opening of the purple-fish shell, it accompanied
her luxuriously curving contour, and there, where the soft, moist
double hump of the lower lip, almost lascivious in its swelling,
was delicately cocked over the chin recess, it was swallowed by
deep cocoa tones covered with a down as delicate as mold. . . . Oh
Lord! to what foolish extremes did I not go in order to make them
burst into a smile, those fat Negro lips, and to watch them rolling
from the ivory of the teeth, brightly shining like hard-boiled egg
white until, at the salmon-colored arcades of the gums, the ivory
turned yellow, like translucent yolk, turned yellow into primordial cannibal strength which was now bared so protrudingly, exposed so bitingly . . . Ahh! but I loved her sword-swallowing,
fire-eating laugh, I loved *nature* in it, crude, unadulterated Nature, loved the laryngological glimpse into the yawning monster-
throat, that multi-vaulted, hortensia-hued grotto, that lilacky Bomarzo, the Art Nouveau arches of pale-lilac lip-flesh, the Gaudí
cornices of pale-pink gums, the purple cupola of the palate over

the dragon's hump of the tongue, which knotted forward out of the rosy-fleshed gate of hell of the esophageal muscle with the bud-like flesh stalactite of the uvula—all this still ineffably fresh and clean, just scoured by surf on palm-fanned spice beaches, still incredibly healthy, full of animal vitality despite her lamentable condition; only, because she was emaciated, her face a skull, it now looked as if she had eaten her own tonsils and was offering them for one last inspection, awaiting an official go-ahead before swallowing them down. Oh, Godohgod, her torso was all skin and bones now, and I did not care to picture what she looked like farther below; but when she, half stretching up, half sinking into the pillows, let her skeletal trunk, covered with a skin like saddle leather, rise out of the billowy nightgown, as frightening as one of the nightmare figures in Picasso's *Guernica*, and when she laughed and laughed, she really looked like a dying horse, a drowning horse, and I thought, She wants to carry it to shore, she wants to rescue it beyond death, this lovely, flawless dentition— indeed it was a pity to take it with her! . . .)

—when she, laughing once again, complained, "*J'comprends jamais c'qu'il veut dire, cet ours—croyez-vous que c'est de ma faute?*" then Professor Leblanc, in the usual Cartesian crystal-clear way, developed his pertinent ideas. Bold, not only because they were articulated at the bedside of a cancer patient but of course especially piquant for that very reason: cancer as a universal phenomenon of the age; the inability to preserve form; hybrid growth of everything and everyone in accordance with physics; modern view of the world, the cosmos, as a monstrous explosion, therefore life as a continuous explosion of cells. Form as anti-Nature, in a word.

At any rate, it's an awful pity that Schwab died so early—I mean, alas, too early to hear my naïve findings in this area being confirmed by a scholar of Leblanc's rank. I will not forget the pain around his mouth when once, on a similar occasion, he quoted Valéry's "*trouver avant de chercher*" (and I brutally re-mised, FOR UNTO EVERY ONE THAT HATH SHALL BE GIVEN . . . BUT FROM HIM THAT HATH NOT SHALL BE TAKEN AWAY THAT WHICH HE HATH. . . . But all this later, later! . .).

MEANWHILE, you can glean from the foregoing, esteemed Mr. Brodny, how the dialogue with my dead friend continues. I mean how difficult—nay, impossible—it is for me to eliminate him from my mind (so that in the end, I have to replace him with you). Which, however, leads—on my part—to an unintentional yet unavoidable, exuberant growth of everything I would like to narrate. Why, that was, as you will hear, the dilemma of my book, and it then, thanks to an enlightening idea that occurred to me a few days ago on the road from Reims to Paris, became its theme. (After all, writing always means making virtues of necessity.)

For example, I just cannot do without Schwab when, as living proof of my (and Professor Leblanc's) views on the relationship between nation (as form) and individual character, I cite the handsome Pole, whom S., for some enigmatic reason, so violently hated (I surmise homoerotic impulses at the sight of the fellow's dreadfully muscular arms).

I am talking about the man who plays night clerk in this lousy hotel—he's probably perched down there now, at his desk, in front of the switchboard in the Rembrandtian light-space-darkness (a turn-of-phrase achievement devised especially for Schwab: a tidbit of annoyance for him, a small vendetta pill for perfidious amiabilities!), perched there in the meagerly shaded beam of the tiny night lamp, so deeply absorbed in one of his idiotic detective pulps that he does not hear the telephone. . . .

well, this outstanding male, who looks like a holy dragon killer on a counterfeit icon—I mean, he's much too handsome, much too lewdly holy, with his egg-shaped face beyolked by archangel-golden curls, with black almond eyes and a straw-whisk of mustache (plus the ever-bared butcher arms)—this hormone-flaunting popinjay, I tell you, has obviously changed since he became a French citizen. You see, he wasn't naturalized during Schwab's lifetime (i.e., five years ago). Back then, he was stateless, like me, but no one could doubt that he felt Polish, was Polish, and would always remain Polish—whatever that might do to one. It was awe-inspiring. When he took my passport upon my first arrival here, he scrutinized the dubious document ("Passport of the Federal Republic of Germany . . . The bearer of this passport does not possess German citizenship"), then scrutinized me with undisguised disapproval (as though I had neglected to wipe my shoes on the mat when entering), and said insolently, "*En voici un autre!*"—as if he had had enough of this sort. And it was only upon my venomous question "*Quelque chose ne va pas?*" that he explained himself: "*Vous êtes apatride.*"

"What's his problem?" asked Schwab, who had come with me from his hotel on the Left Bank (he was his old self again, of course, namely drunk, and held his head, slack mouth half open, so far back that the eyelids had tilted over his carp-gaze behind the thick glasses, like the lids on a baby doll placed on its back; he looked as if he were asleep standing; nobody would have guessed that he was listening to the dialogue with the archangel by the switchboard).

"He's delighted that I'm stateless. It's called '*apatride*' in French," I said. "He probably thinks it's something mythological. A race that devours its children."

"*Ce n'est pas commode,*" said the mustachioed angel-head over the rower's thorax. "*D'ailleurs, je le suis aussi, moi. . . .*"

"What's his dialect?" asked Schwab, his head raised toward the ceiling, like a blind seer.

"No dialect, an accent. Some Slavonic snail's dish of labials and sibilants."

"*Vous êtes polonais d'origine?*" I asked the holy athlete.

"*Oui, monsieur,*" he said, growing a foot taller: male beauty from a pulp romance, the far too short sleeves of his cotton T-shirt (Americans, as you ought to know, J.G., wear this as an undershirt) constricting his muscle-packed arms.

"There you have it," I said to Schwab. "You can really witness the way the national pump-thrust into the asshole bloats out the chest. Enviable, eh? At least, *one* assurance."

"Yes," said Schwab up to the ceiling (he was already having a hard time speaking). "The self-assurance of morons."

But it's really not so simple, I think. The issues require our careful attention. For instance (I still see this anthropologically, in terms of a nation as a form), the relationship between aggression and form. Take the handsome Pole. Having ceased being a Pole and become a French citizen (thus arriving in the refuse heap of the nationalized non-French, all those *bicots* and *pieds noirs* and so forth), he no longer swells up his body half so awe-inspiringly. Something gave him a fine pinprick; he no longer holds air. The perfect egg-oval of his apostle-head has become a zero enframed with angel hair and showing a yellow mustache—his face is a big nothing, a child's drawing on a clouded windowpane, to be wiped away by a hand. Honestly, I believe I could beat the hell out of him now. I could punch him straight in the mustachioed egg, *un direct en pleine gueule*, without having to fear his butcher-arms.

What's happened to him? He's lost his self-assurance. Yet not his stupidity. Has he grown smarter as a Frenchman? Or by doubting whether he is really French and not still Polish? Are we, Yankel G. Brodny (*à propos*, what does the G stand for? George? Gilbert? Ganef? or ultimately even Goy?), are you and I so unpleasantly smart because we are nothing and everything, because our heads hum with doubts as to what we truly are and where we belong? Have we in the course of one lifetime achieved something that took Signor Lombroso at least two generations to reach—genius (and madness)—by migrating and settling in a new environment? How is it in America, where such migrations are the rule? A nation that has its origin in immigrants? Madness galore, no doubt; and where is genius? . . .

But I'm already playing the Roman candle again, as Schwab ironically put it. I'm pulling your leg, sir. Still and all, you have to admit, it's an extraordinarily piquant theme: the sublime interrelationship between stupidity and form. The interrelationship between stupidity and self-assurance is far too obvious, and it isn't useful to ponder whether stupidity grants one assurance. But what about the converse notion: that assurance makes you stupid? (Is French self-assurance a sign that French intelligence is biologically a stupidity? The seal of a lethal factor?) And what about religious assurance? The certainty of a spiritual vanishing point that keeps the chaotic world in a safe perspective? Or an intuitive certainty, a leaning toward the feminine, as it were—female self-assurance, I'd say, is a form of intelligence more safe and secure in the lap of Mother Nature, more in harmony, in a sort of clinch with this dangerous lady. Madame, for example: the boss and owner of this hotel, the handsome Pole's employer.

◻   9   ◻

EVEN WHILE SCHWAB WAS ALIVE, Madame played a key role in my reflections: the perfect Platonic ideal of Frenchness, the image incarnate of the French Idea. Accordingly, Madame's self-assurance—for she is French in this especially—also has flagrantly physical causes: Madame was a beauty queen, Miss Cannes of 1939, an obviously well-preserving vintage year.

Had I, dear Yankel Gilbert, earmarked you for the privilege of seeing Madame *à poil,* such as was granted Schwab and myself on one of those days five years ago— Oh, not amorously in a merry threesome, alas, but only with an indiscreet glimpse from an open window across a rather narrow airshaft into another window that likewise happened to be open. In the room beyond, Madame was stretching in front of the mirror in the wardrobe door, surveying her gorgeous nudity—oh, God! She too, I grant you, seemed to find the sight satisfying. She threw out her chest—a wow of a chest, godammit! Keeping her head high, with the henna-hair monster (known as a *boudin* hereabouts) at the back of her neck, and casting a proud look over the splendidly round shoulder at herself in the mirror, she propped her hand on the tightened waist over the plump behind—a true bliss of hips, sir—and threw out her torso with the double exuberance of boobs like a wedge in a heart-shaped socle (Brancusi's design, Modigliani's contours). And then did a tango step with a half twist in the mirror ... then turned toward us full face, goddammit, and saw us, saw us in the window facing hers, saw us drooling, gasping, our eyes leaden-gray with lust, *les deux chleux,* the prematurely senile men watching Susannah bathing (I adapted the scene for one of my best movie scripts).... She fled from our field of vision and, invisible now and quite explicitly disgruntled, furiously slammed her window shut....

I say, had I, in creative generosity, granted you too this feast for the eyes (but that wouldn't do: even we must obey certain laws), you would understand what I mean by the incarnation of the French Idea. This peony plumpness, this stretching sump-tuousness—"as slim as a scepter and as mighty as a throne"— that's what their cathedrals are like: the black-haired aristocrat of Amiens, the ripe blond beauty of Madame de Chartres, the red-head of Reims with the jewels on the white skin, the arrogant pa-trician of Bourges, the incomparably elegant grace of the brunette of Coutances, the applefreshness of the Norman in a peasant girl's costume, the mermaid Honfleur . . . and that's what their women are like: artworks with which a nation pays tribute to itself, in Delacroix, Ingres, Renoir, Maillol. And in Madame's case this was of special ripeness, godammit! Even rounder, even plumper, even tastier—plus the hard lithographic colors of Toulouse-Lau-trec. You, being a connoisseur of women (I've pegged you), must know what I'm talking about: *"Vecchia gallina fa buon brodo,"* say your friends the witty Tuscans. *Madonna mia santa, che paio di poppe!* Is the handsome Pole allowed to play with them after hours? In German you could make a pun of it: Pole Poppen-speeler—who's that by, anyway? Theodor Storm, yes indeed. Nobody reads him anymore. Schwab—yes, Schwab loved Storm. Reread him regularly. Of course, he also loved Delacroix, Ingres, Renoir, Maillol, and all that crowd. A culture vulture— Schwab, I mean. An alcoholic too, alas. But the two often go hand in hand: a disturbed ego and an artistic sensibililty. What do you think? Is he finally self-confident, my brother Schwab? Self-confident in a definitive blissful state of stupidity, in a triumphal one-upmanship there, or up there—somewhere in the icy blue of the sky, in his now unlosable Godly Fatherland? . . .

But this is quite uninteresting. Back to Madame—the more edifying subject, God wot! Madame is, for me, France, even as France, for me, preserves the stylistic essence of the lost half of my life: erotically determined by the anima of the ripe woman. Don't be led astray by the ephebes of the fashion magazines. Those ephemeral phenomena, fashions, reflections of the era. Creations of latent homoeroticism, of children who are being al-lowed to play. Behind them, France is still the motherland of mother sons. Oedipal Neverneverland, supervised by Mama's benevolent severity. . . .

And now I want to tell you something that should make your eyes go round with amazement like Schwab's when I chatted to him about my adventures hereabouts. So just listen like a good boy:

That Madame is of sovereign intelligence is something I need not emphasize: Madame is French. She displays this in the ineffably scornful hardness with which she keeps this crummy joint afloat. (Madame's *établissement*, called Hôtel Épicure without false modesty, is frequented, thanks to its half-peripheral, half-central location, by a very special kind of human refuse, a bourgeoisie of the marooned, so to speak, who have found a status of their own and even something like a special dignity in being failures, losers, hopeless beginners from the start. And they jealously preserve that status and dignity. Perhaps you know this genre from the petit bourgeois neighborhoods of Warsaw or Budapest. Professions like that of a traveling salesman in colored fountain pens for first-graders; retired tax officials who become provincial tax advisers; unemployed theatrical hairdressers; an Algerian silversmith's family, eight or nine generations altogether, with a passion for sunflower seeds; on occasion a freestyle-wrestling manager with his warriors, "Haarmin Vichtonen the Finnish World Champion," "Costa Popovitch the Bulgarian Buffalo"; now and then, one of the old hookers who have wafted around the Place des Ternes like autumn leaves and whose final lure is despair.)

Madame applies to everyone the cold neutrality of that ironclad law which says there's nothing free in life except death—and even death costs you your life. In pecuniary matters, Madame's severity has something sacerdotal about it. She is inexorable with tardy payers (including me, who have actually managed to get credit at German post offices!) even if the poor devil, begging in vain for just a little more time, is losing his last chance for the business deal that will save him, or the toothless prostitute is losing her last client. But then it may happen that Madame unexpectedly issues a merciful verdict, maintaining a desperate person in his desperateness, pickling and preserving him in his hopelessness—as if to show the others, who believe they might escape their fate, that *their* fate is ineluctable.

And in a miraculous way, these latter, floating belly up and wriggling only every now and again, reflexively, are aroused by Madame's hardness to writhing life—like a pailful of whitefish that you dump back into the creek because they're not worth frying. They get together and bitch. Among Frenchmen, this is an act of communion—the only one they have left. There's no other way for them to find human contact with one another. By bitching, they fuse into a community, a community of choice equality: Frenchmen.

This makes Madame's *établissement* an out-and-out national shrine. Every day, a handful of her clients get together and bitch in the furiously chopped-up cackling of French *éloquence*, in rising and falling and again rising and falling chains of words, tinkling without start or stop, like Czerny piano exercises. They bitch at Madame and at her inhuman inexorability, her shameless bamboozling and penny-pinching. Naturally, they also bitch at the defects of the hotel, the lousy beds and the rarely changed linen, the lack of service; aside from the night clerk, who never hears the telephone, there are a few cleaning women, mild loonies or alumnae of penal or drying-out institutions, who show up in the morning to do something or other with brooms, pails, and mops: that's the whole staff. Madame's clients even bitch at the disturbance caused by these more illusory than effective cleanliness measures. They bitch at the universal mismanagement, politics, the world situation, existence, creation, God the Creator, and His Only Begotten Son, little *Jésu*. And lo and behold, their words visibly blossom. They want to say what they have to say in a better manner, and they always do say it better and better. The strings of pearls of their sentences intertwine and intertwist into arabesques, from which leaves break out and buds open up in resplendent, sensual fullness. The glory of language proliferates among them, a glassy rosebush, enclasping and fettering them, beguiling and bewitching them with its fragrance. They themselves grow into it, become part of it, like the human effigies in the ensnarled illuminated initials in a medieval Bible: iterated and reiterated, their heads peep out of the rosebush's tangles, and its blossoms spring out of their mouths. And each of these blossoms is ennobled by literary usage, has at some point flowed into a sublime pen, has been purged by it, polished, and artfully mounted to be presented to the Nation as a jewel for its treasury.

The speakers sound as if they know this and are proudly aware *that* they are quoting and *whom* they are quoting, and as if they are honoring the quoted by quoting him. Thereby and therewith, they become taller, tauter, more dignified—*oui, on rouspète, mais on rouspète sur un niveau très élevé.* . . . Their bitching has long since lost the hatefulness of anything personal. It sovereignly detaches itself, turns into Truth and Art. And thereby and therewith, they too, the bitchers, detach themselves from one another, become more and more impersonal, more and more formal, more and more stylized, more and more French.

There they stand, clustered in Callot grouplets on the dark landings or in the narrow, shabby stairwell corridors of the Hôtel Épicure, a third-class hostel for the homeless in one of those boglike, stagnating corners of the city, whose maelstrom dumps out its slops here: a handful of castaways and failures, washed out by weather and life, wearing the rags of long-past prosperity, which was probably never theirs, the tatters of long-past fashions, hung with the improvised and converted implements of solitary existence, the seat-cane umbrellas, thermoses, the multifarious pouches and pockets: each man a Robinson Crusoe in the frightful desolation of the metropolis, Paris, isle of the marooned. . . . For a few minutes, language has broken open the crusts of their isolation. They can speak with one another, communicate with one another. And now, this same language, in its refinement and perfection, is tearing them away from one another, pulling them apart in the same powerful flight in which it brought them together: the plunge and upswing of two hyperbolas arch toward, and then away from, one another.

And yet, among these castaways into, and castoffs from, life, something wonderful has happened—something that solidifies, edifies, and elevates them. The riffraff have become Frenchmen, self-assured children of the Nation until old age, worthily wrapped in the bunting of claptrap, swathed in it like mummies, isolated to a compulsively neurotic degree, stiff and proud. Proud

:: 126 ::

of forming, along with millions of other isolated beings, the collective that bears the sublime name of *La Nation Française* and that, in an abstract yet effective way, gives their existence a dimension in which it is invulnerable, ordered, tested, and gloriously transfigured for all time. Each individual is a choice blue-white-and-red morsel in the aspic of their National Culture (an image that would not have failed to arouse an involuntary snort from Schwab).

Like the crest of a municipal coat of arms—Marianne's Phrygian cap—Madame's burning red *boudin* hovers above all this. Below, in the white field: the blue shadows of her eyelids and the harsh lipstick of her Toulouse-Lautrec mouth. Oh God! . . .

Schwab was the first to make a reverence to the high rank of her intellect; this, in recognition of her keen discernment that he was a man of quality, even though the two of them never managed to exchange a word beyond a conventional *"Bonjour, madame"* and an icy *"Bonjour, m'sieur"* (the rest of Schwab's French vocabulary, including the singing of *"Allongs angfanz della patrieyeh,"* never found employment).

To be sure, he had every reason for thankful wonder at how sovereignly Madame ignored his drunkenness. This meant: she understood. Once, after accompanying me here, when we were about to say good-bye at the entrance, he slipped out of my energetically supportive hand. Through the glass panes, he had spied the rubber tree in the vestibule and imagined he was inside and the plant outside. So he splintered through the door and staggered toward the tub in order to unbutton his fly. Whereupon Madame said a brief word to the handsome Pole, who came from behind the desk, grabbed a chair, and shoved it (to my great surprise; I was just about to come to Schwab's defense) into the hollows at the back of S.'s knees. When S. crashed down on the chair, the Pole swiftly left, then returned with a bottle of Calvados and a glass, which he filled and handed to S. Incidentally, Schwab's reaction was no less sensitive. He did not toast Madame, as any other drunkard would have done with gross familiarity. No, indeed. Schwab tipped the glass very elegantly and skillfully over his projecting lower lip, handed it back to the handsome Pole, rose to his feet, peered around, looked into the corner of the vestibule, spotted a broom placed there by the charwomen in preparation for the morning cleanup (it was well after midnight), grabbed the broom, and presented it to Madame, as he had learned to do in the army—ah! after a fashion, though not much of one, the hopeless Pfc. arsehole, the screwed-up, fucked-up intellectual, the wearer of thick glasses—presented the broom, skewily, awkwardly, touchingly, and managed to blurt out, "*Madame ... le boche ... présente les armes ... à vous....*" Sheer agony was glazed in his eyes.

I do not expect you to show emotion, Jaykob Jee. I mention this minor incident simply to give you as graphic a picture as possible of Madame. Rhetoric—especially national rhetoric!—creates reality, after all, creates its own flesh, which in turn creates its own mind. As for myself, I could prolong the list of unusual and intelligent things that Madame did in these years, as proof of her French mind, her superior mind, starting with her surprising sympathy for Dawn, for the progressive abstraction afflicting the Daughter of the American Revolution, and the resolute way she took the soon batty girl into her maternal custody and ultimately into her arch-feminine, anti-male protection against me. ("But she must know that I'm ready to do anything for Dawn," I complained. And Schwab replied, "Yes. That's just it." "What?" I asked, obtusely. And S., "You're playing Ariosto. You're leading her into the Valley of the Moon, where they keep the time that is wasted in dreams. Madame realizes it. And that's what she wants to shield Dawn from.") But the list of Madame's wise and wonderful deeds would be incomplete if I neglected to mention that every so often, even now, she leaves her window open—of course, without standing naked at her mirror, but for occasional little snapshots of her physical merits all the same. As though she knew what delicious morsels are prepared from such inspirations in a writer's alchemical kitchen.

Back then, after our ignominious exposure as juicy voyeurs, leaden with lust for her gorgeous nakedness, Madame outdid herself and all expectations of her: like Bonaparte she crowned herself with her own hands. . . .

I am speaking about her majestic assurance the next day, when returning our artificially un-self-conscious salutes. Schwab had come over from the Left Bank to pick me up. As he came through the entrance door, I arrived at the bottom of the stairs in front of the vestibule. Madame, as usual, was enthroned behind the desk, in front of the switchboard. (There is, as I have said, no clerk during the day; when the handsome Pole is off in some corner snoring out his fatigue after performing his multifarious duties, Madame receives and bullies her guests herself.) Both Schwab and I said, "*Bonjour, madame!*" at about the same time, and she replied with her icy "*Bonjour, m'sieurs!*" watching as we greeted one another. Her gaze was so clear and forthright that we realized she knew what made us boyishly self-conscious and, under her basilisk eyes, almost embarrassed. Namely, that the sight of her yesterday, her female body eavesdropped upon and lecherously felt and fingered by our desire and secretly enjoyed, had been an erotic catalyst, precipitating the essential matter from the delicate state of the friendship between S. and myself. As though, by witnessing us jointly lusting after her, she had, in some abstract way, blessed our wedding.

□   10   □

IT SHOULD NOT STRIKE YOU AS ODD, Mr. America, that I confess these intimate events to you. The consensus, I know, is that Anglo-Saxons are easy to shock in erotic matters. The least protrusion of intimacy will elicit embarrassment— profound reddening, and flickering winks. But let me tell you this is true only of the social strata my paternal friend and patron John referred to as the "bloody fucking middle classes." Strata less tensely self-conscious appreciate candor (*désinvolture*, which Schwab used to talk about so much; tell me your ideals and I'll tell you what you're lacking).

John (later Sir John, after distinguishing himself so awkwardly at the Nuremberg trials and then being cold-storaged as His Britannic Majesty's ambassador in Manila, where he is probably still stranded today, God rest his soul! . . . but at that time, in our

Nuremberg days, and before that in Vienna, simply the Right Honourable John William Robert Derek Russel Quincey Fogg)—well, John gave me an impressive object lesson in elegant unabashment. In regard to his deceased spouse Stella, for instance, with whom I, at nineteen, had maintained amorous relations, which I strove to conceal from him at any price, he expressed himself as follows: "An excellent poke, indeed, a most exquisite fuck—didn't you think so? Poor girl, what a shame she had to die so soon—though she, too, would be fairly close to her forties today. And you know, they don't age so well, those Bedouin Jewesses; they become skinny and grow mustaches—oh come on, you wouldn't roll her as eagerly now as you did back then, would you?"

Probably not. Though I had sworn I would always do it with her until the last breath I drew, with her alone, and never, no never, with anyone else. Stella was the first of my great, final, only, real, and true loves, the latest for the moment having been Gaia (and, by the way, my desire for a new one is urgent).

But Stella was actually more, was different, was more powerful, more divinely generous than any other woman after her. Christa, for instance (an experiment with inadequate means on an unsuitable object, to put it in legalese; to be a legitimate wife in an unimpaired legal position was ultimately the only demand she made on me). Or later, Dawn (likewise, an enterprise doomed from the start, albeit with more poetic, more hazardous, more insane, quixotic traits). Yes, even Gaia (chocolate-brown Princess Jahovary, sumptuous fulfillment unto death). And in between, before Dawn even, long before Gaia, and since then over and over again in almost dipsomaniacal repetition, the fading movie star Nadine; when I'm totally confused, estranged from self, tangled up in hopeless movie projects, incapable of taking refuge in my book (the other act of insanity), close to the worst of despairs, apathetic, when all my fuses have blown and my pity for her—for myself—becomes so ardent that it kindles a sort of passion in me ... well, I don't want to exaggerate; a repeated flash in the pan, as Christa would have put it, and swiftly gone, granted: *tout de même* ...

Stella was—yes, she was "reality." She was the day. I wish I could have explained it to John—but what for? Besides, he probably knew about it anyway. He always knew more (true to the traditions of perfidious Albion) than he admitted or even hinted at. In every way, at every closer look, he was surprisingly denser, richer in dimension, and of course more inscrutable. (My ludicrous guilt feelings toward him back then! The poignant conflicts with my boyish honor, despite Stella's semi-amused, semi-annoyed laughter, her impatient shrugging when I persisted. . . . "C'est jeune et ça ne sait pas," Gaia would have said.)

Needless to say, I also loved him, and naturally John knew that, too, as he knew everything else. Just as Stella knew that he knew everything and hence this, too. It was a game I did not want to join, I was quite simply foolish and young—and that means barbaric. I did not catch the essence of the situation. As a good philistine, I merely saw the scandalous surface: an elegant woman keeping a nineteen-year-old gigolo with her husband's okay. And since, according to convention, I was the most despicable of the partners, the gigolo, I refused to admit that our unconventional relations were absolved by honest, noble, even passionate feelings. Hence, John was not a cuckold, Stella not Messalina, I not a kept stud but rather the love object of two beautiful souls, an ideal son and thereby a lucky fellow. . . .

And I certainly didn't see what John and Stella presumably cared about most: *style*. The neat arrangement, the elegant and civilized behavior that puts such a triangle—forget about the feelings—beyond banality: Art Déco, lived, loved, lauded. . . . Back then, in the lost first half of my life, even such matters had their form.

To say this to John later, in Nuremberg, where he was preoccupied with his poetic deed of madness in presenting to an astonished world Stella's death as a sacrifice of love, to make him somehow understand that now I finally knew how delicately we had danced, all the way to the threshold of the Third Reich, in step with the music of a cherished *Zeitgeist*—well, my efforts would have been superfluous if not embarrassing. A characteristic of the German, he used to say, is to emphasize the obvious. . . .

And besides, how long ago it all was, faded, vanished, buried by the dust of the many, many years we have lived through since then! . . .

Only one other of my great, uniquely true, and final loves—told here for the sake of completeness—might possibly be compared to my love for Stella, I mean in the wealth of experience, in the grateful bliss with which I felt and practiced and ultimately buried it within myself as an undying memory, as the pretty expression goes. (Incidentally, it was for the longest time the only love that toiled not nor spun, the only love that poured out of me without being performed, without cerebral or—if you will—psychoanalytic help, without the Sisyphean labor of loving; the only love that flowed from me with the undemanding naturalness of a forest wellspring, watering my spirit as it bloomed.) My bliss lasted for fourteen years (a magic number for me in many ways: two times the evil seven makes a good number). But needless to say I destroyed this love—out of a need to perform, precisely because I wanted to love so diligently.

It is a dramatic story, which I jotted down somewhere and then threw away. My interpretation did not fit; the reason I gave for the breakup (jealousy of the most abstract, artificial of my loves: Dawn) was quite unnecessary, could just as easily have been entirely different or altogether superfluous. It is nonetheless interesting that during this ideal love, I could still feel a need for that other, abstract, artificial love (for Dawn). Nature, esteemed Mr. Brodny, does not suffice for us, even in matters of love; here, too, we want, must do, something artificial. . . .

But I realize I could be suspected of playing a coy game of hide-and-seek. Nothing could be further from my mind. I am speaking of my love for my (and Christa's) son. He is now twenty years old. A hectically, indeed hysterically new generation. *Plus de pères, rien que des fils.* To play it safe, he no longer speaks to me, and he has taken his mother's name. I wish him love, beauty, the very best. At odd moments, even now, when (with a pang in my heart) I understand him: during his first fourteen years, I must have been for him rather as my mother had been for me half a century ago or Stella almost thirty years ago, except that I was fortunate enough to lose both those figures at the right moment. I have been (biologically) preserved for him, and it must have been painful for him to learn something I didn't have to learn: namely that a parent or a lover is a human being, and that he was not exclusively the god next to whom there could be no other gods as I was for him. *The old, old trouble.* Always comes right before the natural end (of unstrenuous love).

But what good does it do us to be so wise, Mr. Brodny, my fellow sufferer? What good would it do if I told him that for fourteen years he was the dearest and most beautiful of my gods and closer to my heart than any of my goddesses?

However, Stella in those far-off days (1938 in Vienna, and then in the Salzkammergut, and then in Bucharest, and then here there and everywhere during the rat hunt of the early war years until her disappearance in a concentration camp) was quite simply everything for me. She was my life, the air I breathed, all the warmth and sweetness of this earth. She bore me anew. She nursed me with her milk. She liberated me from the dreadful confinement poverty stupidity density of my formative years in Vienna. Thanks to her, my "family" evaporated: my foster parents (Uncle Helmuth and Aunt Hertha—those names!), my real foster mother (Aunt Selma, spellbound, and thus the only one truly related to me), and my cousin Wolfgang (my brother Abel, highly gifted, earnest, blond, youthfully robust, industrious, reliable, all the things that I'm not and wasn't, the born sacrificial animal, the smooth slaughter-sheep with the lovely, gentle eyes and the warm, meadow-scented breath). All those exemplary petit bourgeois people escaped from the narrator's box of toys, which had weighed on me like Füssli's *Nightmare* after a bright, spoiled, suddenly and cruelly interrupted childhood with my beautiful mother (safe and secure in the sumptuous households of her Balkan-prince gallants; lovingly cared for and tended by my lavender-scented nanny Miss Fern—sounds good, doesn't it?), weighed on me through a dozen horrible years in Vienna, weighed on my so-called youth, my dully brooding puberty, my tormented, masturbatory, straying and strolling adolescence—all those petit bourgeois people disappeared into the fableland of memory, became the specters of a bad but happily concluded dream; at best, they were mere puppets from the trash bin of anecdote.

Stella liberated me from what she, in the finest harmony with her husband, John (and perhaps because of my scruples concerning him), called the appalling hypocrisy of the bloody fucking middle classes. "Life in dark waters, fishing in them at second hand, a deceived hand, the pond already empty; life cowering under the whip of imperative shalls and musts that no one believes in but everyone clings to, because it gives a few not entirely stupid people the chance to do business and everyone hopes that some will fall his way; the inveterate dishonesty that tries to rig up a solace in every oppression and humiliation; the unnatural, invented, insane quality of existence in a constant as-if; the envious, mistrustful creature, concerned with and demanding rank and position. . . ."

(we know it all, don't we, know it by heart: all the qualities that make intellectuals and artists) . . .

but let us not speak of that now. Stella, in any event, saved me from petit bourgeois morality, which sourishly ferments everything; saved me from—even worse!—the insinuatingly intimate, pseudo-artistic soul of the philistines into whose hands I was delivered after my mother's death. She released me from the shameful ignorance into which my Viennese relatives had plunged me when they pulled me down to their level. To Stella, and to her alone, I owe my living through the first half of my life, consciously, with open eyes, as lived life and not just as a literary phenomenon, part fairy tale and part tenement story. She brought me to; she brought me to myself and brought me my self—myself as I had been meant to be, as God, the Creation, or Mother Nature, or whatever had originally designed me, and as what they had meant me to become. Stella revived in me the possibility of becoming what I, as a child, should have become, basking as I did in the happiness of my mother's cheerful, kindly, tender, and intelligent nature, and, under the auspices of my various nominal uncles and godfathers, enjoying the finest conditions for growing up: a free person without bitterness, rancor, resentment (admire the result).

Stella aroused this vision of me, a vision horribly frustrated for twelve years, of my original destiny as the Son of Man (how appropriate! how true to the *Zeitgeist!*), and she let me live that vision for a brief while. At the last minute, so to speak, before the era that could afford the luxury of such ideal notions went under in the icy blue-gold of a March day—or rather: froze at first. . . .

For the moment, you see, it froze, congealed, became alien and distant, as if no longer belonging to us, as if it had never belonged to us nor we to it. From now on, we knew the era and recognized ourselves in it by hearsay, as it were. And Stella opened my eyes to this time, too—the time that would soon form the last half of my life. Stella showed me not only that it was a gray, abject time, a dismal, impoverished time of wretched need and humiliating necessity, scarcity, envy, malice, anxiety, constraint, but also that one could still find, in this time, the "reality within reality," as she put it, the world that had made my childhood bright and brilliant and given me an inkling of what man is meant to be. We experienced ourselves as history (which I had already experienced in my childhood). From now on, we lived with our past like Nagel with his shot-off arm—without it and yet with it in some abstract fashion. (Incidentally, to be precise: the day I am speaking of was March 12, 1938, in Vienna, the sky was Adriatically blue, the sunshine sparkling, and the temperature eleven degrees below zero Celsius.)

11

AS FOR THE PHENOMENOLOGY of that era, which has been preserved in me like an alien life: its light.

In my childhood: a bright, clear, wind-stirred, wide-open spring light. (Not an Art Déco light but rather the light of the Jugendstil; our first impressions are not only our own: they are bathed in the light of our parents' heyday.) My mother sometimes sang in her delightfully airy sunlight-dappled-sprinkled mood (Bonnard), and I would ask her over and over again to sing the one that began

Mach mir kein bitteres Gesicht,
Es geht nicht, lieber Schatz,
Denn was dein Herr Papa verspricht,
Ist alles für die Katz!

A frivolous song. My mother sang it for fun. Of course, I took it very seriously; I suffered it, as I later suffered my Rilke. The stanza I loved most retains even now the entire mood of those happy days:

The poplars on the highway there
Sway in the wind of March.

That was it: the mood of my early days (1919–26). Still living in the Art Nouveau past: distance, urging, promise. And light, conjured up in another stanza:

The bluish distance calls for me
Pale-blue like your corset ...

Pale-blue. Silk-blue. Intensifying in the yearning:

And if it weren't for Paree
Then I might dream of you and me
In your most decent bed.

Do you hear it: Paris the goal of migratory birds, the nerve and energy center, the exemplary city, the capital of Europe. But no matter: the *Wanderlust* of those days. The lure of the horizon. Always a Beyond beyond whatever. The only anguish of my childhood: the pale-blue promise beyond the birches and beeches and alders and spruces and all the other dendrological bric-à-brac of the park in Bessarabia; there, way way beyond the fields, along the forest tracts and meadows of the river Pruth, where poplars, strung far across the land, lie westward on the great highway—*îţi mai aduci aminte, domnule Brodny?* ...

March-weather yearning. The land wide open in the fresh light. Spring once again lets its blue ribbon waft through the air. The threshing machine stands in the barn: be patient until autumn. The naked twigs still drip in the morning. The fields lie fallow. There is a powerful rush under the willows along the park wall. In the village, tiny brooks shoot along the paths. The village children send reed boats over their rapids, and I envy their freedom. Miss Fern tugs me past them. "Come on, you must not stare. It will embarrass them."

Uncle Ferdinand's bags are being packed, the servants drag them into his dressing room: huge calf-leather trunks fitted with brass latches, brass corners, buckled with straps, girded with the blue and gold ribbon of his armorial colors. Through the corridors the chambermaids cluck like big black-and-white brood hens, bearing piles of shirts ironed so smooth that they are slippery, balancing them firmly under their chins, the tissue paper crackling (a superfluous protection: Uncle Ferdinand will have his laundry rewashed and re-pressed in Paris anyway).

He struts enormously before us, up and down, past the open window, which contains treetops, bright spring breezes, and yearning. At regular intervals his shadow falls across the tea table where we are sitting. I in the Norfolk jacket with a bow under the broad, striped shirt collar, and I can't bear the bow because I find it girlish and it makes the village children laugh. My mother in a frock of light brocade as iridescent as snakeskin; her dress closes under the armpits in an intersecting line, leaving the throat and shoulders bare, as if placed upon it (this too is quite Art Nouveau—ivory inlaid in cloisonné, imitative of Luca della Robbia terra cottas; in Art Déco, the dress would be batiked, the superimposed bust would be plastic, the hair japanned).

When Uncle Ferdinand's large shadow falls across the tea table, the firmament of sunlight reflections on the silver—the samovar, the sugar bowl, the butter dishes and toast racks, the honey pot, and various containers in which tarts and pastries are kept warm—is for a moment snuffed out. My mother fiddles with the tea things, her movements uncommonly light. She is slender, erect, and wears a hothouse blossom in her hair: a Balinese gamelan player.

Uncle Ferdinand struts around us with solemn, almost ceremonial steps. He is celebrating himself. At each step, his powerfully vaulted torso—and the elegantly sloping bon-vivant shoulders, the alert head constantly turning to and fro, the sharply protruding nose and uncommonly powerful mustache, twirled thread-fine at each end—his torso nods, awe-inspiring, self-assured, self-confident, earnest: an immense rooster.

His eyes are rooster eyes: perfectly circular, light-brown, with piercing black pupils. When he ogles at the cheese- or mush-room-patties, the currant tarts, he tilts his head as though taking aim, then stalks step by step to the tea table to seize the goodies with a nimble whisk of the hand. He balances the teacup very delicately before the vertical line of his vest buttons, then goes over to my mother to have her pour him more tea: "*Comme c'est dommage, mon ange, que vous n'ayez pas envie de venir à Paris. Vous nous manquerez à tous et surtout à Anne, qui vous aime si tendrement. D'ailleurs, je crois qu'il y aura John—cela ne vous ferait pas changer d'idée? . . .*"

He stands close to the tea table, arching his rooster chest to-ward the samovar; and the samovar belly, arching too (convex where he is concave, concave where he is convex), reflects him mockingly, caricatures him, distorts him grotesquely. He is sud-denly drawn upward, as thin as thread, and then is collapsed into a broad sphere. . . .

Fourteen years later, I was to see him like that again: in Febru-ary 1940; I was a Rumanian soldier, a defender of the Fatherland, a Fatherland in which I had become an alien; after returning home to Bessarabia from Vienna I was taken in again by the for-getful patron of my remote childhood as if I had been gone for only a school year: "*Ah, te voilà finalement. Il était grand temps qu'on te voie. Va vite te changer pour dîner. Ta chambre est celle sur la cour, comme d'habitude.*"

He is still Uncle Ferdinand the Magnificent. But something strange has happened to him; a bizarre retromorphosis has oc-curred, a development back into the species and genus, which makes the individual recede and the type come to the fore—and not the rooster type. He is no longer the giant cock-of-the-walk of yore.

I have achieved twenty-one years with God's help, and I am still inexperienced in what age can do to a man—I mean, how much it brings him home, brings him back to his origins. Is it that my eyes, after twelve years of Vienna, have been weaned from the Balkan surroundings and are more sensitive to them? I wonder, terrified. Uncle Ferdinand looks to me as if whole phalanxes of Levantine ancestors had marched right into him—all those Greeks from the Phanar of Constantinople, who ruled for the Sublime Porte as princes over Moldavia and Wallachia, who married the daughters of the land, uncommonly black-haired daughters of Boyars, with noses as sharply curved as their scimitars and the plumes of their otter caps. Uncle Ferdinand's nose is so crooked now that, like a parrot beak, it presses down on his (now yellowish white, now sparse) bristly mustache (as if the nose were devouring a narrow sheaf of bleached straw; similar tiny sheaves are proliferating in his nostrils and ears). This nose arches from its tip (overshadowing the chin and double chin) in a resolute curve right around the entire arc of the skull, between the eyes (now slightly bulging and mounted in reddened lids and pale lashes), seamlessly (with no notch in the root of the nose) into the receding forehead and then the dully shimmering parchment spheres of the cranium, over which a few damp, grayish-white strands are still combed (remnants of patent-leather-black hair, once brushed back from the forehead smooth as a mirror).

A balding old cockatoo, I would have been tempted to think, if Uncle Ferdinand's head alone had developed homeward into the Oriental and thereby into history. But the intrinsic, typical quality now coming to the fore, the element that makes a personal feature a revelatory mark not only of race and class but also of a specific human condition, the potentiality of man in a specific form—this quality has been elaborated (with admirable thrift in the use of artistic devices) by means of a contortion and distortion of the entire figure.

It is the same grotesque distortion that I saw in the fun-house mirror of the samovar belly, during the remote childhood days of 1926: Uncle Ferdinand is both elongated and compressed at once. His stilt legs are drawn out; exceedingly long and skinny, they seem to go all the way up to his shoulders, on which his ears are set (with the yellowish gray-white sheaves of hair now sprouting from them). Once, the high rooster-chest was tremendously vaulted, and the horned pearl-string of waistcoat buttons ran down it like a seam in a bold self-assured curve to the artificially tightened waist—like the trill that Miss Fern, a *Schnitzelpolka* piano virtuoso, fondled out of the keys at the end of the piece, her middle finger rigid, a trill like the energetic gondola arc in an emphatic underscrawl of a signature. But now, this conceitedly bloated, girdled, truffle-fed bon-vivant body is broadly squashed and billowed like a melon, precariously thrust on the spindly legtrestle like a hunchback's torso.

There will soon be nothing human about this at all. It is merely a caricature now, and its essence has developed perfidiously. Uncle Ferdinand's personality has not been rendered harmless by the change, or banalized into cheerful reconciliation. On the contrary, it now emerges in all its sharp certainty. His incontestable authority has intensified, is now uncanny, but is no longer expressed by the complacent power of the rooster: it is as if the rooster's pomp has risen aloft and been suspended. Uncle Ferdinand is now devoid of pompous gravity, is virtually hovering in air, light, weightless. . . .

In short: Uncle Ferdinand has not simply aged but taken a step beyond himself into the timelessness of symbolism. No, no: he is no longer the proud rooster on the hilltop who greets the radiant new day with the drawn scimitar of his crowing. He is something far older, more archaic, more archetypal; something has shifted him to the dawn of creation, as though he were perched at the beginning of time, still bringing his mythic influence on Today, spinning threads of destiny. . . .

Of course—that's what he is: *Arachne*. He has become a spider. Uncle Ferdinand has turned into a gigantic, gray-yellow-white spider.

□   **12**   □

YOU UNDERSTAND MY DILEMMA, Mr. Brodny. I am telling you stories not just for my personal pleasure. I am not letting my figures stroll across paper just for my fun. No sooner have I drawn the picture of Uncle Ferdinand as a spider than I feel compelled to extend the metaphor wherever Uncle Ferdinand leads us—he too a phantom of the narrator, to tell about telling.

The figures have to work out—arithmetically. Otherwise, they will not be right—and do not seem right, at first glance. Uncle Ferdinand is an aristocrat, and the spider is no image for aristocracy. No one has a spider in his escutcheon. On a coat of arms, a spider would be the out-and-out negation of the knightly spirit: not just the symbol of treacherous ambush but a token of shameful stagnation. Only old rubbish that's been stored away gets covered with cobwebs, dusty stuff, now useless and worthless.

But as we know, life is a constant transvaluation of values. Something that may be old junk today, because it is useless, can be doubly precious tomorrow, because it evokes the mood of a yesterday that seems increasingly rich and pure, a life more pleasing to God

(presumably because we feel—through no special fault or guilt today, simply the fault or guilt of existing—that we were more innocent yesterday than we are today and than we shall be tomorrow. . . .)

True, in 1940 we were not so Americanized that we piously placed a cowbell of old-fashioned iron on the coffee table, as an antiquarian relic, thereby placing ourselves as aesthetes one rung higher on the cultural ladder. But still, even then, aristocrats were being fitted out with an antique value that was entirely fictive, to be sure, yet burdened with ethical demands that should not, in fairness, have been made on it. Throughout his life (he was born in 1872 and probably died soon after my coming home to him and the arrival of the Russians, to whom Bessarabia had been ceded; i.e., roughly in September 1940), Uncle Ferdinand, who had a line of ancestors going back to the emperors of Byzantium, found himself in historical situations that made it impossible for him to exercise the virtues that troubadours and minnesingers idealized in the beautiful legend of King Arthur's Round Table as the Mount Olympus of chivalry. You have to make allowances. In the capitalist era, the image of the aristocrat, even if he was one to let chivalrous notions of Honor, Truth, Courage, Sacrifice, and so on flutter over his head like banners, could no longer be that of Parsifal or Lancelot. The feudal lords of the epoch were really Napoleon III and Edward VII—sovereigns whose peers and paladins were the Rothschilds and Sassoons—no longer Gawain and the seneschal Kew.

My mother would accompany Uncle Ferdinand to the Riviera. That is to say, we moved into the house at Antibes, which, as a matter of course, I regarded as one of *our* houses, intended solely for my mother and me, as well as Miss Fern and the rest of the staff (the *maître d'hôtel*, the housekeeper, the lady's maid, innumerable parlormaids, the chef, a few kitchen helpers, the chauffeur, the gardeners). There, after weathering the somewhat eerie merriment of the Mardi Gras, we looked forward more calmly to Uncle Ferdinand's regular visits from Monte Carlo, where he occupied an entire hotel floor. At that time, the Roaring Twenties, among the intimate friends who accompanied him, the percentage of names listed in the old Almanach de Gotha was almost infinitesimal compared with the names of Bolivian tin-mine owners, Argentine cattle breeders, Irish beer kings, Dutch petroleum magnates, and Levantine gunrunners. This disproportion could not even be balanced by a number of penniless Russian grand princes.

We should probably renounce certain compulsive ideas in the concept of aristocracy; the intellect and nonintellect, virtues and vices, of the caste that had been manipulating the fate of Western Civilization for more than a millennium, especially its will to survive, continue (like certain streams that suddenly vanish underground only to bubble up unexpectedly somewhere else, perhaps on the other side of a mountain range) in a new and entirely different form and manner, adjusted to a new and different *Zeitgeist*.

In other words, though you might find all kinds of aristocrats and all sorts of odds and ends testifying to the legends of chivalrous origins—in Sleeping Beauty castles belonging to mediatized German princes; in Baroque palaces flanked by black cypress torches and bombarded by sunlight, belonging to Spanish and Sicilian grandees; in the *manoirs* of certain deeply provincial French nobles, as solemn as though risen from ancestral tombs; and, needless to say, on the poor farms both east and west of the Elbe belonging to Junkers in leather leggings—the aristocracy as a still powerful upper class were now fraternizing with the "upper ten thousand" of the international business world and gathering at places that grossly contradicted the ethos of chivalry. They frequented the boardrooms of banks, industrial concerns, and insurance companies and, for relaxation, nightclubs and gambling casinos as well as yacht marinas on southern shores. These are the meeting-places for the tiny group of men who manipulate not only movie starlets, playing cards, and polo mallets but also the fate of Western Civilization (and hence mankind).

So I need not cudgel my brain about the heraldic validity of the spider as a vision of Uncle Ferdinand's phase of completion. His aristocratic quality leaves every branch of zoology open to this possibility. Had not my fairy-tale childhood been suddenly aborted and had I not been cast out into the grayness of life as an eternally duped poor wretch, I would never have so much as dreamed of viewing Uncle Ferdinand as a standard-bearer of the chivalrous spirit, or his breeding as an ideologically acquired quality to be analyzed in the light of intellectual history. This was middle-class thinking, not only in its categories but also in its abstraction, in its remoteness from life. Uncle Ferdinand himself would not have given it a shrug; he would merely have stared into space for a moment and then changed the subject.

Still, it is interesting to picture what might happen if I retained any of the intellectual restraint acquired as part of polite behavior, and it occurred to me to ask Uncle Ferdinand point-blank (alluding, perhaps, to the similarity between certain notions of the ideology of chivalry—for instance, that a knight must always test his mettle anew; i.e., constantly realize himself anew—and analogous interpretations of existence in existential philosophy): the blank astonishment in the three circles of eyes and mouth in his countenance would be stupendous to behold. But this astonishment would promptly give way to an expression of great weariness and melancholy.

With the touching kindness he always demonstrates when he has to instruct youthful ignorance, Uncle Ferdinand would reply that human beings are not like our minions the dogs: dogs, he would say, are developed into breeds having different functions, so that the physical and mental characteristics needed to perform those functions are passed down not only unadulterated but actually intensified—e.g., the pointers' and retrievers' fine nose, the hounds' stamina, the powerful fangs of the mastiffs, and all the other useful and beneficial qualities of hunting dogs, as well as the extraordinary character traits of the various sheep dogs and watchdogs, and finally the droll, affectionate qualities of the breeds developed for playing, pleasure, and companionship. . . . On the contrary, Uncle Ferdinand would say, man himself seems to be a breed with a highly developed specialty, a function that he probably does not yet understand but that is beginning, eerily, to crystallize: he is a kind of cosmic microbe, a bacillus or virus with the mission to destroy the planet Earth—and perhaps not just the planet Earth.

Any further special function could probably no longer be bred, Uncle Ferdinand would continue. Every newborn baby has all the possibilities of human life available—some quite unexpected, even surprising, and some so amazingly pre-progammed that one is tempted to believe in transmigration (of a very desultory kind); however, any further shaping of these pre-programmed possibilities is left, Uncle Ferdinand would say, to environment and education . . . and, naturally, generations of belonging to a given milieu would also develop certain traits, features, and if not characteristics then certain tendencies that would, overall, identify the individual as belonging to this milieu. But nothing more than that.

Just as a peasant can be identified as a peasant, a seaman as a seaman, a boor as a boor, quite independent of that fact, Uncle Ferdinand would say, each one of them—just like each one of our beloved companions the dogs—has his specific character; that is, he may be either a very darling or a very ferocious dog, a poor dog or a stupid dog.

Very few members of the two latter categories were to be found in Uncle Ferdinand's circle of friends—which was quite simply the world for him, the Middle Kingdom.

Even rarer than a poor or stupid dog was a darling dog. Most of them were ferocious dogs.

Of course, Uncle Ferdinand and his friends knew how to make their world seem like a game—innocent, charming, played entirely and exclusively for the purpose of the utmost enjoyment of life.

This was disarming and would quite appropriately confirm John's statement that if everyone got to know the so-called exploiters of mankind personally, there would be no such thing as social envy and class struggle. These things really didn't exist, he said, when the common people had free access to the dining rooms and sleeping chambers of kings, and could gape to their heart's content at the great people of this world in their ordinary humanity (rather like the good citizens standing at the wolf cage in the zoo on a Sunday afternoon: "Just look at him scratching himself—just like Rover!").

And indeed, my memories of Uncle Ferdinand's friends (some of whom, incidentally, were as close to my much-beloved mother as he was) were heartwarming. Our spring sojourns on the Riviera—when Bessarabia still lay under snow but the small pond in the park was beginning to thaw—contributed in no small measure to the radiant effect that entire lost half of my life had on me, not only the brilliance of those glorious early years but virtually the illumination of an era.

□   13   □

NEVER HAVE I MET ANYONE so effervescent, so funny, so eager for the craziest jokes and pranks as "Bully" Olivera, a tiny, roly-poly, mercurial South American who played outstanding polo and poker and, it was said, owed his immense fortune to the slave labor of entire tribes of half-starved, lice-ridden Indians. (One of his ideas, which would have delighted the pataphysicists, was to go to the Casino at Monte Carlo in the few hours between closing time and dawn—when you hear the shots of suicides—sugar-frost it, and then top it, at sunrise, with several tons of whipped cream and strawberries.)

And never will I forget the kindness, the tireless concern, the unabating efforts for the welfare of his neighbors, the warm, active humanity of Sir Agop Garabetian (known in the financial world as "Mr. Choke" because of his cutthroat methods). Aboard his steamer yacht *Nereide,* where Uncle Agop was the most solicitous of hosts at famous "little" dinners (which, needless to say, were far more intimate, more exclusive, and therefore more sought after than the great "galas"), he personified the highest degree of civilization a human being can possibly attain. Unforgettable to me are the charm, the tenderness, the cordial white-toothed smile in the pomaded, parted, twiddled coal-black beard that framed his Arabian Nights head like a rococo cartouche and gave him exaggerated pomp and *opera buffa* menace, heightened by a sparkling monocle wedged in the left eye socket and precariously clutched by the black caterpillar of an uncommonly mobile eyebrow. (Privately, my mother called him Monsieur Raminagrobis, which I, as an avid reader of Madame la Comtesse de Ségur, found quite accurate.) In contrast, the deep, Orientally wise melancholy of those almond-cut eyes whose pupils floated in the globes like black olives in oil. The blandishing melody of his voice, its sonorous strength nevertheless making the blood-red petals of the carnation quiver in the silk lapel of his white tuxedo. The gentle, skillful movements of his blue-flashing beringed *bayadère* hands when he placed a chinchilla around bare female shoulders that might shiver in the night wind; or when he raised a glass of wine to scrutinize it against the candle flames of a girandole (spiriting a ruby onto the diamond-sown indigo velvet of night over the forest of masts at the marina); or when, with positively scientific devotion, he helped a friend (and no less well versed connoisseur) to select a cigar, or pushed over to him the crystal carafe of port that (according to those privileged to taste it) was in no way inferior to the magnificence of the Easter Mass in a Russian cathedral; when finally he stroked my head with fatherly solace because Miss Fern, to my ineffable regret, insisted on detaching me from my mother's arms (in which, ringleted and cherry-eyed, I lay like the daughter of Madame Vigée-Lebrun) to take me belowdecks to our cabin and get me into bed before the charleston band began to play. This band, which along with the Venezuelan tango orchestra was a part of Uncle Agop's household, had several soloists who today are counted among the classical musicians of jazz: their art having been immortalized on records, they are the teachers of a generation of performers whom

Gaia managed and commercially handled; the money she earned was largely devoted to creating the atmosphere of suitable comfort and elegant freedom from care that I needed to write my book. . . .

yes, indeed, Brodny my friend, the world is small and round, one thing rolls into another. A whore's son simply can't become anything but a whore-schnorrer; the literary laws are more severe in this respect than life itself. . . . But that should not prevent me from finishing the paragraph and returning to my reflections, to illustrate which I have invented Bully Olivera and Sir Agop Garabetian (and so full of beans that their healthy appetite for life threatens to chew up the thread of my story). . . . I mean to say: Uncle Agop and all my other elective and nominal uncles and godfathers (and possible fathers) had a robust appetite for life during the era between WW I and WW II, when they lived in a reality within reality, and it was this that provided the brilliance that makes the lost half of my life seem illuminated as though by a promise of spring. Their irresistible charm and fascinating manners reveal not only that, as true masters of the art of living, they grasped the virtue of humanness as an aesthetic commandment but also that they were indeed great gentlemen.

They were the princes of their time, whether or not their names were listed in the Almanach de Gotha. Their courts were no less arabesquely and hieratically composed of officials, sycophants, favorites and minions with kith and kin, flatterers, jokesters, porters, couriers, stooges of all kinds, than any duodecimo court at the height of the Renaissance. And these courtiers were no less devoted to the enjoyment of life, albeit less ethically ideologized, than any court of love in the days of Chrétien de Troyes.

Only, in the year 1940, all this was no longer so concrete. It was its own self in a different state, so to speak: like ice thawed into water, or water boiled into steam. Even this world within the world and this reality within reality were subject to the process of rarefaction, of abstraction, which affected the entire world of humanity, as though its molecules were flying apart (just as, supposedly, according to modern physics, the whole universe is flying apart).

Likewise, Uncle Ferdinand's world of games and gamesters, the innermost circle of the shrewdest, hardest, most cynical possessors of reality, no longer held together on its own. It would now take a Chosen Being (a new Scott Fitzgerald, for instance) to integrate it in its new state and make it real in another dimension.

□   14   □

THE VISION OF UNCLE FERDINAND as a spider is thus perfectly valid as a symbol. Indeed, he is weaving the myth of his world. He is working on his Middle Kingdom, which needless to say is the middle of a Ptolemaic world; not a middle position between some higher and some lower world but a nuclear pole, from which the closer and farther circles of friends radiate and intersect and intertangle with the farther and closer circles of friends of other centers on the same social level. A kingdom of the extraordinarily wealthy, extending across many lands and girded by the Great Wall of Money, beyond which live those whom Destiny or Divine Providence or the random blindness of nature has denied the truly liberating, really propitious goods of this earth: teeming nations without money or happiness or names, without memorable faces, dwelling in areas that are unrecorded on the lovely maps and charts in the atlas of deluxe living—*on sait que cela existe et on s'en fout.*

This is the reason that Uncle Ferdinand does not even now (it is February 1940; the trees are frosted, the pond in the park is frozen, I could blissfully skate upon it like young Goethe on the Ilm, if I found pleasure in doing turns and waltz-wave-welling curves on my mother's deathbed) . . . I say, this is the reason that Uncle Ferdinand does not even now realize how abstract, how virile, is the activity on which he concentrates all his high intelligence, his energy, all the persistence of his domineering character—a princely character that is accustomed to giving orders, brooks no contradiction, and will not be discouraged by any obstacle. As a real aristocrat, he *serves.* He serves his beloved Middle Kingdom by giving it a new reality: by re-creating it as a myth.

He therefore already lives in a different dimension. He himself has become unreal in some way, made of some lighter, less dense matter. The real world around him means nothing to him. He lives as if solely and exclusively for the task of re-creating his world—always a "reality within reality" and now about to be given a new reality in a different dimension. He lives as if he had been invented like a fictional character only for this specific theme, finding his own reality only in the myth of the "upper ten thousand," as his kingdom was called in his day. He serves the myth of the *beau monde* of the immensely rich, whether they always have been and are still or have just recently become rich and are newly settling into it. His theme is the kingdom of the monstrously rich, and among them especially the inner circle of dynamic enjoyers of life at Deauville, Biarritz, and the Côte d'Azur, with their many beautiful houses in all the most beautiful places on this wondrously beautiful earth; their parks and shooting grounds; their ocean-going yachts, polo ponies, Rolls-Royces, and Bugattis; their wondrously beautiful women, spoiled, sheathed in brocade and precious fur and hung with legendary jewelry; the expensive whims, jokes, flashes of inspiration; the captivating manners and the powerful carnivore teeth, in which (as Uncle Helmuth and Aunt Hertha alleged) the bones of the disinherited classes splintered so crunchingly (as I, in contrast, can assure you) that it was a delight to watch.

Uncle Ferdinand hasn't given up this world of his for lost, even though one can hardly conceal the fact that it is threatened in its core. On the contrary, his will to raise it to the dimension of myth springs from his unbroken confidence in his strong-toothed playmates from the greens of polo fields and chemin-de-fer tables; these are people who will not easily give up the succulent morsels for which they waged such bloody battles, even if the devastations of Doubleyou Doubleyou II were to prove even more catastrophic than those of Doubleyou Doubleyou I. There is something like a quantum law even in danger, a law that those who have a great deal to lose will ultimately lose even less than those others who from the very start had little to lose—and men like Bully Olivera and Sir Agop Garabetian weren't exactly sleepy, even though dawn usually caught them in a swallowtail or a tuxedo. Indeed, one could expect that, like most of the people in the inner circle, these men, thanks to the huge and general postwar devastation of receptive marketing areas (first, emergency rations, bandages, medicine; the rest follows automatically), would simply seize even larger morsels in their teeth (as experience taught in Doubleyou Doubleyou I, to be confirmed after Doubleyou Doubleyou II by the various Economic Miracles of defeated fatherlands in Western Civilization and newly created fatherlands in Africa and Asia). But still: these men would most likely not be able to chew on their morsels as unabashedly as before. And this—the lost assurance of what they had once taken for granted—was the true reason that exhaustion consumed them.

Meanwhile, however, these marvelously unchallenged consciences, with which my diverse nominal uncles and godfathers (and fellow travelers of Uncle Ferdinand's) managed to enjoy everything that their unscrupulous *Weltanschauung* permitted them, are probably the reason that Uncle Ferdinand appreciates them not only individually but all together, as a group, a troop, a swarm, a cheerfully ringing, eagerly sniffing, keenly hunting pack. Well, the sharp and shiny toothfulness of carnivore jaws is as old as mankind, as life itself, and will probably perish only when life itself does; yet in the unadorned fashion of the Bully Oliveras and Agop Garabetians, it belonged specifically to the most beautiful period in Uncle Ferdinand's life (a period whose late flowering coincided with my first flowering). He especially loves the era bestowed on him and his kind, the era of precarious armistice between two phases of a Hundred Years' War (for Uncle Ferdinand, just like John, sees Doubleyou Doubleyou I and Doubleyou Doubleyou II not as two distinct conflicts having distinct causes and goals and carried out with murderous weapons among European nations but as two skirmishes of one and the same European civil war, fought with all means and methods and bestowing on him and his kind a wonderful hybrid blossom during twenty-one years while the armies, aggressions, and weapons were renewed).

No doubt, the thing that Uncle Ferdinand most loves—as I do—about that reality within reality and its era, the thing that gave its style that incomparably piquant mestizo character of refinement and violence, making it quite unforgettably vivid, charming, promising, as the time of our lives, was: *the American touch*.

You may not believe it, Mr. Brodny, but that's what it was like. Uncle Agop's Venezuelan tango orchestra and nigger band as well as Dada and the Constructivist vision, bobbed hair and Expressionism as well as conveyor-belt production of superfluous consumer goods and political street scuffles, transvestite nightclubs and the "simple life" reform movement, Einstein's theory of relativity and Fascism, Greta Garbo and Dr. Joseph Goebbels, Mistinguette and James Joyce, Mayakovski and various secret police (*et quelle est la différence entre le Négus et Léon Blum? Aucune: tous les deux ont une barbe, sauf Léon Blum*)—all the things that now make the years between WW I and WW II seem like a paradise lost we owe to the return of the prodigal daughter America.

The delicious blend of chaos and extreme stylization, of decadence and tempestuous promise in time; the suspenseful adjacency of gangster violence and pure, self-sacrificing faith in man and his right to light, beauty, happiness—the myriad contradictions, the perilous extremes, the explosiveness of all the legacies and tendencies of the *Zeitgeist* made those years a time, a lifetime, more stimulating than could ever have been experienced before or after. It was most likely, as Stella maintained, Europe's most European hour. And just as she, Stella, realizes it, so too does Uncle Ferdinand realize (both of them, presumably, from the proclamations dropped by John in his relative clauses) that this historic hour of Europe could not have come without the return of Europe's prodigal child America, without America's intervention, interference, in European history. Be proud, sir. It's your century, your world.

Certainly, Uncle Ferdinand is an aristocrat and a European, a European's European, sated by the spirits not only of Roman civilization but also of Byzantium; were I to attempt to draw up his spiritual pedigree, I would have to show Irish apostles crossed with Moorish mathematicians, and Venetian seafarers with German philosophers. Nevertheless, or perhaps for that very reason, Uncle Ferdinand loves the American touch in the years of precarious armistice between WW I and WW II. He is delighted by the fedora's smart bootlegger look: the crease in the hat brim, so to speak, the brim clapped down at a slant over the brow of a killer's eyes. He enjoys the new style in the spirit of adventure that, together with the crudeness of the polo-playing tin-mine owners and poker-playing oil magnates and arms-runners, was taken up by the remnants of the *beau monde* salvaged through WW I, a high society in which the coteries of the Guermantes had long since become intimately entangled with those of the Verdurins as well as those of the Astors and the Vanderbilts.

Uncle Ferdinand is neither a moralist nor a romantic. He is really an aesthete of a school for which antiquarian value per se does not exist. A man who has grown up among Gainsboroughs and lives with Roentgen furniture will appreciate even a Sumerian cowbell or an iron spoon from the Fu-Ku or Shen-Si excavations, but only if it's an especially beautiful example. And he will, incidentally, always prefer the latest model of a first-class make of sports car.

□   15   □

WHICH, OF COURSE, does not explain why Uncle Ferdinand, now, in the heart of winter 1940, is still here in Bessarabia, no doubt in the most uncomfortable, most badly heated of his houses, and the most remote from civilization. Only the bone-hard frozen Dniester and thirty-five kilometers of hand-flat land separate him from the Russians, who are lying in wait to march in here and clean up his sort, as they did at home after 1917. In back of him lies a fatherland, Rumania, which in 1919 welcomed Bessarabia's return to the Kingdom of Greater Rumania by dispossessing my uncle of the best of his estates. Now, Rumania will soon be blackmailed into putting up no resistance to the new invasion of the Russians; then, forcibly allied with her natural enemies, she will plunge into an adventure that can lead only to losses even greater than that of a single province.

Thus, Uncle Ferdinand would not need to stick his neck out for the heritage that his forefathers have left him here. This legacy is all too wretched compared with what these sage gentlemen have long since taken to more reliable countries like England, Holland, and Switzerland. And it is all too meager next to what he himself (vying here, too, with his friends from the polo greens and baccarat tables) has multiplied and invested in safe valuables and bank accounts throughout territories with a great future—like Brazil, South Africa, and Canada. Uncle Ferdinand certainly doesn't have to fear the hard fate of a refugee like myself, or (initially, no doubt) like you, too, Mr. Brodny, my comrade in fate. If he wanted to sell just his coin collection (now in the vault of a private bank in New York belonging to one of his closest friends), the yield would allow him to live tolerably well till the end of his days (which end would no doubt be happily deferred by the necessary restriction of alcohol and luxury foods). But, for the moment, such an emergency measure does not have to be mentioned. Even after the loss of his Bessarabian immovables, Uncle Ferdinand would still be frightfully rich and could thus live carefree in California or the Bahamas, in Mexico City or Rio de Janeiro. Furthermore, he would be meeting a good number of the people about whose well-being he is occasionally anxious, cut off as he is from their cocktail and dinner parties and galas and often without even news of such events.

Meanwhile, Uncle Ferdinand is staying on in Bessarabia. He prefers it where he is, isolated and exposed, living in rustic simplicity—even without his French chef (who, as a defender of his fatherland, sulks in some bunker on the Maginot Line). The temperature here would freeze the radiator of his Cadillac and is even turning the shooting of wild geese into a dubious pleasure. But Uncle Ferdinand holds out, though without cheerful camaraderie or female companionship he is bored to tears every evening. His life is downright monastic—in a lovely, crazy, lordly gesture toward his friends, as though, by eschewing the chance to be in safety with them, he could deny the very idea that for them, for their world, for his world, for their Middle Kingdom, a certain danger is now approaching: the terrible danger that henceforth they will have to camouflage themselves; they will no longer have the security of an unimpeached conscience in enjoying what they were, what they are.

In the meantime, Uncle Ferdinand is doing what he would do if he were with them. Only he does it in another way. By conjuring up his various friends and circles, he is weaving this world of his friends together, re-creating it in a new dimension. He takes it out of time, present as well as past, and resurrects it in a sort of no-man's-land of time: the eternity of myth. He lives in it once more, and all the more systematically for that. He pursues an enormously ramified, no doubt mostly one-sided correspondence with addressees in all countries still in postal communication with Rumania. He instructs these people in minute detail about himself and his present circumstances, his social calendar as it would be if the circumstances were different, if it were as it once was— hunting, travel, and vacation plans in countries lying well out of harm's way. He reports on everything—no matter what—that he knows about his and their kind, and he requests equally detailed and precise answers. He has the caution, methodology, and pedantry of a general staff officer (which he was—in Russian uniform, piquantly—during an after all halfway chivalrous WW I). And whatever information he picks up he tries to supplement out of his own (phenomenal) memory, photo albums, older correspondence, and newer memories and biographies, as well as items snipped out of society gazettes that manage to arrive every now and then. Moreover, he excerpts all pertinent notices from the most recent arrivals and departures in Lloyd's Insurance Register of Private Yachts, in the membership lists of the Cresta Run Club, the Jockey Club, the Circolo della Caccia, the Royal English, Dutch, Spanish, Belgian, and Italian automobile clubs, the Almanach de Gotha of Princely Families, Burke's, the Libro d'Oro, and Who's Who. With the material thus gained (makeshift, to be sure, but as good as circumstances permit) he keeps his people up to date on the thing that bears the most infallible witness to the existence of a world of friends: the roster of their personnel.

Amusingly enough, the introverted quality of real aristocracy is thus more purely expressed in spiderlike Uncle Ferdinand than in the extroverted big rooster of his bon-vivant heydey. In high nobility, a more frequent type than this is the elderly gentleman absorbed in some kind of abstruse (even serious) research or collecting, and so neglectful of his obligation to present himself as a nobleman that only very sharp eyes can distinguish him from the next-best white-collar worker. And indeed, the intellectual disciplines in which aristocrats excel are the ordering, catgorizing ones rather than the analytical, speculative ones. (Schwab tried to talk me into writing an essay on the difference between aristocratic and non-aristocratic intelligence.) Uncle Ferdinand's close relations include ornithologists, shell collectors, and lepidopterists of the highest scientific rank, an important genealogist (important because he specialized in the multinational aristocracy of the former Ottoman Empire), and (lovingly esteemed by one and all) a princely cousin who had raised the aristocratic mastery of timetable perusal to such an art that he could reel off both the summer and the winter schedules of the entire national railroad network (à propos, as a true scientist, he was not content with this abstract lore: he traveled throughout the land, stationed himself on various overpasses, and, watch in hand, checked whether the timetable data corresponded to the facts).

In earlier years, Uncle Ferdinand made a nice name for himself as a numismatist. But what he is doing now is something more general, more profound, more fundamental. He is transcending into the metaphysical. Uncle Ferdinand is immortalizing the world he lived in. He thus makes himself immortal, takes himself out of time as a post-inventor of his own lifetime. He would never have existed if he did not exist in its chronicle.

The spider at the beginning of the world. Weaver of the world. Squatting in the no-man's-land of eternity and drawing its threads from time into timelessness, knotting them together there, weaving them back and forth and up and down, making sure that no tiny thread is disconnected from all the others—and waiting for whoever is caught in the web.

He has truly given himself up to his mission. (Naturally, he no longer reads a newspaper, no longer concerns himself with the administration of his estates, his foreign possessions, his business dealings; indeed, he no longer even entertains.) As narrow-minded as a spider that builds its web in a cranny where no fly would ever venture, Uncle Ferdinand has withdrawn here, to a remote, wintry, icy Bessarabia, in order to weave the myth of his radiant bon-vivant world, shone upon by an everlasting spring sun. It is an image of utmost faith in God: the spider hanging its web like a sail in the wind of destiny. . . .

and lo and behold: his web was well woven, and the wind of destiny bore me into it.

□   16   □

I REPEAT: it is the heart of winter in early 1940, toward the middle of February. Earth as hard as iron; one can scarcely believe that it will ever thaw again. No traces of spring breezes, of spring winds shaking the poplars, of pale-blue distances arousing yearning. True, the sky is silky blue now—the same Adriatically deep, spotless, ice-cold blue as over Vienna two years earlier, in March 1938. It is the sky under which the first half of my life froze, God alone may know how and why; I can't explain it, I can only tell about it . . . the fact is: this country, Bessarabia, the landscape of my childhood, has also frozen, a land of hoar and frost, with white foggy mornings before the icy blue of the sky stiffens the mist into feathery star crystals.

I am walking through an abstract world, therefore, a world preserved under the glass bell of a well-nigh-metaphysical coldness that I recognize and acknowledge as the world of my childhood. I am living again in my childhood home, from which I was torn away (virtually overnight, and not very considerately), from which I was driven for fourteen years (my entire youth, from the seventh to the twenty-first year of my life). Some of the domestics (a blathery lady's maid; a flatfooted footman, his head and body shaking; a gardener palsied with age) claim to recognize me. It's not true; they're just imagining things. One does not recognize the little boy who resembled the daughter of Madame

Vigée-Lebrun in this cavalryman who screws the night away through all the hooker hangouts of Kishinev and spends a rueful morning scouring his pubic hair for crabs.

I stroll through the village, and I think I know every house, every crooked, willow-plaited fence, every mushroom-shaped, snow-laden, icicle-hung thatched roof, and also every face that gapes at me without knowing who I might be, and every eye, sparkling with curiosity, peering through the panes of the little windows: but not a single eye can see me one third my present size, in a small gray coat with a tobacco-colored velvet collar, a round gray hat on my curly head, and the hated bow—enormous, toadstool-dotted—under my chin; no one sees me holding Miss Fern's hand, nicely lifting my little legs in their buttoned leggings over the beer-colored puddles in the mire of the village street. No, I am no longer Christopher Robin, Mummy's adored darling, Uncle Ferdinand's pet.

I walk through rooms so musty, dusty, seedy, that my heart contracts. I think I can still sense a breath of my mother's perfume—a sentimental delusion, of course. Only after a few days do I realize that some of the rooms have been completely repapered, refurbished, rearranged. . . .

I listen to the huge, mysteriously chattering stillness of the park, whose floods of summery green were always filled with invisible life: busy birdsong and birds whooshing in the boughs, needle-fine squealing of a dormouse in the foliage of the bushes, a rocking branch from which a squirrel, a marten, has leaped, an owl has soundlessly soared, bits of bark dropping down from heaven knows where, the soft gurgling of frog heads peeping out of the water and then vanishing in the reeds around the motionless water lilies on the pond, a rustling in the leaves, perhaps from a hedgehog or a ring snake. . . .

I have always, all my life, carried it in my blood, this park. It was my Garden of Eden, my paradise promised and lost. Missing it was the bitterest part of my exile. I traveled toward it as toward a beloved, its image in my senses: the soughing of its treetops in the night wind, its sun-sprinkled shadowy coolness, the damp fresh moldy smell rising in autumn from the leopard skin of the forest floor, its mushroom taste of fern and moss and bark. . . .

I regard myself as its creature. Whatever is in it I find also in myself: as the decor of my childhood legend, the proper grooming of its gravel paths, and the vain complacence of the Russian pavilion with the ornamental stained-glass lozenges in the birch woods; the Mondrian severity of the rolled, red, white-lined subdivisions of the tennis court, and the sumptuous flowering of the high shrubs around it. . . .

and above and beyond this (always there, not simply aroused after years of exile in Vienna) the air of adventure: the sudden stench of carrion in the blackberry thicket of some remote unsupervised corner; the romanticism, true, of the huge cedars along the ramshackle wall crumbling under burdens of ivy, but also the sinister and disreputable quality of the black soil of the creek banks, hollowed out by rats and crayfish under the giant hairy umbrellas of the coltsfoot leaves. . . .

I walk toward it, my park, and, within, toward all the vast, rich safeness of my childhood: the park receives me and has become abstract: white, rigid, transparent all the way to the far countryside, glassily sparkling under the silky deep-blue sky, tinkling in the frost as if transposed into another dimension, abstracted, its own myth and legend.

And for the first time I see it, see its skeletons, its structure, the way it is set in the countryside: a landscape garden, a piece of idealized nature within nature (*a reality within reality*); fanning out into the flatly troughed and then gently rolling and rising terrain, with the first signs of formal severity showing in the now frosty snowed-in ornamental scrolls of the flower beds, between which the beeline central path leads to the gates with the snow-capped stone greyhounds on the pillars . . .

and directly beyond, in greater freedom: a spacious English park with goodly proportions between the open lawns and the dense foliage of the summertime trees. To one side, then, toward the dell, a peasant garden full of folk mock-heraldry in the ostrich tails of the black cabbage and the halberd leaves of artichokes, along the parallel rows of fruit trees, whose rounded tops are now dusted with snow and transparent, like the seed tops of dandelions (which my mother used to call "Larousse"). And on the other side, on the rising slope, a game preserve: the small herd of fallow deer that always stood there in the coppice are standing there now, finely drawn in the snow.

Signs in the snow: it's still alive, my park. Mystery is still stirring in it, making a frosted branch snap up so that its white fur drops off and sinks into the down of the snowbed, which receives it glitteringly, everywhere the snow bearing the fine script of life so quick and shy that it would almost not have been, but for these traces (the most eloquent: a deathbed of powdery snow crystals, strewn with half a handful of downy feathers, three or four drops of blood, a yellowish spot ... the Chinese ideogram for Life, drawn by Death). . . .

It lives on unchallenged, my park. Everything in it is precisely as it was always and even twice seven years ago—except that I am no longer here.

Or rather: I *am* here, as if I had been placed into a different dimension, abstracted, my own myth, my own legend . . . I am here in a dual, abstract way that can be mirrored back and forth at will: I as a child, and my own legend of myself as a child, and I now, likewise detached from myself. I gaze at both of them, first through one at the other, then through the other at the one. I gaze through my present self at the child who in his curly-haired, cherry-eyed charm, his well-bred, adorable moodiness and precociousness, was already, all too consciously, his own legend and probably deserved to be slapped. And I gaze through the child at the lightly built young man, scrawny, pale, shot up too fast, but visibly tough as a whip, wearing his uniform like borrowed clothing, a strange watchfulness and, if you look him square in the face, something of Aunt Selma's enchantment in his eyes (and another, more modest garden in his mind).

I put my two selves side by side, testing them for this or that aspect, this or that value. I find that the twice seven years of exile, the hateful Viennese formative years with Uncle Helmuth, Aunt Hertha, Aunt Selma, and all their bloody fucking middle-class thinking and feeling and reasoning and arguing and praising and condemning and accusing, as well as the diabolically tempting Cain-like brotherhood with Cousin Wolfgang, were in many, many respects a wholesome testing, a hardening. And the no longer so finely groomed attitude, the no longer so sheltered and protected nature, the slight air of neglect—all these things they have so clearly left with me are balanced by a keener sight and a certain nobility in being able to hate.

But not even this has anything to do with me, really. This too is already a legend, which someday I may have to cultivate—like the other legend of myself in my childhood, the other myth with which I deliver myself into timelessness; I could not have existed otherwise. . . .

Now, here, returning home to the land of my damnation to form myths of myself, I am once again new, different, which I have never been before: a man who is a stranger everywhere, but most of all at home.

□   17   □

MY BOOK (which, as you know, was unfortunately never completed) was also supposed to describe a different cold world: the Ice Age five, six, seven (there we are again!) years later in Hamburg-on-the-Elbe, Germany: WW II's aftermath, known as the Age of Rubble, or the Age of Reichsmarks.

This period is experienced by the same person, an alien everywhere, soon at home everywhere, and most alien to himself in his own home—

experienced by a person who has virtually come out of himself and is beside himself, for whom, to be sure, this schizoid split became so much a part of his nature even then (1947) that it produced a peculiar, gleeful well-being, a feeling of immunity, of invulnerability—not a resistance to surprises, which our cherished life always has in store for us, but an ultimate inviolability in regard to surprises (the result, of course, being a totally abstract relationship to existence, to the world, and, last but not least, to morality).

In my manuscripts, I have gone to great pains to explain and clarify how this trance-like state was induced by the experience of March 12, 1938—the day Adolf Hitler came home to his homeland, Austria, which German troops occupied amid the jubilant delirium of the people. But even the most conscientious analysis boils down to inexplicables. It was the day when one era ended and another began. A day of solstice, when the sun stood still in the heavens. It is easy to write this down, of course, but proving it will be far more difficult. However, that will be done elsewhere.

What I wish to say here can probably be best expressed in a description of the climatic conditions.

March 12, 1938, was, as we all know, an unusually cold day. Arctic iciness plunged like a guillotine blade into the loveliest and most promising spring. Yet the sky remained blank and blue, not a breeze was stirring. The sun's smile was caught, like that of a beheaded man. And because the saps of spring had begun to rise, buds and shoots and perhaps also hopeful hearts so suddenly froze to ice that they shone; the world looked as if it had been placed under a glass bell: extraordinarily smart and delicately pretty and well-nigh varnished all over. The springtime seething was cut off, naturally. And with it the mood of the first half of my life.

On that March 12, 1938, I was in Vienna with Stella. She had long since taken my destiny in hand and was already preparing my return to Rumania, my call-up for military service there, and my visit to Uncle Ferdinand in order to enter the sphere of influence of reliable friends; thus, she had already launched the entire intrigue that made me unreachable, lifted me over the coming events, kept me hovering, as it were, between heaven and earth throughout the war, but ultimately cost her her life.

We spent an exemplarily beautiful summer in the Salzkammergut and managed to enjoy many more hectic days of sunshine in the following year, 1939, before the first shot for Europe's suicide was fired in September. But, retrospectively, the iciness of March 1938 passed directly into that of February 1940 in Bessarabia, and then, fairly uninterrupted, into the diluvial period of Hamburg until 1947. And it went on visibly losing light, turning grayer and drearier, more and more wintry. I cannot recall a single bright day during the so-called Age of Rubble or of Reichsmarks from 1945 to 1948 in Hamburg-on-the-Elbe, Germany. Never did the sun shine but through aseptic gauze, even during the brief Arctic summers when trees and shrubs were greening amid the yellow tundra grass in Pöseldorf or Övelgönne.

At any rate, by February 1940, which I am now telling about, it has been going on for almost two years—this Ice Age that keeps getting grayer and grayer, perhaps because it keeps filling up with gray iron men and smoking, fire-spewing iron weapons, and more and more gray men keep dropping and turning into phantoms under the smoke-and-fire spewing of these weapons, many many hundreds and hundreds of thousands of gray phantoms, flowing together in a denser and denser wintry fog that shrouds the world and veils the sun so thickly that it hangs as a small, pallid, powerless disk in the grayness, even after the thundering of the fires has been snuffed out.

I, too, in my nettle-cloth uniform, yellow-green like dried peas, am now (in February 1940) one of the iron men. I, too, occasionally wear an iron helmet with a chin strap, and I handle iron weapons that are ready to spew fire. My regiment is ready for action. Each one of its four thousand young men secretly prays to God that, in a pinch, he will be among the few hundred survivors. We have sworn to serve our Fatherland unto death with our weapons in our fists, and the makers of this rhetoric and these weapons are trying to harden our mood, our combative will, our readiness to die—harden them like iron. But nonetheless we are a rather sorry lot, shaking with fear whenever things look serious for us, too, fatalistic whenever the immediate danger is merely put off until tomorrow. And terribly hopeful, by the way: the Germans'll do it.

The Germans. They've got a kind of warfare, called *Blitz*, that rips enemy armies open like a zipper. They spliced and crushed the Poles, they'll do the same to the French. And when the time comes—that is, when they can free their dreadful hands for the job—they'll work the Russians over in the same way. All we'll have to do is storm after them, spurt a little fire here and there, stick a couple of bayonets into anything that resists. Perhaps we, the cavalrymen, can even mount again and chase our fleeing foes, slicing and smashing them with lances and sabers, so that war will regain something of its old, colorful fun. . . . But the war hasn't reached us as yet. The war too is temporarily frozen; the adversaries are lying opposite each other like dragons, showing their fangs before charging and entangling themselves in one another and tearing one another to shreds. Even the Russians are paralyzed in this hostile lockjaw, prevented from invading Rumania by the nonaggression pact with Germany. Accordingly, the weather here is still bright and beautiful, almost festive. "Hitler weather," it has been called since March 1938: days pearling along crisp and cold, under an azure sky, yet the woods and fields and meadows, the trees and bushes and groves are covered with a fur of frost, which is not meant to create an illusion of warmth. . . .

I, at any rate, can still play the peacetime soldier, the toy soldier. Uncle Ferdinand has got me an apparently unlimited furlough. Naturally, he knows the brigadier general. My regimental commander clicks his heels at the sound of his name. For his sake, I was simply shoved up the ladder from a one-year volunteer recruit to master-at-arms and finally second lieutenant. In his honor, instead of the dried-pea yellow-green uniform at dinner (we are two, served by four footmen) I can wear the plum-blue, gold-frogged, red-braided officer's uniform, in which I feel like the lothario in a high-school performance of a classic Viennese operetta.

Uncle Ferdinand goes to bed very late. He finally has somebody to talk to about his Middle Kingdom, tell stories to, show letters, photo albums, and news clippings to. In short, he can now discuss the most urgent matters of the inner circle, the nucleus of this distant reality within reality. The discussion usually goes on until the gray hours of dawn. Even then he would release me reluctantly. Liberated at long last from my high boots and the throat-tightening collar of the hussar tunic, drugged with fatigue, numb with much-too-heavy food, far too much wine, coffee, kirsch, whiskey, my head spinning nonstop like a mill wheel, I tumble into the pillows of an English brass bed, which, I would swear, my mother ordered from London during my childhood. And now, the memories slosh over me, inundate me . . .

but the images, the scenes, the moods, colors, sounds, smells that I have carried about, as precise as if engraved in steel, that I have so poignantly preserved, like flowers pressed between book pages, like ribbons, locks of hair, and *billets-doux* stored through decades in splint boxes—now, all these things turn out to be inaccurate and deceptive; they tumble chaotically, dissolve, flow together and away. . . .

I lie in the bed in which my mother (if memory serves me and this really is the extra-wide bed that she ordered from London before 1926) presumably received Uncle Ferdinand, the rooster. . . . I am no longer a child and I can imagine what happened then. Nor do I have any illusions about my beautiful mother's professionalism in this respect: I can exchange Uncle Ferdinand at will with any of my numerous godfathers and nominal uncles and leave the scene unaltered. (Mama, after all, had ordered not just one of these brass beds but several, dispatching one to our house on the Côte d'Azur, one to Uncle Bully's house in Biarritz, one to Uncle Agop's house in Ireland, and God knows where else.)

Here, as everywhere else, it was the same. A high-class whore (*poule de luxe*, as the term was in those days) always serves her present backer. My mother the whore. I, the son of a whore. A suicide's bastard. Stella the Jewess's gigolo, kept by her husband, the spy. . . .

I say this out loud to myself to test the effect that the echo of such a disgraceful sentence about my mother might evoke in me. But there is no effect. Quite the contrary: it amuses me to imagine her irony when performing her lofty craft, providing any sort of pleasure for her lovers.

But what really torments me is the discovery that I know as good as nothing about her, don't know her at all, don't know myself as I used to be; that I'm but a hypothesis of myself based on a hypothesis of her. The image of her that I have been carrying around might, on the whole, correspond only hazily and casually to her actual reality, despite the sharpness of countless details—like the images I preserved within myself of this house, the village, and even the park (images that here and now I find myself forced incessantly to correct). I have found photographs of her: they do not fit the legend of my sweet mother in any way, and yet they complement and complete it, as though I were now discovering an unknown dimension of her that might conceal yet other dimensions. . . .

I know and have always known that the radiant maternal goodness that I think I recall, the smiling-Madonna quality (without the crushed suffering of Our Lady of Sorrow), the lightness, the serenity that made me think I was a favorite of fortune—I know that all these were figments of my imagination, daydreams, retrospective projections of eternally unfulfilled wishes into a concocted phantom that could not resist them. But that is not what unsettles me now.

Gazing at the extremely elegant, extremely fashionably stylized young woman on the (incidentally, masterful) photo portraits I have found here (they are signed: Bill Brandt), I cannot learn anything about myself. But I can learn a great deal about an era that haunts me like a ghost stalking a house.

To my small surprise (and secret satisfaction), it is not an era of mothers. The young woman embodying it is not a mother. With her steep, narrow shoulders from which the fur has slid, with her stem-like throat displaying the severe emerald necklace, with her shingled black hair like a patent-leather cap, her oval face with the small corrupt mouth, and the radiantly innocent eyes under the thin, high brows—this is the most feminine form conceivable of an ephebe. If someone like this bears a child, it must be either a demigod or a monster. . . .

At first, however, this strange, beautiful creature in which I only very remotely discover familiar features similar to my own, as if in ironical reflection, is as desirable as a sister brought up somewhere else and entering my life as an adult: I know both everything and nothing about her, but I can vividly picture her as an excellent lover, with expert hands, like a Japanese flower arranger.

What I see is the Eros of an era, and I—or perhaps that stratum of my existence that felt itself to be "I" (and that I now feel *was* myself at that time, as remote, to be sure, as abstract as Nagel's shot-off arm, my venerated Djakopp Djee)—am a child of that era and belong to it more than my *I* of today does . . . and *am* no more and am merely an echo of something that has long since waned, just as tomorrow my "I" of today will belong to the echo of 1940 and will have waned and faded with it . . . if it does not emerge from me as an image and myth and live on as such.

And just as I am about to doze off with this new image (and this new myth) of my mother in my mind, there is a banging in the big tiled stove, which is heated from the corridor. An old, familiar, deliciously cozy noise, announcing that Miss Fern is about to come in with a fresh, warmed-up bath towel in order to—

but no. It means that fourteen years have passed; that my mother and ideal beloved is dead, drowned in the pond; and that I will now have to pull on my boots again, because Uncle Ferdinand, the spider, is waiting for me downstairs at the breakfast table (he hardly sleeps anymore) in order to weave me into his Middle Kingdom.

□   # 18   □

HE WAITS FOR ME with the cruelly loving patience of the spider waiting for the fly that strays into its web. He has long since had his tea, and his long, yellow teeth under the straw whisk of his mustache and the parrot beak of his nose are gnawing on a fragment of zwieback. Now he watches as I, with the ravenous hunger of an exhausted young man, wolf down bowls of oatmeal and milk (Miss Fern's long-missed porridge) and bacon and eggs and black bread and piles of toast with butter and honey and currant jam and orange marmalade. My exceedingly healthy appetite in my drowsiness, my visible freshening with the gradually rising day, the animal physicality of youth in me, must repulse him, the rapidly aging man with the delicate stomach and weakened liver. But he doesn't show his disgust. His round eyes, still gazing sharply with piercing pupils from under the wrinkled, eggshell-thin lids, follow my every movement while his voice speaks to me: gently, in an elegant, tenderly ironic, lightly entertaining, conversational tone, changing language at whim or to fit the topic. Normally, he speaks a Balkan French much too literary, and pronounced with affected purity. But occasionally he uses the English of his generation, who, innocently believing that one must speak the King's English, mimicked Edward VII's German accent. At times, he lapses into his startlingly natural (albeit borderland hard) Austrian aristocrat's German, or even Rumanian, whereby an earthy, peasant-like vitality colors his diction.

I cannot escape him and his murmuring talk. He will follow me after breakfast when I stroll through the park, and the trees cover the tangerine-edged mother-of-pearl tones of the winter morning with the fine craquelure of frosted twigs and branches. He will have a servant help him into a fur coat that will enshroud him in otter from the ears to the ankles; and the tremendous collar will prevent a heavy cap of the same otter skin from sliding over his eyes down to the nose. And he will walk along with me step for step and talk to me. He will accompany me when I take a shotgun and a couple of hounds and comb the river meadows for wild duck and hares. Why, he will even be at my side when I try to escape him on horseback: two stableboys will lift him into the saddle of an age-toughened, Roman-nosed hunter; his endless skinny legs with straightened locked knees will be rigid in the stirrups, and the globular spider body will still rise bolt upright on a steely spine. Clearly indifferent to the grim cold that brings tears to my eyes, he will stay at the right edge of my field of vision in the swiftly passing winter landscape. He will sway gently when walking his horse, seesaw up and down when trotting, and finally vibrate at a high frequency when galloping—and his voice will be unremittingly gentle, elegant, tenderly ironic, and casually conversational as it murmurs past my eardrum.

There is nothing thematically or even chronologically coherent in what he has to tell me. His talk does not follow the laws of axial structure as in a crystal; it has no beginning and no foreseeable end. This is life immediately rendered; illogical at a longer, wider range, randomly experienced in a fusillade of impressions, arbitrarily plucked out, reproduced in mental leaps and fragments. And yet all these things make for a full world and for reality, so fascinating that I am soon spellbound. I find myself woven into them, more and more densely, and paralyzed by them. I keep thinking of the flies that Stella and I tossed into the cobwebs of an old lakeside bathhouse a year and a half ago (summer 1938) in Salzkammergut, and the loving and tender care with which the fat garden spiders wrapped them in their threads until they were swaddled like mummies. . . .

Uncle Ferdinand reports on his Middle Kingdom even at lunchtime, when we eat a light repast of four courses and three wines, still in the bright breakfast room. But the age-palsied footman playing the maître d'hôtel here is already wearing his tails. (Is it the same man about whom my mother used to say, when talking about faraway Bessarabia to the amusement of the entire Côte d'Azur, that it was easier to squeeze him into his tails than to teach him not to appear in them barefoot?)

And afterward, during the demitasse that we sip in the library, Uncle Ferdinand will open out the perspectives on what he told me during the morning. He will show me the albums, the photos of houses, yachts, hunts—the scenes where it all took place. We will contemplate various snapshots of the people involved and study their genealogy, their relatives in the Almanach de Gotha, in Burke's, in the Libro d'Oro, their business connections in Who's Who. . . .

I soon know the personnel of the Middle Kingdom by heart. After all, I'm well prepared: I recall many of the names from my childhood; I know the personalities, characteristics, spleens, likes and dislikes, vices and virtues, thanks to the social chitchat that I snapped up as a child and that was recently brought *à la page* again in conversations between John and Stella. Why, I even know some of these people; I can quite vividly recollect them; I used to call them by their first names, address them as "Uncle Bully" or "Uncle Agop." Even if they only barely recognized me, they might still remember delightful Maud (my mother's stage name, her real name being Ilse; but I am convinced that she plied her loose trade with sufficient artistry to have a certain right to a *nom de plumeau*).

In short: I am predestined for the legacy that Uncle Ferdinand wishes to leave me. Not his name, his fortune, his position in the world, of course, but that which can remain of those things when all their earthliness has crumbled into dust that the wind carries away: the *myth* of his bon-vivant world.

For simplicity's sake, we also have tea in the library. The table is set with the same silver as it was in the days of my childhood. My mother loved the intricate and practical odds and ends: the toast racks and beehive-shaped honey pots, the hot-water-heated plates and bowls for pastries and canapés, the little silver muffin baskets. She was responsible for the English look of the tea table, while Russia and the Near East prevail in the huge samovar and the Sèvres porcelain fabricated *pour l'Orient*.

Aside from the chintz sofas and Queen Anne furniture (which I presume replaced the rug-covered divans and Boulle consoles that, before her time, adorned a country estate in the realm of the Sublime Porte), I wonder whether her taste has left its mark on other things in and around Uncle Ferdinand, starting with his tweed jackets, going on to his not really East European passion for ocean sailing, and ending with the liberal choice of his friends.

Incidentally, Uncle Ferdinand has an interesting historical explanation for the latter. He says, "We, the survivors of the cataclysm of the First World War, who were clever enough to amuse ourselves until the outbreak of this second one, have been accused of toppling the boundary stones of morality and opening our homes to people of questionable background and contestable reputation merely because they entertained us. By so doing, we supposedly undermined the foundations of society. But one can see this in a different light. Putzi Cottolenghi told me that when his grandfather was a young man, he called upon the Vicomtesse de Fegonzac in order to present himself to her. She was already eighty years old, and she received him with the words 'Don't you find, monsieur, that the nicest object on earth is a sturdy erect penis?' That was still in the best eighteenth-century style, aristocratic through and through. *We* tried to win back the same freedom after middle-class Victorianism had so dreadfully strangled any natural expression of rapport with life. *Épater les bourgeois!* was *our* shibboleth. And today, no one is grateful to us for our efforts. . . ."

And, having become truly pensive, Uncle Ferdinand adds, "A society preserves its ethical landmarks by ruthlessly expelling anyone who dares to transgress them. He is henceforth cut by one and all. But how can you do that in an era when people have taken up the American custom of drinking cocktails before meals, so that before dinner is even served, everyone is so drunk that no one recognizes anyone, or everyone is ready to hurl his arms around the nearest perfect stranger? . . ."

Uncle Ferdinand stares at me with his round, hazelnut-brown

eyes nailed fast by the black pinheads of the pupils. His gaze does not exact agreement; it is downright commanding. After all, he is presenting his Middle Kingdom not for my critique and analysis but as a costly gift, and despite the exposure of its internal dynamics, he is delivering it in its wholeness and unique givenness, as a *happening*, so to speak. I succumb unresistingly to the experience.

I gaze at the happy-go-lucky rich of the blissful years of truce between the two world wars. Not only do I peer into their lives, backgrounds, pasts, into their brains, their nooks and crannies, their bank accounts, their businesses and business methods; I am soon initiated into their games with their often intricate rules, including those games that are not played at polo grounds, tennis courts, golf courses, or roulette and baccarat tables. I know the internal structure of this easygoing world of players, even the view from within this world to the world outside. (For instance, the geography that is a phenomenon of "seasons." "There are," says Uncle Ferdinand, "people whom you see on the Riviera in spring and then in London for the season, and afterward, of course, for the grouse-shooting in Scotland after August 12. And in between, there are others whom you see in Biarritz or on the Lido or sailing in the Aegean or in Scandinavia—it all depends on whether someone prefers the sun or the rough sea. And then again, you see others in Deauville for polo or in Merano for the races, or at the autumn hunting in the Ardennes and in Hungary and God knows where else. And others in Egypt during the winter or for skiing in the Engadine. Yes, and then there are people whom you see all year long and everywhere—your friends, in short, the ones who really count. . . .") I am also familiarized with the secrets of those spherical hierarchies: the innermost circles from which the closer and farther circles of friends radiate, intersecting and intertwining with the closer and farther circles of other inner circles—I know them all as intimately as if I belonged to each circle right at the center and nucleus. . . .

of course, I know them so intimately only from hearsay, albeit very thorough hearsay. After all, John and Stella talk about them constantly, naming, mentioning, quoting someone or other whose renown and guaranteed wealth plus no doubt quite reliably similar outlook on the world and on life would place him, as a matter of course, in some system of rings of friends in the Middle Kingdom (the manner in which they are named, mentioned, quoted, hints at differences in rank and degrees of intimacy down to the finest nuance). . . .

And this could mean that even John and Stella, incessantly and almost against their will, at any rate without the slightest intention, are weaving away at the myth of the Middle Kingdom—

—John and Stella, the independent ones, the completely unconcerned ones, without the slightest social ambition, who demonstrated ironic indulgence, at best, toward the conspiratorial innermost circle of Uncle Ferdinand's playboy world, and who do their assiduous best to avoid other, more rigorously closed systems of circles of friends of the upper ten thousand (for instance, with a very few exceptions, the North German aristocracy)—even John and Stella, I say, did their bit in weaving away at the myth. . . . I can't believe they did this only because their wealth, background, and education automatically made them part of the cosmos of these rich, renowned, and influential people and sent them wandering like nomads through the closer and farther circles of their world within the world. There must be still another reason.

□   19   □

THIS MAKES ME PENSIVE, and I have the leisure to brood about it when I am permitted to retire for three quarters of an hour before dinner in order to bathe and change.

A guest of this "reality," which seems more and more unreal (hostile armies are deploying behind each of the inner circles of Uncle Ferdinand's Middle Kingdom), I lie in the huge, old-fashioned tub in the middle of the bright, cheery, spacious room that my mother fixed up as a bathroom for me. In the fourteen years of my exile from the world of wealth, I never tired of describing it in detail to my cousin Wolfgang, because it was so utterly different from the damp, narrow hole in the wall, smelling of detergent, with its cold tiles and the dripping, half-rusted water

pipes, in the dark Viennese apartment where we bleakly vege-
tated through our dreary days (together with Cousin Wolfgang's
parents, my foster parents—Uncle Helmuth and Aunt Hertha—
as well as Aunt Selma, my real foster mother). There, the bathroom was a place in which the tasks of physical cleansing, though
conceived as belonging to the ethic of *Weltanschauung*, had to be
performed behind locked doors as an embarrassing necessity to
be discharged quickly and prudishly. Here, it was an almost sen-
suously cozy room filled with comforts, and you left as if you'd
just stepped out of a bandbox, with an aura of fragrant freshness,
whereas there, you came out steaming and scrubbed red but tired
and tending to sweat. Chattering with Cousin Wolfgang, I gushed
on about my childhood bathroom in Bessarabia. I was no less enthusiastic about it than about the park "in the faraway Balkan
land," as Uncle Helmuth called it, sarcastically. I described the
sumptuous delights of that bathroom: the huge, pre-warmed bath
towels, in which one could wrap oneself from head to toe; the gigantic sponges, feather light and crunchingly brittle when dry,
heavily dripping when soaked in water; the fragrant soaps and
pungently prickling colognes ... but this, of course, elicited
merely a disparaging shrug from Cousin Wolfgang, who was
above such mollycoddling and used the toilet as a study where he
could be relatively undisturbed.

Nevertheless, while cozily soaping my limbs in the perfumed
water here, I cannot but be moved at the thought of my Viennese
relatives. I think of the prophetic threats that Uncle Helmuth uttered—to Aunt Hertha's and Aunt Selma's chorus-like approval
and even Cousin Wolfgang's tacit agreement (he has, alas,
perished as a hero)—ranting on against *plutocrats:* those corrupt,
degenerate exploiters of the have-nots, those diabolical capitalists
like John and Stella who pulled me back, despite all my enlightened upbringing with its sound views and true values, into the
debauched world where my mother had gone astray and given
birth to me, a fatherless child, and where, when she soon perished
justly and shamefully, I would have been callously left to starve
had not they, my Viennese relatives, taken me in.

In fact, there was little to say about this other than that it was correct. But it would never have induced me to hate that admittedly vile but nonethless bright, cheery, spacious world of the rich, whose bathrooms I yearningly recalled, or to love the hard, confused, detergent-smelling uprightness of the benefactors forced upon me. Nor did it stop me from observing that Uncle Helmuth's upward tantrums, against the plutocrats, were no more violent than his downward ones, against the proletarians, and that we, the educated have-not bourgeoisie, were hated from below, in the concierge lodges and back courts of our apartment house, as much as Uncle Helmuth hated the still aristocratic *society people*, the *snobs*, as he wrongly called them.

In this respect, too, I disappointed if not betrayed my foster parents. If they assumed that I, the bastard who had popped into their home from the taboo world of the rich, would become at least an ally in their even more violent dislike of the back-court proletarians, then their hope was lamentably misplaced. Aunt Hertha admitted this frequently and bitterly. How could she have known that Miss Fern had cautioned me to stay discreetly aloof from the "simple people" because I might otherwise embarrass them, and that these constant admonitions had aroused my burning curiosity to get to know these susceptible, hence obviously extremely sensitive people, get to know them as soon and as well as possible, and to find out what there was about me that could make them lose their composure, perhaps even assure them that there was no real cause for their response. Now that no visible social barriers separated me from them, I had the best chance to do so. So much childlike naïveté was bound to be beyond Aunt Hertha. And of course she could not know that the gray-faced men with collarless shirts, the haggard women in aprons, the snot-nosed children from the bedbug caves in the apartment house to which I was now exiled, were paradoxically the only people who had any sort of connection to my past life. Aside from the princely households of my mother's friends and patrons, I had known only such "simple people." They were far more familiar to me, far more of a homeland, than the almost equally limited, equally gray-faced, grouchy, but demanding and overpowering philistines with their baroque moral code and their egotism, who, arrogating the right to control my thoughts, feelings, and actions, styled themselves my benefactors and exacted gratitude from me.

I needn't bother saying that my actual attempts at approaching the "simple people" merely unleashed a fusillade of insults and vile imprecations. One of the mothers whose children I ventured to speak to pounced on me because their screams made her think I was trying to attack them. Furiously she grabbed my hand, yanked me up the stairs, and delivered me at our apartment door to the offended-lady rigidity of Aunt Selma. The mother poured out a verbal torrent, and since my German was defective in those days and the barked-out Viennese dialect rendered it all the more unintelligible, I could only just make out that my relatives were well advised to keep the piss-elegant young dandy under control, otherwise there was no guaranteeing my safety.

Two or three years later, I did manage to break through after all. This happened in the course of a friendship I quickly formed at school with a boy who, to Cousin Wolfgang's endless and scornful delight, was the son of a trolley conductor and lived, not far from us, in the back court of another tenement. By now I recollect very little about this friend; I can barely remember his face. I recall only that his features darkened sadly when Cousin Wolfgang, who, as a *Gymnasium* student, also despised us for attending the much less highbrow *Realschule*, shouted after us, "Next stop Wieden, transfer to the Circle Line, please don't push, keep the aisle open! . . ." But I will never forget a summer Sunday that I was permitted to spend with the trolley-conductor people in a suburban garden near Mödling: a day of Maupassant-like nostalgia and enchantment, woven entirely of trivia, with a picnic on the grass, during which the father's undershirt and the mother's stockings, rolled up under her fat knees, did not arouse any feelings of social repulsion. Rather, they made me forget about the bad clothes I had to wear after outgrowing the Little Lord Fauntleroy outfit I had arrived with from Bessarabia. We had a hearty glass of new wine with the sausages and munched green apples from a tree and did airy gymnastics on a shed the roof of which Father Trolley Conductor had nailed down with fresh tarpaper. We spent hours fishing for tadpoles in a small brook and then

drank a delicious glass of clotted milk in the evening, while
Mother Trolley Conductor hollowed out a pumpkin for us, cutting eyes, a nose, and an enormous, toothy mouth, so that we
could stick a candle inside and frighten the neighborhood children. First, however, to my great delight, Father Trolley Conductor gave an artistic performance. He placed the candle in front
of the wall, and his hands created the most entertaining shadow
pictures: barking dog heads and ear-wriggling bunnies and similar delightful things.

When I returned to my relatives, who excitedly reported about
a hike through the woodlands of the Rax, I had my first fistfight
with Cousin Wolfgang, which made Aunt Hertha say I had the
makings of a criminal. All that had preceded it was a remark that
Wolfgang had arrogantly tossed at me when I finished the blazing
description of my day: "From a castle park to a garden plot—
should this step be viewed as descent or progress?"

Cousin Wolfgang now lies in the Central Graveyard of Vienna.
I think of him often and with sincere affection. In those last few
years, when it tortured him to see me reading Nietzsche as a
matter of course while he wrestled with the same text like Jacob
with the angel—

("For you, it's a cowboys-and-Indians story!" he said angrily.
"And for you?" I asked.

"But this shakes one's whole being! This bowls a person over!
It forces your inmost nature to make an ultimate decision. . . ."
And then his voice trailed off before my ironic look. Ach!
Schwab!)

—in the last few years, I say, when he was standing up more
and more resolutely for the *Weltanschauung* of the National Socialist German Workers Party, which was outlawed in Austria
but was celebrating triumphs in the "Old Reich," he would speak
starry-eyed about the *Volk*. We used to talk a lot in those days,
just before and just after John and Stella entered my life (until
his *Weltanschauung* no longer permitted him to watch unpro-
testing while I lived as the kept lover of a Jewess). This was the
era when we had drawn so close through our fistfights as to recognize our brotherhood despite our incompatibility—good Lord
in heaven! Fourteen years together in one room, at one table, in

front of the same emaciated faces, in the same dripping, steaming bathroom. . . .

Too bad he departed from us so prematurely, my dear cousin Wolfgang! He has been lying in the ground for six months now (it's 1940)—a martyr to *his* "reality within reality," which he regarded as the only reality: as if its standards, its weights and laws, were valid for everyone. . . . I should have done more to convince him of God's approval of better bathrooms. . . .

□   <big>20</big>   □

ANYHOW, there in Bessarabia I stretch out my bath pleasurably. I feel it's important to mull these things over while I cover my chest and arms with the sumptuous, spicy foam. Despite the four-course lunch and the opulent afternoon tea, I feel hungry, which adds a degree of poignant warmth to my affection for Uncle Ferdinand, for I know how carefully he will arrange the dinner and the accompanying wines. I am tense and overtired, but quite thoroughly happy. I feel as if once more I had escaped into another, new, unexpected state, a new, abstract reality. My frame of mind must be similar to that of the souls who, at the Last Judgment, have managed just barely to slip under the angel's dividing hand to the right side of God—only to realize that they float in space because they have lost the ground under their feet.

I would have liked to chat with Cousin Wolfgang now. I enjoy picturing him seated here on the edge of the bathtub as he so often did on Sundays in the bathroom of the apartment in the Twelfth District, when Uncle Helmuth and Aunt Hertha and Aunt Selma had gone off to the woodlands of the Rax, and he and I, claiming we had to study, enjoyed a quiet day of ample loafing and undisturbed bathing joys. Our brotherhood was unclouded at such times.

Now, here, I could talk to him "properly and justly"—as we said—about John and Stella: with more thorough knowledge and greater insight into the ways and dynamics of their world. I could explain to him why it made no difference at all whether they were the exploiters and oppressors that Uncle Helmuth made them out to be (and that he, Wolfgang, agreeing with his father for once, saw them as being): John, the second son of the second son of some high-ranking peer, who went through the typical education process at Eton and Cambridge, who, casually and peripherally, as it were, became a linguist, highly esteemed in the professional world for his knowledge of Sanskrit and ancient Persian and for his translations and editions of rare manuscripts from the early Sufi period, but who one day chucked his bookworm life and entered the British diplomatic service with very special missions; and Stella, the daughter of a Bucharest department-store millionaire, a woman for whom squandering money was an inner compulsion, a redemption of her socialist conscience from the guilt of being a capitalist's child. Stella, who, in Berlin—the legendary Berlin of the late twenties!—had been friends with Paul Flechtheim, Gottfried Benn, Max Reinhardt, George Grosz; who had studied sociology in Heidelberg, psychology at the Sorbonne, art history in Florence and Freiburg, and was as well known in Prague as in Madrid. Stella, who had her winter chalet at Saint Moritz, her summer villas in Saint-Jean-Cap-Ferrat and Biarritz, and regularly won the prize for being the most elegant "Lady in Her Car" at the autumn races in Baden-Baden as well as first prize in the golf tournament. Stella, the indefatigable denizen of nightclubs, the chain smoker whose collection of lovers was as important as her collection of Futurists. Stella, who had read her Marx as passionately as *The Divine Comedy*, who knew her Einstein as thoroughly as the writings of Lilly Braun. . . . Whether it was correct to call these two people plutocrats, cynically knowing participants in and promoters of an inhumane system, even its parasites—this made no difference whatsoever; it wasn't the issue, any more than to what extent and in what manner they would have been able to open new horizons for Cousin Wolfgang, too. Eventually they could have done for him what they did for me: expand the world by adding a different world, freer, roomier, airier than the petit bourgeois confinement in which we spitefully crammed our Plutarch and Hölderlin in order to be *something better* than the uneducated. They could have opened to him a world that was cheerier, brighter, more humane than the sweaty, anxiety-damp world of Uncle Helmuth, Aunt Hertha, and Aunt

Selma, this probity made insipid by mousy hopes that were never fulfilled, the petit bourgeois probity about which we boasted because it cost so many sacrifices, though it brought us nothing that did not feed our arrogance; in any case, a world in which the bathroom pipes weren't rusty from the wet laundry that always hung from them. . . .

He hated all these things as much as I did, my brother Cousin Wolfgang. He suffered as much as I did from the stench of cabbage and watery soup in the stairwell of No. 14 in a long line of tenements built in the same ugly way, dilapidated in the same grease-smeared, gray, filthy decay. He felt as much as I did how our vitality was suffocated under all sorts of lamentable restrictions and shameful renunciations. He felt as much as I did—like a lead band around the mind—the eternal anxiety about that cherished bit of breathing space beyond sheer existence, threatened daily by rent rises, potato prices, job dismissals, forced evictions. He was as ashamed as I was of the rigid demand for recognition, the jealously alert, distrustful class arrogance and cultural *hauteur* with which we looked down on the "trash," the "little people," the proletarians and semi-proletarians from the back-court and basement holes. We, the educated ones, strictly brought up with so-called good manners ("Would you please stand up, you moron, when a lady enters the room!"), as poor as church mice but clean ("Did you wash your neck? Show me your fingernails!"), bypassed by Fortune, stepchildren of life, intimidated by a hundred taboos but proud, arrogant, haughty. Uncle Helmuth, a native of Thuringia, the son of a pastor with innumerable children, respectably starving as he worked his way through college, getting his degree in electrical engineering and occupying a low industrial position only because research was paid even more poorly. And Aunt Hertha and Aunt Selma, the stiff-necked soldier's children, born somewhere between Przemyśl and Udine, the daughters of a Lieutenant Colonel Subicz, who (successfully emulated by Cousin Wolfgang a quarter century later) promptly died in action in Galicia in November 1914 and turned into a myth. A myth, to be sure, that no one beyond our four walls cared a fig about and of which no other token was left but a yellow photograph showing a waxed mustache over a uniform collar, a saber with a thickly knitted gold-thread sword knot, and a medal earned by a legendary saber scar across the forehead. That was all that remained, or could be learned, of Lieutenant Colonel Subicz. But his spouse, who likewise had died prematurely, was a *von* Jaentsch, and that sufficed to give Cousin Wolfgang his rigid spine and his scorn for trolley conductors, and Aunt Hertha her occasionally breezy but normally wry and caustic complacence, and Aunt Selma the bewitchment in her old-maid boniness; and it never let any of them forget what a disgrace it was that the third daughter, born in Dornbirn of Lieutenant Colonel Subicz and his spouse *née* von Jaentsch, beautiful Ilse (who characteristically called herself Maud!), went astray and perished by her own hand, leaving behind a bastard as a stain on their escutcheon.

My brother Cousin Wolfgang had all these things in his blood just as I did—like a disease, a wasting toxic (which, however, if you overcame it, made you especially robust and immune to susceptibilities). For him, too, it was a salvation to leave all these things behind and manage to forget them. For him, too, the lure must have seemed irresistible: to exchange the world and find a different world within the world. But no: Cousin Wolfgang was one of those people who prefer to *change* the world—lock, stock, and barrel. He did not live in life, he lived in ideas and convictions. And suffered because a sharp-toothed doubt gnawed on the most sublime ideas, the firmest of his convictions—

and it would be idle, invalid, to perceive in this doubt some possibility of hauling him into my camp: for the camps are long since indeterminable, the fronts vague, shifting; everyone is entangled in everyone else, no matter what ideas or convictions a person was once moved by—

and thus it is also idle to brood about the philosophy underlying the subtle distinctions in John's and Stella's social likes and dislikes. The resulting valuation seems strange. For instance, they take a lively interest in the fates and concerns of the working classes, and not just theoretically, they naturally *adore* their chef, spoil their caretaker's wife, treat their chauffeur, John's butler, and Stella's chambermaids with patriarchal caution and kindness, heartily shake hands with their dentist when encountering him in the lobby of the opera, greet his wife with explosive recognition whether meeting her for the first or the tenth time; however, they display ethereally remote *politesse* toward the wife of a bank director, because the borders are so fine here as to be all too easily crossed; and, with vigorous cordiality, they are icily neutral toward the wives of those of John's diplomatic colleagues who cannot deny a background that is, no doubt, highly respectable but simply not quite to be counted as part of Society.

A year and a half ago, I recall, all this was terribly interesting to me. I felt the bliss of a butterfly hunter who has caught an especially rare and beautiful specimen when, for instance, I discovered that it was still the wives who determined the final place in the social hierarchy; for the time being, bachelors were uncategorized, with every opportunity open. . . .

but it is winter 1940, the first Ice Age commenced two years ago and is about to climax, the butterflies are dead on their pins in the glass cases, my passion for lepidoptera has deepened into a passion for deeper biological dynamics: now, for instance, I would like to open Cousin Wolfgang's eyes to what the stylistic difference between John's and Stella's informational conversations and Uncle Ferdinand's overflowing chitchat signifies for their joint world.

When John and Stella exchange information about the *beau monde* they belong to, they do so in a businesslike way, which is cool, terse, and precise. Their membership is presumed by their social prestige and their financial standing, matters that must be administered both cautiously and soberly if they are to be well administered. John and Stella, in the web of the higher and highest circles, hang on the threads of innumerable commercial, social, familial, and, last but not least, simply human interests. Unavoidably, they talk about their world. But only privately. They leave no doubt that it is a closed world. They even lower their voices as though fearing that outsiders might be eavesdropping. Even when they are alone—or privately with me—they speak quickly, in shorthand and ciphers: they refer to people either by nicknames and pet names (Maxi, Bully, Manetti, Coco, Toto, Cloclo) or by titles that reveal nothing to the uninitiated about family connections and that conceal degrees of kinship like that between the Baron Charlus and the Duke of Guermantes. Or else they speak about their friends by using—even more mysteriously—the names of their estates, which are not always identical to their family names. John and Stella practice utmost discretion. Even when directly asked, they avoid exposing all too intimate facts. And they handle anything beyond the sparest information with a certain blurry sketchiness, which one can follow only with precise and comprehensive knowledge and which is therefore accessible only to true initiates (even though the subject matter is usually something that anyone might just as well know). Even I, who live with them in a way that one could—God knows!—call intimate, am sometimes afflicted by a vexed impatience at this hush-hush business over banalities. And though Coco's wheelings and Cloclo's dealings are largely matters of indifference to me, I do find that when John and Stella exchange their quick and quiet seals and ciphers, I am as spellbound as someone trying to divine the hushed cooperation of face and gesture between two deaf-mutes.

Still, this never happens without John and Stella's instantly apologizing and hinting that these are matters that could not possibly be of general interest but that must, alas, be briefly discussed (by them). They leave no doubt that only one part of their existence belongs to the special world of the rich—the secular part—and that neither their egos nor their true interests have settled there. John and Stella wish very much to be treated as individuals and persons, quite independent of membership in the *grand world* of society (which is actually a very small world)—even if they can't deny that they *live* in this specific world within the world and its reality in an increasingly abstract and unreal reality. That is, that they are speaking about something that is alive.

Uncle Ferdinand is altogether different. He identifies fully with his Middle Kingdom. For that inner circle of the monstrously rich who so utterly enjoyed their merry life is already historical; even more: it is a mythical kingdom. Yet never for a moment does Uncle Ferdinand think of himself as outside it, for he is intergrown with it in every fiber of his being. And yet—or probably because of this—he speaks of it with utmost indiscretion. He exposes the most humiliating facts, reveals the most compromising circumstances, does not spare the most personal and intimate details; but he does all this with a reporter's sobriety, which is disarming. He narrates even the worst scandals in a matter-of-fact way that allows any judgment, makes no moral or aesthetic evaluation, but simply testifies to something that exists, like life itself.

Uncle Ferdinand speaks with this relentless scientific detachment to me—an outsider. True, he pretends to take me for granted as one of his own kind, to whom he may assume that his world is not alien and whom his tales would not strike dumb, like the fables of Sinbad the Sailor of the copper city to which the roc carried him. But the thoroughness with which Uncle Ferdinand exposes each bit of trash (Toto's wheelings and Cloclo's dealings) in every kind of connection with other bits of silly willy-nilly information—demonstrating, explicating, expiating— merely betrays how well aware he is of dealing with a nonmember who must be taught the rudiments. Moveover, I am an outsider not only sociologically but also in time.

Uncle Ferdinand is deliberately telling tales out of school because he wants to transmit what went on *in* school. He wants to instruct me about his Middle Kingdom as minutely and precisely as possible so that I may carry it on in my time. Whether he understands his aims and motives is debatable. He probably never asks himself. When Uncle Ferdinand feels the urge to talk about the Middle Kingdom, then it is not really *he* speaking—something speaks out of him. *The Middle Kingdom wants to speak through him.* And I here, at the ebb of my bathing joys, do not have to brood about what this signifies. To me, too, it reveals the flair for the *Zeitgeist*. Uncle Ferdinand must *speak* his world, for otherwise it no longer is, or will be. True, the kingdom of the rich and richly influential has not gone under. WW II, expanding more and more icily, more and more lethally, in this heart of winter 1940, may have disrupted the overlappings of the circles of friends. But Maxi, Bully, Mutzi, Putzi, Manetti, Coco, Toto, Cloclo, or whatever their names, are still physically alive. Restricted perhaps, cut off from their own kind, without galas, dinner parties, cocktail parties, treasure hunts, but certainly not in dire straits. Some of them may even die; but they have heirs to their wealth and spirit. The carnivore teeth have not been blunted. Once the deluge is past, they will weave themselves together again—probably tighter, tauter, finer-meshed, and richer in booty than before. Nevertheless—or rather, for that very reason—their world will never again be what it was in Uncle Ferdinand's time. For it is already a world of shadows and will remain a world of shadows, albeit occasionally moved lifelike by a shadow player and evoked for his glory.

□   **21**   □

THAT IS WHAT I WOULD LIKE to explain to my dead cousin Wolfgang: Uncle Ferdinand's innocence. The greatness of his innocence. His eminently creative inability to act otherwise. His wovenness in his time, his unity with the spirit of his time—an involvement so intimate that he will pass away with it but singing of it, telling of it. Its bard, its dying swan.

I admire him beyond all measure. I study him as a knowledge-hungry scholar studies a profound and fascinating author who is brimming with ideas. I joyfully and eagerly look forward to our meeting again, to our dinner. I am as excited as a paleontologist who has been given the chance to dissect a perfectly preserved dinothere.

Uncle Ferdinand no longer belongs to our earthly period. His species is dying out; the Middle Kingdom is perishing. It will be destroyed not by Doubleyou Doubleyou II but by the new breed of a new age. This will be a breed that will no longer watch the days festively link up in a garland of seasons (the *"saisons"*), will no longer watch them in harmony with the world and its (and their own) nature, will no longer be innocent and God-affirmed like Bully Olivera, Agop Garabetian, and Uncle Ferdinand. It will itself be a race of dichotomous beings, self-doubters, self-fleers, like John and Stella. True, the teeth of the carnivores will be as sharp as ever, ripping more greedily than ever before. But consciousness will hold a mirror up to the carnivores when they tear their prey: they will realize what they are doing.

Thus, never again will the Middle Kingdom be what it was in

Uncle Ferdinand's day: a world within the world, taking itself for granted, in harmony with the world; a reality within reality, accepted as God-given and natural even by those who did not belong; attacked, to be sure, denounced, derided, contemned, condemned, but its existence never denied, never questioned as a reality of life, without whose wealth of colors and stimuli life would be poorer, thinner, emptier.

Uncle Ferdinand's world is going through what the *Zeitgeist* is making the entire world go through: his world is flying apart, going out of joint, dissolving, passing from a solid state into a liquid and ultimately a gaseous state. In a word, his world is becoming abstract. And Uncle Ferdinand knows it is. He sees it not in an abstract way but with the sharp eye of the man of the world (a still materially palpable world). He says:

"When I think back over my life, then naturally my youth at the imperial courts in St. Petersburg and Vienna and London was incomparably more brilliant than the period after the first great war. However, life was almost more entertaining after the war. Before the war, it was like going to bed with a duchess: God knows what discretion it required, what complicated preparations you had to go through, and then all kinds of obstacles and dangers, with her having pangs of conscience that in the end she'd have to confess it all. And then when it happened it wasn't very different from normal. That was the old world. The new world was like hopping on the *Orient Express* in Paris and looking around to see who else is on board and spotting a fiery female and not knowing whether she's a *cocotte* or your cousin-germane, but either way you make up your mind to spend the night in her sleeping compartment: it'a a lot more fun, a lot more adventurous, don't you think, even if she turns out to be married to your dentist, even if you've once again hung about with people with whom you shouldn't really have any personal relations; it's irksome enough to endure her husband's fingers in your mouth. However, this became unavoidable after the war; I mean, associating with such people. They were suddenly there like flies in summer—the snobs, you understand—and I must say, a new tone came into the world with them, of course, and thereby a new taste into life. I don't even mean a bad taste, although this went without saying.

Yet it was somehow more enticing, more *piquant*. . . . Now, there are two kinds of snobs, after all: one kind are sometimes even *simpático,* and quite useful too—like courtiers. In our day, these are courtiers *sans* courts, alas, but with the same qualities: pushy and boot-licking, ambitious and groveling with their superiors and snappish with their inferiors, but always so poignantly helpful, so pleasantly assiduous. . . . These are simply people who always want to be on top but don't quite have the grit for it, nor can they be alone. They're dependent on you; you have the impression that they look up to you, like children to grownups; it breaks your heart when you have to send them off to bed. . . . However, there are also very unappealing people among them; that's the second category. You have the impression that they clamber up to you like mountain climbers, sweating terribly the while, and so you are cold to them and treat them badly, thus taking on snobbish manners yourself without meaning to do so. Or else you feel involuntarily tickled by the thought of being something like the north wall of the Eiger, you feel flattered that they would risk their necks to climb up to you, you recognize the athletic ambition. So you tolerate them. A kind of mutual complacence develops: while they ecstatically inhale the ambrosia of their gods, one of whom is you, your nostrils suck in the sweat of their brows like a sacrificial smoke. And in this way, too, all sorts of bad manners evolve, don't you agree. When one is with one's own kind, one would never dream of thinking oneself better than anyone else. But if you're incessantly surrounded by people who suck up to one person and snub another and make someone else realize that he is more than someone else or less than someone else or is doing something or other that is better or worse than what someone else is doing, or that he has more than other people or less than other people—yes indeed, then you too involuntarily start thinking about what you really are and do and have. And then it occurs to you that someone or other may be more or have more or do better things than you. He can be anyone and anything, a scientist or a *nouveau riche* or a film star. . . . And then, of course, the whole thing blows away; you no longer have a society in which rank and fortune and kindred opinions and manners go hand in hand; you've got a motley crew consisting purely of people about whom the same can never be said except that one talks about them, no matter why or in what terms, whether it's because a man may be a prince or a jockey or an adventurer who hopes to break the bank at Monte Carlo—so long as people notice him. For, after all, that's what snobs are all about: they want to be seen moving about quite casually among the noblest, the richest and the brightest and the best. And for this reason, of course, everyone has to know who they are. The snobs then make sure that the group keeps getting smaller and smaller and more and more exclusive. And anyone who doesn't get fed up with taking part in this everlasting exhibition, or who doesn't suddenly feel ashamed of having so much more than the others, and doesn't withdraw, will, of course, do his best to belong to the select few and will show the others that he is and knows and has more than they—and thus the world will ultimately consist of nothing but snobs. But you know, the way they started hanging around us, the snobs, it was often very entertaining. . . ."

Thus, Uncle Ferdinand says it all: the finest blossoming of the Middle Kingdom occurred precisely when it began to grow conscious of itself. Never again will it have the same light as in the days when the friends in the closest, most intimate circles went out to taste of the Tree of Knowledge and to gain an inkling of who they were—thus realizing that their paradise was lost, that they would have to find a new one. Even Uncle Ferdinand's paganly happy playboy world was ruffled by a springtime wind of longing for faraway places, the wind that had been so promisingly aroused by Doubleyou Doubleyou I in Europe and that then came to an icy standstill one day in March 1938.

□   22   □

UNCLE HELMUTH, too, is innocent in his fashion, namely in the fashion of the damned. He is condemned to hate himself. He doesn't realize it, of course. He thinks he hates others.

Uncle Helmuth feels challenged day in, day out, from above and from below and from all sides. He sings the loudest part in the chorus of those who have been given a dirty deal. Above him stand the rich, the plutocrats, the undeserving happy, free, frivolous. For them he doesn't count; they look down their noses at him. He wants to hate them, but actually he gazes up at them in worship. He nurtures a childlike admiration for his factory director, who, until March 1938, played not only a leading role in Austrian industry but an even greater one in preparing the annexation of Austria to the Third Reich of our compatriot Adolf Hitler, and then of course vanished from the scene. (John and Stella once met him somewhere and called him "a stupid arsehole.") And as for a certain Countess Kannwitz, who was interested in spiritualism, Uncle Helmuth absolutely gushes about her, calling her "one of the most important women of the century, probably the reincarnation of a very high luminary of mankind, like Jesus Christ, Buddha, or Madame Blavatsky." She was an old bag who used to run after girls with high heels, bang her umbrella on their shoes, and rant, "Don't wear high heels, they're only for whores!" Which regularly led to highly unpleasant scenes.

Uncle Helmuth's hatred is even purer downward, toward the "undisciplined riffraff" of the "proletarians." Granted, they are poor and ought really to be his allies against their mutual "exploiters" and "slave drivers." But Uncle Helmuth feels separated from them by a class barrier. He is an "academic"; he attended university (making sacrifices that he talks about like his wounds in WW I). Uncle Helmuth wears a collar and tie; he has a doctorate in engineering and is married to the second daughter of the late Lieutenant Colonel Subicz and Frau Lieutenant Colonel Subicz *née* von Jaentsch. This separates him everlastingly from the ignorant and dirty rabble in the back courts. And yet he has to admit to himself that, unlike him, this ragtag mob have no prejudices, are not ruled by fictions, and thus in many respects live more freely, happily, frivolously than he.

Since it is basically the envy of the unredeemed that makes Uncle Helmuth hate both upward and downward, one might think that he sees redemption in America. The United States appears to be a society that has succeeded in making social envy the driving element of the national dynamic. In a land where every shoeshine boy is a potential millionaire, one had better not treat him scornfully. And if his road to riches is a little longer than Mr. Rockefeller's, then the distance serves his self-respect as a measure, even if he breaks down en route.

But no: Uncle Helmuth does not feel challenged by American competitiveness. He says too many "values" are lost in it. Americans are "uncultured materialists" with no respect for the "spiritual side of life" and its values—so bitterly hard for him, the eleventh son of a destitute Thuringian pastor, to secure.

In reality, Uncle Helmuth embodies the spirit of "uncritical social criticism," as John calls it—and in this respect, he is a potential Nazi. Criticism, says John, was the intrinsic forte of the Nazi movement. In criticizing, the Nazis were always right—like everyone else nowadays, by the way. But, like the criticism voiced by the German National Socialists of that time, Uncle Helmuth's is too general, too universal, and thus ultimately not maneuverable, an overcanvased ship. His criticism comes not from sober analysis but from resentment, from a general sulkiness about life, an ill humor that only imagines most of the insults and injuries that nourish him, and thus has no solid goal, no concrete object. Uncle Helmuth reacts instinctively against any stimulus that he views as characteristic of something opposing him. It may be a lady in sable or a whistling tramp, a speeding car, a silly advertising slogan on a poster, a kiss on some woman's hand, a certain way of donning a hat—particularly anything testifying to a way of life that strikes him as freer, lighter, cheerier than his own, thereby putting his own in doubt.

And because he feels like a victim, he stuffs everything possible into this hate: blame for the whole dreary monotony of his existence; the probable disappointment in his thwarted professional ambitions (he really wanted to go into research and not industry); his concern about the state of the world, which his newspaper makes him worry about every morning, reminding him how helpless he is, how at the mercy of the powers. Perhaps he also tosses into this garbage can of his choleric emotions the sexual frustration of a man who has Aunt Hertha for a wife, and in adjacent rooms Aunt Selma on one side and Cousin Wolfgang and me on the other, all as possible eavesdroppers; and certainly he adds his spiritualist notion that there is a true, non-earthly hierarchy of nearness to God, or rather farness from God, in which he occupies a totally different, much loftier rank, roughly at the level if not of Jesus Christ or Buddha then at least of Madame Blavatsky, with no one realizing this at all. . . .

He has a collective name for everything he hates. The species that he imagines as enjoying a more carefree way of life than his own (and this comprises proletarians as well as plutocrats, also "society people," and "snobs" like John and Stella) is summarily known as "they."

"They" are the people responsible for (or rather guilty of) the fate of mankind—the powerful (oppressors), the rich (exploiters), the undisciplined uneducated (anarchists)—and are pilloried in sentences beginning *"They*'ve got us in another mess . . ." or *"They*'re grabbing the lion's share, of course . . ." or *"They* can't bear seeing something in order . . ." The obvious flippancy, frivolity, unscrupulousness, inconsiderateness of these plainly well known but unnamable anonymouses inspire such rhetoric as *"They*'re amused . . . *they* skim off the cream and relish it . . . *they* laugh up their sleeves, of course . . . *they* just let you kick the bucket. . . ."

And this *they* is elastic enough to cover whole strata; nay, whole nations: the British, for instance (*"They* imagine they're superior"). It extends to writers of popular songs (*"They* give people highfalutin ideas") and to Jews (*"They*'ve known how to cheat our kind for two thousand years now"). In addition, there is room for the traditional whipping-boys of middle-class resentment: *they* (aristocrats), *they* (Reds), *they* (priests), *they* (Freemasons), *they* (journalists). . . .

Thus, we can hardly assume that Uncle Helmuth has Uncle Ferdinand's Middle Kingdom in mind when he says, with specific emphasis and an indignation-bloated ring in his voice, "They"—meaning "plutocrats," "society people," "snobs."

I remember the time when I first moved into his home. In those days, the smart set of the upper ten thousand did not have the publicity they enjoy today as the so-called Jet Set (or Café Society)—an unwanted publicity that was to be so prophetically foreseen by Uncle Ferdinand. Uncle Helmuth could at best get some impression of it from my childish blather. (Incidentally, I soon stopped the blathering, when I noticed the frosty rejection concealed beneath the artificial irony with which it was received.) Perhaps Uncle Helmuth's imagination was assisted by the fashion magazines and society gazettes that Aunt Selma sometimes bought on the sly; she dreamed whole afternoons away with them in her darkened room, but somehow or other they came to light and were then devoured by Aunt Hertha and Uncle Helmuth (albeit more hastily, more sketchily, more nervously). This wholly inadequate reportage presented yearning eyes with the dream life of the happy rich at the North Sea, Mediterranean, and Alpine resorts of high-society geography—a life lived in the chandelier brilliance of casinos, at racetracks, on the decks of huge white yachts, on the lawns of birthday-cake-like country villas and bougainvillea-flooded terraces on sepia-blue, pine-shielded shores—yet could only give a hint that this was where the true focus of his social hatred might be found: the nucleus, the axial pole of that other, blissful way of life that was so sneeringly opposed to his own, which made his own seem less worth living.

The images that Uncle Helmuth saw in those smart-set periodicals treacherously smuggled into his four-room household were, at worst, the listing sails of an ocean-going regatta and, mounted like medallions in the sky overhead, the not very informative portraits of the ship owners in breezy skipper's caps, white turtlenecks, and stylish navy-blue blazers; racetrack bleachers crowded with ladies in flimsy frocks and enormous heron-feathered hats, and gentlemen in gray toppers and polished leather binocular cases hanging sprucely from narrow straps on their chests; or else a snapshot series of men and women standing in the same cataleptic convulsion, the right leg twisted and the knee turned in, the left knee bent, toes pointed inward, the arms yanked over the right shoulder, head stretched to the left, eyes peering down toward the feet at a small white ball that is to be struck by a golf club that is swung against the backdrop of a cascading weeping-willow branch; or else a saber-legged grouplet of four, each man wearing spurred boots and a cork helmet that casts a shadow like a mask over his suntanned face, in the sportily gloved left hand the grip of a casually shouldered polo stick, and in the right a silver cup—Messrs. Bully Olivera, Putzi Cottolenghi-Strazza, Bruce Spencer-Fox, and Jean de Fegonzac (grandson of the beauty-loving vicomtesse)—and below, perhaps, a close-up of Sir Agop Garabetian, who donated the cup and whose monocle, in the Arabian Nights face with the twirling black beard, flashes sheer benevolence toward all mankind.

Such photographic documentation preceded detailed descriptions of the subsequent *soirées*, with exhaustive lists of names. But when it came to precise particulars of the ladies' toilettes and jewels, the reporting was taken over by draftsmen who knew how to render the essential better than any writers or photographers. Now, it may be astonishing to realize how much can be deduced from even the meagerest external signs of a human being's condition (thanks to a perceptiveness that should interest novelists), yet such vision-restricting peeps into the world of "the beautiful people" could not possibly have permitted the insights that empowered Uncle Helmuth to snort, "*They* are to blame for everything! *They* have all mankind on their consciences! People like us have to drudge for *them!* It's for *them* that people like us had to risk our necks for four years! ... Bu-u-u-t"—his voice trembling in the bombast of indignation, giving the ominously drawled vowel a wavy, swinging staccato "bu-u-u-t, if the whole business starts again this time, then it will go against *them!*"

◻   23   ◻

THERE IS NO DENYING that now, in February 1940, it looks as if Uncle Helmuth will turn out to be right. Of course, at first blush, such a positioning of fronts is not clear-cut. One has to see the situation with John's eyes, too: agreeing on this point, as on so many, with Uncle Ferdinand, he regarded the First World War as class warfare and views the Second as merely and certainly an intensified continuation of the First, with a more decisive focus on the true goal.

According to John, it is both a tragic and a grotesque (i.e., tragicomical) error that Doubleyou Doubleyou II is likewise being waged among nations, peoples, states, rather than, by unanimous international consent, between the representatives of a coming new world and those of a dying old world (among whose representatives John certainly counts himself). With incomparably fewer losses, he feels, they can achieve the same end that will ultimately come out of the slaughter and that (with the exception of Russia) did not emerge fully from Doubleyou Doubleyou I: namely, the extermination of the old upper crust and the takeover by the bloody fucking middle classes. Not by the proletarians, mind you, as the latter have always been promised, but by Uncle Helmuth and his bloody fucking kind. But out of this kind, too, will emerge another, much worse upper crust.

This notion has been haunting me for some time now (namely, since the post-March days of 1938 in Vienna, in their abstract vacuum). The gray iron men who came to us down the Nibelungen river, pouring into a human sea that surged with enthusiasm, these young men with the heavy, stamping boots, the wonder-craving eyes under gray helmets, and the gentle names (Adolf Emil Wolfgang Helmuth), were civil-war soldiers. And though it never came to a German civil war at that time, and for the moment brothers and sisters embraced jubilantly, people soon realized that once again an hour of vast, useless blood sacrifice had come.

You didn't have to hear the Führer's speeches on the radio or to read the newspapers. You sensed it, the way animals whiff a storm, a flood, a fire. It surfaced when the intoxication, the delirium, the yowling, howling ecstasy of the first few days (or rather, the three-day-long day), subsided. The roar, in that shiny blue Ice Age coldness, was followed by a sudden, huge silence. You sensed it the way a murder victim senses his murderer's breath on the back of his neck even though the murderer is still far away, not yet visible: when you turn your head, the street is empty, he is still skulking along somewhere far behind you, around a corner, hugging the walls, but he is coming, he is coming, he is drawing closer to you and closer. . . .

Thus, too, the hour of vast blood sacrifice. No drums were booming or trumpets blaring when the hour finally came on September 1, 1939; it came as if it had been sneaking up for a long time and had finally arrived. And no matter how hard you tried and how willing you were to find some historically meaningful necessity, you couldn't come up with an obvious one. Unless you sensed that the Adolfs Emils Wolfgangs Helmuths had made up their minds to exterminate anything that was not of their kind. And, indeed, you sensed it. *They* were in power. Thus, the fronts are clear. Clearer, at any rate, than in WW I. But not completely clear. For instance, Uncle Helmuth's comments since March 1938 reveal that not all of *them* emigrated when the brown brothers of the Reich marched into Vienna, not all of *them* fled like bats from a cave when a light is carried in. He had always called *them* "shady elements," alluding to *their* "obscure machinations." Now, evidently, a certain portion of *them* who were not so allergic to light had remained, and occupied his imagination more keenly and more intensely than ever. They were now personally closer to him, so to speak, were more of his ilk, and in donning brown uniforms had changed their identities but not their power and arbitrariness, not the infinitely freer existential form that towered over his own and made it appear subordinate. But because they were of his stamp, he looked up kindly at them for the moment. He knew and named individuals (Reich Field Marshal Hermann Göring, Reich Propaganda Minister Dr. Joseph Goebbels, Reich Labor Leader Ley). But by some strange alchemy they too became *they* for him. At first he spoke their names in a different tone, of course (as Cousin Wolfgang did about the "New Human Being"). With stars in his eyes and the booming of unconditional trust in his breast, he would say, "You don't have to worry about a thing; *they'll* take care of it properly!" But this gradually changed again. The intonation became flatter, more sober. Soon the individuals melted back into the old collective term; the names gave way to the anonymous expression his powerlessness used for the possessors of power: *they*.

The more the days plunged, light and blue, into the great iceblue vacuum of a present that promised to become a greater future and in fact became an even greater past, the more taciturn Uncle Helmuth became. I saw very little of him then; I had already moved out of the apartment and was chicly installed in a *garçonnière* (paid for by Stella) in the center of emptied Vienna, so I saw Uncle Helmuth only when I visited Aunt Selma or

Cousin Wolfgang, who refused to meet me anywhere but in the "joint parental home" ("If you want to see me, then the place that was your home for twelve years ought to be good enough, right?"). But by early 1939, one could catch the irked overtones whenever Uncle Helmuth mentioned *them*. ("*They* seem to be forgetting that we people of the Ostmark are Germans, too, after all.") And then the hour of vast blood sacrifice began palpably to advance on him, too. It must have been around this time that I last saw him, but I can imagine that by September 1939 everything was back to normal: "*They*'ve put us in a fine mess!"

□ **24** □

FOR UNCLE HELMUTH and his iron men, I am now in the enemy camp, even though I too am standing as an iron man to fight side by side with millions like me against some kind of "*them.*" This is paradoxical, but I enjoy every moment of it.

Having bathed nicely and rubbed Geo. F. Trumper's West Indian Extract of Lime into my skin, having slipped into my exquisite, freshly ironed linen after sprinkling it with a few drops of Kniže Polo, and having donned my plum-blue gold-frogged and -braided operetta-hero uniform, I will go downstairs. Uncle Ferdinand will be waiting for me in the drawing room. He will be wearing pumps and black trousers, a starched shirt with a tuxedo tie, and a velvet jacket, in prince-of-the-Church violet, that is no less imaginatively frogged than my uniform. His Russian greyhounds will be lying next to him on the sofa, and when I enter, they will raise their bored lady-in-waiting heads and graciously bang their tails twice. On the low Chinese enamel table in front of him, there will be a large silver tray with a battery of bottles and carafes and all sorts of high and low, smooth and bellied, stemmed and flat-bottomed glasses. And he will brusquely tell me to have a drink, for he will be impatient to talk about his Middle Kingdom, against which the iron men have gone to war.

Outside, in the world, there's war. Two hours ago, we were having tea in the library (Indian, not Chinese, tea, like Mama), and for a few minutes it looked as if a huge, soundless battle were being fought in the west. The acanthus jungle of frost flowers on the windowpanes was blossoming as if on fire. The ribs of the leaf plumage were going up in yellow flames. But it was only the sun in a flawless heaven, at sixteen degrees below zero Celsius, gliding into its molten-iron bed.

Now, it has long been dark behind the frosted windows. A cold, heavy, ruthless darkness, such as one learned to fear in childhood when hearing about death and graves and tombs in horror stories. (Miss Fern didn't want these stories told to me, and it was all the more sinister when the servants whispered them into my ear when she wasn't around; I was scared numb, and yet happy to belong to them by sharing their terrors.)

The cold, heavy darkness must be in people's hearts, for the night is pure. Surely the sky is filled with high stars. The knotty acacias by the courtyard gates are throwing their naked branches up to them. The village lies hunched in the blue snow. In some of the black walls of the houses, under the snow bonnets, yellow window squares are spaced out, pricked by icicles hanging from the edges of roofs. It is so cold that all the dogs have crept away, silent. And perhaps, from the dark thicket of sloe bushes along the cemetery wall, where the three birches loom, a slim figure swathed from head to toe in a black cape will now emerge and come up the village road without visibly moving its feet and float to the pond in the park, where it will vanish. . . .

I have to think about Aunt Selma, my dead mother's sister. There is little likelihood that she ever told me horror stories, but she has their romantic poetry within herself. In all her being is the tomb-like darkness of a well shaft. Deep down lies a pure surface, dark and round, a hare's eye staring at the heavens. Of course, you have to catch her off guard. This is not easy, considering her harshness. The image of her afternoon nap blots out any other image that I have of Aunt Selma. There was no way of talking her into lying down. As if to demonstrate that it was her accursed destiny to drudge for us and allow herself scant relaxation and no full rest, she took her nap sitting on a kitchen chair. Seldom did she sleep tight. She dozed like a horse in its harness. Her head jerked forward, eventually swaying back and forth as though to a mute internal singsong. Earlier, we were told, her hair had been extraordinarily rich and lovely. She had cut it off because "it got in the way during housework." The part in it, dividing the ashen strands down the middle, expressed a harsh humility. If you touched her shoulder to suggest that she lie down on the living-room sofa or the bed in her own room, the weary draft-horse head yanked up and murmured with closed eyes, "Just wait—I'm coming. Let me rest a minute." If she intended to arouse our sympathy, then it was only to reject it gruffly. Fate had decreed that she be our menial. She used up her life for us in a clannish feeling rooted deep in peasant blood, a sense of responsibility: for her sister Hertha, whom she really didn't care for that much and toward whom she acted as a quarrelsome older sister; for her brother-in-law, whom she despised; for Cousin Wolfgang, to whom she felt indifferent even though she thought he had all the qualities of a "dear, well-behaved, hardworking boy"; for me, whom she regarded as her booty, something of her own, the sole property ever granted her. She worked her fingers to the bone for us in stolidly monotonous housework, performed with an anger that was more or less part of the routine and that she put on with her kitchen apron, laboring with tooth-gnashing gee-up, with the cumbersome creaking and obstinate squeaking of wheels on the cart she dragged over her life's stony paths.

It was, as she revealingly put it, a "cherished ordeal." She rose with the chickens, at dawn, got us all up, prepared our breakfasts, made sure we left the house on time. And then, all alone and probably with odd bits of incoherent monologue, she drudged the morning away, airing the beds, hanging out the rugs, washing the breakfast dishes, sweeping the floors, straightening up, making the beds, replacing the rugs, peeling potatoes, scrubbing vegetables, slicing onions and wiping the tears from her eyes with her apron, putting water on, handling pots, pans, plates, left and right, up and down, like a percussionist, dropping the gas ring, swearing at the gas, cursing the gas company, accusing life, wiping the hair out of her face, tearing the lid from the pot that had boiled over, sucking her scorched finger—that was how she spent the morning until lunchtime, when Cousin Wolfgang and I came back from school, I from the *Realschule*, he from his stuck-up humanistic *Gymnasium,* Uncle Helmuth from the plant, and Aunt Hertha from the office (she was ; bookkeeper in an ancient, oddball, lopsided little music-publishing firm). Aunt Selma set the table and served the loveless food, which was cooked from thrifty recipes. She hardly allowed herself time for even a bite: every day for twelve years I heard the sentence "Selma, would you please finally sit down!" alternately from Uncle Helmuth's and Aunt Hertha's lips. No sooner were we fed and the table cleared than she began to do the dishes, and at times it almost came to fisticuffs when Aunt Hertha caught to help her. "No, I simply won't hear of it—please! You're tired and overworked yourself; you're in the office all day long; please let me do it!"

Uncle Helmuth and Aunt Hertha caught the trolley back to the plant and the office, and Cousin Wolfgang and I started our homework (only during my boyhood and early adolescence; later, I broke out, ignoring threats and rebukes, playing hooky and strolling through the adventure of Vienna). Meanwhile, Aunt Selma spent the afternoon waxing the floors, watering the flowers, polishing the silver, doing the major laundry, the minor laundry, patching linen, sewing, ironing, darning, until Uncle Helmuth and Aunt Hertha came home for supper (always cold: usually sliced cold cuts with mustard pickles, a hard-boiled egg, kippers, vegetables left over from lunch). Her years thus passed, like the potatoes with which she prepared Bohemian dumplings (Cousin Wolfgang's favorite dish), vanishing between her fingers on the grater. And it was "only for a mere quarter of an hour" after lunch, when she had cleared and washed and put everything in order, that she permitted herself some rest in the harness. Seldom did she let herself go so far as to put her folded arms on the table and drop her head on them like a sobbing woman.

I was the only one who knew that she was different from this: that she was really indolent, work-shy, and moony. I was her property, the fatherless orphan-boy of her dead sister, placed under her guardianship by the court, her booty; but that was not the only reason she favored me wherever and however she could, sacrificing herself for me even more thoroughly than for *the others.* Whenever she winked, luring me into the kitchen to slip a penny into my pocket or spirit a piece of cake topped with whipped cream into my outstretched hand, I would sense that this was also a bribe. She knew that I saw through her. We were the same sort.

More than once, I managed to catch her unawares, but each time, it was as if she were catching me. I recall the first time precisely. We were alone in the apartment, a delicious silence. I lay in bed with one of those marvelous childhood diseases that are painless but that keep you out of school and free from responsibility. The adults are full of loving care; they don't criticize, threaten, or demand. Moreover, the fever gives your thoughts a gliding lightness, as if in slow motion, and the least exertion changes them, like images in a kaleidoscope, into something totally different. Words are transformed into numbers, just as they are in the minutes before you drop off to sleep, or into images, entire sentences standing there abruptly, like totem poles looming out of slow waters, while at the back of the neck, at the base of the skull, a small, sticky knob like a medlar fills the mouth with a lukewarm taste of brass. I was thirsty and I wanted to pee, too. So instead of calling Aunt Selma, I got up and went to the bathroom. And that was when I saw her through the open kitchen door. She was standing at the window, gazing out into the courtyard; or, rather, she had been gazing at the courtyard (or the sky above it), but, upon hearing me, she shifted her eyes to me. And even though there was absolutely nothing to see outside but the ugly wall of the left wing of the apartment building and a patch of indifferent sky overhead, her gaze was full of something very definite, something she had viewed with great clarity, with a hungry, wolf-like sharpness, even. And she was smiling. Of course, it was just the vague start of a smile, its tenderness contrasting poetically with the danger in her gaze. Since then, I have often thought that La Gioconda's smile, which people make such a fuss over, can be understood only if one imagines that she was peering into the distance a millisecond earlier and the smile remains as she looks over toward us.

Later, I often lurked about to see this distant gaze of Aunt Selma's. It was never in her eyes when she drudged. Her entire nature was confused at such times, bewildered and jittery, quarrelsome and vehement. She had a way of wiping her forehead with the back of her hand as if she had run into a cobweb and was whisking it out of her face. But no sooner did she drop her arms than that gaze came into her eyes. Her truer being now seemed to be flooding over and into her, and it was silent and listening. Neither Aunt Hertha nor Uncle Helmuth nor even Cousin Wolfgang noticed this strange presence of Aunt Selma when her mind was absent. (Even though, for Uncle Helmuth, this must have been one of the most ordinary circumstances of his weekly spiritist séances. But, of course, when Aunt Selma's spirit was absent, no spirit of a departed man or woman entered the momentarily vacant shell of her body; it was *she herself* who entered it—and that should have provided the mathematician in Uncle Helmuth with food for thought.)

Aunt Selma is bowed over a darning egg and darns stockings. (It was incredible to see her achievements: there were holes that had ripped into the darned areas and been redarned again and again, so that archaeological strata of darning work covered our toes and heels.) She sits and holds her head at a slight angle, and I know: she is now listening to *herself.* She hears herself like a faraway melody. I think, Now that strange, almost Gioconda smile is budding in her. But she senses that I have caught her unawares, and she turns her head to me. And no matter how quickly I look away, she catches me lurking. (I once heard her saying to Aunt Hertha in the kitchen, "The boy has something shifty about him; he's not open and straightforward, like yours. Sometimes I find him downright sinister.") The others live in the empty rooms of their terribly lonesome indifference. Even Cousin Wolfgang. My brother Wolfgang. The open, honest, dear boy, already reading his classics at twelve and thirteen (while I was struggling to understand what logarithms were, and, because I didn't believe I would ever succeed, instead of consulting Mocznik-Zaharadniczek's *Mathematical Textbook for Realschulen*, perusing penny dreadfuls under my schooldesk, fleeing into a world of wholesome archetypes); Cousin Wolfgang, who at sixteen began his enterprise of absorbing all the great thoughts recorded during six thousand years of history (which barely allowed him to have a single thought of his own but which did not prevent him from exhausting the prime of his mental energy in the dissolute fantasies of masturbation); my brother Wolfgang, which whom I had grown up in the hellish intimacy of a room shared day and night for twelve years, in the brotherliness of mutually smelled farts and mutually knocked-out teeth, in the shared torment inflicted by adults and parents and guardians, in the agony of our impotent and useless hatred of them ... even he never lost his gaze into nothingness.

Yes indeed, he too sometimes daydreamed, said he when I asked him. What? Oh, you know what. You imagine you're going to do something important (a gymnast's dreams, so to speak): contribute to the welfare of mankind (the gigantic swing on the horizontal bar), become famous, respected, loved. . . . Rich, too? Yes indeed, if possible, rich too. But that's not the most important thing (leaping from the horizontal bar, elegant knee bend with arms stretched level, straightening up elastically; the palms slap against the thighs; body frozen at rigid attention: bravo! *mens sana in corpore sano!*). What do *I* dream about? he returns the question. What do I mean—nothing? You can't dream about nothing. A mood—eh? Okay, then, no mood, but what? A sensation with no object, a listening out into the stillness, a peering into nothingness, is not a dream. . . . Fine, I'll spare you the quotations from Freud and others, but even the contemplation of the mystics . . .

It was after this conversation that he began to treat me a bit condescendingly, my brother Cousin Wolfgang. Every so often, I saw that his high forehead under the blond German adolescent's shock (the steeple head that he had inherited from Uncle Helmuth along with the slightly short legs) had become more arrogant by a few dozen important books, his eyes more and more bewildered, more and more tormented. At such times, I felt sorry for him in his emptiness, in his terrible indifference, which was filled only with himself and the great thoughts from six thousand years of history. My pity was so deep that I yelled at him, shouted some obscenity at him, which provoked him into pouncing on me. He was a lot stronger than I, with his gymnast's muscles, but I always managed to get the better of him with cunning tricks and dodges. And I was anything but a generous victor, thrashing him without mercy, and was then treated accordingly

by the rest of the family ("He shows an outright sadistic venge-
fulness against anything better than him; it would be no surprise
if this soon turned into genuine criminality!"). But why didn't he
too occasionally stare into space, my brother Cousin Wolfgang?
Why did he always have the rim of a helmet shadowing his
eyes? . . .

Whenever he realized that along with all the great thoughts of
six millennia he had also absorbed all the great doubts, he would
get nervous ("jumpy," Miss Fern would have said). Something
of the bewildered fidgitiness of Aunt Selma the cart horse came
over him. He made faces as if cobwebs were sticking to his nose
. . . granted, that too reveals a kind of inner life: the inner life of
people who always have shining, watchful eyes that never deviate
from the object and the purpose and the meaning. A truly lov-
able, fabulously decent, warmhearted, magnanimous, even intelligent fellow, my cousin Wolfgang, God rest his soul! He lies in
the Central Graveyard of Vienna. Not exactly a soldier's grave,
but the stone says that he died a "Hero for the Führer and the Fatherland." (Aunt Hertha, who, as she put it, "does not change her
flag as quickly" as Uncle Helmuth—he inadvertently sobbed,
"*They*'ve got my boy on their conscience"—was supposedly the
one who insisted on this inscription. Incidentally, Wolfgang too
believed firmly in written words.)

□   25   □

So that was what we had been living toward, as things
turned out historically. The five of us penned up in a four-room
apartment on the fourth floor of a tenement in the Twelfth District (Schönbrunn in its abstract glory before our noses). Each of
us in his enormously empty space, casting a long shadow, a monument to his own lonesomeness and indifference. Around us
roared the city of Vienna—it too an empty space, its roaring similar to the kind one hears in an empty seashell. To be sure, each of
us filled his space with some kind of activity, fiction, illusion, even
with ghosts. Not just Cousin Wolfgang, who sought out the plaster busts in the corridor of his humanistic *Gymnasium* for this

purpose: Socrates, Plato, Artistotle. . . . Uncle Helmuth, for instance, had real phantoms. Every Saturday evening, he would frequent them in his spiritist circle, the way other people went bowling or to a tarot game. When the medium went into a trance, her eyes rolled under the lids and the whites peered out like the ones the good soldier faces when his bayonet plunges into the enemy's body. From her lips (she normally stammered, heavy-tongued, and in shredded sentences), Uncle Helmuth had received many an interesting tiding from the beyond, which he repeated to us. As early as 1937, when nothing as yet hinted that he would one day tend in this direction (although he often remarked upon the miraculous doings in the Reich, as opposed to the slovenliness here in Austria), he aenounced something to us in conspiratorial secrecy. He had received a revelation from *over there* (the beyond, I mean, not the Reich). He had learned that *there*, in the immaterial and actual Reality and Truth beyond ours, Adolf Hitler occupied a much higher rank than here on earth, higher even than Buddha's and Helena Blavatsky's, and his, Uncle Helmuth's, as well. And he, the Führer, had taken the ordeal and degradation of an earthly, material existence upon himself only in order to bring mankind one level closer to God. (Of course, Uncle Helmuth asked us to keep this to ourselves for the time being. The spirits, he said, pursued their goals in a very complex manner, which we earthlings could scarcely comprehend. Their intentions could be discerned by us only after they were carried out and on the basis of the results. We therefore had to be careful not to interfere rashly in this delicate spinning and weaving. . . . Incidentally, Uncle Helmuth was extremely annoyed upon learning that Wolfgang had joined the illegal Nazi movement, and he declared his membership null and void since Wolfgang was still under age.)

I say: that was how we lived back then (three years before this winter of 1940). Aunt Hertha (to remember her too with piety) filled out her emptiness (and, one hopes, other of her hollow spaces) entirely with Uncle Helmuth. She worshiped him, but not for himself. She worshiped him as her dual.

For, you see, Aunt Hertha too had relations with superreality.

She had heard from over there, an indisputable source, that every *I* materializing here on earth is merely one half of a spiritual unity whose other half is embodied in a different *I*, usually of the opposite sex. Every *I* seeks this other half, and when it has found it, then there is no end to bliss. Such was the case with her. She had found her dual in Uncle Helmuth and henceforth lived only for him.

It didn't bother her that Aunt Selma despised her for it ("Why, you're in bondage to the man!") or that Cousin Wolfgang visibly suffered from it. Her mind was fixed on the sublime. A person who has found his dual has not automatically arrived in the Nirvana of bliss. On the contrary, he (or she) is chosen for special tasks. For when such a unity is completed as itself, then in its fully restored spiritual capacity it naturally understands the mission it must carry out through its materialization. By means of brotherly love and the announcement of the True Doctrine, it must build the ever more spiritual, dematerialized City of God on Earth. Superfluous to mention that she, Aunt Hertha, as the female (i.e., more tested, more earthbound, hence doomed to greater suffering in material existence, and thus, of course, more sublime) half of the Helmuth/Hertha duo, believed in Adolf Hitler's mission of salvation long before Uncle Helmuth did.

Now, Cousin Wolfgang believed the same thing more and more resolutely and was more and more ready for action. In the evening he would disappear without saying where he was going. I alone saw him in our room girding himself up and pulling on shoulder straps. I also found brass knuckles and rubber clubs and once even a pistol on our bookshelf—behind the Spinoza, comically enough, which he must have felt was secure from me, despite the fact that Spinoza was a Jew. But even though my brother Cousin Wolfgang now daily armed himself to flee the emptiness of the house and submerge himself in the bliss of Nazi comradeship, he could only shrug at his mother's ravings. He believed that if she had read her Plato, she would know that with her silly notion of a dual, she was making a gospel out of the joke of a drunken comedy writer—the silly goose!

Still, Cousin Wolfgang was fair enough ("intellectually hon-est," he called it) to admit that the reason his parents' no doubt basically harmless spiritualism enraged him so much was that he was jealous of his father to the point of occasionally murderous hatred. This realization (especially the insight that his own spiritual ambitions sprang from the desire to expose the knuckleheadedness of this "cross between a mechanic and an Anabaptist" whom to his great disgust he had to acknowledge as his procreator) annoyed him doubly because it required him to recognize a so-called Oedipus complex, thereby corroborating the obscene theories of the Jew Freud. To be sure, Germanic mythol-ogy also had . . .

Thus we lived, with our spooks in our heads and our webs across our eyes. Or with eyes that saw through them, and thus stared into space, into sheer nothingness.

Twice a day, the dining table united us in a group of five, and not even quarreling could lure us out of the terrible indifference and solitude within which each of us kept his league-long shadow. When we had been fed lunch, the table cleared and the dishes washed, and the Helmuth/Hertha dual was happily gone, then Aunt Selma would grant herself her cart-horse snooze in harness (hardly ever more than fifteen minutes). Next, while Cousin Wolfgang and I got down to our homework, she would go back to her drudging. Usually, but not always. And I caught her unawares one last time.

It was one of those wasting, silent afternoons that only a large, teeming city can produce (according to the stereotype, I should have someone practicing the piano on another floor of the build-ing). Once again, I had failed to understand something (let's say it was differential and integral calculus this time), and I wanted to pee, or drink a glass of milk in the kitchen. Cousin Wolfgang, in order to be completely undisturbed, was probably cramming in the shithouse. I did not hear Aunt Selma drudging anywhere, but the door to her room was ajar, and I peered inside. She was sitting on her bed, looking through a couple of magazines. This time, she did not sense my eavesdropping, so I found her entirely out of her well shaft, so to speak. She was slowly turning a page. I could see by the covers of the other magazines strewn over her bed that these were fashion and society journals ("smart-set gazettes," Uncle Helmuth would have said indignantly; she had probably pinched and scraped to save up the pennies to buy them). As she sat there on the edge of the bed, very straight, her legs in front of her and her knees scarcely bent, her posture very noble, I saw for the first time that she was tall and slender and had full, firm, high breasts. Her throat, her neck, which I had always seen in the draft-horse collar, was now free and lithe, and her slightly bowed head perched on it gracefully. I saw that she must have been very attractive as a young girl, equal in beauty to her frivolous sister. But I saw this well nigh at the edge of my gaze. What my eyes grasped fully was that she was dematerialized and thereby entirely her true self.

Again she had the vague Gioconda smile hovering around her lips, but now it showed no cruelty, was gentle, shadowy, charmingly dreamy. She turned a page and, before looking down, lifted her head and stared out the window with her distant gaze, as if her eyes were holding their breath. She seemed to be listening for something, something that was not sound and certainly not speech, notion, or thought. The smile stirred her lips to the bare extent that the surface of the well water is ruffled when, from above, from the small blue disk of sky at the end of the shaft, a voice calls.

I thought to myself, She's a mermaid. Some terrible curse forces her to dream that she is a household cart horse, and only when she's completely oblivious of herself, and no longer has the nightmare of herself as a draft horse, only then can she emerge from her well shaft, can her mermaid eyes look upon the alien world of human beings, can she see the faces and visions of her dream and brood about what they might signify. I said this to myself thus, poetically, because I saw how profoundly her Dalmatian-hill-girl head, in this moment of objectless dreaming over some banal object, had been transformed into something that struck me as the epitome of the German.

And by winter 1940, in the tub of my bathroom in faraway Bessarabia, I knew that a further precious element from the lost half of my life was thereby irretrievably lost in an icy, submerging Europe.

I HOPE IT DOES NOT IRRITATE you too much, esteemed Mr. Jay Gee Brodny, if I do not unravel the thread of my narrative chronologically but instead, in order to procure you an insight into the various paleontological layers of my existence, draw it back and forth, pulling out a piece now here, now there, in order to revive some significant moment or other, some informative situation or episode, and thus perhaps to display something that strikes me as worth narrating for a very specific reason. What I envisage is an *I* that keeps emerging out of itself in constant regeneration, like horse willow, yet becomes more and more self-alien, more and more self-inscrutable in this phased growth, so that ultimately time experienced and world experienced seem like a theatrical stage during the continual set changes and scene changes in a play whose author has in no way adhered to the classical rules of unity of time and place—whereby, of course, the protagonist of this tragicomedy is always a different person, although spectrally the same, as it were. This can hardly be depicted except as a literary equivalent of looking at rushes, but I admit that this unsteadiness in storytelling is, no doubt, due to many years of watching movie editors at work and witnessing their laudable persistence, the way they scour through the "takes," the way they comb through the wealth of filmed events, forming a new series that is often the opposite of the original outline, until the intended meaning of the whole becomes acutely evident.

The work of a good film editor, sir, is what a soundly functioning memory should perform, given a measure of intellectual discipline: the selection of personal and intellectual experience that makes the essential rendering of such experience possible, the most effortless conservation for the purpose of the most rational utilization. Alas, that's not quite how my memory works, for it plays the most distasteful tricks on me. I have to be extremely careful. For, as Nagel has his leading character, the narrator, say in his latest (plainly rather autobiographical) best-seller, "What we imagine we are expressing is not always what we are actually urged to express. That is why the writer's labor commences beyond language, where one confronts oneself eye to eye. . . ."

And here lies the reason I am telling you so much, so meticulously, about myself, sir. In fact, it's the reason that I, unfortunately, cannot tell you my story in three sentences. After all, that *was* what you asked me to do, wasn't it?

Needless to say, you did not expect to hear my life story. You had learned that I was writing a novel. A book for which Big-Time Publisher Scherping (heeding the literarily expert but commercially catastrophic advice of his editor Schwab) had paid considerable advances in the course of fourteen years (until he fired S.). Yessir, poor Scherping had committed himself to a lot of money invested in one author. By such commitment from a publisher, any author becomes more and more valuable, more and more desirable. If the chance arises to foist him off on some other sucker, then he advances to a genius and potential Nobel laureate. I assume that Scherping deployed all his eloquence when he told you about me. But you, Mr. Brodny, are too much of an old fox in this business not to smell the rot in the overly fat bait. When you asked me to tell you my story in three sentences, you asked me not only about the commercial value of what I *wanted* to narrate but also about the value of what I was *urged* to narrate. You didn't want to know whether I had it in me to write a good book. You asked outright whether this book *could actually be written.*

One could not ask in a more intelligent way. *Chapeau, monsieur:* if I were wearing a hat, I would doff it to you. In fact, I should have done so when I met you at Calvet's. Unfortunately, I didn't have a hat with me. I feel ashamed. For you, Great Brodny, are not just a pike, a shark, but an *Orcinus orca*, a killer whale, in the carp pond of international publishing; you know all too well the kind of writer you have before you. You recognized at first glance the fateful personality split that took place within me—back then, during a different paleontological era. It actually took place in 1949, at the end of the second Ice Age in Hamburg-on-the-Elbe, Dgeoimanny, when I felt as if I had been cast away among the lotus eaters, and Big-Time Publisher Scherping, in the bosom of maternally strict hookers, chanced upon a movie treatment left in the brothel and sent his blessed editor Johannes S. to seek out the author and talk him into writing a novel—*the* novel of the year, of course, the masterpiece of the century. Since that time—a period now of nineteen years of my life—the screenwriter who works his fingers to the bone for the piglets of the postwar German movie industry (as Aunt Selma, R.I.P., used to slave in the household during my formative years in Vienna) has been led on by the dreamer with lurking eyes lost in the distance, and he has been working on a book. On *his* book: *the* novel of the era, the masterpiece of the century. And while the screenwriter, the assiduous servant of the lively producer-piglets, keeps pouring more and more stories into the feeding trough (stories that can indeed be told in three sentences, goddammit, and occasionally even made into cinematic works of art, which may even win a gilded palm frond at the next festival on some sunny coast, but will, alas, in spite of all, never become a box-office smash)—while the screenwriter humbly works in the sweat of his brow, the other one, the brilliant novelist and potential Nobel laureate, is chasing after his *fata morgana* and dreaming of writing the masterpiece of the century, and writing his fingers to the bone and going blind and turning his mind into sauerkraut, in vain, in vain, because his work begins *beyond language,* as Nagel says: *"There, where one confronts oneself eye to eye."*

And over there, friend Brodny, no story can be told in three sentences. That's what you know and what you asked me about. There, where one confronts oneself eye to eye, you merely unearth black bugs. You know what I mean. What made our encounter so unfortunate was that I saw the black bug within you, J.G. Black bugs are dangerous beasts, fruitful as termite queens; they give birth incessantly to many, many other black bugs— stories in my case, which give birth to new stories, which, in turn, give birth to new stories, so that they teem and swarm. It's hybrid growth. It's cancer, dear J.G. There's something like a metastasis of stories. Their narrator drowns, suffocates in stories, and every single story wants to be told, has to be told, if (as Cousin Wolfgang demanded in his *Gymnasium* ethos and Schwab, infected, repeated twelve years later) he wishes to speak *fairly* and *hon-*

estly about an era and its people ... and if the writer wishes to write all his stories down and put them into a form, it will lead to the madness of the *chef-d'oeuvre inconnu,* to total chaos, to a progressive division of cells proliferating in more and more metastases.

Tell me a secret, dear Yankel Brodny. How does Nagel do it? Confront himself eye to eye while writing and tell a story whose essence can be summed up in three sentences? I don't doubt his fairness and honesty for even an instant. I know the man; he was my friend. But he's fooling someone: either himself or us, his readers. There is something shady somewhere in the way he lays the eggs of his stories and hatches every one of them into a novel. To his credit, I have to say that he is less infected than anyone else by the narcissism of the time, less spellbound by the utterly amazing mystery of existence, even when confronting himself eye to eye. Thus, he appears to succeed in peering through and beyond himself and perceiving his fellow men and neighbors Tom, Dick, and Harry. Okay. No one is saying that novels have to be ineluctably autobiographical. On the contrary: there is a widespread opinion that there is no such thing as a true autobiography. Even more unavoidable than in everyday life is the flimflam of *as-if* fiction in literature. Now, let me tell you a secret: *Nagel iz a firstrayt fikshin-riter. I am an even better fikshin-riter. But Nagel has the colder heart.* He does not sufficiently *love* his fellow men and neighbors Tom, Dick, and Harry. Otherwise, he would go into them more closely and turn them into human beings, not marionettes who are just little Nagels. Thus, they function purely to present the events of which "reality"—according to his steadfast troglodyte opinion—is woven. Sure, this method produces stories that can be told in three sentences, but one wonders why he bothered to use more than three.

And that is Nagel's flimflam, Mr. Brodny. For reality does not consist of events. It consists of existences. Believe Uncle Ferdinand. In his Middle Kingdom, only the same things keep happening: champagne breakfasts lunches polo games golf tournaments hunting parties Mediterranean crossings cocktail parties intimate dinners galas poker chemin-de-fer roulette movie stars duchesses and other whores. These things keep repeating themselves from here to eternity—and thus, nothing happens. However, Bully Olivera and Agop Garabetian—what full existences they have! Tom, Dick, and Harry, if one takes them lovingly and thoroughly in hand—what miracles of creation! If Nagel succeeds in letting Tom stroll through a novel without supplying the total content of his skull, the myrmidon teeming of Dick's thoughts ideas impressions experiences reflections, the entire meteorology of Harry's spiritual life, then I can only repeat: *Chapeau, monsieur!* This strikes me as neither fair nor honest. It is just a narration of events, not of people. I love people; I encounter them wherever I go. All I have to do is stick my nose out the door and I run with the pack. There are crowds of people around. They populate the towns, the highways, and every one of them wants to *exist.* . . .

But I see I am boring you. You've scarcely got a shrug for my problems. As far as I and my novel are concerned, you knew at first glance: this guy is cradling a dead child. You don't want to squander your time on my adolescent writing problems. Allow me, however, to take them seriously. They are the problems that caused the death of my friend S., my brother Schwab.

□   27   □

FIVE YEARS AGO, in 1963, shortly before I saw a white rose eaten from its stem and before I was smart enough to view this sight as symbolic of the fact that my romance with Dawn had no future (I am speaking of a past that seems more remote, more past, more legendary to me than any other, even more alien than the present), I finished dreaming my dream of myself as the author of the literary masterpiece of the era and future Nobel laureate. This was the time of my increasingly hectic dashes from Hamburg to Paris (via Holland, where my son attended boarding school, and where I would hurriedly insert a visit that was probably disappointing to him). I dashed up and down until I finally stopped going back to Hamburg. I did return once, in early 1965, for Schwab's funeral. But before he died, I kept on dashing. And, oddly enough, I retain the memory of those days as a happy period, despite all the ordeals that Dawn inflicted on me. I served my piglets fairly and honestly, was even more useful to them here in Paris than in their country, but of course was not fairly and honestly rewarded for my services, though I lived well on their expense accounts. Paris, the bright and beautiful underworld, into which I had descended like Orpheus to bring Dawn/Eurydice back to the light of day, turned out to be a rather comfortable place to live. I enjoyed the renown of a man having a romance with a setting star, Nadine Carrier, to whom I ran back after sporadic abstinence like a dipsomaniac to his bottle. My name haunted the gossip sheets ("WILL NADINE BE UNLUCKY IN LOVE WITH HER SCREENSCRIPTER?"). Whenever I visited my son at his Dutch school, his classmates asked me for autographs, and here in Paris the news dealer in the stand outside the Deux Magots treated me like a familiar and an intimate friend. But this was the harvest of a fertile past. Actually I was in love with Dawn the mad model. So much was I in love with her that I didn't feel the urge to escape into another, self-created reality. My cases, crates, and cartons were crammed with the starts, the commenced and uncompleted chapters, the drafts, notes, and all the possible sketches for my book that I had carried through life for fourteen years, and now I was about to dump them into the nearest dustbin and finally be liberated from my obsession. It was only with Schwab that I kept up the fiction that I was still writing, and I construed his farewell gesture, when I last saw him, in October 1964, as a desperate request to keep going, undaunted. After being fired by Scherping, Schwab could no longer get me advances for my book, but he urgently wanted me to finish writing it. He stuffed into my pockets the money that was bursting out of his, in order to obligate me, the bastard: he surely wanted me to write the book through which he might have survived.

A little later I didn't need him, for Gaia had entered my life, the chocolate-brown Princess Jahovary, God bless her in her weightiness with its vanilla fragrance. It was she who from then on identified with my masterpiece, and since my need for love had not been fulfilled by all the previous one great only and exclusive loves, I loved her ardently and did whatever she wanted. Thus did my suffering begin anew. I unpacked the cases, crates, and cartons and started writing my book again from the beginning.

At this time, Nagel was at the height of his fame, and, with the nasty alertness of a rival secretly arming himself, I studied his lean style, which was learned from Hemingway. Next to it, anything I wrote seemed like Gaudí's *Sagrada Familia* next to a utilitarian building by Adolf Loos. I was green with envy. I would tell myself, every morning, noon, and evening, "Save! Pinch! Scrape! Be picky, like an old maid. Look at what is offered, at what you focus on, at all your experience, and then select only what contains and renders the essential. Nothing superfluous! A book is a masterpiece if it contains not one syllable more than its table of contents!"

However, I probably had a different notion of the contents of a book than did Nagel and Mr. Hemingway. Which was what I told Schwab. I said, "One has to make up one's mind; you too have to make up your mind, dammit; after all, you too are thinking about writing a book. Don't deny it! I planted the idea in you, just as you planted the idea in me: like a parasitical hymenopter's egg eating up its host. Well, stick to business. No more excuses. Don't be an alarmist—especially with yourself. Even if you tell yourself that everything around us is totally chaotic and that chaos can't be turned into form, your heart is still tormented by a thorn: the feeling that it would be your human duty to arrange chaos in your way. Didn't the notes of a flute build the walls of Thebes? Or was it singing? Words? . . . My cousin Wolfgang knew. He was a humanist like yourself—and you don't know it any longer? Regrettable, but of no importance, for the moment. What I want to say is that even if your pride commands you to claim that only silence is possible against the wealth of absurdity around us, your noble insatiability will demand that you find the word to *name* such a stance. *It* will force you to do so—the *it* that also urges Nagel to express himself. Even though his banalities, puffed up as literature, do not quite express what *it* urges him toward. Do not try to hide how greatly *it* urges you, dear friend; one can tell by the tip of your nose. Of course, not to tell some trivial story artistically, as Nagel does, but to create a reality out of existences, a reality reflecting the reality we live in and through—to a frightening degree. In other words: the reality within yourself. You do understand me, don't you, as a humanist? Perseus had to look at *a reflection* of the Gorgon in order to slice off her head; the direct sight of her would have turned him to stone . . . and isn't it wonderful that Pegasus sprang forth from her dripping blood? Soar up, friend! Undaunted! Do tricks on horseback! You are of the fearless breed who never hesitate to keep their eyes open. Staring into nothingness, like my aunt Selma. Dreaming in the *néant*, as Sartre would have it. You are not of the bluffers and barkers who lull us to sleep with fairy tales, as nannies do to little tots. And do not be discouraged if you can wrest the word from yourself only in tortured efforts: your stammering will be all the more poignant. . . ."

and while I chattered on, friend Brodny, filtering such shallow tidbits through the dull eardrums of an alcoholic into his extremely sensitive mind, I myself was afflicted with the most absurd anxieties about how I would never finish my book, and I invented a new reason every day to tell myself that I couldn't possibly write it. No, it couldn't be written—not as I wanted to write it. It could not be told in three sentences.

In Gaia's time, when I was living a luxurious life at her expense (I was accustomed to such a gigolo existence by Stella), I had again hit upon the amusing idea that the novel of the era, in which everyone was to recognize himself, recognize his era, his destiny, was something I couldn't write because I lacked the essential experience of my generation: the war. Yes, you heard me correctly, sir: I lack the experience of war. As far forward and as close to the whites of the enemy eyes as possible. An experience that had, after all, been granted to my colleagues Nagel and Schwab. Nothing of the sort had been allotted to me. I had laid down my arms when Bessarabia had been peacefully handed to the Russians. While Nagel was gathering material for his stories, losing his arm in the process, and meeting God, I was carrying out the struggle as my inmost experience in Berlin in the beds of homebound wives of warriors. The steel storms came down as aerial bombs upon a man with the most peaceful of intentions. Of course, Schwab (to whom I once indicated my qualms in this respect; to be sure, only in order to explain to Scherping why my book was making such little progress)—Schwab argued that this inexperience should have made me even more aware of the essence of that event of war, that madness that had torn the once so beautiful world to shreds, that corruption into which my beloved first half of life had decayed, that enormous void whose suction had demolished the entire past and driven apart the very molecules of the entire present and future, thus dematerializing them, making them unreal, implausible. But Schwab's argument was, of course, merely one of his charming civilities, inspired on such occasions by his lovely envy. I rejected his amiability. Apperceptive occurrences that had to be explained with the aid of epistemological metaphysics were too abstract for me, I said tersely.

I also had fun refuting my own theories. By trying to show that it was madness to invent a reality out of causal connections in order to have it mirror a reality determined solely by chance, I set up a collection of crazy causes with completely nonsensical effects. I also looked for them in my own background and found a goodly number—for instance, my marriage to Christa, which had come about because her devouring mouth had so tormentingly drawn my notice in Nuremberg, in the canteen for German attorneys and witnesses at the Fürth Court of Law. This then led to fourteen years of mutual torture and a son who hates his father. What an absurdity! Still, it led to "multiplying" me, to fulfilling my biological duty. From this, too, metaphysical connections can be deduced: a devouring mouth, the symbol of Great Mother Nature. . . .

□　　　**28**　　　□

AND THUS THE YEARS WORE BY, highly esteemed Mr. Brodny; autumn leaves and calendar leaves flit through the images left in my memory. Soon those leaves will be as dense as the leaves of the countless manuscripts I have gathered for my book, rejected and abandoned, ripped up and patched together, shredded and stored away for later use in folders, cartons, and cases—for nineteen years, to be precise. And meanwhile, the other half of my split personality served the movie piglets and snickered derisively whenever the future author of *the* novel of the era, the potential Nobel laureate, gnashed his teeth in envy at the expressive devices of cinema, its immediate visuality, its freedom from place and time, its multidimensionality ... and all these things merely to present pulp novels and granny fairy tales! ... while our sort are supposed to depict the most sublime, the most complex, the most multi-vocal, the most fragile things in pale words within the rail network of grammar. Words, man! The paramount abstraction. (A snort of protest from Schwab. He turns red with anger at such statements; he believes in words; yes, he believes in literature, but he is scared, too: the blood drains from his cheeks as, in annoyance, the thrust of air driven from his nostrils loses strength, eventually being taken back in a B-flat-minor sigh.)

In those days, when brooding on the problems of writing novels, even far below the intellectual stratosphere of Messrs. Lukacs and Robbe-Grillet, I (and my brother Schwab) did not find those problems as childish as perhaps you do, esteemed Djakopp Djee. Being fed up with theory and ideology, we did not tackle the issue on the soaring level of the essayists but rather on the pedestrian level of the pragmatic writer, usually ending up at the dead point where the psychology of the writer coincides with the question of the significance of what is to be written. Why bother with a novel today? Aren't there enough good ones to keep you reading for a lifetime? What else remained to be said? And was it of any importance how it was to be said? The aesthetic was indisputably of secondary interest.

There was one thing we did agree on, though, Schwab and I: it was no longer possible not to include the author when writing. Even in scientific experiments, after all, the person of the experimenter is largely taken into account nowadays. Intensifying our self-observation, we soon realized that it was probably this that *it* (Nagel's *it*, presumably borrowed from Freud's *It*, Id) urged us to write. To put it in plain terms: what *it* urges a fair and honest writer to write is *himself*.

This conclusion instantly stirred up a whole swarm of further questions, and I had a devil of a time luring poor Schwab into their midst and watching him flail about with them. I did it with vile pleasure. After all, he was acting as if the business concerned him purely in theory and for my sake. He was professionally interested only insofar as he was an editor for my publisher Scherping and thus obligated to dispel my doubts in myself and my work. Dispel them so thoroughly that I would speedily finish that book and earn back my advances. The fair man! The honest man! How bravely he tried to conceal that I had my finger in his bleeding wound! Yet he never concealed his distress when noticing how utterly I saw through him. He never resented me for using the grossest city-slicker dodges (always pretending I had something far more profound in mind) to lead him to some relevant theme and snidely wait and see how long it took him to realize that he was dealing with some commonplace—after all, he was usually quite liquored up. He gave me a lot of moral credit, my brother Schwab. For it must not be forgotten that in those days I was at the peak of my dichotomous existence. The potential author of *the* novel of the era and the future Nobel laureate—incessantly constructing new arguments for why it was superfluous, impossible, sheerly arrogant and hubristic to want to write and yet never ceasing work on his book in his mind and on any available scrap of paper, nourishing his parasite's egg with himself—this author lived in the most intimate symbiosis with the eager servant of the movie piglets so much despised by Schwab. And my dear friend also knew that each of the two personalities within myself kept an eagle eye on the other, slyly learning useful things from the other—

and thus, in my existential form as a servant of piglets, it warmed my heart to watch what happened to certain scenes of a script I had written, scenes written in the sweat of my intellectual's brow and fixed on celluloid after murderous financial sacrifices, scenes tugged back and forth, back and forth on the editing table, and then, after a quick snip of the scissors, twisting and hissing into a wastebasket ... scenes for which I had struggled with my producer piglets in the thick blue cigar smoke of all-night script conferences, had wrestled over like Jacob with the angel; takes for which directors had suffered cardiac crises and world-famous actresses fits of hysteria; image sequences in which cameramen of international renown had seen the crowning of their careers; shots in which lighting artists had expected the final recognition of their earlier, so wretchedly neglected work . . . and snip! It was as if it had never been, a burst soap bubble, a vanished illusion, damn it, like so many important, significant, decisive moments, episodes, situations, loves, hatreds, in our lives. Gone down the drain. With no harm to the plot and no damage to its artistic value. . . . When I told Schwab about it, he got very excited, and it was child's play leading him to the idiotic question of whether and to what degree people like us can rely on our apperception. Could we really trust our conscious minds to make the proper selection from what they perceive seamlessly and to retain whatever is worth remembering, to forget trivia and only trivia? . . . In what way, then, was that ominous *it* involved in this process, the *it* that urges us to express things we may not have had the wish to express at all? No doubt it is a demon pledged to the *Zeitgeist,* determining our ideas in a manner that *happens* to us, so to speak, and leads us, much to our own amazement, to make statements revealing thoughts that are peculiar to the present era, thoughts of the *Zeitgeist,* notions, insights, intentions, in the style of the era, children of the *Zeitgeist* as much as we ourselves.

"In a word," I said to Schwab, "something in the *Zeitgeist* wants to be said and pushes out from the lips, pens, and typewriters of those who feel impelled to speak. And they think it's *they* who invent what they express! They may think it's a great idea, and maybe it is. But the *it* forces it out of a pen not only here and now but perhaps only a few moments earlier out of some other yokel's pen in Pearris, Freanss, or in Hamburg-on-the-Elbe, Dgeoimanny, or out of another nightwalker's mouth in Athens, Wyoming. You can be sure that when you have an idea that is extraordinarily interesting because it is new and previously unuttered, at the same moment several dozen equally clever men all around the globe are having the same notion. And when you are about to write a particularly original and topical book, you can go right ahead and prematurely bet your probably meager income that at the same moment a good dozen other authors of the masterpiece of the era and future Nobel laureates are about to set down an almost identical book."

and by saying all this I had got Schwab to the point of letting the *it* in him, the demon urging him to do something different from what he was planning, to drag him into the next bar in order to work out his spiritual equilibrium with as even a number of glasses as possible. While I, with innocent eyes, set about offering him various examples of the scurvy, often tasteless pranks played on me by my memory (so often admired by him).

□   29   □

INDEED, my esteemed patron Brodny, I cannot bank on any sort of selection being made here. I distrust my subconscious. My treasure chest of memories is filled by sheer chance. I have an excellent example of this, an example I held up to Schwab with great effect. An impression taken up quite by chance but, inexplicably, with extreme keenness, and preserved down to the last detail—I am haunted by it even today. It is the image of a family filling their faces at a roadside café, something I saw during one of my dashes to Dawn in Paris, accompanied by Schwab. The scene is branded in my memory. Quite ineffably horrible contemporaries they were. Schwab, needless to say, did not perceive them, happy man. (Or else his subconscious functions more selectively. I suggested this to him when he showed some anxiety about his forgetful ways; however, his answer was a desperately derisive snort.)

I, for my part, see them even now: informally grouped around the adjacent table among sprats, sandwich wrappings, plastic bags full of orange peels, beer glasses, and Coke bottles. Smalltowners on a weekend outing or something of the sort. (John would have said "white trash.") They were eating. Wildly relishing whatever it was they were feeding on.

and they clung to me like burrs; I couldn't get rid of them, people who didn't mean a thing to me, unable to arouse the slightest interest on my part: a paterfamilias with a beefy neck, chewing disgustingly, in a Lacoste shirt with a crocodile logo; a materfamilias, shoveling repulsively, with curlers under a kerchief turban; an aunt or housemate or friend, crocheting with a knife and fork, sporting pubic hair under her hat; four children like organ pipes, chomping dreadfully: in short, roadside-café people, humdrum faces taking nourishment, the kind of people that pass us daily, hourly, by the tens of thousands, sucking on the caries in their teeth. People that one looks at without seeing, hence that one has never seen before and, if God be gracious, one will never see again

and these people had been photographed by my obviously rather automatic memory. Photographed more sharply than any other face ever stamped on my mind; not the face of a beloved, not the face of my little boy, not Schwab's face ... and I don't know why, I still don't know why today.

All I know is that I carry the image of these feeding anthropoids around in me like the Zadir. I could have committed a murder and forgotten it, but I can't get *them* out of my brain. My head could be chopped off—*they* could be detected in some sediment in my blood, my tissue.... For God's sake! A man has been around during his forty-nine (going on fifty!) years of life, especially since these years span the core of the twentieth century, from Doubleyou Doubleyou One through Doubleyou Doubleyou Two, until today: forty-nine years, up and down and back and forth through Yurop, the heartland of our civilization, from the meadows of the Dniester to Pearris, Freanss, from Scandinavia to Syracuse, Sicily, yes sir.... Years in which a great deal has happened. Admit it, Djay Djee: a thing or two has happened from 1919 to 1968, hasn't it? Now, if one didn't make a ruthless selection from among the accumulated material, what would become of one?

To be sure, one simply can't sum it up in three sentences. Believe me, governor! Not in our time. Not since everything has been growing frighteningly, running rampant, running riot, devouring the people, the cities, the objects, the events, the stimuli. Hybrid cell growth is also an explosion, after all, isn't it? To be sure, a slow-motion explosion. Describing this sort of thing requires details. Professor Leblanc had his ideas about that—but this is not the moment to dilate on them. *Abbia pazienza!*

Needless to say, one strives to restrict oneself to the essential. One sticks to the tersest, most economical outline. One focuses on what one would like to say, as transparently and graphically as possible, and so one plies one's craft decently and honestly, until—well, yes: until you suddenly have to say something that was not even foreseen in this outline, that does not even go into it, that has nothing to do with it, and that no amount of effort can visibly connect with it . . . and yet it has to be said and it drives you until you finally say it.

One can only hope that the *it*, which urges us to say the so-far unsaid and ultimately confronts us with ourselves, is wiser than we are. That it says something more essential than what we are trying to say. Something we did not realize, whose meaning we did not grasp but is instantly grasped by everybody once it is said because it is in the *Zeigetist* and was as yet unborn—and if you hadn't said it, then someone else would have done so a moment later.

"I hope I don't have to depict what consequences this has for the nervous system," I said to Schwab. "People like us live like someone who's hard of hearing, always tormented by the fear of missing something. The fear that something may be spoken of that we don't know or aren't supposed to hear. I tell you: our eyes aren't red just from alcohol and scribbling by lamplight. Mainly they're red because we keep peering around to see whether something is going on behind our backs, something we don't want to admit or something we perceive but cannot instantly interpret. Imagine what I am going to have to endure until I figure out why I carry around the image of that family eating at the next table in the roadhouse where we stopped once on one of our trips. Had to stop, because you, of course, had been without alcohol for two hours and had to have a drink; otherwise the withdrawal symptoms would have hit you like epilepsy. A pleasant travel companion indeed. It was *you* who lured me into that bloody roadhouse, man. Now it's up to you to explain to me why those chewing *horlàs*, those anthropoids who must have already anticipated the posthuman evolutionary stage—explain to me why they've stuck with me so solidly that I can't get rid of them. It will probably take years now for this crop to grow before I can harvest its meaning. And until then that little group of highway people will stay with me: father, mother, aunt, four children, shoveling, chomping, chewing, swallowing—making me wonder what they signify.

"One has to be prudent as a writer. Live cautiously. A poet, as we know, because Goethe told us, is a mouthpiece through which a god speaks (mainly to tell what he is suffering). But even simple people like us, who don't count themselves among the mouthpieces of God but only of the *Zeitgeist,* are frail, vulnerable, easily exasperated. After all, our kind too lead lives of devotion: we are tense strings over which the *Zeitgeist* passes, making us quiver. And the *Zeitgeist* strums quite vehemently, does it not? *Il nous joue de la belle musique;* we do not even know where to flee. However, the intrinsic feature of the *Zeitgeist,* its exclusive peculiarity, which determines its style (and thereby ours), is something we do not hear so long as we remain in its tempestuous contractions; this is recognized only by those who come after us. Even we who are chosen to speak know it at best after *it* has urged us to express this knowlege. And he who wishes to hear the mystery of the *Zeitgeist,* that which says itself through us but is not yet named—he who wishes to *name* it must make himself so taut that sooner or later he will snap. For the *Zeitgeist* only whispers it; you have to filch it from its breath. . . . Yet when we ultimately reach the point of boggling at every fart because we mistake it for a breath of the *Zeitgeist,* thinking we can hear something in it that no one else can hear, and when we absolutely want to be the first to express it . . . when our throats tighten with fear lest we are late with everything, forgotten by our *Zeitgeist,* never its mouthpiece, when we are *epigoni* after all, adding only frills, unable to say anything fundamental to our era, then our situation will affect our minds, dear friend. No one could be more aware of this than you."

□   30   □

NO ONE KNEW THIS BETTER than he, my brother Schwab, and he took the logical consequences and kicked the bucket. I, however, have survived. Even though the parasitic egg of having to write was laid in me and has been devouring me for nearly two decades, I have survived. I have survived him just as, to his consternation, I survived my romance with Dawn and, two years later, with Gaia. Just as I survived Cousin Wolfgang and Uncle Helmuth and Aunt Hertha and Aunt Selma. And presumably Uncle Ferdinand and ultimately John too. Just as I had survived Stella, although surviving her was the most shameful of all.

That is what prompts me to think back so often to the winter of 1940 in Uncle Ferdinand's home: my innocence back then! The wealth of a world alive, lived in by live people. A world that had not yet gone under in the Ice Ages. The world of the first half of my life, which I had not yet survived.

Uncle Ferdinand is still alive. I sit across from him at a long table. I am wearing the uniform of a good regiment, which may not be the same one in which he once served his old Fatherland Mother Russia—a Fatherland that is no longer his and indeed is hostilely facing his (and thus my) present Fatherland Rumania—but no matter! Uncle Ferdinand's real Fatherland is the Middle Kingdom, and he counts me as part of it. He treats me with the paternal camaraderie that the commander of the Imperial Russian *garde à cheval* would show toward a cadet who had just been promoted to cornet.

I am grateful to him, with mixed feelings. True, I am sitting at a table at which I sat as a child, waited on by servants some of whom claim they knew me back then. I sit beneath ancestral portraits that in depicting Uncle Ferdinand's forebears may possibly be depicting mine—but none of this matters. We haven't seen each other for fourteen years. Uncle Ferdinand is certainly enough a man of the world to see right off how much or how little is left of Miss Fern's upbringing, but he cannot really know who I am. Anything may have become of the child that was once troublesome enough as a hanger-on (or even worse: a love gift) of a delightful mistress. The child that once annoyingly ran underfoot and has now surfaced again is a lad in a cavalry lieutenant's uniform, a young blade sent to his home by his old friend and playmate John, to whom he is deeply attached, whose father he once knew and on whose estate he, Uncle Ferdinand, shot the most unforgettable grouse of his life, but a man whose diplomatic missions have always been rather obscure, suspect particularly now that he is married to this bluestocking Bucharest Jewess. Pretty, yes, spirited, and to be seen everywhere, elegant, witty, quick, but—well, you know.

I wonder if Uncle Ferdinand knows that I am Stella's lover. I wish he did know it. I have a bad conscience toward John, but I'm proud nevertheless. I love Stella. Love her intelligence, her wit, her maternal tenderness, her unerring frankness, her fairness and honesty. I love her with all my senses. I love her taut body, the dull-shimmering olive tone of her skin. She is fourteen years older than I, and I love her ripeness, her experience, the mellowness of her beauty, her sharp spiritedness, the first gray threads in her black thick-stranded desert-Jewish hair. (Absalom supposedly was blond, but one of my most beautiful erotic fantasies is to see her dangling from a branch by this black shock and to ride toward her to bore through her with my lance.)

I was just thinking of her, in the bathtub. I was looking down at my thin, tough body, still tan from the summer. It lay in the water covered by a floating galaxy of dissolving soapsuds. But from a dark moss bed in the sepia skin, a sturdy stalagmite grew through the greenish transparency of the water. Stella, my star (indeed, that was her maiden name: Stella Stern).

It would not surprise, much less scandalize, Uncle Ferdinand if he knew that I was Stella's kept lover. Along with the abstract glue of gossip, the Middle Kingdom is held together by two concrete glues: money, and a sperm thread industriously spun by everyone, everywhere, up and down, back and forth, in and out. Everybody has slept with everybody. Everyone, thank goodness, is rich enough to think of money as a means to the most exciting, most amusing games, and to leave moral considerations out altogether. Every man and every woman have satellites, escorts, parasites, flatterers, whores, floozies, gigolos, catamites, henchmen. Everyone has his little court, and it's in a courtier's power to be treated as a lackey or to command respect (yes, experience teaches that members of the Middle Kingdom at some point like being treated rather insolently by some such creatures).

Uncle Ferdinand could not treat me with more exquisite charm and paternal kindness if the ancestral portraits along the walls, the pale Fanariots with the saber-crooked noses and the fiery-eyed boyars with the crooked feathers on otterskin caps, were truly my forebears too and he were really the commander of the *garde à cheval* in which I had been freshly promoted to cornet. He sits opposite me, watching me dine. He himself eats almost nothing anymore; he briefly pokes his fork in the meager food on his plate and then leaves it untouched. His yellowish-gray spider head over the stiff white shirtfront, which has pushed the bow tie all the way up to his earlobes, is mystically transfigured in the glow of the table candles, like the head of a pagan priest. The glasses of wine before him sparkle like test tubes containing re-agent fluids of different colors. He does not touch them, either. His round, thin-lidded eyes with the rooster's needle-sharp pupils are nailed to me. And I sit opposite him, bolt upright, in my operetta uniform, striving to appear as relaxed and casual as possible. I use elegant John as my model—he is a model for me in many respects—and I deceive him.

Yes indeed, Mr. Brodny: such is my innocence back then, twenty-eight years ago. Stella is still alive, and I love her. I don't as yet know that I shall never see her again. She is with John in Bucharest, and I fancy I can hurry into her arms at my next fur-lough (which Uncle Ferdinand effortlessly obtains for me by way of my regimental commander). Stella, my star! . . .

And all the while, I also love John. I measure myself against John; I compare myself with him. I know that of all the countless lovers of my mother, he was the only one whom she loved pas-sionately. I would like to be like him. He is a fine nobleman. His breeding is better than anyone else's. No trace of the Sublime Porte. No trace of Lieutenant Colonel Subicz's heritage in him. His profile and his hands are finer, his eyes are brighter, larger, more sincere, less cunning than mine—yes, it is that cunning which reveals Subicz's lineage from a tribe of mountain Dalma-tians (it could be traced in Aunt Selma's beauty). John has smoother, less unruly hair, which lies more naturally on his head—the hair of a model child, the kind of hair Miss Fern tried to make mine be with furious strokes of the brush. John must have been an exemplary child from a splendid home, *un ragaz-*

zino molto fine, elegante, intelligente, perbenino (I am grateful to Lieutenant Colonel Subicz that I am not such a brat).

John has the best manners a person could possibly have. I am fascinated with the way he takes me for granted; that is, the way he, almost thirty years my senior, treats me as a perfect equal in every respect (in contrast to Uncle Helmuth's Fafnir-like, menacing demand that we *respect our elders*). "Hello, dear boy, awfully glad to see you. Let's have some booze." (Two years before Uncle Ferdinand's *"Ah, te voilà, finalement. Il était grand temps qu'on te voie"*: chips of the same block). I was delighted with the way John took me for granted from the very beginning—or new beginning—when I met him again after twelve years: no longer Miss Fern's spick-and-span, combed-and-brushed, piss-elegant little boy, the bastard of sweet little Maud; now a scrawny, towering youngster, wretchedly dressed, aureoled with the odor of a tenement apartment, dissipated because of certain backcourtyard experiences, with a dreamy and unreliable lurking in his eyes. I am enchanted by the way John took me for granted then, welcoming me as though not a single day had waned since last he saw me with my hand in Miss Fern's; and I am fascinated by the elegance with which he tolerates me now as his wife's lover.

John's cordiality toward me has not diminished for an instant. I know that he is too rich to worry about the tailor bills that Stella pays for me (especially since he can tell himself that Stella, who is even richer than he, probably pays them out of her own pocket). Not the slightest shadow of a smile, not even a millimeter-high twitch of his eyebrows, an involuntarily accelerated blink, ever betrays his thoughts when he suddenly sees me all spruced up as if I had stepped forth from the latest issue of *Adam*. I virtually live in his home. Although my official place of residence since I left my relatives is the *garçonnière* in the middle of Vienna (my rent paid by Stella), I am at John and Stella's house in the Rennweg from dawn to dusk. I drive his car, drink his whiskey, screw his wife; his chambermaid washes my shirts, his valet presses my trousers—and John treats me as politely as if I were His Britannic Majesty's ambassador. His savoir faire is enthralling; he is indefatigably attentive, obliging, friendly—and completely invulnerable to intimacy. I am in awe of his tact (and almost incapable of looking him in the eye ever since Stella told me that he is delighted with my tact). We are such an exemplary, civilized clover leaf that I often cramp up and hold my breath to keep from vomiting.

□   **31**   □

ALL THAT I HAVE SURVIVED. And not only that but also the farewell from the park of my childhood, when the Russians came to Bessarabia with the summer, peacefully, invited by the Germans, who had promised us to help defend every crumb of Rumanian soil against our foe. A little later I survived the bombs on Berlin when, in a highly suspicious pseudo-diplomatic mission, I avoided a heroic death defending my or anybody else's Fatherland with a weapon in my fist against a foe that was not quite the real one. I survived Stella's disappearance when she—the Jewess, the wife of an Englishman in a both important and mysterious position—hit on the insane idea of trying to enter Germany unrecognized from Switzerland in order to see me once again. . . .

and I also survived the shameful rat-flight the length and breadth of the German lands, the ludicrous game of hide-and-seek with the authorities and draft-dodger hunters: I survived the second Ice Age in Hamburg-on-the-Elbe and Nuremberg, Franconia, where John hit on the insane idea of calling me as a witness to Stella's murder. . . .

And in Schwab's eyes all these things were a remarkable wealth of enviable experience, which I absolutely had to get down on paper. I began to believe him and divided myself (which had already been reduced by half a life) into two further halves, of which one half, the potential author of the masterpiece novel of the era and future Nobel laureate, set about systematically to undermine the life of the other self-half, a pioneer in the reconstruction of the postwar West German film industry. I undauntedly survived the marriage to Christa and an affair (which rocked the worldwide public) with the fading movie star Nadine

:: 226 ::

Carrier (including several relapses); and I survived my son's scorn. (A young man a father could be proud of, by the way: *un ragazzino molto fine, elegante, intelligente, perbenino.* The Dalmatians have mendeled out. Christa's clear, corn-blond brightness. Her better-bred hands. Her small mouth. Her eyes, brighter, larger, more sincere than mine. No cunning in them. Her hair, smooth under the brush stroke. John's grandchild, in short.)

No use imagining that if Uncle Ferdinand were still alive, he might be interested in meeting my son, grandson of beautiful Maud and possibly his own. Except for the data put down once and forever in the Almanach de Gotha, the only genealogies that interest Uncle Ferdinand are those of horses and dogs. And even they did not interest him anymore during that faraway February 1940 when I saw him for the last time. The only thing that interested him then was the *act of handing down.*

I still sense the unerring gaze with which he watches over my table manners. In them, he does not read my aptitude for someday entering the ranks of the Middle Kingdom but only whether my polite willingness to listen to him is false or true. My powerful appetite evidently pleases him; I won't tire easily. His fatherly concern, his elegant, seemingly unconditional familiarity and comradely intimacy, should not deceive me. I would make an embarrassing mistake if I presumed to derive any privileges from them. "I like to treat everyone as my equal," says Uncle Ferdinand. "But that doesn't mean that he may treat me as his equal."

The elegant as-if of our equality is quite naturally due to his not asking me anything. He does not wish to know why I am not seen in the right places at the right time through the annual course of the "seasons." Why I do not play polo near the Pyramids in January, zoom down the Cresta run on my knees, belly, and elbows in Saint Moritz in February, play in tennis tournaments on the Riviera in March, sail near Ragusa in April, dine with Lady Diana Duff-Cooper in London in May, attend the night races at Auteuil in June, waltz with Geraldine Apponyi on Budapest's Margaret Island in July, shoot grouse in August with our many friends in Scotland—and so on through the moons until the graceful cycle concludes and recommences. It is tacitly assumed that only private reasons are holding me back. In case of doubt, at my age, a romance that must be discreetly handled (and then indiscreetly gossiped about). Otherwise I would quite obviously be doing all those things, though to be sure WW II is, to some extent, a hindrance.

Nor does Uncle Ferdinand ask to hear where and how I have spent the almost one and one half decades since my short pants and long, buttoned gaiters, and little Norfolk jacket with the tremendous navy-blue and white polka-dotted bow under the Eton collar, and Miss Fern's admonishing English dove-cooing in my ear. And even if he became absentminded and let the question slip out, he would not wait for my answer. For if he doesn't know the answer, then the events must have taken place outside his world, and anything happening beyond Uncle Ferdinand's world has but remote significance for him. There is no room in the Middle Kingdom for the people, things, circumstances, incidents I could tell him about—except, at best, Uncle Helmuth's spiritist séances. And Uncle Ferdinand would know about them from Countess Kannwitz without Uncle Helmuth's making an appearance.

But perhaps Uncle Ferdinand himself does not even wish to hear anything about his Middle Kingdom. If he wants to keep informed and up to date, it is probably only for the sake of inventory. Like the task of the ornithologists and shell collectors among his princely cousins, his true chore is to sift, count, arrange, and name. The world is as God the Almighty has created it: *è così perchè è così.* All we can do in it is enjoy being in it and, perhaps, take its inventory. Uncle Ferdinand has already told me everything basically worth knowing about his Middle Kingdom—its structure, its mechanics, its functioning. Now he goes into detail. I already know about habits and conduct—say, that the toughest hunts are ridden not in England in pink or in France in green but in Ireland in glen check and brown boots. I am told of Count Dankelmann's famous five driven partridges in Upper Silesia: two shots at the approaching covey, change guns, shoot only *one* barrel, change guns again lightning quick and take the last two shots at the flushed fowl. . . . But all this is of secondary importance. More urgent is the full inventory. Anecdotes likewise recede into the background. (For instance: "She was terrified of having a baby, but she didn't want to do anything to protect herself because she was afraid that some birth-control device might injure her and then she couldn't have the child that she wanted someday from a man she really loved. And that was why—" I understand. Expressed in the floweriness of folk poetry:

> And there you see the reason why
> it's only through the arsehole by
> which narrow passage for the fart
> he finds the entrance to her heart.

Although Uncle Ferdinand is so prudish that he freezes at the slightest obscenity, he now has a good laugh. If an off-color joke is heartily ribald, he appreciates it as he would a coarse dish that occasionally interrupts the monotony of his daily *haute cuisine*. He has me repeat it twice: "How did that go again? 'And there you see the way—' Oh yes, of course, 'the reason *why*'—otherwise it won't rhyme. It's only through the arsehole by—well, well, very funny indeed—she lets him find his way to her heart. Very funny, really very funny!")

But this is only a short digression, after which we return all the more assiduously to the business at hand. He rapidly becomes impatient whenever I show lacunae in my education. He is slowed down by having to localize every last detail and connect it to the others: "Well, naturally, they got to know each other better at Titi's wedding, because he's a cousin of Mutzi's—in Rome, of course, where else!" An intake of breath, with which he controls unruly stirrings. Then relief, because he thinks of something that excuses me: "But I keep forgetting how young you are. *J'ai une mémoire admirable, tu sais: j'oublie tout. . . .*"

Which, needless to say, is pure *coquetterie*. In fact, his memory is fabulous, worthy of a cabaret act. It enables him to focus on the titanic chore of keeping the inventory of the Middle Kingdom. The material is gigantic: "*une mer à boire*," as he himself admits. Scientific meticulousness requires that every detail be recorded of the happy inhabitants of that reality vanishing into legend: the tonnage of their yachts and the horsepower of their sports cars;

the names of their horses and dogs, their pedigrees; the jewelry, hair color, and liver spots of the women; the cock sizes of the men; the quality of the silver used at this or that gala dinner; the names and vintages of the wines that were drunk; the bizarre wanderings of the jewels important enough to have destinies of their own ("Well, first Toto inherited it from his mother, an Aldobrandoni, and he gave it to his wife, Nini, and then she gave it to Lazzi when she had an affair with him, because he had gambling debts, and that was why Lazzi sold it to Joshi for a song, and then Joshi gave it to a Parisian dancer at the Lido; he was madly in love with her, a girl named Yvonne; and then she . . .").

The catalogue of the Middle Kingdom is like the marquis de Sade's *120 Days of Sodom*, and, like this key opus of modern literature, it is bound to end in sheer mathematics. Uncle Ferdinand's reports grow more and more abstract. The Middle Kingdom is dematerializing. It makes no difference that its de facto survival is endangered. Uncle Ferdinand appears less disturbed by the realization that Poland is lost once again ("despite the stubborn assurance to the contrary in her national anthem") and that he will probably have to write off Stash and Wanda, Kotja and Olga, once and for all, and with them the fantastic wild-boar hunts in Volhynia. He is much more worried about whether roulette and other games of chance are really still elegant. Who is still playing them? Of the friends in the innermost circles, only the Greeks and a couple of Sicilians and Spaniards (he lists them by name).

The tide of gray iron men, rising all around Europe, is of no concern to Uncle Ferdinand. He knows that they have massed just a few miles across the Dniester and are menacing him directly and personally, but he doesn't care. Nor does it matter to him whether others are about to blow up the Maginot Line before pitching into one another. Nothing, incidentally, says that they won't make a detour and invade France via Belgium (as a former member of the general staff, Uncle Ferdinand thinks of General Schlieffen with great respect). In other words: Jacqueline and Guy and Alain and Marie-Jeanne and with them the stag hunts in the Île-de-France and the pheasant shoots in the Ardennes and in Sologne are as much at the mercy of providence as, perhaps, Ian and Daisy, Hugh and Elizabeth-Anne, in their splendid country houses and play parks full of first-class horses, dogs, sailboats, on the other side of the Channel. But more than anything, Uncle Ferdinand is haunted by the observation that for some time now—that is to say, increasingly since the last decade, from the end of the delightful twenties till today—more and more friends of the innermost circles have been complaining of boredom or (usually this goes hand in hand) have become boring themselves.

"If you can still remember good old Nicki—he was absolutely mad about your mother, and she liked him because he was so entertaining—I'll never forget what he said at Stefanie's funeral: *'C'est commode, un enterrement, tu sais: on peut avoir l'air moussade avec les gens, ils prennent cela pour de la tristesse. . . .'*" (Stella calls this kind of *esprit* provincial.) "And then he married that person, that former actress. There was nothing to say about it. After all, in our day, the king of England stepped down from the throne because of a love affair with something similar. Now, Nicki didn't become as boring as the duke of Windsor. Quite the contrary. But poor Nicki did become a different man. He loved her so much, and they were so happy—a real bourgeois marriage. And when that person died in the bargain, he never stopped talking about her. He was unbearable. No matter where you ran into him, he talked about her. Eventually, nobody wanted to have anything to do with him. Who wants to hear about such matters all the time? People have enough problems of their own. If everybody carried on like that, it would be the end. And so ultimately we quite abandoned poor Nicki. Sandro as much as said so in his eulogy when Nicki died. And he talked about what a valuable person Nicki had been. Oh, well? *Éloge funèbre. La moitié de tout ça lui aurait suffi de son vivant.* But poor Nicki had really become unendurably boring. . . ."

This reminiscence has unforeseeably arisen during the recitation of a long list of cocaine sniffers among his friends, and he terminates it with a necrologue: "I can understand old Silvio Francalanza. When he turned ninety-five, he simply shot himself. Things had got too boring for him. *Basta, fini,* good night, everybody. I can understand him perfectly."

IT IS MIDNIGHT. The witching hour, Mr. Brodny. Back in Vienna, at twelve midnight, Uncle Helmuth and Aunt Hertha would exchange intimate glances at every creaking of an ancient and decrepit piece of furniture (almost pure Biedermeier, a *von* Jaentsch heirloom). They knew what was happening: visitors from the beyond. The departed were going about. Uncle Helmuth even knew them by name. During the séances of his spiritist circle, they would materialize in the temporarily emptied physical shells of the mediums, identifying themselves and revealing from which sofa nook or dresser corner they were creaking. You should not be surprised, sir, that I, familiar at an early age with such occult phenomena, have got into the habit of evoking ghosts. We live in the era of historicism, obsessed with the notion of rationally comprehensible causal connections; they alone guarantee our "reality." I, for my part—I never tire of repeating it—am afflicted by the loss of a full half of my life. I would like to conjure up the vanished reality of that half. I have to do so. I ask for your sympathy: it's not pleasant living amid the realities in the no-man's-land of time. To feel comfortable here, one must be dead, like Uncle Ferdinand, like Cousin Wolfgang, like Schwab and all my other loves. They still exist marvelously as heroes of their myths. Which, of course, also means that they have to put up with being summoned forth by any shaman. People like us have the power to call them from their shadowy existence into time's no-man's-land and to materialize them in the magical element of writing. Just look: all I have to do is use my quill, my ballpoint pen, the keys of my typewriter, to place a few hundred letters on this sheet of paper, and Uncle Ferdinand—the Uncle Ferdinand of winter 1940—will live before our eyes. His yellowish-white spider-head is wedged deep between his high-thrust shoulders. The straw whisk of his mustache bristles out horizontally on either side under the parrot's beak of the nose. The skin on his forehead is so smooth that it rosily mirrors the glow from the fireplace. I sit opposite him, listening attentively. The reflection of the fire's glow is fitful in my boot shafts; the boot tips are in a pool of red light. Uncle Ferdinand is also staring at this. Though physically still very much alive in that winter of 1940, he is no more of this world. He already belongs to another dimension. He now belongs to the marvelous no-man's-land of space and time in which stories, History, and histories gloriously exist. He is already with his ancestors, whose pictures gaze down at him from the high walls of the dining room. His faith in immortality has placed him among them. Perhaps Uncle Ferdinand does not really believe in the immortality of the soul in God, even though he has been brought up in this faith and would regard it as poor taste to doubt it. But he does believe in the immortality of fame. His ancestors did not die because they entered history. He too will not die, for he will become history. Stella says that he is one of the modern princes who do not determine the fate of the nations with an open vizor but manipulate it surreptitiously, rather in the way a man rummages under a girl's skirt. Hence, says Stella, his proper place is not in the history of the world but in the history of manners. Nevertheless, when you consider the people in the roadside café, this is still the history of the manners of gods: mythology. Meanwhile, he thus placed himself in my shaman power. I need only a few dozen letters again, and he scurries over the glossy curvature of the samovar, withdraws into the constriction under his belly, telescopes into his spindly legs, is caught by the ring over the samovar foot and is dreadfully flattened out; then, extended into a serpent, he slithers around the base of the cone over the heater flame and, as though liquefied, pours into it—

and he steps back from the tea table of 1926. He has got hold of his watercress sandwich, mushroom patty, currant tart, or cucumber sandwich, and struts once again as a giant rooster through my childhood day—

and in the silver on the tea table, as his shadow moves away, the springtime rises again, a hundred times in a hundred radiant stars. Spring, outside the window, wafts through the air, blue and full of distressing promise.

It is the springtime light, the sweet core, of the lost half of my life. In the marvelous no-man's-land where legends live, it has not even been snuffed out by the years of my Viennese upbringing with Uncle Helmuth Aunt Hertha Aunt Selma plus Cousin

Wolfgang as a dowry of the spiritualized philistine world. The dismal gray of those fourteen years was still lined with that light—as was yesterday's fog (the day before yesterday's fog? or that of how many nights and days ago?), through which I walked from the Place des Ternes to Calvet's on the Boulevard Saint-Germain-des-Prés in order to meet you, Mr. Brodny. Don't think me certifiably mad if I repeat that this was the light of the old Europe—behind the fog even here, in Pearris, Freanss, in the year 1968. It froze on a day of solstice thirty years ago, in March 1938, in Vienna, Austria. The first phase of the Ice Age then commenced. Now, the second age is already long since past. But the ice doesn't seem to have thawed completely. The gray mist is still hiding that golden light. How long will it take the mists to dispel altogether? And will the light that finally breaks through be the old light again? What do you think?

◻   **33**   ◻

HOW REGRETTABLE, dear Mr. Brodny, that our meeting yesterday (the day before yesterday? the day before that? I can't remember which day it was; since then, I've been living behind closed shutters and without a timepiece; I write; now and again I sleep for a few hours and then continue writing, and I shall not stop until I have explained to you why what I have to say cannot be said in three sentences)—how frightful, I repeat, that our meeting took such an unfortunate turn! I would have very much liked to talk with you. As a compatriot, so to speak. You see, I insist on imagining that you too originally came from Bessarabia. I insist that I saw you when I was a child in there. You were one of the men who purchased Uncle Ferdinand's harvest. We had gone on a carriage ride, Uncle Ferdinand, my beautiful mother, Miss Fern, and I. It was still very warm; and my mother held a white parasol over us. Uncle Ferdinand told the coachman to turn into a field. There you were, standing by a fiery-red thresher that puffed small white clouds of steam into the spotless sky. You were wearing a linen jacket and leather gaiters, and you greeted us with such élan that Uncle Ferdinand automatically and irritatedly waved you off, telling the driver to keep going. Thus, our first meeting was unconsummated, Mr. Jacob G. Brodny. And, at the second meeting, it would not have surprised me to discover features in you that I had not reckoned with—for instance, the dismayingly clear singsong of your angelic voice. I was quite taken off guard by this cantorial tenor.

But all this is nonsense, of course. Sheer fantasy. A fancy of my overstimulated imagination. If this were true, then you would have to be over ninety years old today, in 1968. And besides— why? There is no reason to assume it. Not the slightest thing to go by. At best, some sort of manipulation by my subconscious. The foggy day outside, from which I came, was edged with a light that reminded me of autumn days in Rumania. Autumn and also spring days. (I myself begin to fear for my mind. *Abbia pazienza!* Be patient with poor me!)

And you greeted me so dashingly, with such élan. Without having ever seen me before. As if you had known me for years. I found this heartwarmingly pleasant. It led me to joke on the spot. I could not guess that you expected more ceremony from me. After all, you are a mighty man on the literary scene and I am nothing but a writer.

But no matter. Right after our first exchange went awry, everything else went awry. But you should not therefore believe, Jaykob Gee, that I didn't like you. On the contrary. I liked you very much: the way you sat there, enjoying a thrush pâté on small pieces of white bread. From the mashing masticatory movements of no doubt perfectly filled molars, your cherubic voice asked what I was writing. Could I tell you the plot in three sentences?

Try putting yourself in my place. I had come from the fog outside, as I have said. From a white-surging ocean. A bright, splendid blue-gold autumn day could be divined at the bottom. The fog was lined with gold. The dove-blue and lemon-yellow city of Paris was completely dissolved. It had turned into gray-whitish steam suffused with gold.

I had walked all the way from my hotel near the Place des Ternes to the Boulevard Saint-Germain. Or rather: I had swum. Along streets that had turned into white-surging riverbeds. Across squares like vast bays. Through the great flood areas of the Tuileries, where tree stumps, planted in the steam, loomed into the air. Across the Pont Neuf, which had turned into a cloud bridge over a steam-filled chasm. As I walked, I was overcome, of course, by all sorts of memories. Thanks to my drifting through the fog, they too were detached from any context. As if moving through fitful half sleep, full of exchangeable and exchanged meanings. They came floating from every place that hovered between Bessarabia and Paris in the torrent of time. They were not in me—I was in them. Dissolved and disoriented. The thing bearing my name was not a person. I was a surging flood of memories. I should have explained this to you, Mr. Brodny. I should have told you that the contrast was too abrupt, too enormous, when I entered Calvet's. I mean, the contrast between one "reality" and another.

There you sat, so unbelievably concrete, so utterly self-assured and American, so—how shall I put it?—so formed, so solidly immured. . . . Yes indeed, in my disheveled mental state, I involuntarily thought of Schiller. I said with boyish zeal:

> "Solidly immur'd in earth
> Stands the mold of hard-bak'd clay . . ."

Yes indeed. There you sat, Jacob G. Brodny, the world's most efficient, the globe's most important literary agent, square-shouldered, square-faced, with iron-gray woolly hair in an angular crew cut and heavy dark eyes under heavy thick lids in your strikingly individual Jewish head. You sat there like a solidly cast iron cube between the wall and the table. And before you there was something that seemed to come from a German fairy tale, all those things straight out of Red Riding Hood's little basket, spread out before you on the neatly folded red-and-white-checkered tablecloth: little plates and little forks and little knives and little spoons and sparkling little glasses. And in a pleasingly shaped little pot of fired clay, half covered by a layer of white fat half scratched away by your knife, the thrush pâté gave off a spicy aroma. And in a little basket next to it lay the wine, half swathed in a snowy napkin, like a dusty, ruby-red-capped and white-bibbed child-mummy: a bottle of blood-red Château Margaux. You, Mr. Brodny, were sitting there, breaking pieces off a stick of fine white bread, smearing them with clay-colored pâté, and inserting them between your greasy satrap lips. You were chewing very pleasurably, earnestly, eagerly, washing down the food mush every so often with a sip of the dark wine. And where your form-fitting, albumen-bluish nylon shirt was wrinkled by your chest hair, a black bug ate at your heart.

I should have taken that into consideration. Likewise, the clear bell tone of your voice. But I was so confused by your request to tell you my plot in three sentences that I forgot the black bug in your heart as well as the one in mine and did not even perceive your voice. This may be pardonable. Going by the purely optical effect of your utterly American appearance, Jay Gee, one expects the usual mixture of senatorial potato-mouthing and lay-preacher sanctimony, squooshed out in chewing-gum cow pats. But not that heavenly milk of a voice. That voice does not fit under a Stetson hat. It does not even go with the Cosa Nostra–boss cigar jutting up toward the fedora brim. I should have noticed that voice. But I was bowled over, *bouleversé*. Once again: *Abbia pazienza!* Forgive troubled me!

□   34   □

CERTAINLY: I have spent nineteen years of my life pouring the bell metal of my memories into the mold of a story. I was, I am, ready to explain in detail how and why. Nevertheless, nineteen years is a considerable stretch of time. It adds up to—I've figured it out—six thousand nine hundred thirty-five days (plus five days for leap years) that I have spent as my own lunatic attendant. Six thousand nine hundred forty days and nights of which not a single one has passed without doubt assailing me, paralyzing me at some point or other: doubt in myself, in my strengths, in my gifts, my intelligence, my knowledge, my memory, my perspicacity, my sincerity, my character, my calling, my good fortune, and everything else one needs for writing. And even doubt in my cause. Was it still worth the trouble to write a novel? . . . Good God, how often was this not discussed with brother Schwab!

How often was it not discussed in the intellectual chitchat of the newspaper supplements! The doubt in the necessity of writing per se, or in its effectiveness. Why write at all, nowadays? Don't the roadhouse people have their fill? Aren't they crammed up to their eyebrows on newspapers, magazines, movies, television, comic strips? Do they still need books, literature? . . . You yawn, dearest friend? I couldn't agree more. Nevertheless, our sort take our profession seriously to the point of self-destruction. Just imagine: six thousand nine hundred forty days, of which perhaps a dozen may have been completely happy, because I didn't think about writing—and afterward they struck me as sinful, as licentiously wasted time.

I can also tell you that, of course, there have been days of fulfillment. Days of euphoria, of creative rushes. The bliss of procreation, you know. When nuptially white paper is irrigated by myrmidons of script and becomes gravid with significance. A magical act of creation (which can bring forth not only Literature but also such crap as newspaper articles, film scripts, cutthroat publishing contracts, love letters, death sentences, declarations of war). Here, however, under my pen, the book of my generation is emerging. Indited by the conscience of our race, Jacob. It is emerging out of such states of self-intoxication. The writing days . . . But these blissful moments are buried in weeks, months, seasons, years of weary indolence, incapability, irresolution, dullness. In days so sluggish as to make the daily life of Oblomov's footman seem Stakhanovite. And he, Oblomov's footman, has a totally unburdened conscience about his indolence. People like us wouldn't. For us, an unburdened conscience is theft of our own work. A carefree spirit is embezzlement. The man who works away toward a quick end is a saboteur.

You can, of course (like beautiful Maud), reply that the art of life consists in relaxing ever new cramps before they actually appear. The same holds for the art of writing. Golden words, assuming that one lived a self-determining life and that for the most part one did not really live. It is not I who write, Brodny-*leben*: **IT** writes out of me. Ask Uncle Helmuth about the torments that a medium suffers before the vessel of her physis is so utterly purified by her that an otherworldly spirit can slip into it and use it for a while as an earthly instrument of expression. But I do not wish to lament. Though hopelessly behind the times, I live the destiny of my era. Anyone who is not a performer in it will, presumably, have an even worse time.

However, you must understand that your blithe request for me to tell you my plot in three sentences touched on deep things in me. It was as if you had met a mother who devotes everything to keeping her child alive despite its simultaneous malignant tumors, scrofula, and consumption, and you asked her in how many seconds the child does the hundred-meter sprint. I found you a bit tactless. A bit all too peppy, Yankele Brodny. I approved of Uncle Ferdinand's slightly vexed gesture of decline in Bessarabia. You were obviously buying too well, too cheaply, from the peasants. We were not certain whether you, clapping us on the shoulder, might not claim that the grain on the stalk was half rotten. I felt you lacked savoir faire in dealing with grands seigneurs—that's right, I said: with grands seigneurs. In six thousand nine hundred forty days of alternating between compulsive expression and juvenile ink-retention—one hundred sixty-six thousand five hundred and sixty hours of testing and rejecting, of anxieties, flickering hopes, blazing certitudes, and ashen disappointments, as well as faith and courage—people like us achieve a certain sublimity. After which you don't squander your grain anymore.

Please try to understand. Just a few days ago—about a week before I received the message that you, the powerful literary agent Jacob G. Brodny, wished to see me and would be delighted to dine with me *chez* Calvet—a few days earlier, I tell you (I had just barely arrived here from Munich via Reims), I fancied I had something to say in my next book. Despite all theoretical and particular doubts. During my drive here from Reims, it had suddenly emerged in front of me quite clearly. I had only to cheat my producer-piglets, who had ordered me to Paris, of a few short weeks; I had only to sneak off for a while, to some place where no one would suspect me of staying. I had only to unpack my papers there and launch into my shaman arts: with the anthracite-gray magic conjuring up spirits by means of black letters on virgin-white paper . . .

Unfortunately, something interfered with my plans.

However, bullheaded as a human being is (dragging the past into presence even in the flight of days ahead, even in the flight of years ahead), I was still not ready to admit final defeat. I became aware of my failure only when you asked me to tell you my story in three sentences.

□   35   □

AND SINCE DEEP THINGS in me were touched by your Mephistophelian demand, I had a vision. I saw with what appetite you ate your thrush pâté. I scrutinized your mouth. I was fascinated by the dumb show it was performing with no spiritual effort on your part. You were relishing the taste with such gusto; one could see that your entire essence was interiorized to the fine-tasting of food mush. After each morsel, your lips closed solidly, like rubber cushions lying snugly on each other, and while your jaws were crushing, your lips kneaded along, stretching and twisting as they assumed an expression now of bitterness and indignation, now of insult, hatred, baseness, and finally of almost majestic scorn. Scornfully, with sneeringly pulled-down corners, your lips suffered a swallowing hop of the Adam's apple; they waited for the rather choky slide of the delicacy down the gullet; then they opened, contorting into a gorgon's grimace in order to give a pale-violet tongue tip a chance to cleanse any pâté remnants from suspiciously perfect jacket crowns.

Please don't misunderstand me. I am not a neurotic aesthete. Business breakfasts in gourmet restaurants with producer-piglets and all sorts of crappy newspapermen are part of my professional routine. I know the expression of involuntary disgust in the comfort of people eating sumptuously. I know not just *your* autonomously working mouth. Incidentally, as you know, I once wed such a mouth. It was, as I have told you, in Nuremberg, at the canteen for German attorneys and witnesses in the gigantic Fürth courthouse. You got the same food as in the Allied cafeteria, but here it was poured out for you like swill. It looked half fermented and maggoty. Still, it had nutritional value, vitamins. Germans were not picky in 1946. That mouth too was detached from the human being it belonged to. It too expressed feelings that the human being did not feel. It too behaved in a most peculiar way, remaining closed and twisting grotesquely while the human being chewed. It too worked valiantly, albeit with the most peculiar clowneries for itself, just like yours. And the chewing, swallowing human being to whom it belonged and about whom it was completely unconcerned, and who was likewise unconcerned about it, was entirely interiorized to taking in nutrients. It was a young girl, corn-blond, with a very lovely posture, like someone who knows how to ride well. Over the capering mouth hovered a pair of aquamarine-clear fairy-tale eyes, seeing nothing. They were switched off, so to speak, or were listening (so far as eyes can listen), likewise into themselves, to the intake of vitamins in the disgusting canteen grub.

A burning pity overcame me at this sight, a pity not for the girl but for the human condition in general: for the human creature and the tragicomedy of its existence. Outside, the city of Nuremberg lay in rubble, as did the rest of Europe. The mass graves from the Don to the Pyramids, from Andalsnes to Salonika, were barely covered. The land was still full of iron men, and children ate from garbage cans as from troughs. Here in Nuremberg, judgment was to be pronounced on WW II: the crime of war, war crimes; crimes against humanity, the crimes of conspiracy for all these things—twenty million victims. The self-assured zeal with which the gallows were constructed for several of the accused did not permit the hope that the twenty million victims would be the last. And amidst these atrocities sat a foolish, lovely young girl, eating with ardor and physical devotion, as though she were eating the flesh of the Lord. I fell in love with her. I married her. I sired a son with her.

That too was in my mind when I saw you eating, Mr. Brodny. The year 1962 was also in my mind, the year when I was at the peak of my fame as the writer of shitty movie stories and completely at a standstill with the work on my book, on which I pegged hopes of my salvation from screenplays. It was the year I finally got divorced from Christa and soon did not even have a place to live. I moved from hotel to boardinghouse and from boardinghouse to hotel, while people in the street pointed their fingers at me because I was the lover of a world-famous star, Nadine Carrier. The escape from Nadine to the crazy love for Dawn was also in my mind—Dawn and the abstract existence I entered because of her: the growing unbelievability, unreality, of my existence (which so fascinated Schwab), while all around me lay a world of tormentingly immutable facticity: millions of people teeming over highways, hundreds of thousands eating in highway roadhouses. Everyone, it appeared, knew what he was doing, how much he was earning by doing it, what he could afford with it, what things cost. The supply of purchasable goods was overwhelming, the choice soon imprisoned the entire individual. Everything was getting better, more perfect, more obligating; you had to have it, otherwise you didn't count. . . .

And I sleepwalked through Paris, the bright and beautiful underworld, with the sorrows of a lover whose beloved has been abducted to Hades like Eurydice (I still remember very precisely a conversation with Schwab on the Pont Neuf), and while I sleepwalked in my love, her beautiful mouth, detached from her, devoured a white rose.

All these things were in my mind, as well as Bessarabia and Uncle Ferdinand and my unhappy adolescence in Vienna, and Uncle Helmuth and Aunts Hertha and Selma, and Cousin Wolfgang and my brother Schwab. And then I heard you speak (without, of course, noticing your angelic voice). Aside from the free and easy "Hi," which, I must confess, got on my nerves, you very soon said, "I've heard about you, young man." (Why so young? At worst, you're only five or six years older than I.) "You're writing a book." (Indeed.) "Tell me the plot in three sentences!" This was said by your hardworking mouth, which lent such original expression to feelings, sentiments, moods that you did not even have, while you consumed pieces of white bread, mashed in Margaux and sputum, with *pâté de grives*. And to my gracious surprise, I heard familiar sounds in your diction. Neither your bellowed *R* in "story" nor the thick *L* of the recent immigrant conceals the slightly nasal Viennese *Kaffeehaus* yiddle of your speech pattern, Jaykopp Gee.

And that really knocked the bottom out of my memories.

There was no stopping now, and I was not solidly immur'd in earth, I was floating away from myself, floating through the catastrophe-land of Europe, back to the lost half of my life.

There you sat. You were a part of my past and yet everything that Europe no longer was, everything that it had meanwhile become, to my sorrow: the same Hilton Hotel from Madrid to Oslo, the same service-station diner, the same airport, the same jukebox from Bückeburg to Calabria, the same supermarket, the same T-shirt on girlish tits, the same hard neon light on evenings when the sky turns to stone over the phallic cities.

And there I had a vision all at once. You, Mr. Brodny, the model American (hadn't gone over on the *Mayflower*, to be sure, but all the more militant in New World spirit for that: a pogrom-tested Babbitt from Galicia), and as the personification of that spirit you were eating not *pâté de grives* but a dish named Yurop. The thing you smeared so thickly on your little pieces of white bread and inserted between your perfectly serviced teeth, the thing on which you closed your lips, leaving them to their so original play of expressions, while you were totally interiorized to a chewer and swallower—that thing was not thrush pâté, it was Europe. Her spirit, her soul, her dream of herself, her self-illusion. Her old skillfulness, her inexhaustible wealth of forms, all her many forms so thoroughly imbued with her spirit. In short, the essence of her being. Indeed, that *was* a feasting! I saw palaces and cathedrals vanishing into your mouth, which closed over them, contorting—either disdainful or offended, mocking or arrogant—while your teeth chewed. Entire cities, lovelier than Nuremberg, were gobbled up by you, for instance Bruges or Siena or Salzburg or Varasdin or Prague. With you, I tasted Paestum still in swampland and a tangle of wild roses, I saw a spring morning in Brabant melting on your tongue. You forked up the Lübeck *Dance of Death* and chewed it with delight; you then inserted Michelangelo's *David* with its oversize head and fists (but what a head, what fists!), promptly followed by a Klimt portrait of a lady. Shakespeare's sonnets tickled your palate. You swallowed the façade of Chartres with all the mysterious queens and angels and granted yourself, last but not least, the concluding chapter of Proust's *Du côté de chez Swann*. And you washed all this down with a wine that got its color from Giordano Bruno's blood and its charmingly virile spirit from Spinoza. And with the sounds of Palestrina, Mozart, Beethoven, and Strauss, your angelic voice now clambered over the threshold of my consciousness: Gaia's first lover. . . .

I had to hold my breath and writhe and squirm to keep from throwing up.

□   36   □

I ADMIT, I ought to have been overcome by the same pity that I once felt for Christa in Nuremberg. Or rather for the *condition humaine* in general: for the human creature and the tragicomedy of its existence. But this would have led only to my suffering, and I have avoided suffering as best I could ever since I lost the first half of my life and conceived the idleness of the second half. There is too much cause for pity; one simply can't manage it. I skipped it almost entirely.

Do credit me, however, with not dragging the past into presence at least on this occasion. Imagine how simplifying and abbreviating it would have been had I been able to give vent to my dichotomous feelings with a gross "Kike!" What a lovely tension, with the possibility of release granted by such short circuits, has been lost to us because of German immoderation! Europe without hatred of Jews—why, that's like faith in God without the devil. The loss of a metaphysical dimension. A loss of eroticism. (Never does my heart fail to quicken at the thought of the caresses I provoked in Nuremberg when I held the black-haired girl from the death camp in my arms and whispered into her ear, "Kike bitch!" and she drummed her fists on my chest and gasped, "You filthy goy!" . . . Incidentally, she knew I was engaged to Christa, blond as sheaves of wheat.)

Scherping would understand this. He knows that even sex becomes revelatory in suffering. But after all, we avoid suffering. With Americanism, the Aspirin Age has come over the Old World. It was sheer cowardice that prevented me from confronting you, Mr. Brodny. I was afraid of the black bug on your heart.

Your bug and mine might have pounced on each other. We w
have had to become brothers, like Schwab and me. Even wit
the clarion fanfare of your voice, I would have recognized G
angel in you, J.G. And I did not want to wrestle with the an
Not anymore.

Cowardice provided me with an armor of irony. And you kn
how garish irony becomes in our days. All the same, I didn't c
you "kike." I left you alone, left Calvet's, walked back into the fo
lined in gold, dropped in on a couple of bistros, and drank. I di
not feel like eating (which you may understand). I even went t
the Crillon and asked for Nadine. Luckily, she wasn't in. A couple of Americans at the bar tempted me to bait them. But they
noticed I was drunk and good-naturedly gave me the brush-off. I
could have got pushy and provoked them into a fistfight, but I
didn't want the bartender to tell Nadine, because then she'd
know I was in Paris. This way, he'd take it for granted that I was
with her in the Crillon and find it superfluous to talk about me. I
wanted to walk across town again. The fog had lightened, but the
golden day underneath had vanished. It was already getting toward evening; I don't know what time it was. At the Madeleine, I
ran into a streetwalker and unloaded my grief with her. I didn't
get home till late at night.

"Home," as you know, is at present the Hôtel Épicure by the
Place des Ternes. I owe it to Dawn. This is where I tracked her
down in 1963 the first time she disappeared. This is where the
scene with the Indian doll (and Schwab) took place, and this is
where she became my mistress. This is where I deposited her for
good after her mouth had eaten the white rose in the Bois de
Boulogne.

Since then, I've been returning here regularly: whenever I'm
fed up with the true-blue folkloristically preserved greasiness of
the deluxe tourist hostels on the Left Bank; whenever the movie
piglets won't foot the bill for the George V; whenever I want to
write undisturbed for a couple of days or read Nagel's latest best-
selling novel; sometimes simply because I want to be alone as I
truly am; sometimes, in Gaia's days, whenever we had fought or I
was overcome with a surfeit of my luxury-consumer existence;
and over and over again when I have the compulsive thought that

I might be pounced on in some hour of grace by the vision of a form for my book (as occurred during my drive here from Reims, as has occurred all too often throughout the last nineteen years; for the *it*, which wants to be spoken through this book, constantly prowls afer me; I can sense it at the back of my neck—only it evaporates whenever I try to make a swift grab at it) . . .

in short: I return to this lousy dump like a murderer to the scene of his crime.

You know the details of my stay this time: I spent over a week here (one day more or less makes no difference) as a voluntary incarcerate (solitary confinement). The cause, as indicated several times, was an illumination during the drive here from Reims: I finally had collared my pursuer. The *it* that wanted to be spoken through me had revealed itself. The parasitic egg that Schwab had once (nineteen years ago!) planted in me had got through its caterpillar stage, had hatched, and was now floating before my eyes as a richly colored butterfly. All I had to do was make a grab. Only—since we're dealing with such pretty metaphors—I had reckoned without zoology and without the relationship between the guest and the host.

The eggs of parasitical hymenoptera, Mr. Brodny, never become butterflies; they are placed in caterpillars which, in turn, nurture the hope of becoming butterflies. The evil guests eat up their hosts from the inside; no beautiful metamorphosis ever comes about. All that remains is an empty shell into which (as into Uncle Helmuth's mediums when they stepped out in a trance) an astral being, freely floating in the beyond, can take up residence and materialize at will. Should your kind interest in me go so far that you muster enough patience to skim through the papers I am sending you with this (far too lengthy, far too prolix—forgive me) epistle, then you will find the faithful notation of such an occurrence.

Any utilization for book dealers—as the first glance will reveal—is, to be sure, out of the question. The three folders, A, B, C, contain dismally fragmentary material. Needless to say, you have long since divined that these fragments are pieces, patches, sketches, notes for my book (the masterpiece of the era, right? the lifework of a potential Nobel laureate). May I take the liberty of leaving them with you as a legacy, not with a thought to any possible publication but as reparation for my regrettably poor behavior *chez* Calvet.

and with the hope that you may find someone to tell you the plot in three sentences.

A

You must realize that writing is one of the most lamentable roads, leading to anything and everything.

ANDRÉ BRETON, *First Manifesto of Surrealism*

The limits of my language stand for the limits of my world.

LUDWIG WITTGENSTEIN, *Notebooks, 1914–1916*

Why did I write? What sin to me unknown
Dipp'd me in ink? My parents' or my own?

ALEXANDER POPE, *Epistle to Dr. Arbuthnot*

Fear is a female faint in which freedom loses consciousness; speaking psychologically, the Fall of Man
always takes place in a faint.

SÖREN KIERKEGAARD, *Fear and Trembling*

□   □   □

HERE I AM, once again rummaging through my papers with an
impatience that nests deeper, closer to the breeding grounds of
fear—worse than the fidgety restlessness I've retained from my
damned formative years in Vienna, a restlessness like a nervous
tic, the involuntary closing of an eyelid or an annoyingly recur-
ring, dribbling twitch of a tiny muscle in a nostril, as if a dwarfish
alarm clock there were soundlessly ringing at unpredictable intervals. Remember! Those were the years of my "deepest humiliation." At least that's what I used to call them when I told my
friend S. about them, quoting a once current phrase of Hitler's
ironically, of course, for who'd take himself that seriously? Yet I
can't deny that in my frail heart I do still resent that time of so-
called education: when my petit bourgeois relatives in Vienna
tried to "bring me down from the clouds" and teach me to "take
life [that is, myself] seriously" the way they did, the poor
blinded creatures! the lamentable suckers! the self-deceiving victims of the narrowness they believed to be *reality!* martyrs to the
mendacity of a small world within the wealth and beauty of the
world! people always mirrored in themselves, always viewing
only themselves, unable to see anything but themselves! Forgive
them, forgive them—even if their so-called good intentions were
an assault on all that is meant to make a growing child become a
bright, sincere, and happy being.

It is night. The eighth since I have locked myself in this room.
Eight nights and a goodly portion of the days (during which I

prefer to get some sleep; the nights are quieter) I have spent ransacking my papers: a chaotic mass of sheets and pages, leaflets, slips and scraps. This is all that has come out of my work on MY BOOK. The result of nineteen years of alas! all too frequently interrupted but maniacally and persistently recommenced labor: two suitcases and a couple of big cartons full of beginnings, sketched or worked-out chapters, fragments, remnants of rejected drafts, essays, outlines, studies, flashes, ideas. Memo-pad slips with microscopic scrawls, letter-size pages maltreated with crisscross penmanship like saber strokes, newspaper clippings, ripped-out book pages with handwritten marginalia by the printed text. There's even a beer coaster among them with a few yellowed comments that today, being wholly detached from any context, are unintelligible. Still, this can't be all. There must be notes I've misplaced, or lost, or thrown away. I sweat at the mere thought.

This is not the first time I've undertaken such a sifting. I do it regularly. Compulsively, I'm tempted to say. Whenever I'm overcome by the illusion of—finally!—having found the FORM for my book. Or when I imagine I can yield to the hope that I might—finally—have enough leisure (or rather freedom from afflicting necessities, like women or movie piglets). Whenever I imagine I'd have enough willpower, enough concentration to bring some order to this heap of eruptively hurled-out literary production, so that at least a vague outline might be traced of where I was aiming when I wrote it down. Needless to say, with each such sifting, irreplaceable stuff is destroyed; and, with the next one, I despair about my rigor in making the previous selection. Needless to say, furthermore, I never advance a new plan far enough to bring any sort of form to the manuscript for whose sake I have so horribly mangled the previous outline.

This time the same, I fear. Although this last attempt (and failure) was undertaken with a clearer notion than ever before, and, unlike the previous ones, was not stymied by some unforeseen and unavoidable obstacle. What prevented achievement was something from *outside;* I mean to say, something that had nothing to do with any practical hindrance or with an insufficiency of my last vision of this book, not even with my shortcomings as its presumptive author. Were I not afraid to come too near to my uncle Helmut's spiritualistic ideas, I would say: it came indeed from *outside this world.*

This was prepared for by a state of unusual exaltation. When I arrived here, eight days (and nights) ago, I brought with me a new vision of my book. It seemed to me exactly what I had been waiting for ever since I started believing I could write at all. It appeared as an award for nineteen years of hard labor. My instantaneous decision was to lock myself in here and do nothing else but put down the new draft and put together the old bits that would fit in and—finally!—achieve something whole and close: in one word, a FORM. I began working in a state of excitement such as had overcome me only in the most enthusiastic (and most humiliating) moments of love. The same mad fixation. The same restriction. The same loss of liberty. Nothing outside the love can count. Nothing is real *but* that love. Incidentally, en route here I had dreamed my dream. I dreamed it in Reims, where I spent the night. In the same hotel where I had spent the night the last time I took S. to Paris, five years ago. It is the nightmare that has haunted me for years (nineteen, to be exact). Not regularly, of course, but at various small and large intervals. I can never figure out what triggers it. This time, too, there was no apparent cause. It ambushed me like a highwayman.

The dream was in most of its features the same as always. I commit my murder for no other reason than a vile wish to hide something. More than to hide: to make it never have happened. By slaughtering the old charwoman, I want to rid the world of a shameful deed that would really happen—and become known through her. I brutally assassinate this lamentable creature of mislived life—mistreated, humiliated humanity, foul flesh and rags—in order to wash the world and myself clean with her blood. And when I am about to bury the corpse, I realize with increasing certainty that nothing can help me, that I have murdered in vain and that the world will know about my deed and people will find out—worse, they will find out the even more damnable reason why I committed such a dreadful crime. . . .

As usual, this dream haunted me in the daytime, too—an insidious pursuer that follows me step by step and disappears around corners when I try to confront it. For, as usual, everything I did during those days was aimed at luring out the terror of the night in me.

An unclean game. Ultimately erotic (our friend Scherping would find it blissful). But I certainly do not play it for pleasure. It inveigles and hoaxes me with the promise that I'm on the verge of some kind of revelation. The paralyzing horror at my deed has a moment of utmost intensity—in the moment in which I awake. I think I recognize in it something that is at the core of my being, the key to it, something dreadful and, at the same time, marvelously promising—and which I lose by waking up.

The hunt to find out what it is goes on for a few days. I act as if nothing had happened, go about my customary business. I see this person, speak to that one, make my reckonings with yesterday and my plans for tomorrow. But secretly I wait for the terror of my dream to ambush me again.

For it is always near—and yet I can never conjure it up. If I think of it, it fades away. If, seemingly unabashed, I busy myself with something different, it skulks after me. If I glance around (so to speak), then the street is empty. . . . But I sense it hiding somewhere behind me. It lies in wait for me, as I for it. Only it is incomparably more skillful, more nimble, more agile. At times, I feel the horror very close. The expectation that it will assault me again softens my knees and makes the hair stand up on the back of my neck. But I am too impatient, I anticipate its enlightening. Even before the blow occurs—the terrible blow with which it might enter me and descend to the refuse heaps of consciousness in which the key to myself is lost—I already relish the rending that would sever me should I finally see what it is—

and thus, everything dissolves into nothing again—as in awakening. The atrocious blow never falls. I feel the crack—but before I can see what was opening with it, I have lost the feeling. Only a faraway echo remains—and vanishes too.

It's even more frustrating when I summon back the events of my dream. One by one they become empty of significance. What had been an image now becomes verbal, and thereby abstract. I can say in words what I have dreamed—but it has lost its reality. My grip on it has stolen its magic meaningfulness. I remain empty-handed, a swindled swindler.

I then try to deceive myself with all sorts of childish maneuvers. I fake guilelessness. I pretend to focus my interest on something else, something peripheral, innocuous—for instance, I count up the women I have slept with in any seven fat or lean years—

for even our wealth of amorous adventures (as shown by the Leporello lists we secretly kept up in triumph and humiliation) is not due to skill in erotics but occurs or fails as naturally as good or bad harvests (of course, the soil must be conscientiously tilled). And, just as our fate, according to the mood or grace of the weather and the ripening, sometimes brings a shortage and other times leads us to lavishness, and perhaps from prosperity soon back again to meagerness, so, too, by sheer biological chemistry, we are granted a fixed quota of erotic success, inscribed in us, readable in our faces, so to say, which, with its clear benchmark, ensures that it is neither exceeded nor unfulfilled. And you cannot trump it with any effort or skill, with any physical, much less mental, quality or quantity. Neither the beguiling eloquence of Cyrano do Bergerac will help you nor his long nose (or whatever other lengths or sizes are deemed relevant), because Nature has created poor and rich in every respect—and hence in this respect too . . .

Such are the things I busy myself with and write down, ending with my papers again; that is, lying in wait for myself (and yet knowing that I cannot escape my destiny; pressured by time: I'll soon be fifty, I could be dead tomorrow, and I haven't done my work, my book lies here, proliferating under my hands in a horrible hybrid cell growth, turning into a monstrosity)—

hence, I yearn for the dreadful, pleasurable *recognition* to pounce on me just once more, one single and lucid last time, the recognition with which (albeit for only a fleeting moment) I can be certain that *it is true*, that old nightmare: that I *have really murdered*, shamefully and for no other reason than to conceal some baseness deeply rooted in me—

but when? how? where? and whom? That's what I can't grasp.

I've suppressed it. Even without consulting Dr. Sigmund Freud, I realized long ago that my forgetfulness suggests disreputable sediment in the dark depths of my soul, and I wisely make a point of not trying to dredge it out with what that great son of the literary nineteenth century recommends as a fishing rod: *autobiography*. Unfortunately, my horror, which I voluptuously fear and desire, cannot be pursued back to my parents' bedroom. It springs from the sheer terror of existence itself. Such a momentary revelation of the totally *unknown* that lies behind and beyond all that can be known is what the primitive man calls *God*.

How marvelously well off I would be if it were simply a matter of confessional biography, something like the early experiences of Freud's Wolf-Man. A cinematic street song. Perfect pap for my piglets. It would convince everyone. Especially when presented in contemporary style, which, in its love of atmosphere—oozing quotations of style—betrays its attraction to the past:

POSTER

(in psychedelic dynamized *Jugendstil* graphics: the linear flow of the rapids narrowing, the spectrum dentated into a buzz saw of nerves—rose-madder, sulfur-yellow, prasine, violet ... with interspersed boutique heraldry: two male hands chopped off at the gentlemanly cuffs, with forefingers stretching like pistol barrels, point from either side at the name)

ARISTIDES
Tunnel of Love/First-Class Mechanic
of
Western Union

(collage: model of early locomotive, its cathedral-bell smokestack sending up as a cloud of steam a distilling flask with alchemical stuff in it—toads, snakes, embryos, homunculi; in the engineer's cab, his booted foot on a female body with a bald head, General Custer with a drawn sword, his left hand waving a fresh scalp)

invites you
on a
TRIP TO HADES
into the
SPIRITUAL INNARDS
of
CONSUMER SOCIETY TROGLODYTES

(newspaper advertisement praises a method for treating club feet and ears that stick out; likewise nose-shapers, body-hair removers, wart, blackhead, and goiter remedies)

THEME:
A MIDDLE-AGED MAN COMES TO REALIZE THAT HE IS SUPPRESSING GUILT!

God grant that I could offer such a thing: I could sell it instantly to my producer-piglets.

the peppy little producers, co-producers, copro-producers who teem and crowd wherever the bliss of financial assistance, government grants, and development prizes pours from the overlapping folds of show biz and kulchur biz:

the bright, alert apprentices soon outstripping the great film sorcerers—and the hatchlings of the movie business, living it up on expense accounts; rosily fattening on petits fours, foie gras, crab claws, slices of Nova Scotia, caviar dollops at the press conference buffets (with champagne, of course!), their tiny eyes sated and wearied by starlet flesh—

yet physically fit, robust; swept along in the process of beauty-construction in the studio and location wardrobes—groomed and bedizened, their little fingernails pared, filed, and polished between the motherly breasts of staff manicurists, their facial skin smoothed and salved by epidermis-solicitous makeup men, their intervertebral disks loosened and their bodies shaken aright by studio osteopaths, kneaded and massaged to firm up their tissue by junior-star gym teachers, their blood circulation refreshed in stars' genuine Finnish saunas, their flesh treated to ultraviolet rays even in the winter months and then tanned to a crisp by the spring sun over the beach promenades of Mediterranean festival settings—

men of the world, of course: well traveled, as they go about preparing unrealizable big projects, and thus surefooted on the grill-room parquets of Hilton hotels—

hence, mentally too at the highest attainable peak: shrewd, crafty, brazen, hard-boiled—and infernally clever at wielding the magic wand that every moviemaker carries in his old kit bag and that opens wide all doors, hearts, female legs—nay, even bank accounts:

so that over and over again by the fictions of uncovered checks and uncashed drafts they manage to keep shooting off a fireworks of life-reality, of adventurously colorful and dynamic, lightly pulsating life; and with swindling promises and insincere assurances they determine destinies (and not necessarily for the worse) without ever being troubled by the law: they do nothing but add more and more possibilities to the everlasting game of the exchange of fiction and "reality." . . .

For two decades now, I have been their partner, their stooge and assistant, in this game, their officious servant and loyal squire. I know them and their needs. I know how eagerly their little ears perk up to the whisper of movie themes, wriggle with every flash and trash therein; and I know that this particular trash would most blissfully tickle their little piglet ears. It would be best to funnel it in through the telephone receiver early in the morning.

SPECIAL PRIORITY CALL, PARIS–MUNICH: *Hello? Intercosmic Film Art? Hi there. May I speak to Herr Wohlfahrt.—Ah, it's you! I didn't recognize your voice.—What? All night? Who with? hahaha!—Who'd've guessed!—What? What project? Jesus, are you ever crazy! But listen, I've got a new project. No, not a package, for now. But it would be a piece of cake making a package out of it.—Anyway, that'll be your problem.—What? Imagine, well just let it . . . by the way, you really put one over on me with the last contract.—You certainly did! But, okay that's water under the bridge. Listen: just picture a middle-aged man—okay?—let's say early to mid forties, close to fifty—well, precisely the generation that's going at it now.—What?—That's right, our generation, right on the nose. It'd be ridiculous if it weren't, right? Anyway, a man in his best years, something for the female audience, okay?—No, I really mean it. Something a woman can identify with. Her*

:: 258 ::

guy, right? Postwar German reconstruction man, head of family, divorced, with a kid and so on, irreproachable life so far, right? Well, one fine day, let's say on a business trip abroad—quite by chance, you see, this man suddenly realizes he is suppressing guilt! He has committed murder and knows it! But he doesn't know who the victim was. Or how it happened. And—Ne coupez-pas, mademoiselle! Ah, merde!!—Hello.—Intercosmic.—Hello! . . . ah, there you are. Did you get it all? Well: he no longer knows when and how and where. Suspenseful, right? But that's only the beginning. I mean, the opening situation.—What? No, no! You know me. I don't like flashbacks either. You know that. No way! Anyhow, that's just the basic idea. Now, the point is: do you want the rest of it to be a genuine German problem film?—What?—Well, so who cares? No, no, don't just wave it off as old hat. The times are changing again. One of my 1958 jottings says:

Autobahn restaurant near Karlsruhe. At the next table, they're overcoming the past: "Oh, you people are always saying Hitler did this wrong and that wrong and so on. But I say: just try to do it yourselves!"

Slice of life, sir. Highly topical not just in Germany, but overseas too. . . . By the way, murder isn't just a political phenomenon—but as you like! The good thing about this material is that it's flexible. We can leave it open as far as the distributor is concerned: Scientifically psychological à la Tennessee Williams, Esther's husband, yes indeed, or espionage à la Bond, with thrills galore. And if all else fails, you can always make it a social satire—No, not a screwball comedy, damn it, a satire, topical, realistic. With a knockout part for Nadine. . . .

Okay, agreed. You'll have the treatment in four weeks. In two languages. German, and also French for the gracious Monsieur le Co-Producer. Do you want it in English, too? It makes no difference to me. People like us are as fluent in the main European languages as a grand-hotel clerk. We speak them, write them, sing them in the morning while shaving. At your service, my dear piglets. Naturally, I'll keep Nadine informed. —What? Of course not. I certainly won't let her interfere too much. What do you think! We want to get the work done. I mean: complete the project. Okay then. If necessary, I'll go to bed with her. It won't satisfy her need for literary expression, but it'll calm it down for a while. Anyway, as I was saying, I'll get to you in four weeks—

With empty hands, needless to say (my name guarantees quality and absolute unreliability). With empty hands stretching out, demonstratively, to receive another advance:

—for Nature creates rich and poor in the movie business too. With the vast offer of beauty and talent, the rise of a star, for instance, can always be explained by many factors; but the ultimate reasons are always a very special aptitude and predestination for success. Likewise, any reward is left to the workings of the Eros that is peculiar to the cinema: either you never get your money or you're inundated by it like Danaë. . . . And this cornucopia shower has nothing to do with quality or punctual delivery. It may be deserved or undeserved, but it never comes like hit or miss in a game of chance. It always favors only the person of means—movie-erotic means, that means.

Here too, we would have to apply the harsh Biblical verse: FOR UNTO EVERY ONE THAT HATH SHALL BE GIVEN, AND HE SHALL HAVE ABUNDANCE, BUT FROM HIM THAT HATH NOT SHALL BE TAKEN EVEN THAT WHICH HE HATH. . . .

For two decades now, I have been relying on these words of the Holy Script, fishing in the brackish waters of postwar German film (with little more than the bait of promise and God's blessing). It will work on, so that my outstretched hands will fill up again this time too—and I shall be right back where I am now.

For this is precisely my situation: my treatment is expected in four weeks. The script in eight. Not only my producer-piglets are waiting for it; along with them, hired by them and ready to make the movie, an entire staff will be loitering in Cannes. At their head, in Nice, at the Hôtel Negresco, Nadine Carrier, a world star in that phase of waning that is transfigured by the nimbus of outstanding thespian ability.

Madame Carrier is already waiting for me here and now, in Paris, at the Hôtel Crillon. Ready to participate in the treatment. Not only artistically (Lord preserve us!) but also personally: with an open Thou-soul striving toward my I (and, needless to add, with hospitably open thighs). She's already been waiting for a week. That's how long I've been gone from the movie world.

I'm playing a risky game. Of the four weeks I've got for the treatment, I'm trying to steal three—the one remaining seems to me enough for my piglets. I plan to use these stolen three weeks for something else. Twenty-three days of peace and quiet! I'd live hidden in some small hotel, closed in, seeing nobody, hearing from nobody—in short, a recluse, a prisoner; an ideal state for a writer. The advance I'd draw would cover Christa's alimony and my son's monthly check; hence I'd be freed from my two most ruthless creditors. My contract stipulates that I'm to be left alone. That means that not even Nadine will seek me out. If I'm to keep body and soul together, I've got to keep her away from both. I'd have twenty-three whole days and nights for my book! . . .

□   □   □

MY BOOK—

That sounds as if I were carrying it within me as Nagel carries one of his, a divine mission. . . .

as if, in the flood of printer's ink inundating us, I were chosen to create the maelstrom that could stir up the human race; I, the *conscience of our race* (as if this race still existed as a race and as if a pang of conscience might help it):

the book that bears witness to man in the second half of the twentieth century and to his heroic effort to save himself from himself:

Prometheus as fire captain: using the brittle hose of humanity to put out the fire whose spark he has stolen in its name;

Daedalus astray in his own labyrinth: shouting warnings to others not to follow him;

Noah in the deluge of overpopulation: doubting whether he is truly the only choosable righteous man, the tragicomical hero of the end of a civilization, who (in order to carry out his mission with clean hands, hands that violence has not desecrated) has no other way out than literature—

literature, which has slid below the mark: as a news-supplement feature along with the mixed items on the development of the cobalt bomb, the strategic importance of space travel, specula-

:: 261 ::

tions on the outcome of the Korean conflict, the state of arms negotiations in the Congo and Indochina, the Vietnam war, the failure of disarmament negotiations.

Stephen Dedalus would have had to be a reporter to make the front page. Otherwise, his self-realization as the "conscience of our race" will remain a highly private affair.

My book *is* a private affair. Professor Hertzog (of Hamburg: Schwab's psychopompous) would say it is the wish fulfillment of my guilt complex

—final justification of an existence which isolated itself with nothing but a promise that cited that very existence. Now sundering and sin are cognates. Hence (just as sinfulness contains an obligation to do penance and can escape itself only by willingly accepting its punishment) the arrogance of such an isolation, such a sundering, can be atoned for only with the arduous demonstration that it was justified by an outstanding achievement—

My book is a promise that I've never made in so many words (not even to Gaia, and she paid through the nose!) and that cites my very existence. A promise that anyone thinks he can demand like a tribute—anyone who is mewed up in the birdcage of my life and out of it on the other side (legitimated and non-legitimated mistresses; growing and still-unconceived sons; well-meaning people of all sorts, with my friend Schwab in the lead). And they all think they have the right because, while never having promised in so many words, I have presumably pledged it with each of my bizarre actions, with each of my peculiar character traits, each of my farfetched qualities; in short, with my disconcerting way of being me-and-not-like-the-others:

—afflicted with the most annoying of all birth defects, which arouses no pity like other strokes of a stepmotherly Nature, such as a cleft palate, for instance, or a harelip, or other bizarre deformations and malformations: a hump, a hydrocephalus, all kinds of nervous and mental ailments, cretinism, falling sickness, and the like. No, indeed. This is a far more repulsive handicap, evoking arbitrary hatred against people who are totally different, fundamentally alien:

the mark of Cain: existential consciousness

stamped on those who are condemned to recognize in themselves not just any human being but man per se:

as if the capsule of their individuality had a crack through which the individual leaked out into the teeming of his species, and further out into the swarming of past generations, along the entire family tree to the root ends at the origins of the genus, and then right into the cosmos: so that every experience has an echo from the universe . . .

but instead of a human specimen of salient character emerging from such profound depths, all that comes out is an uncertain, unsteady, unsettled seeker, who listens beyond things and cannot accept empirical reality in its givenness and its causality as a complete world, and who keeps countering it with skulking nonconformity, a pigheaded if-and-but, which in an insidious way dislocates all that's conventionally established, universally believed,

until eventually nothing is reliable anymore, and reality knows as many alignments, subterfuges, and loopholes as a lawyer;

and thus, it is only fair that such a misbegotten troublemaker (if he does not wish to be counted among the dangerous fools and recalcitrant villains and be truly isolated behind bars) must ultimately accomplish something that will turn his stated ideas of interpreting the world and life into a model for a new kind of life, expanded by a new dimension

whereby, of course, my book should not have remained a private affair—and this is the dilemma that can destroy a conscientious man (for instance, Schwab).

I have been working on this book for nineteen years. Sometimes it blazes out of me. Then I can't do, or think of, anything else. I drop everything else, I ignore what's happening around me. Everything gets delayed and disorderly. Important deadlines are forgotten, excellent opportunities are lost. I fail to deliver promised work, I neglect bills, I'm sued, creditors beat down my doors. I won't see anyone, I open no mail, I disguise my voice on the telephone. I barely sleep, I eat on the run or on the edge of my desk, I stop shaving, I don't even scratch out the dirt from under my fingernails. I'm in a trance, the hours fly . . . until my writing stalls, until eventually I can't go on, and my doubts about the whole thing return, and fear, rebellion, surfeit, and finally all sacred enthusiasm is snuffed out.

Sometimes, the blaze is steadier. For a happy span of time I work a few hours every day with a clear mind. I don't have to strain my mind, I have nothing to invent. There's material galore, in heaps, in piles of paper covered with writing. I link up fragments, fill out joints, smoothen bumps. The sober craft of working and reworking makes me feel my growing abilities and capabilities. I am pumped so full of faith and confidence that I soon burden myself with other work—work that brings in cash. I then spend the money right and left: it is a light currency and I'm on top. I feel I can do the impossible, I dare to make all sorts of ambitious plans, I accept obligations I cannot honor—and I soon find myself so entangled in promises and agreements, contracts, coercions, warnings, dunnings, final notices, that I have to apply all my time and energy somehow to complete things I have hastily begun, finally to tackle things that are long overdue, further to delay things I have frivolously promised. . . .

most of these matters drag on forever; I dare not even think about my book. And the weeks wear on, the months, the years . . .

There are also periods when I am incapable of anything. I brood obtusely and stupidly over empty pages. I am unable to form a sentence out of a subject, verb, object, predicate. Nothing comes to me. Even my worst spirits abandon me: my impudence, my wit. Doubt in myself, in what I have to say and in my ability to express it, devours the energy that drove me to the desk to make a stab at it. Discouragement assails me, impairs my other work. Even (and especially) the movie scripting, long since a cynical routine, is now impossible. I dawdle through the days, grow restless, swell with impatience, long for action, want to be among people and thus avoid them. So I leap over not only my own inhibitions but all assuring distances as well, smash the neutrality of noncommittal relationships and make them personal: I soon find myself entangled in disagreeable friendships and insignificant love affairs from which I can extricate myself only in the most brutal fashion. I go on sprees, I can't get out of bed in the morning or into it at night (at least not my own). Suspicious passions break out: I collect all kinds of superfluous stuff (deluxe editions of books I won't read and sinfully expensive objects I don't know what to do with and soon give away). I tend to my appearance with the vain punctiliousness of an aging pederast, I shower my tailor, my shoemaker, my shirtmaker with orders, I spend a fortune on neckties, ascots, dressing gowns, slippers, soaps, toilet water, brushes, files, and I reach under every skirt I can find. I feel time flying by, and I run a race with it: no car is fast enough for me, I drive heedlessly at breakneck speed, I invent the necessity of dashing from place to place: the experience of speed both calms me and tires me, both whips me up and wipes me out, leaves me unfeeling and unthinking.

But my book still glows in me. It has burnt to ashes nearly a third of my life.

It screwed up my marriage with Christa and drove Dawn to the madhouse. It was the lie (never fully exposed, yet shining through everywhere and soon filtering into everything) that kept Gaia from trusting me (and thus probably helped cause her death). It turned my son (a child with eyes like well surfaces in which I was a star) into a bitter little bookkeeper of my unkept promises and unfulfilled assurances—hence turned me into a shrewder and shrewder swindler, a craftier and craftier liar, a man of no responsibility whatsoever. It turned my existence into a more and more threadbare as if.

For whatever I write, it ultimately writes *me*. Whatever I narrate, *it ultimately narrates me*. In other words, it is not *I* who live my life, *my book lives me*. And what I live and how I live are determined by the success or failure of my book.

So I live my life dissolutely, banking on the fact that my book (should it succeed) might not earn out its account but will in any case justify the expense (none of it will matter if the book does not succeed). I live into the notebook of drafts, so to speak: toward a still-incomplete fair copy. I cannot let myself be pushed by a given chance, a given state. Even in a no-exit situation, when all bridges are burned, I am exempt from decision, because decision comes not with what immediately happens but on the pages of my books.

Thus, my book lives me over and beyond the dramatic high points of my existence, from which peaks I may survey a battle-field not necessarily a field of honor, for the time being, and on which (for the time being) only others are killed in action. I myself tarry outside the events until the decision has been made, has fallen, with my book. Reality presents itself to me in two alienated ways; on the one hand, delayed in the weightlessly weighty movement of slow motion, in which my seeing eyes perceive "reality"; on the other hand (experienced by me as lived) as arbitrarily swift, uninfluenceable, and inevitable as if filmed in fast motion.

And all this has the ineluctabilty with which I, terrorized until I scream in primal horror, and yet voluptuously paralyzed by curiosity about the foreknown, dream that I am luring the old crone across the threshold of my cellar in order to murder her brutally.

I have not left this room for eight days and nights. Madame gets me wine, bread, cold meat, and eggs (which I drink raw from the shell). The handsome Pole brings the food to my room, sets it down at the door, knocks, and is usually gone by the time I open. The chambermaid comes every morning, makes the bed, and finds little else to tidy up. I don't let her touch my papers.

These papers drive me to despair. Each one directs me to another, which it refers to, which it adds to or is added to by—and which is not at hand. Because, with some other junk that I have left behind, it lies in some trunk in Hamburg, Munich, Barcelona, or Rome or some other place where my movie-parasitical hotel-lobby-loafing life has cast me away. Or even worse, it has been destroyed in some auto-da-fé like the one I have instituted here.

I find chapters that I am sure I have written down in a tighter, clearer version. But that version is lost: entire folders are missing.

I am often so sharply beset by impatience that I rip up wads of papers: sketches that strike me as totally absurd, first drafts that demonstrate my most lamentably unimaginative, inexpressive periods, unrelated notes—whatever they refer to is lost. A bric-à-brac of documents testifying to practically anything—but not the definitive shape of the book, crackpot structural designs, dozens of beginnings. . . . It all strikes me as crazy, chaotic, erroneous, and useless. I regret the time, energy, ink, and paper that I've squandered. I destroy it like something very shameful, like the trace of a scandalous past. A few hours later, I stick my head in the wastebasket, rummage around, pull out the crumpled tatters, smooth them, and arduously glue them together again. Once, I almost beat up the chambermaid (a half-dotty, gentle-eyed old woman from Brittany with the dreamy name of Monique) because she emptied the wastebasket before I could salvage a couple of irreplaceable jottings.

Sometimes, I write. I often toss out pages with rough sketches I think I have already completed. But they also contain drafts for later sections, notions, discoveries, comments, the order of the subsequent chapters—and only when I reach them do I realize what is lost.

Thus do the days go by. At night, I murder.

Yet I could have a marvelously simple time of it. Put my book aside, as so often in the past, and serve my piglets. Not just one week in four but a full eight weeks—of which still seven are left—however: seven fat expense-account weeks in Paris.
(To Schwab, in the style of a music-hall ditty:

> Oh, to be in Paree!
> And pee on the boulevard so free!

and his face: the twisted, tortured smile and the abrupt, simultaneous bloating of the cheek skin in disgust—)
Fifty-six late-summerish early-autumn days in Paris:
Slept my fill nicely in the morning, bathed nicely, bedizened myself nicely: not in the usual mobster outfit of filmmakers—turtleneck sweater, sailor's trousers, tam-o'-shanter, cowboy boots—but as a gent with a cineastic note, Douglas Fairbanks, Jr., style: café-society denizen on studio lots; a gentleman with graying temples, racing driver and record-album expert, Playboy Club member, and St. Tropez yachtsman: elk-leather coat and gold-buttoned Dunhill blazer, Battistoni shirt, Hermès necktie, Gucci shoes.

Dressed like a hack and writing like a hack.

A stroll on the Faubourg St.-Honoré: swimming through display windows: the smoky reflection of the sentries at the Élysée: *Petit Larousse* heroism: in the *rouge et noir* of the uniforms the symbol of the *hasard* of politics.

Viewed through their transparent astral phenomena in a different dimension (permeating theirs), the harvest festival of *de luxe* clothing:

feuilles d'automne in silk and velvet; over the hair-tips of fair mink the brilliance of ripe grain; bucolics in the tortoise-shell inlays of Boulle furniture; fruit splendor petrified in rock crystal and rose quartz; oxblood in the gold-embossed leather of old book bindings . . .

Interspersed: the bright, smoky-marbeled evergreen of malachite: *La vieille Russie:* hunted around for Fabergé writing paraphernalia: Monsieur collects.

(to Schwab, in a parody of Nagel:

"—*in the insatiable hamster-bustling of the battened and fattened, whose hunger grows as their larders fill, as though they knew instinctively that soon they will face a winter that knows no mercy . . .*")

Next: lunch at Prunier's: surrealist food (the corpse flesh and vaginal forms of mollusks; the barbed armors, nippers, pincers, antennae of crustaceans: horror-movie material) . . .

The afternoon outdoors, to mull over the treatment.

Versailles (the castle in the glass coffin of autumn air: Disneyland) or Fontainebleau (park landscape in Technicolor: the foliage colorfully discolored—pretty much the only thing that, along with the breasts of aging international stars, still fills the word "resplendent" with substance);

Occasionally, a quick and useless visit to the Boulogne studios to view the newcomers: new faces inspire new ideas. . . .

Sometimes, scribbling a few notes on some café terrace, for instance Fouquet's—for sentimental reasons—if the tables are still out. (I don't know if they really are. I've been locked up here too long, and it's October);

Once, at most twice, a week, dinner with Nadine, a chat and some fornication to avoid creative differences about the movie;

And in the very last week, a week of unleashed, unreflected writing: it wouldn't be the first time, God knows;

In short, the life of Riley.

After which, to be sure, I would reach the far end of Never-neverland: where you have to eat your way out through the enclosing mountain, and it's not made of rice:

for six solid weeks: critical objections from the piglets (compared with whose artistic empathy Nadine's is a gift of the Muses);

at least six more weeks: changes from the distributor (it is not true that man is descended from the ape: the ape is a man who has evolved himself back to nature because of his embarrassment at being human);

another six weeks: changes from the director (who, soon united with Nadine in spirit and in bed, has a dreadful say in the matter)—

summa summarum: four and a half months of coprophagia.

But that's the normal overhead: I have to reckon with it. I had reckoned with it when planning to do what I had originally intended to do: misappropriate three of the four weeks from the movies (and from cineastic existence) and write in monastic isolation through the blue-gold days and the quietly misty evenings—

not the agreed-upon treatment, but my book. . . .

I had pegged all my hopes on being able to do it. Finally to put together a part of this book large and lucid enough to convince Scherping that I still was worth another publishers' advance. That way I could have sent the piglets and their goddamn cinema to hell and I'd have been free for my book—

if my dream had not afflicted me—and with it Schwab. I've squandered the last seven days and nights with the two of them—and thereby all the hope I set in my book.

◻   ◻   ◻

MY ROTTEN EXPERIENCE in these past few days and nights teaches me that I cannot be precise enough in my jottings:

I write this in Room 26 of the Hôtel Épicure on the rue du Roi Philibert, a filthy little side street off the Avenue des Ternes, veering acutely from the end of the last line of houses on the avenue and forming a sharp angle with the Place des Ternes.

At the point where it crosses the avenue, a couple of vegetable carts supply Parisian coloring: the color splotches that we (not unversed in art history) experience as *Impressionistic;* and, in the spider-legged spokes of the cartwheels, that *certain French frothiness* of all kitsch practitioners since Dufy:

—a piece of so-called genuine and typical Paris, which, in folkloristic sentimentality, we ramble after, seeking it in more and more hidden, more and more remote corners, in order to feel the melancholy of watching it disappear here too—whereas it is no longer so much Parisian as just suburbanly colorful and provincially contemplative and characteristic of a vanished era that has produced a similar atmosphere everywhere in the once not yet metastatically proliferating metropoles and that survives most tenaciously where the dreadful development is slower, so that sporadic impressions caught today in Copenhagen or Turino often seem more Parisian than Paris itself—

Thus the rue du Roi Philibert is a so-called picturesque nook. During the day, garbage is dumped on the sidewalk. Once in a blue week, a pack of Chaplinesque slapstickers in baggy overalls show up, municipal street cleaner's caps on their curly hair, cigarette butts behind their ears, and gigantic, cumbersome brooms like halberds under their arms. They turn the hydrant on at one corner of the street and send the filth swimming to the other corner. At night, a couple of cheap hookers come roaming around from the Place des Ternes, withdrawing into doorways at any sign of police. After midnight (like now: it must be close to one A.M.), the area is perilously quiet and empty except for occasional auto tires whimpering around the dead square—spookily, as though ghosts were having a drag race.

I'm well concealed here from my piglets and Nadine: isolated in the dense, close square of the walls of this room, deep in the narrow-chested, box-like structure of the shabby hotel, whose fire walls are slapped on the half-timber gables of the houses behind:

former stables converted into petit bourgeois homes, presumably; their yards—with mangy geranium window boxes, atrophying jasmine bushes, and oleander saplings in weathered tubs—preserve the defoliating poetry of the horse-and-buggy world, the autumn efflorescence of mankind preparing for a journey of no return.

From the wallpaper's sharp floral pattern (once a playground for bedbugs), repeated in the bedcover and the slipcover of the upholstered chair, a thousand round eyes peer at me—wondering whether I can muster the patience to remain by myself. . . .

they too whoosh away when I glance up to catch them unawares, and all I see are insignificant roses badly printed on bad paper and cheap cretonne in the tight-meshed tangle of their thorn twigs. Oh, no; no prince will break through them and stagger back in disappointment upon finding me here instead of the Sleeping Beauty.

Here, I am finally at home: nestling in my murderer's den like a fetus in its swollen womb, lovingly designed by Professor Leblanc's freckled hand: a ghastly little creature cozily curled up for the somersault of life from the mouth of the womb into the crouched burial position of Stone Age people, woeful little legs drawn up to the blistered forehead, webbed little fists furiously clenched against the blind pug face . . .

In general, there's a lot of homey secrecy here, in Leblanc's terms: the brutal iron coat hook on the door (clinical white enamel) is waiting for cattle to slaughter, as if a halved woman were hanging from it, meticulously prepared by the professor's artistic, carrot-haired hand:

Gaia's splendidly fleshy, exotic leg (slightly bent at the knee, the foot in the high-heeled shoe of society whores), testifying to the humanity of the fallow anatomy above it:

over the massive thigh, in the evening-shadow tones of the shiny mulatto skin, pouring, as if smoked, from the tender, mucus-glistening constriction of the silk stocking, the elegant arc of the abdominal-wall cross section curves into the intensely downy parabola summit of the vagina, tipping inwardly into the blossom pistil of the uterus—

"Et je vous assure, mon cher ami: c'est pareil chez les noires comme chez les blanches—d'ailleurs, ne me dites pas que vous avez senti la moindre différence"—

over it, the concave red-white-red stripes of the rib cage—

"Et voyez-vous: l'intérieur du thorax est tout à fait—mais tout à fait égal chez les unes comme chez les autres: bien entendu à l'extérieur il y a quand même des variantes. . ."

and from the throat, as if blown by the pipe of an art-glass blower: a wolf-toothed grin, forcing its way like cigarette smoke through the labyrinth of the frontal sinus and nasal cavity.

"C'est ça, mon cher: ce que vous avez aimé!"

I sit like a maggot in the core of night.

The glow of the lamp on the dresser where I write (I've covered the mirror) peels a slanting hollow cone of yellow light from the darkness:

in it, I huddle over my papers (a spider caught in my own web).

The light gathers around my feet in an elliptical puddle; in it, I suck in my shadow.

Here I dwell in the core of nightly stilless. The telephone at the switchboard (two floors below me) futilely bores into the stillness with its dull buzzing. It is doomed to be ignored. The handsome Pole is asleep, or reads, with world-remote ardor, one of his detective stories. (Or is he with some woman somewhere in the box contruction of rooms? It's none of my business anymore.) The silence is too thick for the buzzing to thread its way through. The sound merely sews it thicker, a small-stitch quivering of desperate impatience, pausing only to resume, like the stickily entangled murmur of a fly on sized paper

(the buzzing fly is surrounded by the cringing black corpses of its fellow flies that have buzzed away their lives into the unrepentant nights of the Hôtel Épicure:

corpses of souls: when I was a child, I thought of flypaper whenever I saw the glow of candles in the old honey-gold of the effigies of saints: it had grown fat with the souls that stuck to it—)

And I try to picture the nights when it was *my* patience that let the buzzing of the switchboard telephone bore across a thousand leagues into the night stillness of the sleepers here and vainly shrill away against the vicious despotism of their dreams.

Back then, I was assaulted by a different madness: love.
I loved Dawn.
I was far away from her: in Hamburg, in the apartment I had set up *for us* in a lover's world-embracing yearning for happiness—
at number 7 Heilwigstrasse:

as if the address were an incantation conjuring up that self-effacing bourgeois happiness that both of us knew would never be granted us, could never be granted us, because of fate: not admitted by our indicated history, because we would thus have lost what had driven us to each other: the other yearning inside us, unresponsive, without a precise aim, making us susceptible to any insanity, a yearning beyond ourselves, steering our lives toward each other in a different way: like two parallel lines meeting at infinity, in the beyond of a story worth telling—

I loved—and as if in this state not only did the primal motifs of nature have to keep sounding but also, along with the leitmotif of personal fate, its full theme, so in this love story there was a cool-jazz repetition of what had been a trumpeted marching song of my love for Christa (and was to be an atonal *valse musette* with Gaia): from building the nest to devouring the male, from the blissful isolation *à deux* to the desperate effort to reattain someone who had become unattainable.

The Apartment

(this time):
A model shell of twosomeness in the immediate present, a space-ship for the icy spheres of absolute earthly happiness. We live in style, the ordinary style of the era. We live in splendid isolation, which screams to be published in all the appropriate big-circulation maga-

zines on the arts of living and interior decoration (Oeil, House and Gar-
den, House Beautiful, Schöner Wohnen): the home of the successful
screenwriter and his enchanting companion on this stretch-of-the-
road-of-life, a star model from New England, to be seen repeatedly in
Vogue, Harper's Bazaar, Elle, Grazia. *Hence, the fragrance of the wide*
world even in the space-efficient kitchenette: Chinese spices, hand-
forged iron pots for Indonesian rice specialties, shashlik skewers,
Swedish designer flatware, health foods (Bauhaus style of nutrition
culture: purely functional wheat germ, soybean extract, sea salt, brown
sugar). A yoga board for bathroom gymnastics. The house bar is a
Hammond organ of luxury consumptions: Drambuie and Izarra, Pass-
over wine, tequila, raki. A record collection with early English church
music, Vivaldi, Earl Garner, Strauss (Ariadne), Boulez. The furniture
(two rooms plus sleeping alcove) showing cultural growth in fast mo-
tion: English walnut (Queen Anne) combined with Finnish pieces
(mass-produced). The knickknacks: pre-Columbian, Gold Coast, Tong
Dynasty, Dada. On the walls: samples of Arabic script, ancient Coptic
woven fragments, and the works of masters in whose names Tarzan's
gurgling jungle shriek is abstracted into the flashing, smashing, crash-
ing of the spaceship when it shatters against the satellite: Braque! Arp!
Picasso! Wols! . . .

I lay in the Corbusier armchair (an abstract warrior of steel,
fur, and leather), holding the telephone (enameled in clinical
white) to my ear:

I was drinking in the vast space of night from it: mythical: like
a man who has to drink the ocean in order to reach an island
where his happiness is exiled:

the space of night that separated me from Dawn.

She was in Paris in the Hôtel Épicure. Why didn't she answer?
Was she ill? Cheating on me? Was she wandering in a daze
through the streets of the *bright underworld?* I believed that my
voice had the power to call her back to me (*Orpheus*—Schwab
had found this image; and I reveled in the way he flinched when I
then quoted that line from Cocteau's *Orphée,* "Go on! Go back
home to your mud!")

During the day, it was easy to get through on the telephone. I
was then told: *"Mademoiselle vient de sortir. Non, m'sieur, elle
n'a pas laissé de message"* (the hated snail-fed indifference in

Madame's voice). "*Et vous même? Vous allez bien? . . . Non, j'en sais rien, m'sieur. D'habitude, elle rentre assez tard*" (*d'habitude* a syntactical formation of perfidious smugness). "*Non, m'sieur, elle était à la maison hier. . . . Oui, elle a passé toute la journée dans sa chambre*" (and wouldn't take my calls . . . and why does Madame's fat laryngophony gloat? Is she, too, jealous of the handsome Pole? Her hatred of Dawn is obvious). "*Certainement, m'sieur: le moment où elle rentrera. . . . Oui, oui, j'ai votre numéro. Non, je n'y manquerai pas. À bientôt, m*—"

I waited until midnight. Then I couldn't stand it anymore. I grabbed the phone like an alcoholic grabbing a bottle.

(Schwab: how greedily he interrogated me about my futile attempts to resist. "You seriously mean"—a puff on the cigarette in the trembling fingers, smoked to a dark brown like an old meerschaum pipe—"you seriously mean that these are self-imposed spiritual drills? Compulsory soul-testing exercises, as it were—to test our powerlessness? Do we not know it precisely enough?")

I was practicing anthracite-gray magic:

By combining letters and numbers in a circle of mysterious correspondences, I evoked the voice of a servant of the spirits into the telephone receiver:

"Hello, this is long-distance operator four."

Language of pure poetry: a key word for the universe

I uttered a magic formula of words and numbers, and the locks to astral space burst open:

The rustle of the vast expanse of night

In its echo the world was dissolved. Like charring paper, the shadows crackled across the earth, melting in the smoke of sounds. Mystery flew in whooshing signals from continent to continent: sounds flashed like quick silver fish swallowed by the leviathan of darkness. Twittering voices slipped like white mice into the enormous hole of blackness. . . .

Then, far, far away, the broken line of a repeated fluting came filtering through: flickering and fading like a will-o'-the-wisp, flickering and fading, it sewed the tiny stitches of its seam into the moor of the celestial expanses:

—utterly yearning—tadpole of the Word: in the seed water of the umlaut—the unborn consonants—

In the great maternal belly of night, it procreated *time-space*

—tape measure of my patiently stretched impatience—

The voices of spirits were startled. They fluttered in chaos like pale birds (the powdering of gulls in the headlight rays when I drove through the night to my son in Holland):

One voice close by: "Are you still speaking?"
Another half remote: "You still don't have a connection?"
One very far: "Paris, hello, Paris?"
Far, far away, another coming toward me: "Le numéro ne répond pas, m'sieur."
Again, the half-remote one: "Hamburg, can you hear me? The party in Paris is not answering!"
The close voice, lunging: "The party in Paris is not picking up."

I said, "Please keep trying. Someone has to answer. It's a hotel." The last sentence stood like a mountain: planted by Faith.

I listened to my own voice passing through the cosmos. My breath had thrust its way between me and the echoing expanses. My breath perched on my chest like a contented tomcat: a purring of the secret called I.

I was no longer a magician. I no longer conjured up lower, subservient spirits in order to awaken a slumbering corpse and have her follow me, somnambulantly. Something more powerful had emerged from me, walking through the night with my voice, like the word of an archangel:

It announced something to the anguished waker: the tiding of *Patience.*

Beneath it, the earth had gone wintry rigid: a poor people's land in the broken poetry of a collage: snowy expanses of paper, forests scattered like shreds of felt; the rusty wire ribbing of the plowland in the stringwork of roads, glass shards, glittering like ponds—and settlements like Bethlehem: humble earth-stars, protected from waning by God's hollow hand.

My voice passed over them, across a thousand leagues, to arouse again the sparse rippling of the strand of pearls, the monosyllabic flute tones:

Tracer trajectory fading in its goal—

the tiding of patience cleaved to the telephone switchboard in the Hôtel Épicure.

Here, it was transformed into a desperately malicious buzzing, and it sawed away ineffectively on the trunk of the stillness

—which had grown into the stairway chasms with crooked roots and sprouted its branches into the corridors and rustled its dark foliage in the rooms over the gaping mouths of the sleepers—

sawed away and dulled its teeth with each of its pulls.

This went on night after night from twelve to four. Then, finally asleep, I murdered an old charwoman in a dream.

The jittery disquiet of love. That beatific state of being beside oneself. High frequency of existence in full, immediate presentness. A sporadic condition, announced by a preliminary stage of amorous inclination; until chance selects a specific woman, every female is a potential love object—which may explain some of my relapses with Nadine.

Meanwhile, the pure gifts of God: cheerful, uncomplicated, noncommittal bedroom episodes (similar to periods of effortless success when writing: gambler's luck: being in harmony with the cosmos: FOR UNTO EVERY ONE THAT HATH SHALL BE GIVEN . . .)

what is spared in such encounters? What remains untouched, unstirred? Does so-called love dig deeper into the mire at the bottom of our souls? Does it unearth things more deeply hidden there—more es-

sential, more fundamental things? And what is it that makes one encounter cheerful, well tempered, pleasant, enriching, carefree, while another, equally random, initially perhaps even more trivial, crashes into our lives with all the impact of destiny?

Christa's devouring mouth in the canteen of the Nuremberg law court . . . and years of our tortured efforts to reach each other, of my tormented attempts to reach her, like a deaf-mute trying to recite a poem taking shape within him . . .

and in contrast: Gisela, whom I first see as she crosses the bombed-out railroad terminal of Hamburg, her head high, her figure tall, slender, unapproachable—a queen. She strides through the mouse-gray teeming of refugees and belated home-comers, the war-damaged and the war-dazed, looking neither to the right nor to the left. More vision than a tangible reality, she passes through the medieval misery of this crowded humanity of mislived lives, through the mob of rags and worm-eaten flesh, like a beautiful ship through brackish water, *le beau navire* of eternal boyhood dreams, a ship's figurehead of whom no longer believed promises of breathtaking experience surge up again—

and I dare not follow her; I want to keep her as a vision, reserved for all possibilities of experience. Nor would it make sense to follow her, accost her: as wild, as adventurous as the time may be, this woman is beyond the vulgarity of such adventure.

It is futile to hope that I will ever see her again: the age is medieval, nations are migrating, the wind of our time is driving them along like chaff, God alone may know where they come from, where they are going . . . only her majestic stride, long, swift, and light, is purposeful; even though her purpose and her destination may be unnamable and far away from here, she bears the certainty of reaching her goal—

and then, several weeks later

(it is the year of OUR LORD 1947, the Ice Age is approaching its bitter end; before passing into the new phase of the world, it sinks its teeth one last time into the survivors' rubble cities, coating their makeshift lodgings and their woeful rags and trash with ice, their hunger swellings and reconstruction dreams, the final hopes of the timid, the finest intentions of the valiant . . .

but the tougher souls will survive this too, will live to see the approaching year of OUR LORD 1948 and thereby the impure miracle of the new epoch:

the pitiless, the greedier and greedier souls, survive ever and always; and with them, those who are eternally outside reality, the eternal dreamers;

the former and the latter are destined to become the founding fathers of the mankind of tomorrow; fools and somnambulists, *criminals and monks:*

this is the stuff with which (on which) they will create the tremendous conjuring trick of the currency cut, the sinister prestidigitation of the bursting-out-all-over economic efflorescence and thus the new reality:

the abstract world of the prosperity-termites in the baleful profiteering, proliferating administration of deranged production and demented consumption: the horrible, abortive total of identical life-drained days in the nightmare geometry of cities of utilitarian buildings, shooting up like crystals in some nasty mother liquid:

Already built into the trashy boxiness are the ruins of tomorrow, the tin-and-concrete wasteland of secondhand Americana, with mange-belts of rust and mortar, seething and teeming with ever swelling, swarming masses of more and more colorless more and more dissatisfied more and more demanding more and more hopeless more and more evil supermarket consumers in ever swifter, tinnier, more hastily glued-together, more and more perilous vehicles. roadside café eaters with empty eyes over munching chewing kneading swallowing mouths . . .

Christa's empty, inward gaze into the emptiness beyond the wall of the Fürth law court, while the kneading, munching, chewing swallowing of her thrifty lips betrayed the secret (guarded by good breeding) of wanton voraciousness: a vision of the future, a blueprint of the world our son was to be born into:

the emptiness in the gaze of the innocent culprits, guilty of losing the wonderful possibilities that were soon to be forfeited forever, with that final start of the new era in 1948.)

the time I'm telling you about is still 1947; once more, after twelve years of bitter biting, the Ice Age has sunk its teeth in: one evening, of a day drawing to a close as the future dawns (the food rations are approaching those of Buchenwald, but the film industry is already resurrected), during one of my aimless strolls through the world of the lotus eaters (the first star is already sharply needled into the turnip-water-stained sky over a starving Hamburg), I wandered into the red-light district of the Gänsemarkt

(long since vanished, this ultimate remnant of the old walkway district, now replaced by a newspaper tycoon's high-rise with a utilitarian geometry towering into emptiness—

but at that time, it was a place of profound Christmastide expectations, a stronghold of seething, sap-driving, vital warmth and the seashell-carbolic-acid smell of whore cunts, an El Dorado of sexual plight and the torment of erotic fantasies,

in the honey light of dim bulbs in windows at the base of the swiftly darkening shafts between half-timber gables on bowing gingerbread houses, the sparkle of promises shimmers like a treasure half buried in a dark riverbed: the Rhein gold of rubble-dwellers, the abstract fabled wealth of association

water-sprite-shiny female flesh bursting through the fish baskets of bodices, smoothly caught in the black nets of can-can stockings; lascivious gaping coral lips millipedes of false eyelashes peacock-blue-green mother-o'-pearl of mascaraed eyelids; blond hair like beer foam, black hair grease-enameled in piglet-tail whorls, painted on floury-powderd skin; cartwheel hats the plunder of ostrich plumes the impudent fire of crab-red wigs over violet feather boas the pale medusas of tremendous breasts fat arms like dragon bodies guarding the grottos of acrid-smelling shaven armpits the lacing of hams of tremendous matron-thighs high-heeled champagne-bottle-shaped boots tightly buttoned up to the jellied-meat of old knees emaciation-larvae of weakness-sweaty-cellar-child-skinniness back-courtyard-vileness of eyes and words knife-sharp voices and the clatter of keys on the salon windowpanes)

and there—I cannot believe my eyes, but there she is: the same woman; the woman I saw just a few short weeks ago, striding as proud as a queen through the tattered railroad terminal.

She sits with her back beautifully straight, gazing imperturbably out into the street. Her full, rusty-brown hair is swept up;

she wears nothing but a lightweight sleeveless sweater with a narrow turtleneck and very short velvet pants (years later, they would be all the rage as so-called hotpants; years later, every woman will dress like a whore); her wonderful long legs are bare; her feet are in flat suede pumps.

I purchase a quick tumble in the hay; she handles it with sovereign and businesslike dispatch, merely stripping off her hotpants; only after I place a bonus on the table is she willing to pull the sweater over her head. She is not wearing a bra, her breasts are magnificent. She knows how beautiful she is, and she is intelligent enough to know that such beauty counts for little here; the important things here are stylization, alienation from reality, denial of "reality," which the imagination puts, unrestrictedly, into the splendors of its creations. This doesn't bother her; nothing fazes her: she is sovereign, utterly self-confident.

Our mating takes place on a narrow, greasy sofa; the room is tiny and messy, repugnantly appointed with teasing effects in the worst petit bourgeois taste; one can smell the bedbugs in every nook and cranny. The thin door cannot be locked, it opens to a stairway that creaks continually under footsteps, voices speak as loud and as near as if they were with us in the room. The whole place smells of chamber pots and disinfectants.

I have to overcome an instant of panic, which brings back a memory

a similarly horrible room in an ill-famed hotel in Vienna: Cousin Wolfgang and I have saved up enough from our ludicrously meager allowance to pay for a cheap hooker. The instant we accost her, our nerves flutter: we are still in school and are tormented with fear of being caught, of not having enough money, of getting into an ugly scene with her pimp, of getting the clap. When we are asked which of us is to go first, Wolfgang takes off: he can't get himself to find the lamentable creature desirable: everything disgusts him: the place, the circumstances, the thought of himself in these lower depths. I am just as disgusted, but more resolute. He remains outside the door, waiting for me. But I too fail. I too am incapable of letting natural drives prevail over upbringing: the girl's Käthe Kollwitz face, her ragged little breasts and pointed shoulders both move and repel me, the bushy triangle of her colorless pubic hair fills me with horror. I stick out my hand, ap-

parently touch something like a big boil, and wince. Since I offer no sign of being ready, she becomes impatient, milking and tugging me, and finally she lets out a string of filthy words, but I am stubborn, I have to show Wolfgang I am man enough to overcome the sentimental philistine in me. My behavior becomes a symbolic act of protest: my defiant renunciation of the spirit of my formative years in Vienna and their bogus aesthetics as I undergo this test to show I am capable of striding unfazed through such filth, freeing myself of Uncle Helmuth Aunt Hertha Aunt Selma and everything they are and feel, think and represent. I would like to penetrate the girl as if I were boring a knife into Cousin Wolfgang's heart. . . .

But the situation of 1947 in Hamburg is different: I am free, virtually free-floating, as if I were on a different star with a weaker force of gravity. The failure of my efforts to get close to Christa has released me from my last tie. Now there is nothing left for me to rebel against. My soul is calm. I can have pure enjoyment; the shining slice of little windows under the Biedermeier gable on the house opposite is beautiful in the reflected golden light from below in the street. The young woman is beautiful. Her soul too is calm. Neither of us feels much pleasure, it is a business transaction. In order to reach orgasm, I have to shut my eyes and imagine following her after seeing her stride through the tattered terminal, accosting her and properly seducing her, against her will, she being overpowered by the eroticism of adventure, swept away, giving in. . . . I am grateful to her for this dream.

We talk afterward for the length of a cigarette. Her speech has an East German flavor: she is from Upper Silesia, probably the daughter of Germanized Poles (she does not tell me her last name). I ask her whether she would care to have a cognac with me; her answer is clear, resolute, and scrupulous: her percentage of the overcharge on a mere two glasses of cognac will not make up for the loss of possible business during the time we would spend drinking them, but if I ordered a whole bottle, she would be willing to chat with me for an hour.

She smiles. Her profession as a hooker, she says, consists mainly of such tourist-trapping. Contrary to the popular conception, there is a great deal more talking and boozing in a whore-house than there is sex. As for the latter, her life here is presumably calmer than that of many a decent Hamburg housewife.

The cognac is wretched and many times more expensive than a select one would be at Maxim's in Paris, but that doesn't bother me; my pockets are stuffed with movie money—an inflative currency, especially when handed out in one as worthless as the Reichsmark. My delight with the girl increases. She merely sips, but tells me with her open, comradely smile that I can imagine she knows all sorts of tricks to make believe she is drinking like a lord while actually pouring the cognac away; so, for my own sake, I shouldn't insist that she keep up with me. Nor can she drink, she adds: alcohol is one of the drugs that wreck the lives of the girls in the whorehouses along this street.

I ask her if she has been plying her trade for a long time? No, she says, only a few months. But you can work your way in very quickly, if you're not stupid. Unfortunately, most of the girls are. Practically any girl who winds up on the street owes it to stupidity or laziness.

And what about her? How did she wind up here? I ask, ready for some tale of high drama.

She came to Hamburg as a refugee, she says obligingly and without pathos, and then she found herself on the street. Her parents had insisted that she get out of Upper Silesia when the Russians came, with the first wave. They themselves were supposed to come later, but they didn't make it; they are still there or else they've vanished; she hasn't heard from them. "But they wanted to get me out," she says, and laughs, "so that the Russians wouldn't rape me." The Russians caught up with her and rolled over her before she was even halfway to Berlin. The combat troops barely had time for raping; that came only with the stragglers, in Berlin.

The early time was bitter in every way: hunger, cold, and constant menace. Still, people were as helpful as they could be—something like an "emergency humanity." (I ask her where she got that phrase; she says she made it up, just now.) She took off for western Germany in fairly hazardous circumstances, but she doesn't go into detail (she doesn't give me the particulars until a later time). At first, she moved in temporarily with distant relatives in Schleswig-Holstein (in a one-horse town near Preetz: a few months later, I remember, we went there to delight in the good people's astonishment at our elegance). But the narrow-minded, intimidated philistines, in a fever of concern about their meager property (they ran a grocery; at night, behind tightly closed shutters, they devoured the sausages they kept hidden during the day), had been so reluctant to take her in that she left after a short time—all the more hastily since the paterfamilias had, of course, made a pass at her. She went to Hamburg.

"Within a week, I realized I'd have to wind up in some bed or die in the street," she tells me imperturbably. "I've never taken such long walks in my life—and never in such thin dresses and on such an empty stomach. One day, I ended up on this street. At first, I didn't know what it was, but soon it hit me. It was morning, scarcely any clientele. I got to talking to the girls, and they were friendly and nice and understanding. After my country relatives and the railroad policemen who kicked me out of the waiting room when, like hundreds of other people, I tried to warm up there, except that I came several days in a row—after all that, I felt at home here. I asked the girls what things were like for them here, and what you had to do to get into one of the houses, and they all told me to do it; they said I should go to the police and register."

She explains that the whorehouses are city-owned. They are run like rooming houses, leased as concessions to veterans of the trade who have saved enough money and have squeaky-clean police records. The girls pay rent and get a percentage of the receipts, plus any personal bonuses from the johns. "But most of the girls fritter away their money and start boozing, or else they play cards or snort cocaine or do it with other women, and that's how they go down the drain—they're always very irritable, and they can't come with the johns. . . . The worst thing here is boredom."

What does she do about it? I ask.

"I observe," she says. "I never get bored. Although I used to."

When was that?

At school, and then later, when she worked for a photographer.

"If you ever want to get out of this someday," I say, "perhaps I can help you find a job. I've got movie connections. For a girl with experience in photography, there must be work in the movies: maybe editing; that's not so boring."

She muses for a while, her elbow propped up, her hand, holding a cigarette, on her temple. "I want to stay here until I've saved up a nice tidy sum. I'm in no danger of going down the drain here. I don't like alcohol or drugs or other girls. I want to be a first-class hooker— one who gets top money. To do that, I have to specialize in something. S and M is a pretty sure gimmick. You wouldn't believe that most of these guys come here for some kind of kinky S and M. They can fuck all they like anywhere else without paying. We make our money off guys with fantasies in their heads and their lower bodies. And homeless guys like you."

I toast her. The stuff she's told me so far is small talk, so to speak. But the last sentence establishes a personal relationship. I desire her intensely. I suggest going to the sofa again. Any time, she says, without stirring; naturally, I have to pay for the second time just as for the first. "Despite the bottle of cognac?" I protest. Despite the bottle of cognac, she replies, unruffled. "But you'll have most of it left." Not even jokes can soften her heart. I shell out the bills on the table, and she instantly rises, pulling her sweater up over her head and the velvet hotpants down.

During the year we were friendly (until the birth of my and Christa's son, when a fit of philistine morality persuaded me to break up this friendly, intimate intercourse with a brothel whore: after all, our son was a Hamburg native; his respectability was all-important)—during that full year granted to us by our foot-loose and fancy-free, often rip-roaring, always stimulating, high-spirited friendship, I never once succeeded in sleeping with her without first paying the set fee. No matter what I did to try to change her mind—cunning, tenderness, violence, even sneak attacks—she was adamant, as if she would be violating an oath by giving herself just once without payment, and as if it would bring the entire structure of her goals and plans crashing about her ears . . .

and I insisted on it stubbornly, obsessively, as if my fate hinged on a victory over her, over her implacable refusal—my entire fate, the realization or failure not only of my personality but of all my goals and plans . . .

for it was then, during the early weeks of my tempestuously erupting friendship with Gisela the whore (the Ice Age was clamping down one last time, and the teeth of the winter of 1947 cracked and splintered: I can recall sudden puffs of soft spring wind wafting unexpectedly through the days)—it was then that it happened, that I left something behind in her room, the copy of my treatment for a big movie project at Astra Film Art, commissioned by my primordial piglets Stoffel and Associates; and one of her clients, the then rather small-scale but later big-time publisher Scherping, found the manuscript and read it and excitedly passed it on to his editor J.S., ordering him to track down its author immediately, so that this genius, evidently as yet undiscovered for *belles lettres* and hence lying fallow, might instantly write a book (to wit, about wartime experiences, which I did not have, to be sure, but which were dealt with in the film treatment) and thus give mankind the masterpiece of the era, the great novel of the waning century . . .

and how we laughed at this, my accomplice, the hooker Gisela, and I! How amused we were when she first described Scherping to me, with his quaint *bonhomie* and transparent slyness, his yokelish cunning when he got her to impose and inflict punishments on him, as if he himself had not invented the reason for them, had not begged to be punished (Gisela now specialized in discipline, and that sort of thing gets around quickly in the appropriate circles) . . . our bliss when she told me about his blubbering ("If only just once I could be beaten, whipped, tormented for something I had *really* done"—for Nagel's best-sellers, for instance).

and S., Scherping's emissary, striding through the red-light district "like a blind seer," head thrown back, fish-blue eyes looking neither to the right nor to the left, pride in the high thinker's brow, humility about the mouth twisted in disgust, slippery desire in the soft, moist flesh of the twitching lips—she described him with the skill of a private eye. Later he would become my friend and fellow sufferer in literary limbo, Johannes Schwab, whose weighty appearance I did not tire of describing. But during those last months of the Ice Age, he was as skinny as anyone else: truly, it was a slender nation of Germans in the year 1947! Gisela masterfully evoked his large, clumsy frame and klutzy Martin Luther head with the wind of culture blowing in the luxuriant (still flaxen) hair, the bottle-bottom-thick eyeglasses and the ill-fitting baggy-seated tweed suit. He was such a model of the world's idea of a German intellectual, she told me, that when he first appeared in the whorehouse street, the cry "the Herr Professor!" leaped from window to window along the entire alley, from one thickly reddened whore mouth to the next . . .

and one of the girls, beautiful Heli, still young and warmhearted, like freshly baked bread, trustingly dedicated to the foolish faith that the world contains a God-willed, occasionally disturbed, but always gloriously restored order, in which a small, well-to-do portion of mankind, better instructed in the spoken, written, and printed word, is, in moral terms, superior to the larger, poorer, less educated portion and determines which among the lower born it will raise to its level—beautiful Heli fell hopelessly in love with Schwab: the "educated man," happily able to read and write. . . .

what a blessing: to be loved by a whore, who submits to anyone, whom anyone uses unhesitatingly, and to be loved by her because of your superior dealings with language, which is similarly a whore, whom everyone (aside from a chosen few) uses unhesitatingly; to be loved by her unreservedly, giving herself with all the power and powerlessness of feeling, beyond the never wholly dissolved remnant of hatred and disgust that lurks in every love, beyond the struggle between the sexes, a battle never waged to the point of purification . . .

how greatly I envied him, Johannes Schwab, the Scherping Publishers editor, sent to me with the evil angelic tidings of literary conception, and how often and how excitedly we spoke of it, Gisela and I—

for what we had—no: it couldn't be called love. It would never have occurred to us, Gisela and me, to call it that. Mutual attraction, affection, great liking—yes: all that. But not the mawkishness of love. Not its moistening need for tenderness. No suffering whatsoever at the withdrawal of affection. No urging and shaking and quaking to find entry into the soul of the other (who doesn't understand what it's all about). No metaphysics, but all the brisker, all the more pleasurable copulation: the fixed advance payment eliminated any possibility of misunderstanding even here; it was sexual intercourse without dross or sediment, an art form with itself as its own subject, so to speak, not "*it means*" but "*it is.*"

No: it was not love, thank goodness, that made Gisela a pure joy for me (and perhaps me for her), more cherished in memory than some of my great passions. We were quite in control of our well-tempered, well-balanced, well-wishing and -meaning emotions. Between our brain glands and our reproductive glands (both delightfully animated), our metabolisms functioned perfectly, no increased blood pressure because of spiritual exuberance, no diaphragm flickering from psychic interference with our calm metabolic rhythms. Our mutual affection was as cool and deep as a well, and we did not even try to wage the battle of the sexes; we confronted each other in an armed-to-the-teeth armistice in which sex did not interfere but ran conflict free on the ball bearings of financial—not sentimental—settlement, ruffled neither by the transcendent nor certainly by the transcendental.

So we were also spared the torments of jealousy; our friendship was purged of this mire. Moreover, the idea that she slept with other men or helped them to achieve pleasure in a different way (always pasteurized by financial settlement) did not deflate my ego; instead, it inflated and expanded my experience, for the ones she found worth mentioning were not lovers glued to her by the mucous filaments of sentiment but interesting cases of sexual psychology.

(*Cousin Wolfgang, taking the volume of Krafft-Ebing from my hand and thoughtfully weighing it, says: "For me, dear cousin, this is nothing but the grossest obscenity," and I, quoting my favorite verse from Romeo and Juliet, "Call me but love, and I'll be new baptiz'd. . . .")*

Sometimes those lovers were authors of felicitous linguistic creations, which we preserved like objects found during a stroll, seashells and colored pebbles (the dockworker, a heavy man, crying out in his ejaculation, "Trials and tribulations!" or the retired cavalry officer expressing his delight at the fullness of her breasts with the words "If a flea galloped over them, it would split a hoof!")

and the endless fun of wandering through Hamburg in quest of adventure. That summer (it seemed like the first summer in decades), when the miracle of the currency cut had taken place, the shops began to fill up; production was not yet going full blast, spewing out junk, like today, so there was still prewar merchandise from secret warehouses, handmade things, absolutely genuine; and she went shopping with me. She had astonishing amounts of money and she spent it judiciously on top-drawer, durable goods chosen to last: leather coats, fine furs, handmade shoes, silk stockings (not by the dozen but by the half-dozen dozen), cosmetics by the carload, jewelry (completely flawless one-carat diamonds); she paid cash for everything and was treated like a princess—

and the shock, the terror, the stupid confusion in the eyes of a salesman or store manager who recognized her, who might have been her customer the day before, the inner struggle in the decent, law-abiding citizen, who was swayed only by business interests . . .

We rented a car, and I taught her how to drive. We motored deep into the Holstein countryside and the Lüneburg Heath, fetched up at rustic inns, lay under firs in the sandy grass (yes, indeed; even when I was overcome by libidinous stirrings there, I had to pay in advance), hiked barefoot through the silt of Baltic beaches, danced at farmers' festivals and on the casino terrace in Timmendorf—

and the incessant awareness in our conversations, in our laughter, in our delightful mutual silence, in our thoughts of one another when we were apart—the heart-lifting awareness of an extraordinarily sovereign, utterly unassailable situation

("What can happen to me now?" she used to say. "Disease, death—fine, that's nature. But otherwise? So what if the Russians come. I'll receive them like anyone else. With champagne, if they want it—and pay me for it.")

the ether-clear awareness of living at the extreme boundary of existence, on the razor's edge, in perfect freedom—this intoxicated us like a drug high.

Once, I was giving her a driving lesson along a country road, and we stopped at the entrance to the highway, where I was to take the wheel. It was late afternoon, and she had to return "to work." We had had fun and were in a good mood. We liked the open car; she wanted to buy one just like it—if she ever needed a car. Before changing seats, we smoked a cigarette. With her head tilted back, so that her full hair dropped over the back of the seat, she blew the smoke into the air. "You once told me that if ever I got fed up and didn't want to work in a whorehouse anymore, I ought to tell you, and you would try to get me an editing job in the movies. I've done a lot of thinking about what I would really like to do; I've thought about what would be fun and what would be sensible. You know what? I'd like to have my own brothel."

Happy days before the Fall of Man; before I was befallen by the passion for writing. Happy days in the Eden of non-vicarious *reality*, of first-hand experiences that were real, even if these concrete experiences were merely a threadbare pretext for the more powerful abstractedness behind them. Days of innocence, before the vice of writing abstracted even the abstractness into material that could be experienced at second and third hand, book-page reality, in which the pseudo-logic of art forges the infinitely multidimensional logic of nature into the theatrical metal of arbitrary, confected artifice. God-affirmed days, in which the world still fell into the self like a summer morning through a window; and it was not mirrored out of the self as a multiply-broken reflection of self, a spectacle making its own producer and lead actor and sole subject, performer and stage at once and in one: the world and the self were identical to the point of loss of the world, worldlessness of the totally isolated self lost to itself beyond measure. . . .

□   □   □

BUT I *loved* Christa.

I loved her even though our marriage had become as bleak, as dreary, as hopeless as the ice-gray diurnal life in the rubble fields around us—which for me, however, for Nagel and our kind, and even for that fussy man Schwab, was a constant adventure, a frontier existence in a no-man's-land to which we could lay claim, a deeper and deeper daily penetration into a state of unconditionality, which seemed delicious to us because in its desert emptiness, open to all winds, it was full of possibility, hence full of promise, an undaunted Promised Land that we would build into a new Garden of Eden once we had fully reconnoitered it, once its borders were established and the claims were staked . . . but for others, of course, for Christa and her kind, it was damnation in limbo, an everlasting routine of poverty, joyless, colorless, with the ever same nagging necessities and sorrowful chores, a trudging in the treadmill of hopelessness, merely to deal with the ever same lamentable troubles and the ever same woeful needs.

It certainly saddened me that I had to count Christa among those others—the poor by nature, so entangled in their woeful needs and lamentable troubles, so doomed to the wretched daily routine that, as Nagel was to write later in one of his best-sellers, "They could not brace their spirits for a festive tomorrow. . . ." Nagel, the flatfooted poet! . . . Christa appreciated him for that, had to admire him for his wonderful verbal power; it was part of her cleaving to workaday routine that she loved artsi-craftsiness; it was the only thing that took her out of her workaday round, the poor thing. . . .

Sometimes I was overcome with pity, like a hot wave, when I saw the despair in her eyes—in the radiant aquamarine of her childlike eyes!—because, of the four pounds of potatoes I had managed to scrounge somewhere, three pounds had been frozen and were half rotten, or because the fuel for our alcohol burner was used up, or because the wall of the room we lived in at the bisected villa on the Elbchaussee was sporting a new crack, and dampness was seeping through. Granted, things like that can be awful, but at closer sight they didn't seem so bad; almost everything was ruined anyway; we could just as easily have laughed at any new problem, especially since I knew that Christa would waste no time routing me out of a wonderful conversation with Nagel (precisely at the point when our spirits were "ardently bracing themselves for a festive tomorrow," of course, a tomorrow that would be hers, too, after all!) in order to get more potatoes or fuel, no matter where or how; or, ruthlessly stubborn, demand that I do someting about the damp wall; remove the crate of ludicrously useless slipcovers and damask curtains from her family's home in East Prussia—treasures that some fool of a fleeing relative had rescued from a fire and proudly dragged west—and replace it with my books and watch *them* molder.

"If you could at least make something pretty from these pieces—an evening gown, for instance. . . ."

"An evening gown?"

"Well, okay—some clever dress. . . ."

"A dress? To wear in this ramshackle hovel? I'm already freezing to death in ski pants and a sailor's sweater."

"Then throw it all out!"

"I wouldn't dream of it! Somebody will take the slipcovers in exchange for beans, peas, turnips, cabbage. . . ."

Ah, no, my pity never lasted long, even though it had been the origin of my love for her: the sudden yearning and understanding of human weakness and humility in a fellow creature and spontaneous identification with it, the physical commiseration of my tenderness when I had seen her chewing and swallowing the American Army chow in the canteen for German witnesses and defense attorneys at the court in Nuremberg—chewing and swallowing with a dedication that was so totally so unconditionally so definitively physical as to leave not a sliver of space for any lofty inner life, for the mind or soul, for the enjoyment of the "bread one doth not eat."

In Nuremberg the sight had moved me to tears, as I've said. I felt I was watching the basic truth of the *condition humaine*. The dreadful existential plight and exposure, the heartrending destitution, of the zoological species *Homo sapiens*, everything this naked and exposed creature undertakes beyond coping with the immediate existential necessities of finding food and shelter, mating, raising offspring, all its grotesque spiritual leaping into the metaphysical realm together with the proliferating madness of its artistry and intellectuality—all these things seemed futile and therefore poignant.

Such an insight (I had discussed it with Christa often enough!)

should have brought us together all the more humbly. It should have made us love and protect each other in this state of exposure, aid and assist each other as much as we could. At those times, people truly met at point zero, as the term goes; thus they could have easily laid down arms, formed an alliance, jointly confronted *an existence under spiteful conditions.* But precisely because we were—albeit only legally—joined in matrimony, the knowledge remained one-sided and hence ineffective. Right after the passage from bridehood into matrimony, that is, right after the legalized transformation of lovingly offered charitable acts into actionable duties, Christa saw me no longer as a fellow wayfarer through the earthly vale of tears but simply as a woman's archenemy, a failure on all fronts, a man who having started the war with his fellow men shamefuly lost it; and now, in this devastation, instead of getting a decent roof over our heads, he was running on at the mouth about a beautiful future—and, to make matters worse, had got her pregnant, thereby adding one more extortionate helpless mouth to the existing hungry ones.

Nevertheless, I loved her very much. Only I saw, alas, that I could not count on her as I could count on, say, Nagel. I could not count on the same understanding, at least. Christa was the kind of woman who not only tries to tie us down to accursed earthliness but also is of a different race: despite her good background, she was one of the poor in blood, the gray-faced, rummaging through the rubble fields, looking for the remnants of their property, instead of being delighted to be rid of it and to begin a new, unencumbered existence. I had no sympathy with these people, though day in day out they were a vivid reminder of the *condition humaine.* They did not rebel against it. To use a literary expression that does not come from Nagel, they even *ate the flour after they themselves were put through the mill.* Instead of expressing sovereign scorn at the tremendous injustice of life, they humbly gave in; they moaned under the whiplashes of real and imaginary ordeals, but then they put their noses to the grindstone.

They were our natural enemies, Nagel's and mine, as it struck me at the time, and they hated us as profoundly as we hated them. It was a time of promise, in which (as Nagel was later to write) "we prepared for the adventure of renewal," and they turned it into a workaday grayness, which ultimately consumed our hope and confidence before the harvest. *We* lived in the frivolity of the saints, like the lilies of the field—for whatever one may say about the ludicrous weakness of the human spirit when confronted with the relentless conditions of nature, that weakness does give us the strength to transcend our plight, however temporarily and with whatever fictions. . . .

So, we lived like the lilies of the field, Nagel and I, and they, the flatfooted people, crapped on our loveliest blossoms. For us they were what those others had been for Uncle Helmuth: the wicked *others. They* spoiled the dreams of the dreamers, the abstract happiness of the enraptured. Even before, when so well housed and sated that the fat on the backs of their necks burst their rubber collars, they had lived shabby, workaday lives, and they would go on like that once they were sated and well housed again. With their world shattered, they did not face events as a challenge to build a new and better world but took everything as a stroke of fate, which somehow had to be overcome with heads bowed till the old order was re-established; whatever was to come—if it wasn't worse but, unexpectedly, better—theirs would be the same mouse-like existence in the same roll of fat. They could not picture, hence could not bring about, anything better. Unlike us, they lived without the Easter promise; lived instead with the tenacity of termites, which was far superior to our childlike-fantasy ways. For them, the future was not a sublime vision, its rays transfiguring even the gray present, but something they trudged toward as pedestrians; it could bring them at best a more sated, more corpulent, more stably housed, although equally dismal life—and they were certain it was theirs, no matter whether the terrors lurking in it were the same old terrors or even worse.

Incidentally, I do not know where we extravagant windbags, we visionaries around Nagel (or rather around the homemade beet schnapps in Nagel's garden flat), got our sense of mission. We truly believed we would find the solution to any conflict, plight, evil, stroke of fate in human existence (we called them "problems"). We played ourselves up as if we and no one else had to find the key to the future of Germany and thereby, according to Major General Baron von Neunteuffel, to the destiny of the entire world. We searched for the "spiritual foundations of a new humanity," even before Professor Hertzog supplied us with this rousing formulation. Meanwhile, the other race, Christa and her ilk, concerned themselves with the rationing stamps for a special allocation of barley. They did not think beyond the next day, but they pettily, sullenly, and tenaciously saw to it that the next day would at least be no worse than today. We dreamers and windbags viewed this narrow-minded scorn of the spirit as a danger for the day after tomorrow. But while we were talking about how to stave off that danger, they kept puttering and pottering on in their obligatory dreariness, creating the foundations for their world—and the day after tomorrow was as empty of hope as are today and tomorrow.

Thus time passed. Time passed over all of us, utterly sovereign. It didn't give a hoot about our conflicts, our different opinions and ways of life. Time did the only thing it is supposed to do: it passed, and made everything that lived in it pass as well. As usual, it did not do so in a steady series of developments but was seemingly inconsistent, leaping unexpectedly, tarrying whimsically now and then, sometimes even taking a step backward after two steps forward, as in a looping procession, and eluded precise observation as it whizzed along.

In those postwar Ice Age years, Time seemed to have made up its mind to tarry; and whether a man brooded dully on his hunger or drew from it the fanatical fire to blather on about the spiritual foundations for a festive day after tomorrow, the harsh time lost nothing of its grimness. Whether we lived through a morose daily round of petty chores or in the Easterly expectation of a new humanity, we all lived in a bizarre state of waiting. Even the most hopeless gray faces in the Quonset huts, for whom tracking down potatoes was routine and gleaning coals on railroad embankments a quixotism—even they were waiting for something, whatever it might be, good or bad. We all were waiting just outside reality, waiting as if we weren't really living but were being lived by someone or something, or simply dreamed of by something or someone, nightmarishly dreamed of by some mysterious "it":

destiny or divine providence or whatever one might call it, or merely a collective spirit that shaped the era—in any case, from somewhere outside of us and our realm of perception.

Meanwhile, time was dribbling away from us without our noticing it. We breathed away our existence, day in day out, and the days, objectively speaking, were truly gray and grim and cold and clammy, like the watery puddles in the bomb craters, whose dead surfaces shuddered and raised goose bumps under the raindrops during the so-called mild seasons and, during the biting ice-winters of those legendary years, froze into blind eyes that gaped sightlessly into the stony sky over the city ruins.

And all the while I loved Christa. I loved her body, even though she let me have it only as if it weren't worth the trouble to refuse me. She developed a new habit: no sooner did I slip into bed with her than she would raise her arms to her face, her right hand clutching her left shoulder and her left hand her right shoulder, so that her elbows stood before her mouth like two bastions in the wall of a fortress: she did not want me to kiss her anymore. A kiss demands spiritual participation or, conventionally, presumes it. This, as she would have put it, was "not part of the bargain." But I was allowed to luxuriate all I liked in her full breasts and further downward. It wasn't even worth the trouble for her to deny her senses an involuntary participation in my passion, and she permitted herself an occasional thrill, sometimes even the churning up of an outright orgasm; thus my nightly masturbation with my spouse often achieved a perfection that almost amounted to a true act of love.

The emptiness of the aftermath eventually made me cunning. It seemed like the most sublime kind of castration, the way she made me so acutely aware of how abstract the role of us men is in a process that, presumably, constitutes the only, in any case the quintessential, meaning and purpose of our existence: the preservation of life by means of the preservation of the species. In zoology, of course, this is known as mating—what mockery! It is actually the separation of *Homo sapiens* into two utterly different species. The fruit that our first parents picked in the Garden of Eden gave them the knowledge of their separation into two total strangers. In the moment of utmost bliss, Christa was as remote from me as Saturn. She let me know what tremendous spaces I was trying to bridge with my ridiculous striving for spiritual union.

Very well: I learned my lesson. Soon (we hadn't been married for a year), I scarcely dared approach her, lest I alarm her with my warmth, annoy her with my tenderness, my need for some token of her affection, understanding, indulgence, some small gesture that would let me sense that I meant more to her than merely the man whose task it was to ensure her physical well-being, to which end after all it was not entirely insignificant that I had something dangling between my legs that relieved the occasional itch between hers more effectively than her own middle finger or the candles of her teenage years.

It could hardly be denied that, as a breadwinner, I was a loser. Soon I no longer even dared wonder about my ability to ensure the rest of her well-being. I was put in my place. My ego shrank to the measure of what I was biologically: a seed carrier, a drone, nothing more. It struck me as presumptuous on my part to have any other claims and to seek any but a purely physical union with a daughter of the *Great Mother*, a world-birth-giver, able to resurrect mankind from within her body—to reduce, inside her belly, the millions of years of protozoan-to-primate development to three quarters of a solar revolution, to mold a human being perfect in all faculties of body, mind, and soul, and to release him into life, letting him become Messalina or Saint Cecilia or Adolf Hitler or Jesus Christ or anything in between.

Gracious, what a difference in "realities"! How unreal, in contrast, was my male contribution to this extension and continuation of the world, of life! . . . How meager, what a wretched crumb from the table: a few angry minutes of dark sweet pleasure, a few moments of effacement, of cramped discharge, while, in several ejaculatory thrusts, that wonderful, even incomprehensible, ever mysterious, essential, actual something took place—beyond our awareness, snuffed out in a few instants of blissful near-death, in the dazzling of utterly sweetened pain . . . and then slam, bam, thank you, ma'am! That was that, once again, thanks a lot, don't worry about anything else, *ci penso io, dottò* . . .

After that, our hunger for reality ought to be comprehensible:

the insatiable hunger for immediate realization, for tangible proof that we men, too, are real, that we, too, can achieve reality, actuality, with our own actions—

". . . but you *can*," said Christa, with her sapphire-blue, round, childlike eyes. "All you have to do is go and find a little wood to chop."

"*Saw*, sweetheart, *saw!* You're misquoting. The original goes 'Men saw wood: one pulls, the other pushes, but they're both doing the same work; by decreasing, they increase.' Granted, a rather silly image from the *Corpus Hippocrates* for the identity of creation and disintegration. But what can you do: statements about the *archai* can't be worded in rational terms, because it is ir-rational and prim-ordial; such statements can only be figurative, isn't that so? . . . But I would like to take part in creation, though in a less destructive way than I am allowed by this perspicuous image, do you understand me? I do not care to limit myself to the male work of destruction in order to contribute to creation. At the risk of sounding like a screaming queen, I'll say it loud and clear: I would like to give birth. Freud gave you women dick envy to explain your inconsistencies. Allow us men to envy your uterus. I do not wish to reinvent, reconstruct reality in order to experience it: I want it to be immediate. . . ."

It was love's labor lost. She understood every word, but not the meaning of what I was saying; she simply thought I was crazy. And I must admit, those were muddled thoughts I was voicing—voicing in my way, furthermore, which was an intellectual decollage, figuratively speaking, a shredding of age-old commonplaces; I am almost ashamed of writing this down now.

Meanwhile, indulge me: that was not yet a time when, like today, people could draw ready-to-use intellectual material from paperbacks and cultural television. We were troglodytes. Those who—like myself, like Nagel and our buddies around the bottle of beet schnapps in Nagel's garden flat (later, the nuclear group around Professor Hertzog; I shall give a detailed account of this elsewhere)—those, I say, like us, of the juiciest cannon-fodder generation for Doubleyou Doubleyou II, whose best years of learning and education were suddenly interrupted by that historic event and who were left behind with the always insatiable hunger of the half-educated and the autodidactic—such people, in their poignant attempts to analyze the spiritual bases for yesterday's catastrophe in order to destroy the seed of evil and perhaps eliminate it from the spiritual foundation of tomorrow and the day after tomorrow, felt like pioneers and rubble-rummagers and refuse-recyclers. We continued to feel the naïve need to explain everything *ex ovo*—even age-old commonplaces and platitudes, even ourselves as well as everyone else. For not only had the commonplaces and platitudes become extremely questionable but we could no longer count on understanding them without an *ex ovo* explanation or on being understood when we explained them. We were troglodytes and lived among troglodytes—not like the spoiled youth of today, in an environment that obtains its well-founded knowledge and reliable intellectual depth in oversize paperbacks and educational TV channels with all the paraphernalia of prefaces, forewords, and introductions, notes, addenda, and bibliographical data (home delivery free of charge). The present still lay ahead, in which the satisfied roadside-café person may, figuratively speaking, transpose the elegant atmosphere of the champagne advertisement into cerebral experience and—in fashionable comfort, aristocratically leaning back on the plastic-bolster sofa, clutching a beer can, listening to the cultivated voice of a moderator—mentally follow the most exciting philosophical paper chase (forgive the shallow metaphor; it forces itself on me!) with a cheerful Husserl, behind the Jaspering pack, cross-country over Heidegger and Wittgenstein; for him, the sovereign self-servicer in all other situations of life, outside the unacknowledged intellectual situation, our lederhosen-boy-scout ponderings in the prehistorical year of 1947 must seem like a quaint folksong.

But, as I have said, time only appeared to be stagnating in those days. What lay ahead in time simply moved one hour closer to us with every revolution of the clock's hand. Of course, the star of Bethlehem was in the winter sky of 1946–47—thanks to a need, intensified by the lack of real bread, for the "bread one doth not eat." But right after the winter of 1947–48, one could tell that this bread would fall far behind in the race with the bread one *doth* eat, as soon as this last appeared in sufficient quantities and thickly stacked with cold cuts. Soon the black market was running smoothly, new democratic parties were a reality, the press and the publishing world were flourishing, and instead of the star of Bethlehem the star of Astra Films had risen over Hamburg. The interregnum of the Quonset-hut intellectuals ended without anyone's noticing.

Only a very few, who were fervently seized with the spirit, as if they had to make reparations with it—a remnant of the nuclear group around Professor Hertzog and, needless to say, the psychopompous himself—kept on, although now they had company pension plans; they were working in radio or in the new magazines, newspapers, publishing houses; intellectual subhumans like your humble servant served the movie piglets. Only the uniquely bold and intellectually pure broke a lance for intellectual freelancing and began to dash courageously into the arms of the windmills that ground for future roadside-café people.

And all my lamentable attempts to explain myself to Christa, in relation to this pregnancy of time, were doomed. To be sure, I tried with what I thought was a great deal of tender care. After all, I loved Christa: I took her in my arms and cradled her like a child. At times, I even thought of interpreting our disturbed or, rather, never properly established relationship not only philosophically, as a symptom of the *Zeitgeist*, but also as a personal failure on my part, admitting that although my stoic attitude toward the general situation in the rubble landscape might be to my credit, I was thereby neglecting those who had bound their destiny to mine, and that this might have contributed to the misery that had developed in our love relationship, which Christa too had originally seen as promising the realization of certain atavistic ideals and expectations: a lifetime alliance of deep mutual affection, kindness, understanding, of unconditional belonging and security, of appeasement in and with each other, hence, a harmonious home, a sunny bearing-and-breeding place for happy offspring, the nuclear cell and fundamental element of future society, a freer, happier, more just, more humane society. . . .

I was speaking not only to Christa but also to our child within her, to our future in her body, which had swollen up with that future, turning white like a fat maggot, but which I loved nevertheless and would always love, even though my love soon threatened to become incestuous—"You're molesting a child, your own flesh and blood," she said, but she let me be, so long as I didn't try to become spiritually pushy and inveigle her into allowing anything more than a lazy letting me be. My goodness, her swinish laziness in letting me be had a certain kindness, perhaps in response to my chatter . . .

she probably didn't find my chatter too annoying—as I stammered into her flaxen hair, pathetically wanting help, a blather zooming into flimsy universals, preposterous metaphysics, verbal gruel of spiritual distress; as I held her in my arms, warming and protecting her—I, who was writhing in pain, I who was flayed, I who had nothing to hold on to in the bottomless pit . . . I held her protectively, cradled her, with my arms crossed over her belly and my hands placed gently on her heavy breasts, cradled her and her child within her and, by cradling our child within her, cradled myself . . . and she didn't think it was annoying, she let my splashing verbal gruel trickle down her; phlegmatic by nature and nourished with nothing more fortifying than turnip juice, she endured my monologues with the same dull equanimity with which the Germans, believers in the spirit, listened into the ether to hear the hissing and honking of educational radio broadcasts or read the Cassandra tidings of articles in the *Kultur* sections of newspapers, as if all these things were part of the sound effects of everyday life, like the clapping wheel of a brookside mill where one has grown up and still lives or, on a more contemporary level, like the traffic din in city streets before a few carefully laid carpet bombs brought silence. Christa allowed me to get at her lower body regions together with the oxytocin, which, triggered by certain stimulations, occasionally flowed into the muscle fibers of her uterus, so it didn't seem to matter that I profited from the tolerance of her tympanums in the upper regions—

and I spoke and said (said the same thing over and over, in all sorts of verbal combinations, spoke of the same thing incessantly):

"You know, darling, you've got to understand me when I tell you that your only duty as my wife and beloved is to keep letting me experience afresh that I am a man—your husband, for you! More than anything, I want to be your man! I am proud to be your man—but I am afraid of the curse of being a man. I am afraid of being made all too conscious of my utterly manly condemnation to unreality, to invention, to feigned reality, to the reality of fictions: in short, to the creation of the world as an as-if. You have me completely in your hands. It's up to you whether I experience myself as a real man: strong, courageous, reliable, above all; overwhelmingly erotic, irresistibly virile. . . . I have to believe this, even if I know it is not true: I have to mean it, in order to have no doubts when I tackle the masculine work of reinventing and rebuilding the world. I need faith in it, in order to endure the fact that even as the strongest, most courageous, most reliable, the most manly man, I am nevertheless merely a manikin of life, a tiny means to an end, a tool. I must delude myself, in order to pretend that I do not have what I am now holding in my arms: the life-reality in you with our child in your belly. I share in that life-reality only in the unconscious moment when you and, inside you, the Great Cosmic Mother Nature use me as a tool—an indispensable tool in the process of creating life, for the moment, but still of a secondary necessity . . . I as such am abstract and with no true reality . . . can you follow me? Can you understand how important it is for me to be strengthened in my self-confidence by your love, your longing, your trust? . . . Granted, I cannot be denied as a part of the world, as a tool in the tremendous process of breeding and perishing; but as a tool, I naturally view the world as a workpiece, something that must be worked on, altered, and re-created by myself. Created on my terms—for you, for all of you, for us and our children. It is my intrinsically male mission to work on the world *as if* it had an order. Unordered Nature threatens us with annihilation at any moment. We cannot exist in chaos; we must oppose it with the as-if of an order. To deck out Nature with the fictions that enable us to exist in it—that is men's work. But it is work that must be done in the security of absolute self-confidence. We sleepwalk across the chasms of insight into our true nothingness, into our fission-fungus role in the events of life: splitting reality into truth and fictions, we deceive ourselves about it with our fragile visions and illusions; but the least appeal can terrifyingly arouse us out of our life-delusion, and we then plunge into despair; we then find our reality and realization only in destruction, because destruction too is a reshaping, a reinventing of the world: a replaying of our own past, only not abstract, not merely feigned, but undeniably real, at last . . . do you understand, my darling?"

She was silent, and I knew she had only a fragmentary and incoherent grasp of a sentence or two in my chatter, but she did listen to the singsong of my voice, catching what she wanted to hear, presumably the important part of my finely ground shriek of distress (that was what later made me so impatient with Schwab: the fact that he always took me at my word) . . . and perhaps she caught the madness woven into the monomania of my endlessly reiterated melody, the gentle eeriness in the obsessive *idées fixes*, all of which was not without its peculiar enchantment and could be, in the compulsive recurrence of motifs amid the overall confusion, as insistently fascinating as drawings done by madmen.

But perhaps she felt and thought something entirely different or was even about to fall asleep in my arms; it didn't matter, I was talking to myself and, over myself, into the world, the world in which our son would experience the same distress and, presumably, be thwarted by the same anxious questions.

I said, "The awful thing is that we men cannot escape despair, even if we recognize the dreadful illusion and fiction of our men's work or perform that labor unswervingly under the constraint of somnambulism. Because we have to reinvent the world in order to experience it in our reality, we also have to reinvent and replay the destruction in it: ourselves in the destruction. . . . We have to become murderers in order to experience ourselves as real . . . isn't that horrible? This comes out in even the most beautiful of our myths. Do you remember the story of Daedalus? Hertzog called him the 'compulsive inventor.' Daedalus built the labyrinth, a symbol of the world: the artistic copy of confusion, in which, as the epitome of the dark and dreadful forces of Nature, the minotaur dwells, half animal, half human, full of demonic might, devouring human beings. . . . Daedalus banished it into his image of the world, and now he, the compulsive inventor, must also invent an image of his own spirit, the spirit of human beings, of males, which aims beyond itself, eternally insatiable, into infinity, heedless of the sacrifices . . . so he makes wings for his son Icarus to fly to the sun, and when Icarus comes close to the sun, the sun melts his wings, and the boy plunges to his death. Daedalus sacrificed his beloved son because of the compulsion to replay, as an image, the manliest of manly deeds: the action of getting beyond oneself to the point of atrocity."

I cradled her gently in my arms, for now she really *was* about to fall asleep, and that made me feel tender in a suffering kind of way, like that day in the canteen of the Nuremberg court, when I saw the embodiment, the incarnation, of creature indigence and human neediness in her chewing, chomping, kneading little mouth, in its bitter heartiness when she swallowed one of the chewed-up, chomped-up bites, in her utter forlornness, her removal from the world, her absorption in her bodily self, her physis, the sheer biological functioning of her anatomy. I realized that she had to pay her dues for the intrinsically female ownership of reality, and that the price was no smaller than what we men paid in our longing for "reality."

I said, "I know, my poor darling, that all my chatter is no excuse for my inability to get you the herring paste that would make the frozen potatoes palatable for us." (There you are: I said "us": I was identifying with her; I was generously hiding the fact that I didn't particularly care for herring paste, and if I did have to eat frozen potatoes, I would prefer eating them without herring paste: out of love of the unadulterated, or rather out of a delight in alchemistic transubstantiations of things, in order to turn lead into gold and derive enjoyment even from the unenjoyable.)

I said, "I know: other men bring their wives butter and nylon stockings, even egg-yolk liqueur, like your cousin Hatzdorff. That doesn't make him any less manly, of course; no, no, that's not what I was saying; on the contrary, he is truly strong, courageous, reliable; and your cousin Jutta must appreciate these qualities in him, despite her teenage swooning over Nagel, who, aside from the liqueur of the eggs that one doth not eat, has little to offer her . . . yes, indeed, I know, my taste leaves something to be desired, but you could overlook a bit of silliness on my part now and then; Nagel would have laughed heartily for at least thirty minutes over my pun. . . . Seriously, though, darling," I said, kissing her hair and caressing her thick abdomen, while I felt as if I were being repeated inside there as my son, "if there is one thing I know for certain, it is that several decisions are being reached here and now in our misery, and that it is important to know where one belongs. I admit it is more difficult and more courageous to get hold of butter than dreamily to give in to the chimerical idea that now, here, in this ice-wind-whistling rubble wasteland of a shattered world, it must at least be possible to lay the cornerstone for the future kingdom of God on earth, but I think one might nevertheless find some sense in the butchery we have miraculously survived (albeit more vegetating than alive); we might at least assume that it purged the world and that the enemies, who bled each other white, have now realized how insane they were and will join together as brethren so that, united, they can transform the remnants of a devastated civilization into fair conditions for a humane existence on earth . . . and not recommence at a point at which the new bad end can be instantly foreseen: a world of profiteers and racketeers, of the horribly shortsighted and blindered, of the fanatics of abstract ideologies and the fanatics of materialism. . . . What I fear, my darling, are the dangers that come with people who are all too efficient in getting hold of butter. They are the human type to whom we owe the most exquisite terrors brought to the utmost perfection of destructivity: the engineers and electricians of my uncle Helmuth's ilk: the professional termites with slide rules, who, in carrying out their male mission of reinventing and reworking the world, are all too crazy about 'reality.' More than anything else, I fear what stands behind them, driving them to self-oblivious work: money, which Nagel so poetically calls the idol and moloch of this godless time. . . . Today, we must decide where we belong if Gottfried Benn's prophecy comes true and, one hundred years from now, the world consists exclusively of *monks and criminals.*"

And Christa spoke a sentence that, to my utter amazement, was intellectually not at all simple, albeit grammatically correct, fluent, and elegant: "If I had a pound of butter now, I wouldn't doubt for even an instant that a hundred years from now I would want to belong among the monks."

She was brilliant. She would always speak illuminating truth whenever—seldom enough!—she was willing to open her disdainful lips and say anything at all. Once again, she was speaking nothing but the terrifyingly pure truth—the very thing that everyone was thinking and feeling. For we dreamers and chatterboxes, we illusionists, we utopians, we intellectuals (the Germans were already starting to put us down as that), were by no means the only ones to perceive the dangers inherent in the way people were preparing for reconstruction. Soon it was possible to turn the act of prophesying a new and final cataclysm into a profession, as a newspaper editor, or as an educational-network director, or even as a novelist; and this was possible because one had only to say what everyone knew anyway; one had only to say it so that it did not stand out as an importunate noise amid the usual sound effects. After all, everyone had made up his mind to do good, and he would have been even more mindful of doing so if the circumstances of life had not forced him to put up with things that were less than good. The reconstruction, especially after the memorable act of the currency reform, had its pleasant sides—this was undeniable—and for the time being, people, as consumers, avoided the alternative of "monks or criminals."

No, no: we were not the only seers who could read the future and foretell to what extent they would have to cut their ideals to the cloth with which time had graciously covered the past. Even they, the people of the other race, the stonehearted burghers whipped by anxiety about life and therefore occasionally irritated, and concerned only with their narrowest interests—even they realized that something was sprouting in our Ice Age winters, something beyond their immediate present. Today's time was pregnant with tomorrow's time, and our universal mission was to make sure that this tomorrow would not be a changeling, as yesterday had been. They nodded when they read such things in the new newspapers, whose pulpy paper lent a touching purity to their contents, as if the words, arriving in hair shirts, could do nothing but tell the truth . . . and the monstrous birth of the future took place beyond or below the threshold of the collective consciousness, virtually on its own, with no visible help from individuals and yet with the admirable assistance of everyone and completely unmolested by the admonishing and warning and morally armoring claptrap of the pseudo-intellectual philistines, who were soon well paid again for making the tiny celluloid balls of their intellectual elitism dance on the pitter-pattering fountain of their eloquent pessimism.

It was given to Christa to sum up this complicated and dismal state of affairs in a single sentence, and I loved her for it, even when this sentence passed an annihilating judgment on us and our impulses for a happy humanity. It was a rather sordid attempt at justification when I told her, "I admit that even we, who do nothing but speak of the devil, know only what must *not* happen, so that the devil won't get us, but do not know how to stave this off—much less what should be done instead. We talk about the new spirit that should inspire us, yet even if we spoke about it with nightingale tongues, we would be incapable of inspiriting anyone. It is as if no one had the spirit, unless it is everyone. Either the new spirit is part of the time and is pouring into everyone or it is not part of the time, and then it is idle to preach the new spirit: the seed of the word will not sprout. . . ."

I could have added, "It is like our situation, yours and mine: I can speak to you with the tongues of angels, and because you are not imbued with the same spirit, my words will be sounding brass for you"—but I did not have to say it; she knew that everything I said referred profoundly to us. It was from the noise of my words, not from the words themselves, that she knew what I meant when I spoke of the plight of those who felt destined to speak: "Those people who are trapped ecstatically in their dreams, the people you call intellectuals, it's true they do nothing but talk; and if it becomes practicable, they will have to clear out and give way to the professional termites with slide rules and, behind them, the profiteers and shamans of money idolatry . . . and yet the chatter of the visionaries is the salt of reality—how can I make it clear to you?—it is the herring paste without which you people could not eat your frozen potatoes because they would stick in your craw. . . . Please try to understand what I mean: the movers and shakers depend on the visions of the dreamers: those for whom the world is real are nothing without the others for whom the world is an idea; the two have to work together to reshape the chaos into a world we can live in: it is an act of procreation, in which both participate, just like you as a woman and me as a man, the sons of the mothers and the daughters of the fathers. . . ."

It cracked one's heart! I might have added that it was for the sake of this cooperation that people *spoke to each other*, but then I would have had to say that the most deceptive illusions came from us dreamers and visionaries: not only was it a dreadful proof of the fallacy of this statement that I had to repeat it to her here, even though it had been iterated and reiterated for thousands of years and already wore a yard-long beard, like all my other philosophemes, but, above all, we could immediately experience how unreal, how purely theoretical, such philosophical sum-and-substance utterances were. Did not Christa and I bear the most eloquent witness to the human distress of being unable to speak together, the horrible plight of always speaking past one another, of using words that signified something quite different from what was meant, words filled to bursting with affects, emotions, resentments, hence achieving something quite different from what they aimed at—semantic explosives, so to speak . . .

but nevertheless, I persisted in my monkey chatter, held firm to the proposition concerning the necessity of speech and the delusion that speech was a means of communication. I believed in the curative power of the word and in the high priesthood of those who force it to produce the clearest expression of its most profound content; and I bombarded Christa in a way that not only made it impossible for her to understand me but was also bound to incense her, turn her against both what I said and me who said it.

I said, "You know, darling, every sentence we speak reveals something, and the revealed can signify the most sublime thing—salvation in the crucial sense, as Kierkegaard says—or the most insignificant thing—the articulation of something random. We should not allow it to confuse us; the category is the same; phenomena have this in common: they are demonic, even if the difference is otherwise dizzying. The act of being revealed is the good thing here; for revelation is the first expression of liberation. That is why we have that old saying: 'If one dares to name the word, the mirage of enchantment will vanish, and that is why the sleepwalker wakens when his name is spoken.' "

I kept my voice low, as a precaution, for by now she had already fallen asleep in my arms, and I was afraid of waking her by talking loudly, or rather, by ceasing to talk: a sudden stop to my verbal splashing might unbalance the gentle transformation of her dozing into deep sleep. So I kept talking, and I secretly kept hoping that she was still listening, or, even better (like the hope that sustains intellectually lazy students when they take a book whose lesson they have not learned and put it under their pillow for the night), that her subconscious, by a sort of intellectual osmosis, would absorb the substance of my monologues; and even though her all too human sleepiness made me feel tender, I nevertheless began to feel bitter that she so mercilessly left me writhing in the plight of my expression-compulsions, she, cruel in the superiority of silence, making the speaker appear an idiot, so that ultimately there was only one way to interpret her hardheartedness: she simply didn't love me, had probably never loved me, or at best only in her chary way, which I did not regard as "true" love, even though, for all its meagerness, it struck me as far more reliable and far more pregnant with "reality" than my importunate and possessive "true" love. In any case, I suffered, because I could not avert my eyes from the fact that my loving had turned into a steady and annoying pursuit of a word of love, of a revelatory gesture from her, had turned into an incessant jolting and jouncing in order to get something out of her, something that (as she put it) was "not part of the bargain"; and thus, I was eventually seized with a hate-filled self-scorn, which I—a true intellectual!—projected into the state of the world and the vision of its imminent destruction. Naturally, I also knew how ridiculous this was; I knew that I would someday take bitter revenge for it. "Don't forget," I told Nagel, "the reason why Robespierre became a mass murderer!"

But Nagel, who had only a rather nebulous idea of Robespierre and the circumstances that had made him a mass murderer, assumed I meant the class struggle, whereas I had meant "excessive virtue and an excessive sense of order."

And yet Nagel was right in a way, with his class struggle—although, then again, he wasn't—because Christa was so extremely highborn, virtually from a gold vein in the bedrock of East Prussian aristocracy, while I was a bastard from a remote Balkan land. I could not have more successfully invented a hero's wife in a novel, the slave relationship that exists between a husband and a wife (especially a wife who is loved hopelessly). It was not only the humility of the hopelessly loving husband but above all the dog-like devotion and uxorious worship, the impotently indignant dependence with which the husband looks up to the totem pole of the "wife" and "mother of his children" while he may hate and despise her with all his heart, the wife whom he has raised to that level—these things often made me gnash my teeth like a serf in bondage.

I said to Nagel, "Do not believe that the institution of marriage, which has been raised to a sacrament, has its origin in an even biologically reliable guarantee of the legitimacy of the offspring. The roots lie much deeper. They go back to prehistoric times, when hunters and gatherers became grain farmers and storers. The underlying goal is to cope with times of dearth, to get through the winter, so to speak. If a man doesn't hunt and gather sex from dawn to dusk, then one day he will come back emptyhanded; the fat times are followed by lean times. Might not then one of our early forebears, upon contemplating the imperishability of a ham smoked by chance and upon recognizing the advantages of conservation, hit upon the idea of dealing with sex in the same way: I mean, legally conserve the steady playmate; the wife as a preserved cunt, to be consumed at any time of the day, the night, the year, even though it may lose a lot of flavor nowadays because of modern deep-freezing . . .

but while speaking so heretically to Nagel, I had the audacity to continue my boundless monologues for Christa's blond-hair-crackling ears, in order to stammer out in entangled circumlocutions things that millions of husbands have been saying to their wives for countless generations: "Darling, if only you knew how easy I am. A little affection, a little tolerance and understanding, a little friendliness and good cheer . . ." and I instantly choked on my own stupidity; terror took my breath away. I could picture her jumping and showing her small, sharp teeth; in dreadful embarrassment, I heard her asking if I had taken leave of my senses, expected her to bubble over in good cheer—with three frozen potatoes and my bastard in her belly and the room temperature a few degrees above freezing. She was right, she *was* right! . . . So I instantly corrected myself: "Of course, dearest, you have no reason to throw your arms around me like an exuberant debutante in a novel when her fiancé comes to her laden with gifts—but now and then, let me feel that I'm not the sole cause of your ill humor. Just a small gesture—anything, you understand. The shadow of a smile, a touch of your hand on mine, a glance of sympathy. That would be more than enough, it would work wonders. . . ."

Yes indeed, it was because of such modest, undemanding wishful thinking that I virtually did a Saint Vitus' dance in front of my wife Christa. With an almost cultic thoroughness, I stylized the male dance before the merciless female supremacy (a dance as old as mankind) into philosophical reflections on civilization; and Christa's unshakable silence seemed to take on a sacred sublimity.

When I discussed it with Nagel, I naturally used modern-day metaphors for my crazy actions. I said, "Damn it, there are people who play chess with themselves—isn't that so? Or with the reader, like Uncle Vladimir. But I'm playing something a lot more exciting. I'm playing soccer with myself; I'm a whole team, so to speak, with a goalie and defense and forwards, and, with the concentrated energy of eleven major-league players, I shove and kick the ball of responsibility into my wife's field—I mean the responsibility for our misery, for our unintended but ineluctable mutual torment. . . . I play it into her field, you know, the responsibility for our terrible incapacity to understand each other, the responsibility for our bleak loneliness in living past one another . . . and my playing is masterful in both tactics and technique: Miller to Meller, Meller to Muller, Muller shoots a GOAOAOAL!!! . . . But, unfortunately, my wife's field is a wall, a solid wall on which I have only painted her players, and the better I play against them, the more sharply I shoot, the more violently the ball bounces off the wall and back into my kisser. There ought to be a penalty for a thing like that, don't you think? Or at least a satisfaction for me: there must be such a thing as justice even here on earth. Sooner or later, the ball has to smash into the face of the woman behind the wall, and smash her good and hard! . . . I mean, sooner or later, the woman has to realize that I want only what's best for both of us!"

but this, unfortunately, was not the case for the time being, and so no little gesture was shown. Christa couldn't understand that I had only pedagogical reasons for throwing the ball at her, the responsibility for our mutual failure: I was only trying to arouse understanding in her conscience and, with that understanding, her feeling for me. She was unable to realize that I did so in order to create order between us, to close a life cycle, in which affection gave birth to kindness, and kindness gave birth to deeper and deeper, more and more ardent affection. To be sure, whenever I was completely honest with myself (and at times I *was*), I did not set much store by whether she loved me still or a little less, or whether she had ever truly loved me with "true" love; granted, I did love her, but more as my wife, the mother of my son, than as the human being, the woman Christa—oh my goodness! My eyes had long since been going after other women—what am I saying? Not just my eyes (and she should have understood this, too: after all, the adulterer is homeless, all too willing to return to his own hearth). But that didn't matter: the important thing was our *case*, so to speak: two people with a basis of positive feelings for one another, right? In any case, two people who did not have it in for each other, who were actually seeking each other—and they did not understand each other, spoke past each other as if speaking different languages, soliloquizing into the isolation, the torture of an inability to express themselves, fell silent with each other. . . . Obviously it was not a unique case; nothing special about it; on the contrary: a rather run-of-the-mill condition for many people, but that was the very reason I didn't want to throw in the towel; I wanted to force her to understand that the soccer ball I wanted to smash into her face was, so to speak, the eternal *ballon d'essai* from the depth of the deepest human misery: the attempt to break out of the imprisonment, the entanglement in one's own self. . . . "I speak to you because I love you," I wanted to say to her, "and even if it sounds as if I wanted to blame you because we are two human beings and not one, because I am I and you are you and

each of us is in solitary confinement in his own self, eternally separated from the other; even if we are banished into two cells from
which we cannot communicate with knock signals because neither knows the key to the other's code ... even if it sounds as if I
were reproaching you for being blind and deaf to all that, listen to
me anyway, listen to me: for whatever I say, it means only that I
love you, and even if the word turns over in my mouth in the bitterness of not being understood, I mean only that one thing ...
and no one should ever say anything else, for whenever there is
no love, demons prevail and speech produces nothing but confusion; no one should ever want to say anything else; all speaking
should mean only that one thing. . . ."

and whether she was listening or had fallen into a deep slum-
ber, she was silent. And what should she have said anyway, since
she did not mean that one thing?

□   □   □

THE DISQUIET that I want to keep dammed up and imprisoned
in this room until it surrenders and dissolves into the blissful torrent of *speaking*—the speaking of everything caused by disquiet—often becomes so powerful that it constricts my throat,
making my temple arteries pound and the sweat bead on my
forehead: the urging of a reversed eroticism, as it were, an eroticism turned against myself. I crave a woman, yet I am not I, my
self; I am I detached from myself; I do not actually exist; I am
merely a notion of myself, a projection of my Self. And I crave
the chimera of a woman, a notion of woman, which corresponds
to my notion of myself. My imagination makes an effort for these
two: it wanders through the numbered cave dwellings of this
rundown hotel for stranded existences; it pictures a woman inside
each cave, on her own, forlorn, helpless. A half-crazy American
fashion model, for instance, who similarly exists in the bright and
beautiful underworld, like a tench in the aquarium of a pederasts'
bar—was it really possible that the handsome Pole sneaked to her
room at night? Is he really sleeping with Madame instead of
guarding the telephone behind the hotel desk? Is Madame being

deliberately cold to me? That would mean that she is playing my game. . . .

For four years now, I've been a regular customer in this lousy dump; and one would think that by now, I and Madame la Patronne, in the splendor of her full-blown tits and her blazing red *boudin*, would have developed if not out-and-out intimacy then at least a certain familiarity. Parisian shopkeepers, flower vendors, newsdealers, waitresses have cultivated such impersonally personal relations and they have evolved into a cordial art—the only and final manifestation of something that has otherwise vanished (if not turned into its opposite): *la courtoisie française.*

But not Madame. Gravel-hard *politesse*, that's all. When I arrive, a nasal *"Bonjour, m'sieur, vous allez bien, m'sieur?"* without a further glance at me while she writes my name in the guestbook. She hands me the key: *"Je vous donne la vingt-six comme d'habitude"*—the room with the windows facing hers. And not the softest flicker in her eyes. (I too occasionally leave my window open, sometimes even when I'm not alone.) We maintain form—and form is abstraction, hence immediately erotic. Things have reached such a pass that I wonder whether I am in love with her.

I need not say that Madame has not only kept all her charms but even quite uncommonly increased them. Scarcely four years, as I said, have passed since Schwab and I were able to feast our eyes on her. The peony freshness of her cheeks is barely assailed by an autumnal breath, by the frost of the first cold night. The black aftergrowth of her strong hair, when it has not been freshly dyed fox-red, reveals two or three white threads at most. The snapshots that Madame occasionally vouchsafes me through the window do not permit any precise examination; but according to an established cavalier saying, a woman's body ages more slowly than her face. Her body must therefore now—now, damn it, at this hour, in this night—be bursting with ripeness (a notion to which Schwab would no doubt have gladly drunk a beer). . . .

Madame must sense what effect she has on me (in me). But no: we do not smile when facing each other. Our gazes meet frankly and coolly and do not slide down to cleavage or fly level. If our fingers touch when I receive the key from her hand, this touch is unheeded, even when one of her nails, lacquered bone-splinter hard, scratches the back of my hand. Once, I came in after a rather lengthy drive from Reims, wearing a cashmere sweater and soft, rubber-soled shoes; the friction of the leather car seat must have made me as electrically charged as a Leyden jar, and a spark leaped between our hands with a perceptible shock. We pretended not to notice. A pleonasm to mention something that was by no means unexpected.

We wish each other Merry Christmas and Happy Easter and also exchange inner feelings through the usual reflections on the situation of the world and the weather: *"Et qu'est-ce qu'il est devenu, vot' gros ami allemand? . . . Il est mort? Tiens, je l'aimais bien. . . ."*

Sometimes, I am seized with the desire to do something unreflected, even violent: hit her in the face, *une bonne paire de claques dans la gueule*, or else clasp a Cartier bracelet on her wrist without a word of explanation. But I know: if I hold my ground and keep as gravel-hard and impersonal as she, then her window will stay open.

I assume I don't have to make myself any clearer. Scherping once told me a pretty Art Nouveau story—a trauma of his childhood. His beautiful mother used to chastise him cruelly for the slightest offense. Once, when he had done some misdeed for which he must expect worse chastisement than normal, she summoned him. She was sitting at the mirror, brushing her hair— very beautiful hair that flowed richly over her shoulders and back. He had stepped in and paused at the door, not daring to take a step toward her, so fearing her punishment that he trembled. She gazed at him through the mirror and did not say a word. She kept brushing her hair, never taking her eyes off him. This went on for a while, which seemed like an eternity to him— an eternity in limbo. Hell, by comparison, was redemption. He could stand it no longer and asked her to hit him. He sobbed and begged her for it. She still said nothing and continued brushing her beautiful hair. And gazing at him through the mirror. . . .

Scherping says that his expectation that she might turn to him, open her arms, and cry "Come! I forgive you!" has remained in him all his life. He will torment every person who loves him until that inarticulate creature is before him with the same harshness—just so that someday someone will nevertheless open his arms and say to him "Come! All is forgiven!" He will demean himself with everyone until he is hated: in order that someone someday will tell him he is forgiven. He despises the women who love him. He worships the unyielding ones (Carlotta, Gisela).

I need Madame's never kept promise. Just imagine if I finally did land in bed with her—or on the divan behind the clerk's desk, on the pool table in the lounge, on a pile of rolled-up carpets in the stairwell. An assault, wordless, brutal, a willingly granted rape, my fists clawed in her arse, my bared teeth foaming between her wonderful tits, the backs of her knees hooked over my shoulders, expertly bestial, in keeping with her voluptuous, sweaty, hennaed female ripeness—

even if we vented our rage on each other, if I made her fizz, burst like a geyser, if she plunged me into a snarling frenzy of destruction and then gasping exhaustion, my back crooked as though whipped, my head dangling between her knees, blind and drooling, we would not forget for even a moment that we were merely play-acting, playing ourselves in the scene, a performance, inauthentic, drilled, put on. We would be playing nature but we would no longer *be* nature.

I lust for Madame. A rammer grows from my groin to smash through the fictions separating us: to smash *it*, the fiction of the *other*, which throws me back upon myself and isolates me in myself; smash the fiction of bodies that imprison us and keep us locked apart; smash the fiction of woman that makes me the fiction of man; smash the fictions of solitude, uniqueness, and unrepeatability, which exclude me from the world, splice me away from oneness with God and His cosmos. . . . I picture myself meeting Madame in some dark corner of the hotel—there are so many! Madame all alone and lusting as much for me as I for her (or even merely guileless, unprepared, so that I could succeed in catching her off guard): I would pounce upon her, yank her skirt high and her underwear off, and thrust my rammer into the blackness between her white hams, bore into her with all my might . . . but for all the pleasure-yelping, all the snarling and gasping, the two-backed animal we would form (in the bed or on the sofa, on the pool table or on a carpet roll in the stairwell), the epileptically twitching package of human limbs, human clothes, human hair, and human flesh, would remain unaltered: Madame and I, each of us hermetically encased in his or her story, which makes him or her hopelessly different from the other. Each one a tissue of his or her memories, a product of the specific, manifold, complex fictions that he or she has lived, is still living, and will continue to live. None of this, nothing, could be shaken off, not even with the wildest fucking. Nothing could be changed, nothing overcome, not even with the fiction of love. After all, everything would still stand between us, keeping us remote from each other!

Madame would still bear in mind that she is a Frenchwoman, and she would feel above it all, even though she were receiving a non-Frenchman into her. *One* pride would still be with her. Dutifully she would place my carefully emptied testicles on the altar of the *Patrie: "Voici! N'y a qu'une française qui baise comme ça! Qu'il s'en rende compte, le pauvre bougre!"*

And I, for my part, would fuck Madame-to-the-second-power, *the Frenchwoman!* I would fuck Marianne with her banner waving, fuck her so that the blue-white-and-red cockade would fly out of the Phrygian blood sausage; I would get my revenge on her. I would humiliate, besmirch the superiority, unflappability, enormity of their national fictions, the legendary, the nonpareil, the incomparable self-assurance of the French. I'd pay them back in full here: *Je baiserais leur Liberté, je fouterais leur Égalité, j'enculerais leur Fraternité* and all their *gloire* and *culture* and *connerie.*

And thus, this would most certainly not have been an individual act but rather all the more a collective act: a vengeance in the name of all those who, like me, nurturing hope for Europe, have lost hope because of the French: because of their fossilization, their cataleptic stylization, their utterly inalterable *form.*

The sexual act, too, is tradition. Our very drives are secondary. Even before we hit on the idea of using our thumbs as pacifiers to drive away the boredom of our baby existence, we are products of civilization, prisoners of our inevitable fictions, mewed up in the cage of our traditions, in the straitjacket of our conventions. In vain do we yearn for a transcendence into naturalness. We mime originality because we want so badly to believe we are real; and all we find over and over again are fictions. No matter how deep we tumble into the chasms of our animal nature, we encounter cultural goods: our shrieks of pleasure, however guttural, sound like opera; the obscenities we stoke our fires with are, at best, a weak copy of Rabelais; the mendacious words of tenderness that we murmur at each other to benumb our despair are classically French, as if by Rostand; and our imaginations, which are supposed to pull us toward unification with the universe, are ruled by the most skillful, the most stylized Frenchman: the marquis de Sade. . . .

and Madame would actually be proud of this. Being a French-woman means carrying French cultural awareness between the legs, too. Kalokagathia is attained when the *culture du moi* matches the *moiteur du cul*. . . .

Thus, if we forgot ourselves with each other, we would be doing nothing but constantly quoting, citing, reciting. We would be declaiming a fuck by all the fine, grand, good rules of the Comédie Française, and that brief moment of snuffing out, toward which we would thereby be whipping ourselves so fiercely, would distort our faces into the two masks that hang over every provincial theater.

And the horrifying aftermath is, at its best, cineastic art. We've met the quota of obligatory biological performance. Now there's nothing left to depict; the take's over. With the last quiver of our orgasm, the scene fades, we are no longer in the picture, we have completed our cameo parts: the well-drilled roles we have prepared for since we first heard about sex with curiosity, anxiety, and yearning; that we have never tired of rehearsing and reiterating; that we have memorized more and more perfectly, more and more adroitly, an imperceptible flicker, a mere grain of light in a movie that has been repeating the same event millions of times for millions of years now, performed in every waning instant—now in the just now beginning, just now passing, just now passed second!—by millions of performers in precious few, pathetically unimaginative variations: in beds, and on sofas, on pool tables and carpet rolls or on the bare ground, in hay lofts, forests, roadside ditches, railroad compartments, lying, standing, squatting, in clay huts or igloos, under starlight and in the darkness of caves, in the palm shade of oases, camping tents, canopied beach chairs, and by the thousands in the roaring wastelands of big cities, from in front, from behind, sometimes with him on top and her underneath, sometimes with her on top and him underneath, or *à l'amazone*, sideways, with the lady crooking her leg.

The possibilities are soon exhausted; at best, there are still a few acrobatic improvements, like those of a horse of the *haute école*, between the pillars. I personally find this extremely uncomfortable, at times even annoyingly comical, but that is a private view; it doesn't count on the global scale; in any case you always take part in a collective enterprise even in the most peculiar luxation. Every individual coitus is merely a partial action in a steady mass course of events, whether or not the participants realize it. Still and all, the theatrical passion deployed is astonishing: every actor or actress devotes *élan vital* and every power of expression—most of all, the pent-up ones, the trembling, bashful ones whose palms break out in sweat before their other glands open. The less naturally gifted ones simply make up for it with artificial means: panting, gasping, rattling, laughing half crazily, sobbing, murmuring sweet nothings or slobbering obscenities, raging fiercely, in ecstasy, in murderous delusion, or fading with the slaughter-victim look of lovers. . . .

all in all, by the millions, as mentioned, recorded through millions of years, the result is a highly interesting, significant, with-it, modern film. The title, needless to say, is *Reality:* Mr. Warhol's undisputed masterpiece if he let me write the script: the history of mankind subsumed as a continuous mass act of procreation.

For we were born for nothing else than to cooperate in the preservation of the human race. To eat in order to procreate and to die in order to be eaten by worms so that the worms may procreate. We occur for no other purpose on this shitty planet than to let only the same thing occur over and over again. We exist for no other purpose than simply to

cooperate in life—in life, which is lived by eating life in order to procre-
ate life. Life that procreates by eating life.

And having done this, having played out our tiny parts in this huge, sublime play of Mother Nature's, we are kindly furloughed from "reality" for a while. We can go and play our own little games. We can whip up our own "reality," some gaudy figment, a merry or dreary as-if. Our little private or collective fictions. For instance, that we are writers and have to write our books. Or readers who have to read these books. Or great actresses, like Nadine Carrier, who gives so ineffably much to millions of people with her mature art of incarnating human beings. (As if there weren't enough of them.) Some gracious or ungracious delusion, according to our taste. It does not count, it is not essential, *it is not real.* The real thing is our biological existence as a minute particle, as a mini-micro-function in the sublimely stolid play of Ma Nature.

For whether we pray or kill one another, argue with, joke with, or gyp one another, kick one another in the balls, deliver weighty thoughts or wet clay for kneading fetishes, whether we laugh weep twist in pain or leap for joy, whether we are awake or dreaming, dancing or sleeping— everything is aimed at only this one thing, means only this one thing, is concerned with only this one thing, leads to this one thing: to procreate in order to procreate procreators. It all has only this one purpose: to preserve life. It has only one reality: the reality of being procreated in order to procreate life-devouring life and to be devoured by Life.

A perfectly meaningful playing together, in order to produce an inherently meaningless duration: the duration of life from here to eternity. Achieved by a gigantic squandering, a continual immense lavishing of myriads and myriads of individual lives. An insane wasting of tens of thousands of genera, species, breeds: the game of a certifiably mad demiurge.

Thus could we perform our mini-parts, Madame and I—our roles, being an imperceptible flicker of a grain of light in a film hundreds of thousands of billions of yards long—and now we'd find ourselves on the shadowy line between horror at the nothingness of this reality and the terror of the fictions that fill time for us between two such acts of biological realization: so-called everyday life and its reality, which everyone takes for granted as reality. . . .

the very thing that drives Nadine into her dressing room after every completed take in order to exult in having some guy (in an emergency: me) between her legs . . .

(then, afterward, the other horror in her eyes, when the veils of orgasm dissolve and those eyes are forced to recognize the fellow lying on her, heavy, as if dead, and are forced to recognize that she, too, has been expelled from this reality of being and has been cast back into nothingness: the immense terror in it, as if she had looked point-blank at the whole swindle, the sheer madness of Creation)

Nagel once told me a story from his seafaring days. Leaning indolently over the railing of some ship he'd signed on with, he watched a pair of mice that had fallen into a vat of syrup on a wharf and were trying to clamber out. It was the image of pure love. The two little mice licked each other with heartrending, nauseating fervor. They clutched at each other with their little paws, slopping and lapping; they drew their little tails through their little mouths; they bored their rosy little tongues into each other's little ears; they kissed the little drops of syrup from each other's every little finger—and for a moment, they stood nose to nose, peering into the black pinheads of each other's eyes, and then sprang apart as if the devil had leaped between then. They had forgotten all about each other, said Nagel; had completely forgotten they were mice, with good reason to be frightened of any other animal, even another mouse; and so they were both frightened when they saw each other up so close. . . . But I believe that Nagel does not have the full image of reality. From my own experience, I believe I can say: each little mouse saw itself in the other's eyes—and behind, the cat.

□   □   □

YESTERDAY, LATE AT NIGHT, in a fit of irrepressible contrition, I began a letter to Christa, intending to explain, although far too long after the event, my disintegration. (Why?)

Fortunately, I didn't get past the beginning. Not only was I embarrassed about making such an apology in confessional form but I was overcome by pure fear: I caught myself writing like Nagel: the closer to self-confession, the more dithyrambic yet restrained the style became. The beautiful soul that does not wish to say outright how beautiful it is—you're supposed to notice by its quivering. The Poet as a taut string, which resounds splendidly even when he scratches his arse—

And even this style is complacently abandoned with an ironic stylistic cover: a wink to the reader, making quotation marks unnecessary—and this to Christa (whom I could best approach spiritually in a street song, if not with Rilke):

> You to whom I never say
> That I lie awake at night
> Weeping . . .

At any rate, I squandered an entire night trying to fathom what the devil it was that kept urging me to make confessions in the first place.

(For the sake of stylistic consistency:

—as if my accusers were drawing nearer and nearer to me, about to confront and unmask me—and I were futilely hurling new masks of me at them, each closer to the Truth than the last and yet not the Truth, merely an image with whose delusion my guilt merely worsened—

whereby the most deceptive of these images would emerge with the confession of the whole truth.)

As always when in the mood for parodies, I was desperate, restless, jittery, mordant particularly toward myself—and this naturally ended once again with my clumsy attempt to stumble across the threshold of consciousness behind which my murder lies in darkness.

It was almost morning by now. I had switched off the light and thrown myself on the bed, and once again I recapitulated the image of my dream in detail. I set up each one in front of me, sneaked around it, tried to attack it from the rear, as it were, take it by surprise and thereby force it to surrender the truth that it was mirroring to bits—but something stabbed me in the back: a horror at myself, which made the marrow freeze in my bones.

I spent the day destroying everything that was literature in my book. Everything that did not reflect the purest verifiable Truth. Any figment, fiction, fancy, fantasy that could disguise or falsify Truth. I thus destroyed my book for good; but I wanted things to be clean and orderly at last.

It is now long after midnight again (I heard twelve strokes from somewhere a while ago; that's beside the point anyway; I feel utterly fresh; I am writing easily again—only I feel a cramp burgeoning in my hand—poor Nagel!)—

I wrote down what happened yesterday and (together with a few jottings I fished out of the garbage with Monique's help —I believe she has become shrewd and stores my refuse in some broom closet) put it into a folder (everything else into Folder C).

To supplement the above, I must add:

If my reckoning of time is correct, then it has been exactly one week since I went back to the Épicure. I'd come from Reims, as I've said, spending the night there while en route from Munich. The day was high and clear, a blue-and-gold early-autumn day; there wasn't much traffic on the roads, and I made rapid headway. I drove through sweet France, toward Paris. Hamlets lay there like primer pictures, small toy towns, and everything about them was utterly French. *La douce France.* The heartland of Europe.

I had it in my blood. It had been in me since my childhood, implanted in me since the first sounds of the language that my beautiful mother spoke to my many uncles. Implanted in me at the same time that Miss Fern's gentle firmness and strict moderation, the scent of Pear's soap, the sharp stroke of a scrubbing brush, and the burning of Geo. F. Trumper's West Indian Extract of Lime on my shivering skin breathed the breath of Great Britain into me. France belongs to me just as, by way of my first picture book, the summer sky over Rübezahl's Bohemia or the pine coast of Pinocchio's Collodi belongs to me. All that was European belongs to me that way. Like my fingers or my voice or the tip of my nose. Just as, presumably, rock 'n' roll rhythms or Donald Duck and McDonald's, and hence New York and the Rocky Mountains, too, belong to my son. France was an element in my chemical makeup, and I wondered if I was capable of putting it into words.

Let's assume, I told myself, that you had to explain what France is to your son, who has never heard of it and doesn't know the usual illustrative material. Or even better: to the wolf boy—not Freud's, of course, but one of a more serious breed, one of the outcasts who have grown up among animals in the wild and scurry around on all fours. You've caught him and you're supposed to teach him about the human world. How will you tell him about France? Her essence: her fragrance, her sounds, her colors, her light, her mood, her unmistakable style? . . . What is this? You carry it within yourself as the impression of a very definite azure air density, golden fields, a little blue-white-and-red flag on neatly banal municipal buildings, tin soldiers in red trousers, buttoned-back jacket tails, and front-squashed shakos or gray-green WW I *poilus* in steel helmets with a middle rib, high coat collars, and puttees, such as you scissored out of sheets of pictures by the dozens when you were a child in Cannes. You carry it within yourself in the *maquis* on the rugged coasts of the Corniche and in the pictures of particolored marketplaces where old gentlemen, wearing berets and carrying poles of white bread under their arms, browse around for the fleshiest eggplants, the ripest tomatoes, the plumpest mushrooms. You find the style of France in the airy lattice of the Eiffel Tower, in the tiny, sharply etched illustrations of Larousse, the classicism of Corneille and Racine, of course, in Impressionist paintings, and so forth up to *La Reine Pedauque* and Coco Chanel, *Cousin Pons* and Jean Gabin, the enchanting eloquence of M'sieur Malraux and the sublime spirituality of Paul Valéry . . . but what can you *say* about all this? How can you crystallize the common essence, the—well, unmistakable Frenchness? How can it be put into words? Oh Lord! *What can be put into words anyway?* . . .

Besides, just what *did* I have to say? Myself— certainly. But wasn't France in me too? It was part of the light that illuminated the first half of my life. Remember:

> And if it weren't for Paree
> Then I might dream of you and me . . .

It was one of the elements in the spectral composition of that French light, as specific, intrinsic, and irremovable as the greenish-golden flickering of the German mermaid-world or the full yellow wine light over the sepia and cypress-darkness of the Mediterranean coasts, the glacier blueness and trumpet flashes of Old Austria in a dying Vienna or the melancholy under the brooding sun of Eastern Europe. I had to be able to *say* these things. I had to be able to say what the light had been like when a spring wind full of urgent promise, the wind of a new era, had blown through it before the great Ice Age—and then, from one day to the next, as in a new pendulum swing of time, the light had tipped over into a different state.

For this European light had been the center of our days, even the bleak, gray ones. This light shone even on the dismal years of my Viennese youth, fed it with hope and confidence about the hereafter; fed the dreary apartment and the houses opposite, which may have blocked our view but could not totally extinguish the brighter, airier vastness of the sky overhead or the park of Schönbrunn beyond. This park had been my comfort in the bitter early years of my exile from the vast stretches of Bessarabia and the light-and-color intoxications of the Riviera, and I went there as often as I could. Sat on a bench, breathed, gazed. Did not know, of course, what it was that calmed me. Only sensed that the vast layout of these imperial grounds and the little garden of the trolley conductor's family, which I had visited one Maupassant-like Sunday, had something in common, which I carried within myself along with my yearning for the park in Bessarabia: a piece of orderly nature—the European legacy, which we were squandering. Here in France, there was something left of that legacy, and this was what I had to say in my book.

After nineteen years, I still did not know how it would shape up, this book of mine. It had always been obvious that it would have to be an autobiographical novel. A novel because its subject was a continent: the period of a lifetime. Autobiographical because it had to be the lifetime of the person telling it.

"It's got around that the world cannot be experienced objectively," I said to Schwab. "The titans in the early years of our century knew that one can no longer reflect reality without showing the person who experiences it. So, the eyes through which they had the reader experience such a world-within-the-world were often those of a narrator, placed next to the narrative, in whom the reader unerringly recognized the author himself. As in Proust's *Remembrance of Things Past*. Other times the eyes belonged to a potential narrator, who to some extent was a projection of the novelist into the plot: a character placed in the midst of the events and trying to unravel their problematics, because he will presumably have to tell about it all someday: like Joyce's Stephen Dedalus and even Musil's Ulrich."

Thus, I felt, in literature that is more than broadsheets and street ballads (a possibility that must be accorded even to us dwarfish epigones), the world is the experience of a character who is, only fictitiously, *not* the person of the author himself. The first-person narrative blossoms. But for the cunning reader, this zealously confessional anonymous narrator, this *I*, is transparent enough to reveal the *writer* of the story. Up to a point, the reader follows the flimflam of fiction, but no further. Fiction is possible only with the reader's tacit consent. A complicity that should not be overtaxed.

This was my firmly held thesis when I talked to Schwab. I chatted endlessly about all this with him. I never tired of drumming my notion into his ears. "We are in a dilemma," I kept on saying. "Especially you—if you really intend to write your book one day. *You* would truly have something to say. Come now: such a valuable, massively earnest man: a top student, completed doctoral dissertation lying in his drawer, not handed in because of his elegant restraint (spiritual hygiene to the point of near-sterility); and what is expected of him but an act of self-exposure or, worse, a glimpse into his spiritual digestive processes? This is sure to be embarrassing. Insuperable for an aristocratic character such as yours. I, on the other hand, am an entirely different type. I have always been narcissistic, exhibitionistic. But let us not talk about me and my effronteries. Let us take Nagel—a model of the up-to-date litterateur. He is not without his discretions either, no, no. Yet he is incomparably more democratic. Deliberately run-of-the-mill in a dignified way. Highly *simpático*. You are disgusted at the thought of being in cahoots with the reader, but it's only half so difficult for Nagel, because he lets it happen on the basis of the universally human.

"Needless to say, he's honest enough to admit that he too has no *message* to convey. Nor does he cover our eyes with rose petals. Even the best-selling author Nagel does not give us beautiful images, lofty thoughts, or soul-expanding emotions anymore; he only hands us problems. Like everyone nowadays, he is nothing but a pile of completely unanswered questions. Like every upright writer, he too stammers on about himself. But he stammers only the stammerings of everyman. He stammers of the questions that every moment of existence holds under his nose, everyday problems. He circumspectly chooses those that haunt everyman. Thus he can honestly go halves with the reader. He truthfully admits that the questions concern primarily him, the writer Nagel. In exchange, the reader accepts his disguise as a character in a novel. Naturally, it must not be too exotic. For example, Nagel transposes his own litterateur-head to Bookkeeper Müller's shoulders. The reader accepts this, especially when Bookkeeper Müller admits that he spends part of his leisure aspiring to higher things by writing short stories. That's a good deal. The reader gladly identifies with Müller because he too doesn't want to spend twenty-four hours a day trudging through his daily round and would love to write short stories himself. He yearns for rose petals. That's why he reads books, after all. What makes him a reader is the escape from and beyond his fucked-up workaday life. Thus, with Nagel's book, in which he identifies with Müller, he can tackle the problems of existence arm in arm with the writer Nagel and, together with him, fail to solve them. But I ask you: does our friend Nagel realize how clownish that is?

When the fiction of Bookkeeper Müller, without Nagel added in, is something one can't expect the shrewd reader to accept, then the half fiction is basically an ironic cheat. Do you believe Nagel gives this any thought? . . ."

□   □   □

IT WAS A DAY like this through which I drove with Schwab, then. A day in autumn 1964. Panic-stricken, I had set out from Hamburg, for Dawn had vanished once again in Paris. Untraceable, no matter how much I telephoned after her. So I had to go back to haul her, in a state of total bewilderment, from some Épicure-like dump and calm her down until she had pulled herself together enough to endure a few more weeks of existence in the bright underworld of *la ville lumière*. Schwab insisted on coming along. At the time, I was busy with one of the movie piglets' usual big projects. So I wanted to get to Paris as fast as I could but have the car handy because I knew it soothed Dawn when I drove her around, with her delicious hair in the wind. I didn't hop a plane; I didn't go by way of Holland, where my son probably wasted a whole Sunday yearning for me; instead I tooled along the Autobahn to Baden-Baden, and, with my then still alive German friend S., followed tradition by penetrating France via Strasbourg. Because I hadn't managed to leave Hamburg until late, we spent the night in Reims, going on to Paris the next morning.

"There's something else that good old Nagel doesn't seem to see," I chatted during the drive, "namely, that with his silly bookkeeper who writes short stories, he loses out on the very thing he would like to write himself: a novel. If he wrote about himself, the writer Nagel, who writes not only short stories but whole books, and indeed so incessantly and uninterruptedly as to make you think that he can't live without writing, *then* he would have a novel! A writer who writes about writing will open the world in a new way. A lost possibility will open up to him: the very possibility of showing a human being in a world with which he has a living relationship. Hence, a world in which one *lives* and not just exists unrelatedly, like some bookkeeper vainly trying to relate to the world by writing short stories. We are told on all sides that the novel is dead, and that's because its last great theme is exhausted—the incompatibility of man's inner world with his outer world, the individual's forlornness in society, the unreality of the world man has created. But these are simply the problems of novel characters, not novel writers. These are the troubles of Bookkeeper Müller, whom Nagel has disguised himself as. They concern the writer Nagel only because he falls for his own flimflam and identifies with Müller the bookkeeper, not with Müller the short-story writer. Okay, through Müller he identifies with the reader—but by way of Müller's intention to write short stories. The reader, in his workaday existence, is totally uninterested in Müller. He's enough of a bookkeeper and has enough everyday problems himself; he doesn't need Nagel in this respect. In order to escape, he reads books and wants to write short stories. So why doesn't Nagel go all the way and let the reader identify fully with *him*, the writer Nagel? With a writer not only of dreamed-up short stories but also of books, day in day out, year in year out. Someone who lives from and for writing books. For whom writing is life. Who can experience the world only by writing. That way, he'd pull off the trick of writing about a life full of relatedness. A writer interiorizes the outer world. The more incompatible he finds the existence of man as an individual, the more it becomes an immediate, burning, living issue for him, and he concerns himself with it. And the more subjectively he concerns himself with it, the more objectively he grasps it, and the more objectively he renders it. The world becomes an object again. One not only swims in it, as among fish in an aquarium, but can confront it, simply by writing, by *describing* it. Admittedly, the writer who sees the world only from his special vantage point circumvents the problem of society. *Il s'en fout totalement;* he doesn't give a shit. He has an easy time of it, after all. He is in the enviable position of getting along marvelously without society. The more isolated he is, the better he works. Cervantes—whom you as a top student must vaguely know, don't you?—wrote *Don Quixote* in a prison cell. Fine: in the prison cell of your existence, you, as a writer, will find your great theme today:

yourself. The self as a reality—in German, *Wirklichkeit*, from *wirken*, to work, act, operate . . . working: writing. Acting by writing. Become real by writing. By de*scrib*ing, writing about, the world the way you wish to de*scribe* it, write about it; and, experiencing defeat, you will challenge the world as a reality. You become a defeated Don Quixote, who, being entangled in his inner world and thwarted by it, reaches the outer world. In this way, the reader Müller, staring bewildered into nothingness, is shown the road from the interior and then out of it into the exterior. You present the world to him. For the writer who writes about himself writing, the world becomes once again a means of experiencing the world—and thus, for the reader, once again a means of experiencing himself. Heed these golden words, dearest friend, for they may contain salvation for you, too. No more roguish acts of lightning-swift exposure. No more brief liftings of the costume so that the reader can see the naked author underneath. What we have now is a grand act of dedication. Hara kiri. Offer yourself as a slaughter-platter to your fellow man bookkeeper reader Müller. No more machinations to go halves. You need not borrow Bookkeeper Müller's costume from Reader Müller in order to hide your nakedness. You don't have to wink at him from that costume: 'Look at me; I know that you know that I, naked underneath, am the author; but a very tiny little thing that wishes to write short stories is dangling between your legs, too.'

"Show Müller what you really think of him. Smash all your innards, smoking, into his face. Show him what you think of his fifty-fifty partners; for instance, Nagel. But no! Nagel is an upright fellow: a Sancho Panza, who, for sheer love of being a lackey, continues Don Quixote's heroic struggle. This is not for you, no, no: show Reader Müller what you think of the great writer Thomas Mann sitting at his desk and giggling into his *fist* (which we Germans call *Faust*) because he, who has just Wagnered *Faustus* out of that selfsame *fist*, is now masquerading as *Felix Krull, Confidence Man*, and cutting capers for us. Pull down those borrowed pants! The Mardi Gras is over. Today, even a child knows that existence can be endured only if existence describes itself. Ask any modern-day child the old, idiotic question, what does he want to be when he grows up? Not a fireman or train engineer, as in our day. No, he wants to become an artist. A circus performer if he is especially talented and in the best of health. But if his gifts are average, then a sculptor, actor, painter, moviemaker. In delicate cases, the brat is already writing. He's had the outline for his novel lying in his little desk since long before puberty, since the age of six or seven. And his enraptured parents are encouraging him. Weren't yours? Just imagine how proud I am of my son's ceramics. . . ."

I waited for his reaction, a sign of agreement or rejection, or else simply amusement or boredom; but Schwab, at my side, remained wordless and gazed unswervingly forward into the road flying toward us. It was a straight-as-an-arrow road through land that surged toward us in a vast breath; intoxicatingly set between the round tops of apple trees, the road dipped steeply into the depressions, like a roller coaster in an amusement park, and then up the other side, straight as an arrow, and the densely green spheres of apple trees continued to accompany it. *La douce France* flew past Schwab's profile, which was strangely delicate for the massive Luther head (a silver-burin drawing, I thought to myself); every acre of soil had been fertilized with French and German blood. I knew his father had died in action here, just before the end of Doubleyou Doubleyou One, in 1918. Schwab had never known his father, but he piously nurtured his memory. German Professor Anselm Schwab (no relation to Gustav).

In those days, one of my delights was to let the landscapes of Europe fly past Dawn's profile. She loved an open car and was very beautiful when she closed her eyes and held her face with its blowing hair into the headwind. I thought of the cruel game I had played with Christa: "If there were two people you loved equally, and you had to sacrifice one of them so that the other could survive and you with him, which of the two would it be?" I loved Dawn. But I never doubted for an instant which of the two I would sacrifice if I were forced to choose between her and Schwab. I sensed I was becoming irritable, and I stepped harder on the gas pedal. I had been driving rather fast anyhow. Now things began to get interesting.

"You may have goodness knows how high an opinion of Nagel," I said (and knew I was hitting a raw nerve, for Schwab held Nagel in very high esteem and regularly despaired when Nagel failed once again to achieve what Scherping ingeniously called the "breakthrough to himself"). "But so long as Nagel does not realize that he is always deceiving himself, that most honest of all men, he will never become a first-class writer. But that's *your* funeral, honored friend. You and no one else have been appointed to tell him that. After all, Scherping pays you to administer pastoral care to his authors. However, there are also purely ethical motives. When a man like you is too prim and proper to contribute a work to literature, then he at least has the damned duty to make sure the general level of culture is raised by the works of other people. A task full of self-denial, I own, but as we all know, it is always the best who fall in the war, likewise the best who perish in the culture business. The survivors write; there's nothing we can do about it. They write to survive, and they survive because they write. But they shouldn't make it too easy on themselves, right? I know you'll have Scherping to deal with if you convince Best-selling Author Nagel that what he writes is shit. But after a dozen best-sellers, even his publisher ought to allow him an excursion into literature. Naturally, that sort of thing might mess up the Complete Works. The Oeuvre. Without failed attempts, it will be more homogeneous, of course. Twelve gentle street ballads by Bookkeeper Müller, who wants to write short stories. Twelve illustrated broadsheet tales, striding like valiant hikers toward their noble goal of assuring us that, despite all the murky confusion, the world is ultimately an orderly structure. It may not be obvious why this is true, but it is comforting to believe it. At least it could be an orderly structure. It should be in any case. *Per aspera ad astra* even for the potential short-story writer Müller. After all, it's always the same story with the same character, and the same destiny, simple and obvious as a child's mechanical toy. The coil-spring tension of some tiny man-in-the-street problem, some common, current conflict—for instance, in the wishful short-story-writing bookkeeper Müller, the bad conscience caused by belonging to an elite—transferred to the gear transmission of our theoretically humanitarian and in fact misanthropic social conditions; and the thing is already purring along its path, joining with others of its kind, creating a tiny world, a tiny as-if, which, minute and simplified, is nevertheless a fair image of the big, bad world, as though it were our dear, bad, workaday life itself. Meant merely to be wound up, reduced to the simplest term, deciphered with the easier multiplication table. A tiny fiction, sharply true to life but so remote in its own reality that if you look at it, your gaze is lost in dreams as in the glass-encapsulated oceanic vastness surrounding a meticulously rigged ship inside a bottle. Happily, you add it to other bric-à-brac in your home, in the culture cupboard, where next to an anthology of short-story writers stand a dozen contemporary novels like peas in a pod. In terms of its skill, this belongs with the little Calderesque mobile whirling overhead. But imagine Nagel understanding that his bookkeeper Müller, who wants to write short stories, is *not* material for a novel, no matter how tragicomically he has Müller struggle through to the light or be doomed with all the powers of earth and heaven. Still, it's an excellent topic for an essay: 'Imagination as a Gamble.' For once, a sober posing of the question whether the courage for this should not be reserved for an elite of more or less violent lunatics. Can't it be consistent with order if the gamble of imagination is also granted to his bookkeeper Müller? What damage is thereby done to his soul? You see, if this is accorded to just anyone, then it would leave the door open to such questions as well. . . . Oh, come on, you don't have to snort so indignantly, I'm quite serious. One is confronted with the question of a sound relationship between fiction and reality. We realized long ago that this relationship is out of kilter among people like us. The dirty-minded psychology boys didn't have to demonstrate the close connection between writing and masturbation. That has always been a source of our arrogance. The onanist is a sovereign. He has the biggest harem on earth, and no woman can resist him. Above all, however, he eludes Mother Nature's dirty game. Who wants 'reality' anyway? Don't we do everything we can to flee it? For instance, by reading books. And certainly by writing books! Even Wishful Short-Story Writer Müller knows that. It is simply human. What gives us a special place in zoology is the fact that we cannot endure reality and incessantly oppose it with fictions. Mother Nature's monotonous game made us sick to our stomachs long ago. We refuse to admit that only one single 'reality' can dominate: the sheer, brutal, infinitely unimaginative reality of being born in order to procreate life-devouring life, and to be devoured for the procreation of other life. We push this reality into the background and cover it up with a camouflage backdrop of fiction. All well and good. But the problem is the mixture: too much fiction blinds us to Nature, while a man is devoured before he can say 'Jack Robinson'; too little fiction renders Ma Nature's unendurable cruelty too evident. Here, too, we who are mentally disturbed because of too much imagination are nicely left out of the game. We know we'll be devoured; in the meantime, we send up the balloons of our fictions, create a reality within reality, valid for us alone, a world within the world, in which we can be happy-go-lucky, a Middle Kingdom in which we are sovereign. If everyone thought and acted along those lines, obviously things would become chaotic. The man in the street must be allowed to go halves with 'reality' and veil it agreeably, and he must be permitted enough consciousness not to be caught unawares by *reality.*"

Schwab was still not perceptibly involved, and I laughed. "Perhaps there is a possibility here to save you, too," I said. "I mean: the essay. If I were you, I would write an essay that would be a consequence and heightening of the essay on 'Imagination as a Gamble' and also a genuine German contribution: namely, 'On Causality and Necessity.' The German contribution would come directly from the German genius: its language. No other language more blatantly expresses the predicament of having to stave off necessity: *Not-wendigkeit:* see the translation of *Not:* need, want, privation, indigence; care, sorrow, misery, affliction; trouble, difficulty, plight, predicament, emergency, extremity; danger, peril, distress; necessity, exigency, urgency . . . and all this wants to be *gewendet:* turned away from us, take a turn for the better, turn out for the best . . . Incidentally, a theological theme. I can sniff the LORD Zebaoth. Our most reliable camouflage backdrop. No, no, I've been talking nonsense again: Nagel knows what he's doing. When he feels like philosophical profundity, he merely sticks a steel helmet on his bookkeeper Müller: not only does this make Müller totally universal and humanly close to everyone, even without the urge to write short stories, but also thrusts him into the midst of the realest events, and Mother Nature laughs at the human beings dancing to her pipe in the name of the most astonishing fictions. Yet all this is necessary if Nagel is to go halves with Reader Müller. Whenever Nagel opens the little treasure chest of his wartime experiences (for which I envy him more and more hungrily), something else emerges in the glowing of the German Cross in Gold, the Iron Cross First Class and Iron Cross Second Class, the Close Combat Ribbon, and Seriously Injured Medals: that something else is the Lord God. From out of the gunfire, HIS eye gives us an encouraging wink, indicating that the whole hullaballoo has been put on in order to help Private First Class Müller find his identity. On a literary level, a steel storm is just sufficient to forge a young man into a Self whose inner wealth (of doubt, of course, but now also self-confidence, thank goodness) will supply an entire generation with a basis for seeing its own portrait in that Self. The fact that the riflemen Neumann, Lehrmann, Meier, and Kunze, all the same age as he, are shot is significant only in that it displays the harshness of this test of destiny. It is part of the drama's background dynamics. Chiaroscuro flatters. Nitpickers are referred to the irrational fraction that remains when we try to divide life by reason. But for the Bros. Nagelmüller, what results is *necessity—Notwendigkeit—* and with it, subsequently, alleged causality. This is then known as: history. *Bravo!* A final European attempt to infer an orderly structure from the absurdity of existence, to make it into a meaningful structure. Does Nagel know this—Nagel, whose intellectual lodestar is Mr. Hemingway? Does he know—however much he plunges into his Europeanized Hemingway imitations while involuntarily rebelling against America's tiding—that life is, more than anything else, irrational and subject to violence? For wasn't that what the New World pioneers brought home to us from the harshness of their wide-open spaces? Dealing the coup de grâce to millennia of frail efforts to put Nature in order? Just what is our culture, our civilization? The tradition that our origin and ultimate bliss are *in a garden.* That unordered Nature can have an order and thereby a meaning and purpose. This is the tiding of Western Civilization from the Bible to Nagel. True, Mother Nature is not overlooked, especially in certain gory and decay-green depictions of man as the Son of God nailed to a cross. Oddly enough, though, despite their spectacular evocation of anxiety, these often sincere, even unsparing likenesses of everyday human life have something comforting and ethically edifying about them, don't you think? This depicted world is no less dreadful, monstrous, devastating than the real world that gets too close for comfort. However, the artist's depicting hand has also gotten himself, man, into the picture, has brushed and stylused him in. This makes it a human world, a world with the dimension of its echo in the human soul. It keeps it in suspense, as it were, hanging from the conceptual balloon like the Saviour on the cross. The image of horror contains horror, spellbinds it. The image of terror includes terror, canceling it somewhat, offering only its outline and not its weight, only the reflection of its harshness and not the harshness itself. The elements of disorder have been sifted through and ordered by the person who put its likeness together. Meaninglessness fills up with the well-meaning-ness of the person who recognized it as meaningless. . . . Oh well, we know that the image of reality is a magic formula that casts a spell on reality itself, in a dialectical equilibrium that gives it a logic in itself, the analogic of likeness. And that's what we're charmed by. We've been charmed by this since our very first primer picture and nursery story—what am I saying: since the Cro Magnon cave drawings. . . ."

Four years had passed between then and my latest trip from Reims to here. I drove along the same French highway, cutting straight across the land over hill and dale; the day was as bright as the day when Schwab had sat next to me in the car. I remembered adding: "Fine, I've sensed for a while now that I'm getting on your nerves. But I've got ants in my pants, I can't get along without the usual *Kultur* gallop. In fast motion, I promise you! I promise you I am heading straight for something that is certain not to bore you. As Uncle Ferdinand used to sing: *Parlez-moi de moi, et exclusivement de moi-même, et je vous aime.* . . . Now where were we? With the shamans. Ever since the Cro Magnon cave ceremonies, man has been—(à propos, back then people must have been a more likable bunch than the riffraff we saw at the roadside café yesterday)—anyway, for millennia now, man has been charmed by the same old flimflam and the same old flimflam men. He's been getting his eyes rubbed by the spell of image, in which man and the world are united as one, fiction and reality in a magic equilibrium. Still the same old devices: drums, geometric figures, mutterings of conjurers, lightning-swift casting of runic staffs—*our* devices, dear sir: the devices of the *Kultur* Association for Art and Literature (a chartered and incorporated club), lyre, quill, chisel, and palette embroidered on the banners by the ladies' auxiliary. And, if you please, we also have to sing the old ditty. The Song of God: *Oh, you beauteous forest you,/Who built you so lofty, who?* Well, who? The Parks Department? No. Ask Nagel, he knows. He'll even tell you. Cryptically, to be sure, and bashfully—a Hemingway disciple in hairy-chested sentimentality—but unmistakably. And he's right. What can we do: like it or not, we are serving God. Working on the most sublime of all fictions. Since the immemorial beginnings of language, we have been filling the names of things with our exultations and lamentations, and we have been speaking of them as if they had found a response within us. Millennia before the chanting of the pre-Homeric rhapsodists, an orderly image of the world had already been conjured up, because the rhythm of ordered words had brought that image into the world. What does a man do if he closes his eyes in a state of idiotic rapture in order to hark within himself to the responses of things to themselves? Or self-obliviously to rivet his eyes on them until their images rise up again within him, forcing him to render them with an added human dimension? Am I then being indiscreet if I ask whether it is the right honorable intellectual timidity of it that will ultimately prevent you from writing your book? I am being presumptuous, but after all, you did talk *me* into writing *my* book—good heavens, fifteen years ago! that's how long it's been!—and I want to wreak a little vengeance. So, tell me, am I wrong in assuming that you are revolted at the thought of dealing with devices that permit intellectual fraud? I mean, the suspect ingredients that turn a sentence into a fetish and a stanza into a revelation of the numinous, a formation of ABC's into a Gospel—let alone a crappy bestseller? But you're not answering me, you're leaving me in eternal uncertainty as to whether I should join the lousy game of asking, once again in my own way, the question about the meaning of existence—a question that, even if I don't find an answer, I will nevertheless have already answered with my own way of asking, with the originality and passion of my asking. . . . Come on, bestow a comforting word! Just say that creation fulfills its meaning in man, and that his existence contains a premeditated plan and an ultimate goal of salvation. Just convince me that the dreadfulness of the world is matched by so and so many sublimities, which cancel the dreadfulness out. Persuade me that anyone who cannot recognize this in Alpine peaks, in sunsets reflected in the Mediterranean, will find it all the more cogently in the *Gilgamesh*, Beethoven's Ninth, or the Angel of Reims. . . . Tell me all these things, I need them as backup. I'm driving to Paris to pull a twenty-year-old American girl out of some dump she's crept into, because her beautiful eyes are still full of the terror of the wide-open wastes in the New World, where she comes from, where an arrow can come whizzing out at any moment from behind the rock outcroppings, and Grandma wears an Indian scalp in her belt; where the pistols in thigh holsters are still as loose as in the days of Billy the Kid; where the ears of sleeping Negro children are devoured by slum rats in the huge stone wastes of the cities . . . in short, images in eyes that absolutely require the optical illusion of God in order to endure thinking about the world; eyes, alas, that did not try to recognize His revelation through European civilization, certainly not in the cancerous proliferation of the Old World, in the horrible teeming of the motorized army ants, the chewing *horlàs* who chomp on their morsels, zealously insalivating them, washing them down with a swig of beer wine Coca-Cola apple juice milk booze mead lemonade club soda—swallowing, jerking-up of the Adam's apple, parting of the lips, the tongue-dragon rolling forward and flicking a few food-gruel remnants from the teeth, a slight burp—excuse me, it's only from the stomach—and then the next morsel is shoved in . . . and behind it lurks the big cat Nature, ready to devour them all. *Against this* I have to tell my disturbed young beloved, make her believe, that this ceaseless gruesome production and destruction of living creatures is made up for by a heartful of love (isn't that so?), and, in case of doubt, by such verses as, Springtime drops her azure ribbon, or Peace lies on all the mountaintops, or a few bars of Vivaldi, or a Cézanne landscape.... I have to tell her this convincingly, so that she will come to her senses and allow herself to be photographed for the spring collections of Coco Chanel and Monsieur de Givenchy and Yves Saint-Laurent for *Vogue* and *Harper's Bazaar* and *Elle* and *Marie Claire....*"

That was fifteen hundred days ago. I survived them, writing and undauntedly loving: loving Dawn loving Gaia loving Nadine still loving Christa—always ready to flee from the terror of life into the gracious madness of love, or rather, from the ungracious hallucination of having to write into the not much more gracious delusion of having to live. Schwab had chastely withdrawn from this neurotherapoetic treatment of alternating hot and cold baths: he was dead, was now next to me only in spirit. The little pile of earthly substance to which his large body had been reduced was probably well preserved in some urn. I still don't know where that urn wound up—at the Ohlsdorf graveyard or in a display cabinet with his Hamburg relatives. Perhaps Schelmy got hold of it and put it on the bottle shelf behind the bar at Lücke's. I couldn't quite tell whether I was sad about it. I certainly must have been in a way, for I was sorry not to see him. But on the other hand, now I had him around more comfortably, especially when traveling. I didn't have to get fidgety with nervous expectation that he might again be overcome at any moment by some irresistible desire for whiskey or beer or a hedge to piss behind or matches for his innumerable cigarettes after burning his fingers on the last one and absent-mindedly tossing the dashboard lighter out the window. True, he had always been at the mercy of my chitchat, and a man who loved to suffer, as I well knew; but now I had him unresistingly at my disposal, and he could never again escape my convulsive monologues. It crossed my mind that a witty Frenchman (I don't know who; one of the spirits whom Stella called "provincial," anyway) described writing as a welcome opportunity to talk without being interrupted—

And in the enigmatic way in which seeming trivia spark the revelation of something fundamental, it came to me with an illuminating bang: I suddenly had my book very clearly before me. It loomed before my spirit's eyes in flawless architecture: a glass cathedral, whose symbolic formula, like the axial system of a crystal, could be read from all relationships of the lines and masses. A House of God to celebrate myself—Hosannah! At last, I had the blueprint.

Naturally, it had to be a book by a writer about writing. "Here we have it at last, our spiritual child!" my spirit called to Schwab's spirit. "But it's too bad that you're pulling it out of me posthumously. When you were alive, it would have aroused your keenest envy: a book about the very writer of this very book. This, of course, completely involves the author.

"And this means that everything that comes up in it has to refer to writing. Of course, it's necessarily—*notwendig*—an autobiography. However, for such a life confession to be of even the slightest interest, it has to tell a life story that is typical of the era, and it has to demonstrate that a man of his time has no choice but to write—and thereby write this life confession of a writer.

"But if this is to deal with writing in a truly transcendental way, then every situation of the confessed life, every situation that necessarily leads to writing, must simultaneously be a metaphor for a corresponding situation *in* writing. This can hardly be achieved with a confusing and also banal biography like mine, dear friend. Once again, art will have to lend life a helping hand. Instead of bare, complex, and paradoxical 'reality,' this too will require an agreeable as-if that is perspicuous in its simplicity and flawless in its logic. We resort to the expedient of a *hypothetical autobiography*, dear friend. In a word: we must not be as honest as we would like to be. We shall have to cheat. In the language of art, you have to say, we must *invent*. Fine! Let me worry about that. For the moment, I'm delighted. My book—or shall I rather say *our* book?—has finally found its form! The structure is given along with the substance. The situation of the writer in the process and experience of writing is prenatal. His intimate incorporation of the world of the incorporatedness in the world; his absorption in things in order to suck out their articulable essence; his wholehearted devotion to what wants to express itself through him—all these things correspond to the embryo listening to its own growth. The writer, in the amniotic fluid of his desire, his urge, to write, is budding. What he writes has to bud. Has to develop out of itself. No dramatics, please. No plot storming forward; the story growing statically out of itself, adding stratum after stratum by wearing out stratum after stratum. Am I expressing myself intelligibly? How did you always put it? 'I accumulate in order to have something to lose.' That's a quotation from me, of course. All yours, comrade. The crucial thing now: the writer buds out in writing. Without it he wouldn't be. After that, we hardly have to talk about the time and the place of the plot. All pastness of the described (and describing) existence is telescoped in the presentness of narrative. The entire story of the person who narrates himself is present in the here and now as that person. But the story refuses to be told in historical sequence; it has to be told as the ever-present historical content of his presentness: he contains himself in all phases of his story, confronts us in any phase and is all phases at once.

"The style too, accordingly, results from this. A life in the steadily changing multitude of its moods demands the totality of possible forms of expression. First of all, the penumbra of the cell situation, the isolation from the world, flight from the world, search for the world in mole blindness, in the light beam of the desk lamp—these subjects require a chronicler's diction that conjures up the atmosphere of the remote past and yet is so present that the envelope of the as-if never opens for an instant, even when it is kept transparent, bearing in mind that this is an allegorical story that is meant to illustrate a universal truth in a chain of symbolic situations. Got it, friend? Just as I must use archetypal imagery in the story without being inhibited by fear of banality, so too my language must risk walking the tightrope between genuine poetry and occasional kitsch, antiquated diction and crassly current colloquialism. A tightrope of language, yet a catalogue of style: from characterizing jargon to the icy neutrality of the literary tongue, from trivial chitchat to the argot of the intellectuals, from the perfidious mendacity of salesmen's eloquence to the poetry of pimps. My movie piglets are finally putting in their two cents. Scherping finally becomes a bard. In short: a style of barbaric *haut goût*, like the decadent Latin texts in the centuries during and after the migrations of the peoples, a style that has something nervous and spasmodic in its incessant changes of milieus and moods.

"What did you always say about a novel? It is a continent in its space-time. This sort of thing should no longer be presented in linear form, can no longer be presented chronologically. After all, as a writer, I do not speak about writing as about something that has taken place; I keep on writing by writing it down. I keep living my writing the way a living man lives his life. I must tell about it the way I would tell about my life to someone who lives with me. Living on. My space-time is an island in the ocean of time. My reader is with me on this island, which still lies in the dark for him. He wants to get to know it—by all means. My story sweeps across it like the beam of a lighthouse. It sweeps along the horizon all around my island, always sweeping across the same areas; but each time the light beam seizes them, they reveal something previously unknown, until eventually the entire topography is experienced. I know: I will have to exercise caution—for instance, the balance of intellectual and emotional stimulations. A delicate matter, eh? But these are problems of execution, additional work to prove our diligence. All I have to do now is rummage through the jumble of papers in the car trunk and pick out the ones that fit in with my plan. And I'll have my book, damn it—*I'll have my book, man. I'll have my book!*

"What do you say? HE WHO HATH WILL BE GIVEN . . . Why the hell don't you say something? It's a bad joke on your part to have been dead for four years now."

Then, suddenly, everything was gray all around me, like the densest fog. I heard a brief, hard bang, and all at once, I didn't know where I was, I got scared, I slammed on the brakes and the car almost whirled on its own axis, with crushed stone spraying up around me.

I stood up. I opened the door. On a stretch of freshly rebuilt, still unasphalted road, I had come close—not too fast, luckily—to a truck. When I sheered out to pass it, he had stepped on the gas. His back tires tore up a stone, which flew into my windscreen. It was like an opaque stroke of lightning that totally blocked my view.

I should have taken this as a warning. But people like us, heroic as we are, do not do such things. I dug a hole in the debris on the windshield so that I could see, and then on I drove to Paris. I was absolutely determined to start work immediately.

□   □   □

THIS HAD TAKEN PLACE—let me repeat it once again—a week earlier. I did not hesitate for an instant. I drove straight to the Épicure, unloaded my suitcases, cartons, and boxes, parked the car in the garage, bought myself a big jar of instant coffee, went up to my room (number 26 as usual; it's always free, seems to wait for me), and got down to my papers. The first slip I took hold of said, in red letters, SCHWAB. That same moment, the horror of my dream attacked me with such power and present reality that I thought someone was actually standing behind me, catching me in the abominable act of my murder.

And while I tried to hold on to the flash of recognition that made me realize that my dream was true, that I had really murdered someone (and that I would soon also know whom and how and when and where), I was overcome with a sense of profound shame:

the flimflam of my actions became so horrifyingly blatant to me, just as a lunatic may realize in a lucid moment that he is a lunatic—

the incredible flimflam of the existence of a writer—a fiction inventor, a man playing his game like an unsophisticated child, in an utterly menacing world—

composing his as-if like a moron who accumulates pebbles and who, babbling and drooling, watches them dribble apart as he tries all the harder to build up the same pile again . . .

What was I doing here? What was I working on?

Schwab—who *is* he?

It is the name of a character I have sketched for a novel, for whom my (now deceased) friend S. was the model. The invented name for one of the many figures (freely recorded from life) in the untold (never fully drafted and ultimately rejected) drafts of my book. Originally, S. had not been given a significant part. To be sure, I had toyed with the thought of letting him stroll across the stage; after all, he was important in my life story, and hypothetical as my projected autobiographies may have been, I nevertheless took from the one reality whatever served me for the Truth of the other "reality." But still, the Johannes Schwab character was merely one of the tinier pebbles from my idiots' game, a so-called *supernumerary*—

so that was what had become of the living man, the human being, my friend and spiritual brother J.S. . . . I still know rather precisely when I had begun to jot down utterances, habits, particular features of his: here, in Paris, one morning on the Île de la Cité, when we were on the Pont Neuf, gazing up the Seine, and he made a remark implying that he was planning to write about me. I wanted to forestall him. Surprise him one day with a portrait that would throw a monkey wrench in his works. But never had I seriously planned to use him as a main figure in any of the countless drafts for my book.

Yet now a certain Johannes Schwab was erupting from every even halfway intelligible sheet of paper. He clung to me like a shadow—and placed me under him. He was not to be shaken off. He was simply everywhere. He dominated everything. He squeezed into the new draft of my book and did not look all that bad in it. But he made it burst: he enlarged it *ad infinitum*. If I gave in to his pushiness and took the character of Johannes Schwab into the story, then he pushed the events in a different direction, way beyond the plot line. With him, the story proliferated all over the place, beyond its original shape, metastasizing in new and entirely unforeseen dimensions. It could scarcely be held under control; it demanded a thorough rethinking; it required a plot ten times longer; it opened new paths for invention.

Without him, the story now seemed lifeless, artificial, too obviously forced to be plausible, too private to be interesting. My dead friend S. suddenly seemed to contain all the life of my book.

For seven full nights and fitfully dozed days, I sought a way out of this grotesque dilemma (always pursued by my lurking dream) until I finally realized that my resistance was futile. Either I had to take Schwab into my book (which meant that I would have to rewrite it; that is, again put it off indefinitely) or else, for the time being, I would once more have to fling my outline to the wind.

The thing that has been agitating me so profoundly since then is the discovery of such a blatant, absolutely undeniable, inexplicable, and sinisterly effective magic.

At some point when S. was still alive and kicking, I found and wrote down a name: Johannes Schwab . . .

and thus a human being is put on paper and is *alive* . . .

he has the features of my friend S. (who is no longer alive), he moves, he carries himself like my friend, he talks like him, he articulates thoughts that *he* could have uttered, he behaves like him, he has his unhappy genius, his stand-offish character, his forcefulness and his weakness, his whims, crotchets, and eccentricities— and in the end his destiny as well. The demonic power of the script has awakened a dead man to life.

Now I have him around me day and night. Since the baneful hour when I re-exhumed him (after a few years of oblivion), he has been my worst tormentor, the most sublime, the most murderous instrument of self-destruction.

He peers over my shoulder when I rummage through my papers; he keeps a sharp eye on me even when I write (yes, even now, while I write this down). It was he who drove me to destroy entire sections of the book. Because of him, I ripped up and threw out the tangle of beginnings, finished and still unfinished chapters, drafts, outlines. Because of him, whenever I continued working on something these past few days and nights, I eventually dropped the pen in disgust, and furiously and desperately tore my scribblings to shreds.

He has infiltrated my thoughts, my soliloquies; he comments

on them sneeringly (for instance, now); he encourages my most abstruse plans, praising them only to undermine them. He sabotages my best ideas; he presumes to judge my abilities, my intentions, my resolutions, my decisions (it's beyond my strength to carry them out, right?); he scorns, mocks, warns, proves, convicts, and shames me—in short, Schwab is willful (probably infected by my own worst manners). What his model (friend S. the graceful: in his lifetime the finest standard-bearer of freedom granted everyone; the sovereign appreciator of any spiritual form or utterance so long as it was at least halfway equal or even superior to his; the proud and happy discoverer of my literary talent and its most ardent defender against infidels and doubters, a man who always practiced the tenderest admiration for me, an admiration deftly concealed and hence all the more flatteringly manifested)—I say, what friend S. would never have dared to do Schwab does unsparingly: he delivers the most annihilating criticism, offers the most cutting, most destructive analysis, paragraph for paragraph, line for line, word for word, expresses fundamental doubt in both the mission itself and the calling of the man who has undertaken it: your humble servant.

The creature from my pen, whom I have called Schwab, carries on like a literary tax investigator, so to speak, an unrelenting snooper who quickly spots the finagling in a balance sheet, ferrets out any tax evasion, tracks down any unlisted source of income—

and, unfortunately, he does not limit himself to that. He uses the literary as a pretext to burrow into my private life, and there he acts with overwhelming power, demands absolutely accurate data on incidents that I would much rather have let lie, confronts me about things I may have once, foolishly blinded, viewed as vile and concerning which I might now blissfully look down, like a martyr at his battered body—if the quondam vileness had not been restored, thanks to his pastoral activity, which drills into your teeth

—as if even the most false, stupid, nay inhumane commandment still contained something ethically valuable in essence, not forfeited with the Expulsion of the Idols, something we have been unable to get fully rid of since the establishment of a new and more radiant God—

Thanks to Schwab, I am surrounded again by a forest of those formerly worshiped totems and feared taboos, with all their terrifying grimaces: I experience the most absurd incidents of my formative years in Vienna under the same moral pressure that made them traumas in the past, not to mention later events.

My dead friend S. (*le pudique*, who blushed furiously at the slightest indiscretion, so that his lips turned pale and began to tremble; S. the broad-mindedly playful man, *passionné des cascadeurs*, enraptured gaper at my feats in the art of life, who released an orgiastic "Ah!" at every volt, every *salto mortale* with which I managed to twist out of the allegedly fateful alternatives of existence; S. in love with whatever I wrote, whenever I wrote; S. the fiery head of a claque in a small but select audience, endlessly delighted by my adventures, my gambles, and their stunning peripeties, as well as my ether-clear somnambulism)—this friend S. was replaced by a man named Schwab: an unpleasant zealot and tough-as-leather moralist, a boorish second-guesser and nitpicking examiner, who continues to live the life of tactful, sensitive, generous S. but in a puritanically narrow-minded and aggressive manner, in annoying, obtrusive, sinister ubiquity—

And I, for my part, find myself embarrassingly obsequious to him. I am at his mercy. I am as submissive to this changeling of fantasy and reality as I was to the "protective spirit" that my foster parents invented to keep me on a string during my formative years in Vienna. (This was allegedly one of the spirits that joined the séances of Uncle Helmuth's spiritist community, the New Star, every Saturday evening: a lofty gentleman in the beyond, I was told, taking care of my dead mother there, hence astrally, as my diverse uncles had when she was alive; however, he was far more severe, more serious-minded, more draconic. With faces stricken lifeless by shock, Uncle Helmuth and Aunt Hertha informed me of his disappointment at my conduct, which he observed very carefully; they scarcely dared hint at his threats of punishment—just the usual, terse "You'll see . . .")—

The pen-and-paper homunculus whom I named Schwab had seized hold of not only my conscience but also, thereby, my book—

but not quite without a deeper meaning. I mean: not just for art's sake: Schwab is not merely a personification of my literary conscience: he *is*. He *is* S., my dead friend. J.S. wants to materialize through him, in him. Fine! I am supposed to write J.S. into life as Johannes Schwab. Of course, I must warn you, my honored dead friend J.S., this is no longer you: *Schwab* is here on the paper. *He* is living his own life here. I cannot do anything for you now. *He* will have your features, your powerful body; *he* will move like you, carry himself like you, speak like you, speak thoughts you could have uttered, reveal feelings you could have felt; *he* will act like you, for he has, I repeat, your unhappy genius, your stand-offish character, your power and your weakness, your likes and dislikes, characteristics, cranks and crotchets, and ultimately your destiny as well: *he* will have died *because he could not write his book*. But he will be *he*, not you.

Nothing can be done about it, alas. He is already here, on these pages, already living on them—and in a sharply outlined figure at that. If I had written down nothing but his name, *Johannes Schwab*, he would already be quite unmistakably himself. He no longer escapes himself—and I could not help him escape. No man escapes himself if he has forfeited himself in the demonic world of writing, whether alive or deceased.

I do not doubt that you, friend S., in that world beyond where you are now, are among the free, the mighty, the illuminated (although it strikes me as a bit suspicious that you feel such a vehement urge to cross back over the threshold, so vehement that you already virtually have a foot in the door, so that I cannot shut you out). But you don't have very much to do here. Someone else has taken your place. And here (I am obliged to point this out to you), here we must apply the harsh Biblical verse: FOR UNTO EVERY ONE THAT HATH SHALL BE GIVEN. . . . BUT FROM HIM THAT HATH NOT SHALL BE TAKEN EVEN THAT WHICH HE HATH.

So I ask your forgiveness. I, for my part, must now join Schwab. For I too am on these pages: I am already placed upon them, pasted on them, and will appear all the more vivid and diversely colored the more I pull away from them—*into One who writes me . . .*

HERE, TOO, I wish to be of assistance. My wanted poster is quickly written.

I write. But I lack the so-called demonic element one expects of a writer. I am (despite Aunt Selma's occasional doubts) a good, soft-hearted, anyway banal person. I love children, dogs, cats, fresh milk, the moon in the evening sky, my friends (Schwab and, especially, Nagel). To be sure, I do not love myself. I find myself completely suspect.

I hate my life-lie. The grand hopes and good intentions I left unrealized because I was supposedly summoned to some greater fulfillment—I would have left them unrealized anyway. The years I have squandered on them—I would have squandered them anyway. The people I have disappointed, the women I have exploited, deceiving and deserting them, my son, whom I have frustrated—I would have exploited, disappointed, deceived, deserted, and frustrated them anyway. The shameful junk I have written for my piglets to scrape out a meager living with partridge and Mouton Rothschild—I would have written it anyway.

For I have this mucus in me and I would have coughed it out in one way or another—if possible ardently believing that it was a tiding of salvation.

Nevertheless, I'm no monster, no freak. No splendid malformation like a medieval curse. Nothing to put me on the level of dwarfs, bearded ladies, Siamese twins in a sideshow. I am simply weak flesh. An average child of mankind. Though a retarded child: a child of almost fifty, playing with its life rubbish while daydreaming that one day it might be used to create a literary masterpiece.

That is what I daydream about every moment, blasphemously, sinfully ignoring the sober experience of here and now. I sneak away from the full reality of Here and Now so as to skulk back along a stretch of the path of life and pick out a tiny, colorfully glittering splinter out of the past from the detritus, turning it back and forth in sheer delight before my inner eye: to see whether it contains the secret that is called *I* and that eludes me when I think *I*. . . .

I embrace a woman, am one with her—her mouth tastes sweetly of saliva, I feel the warmth of my skin on her smooth limbs, I feel sensual pleasure, physical happiness concentrates into painfulness—

and my thoughts wander through a day of my childhood: what was it that I lost (or won) back then?

I sit, leaning back in the leather easy chair of an executive office, portentously splaying my cigar between my index and my sexually experienced middle finger, cognac in a snifter, leg over leg (my comically abbreviated reflection in the deep brilliance of the polished shoe tip: a towering microcephalic with elephantiasis of the outer extremities: knees like a mammoth, hands like barn doors, a newspaper advertisement of the man of success: a caricature of five-and-dime splendor). I witness another act of modern magic: the breathless voodoo rite of the conjuration of money. The counterfeiters drum out their mumbo-jumbo. Language foams under the strokes of their witches' brooms, sentences tangle up into serpents' nests, numbers are encrusted with the lecherous spawn of zeros, individual words bubble out from the sputum of mouths, float through the room, the air delicately traced with cigarette smoke and fragrant with secretarial secretions (a hazy stretch of surf coast: on the ribbed sand in the crumbling foam, the purple-fish aperture of a vagina), and sentences, numbers, words launch into vicious pursuit of one another: the iridescent bubble of "cultural mission" hits "box-office receipts" and both burst in a soapy flash; the "level of quality," which "absolutely must be maintained" (how? where? by whom? for what?), collides with "production costs," which tears its own and the "level's" membrane from the nothing they are made of; "artistic creation," "universal human problem," and "topical issue" concatenate in a mucous cluster—and furiously the "co-production considerations" pounce upon them and shatter with them. . . .

and all this floats over a roaring surf of chitchat, waves cresting, agitating, foaming, only to vanish in the sand: a crumbling squandering of words, hissing and seething foam, seeping of mirages and phantoms. . . .

nevertheless, the surging, heaving rigmarole brings something forth, for mightily and magically, the totem of the Project grows, and it will both create and determine life reality. . . .

and meanwhile, I walk up a mountain slope near Lake Zurich, hand in hand with Dawn, and brood about what makes the nervous texture of this hour as heavy as a honeycomb—Dawn's profile against the sparse backdrop of the firs (trunks as rusty as her hair)—or the restriction of Nature, which painfully jerks up the memory of a late-summer park somewhere between the Pruth and Dniester Rivers: a park with a little pond where a frail old-fashioned boat is rotting:

> Si je désire une eau d'Europe, c'est la flache
> noire et froide où vers le crépuscule embaumé
> un enfant accroupi plein de tristesses, lâche
> un bateau frêle comme un papillon de mai—

(And Schwab, dismayed, pausing at the little Sisley in Hamburg's Kunsthalle, the almost foolishly poignant expression with which he looked at me in order to say, "There really was such a thing once: such a summer garden")

There really *was*. It belonged to very simple people. The man was a trolley conductor, the woman carved a lantern for us from a pumpkin, the son was my friend in times that have wafted away. There really *was* such a thing, this little garden, a piece of orderly nature. And I find myself in it again, the way I may have once been and no longer am (even though, or rather because, I now am only in such pictures).

I seek myself in it, madly in love with the various images of myself, a mythological caricature (damnable expression of misanthropy in the great Daumier): Narcissus as archaeologist, mirroring myself in the shards unearthed from various strata of my prehistory (even before I had begun to think about my book) and, in bewilderment, comparing them with the images of my subsequent existences

> —in search of the innocence of a time
> when my life was still a first draft of a life,
> within the myth of its time—

I see my Fall and Original Sin in the reality that has sprung up around me, a reality betraying the myth of that time. I am a foundling of this myth, an afterthought in an era that dreamed the dream of man as a blissful inhabitant of ANTHROPOLIS but was born into the age of maggots teeming in the carcasses of cities. Through my veins runs the nostalgia for the promise of that time of beginning, and it gives me a pride I feel guilty about—

and that is why I must believe I could write my book. In it, I hope to find what I no longer am and no longer have. I know I'm thereby robbing myself of the present, destroying it, so that it can become only a rotten future. My past lies before me as my future. This is no mere wordplay: it is my ultimate innocence, and I do not want to lose that one, too.

My book is my chaste vice. Whenever I think of it, I blush like a whore in love. If I sit down to work on my book, I don wedding garments. I slip into a different, a purer, existence. I become timid and high-strung (like Schwab, my dead friend).

In my book, I stop deceiving. I renounce my cheap (and sturdy) irony, all my tricks. I jettison my imaginative faculties (almost proverbial in my piglets' movie business). I put aside my shrewd way of combining an accursed knack for the "depth effect" in "the art of spinning a yarn," the "interesting and yet lucid architecture," and all the other legerdemain, for whose sake even so-called serious producers (not to mention the piglets) overlook my breaches of contract, my failure to meet deadlines, my constant revision of outlines, and instead go on (as they say) paying me "top fees."

In my book, I am humble and confess my poverty. I have nothing to offer but my bare self. And this self becomes more and more wretched with each passing day. I am no longer who I was when I began to write my book. At that time, I was rich: I lived on the dividends from my innocence. Today, I live guiltily, hand to mouth. At that time, I was able to dream, and I fed from the honey pots of fantasy. Now, I gnaw on the bare bone of reality. Whatever I suck from it merely increases my hunger.

Never in the preceding days and nights did I so ardently long for "reality" as at this moment. Somewhere in the marsh of my consciousness, a drifting memory had sunk to the bottom, and every so often (in the fidgety stroke of overexhaustion, or after an evening of stomach-stuffing, or under the new moon, or the devil knows what), the wraith-like, dissolving image of that memory rose to the surface—and it looked damn near like a corpse—

and I screamed with longing to recognize that memory. As on my first day here, in the terror that befell me when I reread the notes on Schwab, I yearned for this recognition. I wanted to have committed this murder, no matter how dreadful, cowardly, and contemptible, and no matter how shameful the reason—so long as it was true, and real. I knew I had the possibility within me. Everyone has the possibility of murder within him. But I needed "reality." I needed it for my absolution. A deed, no matter how cruel and vile, can be acknowledged and admitted as a misdeed, can be regretted and expiated. But there is no absolution for the mental predisposition to be a potential murderer.

I needed something solid as testimony for myself. I had to be able to grasp who *I* was. I could no longer be merely a possibility of myself. Schwab had put a bug in my ear when he said that if he were really going to write his book, he would begin with my eyes gazing up the Seine.

He had wanted to write me before I did so myself—my cunning friend. He had wanted to forestall me with *his* book, as much as he allegedly wished that I should write *my* book. But *what* had he wanted to write about me? What could he write about me? My story—what was that? The story of a checkered life. Was that *I*? A chain of more or less loosely connected incidents. A pattern of circumstances that had produced their consequences in me. A cooperation of more or less causal processes that had led to me. What did that mean to him? What did *I* mean to him? Just what can anyone mean to anyone? He can be his brother or opponent, friend or foe, his slave or his master, his model or his horror . . . but those are projections, ego-centricities, metaphorical assimilations of the other into one's own self. In other words: fancies, figments, fictions. How does one break through the web of deceptions and truly reach the other person? Only by murdering him (or being murdered by him)? With what can one really still identify? Only with a murderer or with his victim?

It was ridiculous. Probably the closest I ever got to murdering someone was my last good-bye to Cousin Wolfgang. 1939: I was already in Rumania to be a soldier myself, thus could not say good-bye to him when he was loaded onto a train to charge into the land of the Poles. In military gray, in which he had appeared a few weeks earlier, poignantly planting himself in front of me ("Well, what do you say now?"). But I had asked Aunt Selma to put a cluster of oak leaves in his rifle barrel (as is customary in Germany in historic hours), and, touched by my tenderness, she had obediently done so. Cousin Wolfgang took the train straight into his baptism of fire. He had no time or chance to pull the oak leaves out of the rifle barrel. He probably didn't even recall they were there. All he knew was that the train stopped, out in the open somewhere, and he was surrounded by splintering and crashing. He thus realized he was being shot at and that it was his duty to shoot back at whatever he could see with his purblind eyes. So he shot back. And since my oak-leaf cluster was stopping up his rifle, the bullet backed out and tore the bolt off the chamber and the thumb off his right hand. Cousin Wolfgang, the lucky bastard, had hit the jackpot. Nagel, with the sacrifice of his entire right arm, was not more thoroughly exempted from further military service.

Cousin Wolfgang was sent back to Vienna with a transport of wounded soldiers on the very next train. En route, he was bitten by a rat, which had sneaked (unscheduled) into the railroad car meant to hold eight horses or forty (damaged) men. By the time he arrived in Vienna several days later, Wolfgang was dying. It was tragic, if you overlooked the comic part. But you couldn't headline it as a murder.

☐   ☐   ☐

I NEVER TOLD YOU THIS, I said in my spirit to Schwab's spirit. Out of tact, of course. And naturally also to avoid revealing all my professional secrets. Now that you're over there in the beyond and know everything that goes on in my mind, it's no use my concealing anything. So, then, listen: I didn't want to confess to you that I wanted to keep myself as a murderer, albeit such a pathetic one, for myself. I didn't want to grant you the possibility of expanding me on a literary level. If you were to write me, then it would have to be *I* whom you drew, not some literary fiction of myself. I refused to give you this possibility of myself—like the Dollar Princess of operetta fame, who reveals nothing of her riches because she wants to be loved for her own sake and not for her money. I wanted to experience myself through you as a pure Self—which, needless to say, is sheer nonsense, or, even worse, self-deception. The feeble-mindedness of vanity. I wanted to see myself depicted as your beautiful envy mirrored me. The admiring envy of the happily unchallenged invulnerability and sovereign frivolity of the foster child of Sir Agop Garabetian, Bully Olivera, and Uncle Ferdinand, embellished with the listening, spellbound eyes of Aunt Selma's adopted child. And my disappointment was consistent with this when I learned that the first of your jottings about me used me only to describe Paris. The expression of my eyes gazing up the Seine was merely a mirror for you to depict a moribund city:

Very intense blue, now lightened by the reflection of the extraordinarily dramatic sky: announcement of the Last Judgment (describe the scale of cloud formations & illumination effects in the Paris sky: from the most transparent aquamarine—"pale-blue like your corset"—to lead-blue and lemon-yellow as in Seurat, and so forth up to the color violences of the Apocalypse). Eyes that have gazed until aching at what he sees: the river now reflecting as if polished and notched hard-edged along the quais, where the roaring lava of the cars rolls in a swift, tenacious, compact torrent that is skin-covered and streaked by a metal virtually oxidizing with spectral colors; the torrent stops at the traffic light at regular intervals, damming up there for minutes at a time, and then roaring loose again in a metallurgic vomitatio. The rows of buildings along the riverbanks have become the real quai walls, a makeshift dike for these evil flows which are divided into two cross-current beds by the mirroring ribbon of the river. The rows of buildings, against the catastrophic sky, seem broken, like gears, streets of ruins; in the garrets a Golgotha of window crosses.

You see that this jotting is in my possession. And I am quite capable of reading it as a literary metaphor—now that I, thanks to the folder Schelmy tactfully turned over to me after your decease, have been able to peer into your professional secrets; now that, thanks to your occult return, the crumbling masonry of my self-confidence has been dismantled stone by stone, and I dare not set a line to paper without first permitting you to test me, punctiliously and painstakingly. With self-tormenting pleasure, I assist you in this game. Enjoy yourself as you hurl my visions, intentions, ideas, emotions, into your mortar, pound them into powder, weigh them on your apothecary's scales and then drown them in aquafortis, only to shrug off coldly the result of the examination and ask me, with a disparaging wave of your hand, to get rid of the residuum:

—as if writing were primarily an act of conscience, and every sentence a touchstone of the moral person of the writer who undertakes to write that sentence down:

so that, with every line, the author's responsibility increases—not only toward the reader (whose susceptible spiritual salvation might be imperiled by the slightest dishonesty in the literary intention, the least impurity in the form), but also toward himself:

because dealing with the magic device of script unleashes not only the demons, who seize other people's lives, but also the devil, who carries off the inattentive writer himself—

The results of the self-investigation, in which you so kindly help me, are not encouraging. My dream is my last hope. Kindly understand this. If my dream is not telling the truth, then I am done for. *I* would not really exist. I would be in no way essentially different from any *horlà* maggot, any roadside-café person. I would then no longer be your brother, dear Schwab. If this dream (and its dark echo during the days) is nothing but a dream, then *I* am nothing but the cluster of concepts to which so-called science wishes to reduce man, nothing but a banal object of town-and-country psychology. A man-in-the-street type, who can at best lay claim to being haunted occasionally by a man-in-the-street trauma, the ordinary aftereffect of some even more ordinary early experience, some silly, deepseated shock from the piss-sphere. For the scientifically enlightened, of course, a key-hole to the soul, into which every degree-holding underpants inspector can insert his skeleton key in order to snap open the mechanism of the causal relationship between the length of the dick, frustration, and the product of wishful thinking, and to ascertain a quite normal, meaningless deformation of the psyche, which should not occasion any serious concern.

If that was the case, friend Schwab, then I was doomed to lower my flag. Then I should give the chambermaid a fat tip for taking my garbage heap of papers down to the furnace. I should pack up the rest of my belongings and go to Nadine at the Crillon.

□   □   □

SHE IS WAITING for me there anyhow. We meet again after a year apart. "Don't say a word! I told you so, didn't I? One day, you'll vanish from my life the way you dropped into it. No explanation is needed. It's a character trait. It was just as obvious that you would come back. Sooner or later, you all disappear; you take out the dog for a moment and you're gone. But sooner or later, you all come back to me."

Tant pis pour toi, mon ange.

Incidentally, she didn't have to put this into words. She would come toward me and *offer me her lips*, naked of lipstick and weary with kissing—the lips of the great tragedienne in a housedress. Wordlessly, she would then walk past the splendid floral arrangements to the folding table with the Second Empire silver tray, which she drags along to every hotel and every location. There, without first asking me, she would mix my margarita just the way I like it (smokingly cold and sharp, with a furry crust of cryptocrystalline salt around the edge of the glass). Then (without the least triumph at the memory feat gleaming in the spiritual bath of her dark-ringed eyes) with a smile she would offer me the drink: the *grande dame*, voice muffled to boudoir level, relaxed, above all sophisticated: "I never forget that I grew up in a slum. The important thing is that other people forget it. . . ."

This is stated so casually, taken for granted so soberly (or expressed mutely with the eyes, mimicry, gestures), that the knot it ties in your bowels will dissolve instantly. The evocation of a child sketched by Käthe Kollwitz gracefully withdraws to the wings, clearing the stage for the present figure: the delicate woman who, by dint of unsuspected strength (and high intelligence), has managed to overcome social inequity and establish her talent—and thus her ripely mellow humanity in a halo of radiant light bulbs.

She knows all this. She would smile knowingly. It was the prelude to what she loved most: sibling togetherness. Perhaps this softly mournful and yet courageously hopeful chamber-music prelude to intimate sibling togetherness had sounded thirty-seven times during the previous twelve months in exactly the same way (although not with a margarita but with a whiskey-and-soda or on the rocks, a martini, a gin-and-tonic, or a bullshot), with thirty-seven men who, like me, had sooner or later "taken out the dog" only to come back again after one, two, seven, ten, or eighteen years. Or perhaps the most recent guest in her life was on the stairs with the dog or waiting in the next room in order to take out the symbolic animal either tomorrow or the day after tomorrow or in two weeks. But none of this mattered.

She lived for the moment, detached from its historical context. She play-acted in life as little as she did in front of the movie camera (or, earlier, on stage). She was always completely herself. In full intensity. She lived only the present situation—which was fixed in space, too, even isolated from even the next room. She lived it whether as Mary Stuart or Phaedra, the madwoman of Chaillot, Fräulein Elsa, Ninon de Lenclos, Mother Courage, or simply Nadine Carrier, the much-tried, much-tested woman: lover, intellectual, courageous endurer, roguish imp.

It did not matter what author had invented the situation; it did not matter if the creator of the moment was named Racine or Kleist, Ibsen, Shaw, Anouilh, Arthur Miller, or the Good Lord, McFate, Providence, or Chance. She snuggled up to him; she filled out the moment and imbued it with her presence, raising it from the stream of events, incidents, occurrences, and nailing it fast to its unique, unrepeatable presentness.

This was certainly not alien to my nature. Oh, no. If ever there was a man who saw the past as a tangle of happenings that was more familiar from hearsay than personally experienced, more ghostly and spectrally illusory than truly taking place, if ever there was a man who viewed the future as an ocean of vague possibilities for such happenings (and thus regarded the present as a free-floating, available dimension open to any myth), if ever there was such a man, then it was I. Never was I so distinctly aware of this as when faced with Nadine's highly cultivated, disarming naturalness. Thus, while I sipped my margarita (and she went to the record player to put on *our* record, the Beatles' "And I Love Her"—her memory was really fabulous!), I would have the chance to mull over the notion that every intensely lived life is veined with *treason:* the blood path of reality. The Arabs, seeing this with profound accuracy, say memory is a sin.

Who is not familiar with that? Who has not held his beloved in his arms and told her in ardent or entrancedly stammering words something that, regrettably, he once (if not more often) said to someone else (and will presumably say again to a third, fourth, or fifth person): that this moment is the fulfillment of his being, and he would rather die than ever betray this uniqueness. . . . Now, whether ten years or ten minutes lie between the confession and its repetitions alters nothing fundamental in the contradiction— nor, paradoxically, nothing in the possible (even probable) truth of each assurance in turn. Only in connection with one another will one or all the others seem like a lie. And who, if you please, will dare to make this connection? The continuous personality? . . . It was Nadine's profession to change her personality as often as her costume, and mine (when I saw myself chiefly as a writer) to carry within myself the entire gamut of possible personalities between Jesus Christ and Adolf Hitler. This was not the difficult part of the matter. The sibling intimacy of our togetherness was thoroughly genuine. ("All I want is to be near you—do you understand?") Yes, indeed. Sure. I, too. I do want something else on the side, but first let's be close.

It wouldn't even get on my nerves. Nadine was an artiste. The gently spontaneous way (she was armed with a glass: I must confess I don't know what mixed drink is her favorite) she would sit down in the farthest corner of the sofa, pull up her feet, and slip them into the folds of her dress (I have long since accepted circulatory deficiencies in the extremities as a hallmark of the sublime feminine) would certainly have nothing aggressive about it. *Being close* really meant nothing but making a moment of togetherness last as long and undisturbed as possible. This was to be understood in terms of time and space, and thereby metaphysically too. . . .

In support of the metaphysical, "our" record would be playing. Its melody, so often hummed back and forth between us in the past, was as insinuating as a suppository, and the straightforward suggestiveness of the lyrics would relieve us of the strain of having to bridge our closeness with spiritual emanations (technology had for once sensibly achieved its purpose!).

I could hold the glass, meanwhile drained of the margarita and licked free of its salt-crystal boa, and turn it back and forth in front of my right eye while keeping the left one shut, and I could mix my memories with the delicate rainbow waves in which the colors of Nadine's flowers dissolved behind the glass: memories of situations that, by means of arbitrarily drawn connections between the foregoing and the following, expose what is lived, said, and done moment by moment in the most sincere veracity as lies, deceit, betrayal. For instance:

I stand stark naked on the scrubbed planks of a grooved and dented floor in a schoolroom in Berlin-Charlottenburg, March 1942. One year earlier, with Stella's help, I stole out of Rumania (and its army). Brilliantly grasping the situation (before Stalingrad, before sacrificing her life for me), Stella advised me to volunteer for the German army, so that I would no longer be regarded as a Rumanian deserter. The red tape took its sweet time (a breathing spell for me). But now the time has come. A notice fluttered into my hands from the military commission, I dutifully reported, presented my papers, and was told to strip to the skin—among a pack of glum, monosyllabic, slightly graying draftees. They peel themselves out of gray clothes, bloated bodies à la Hans Baldung Grien, crooked hip bones, shoulder blades, the battered, constricted rib cages à la Egon Schiele. Among them, my nakedness radiates like an Apollo's. A coarse person in a veterinarian's smock has placed me against a rod with centimeter notches, screwed a sliding peg hard against my skull, measured my height, peered at my soles, into my throat and larynx, as well as deep into my anus, tugged up the fore-skin from my glans, questioned me about diseases and possible com-plaints, then pushed me in front of a long table, where the members of the Conscription Commission sit before heaps of papers and a collec-tive ashtray filled to the brim (with the butts of collective cigarettes that are handed from man to man like a calumet). At their center, Chief White Horse, a hoary colonel, who (if he weren't sitting) could presum-ably keep himself erect only with the help of his high riding boots. A terse, snappy dialogue develops between him and me.

Colonel, turning to the puffy medical corps captain, who, it is pain-fully obvious, has been dispatched here from the reserve post in Berlin-Wedding: ". . . Except for a couple of fillings in the teeth, he's perfectly intact. . . . Something you don't find nowadays. . . ." *To me:* "A born infantryman, my lad! . . ."

I, blushing: "If you will permit me, Herr Colonel . . ."

Colonel, unpleasantly impressed; White Horse pricks up his ears: "Yes?"

I, modest, but firm: "In Rumania, I was trained as a cavalryman."

Colonel, paternally clearing his throat à la Papa Wrangel, his ears now alertly playing forward: "Oh, yes . . . I understand. . . . But then the cavalry dismounted, unfortunately——"

I, trumpeting a confession: "I would like to request permission to join the paratroopers!"

Colonel White Horse, raising his head, his eyes shining, his mane waving in the wind: "Good lad; yes . . . officer's child, oh?"

I, simply, but loud and proud: "Yessir, Herr Oberst. My grandfa-ther."

Colonel, spotting a mental obstacle: "Hmmm—yes. Training takes a long time." *Accepting the obstacle, increasing his tempo, intensify-ing his volume:* "We don't want to wait that long till the Final Victory, do we?" *Emphatically digging in his spurs:* "And you want to be there when it comes, don't you?!"

I, wildly enthusiastic, helping along with a whiplash: "Before then, Herr Oberst!"

Colonel (yohoho!): "Well, then, how about the tank gunners—brav-est lads on God's earth!"

A splendid leap: the horse and the rider snort blithely.

I, radiant: "My most obedient thanks, Herr Oberst, sir!" *My naked arm jerks out, exposing the underarm hair, its manliness so poignant on the adolescent body: "Heil Hitler, Herr Oberst!"*

My about-face is so snappy that a thick splinter from the cauterized floor shoots into the ball of my foot. Ignoring it, I stomp smartly, back stiff and tin-soldier chest globularly vaulting, into the next room, where, after receiving my papers, I pull the splinter out and my clothes on. I am blissfully certain that it will now take at least seven weeks for the certificate of qualification to produce its results and for the official order to be issued, and for me to submit it to the Reich Ministry of the Interior together with the other documents required for attaining citizenship in the Third Reich. My papers will then be handed to me by the postman against a receipt at my apartment (subleased) at 14 Wielandstrasse, Berlin. Whence, unfortunately, I will have moved in due order to Klein-Klützow on Lake Papenzien, in the district of Deutsch-Krone, Pomerania. Whence, after a sojourn of thirteen weeks, I will move once again, this time to Stedlinger in the Franconian Jura. Now the precarious document might have to take a further detour by way of Kienberg on the Erlaf, in the region of Scheibbs in former Lower Austria (now the Danube Gau in the Ostmark) and Illerstein near Crossen, in Neumark, Prussian Silesia. And if it then circuitously catches up with me back on Wielandstrasse before the Final Victory is won (without me)—a further delay will be open to me (and this was what Stella farsightedly foresaw): in order to enter the German Wehrmacht honorably, I had to be a full-fledged citizen of Greater Germany, and in order to become one, I had to prove my pure Aryan extraction—certainly an extremely time-consuming enterprise considering that I, regrettably, cannot explain who my father was. Meanwhile, however, my already invalid Rumanian service pass (which Stella also procured for me) certifies my voluntary registration with the German tank gunners: proof of a commitment to the German Victory, which will make everyone who checks my papers click his heels automatically and send his hand racing up to his cap visor. . . .

"You're smiling? What's so funny?"

The wide sleeves of the dress have glided away and now she places her folded arm on the back of the sofa, propping her temple on three fingers of her hand. Her hair splendidly ruffles: light, soft, fiery (her *coiffeuse* spends two hours a day on it). Her dark eyes with their blackish blue circles rest moistly on me.

"Nothing, darling—something silly. It has nothing to do with us." (This "us" is a hand stretching out to her, mercifully arching toward her as a deathbed for the small, cold bird of her hand. Soon the bird will lie in it with tiny, rigid, fragile claws.) "Well, no. It does have something to do with us, insofar as we're brother and sister. . . ." Only we can't stay that chaste, goddammit! ("Whatever you do," my piglets say, "don't forget that if Madame Carrier doesn't bite, then we're screwed—okay?")

Okay. That was the difficult part of the matter. For what Nadine esteemed more than anything else was sibling love. ("Why do you want to destroy that? The bond between us is so much more than sexual, isn't it.")

Exactly. If only she knew how passionately I'd love to remain her sibling! But, alas, as a little sister, she had a penchant for precocious sophistication. The effect was humanly delightful but scarcely conducive to the smooth development of movie projects (many a poor fellow screenwriter could tell you a thing or two about that). However, if the relationship was not purely one of a brother and sister, then, as the professional terminology put it, you could get down to the nitty-gritty with Nadine Carrier. If she waxed poetic, then you had to hop into the sack without further ado. If she wanted to hop into the sack, then you could beg off, pleading work on the script. But it was I, alas, who had to make the first move.

The first move was to convince her about the material for the screenplay. It's easiest to talk about it in bed. You had no choice: the orphic melos of artistic inspiration that would soon permeate her entire being, swell up in her into a dithyramb and become a hymn, was commenced in her uterus. And this uterus was temporarily blocked by elements alien to art. ("I have to tell you that there is someone in my life who means almost as much to me as you once did.")

This didn't necessarily mean very much; I had had to learn it, and I would soon have it reconfirmed. Still, one had to be considerate of her notions of order in these matters. (Please don't push! everyone'll get his chance! everyone in his time! An orderly line makes it easier to take care of everyone, so if you've had your turn, then please go to the end of the line!)

The trouble was that I quite sincerely liked her. I suffered with my little sister when I raped her. The very thought of it tormented me. Her face torn back into the crackling, spraying fox hair, the face staring with large, childlike eyes into the dreadful resolution of my face, trying to understand what brought this wild, sudden change over me ("Is that really you? Tell me that isn't you!")—

the thin eyebrows rise into a gable of terror as though under a threatened whiplash, and amid unuttered words ("You can't really want *that?!*") the mouth tries to bring out a "No!" from the fear-choked throat, a "No!" that finally, since it is not granted verbal expression, forces a prematurely senile shaking of her head. The face—still anxiously investigating, the eyebrow circumflexed awaiting a blow—begins to turn back and forth in front of me, first gently and swiftly, like the mechanism of a fine clock, then swings out farther and farther, more and more unsteadily, teetering more and more, thereby coming closer and closer to me (hobbling on its knees, so to speak) until, rolling under a wild and desperate kiss, it suddenly buries what the lips do not wish to say ("Why do you torture me?! You know I can't refuse you!")—

a kiss with which negation virtually tries to burrow into me, whereby our lips curl over our teeth in all kinds of overlapping folds, like blotting paper loosely drawn over a roller, a kiss with which negation is minced as fine as chives under a cleaver . . .

but then the head just as suddenly tilts back again, as though a karate chop had cracked it at the cervical vertebra. The splendidly trained hair now flies out from the lunar arch of the forehead. The mouth stays open. From the eyes, an Edvard Munch gaze breaks like a final shriek. Then the eggshell-thin, bluish-brown lids drop, form two moist, narrow slits that shimmer lasciviously from the thicket of lashes, while an unusually skillful shift of the pelvis receives the inevitable, point-blank, and her legs fold in surrender over my back. . . .

and in spite of all that, I really did like her! Sporadically, I even imagined I loved her! I could have beaten her up. Why all this fuss?! Her performance needed no fancy dramaturgical contrivances. It took place quite like an epiphany. The effect was already in her physicality: her body at thirty-three was nearly juvenescent, much as it might have been at thirteen. She could grow as old as a tortoise with it; she had been born as old as stones—two or three hundred years would scarcely work any changes. That infantile leptosomia destined her for stylistic reasons to lie there like a drowned woman cast up on the beach, with waves smashing over her, man for man. . . .

No, no—this was no violation. It was the ocean of eroticism to which she surrendered and in which she drowned, and by which she was borne ashore—

she could not sink into it, of course. Pacifying orgasms were denied her. But she could not help being moved, carried, will-lessly washed back and forth. She was meant to embody the female destiny, and this gave her a tragic sublimity pleasantly reduced for wise domestic use—and I could look and look until my eyes ached and see what I had done again:

the gigantic eyes in the small, wan face, blurring black on the edges, like coals in the head of a melting snowman, eyes that were so eloquent in expressing the variations on the basic anxious question ("Is that you?" "Is that really you?" "Who are you?"); the aureola of her hair, ruffling lightly and yet flowing, peacefully sunset-like and yet blazing ("Don't forget, I'm a witch!") . . .

her thin, fragile neck; the even flute melody of her clavicles; her disarmingly adolescent arms, hanging childlike from the thin shoulders (one was involuntarily tempted to see whether a pair of dragonfly wings had not grown from the shoulder blades) . . .

the poignantly yielding melancholy of her tiny breasts like bloodhound whelps, and the quite powerfully forested triangle above her crotch . . .

then again, the parenthesis of the thighs now clasping me so poignantly (often, when lying on her bath towel in the swarthy sand of the Dalmatian coast while she came striding toward me after a shooting session, I had seen the prettiest landscape pictures in the bronze-sword-shaped air space between her thighs: a clump of black cypresses over a fragment of fieldstone wall; an upside-down blue triangle of Adriatic Sea with the right-side-up white triangle of a sail; the smoke-colored silhouette of the isle of Rab) . . .

her dance-of-death knees; the calfless shin bones, then the surprisingly large, broad feet—bone cartilage and strings of sinews marked reddish through the white skin, so very much a déjà vu of some other pair humbly folded together under a nail—just where was that? . . . when was it? . . . That's it! An alabaster insect with yawning wing covers, skewered in an insect cabinet, lifeless in its terrible liveliness. One would have to consult Uncle Vladimir to pinpoint it zoologically. . . .

Truly! My Supreme Piglet Wohlfahrt hit the nail on the head: "What does she have to act for? The woman simply brings everything along."

Indeed, she brought everything along in order to make me suffer, even her evocation of the early part of the lost half of my life (which made her a sort of mother for me). It was certainly no accident that this daughter of Pre-Raphaelites, who had ascended from a manger in the coal district of Belgium, rose as a cinema star at the very apex of the new era, when the sensitive vanguard of art consumers began to sniff out the triumphal renascence of Art Nouveau. This certainly was not the crowning of a thespian career but an epiphanal consummation. With gentle abruptness, like the evening star, she was there, in the screen firmament, surrounded by the dancing and flickering of sparks. But, alas, she also shared the uneasy destiny of the evening star, which soon gets lost in the magnificence of astral space. . . .

But I had no choice. My work had to be done. It was part of my assignment "to be carried out at the place of destination." *The Prodigal Daughter*, a Wohlfahrt Production of Intercosmic Film Art, was at stake.

"Well, you can take my word for it, old man, the material isn't at all bad per se—right? Of course. We still have to talk about the ending, it's not convincing, we've gotta come up with something, but I will, I will, you can count on it. Anyway, where would you be if it weren't for your pal Wohlfahrt, who had the brilliant idea of getting Nadine Carrier (though

it was pretty tactless the way the exposé was tailored to her), where would you artists be, I ask you, without the lightning-fast mind and vigor of the entrepreneur, the manager, the producer—if you want to be ruthless enough to use those words, I don't have anything against being called that, at any rate being called a businessman, whom you so greatly despise; I admit I'm one, not that I blame you for it, you're an old hand in the business, you know the responsibility weighing on our shoulders. I'm talking about intellectuals in general. Why, they wouldn't even know where to steal ballpoints if it weren't for us, with our all-inclusive production organization. And yet they imagine that we, the people who make their brainstorms come true and also let them get a nice fat share of the money—why, they imagine that we brazenly exploit them! Let them think what they like for all I care—forget it, I don't want to discuss it anymore. But there's one thing you can't say. You can't say Wohlfahrt does not respect the mind. Please, be my witness. When the mind creates something that can be realized as something beautiful, making not only an economically important industry like the cinema blossom, we are ready to make any sacrifice—have you ever looked at the statistics?—yes?—you haven't? then I advise you to do so, it will open your eyes about the situation. And with all this we independent producers give the masses the possibility to escape their dreary livelihood by enjoying first-class quality entertainment. That is our cultural mission, which people always use to put a noose around our necks. And yet all you have to do is mention the present case: here is a subject that's fairly alien to the general public, but it's got possibilities for artistic development. For this kind of thing, we're always here, we hold our own, which you can see once again with this project of ours, The Prodigal Daughter. Here we have a treatment that, among so many hollow nuts, makes me, Wohlfahrt, realize right away, damn it, Wohlfahrt, you can make something out of this! Put together with some concrete possibilities, and I'm already surveying the field: who're the good distributors? which performers are great box office? which popularity poll do theater owners send me? Market research is the name of the game—who reacts to it like a seismograph at the slightest tremor? Wohlfahrt! Let's get cracking! Here's my offer, I say to the money guys: a subject—right?—not ideal as yet, but it's sort of got the makings of an interesting screenplay. So that's why we two are sitting here together, to develop it. Movies are teamwork. In you, we've got a writer who knows the business, your name is not unknown to the public, no one remembers the old flops, and if the distributors start bitching, I'll tell them, Let the dead bury the dead. I, Wohlfahrt, will vouch for the man and for his total cooperation with the production. In life, you've got to be able to make decisions. I'm known as a man who's willing to gamble—always on a solid artistic foundation, needless to say, that's the opening move, now we're gonna play our trump card with a bang: a lead actress who's all the rage, a European star. If you read 'Nadine Carrier' in the movie ads, then you know nothing can go wrong here. The screenplay may be pure shit, like so many of her movies, but the audiences will run to the theater anyway. Now the problem is to hire the up-and-coming young director. Who's got him if not Wohlfahrt? Dennis Kopenko created a sensation in the industry with his first opus. That's no longer Grandpa's Hollywood. This is avant-garde. And it's not kid stuff either, with fucked-up leftist ideals. This is solid work, I can market it as a commodity. Two or three big names in the featured roles—and you've got a first-class package. Now that's a reality, not a pipe dream. The moviegoers will bite, the coproduction with a foreign country—France at the top, as usual—makes the enterprise foolproof. And if we can talk the Americans into it, then the project will gain a global dimension. The ruble has to roll, my friend, what else can it do! We all wanna live, and so do you, after all. Don't act as if the financial part of the affair doesn't concern you. I've seen your new car—damn it, you won't get that with pure intellect. I, for instance, can only afford a car like that to put on the dog. Nowadays, people like us have to know how to present ourselves—if for no other reason than to avoid intimidating those little bureaucratic shits in the government-subsidy office. Those guys wanna see prosperity, the economy's gotta advance, especially when our industry goes through hard times. The thing that convinces them is the grit of the entrepreneur. Don't give in. Attack the enemy resolutely. That's my motto. People today don't want a depression. People today want the welfare state. Let it ring in your ears: Wohlfahrt knows his onions. The main thing is for you to know your onions too. We're fast workers. That's why I'm assigning you the job of going to Paris and convincing Madame Carrier that you've written the role of a lifetime for her. The end, as I've said, will be taken care of as soon as possible. It's got the right makings, as I've said. The woman'll see it at first sight. She wasn't born *yesterday. But it's your job to make sure she doesn't turn everything upside down. The methods you use are your business. I'm just telling you not to waste even half a day. You've got to have a treatment in four weeks, ready for a screenplay, something I can hand in for a government prize. Without the 200,000 subsidy, we're screwed. I've already got Kopenko and the other artists under contract. Wohlfahrt works fast and resolute, before anyone else can grab anything. I'm no dream dancer, and I don't expect my team members to be dream dancers. The responsibility is yours. The Paris co-producers have been notified, they're not forking over one red penny without Carrier. So everything depends on your script. I've told them: what's today? Today's October 11, I said. My author's got exactly four weeks to put a first-class treatment on its feet and four more weeks for a first-class screenplay— something with which Madame Carrier can expect the hit she hasn't had for a long time and urgently needs. I'll be working here parallel with you. On November 11, my writer will deliver. It'll take the prize commission another six weeks to decide. Meanwhile, I've set up the shooting staff, the assistant director and the cameraman are already out looking for locations. I'll take care of the sets and so on right here. The studios are ready for February. The trailers'll hit smack dab into the Christmas market, and by January 1, at the latest, the first shutter on the outside shots will come down in Cannes. So get to work, comrade. I'm counting on you. Our project will rise and fall with you. You know what it'll mean—especially for you in your financial state. I don't have to point that out. I'm just reminding you that according to the contract you've just signed, your expense account is also limited to four weeks. . . ."*

There was nothing I could do, alas. I had to take up the burden: along with the slow awakening of the woman drowned in the sea of senses—even though she had remained wide awake between the crescent line of the hair torrent and the eyebrows painfully drawn into a pointed bracket . . . *I,* who was actually the shattered castaway on the beach, *I* the somersaulting breaker, hurled into shallow water, feebly running off on her childlike body, the reflecting trail drying in the sand . . . *I* had to overcome it along with the gaze coming sore and dark from the wet thicket of the lashes: the gaze first seeking a hold on the ceiling and then, as though involuntarily following a transparent fiber on the retina, sliding down to me in a slanting arc and clinging to me with the anxious question "Who are you? Is that *you?*"—

together with the awful silence with which we would both reply to that question . . .

and finally with her kiss of reconciliation, chastely offered with corrupted lips.

I would respond to the kiss warmly and gently, humbly knowing that this moment, bursting with betrayal, would later be recognized in connection with the past and the future and might thereby become one of those rare moments of reality possessed, the memory of which inveigles us into continuing to endure life.

□   □   □

STILL AND ALL, this would enable me to withdraw from an ever more painful affair. I would not need to occupy myself with my book—which means, with myself or, worse, with Schwab. I wouldn't have to hide in the Épicure and try to find reality in my papers—if not in the dream. Questions about my identity would dun me no longer. I wouldn't have to worry whether I was a simple *horlà* maggot, a diner in a roadside café, a bookkeeper Müller with an urge to write a short story one day. No need for me to break through to the Other and escape from the cage of my goddamned ego, because I would be completely dissolved in him, completely assimilated to the collective of the species. Just an ordinary zero within a world of zeros, spaced out between a stiff collar and a bowler hat. I would not need to *write myself* in order to *be*. No book would contain my *self* in its purest form. I wouldn't have to care whether I were or were not a spark in the immense darkness, a will-o'-the-wisp lighting up for a brief moment in the gigantic process of procreation and annihilation. I wouldn't have to wonder whether my nightmares were true or not true.

But, on the other hand, if my dream were true (and I wished with all the ardor of despair that it were)—if it were true that I was a murderer, and the *recognition* on the first day here when I saw the name Johannes *Schwab* in my papers kept what it had promised me (not just like a conjurer, who draws gold pieces from one's nose and triumphantly displays them only to make them vanish again, but with the award of reality)—if my old nightmare, last dreamed in Reims, was indeed the horrifyingly and essentially truthful reflection of a murder that I, my *self*, had undertaken and committed to the very last gasping and twitching of my victim, then I could still hope. For then I had something to tell, after all. Something concerning not only me but everybody. I would have something to write about that could be told in three sentences, either as a shadow play on a motion-picture screen or as a book of several hundred pages, something that would link me with the Other. I could tell about real guilt, not just the nameless guilt of sheer existence but the very core and essence of guilt.

A murder, no matter how vile its motive, no matter how despicably committed, no matter with how much literary hedonism it may be grasped, goes beyond the private and the literary sphere. A murder (and presumably only a murder), despite all modern-day problems of interpersonal communication, establishes a relationship with the other—and indeed one that instantly becomes transcendental:

—for everyone carries the murderer inside himself and is simultaneously a murderer's victim. And thus the terror aroused by a murder is a primal terror, the immediate realization of the Evil that dwells in us— more thorough, more intrinsic, more involuntary than all drives (and, incidentally, contained in all drives). And such a confrontation with this terrible thing in us, bloodily witnessed by a martyred victim, who is I, and a murderer, who is I, instantly raises the question of the why and the wherefore and, thus, of the how of creation. Why is man born with this terrible thing in him? Who created him in this way and for what purpose?

For this reason, every street ballad about murder is actually primal history, and even the most inane whodunit (beyond the silly hunt for the murderer, who could be anyone, and not just for the sake of suspense) is a circuitous search for God, a search left to the acumen of

*the reader (who can draw his ultimate conclusion from the struggle be-
tween good and evil in the intellectual dual between the detective and
the criminal)—*

□   □   □

I HAD DREAMED MY DREAM in Reims, on my way from Munich
to Paris. For a couple of days, I tried to tell myself that I had interrupted my trip in Reims because of exhaustion. That's not
true. *It* lured me there.

I like driving long stretches at night. The roads are emptier,
and I'm more lonesome, more intimate with myself. I love being
encapsulated in the spaceship of the car, which hums and zooms
like a hornet into the foresprayed glare of the headlights. This has
something of the boyhood delight in concealment, in caves and
grottoes—I love my snuggly isolation in the big womb of night.
Nowhere else—not even here, in the glow of the lamp over my
papers, while Paris snores all around me—am I so autocratically
isolated. In my car, I am a sovereign who detaches himself from
the profane bustle of the surrounding world with a few shifts of
the clutch. A bold isolationist who holds his fate in his hand and
races toward it, tracking down the etiological secret of the Alea-
tory. Anything Chance may hurl at me has the character of necessity.

And I don't have to be alone if I don't want to. Sometimes, by
pressing a few buttons, I invite abstract guests in: voices that
speak to me in many languages, music whose sounds I pull along
with me over wind-swept hilltops, through the ravines of black
forests, past dead villages with their rows of houses that fall back
as though mown down. I press a button again, which cuts off my
visitors, denying them entry into my spaceship. While the world
around me is as silent as in the Carboniferous, I fly, I dash
through its blackness: hovering in the shimmer of the dashboard
lights as though I were lying in the sickle moon that cuts through
the rushing clouds of an autumn night.

No, no, it certainly wasn't exhaustion that made me strike the
sails of my flagship (the Dutch Schout bij Nacht) in Reims.

Quite the contrary. The truth is so trivial that Kapudan Paschà is ashamed to write it down here: I was horny.

I had already been horny in Munich. During my Hamburg days, at the start of my ignominious career as a screenwriter, after the endless, confused, sometimes dreamily bizarre, always traumatically reverberating script discussions with Stoffel & Associates, I would flee to Gisela in the hooker alley. And now, during the last seven days of daily hot air in the leather armchairs of the Intercosmic Film Art office, with cognac and cigarettes (the piglets called such meetings "conferences") in between, a thinker's brow, a smoker's cough, heartburn, and my trouser fly, I had only one wish: to lie with a woman, not to think, to feel only female skin, to smell a female, to knead female flesh; briefly and brutally to unleash latent atavisms (murder instinct, anthropophagia) and then to sink into beneficent stupor (the copulation numbness of certain species of mice). The Chinese definition of happiness: warm, well filled, dark, and sweetly drained.

Naturally, I had tried to satisfy this need. I got plastered in Schwabing's abstract cellar gloom, in vain. I'm too alientated from the local customs; I used the wrong semaphore: my British necktie and the wretched shoulders of my jacket look antiquated, miserly, devoid of department-store reality; repel rather than attract, elicit distrust and mutual clumsiness. Language too no longer obeys me. Not even liquor can reduce it to simple communication, much less to conveying my physiological desires. It strikes either under the target ("All I want to do is screw you, my child") or over it ("You probably can't even love").

Only once did I get my hands on a platinum-blond wench. After the bar closed and I paid a tourist-trap bill, after shouting in the street and an unpleasant scene with a policeman ("I insist on having your number! I'm a foreigner and I will not be spoken to in this way!"), after a bone-quaking cab drive and then a wild *Weisswurst* gorging in the din of Donisl and another taxi trip, she turned out to be a biting albino rat. We wound up in a room in Harlaching that looked as if a tornado had whirled through it. She was equipped with the clitoris of a hyena, which, however, hysterically yelling, she wouldn't let anyone approach—and certainly not me. Despite a numbing quantity of whiskey from a bottle that I had haggled for at a brothel price, and despite a tumultuous rolling around in bed—which woke up the next-door neighbors and made them bang their protests against the door and the walls—any peace-bringing discharge of my neuromuscular tensions was out of the question, not to mention any appeasement of that erotic urge that wants to absorb the feminine and make it an integral component of one's own being, like the wonderful *Schistosoma haematobium*, which, a velvet-lined casket, carries its beloved lifelong within itself and releases it only temporarily, to lay eggs.

The matter ended badly, of course, with a couple of resounding slaps, which did not produce any meliorating effect. On the contrary: now the neighbors were properly mobilized, and they did not take my side at all. . . . It took me several days to suppress the incident.

Came the tormentingly long day that the piglets required for what they term "concluding the contract": drawing up and finally signing a document that reduces by half the agreed-upon honorarium and stipulates all kinds of loophole contingencies for further reductions. When it was over, I left Munich. My car had been waiting since noon with freshly changed oil, a grease job, a full tank of gas, and the tire pressure carefully checked. Packed with my suitcases, briefcases, portfolios, and the cartons of papers for my book (I dragged them everywhere, as Nadine did her deluxe tray), the car stood ready in front of the hotel. It was a flat, low monster, like a predatory bug, and a small pack of more or less expert observers were always gathered around it. In the grouplet of scraggly-dressed young Germans (even in Gypsy garb, they manage to have something stiffly awkward about them), I was struck by the gaze of a girl: dark, beautiful, relaxed, wide open in the eternal, primal question: "Is that you?"

I took this gaze along into the smoky turquoise into which the blue of the Bavarian sky had faded on this October day, gilded with autumn foliage. And now the turquoise also filled the roads with magic spaciousness. It hinted at a night frost; pale, wan, and hazy, it shimmered around the dividing and hardening contours of the neo-Gothic gables and neo-Classical moldings and the Baroque-capped twin church towers. My curved windshield sucked in pallid strings of light and split them up. To the left, the massif of the railroad station, star-studded red and green, accompanied me for a while. White-waving columns of steam with capitals edged in a dawn-red blaze tumbled up into the blue, rolling with a fiery glow—the romantic early period of technology, when it still had a volcanic character. On the right, tooth gaps in the line of buildings recalled the bad wartime and worse postwar time; architectural horrors of the Age of Promoterism and the Age of Reconstruction glided past, then, while the rail strings frazzled out under black Egyptian tau symbols with emerald and ruby eyes, flattened out into suburban bungalows. A square, with a trolley shelter painted Josephine-yellow and decorated with peeling geraniums, evoked a children's-book illustration of garrison bandstand concerts. One breach farther, and the *Spiegelfuge* of a church façade, carved of plaster, sprang back into the lilac-blue of shadows. On the left again, a landscape-shaping dimension of depth yawned open for an instant: a perspective bordered in black-silver-black by two canals between tree-lined avenues, shooting out straight as an arrow toward the façade of Nymphenburg Castle at its focal point, as if carried off at the wrong end of a telescope. Next, housing-development row cottages and crumbling suburban villas hid behind front-yard thickets—a couple of big Technicolor gas stations. . . . I turned into the Autobahn—and the gaze of the girl whom I would never again meet hung over me like the Star of Bethlehem. But I hurried away from it.

I did it without melancholy. I was even exhilarated: faithless by blood. I love to leave towns in gathering twilight. Then I don't have to say farewell to them. I just wait for the moment when the broken light disintegrates their density, pulling them apart as though with a magical molecular expansion and thus canceling their gravity. I drive for a while into the darkening countryside. The evening is a sigh of relief. The earth is liberated of the bad dream of another wildly marauding human day. The city falls back. Gradually, the mange that it spreads along its outskirts is healed. Once I'm beyond it, the city's magnetism lets go of me; I too can breathe more freely again. Behind me, the descending night swallows up the city. It no longer exists; it was never real, only a dream: the echo of an existence I attempt to escape.

Soon, I had uncoupled myself from the evening suburban homecomers on the Autobahn, dived beneath overpasses that hissed away above me, and plunged into the denser and denser texture of evening, which, after a few precarious minutes of sharply dividing sky and land, caught them both in its veil and let them blur into each other. The huge deep-sea eyes of my diving bell were switched on. In its interior, the lights on the instrument panel were already glowing. The speedometer needle had quickly scaled past the apex of the dial and scurried down its right half; now, reeling slightly, it hung over the final marks. The tachometer needles hovered calmly beyond the border span that a red segment ordered it not to cross. To my right, in the scattered, powdery glow of my lights, fields and meadows flickered like the blue-gray checkered backs of cards fanned out in the hand of a nimble-fingered player, then were swiftly raked in by the edge of my side window. To my left, like bristles under a sharp stroke, the trunks of a forest bent toward me.... All this broke off, changed, jumped back and forth and up to hilly terrain in cringing, hunchbacked leaps, and then out into uncertainty; came soaring down, leveled off again, smoothed out. The sagging darkness trussed up the scattered beams of my headlights, squeezed them into two intersecting cones in the hose of the road, ripped out a hollow space, at the end of which it was swallowed by the pent-up blackness. I was hurled into the dark space and toward that place of uncertain encounters dashing ahead of me. Its harbingers were the pale tracer bullets of the dividing line, sometimes the red-glowing rectal eyes of a truck, which I signaled to before the shadowy monster loomed and towered to my right and whooshed past me.... I was warned. I was holding my destiny in my hand. I was sovereign.

But I was not alone. I had invited a friend in: Schwab, who was dead now. And I chatted with him, in the manner that had always irritated him the most: in the parodying rattle of culture-vulture chitchat, in which I could insert the barbs of my malice, which had to lodge in the matters he took seriously

—*for instance, the European heritage. Can you tell me why you take it so seriously? It's a sackful of fictions, that's all. With some mental hygiene, one should be able to shake it off. Sentimental values at below-cost prices. Nowadays, any self-respecting person has a Biedermeier dresser in his assembly-line bungalow. Even in America. There, it's Colonial Style, of course. Very popular lately. Those fellows used to be way ahead of us, lacking a past as they did. But now they're spending their advantage on dubious antique furniture. They too are discovering their history. Not as a trauma, you understand, but as a Western. Living in the past in sentimental re-creation. The Western is timeless. The eternal song of man creating Civilization against Nature. The Biedermeier dresser in a vacation bungalow is a barbaric booty: a souvenir plucked out of Civilization's refuse. The Western is life; the Biedermeier dresser at best a genre picture. The thing that gave the American myth its persuasive strength was the kick with the boot heel, which is all that the hero of the Western has to offer the Biedermeier dresser when he wants to push it to where it can catch the bad man's bullets. Could people like us do that? What would you do if bullets started flying? You would spread out your arms, and throw yourself in front of the Biedermeier dresser. A martyr to the memento industry. Shall I confess something to you? I'm disgusted at myself. I'm sickened by the evasive way I sneak out of cities at nightfall as if from the scene of a collective infamy which I have taken part in but would like to be absolved from. I share the guilt for transforming our world into a heap of gravel, but I carry off a small booty. I've spirited away something of the museum exhibit, and with it I slip into the black sack of night, which draws tighter and tighter around me. I steal away with a voluptuously tickling fear in the back of my neck, a fear that may drive the sentimental value away again. My memory breaks the precious stones from the now worthless settings. I carry the city along, virtually purged of artistic invalidity: for instance, a Munich consisting of nothing but spicecard cottages, gingerbread palaces, wax-dip churches, crowding around color-splotched squares on which mushroom-cultures of parasols proliferate, among which rustic market women peddle their tiny witchbrooms of soup greens. A Munich of jovial, house-proud streets, which lead to the water-lily tangles of Schwabing's Art Nouveau landscape garden jun-*

gle. A Munich, consequently, no longer existing outside my imagination, which utilizes old postcards and fairy-tale illustrations as cut-outs placed in front of a totally different reality. But I imagine I have taken along its soul, the soul of a burghers' city aware of being a royal residence, aired by mountain breezes and set with Hellenistic serenity in pleasing farmland, and granted forever the sweet melancholy of an autumnal fin-de-siècle summer resort where the arts abound in fruitful liberty. I envisage this under the glass bell of a delicately fleecy sky, powerfully blue, with the lace of snow-covered Alpine peaks along its brim. And I visualize it for solace, when I realize I am breathing a sigh of relief to leave Munich, the real, present one, which transmits entirely different, nightmarish impressions: an unreality confusedly spun into the steel-brace network of high-rises, the display-window unreality of department stores, an unreality that, from behind the reflections of swarms of contemporaries and torrents of traffic-lava—reflections insanely reiterated as in a fly's faceted eye—offers the instrumentarium of a modern-day deification of Nature: the tents, raincoats, hiking boots, sleeping bags, folding boats, snowshoes, loden coats, felt hats of the bawling backpackers:

> Oh, just see the archer stride
> Over hill and dale,
> Bow and arrow at his side. . . .

We suffer, we sensitive people, because our history runs counter to our civilization. . . . Do you see the difference between us and the Americans? I mean, the difference in self-esteem, which gave any gum-chewing GI the right to kick us in the arse with the heel of his boot when we bent over to pick up his cigarette butt? Not because we were beaten but because we had given ourselves up, because we had betrayed our dream of ANTHROPOLIS. We Europeans, heirs to all the dreams that built up Western Civilization, we slip like marauders from the cities, where bulldozers are still digging out the last bombs of WW II. With full camping gear, we throw ourselves on the bosom of Mother Nature in order to escape the decay of our heritage. The hero of the Western rides toward the city—the city he wants to help build, to cleanse of all evil, to turn into ANTHROPOLIS, city of mankind. These are two entirely different attitudes in the world. No wonder our city gnaws at our hearts like a black bug. . . . We woeful heirs! We need Nature for recreation, every time we have betrayed the dream that we could stand up against her merciless greed. Every time she has devoured another bit of what was built up against her throughout millennia, we seek comfort in her bosom. And when she herself has had a little feast of several million corpses, then we seek for the crumbs under her table; then once again we recall our heritage, our priceless antiques. Slightly irritated because so and so much of lesser artistic value is handed down along with them. Just think, for instance, what incredible clumsiness it took for life to alter, diminish, or add even the slightest thing in Tuscany after the blessed moment of two and a half centuries from the birth of Cimabue (c. 1240) to the death of Piero della Francesca (1492: also the year of Lorenzo the Magnificent's death). The very idea! What misled historical development to continue in its natural way of growth and decay! Here, it produced a masterpiece. Couldn't it leave it alone and turn to another region that had not yet fully flourished? Michelangelo—fine. But in Florence, he was already stylistically out of place. Far too Baroque, that man, far too lush, too un-Tuscan. Rome, all right. That's his home. That was his true hometown. There he could let off steam. Even at the risk of depriving Florence and the world of a wonderful tomb, he should have limited himself to Rome. It would have spared us some of the worst horrors of the nineteenth century. But certainly after him: from the seicento to the settecento (which had quite delightful results elsewhere, for example in the Veneto) they should have simply prohibited any artistic attempt in Florence. Just imagine if you and I had got control of the matter in time. What a Disneyland of cultural history Europe would have become! An Italy without the Risorgimento The Netherlands, where after Vermeer anyone who touches a brush has his right hand chopped off. In Germany, the natural development would have been halted shortly before the Thirty Years' War (although I have to admit: Grimmelshausen was worth that little feast of Mother Nature). And of course, without this barbarity, all those highly gifted sons of pastors would never have turned up, the later writers to whom your Fatherland owes so much—nor would I have had the benefit of the spirit of my uncle Helmuth. The profession of private tutor might have blossomed even more richly, although less protestant. It might also have produced important pupils and not just poetry and philosophy. But I am speaking of the truly plastic arts, the "formative arts," as they are known in German: pleasant to our senses, and therefore truly civilizing, arts that, unlike literature, do not stir up our brains. Intellect is a precarious thing, after all. It testifies to a high aesthetic sensibility that the old aristocracy had domestics to take care of thinking. Be that as it may: we'd know how to present this Wonderland of Europe, varnished like the color prints in the Propyläen History of Art, neatly cleared of the refuse of cultural decline here and there, the corners swept clean of the feces of epigoni. In short, a U.S.A.-perfected Yurop: a gigantic museum, splendidly lucid in its arrangement, its inscriptions intelligible even to the semi-literate, purged of the stylistic anachronisms committed by those who are behind the times, the latecomers. Just think of the treasures of Europe's landscapes as designed here by Lorenzetti, there by Altdorfer, there again by Breughel, there by Le Lorrain, here by Caspar David Friedrich, there by Constable and Turner, here by Courbet, Corot, and Cézanne! Imagine this pleasure adorned with Piranesi ruins and crowned with hilltop towns à la Matthäus Merian, towns by Paolo Ucello, by Dürer, by Canaletto, on whose squares we are greeted by Praxiteles and Brancusi, and whose halls relieve us with frescoes by Giotto and Picasso. Gardens by Lenôtre, where we ensconce ourselves with Hanau porcelain and Gothic two-pronged forks to feast on nightingale tongues prepared according to Lucullan recipes, and to sip at our Mouton Rothschild from Cellini's crystal goblets, while behind the ornamental shrubbery, following a libretto by Herr von Hofmannsthal, a Klimt-costumed lady of the Viennese haute volée surrenders to a Böcklin faun. Is this not precisely the image and musical theme of Europe that you carry within yourself? Admit it: cultural history—that's as surprising, as frightening, as the garden of Bomarzo. No matter where you go, no matter where you turn, the monsters of arts and artists come toward you, insanely multifarious, and shoo you from reality into nightmarish unreality. Perhaps you now understand what makes my film piglets so dear to me. Too much culture is harmful to mental health. Just think of the sad fate of Huysmans's des Esseintes. I, for my modest part (born under the sign of the Ram, with the Archer in my ascendant and half a dozen sputniks in my first house)—I was not made to live à rebours. I cannot exist in a world that haunts me with its rubble. I would rather do without the European heritage. I don't want to sneak out of the cities like a marauder. I don't want to shut my eyes in the suburbs, in the residential districts and principal avenues, only to open them at the Renaissance town hall, the Gothic cathedral, and the cement-propped remnants of the Roman walls. Memory is a sin! Our kind is already *sufficiently afflicted as it is. There are things I haven't even told you. For instance: the way the trauma of art worship was inflicted upon me at an early age, thanks to my beautiful mother, whose life was so brief, and to my aristocratic uncles, so well versed in many kinds of splendors. Starting with Uncle Ferdinand's coin collection and the uncounted pilgrimages to historic monuments in the hinterland of the Côte d'Azur, I was infected with the black bug of art idolatry. At first, these trips got me excited mainly because I was allowed to sit next to the chauffeur in Uncle Agop's Isotta Fraschini or in Uncle John's Rolls-Royce (Mama herself drove a Stutz). I would wear a little raccoon coat, a leather auto helmet, and far too large, simply enormous goggles, in which my head looked like a horsefly. In the front seat, I watched the landscape shifting, sliding, blending, Proustian early experiences that put me on the dangerous road. Soon I zealously leafed through the art books lying around everywhere—of which Gobineau's Renaissance, in a deluxe folio edition with tissue-covered illustrations, has remained vivid in my memory. Then the magazines—including one named La gazette du bon ton and published by a M. de Brunhoff, the same man whose King Babar was to snatch forth my four-year-old son's first aesthetic judgment twenty-seven years later: "Daddy, this is so beautiful!"—strange words in the mouth of a four-year-old, aren't they? But more and more, kids get infected at a tender age. . . . By the way, the numbers of the Gazette du bon ton I saw as a six-year-old must have been old issues. The magazine no longer appeared in the time I am speaking of—1925. It had ceased publication in Paris in 1916 and was continued, strangely enough, in Berlin until 1919 by Flechtheim. I once found an issue in Aunt Selma's room. Thus does the cultural heritage intertwine generation with generation. It was only natural that I fell in love with a Vogue fashion model. . . . Last but not least, Miss Fern's brazenly acrid bell tones and rolling R's also transmitted culture, especially when she spoke about Florence, a name that sounded like a flourish of muffled drums. Before the war, she had looked after a little girl "of a very noble family" there, and she always held up her charge's exemplary breeding to me. In a strange blend of desire, envy, and hatred, I was secretly and hopelessly in love with the little girl: in the future, my Beatrice, my anima: Dame Cultura in person.*

Only a year later, in 1926, after my mother's death, I was in for it, my friend. I spent the following twelve years in Vienna: the first four in a totally idiotic school in the Twelfth District, then eight in the dreadful obtuseness of a high school in the Thirteenth District. Until Stella rescued me: taking me to the commencing summer-solstice festival of the year 1938. And you know: what kept me from going completely obtuse during the twelve bitter years of this apprenticeship in triviality, mere usefulness, or pure decorativeness (culture as a status symbol), what protected me from becoming a will-less instrument of the Zeitgeist, chaff in the wind of time—it was the CITY. The City as a promise and as an object of hatred, you understand: the Jerusalem still to be built: ANTHROPOLIS, city of all mankind. . . . The promise of the city comforted me first for the loss of my mother and all the luxurious circumstances and happenstances of my previous life. Of course, I was despairing, disturbed, disoriented. But even as a child, I wasn't exactly sentimental. Despite any disquiet, I did find the change extremely interesting. I lived in a twofold awareness, a dichotomy at least as exciting as the wonderfully scary and shivery moments at home in the evening before my leap into the crib: when I eerily imagined that the wolf would now come shooting out from underneath to grab my naked legs, even though I knew there was no wolf under the crib.

This, of course, with effectively exchanged emotional values. I convinced myself that the things I was told were true, and that my mother really had gone off on a long trip from which she would return one fine day and take me home again—yet I simultaneously knew that this was nonsense: that my mother had died and the truth of her death was merely lying in wait in order to shoot out from its hiding place and pounce on me, as the paralyzing terror of reality pure and simple. But in the meantime, there were so many new and exciting things to see, to hear, and to experience. The city of Vienna was around us—a promise as stimulating as life itself at that time.

Incidentally, I must say to their credit that my Viennese relatives made an honest effort to ease my adjustment. Uncle Helmuth very plausibly explained to me the principle of the steam engine and (I suppose because he was taken in by my precocious powers of apprehension) recommended that I read Helena Blavatsky's Isis Unveiled. Unfortunately, the text was beyond me; aside from a few descriptions of occult phenomena that terrified me to the marrow of my bones, it left no trace in my mind. Aunt Selma, ranging hungrily about, seized hold of my need for affection—with moderate success, I'm afraid to have to say. Aunt Hertha, lecturing me in a soft, sugary voice laced with philistine vinegar, did not succeed in hiding a certain petit bourgeois insecurity; yet, despite her nagging, the liberation from Miss Fern's discipline was at first agreeable, even though I vaguely missed the support, like someone accustomed to a tight corset and now released from it. And Cousin Wolfgang was, simply, a gift from heaven: my first buddy and fellow rogue for my first mischief—also my first audience, breathlessly listening, in the dense blackness of the room we shared; as we whispered from bed to bed, I would tell him of the glittering tumult of the carnival in Nice: the staggering, shaking, hopping, reeling, whirling dance of the giant puppets through flurries of confetti, explosions of paper streamers, and crazily screaming, teeming, frolicking masses around the slowly moving caterpillar procession of floats. Or the automobiles gliding along like state carriages, heavy and majestic, their wheels rolling over the Promenade des Anglais with the sound of a bandage being slowly pulled off your skin. Or else about the very gently swaying maze of sailboat masts in the harbor at Monte Carlo. The purple bougainvillea cascading over white terrace balustrades. The green, white, and red of the tennis court in Cap d'Antibes, feathered in palms and embedded deep in the intense blue of sky and sea, behind the magnolia boulevards and laurel hedges. And naturally, too, our park, in the distant land of Bessarabia (whose name sounded dappled, like a guinea hen) and the pond in the park . . .

whereby I was already, if you please, animating the accounts and experiences, which were not necessarily always mine (Typical! Christa would think). Besides, please do not forget: the dark bedroom that we shared for twelve years, Cousin Wolfgang and I, may have been uniformly murky at first, but on closer view, once the eyes had adjusted to the finer light values in the darkness, something shimmered through the narrow cracks between the blades of the window blinds, shimmered regularly, now brighter, now darker, now more reddish, now more bluish, casting a dim reflection on the linoleum-covered floor. This shimmer was Vienna, one of the legendary big cities (ineffably more adventurous, more variegated in its population, more confusingly tumultuous than a Mardi Gras with its frivolous fireworks), whose name had echoed in the conversations of my divers uncles whenever they brought my beautiful young mother all manner of splendors (returning Conquistadors, laying gifts at the feet of their empress): dresses crustily embroidered in castle-garden-bed patterns and glittering with diamond clasps, gigantic circular boxes containing hats adorned with feathers (I believe they were called aigrettes) from ospreys and birds of paradise, diadems from Cartier, red-white-and-green eardrops (baked out of rubies, diamonds, and emeralds) from Buccellati, furs from Revillon, deliciously soft, tenderly flattering the cheeks, still dimly redolent of a sweet little animal through the hint of lily of the valley, greasily polished heavy leather bolsters from Brigg, filled with clattering, from whose throats (opened by a sensationally modern zipper) the steel-and-ivory heads of golf clubs stretched like starving nestlings, umbrellas from Hermès (their slender handles: a small forest of miniature totem poles with dog and parrot heads); simply all manner of cunning barbarities: crocodile-leather vanity cases from Hies, for instance: marvelously space-efficient, filled with a multitude of objects (doubled by the mirror inside the open lid) fitting precisely into the furrows of the chamois lining and crowned with monogrammed ivory tops: perfume vials, powder boxes, cold-cream jars, soap dishes, ivory combs and brush handles, and the inevitable, never utilized manicure set, which could not lack the tiny obstetrical hook of a shoe-buttoner; in a word: luxury articles. I do not wish to irritate Christa with them, her aquamarine gaze is already deeply sunk in the trout-blue of your gaze in order to fathom whether you share her thought: namely, that I mythologize my background as a whore's child. . . .

What I meant to say was simply this: I had been able to watch the ambassadors of the great cities lay their patterned splendors before my mother. (There was usually something for me too: a deeply loved cloth dog named Bonzo, for instance, but let us forget these details, our chat is already overladen with them, yet shouldn't a good novel also be a cultural catalogue?) In any case, for me it had been only a matter of a time before I would visit these cities and probably even live in them. Soon, I would drive through seething streets in Uncle Bully's Delage, be led by Miss Fern through vast parks to fountains spraying their water up to the clouds—so close that a puff of air, bewitchingly redolent of autumn leaves, fresh garden soil, gasoline, and roasted chestnuts, would carry a fine shower of the rainbow-flickering spray over me—and soon, one night, I would be in one of the luxury hotels of these cities, and could listen to the roaring surf of the streets while, with a beating heart, I tried to envision the images that would be unfurled tomorrow. . . .

Previously, I had, so to speak, viewed only the covers of their paperback editions, and very casually at that: with a glance, say, through a wagon-lit window into the sooty pigeon-blue of a railroad station where, under the title (Bucharest, Budapest, Belgrade, Trieste, and so forth: édition spéciale, bonne pour les Balkans), red-capped (incidentally, extremely ragged) porters dragged baggage around, and the little wagon of oranges, chocolate bars, and lemonade bottles was always too far away for someone to call it over. . . .

and sometimes, as under a thumb cropping over the edge of a book, a brief glimpse of an open page: seen through a dueling network of struts and stays (while the train lumbered dully across a bridge), a street filled with bug-like vehicles and teeming ant-like people . . . and even this image had been alive with anxious promise. . . .

Now I was actually in one of the truly big representatives of those big cities. I had not yet penetrated to where its heart, beating red and blue, seemed to glow in a melting pot—but it was really just a matter of days. I had only to run the length of my nose (I eventually did just that, but that's another story) . . . in any case, I hope you understand that for the time being, I had no time to take precise stock of my losses. The world that had sunk away from me was still lying about me (if no longer quite intact, it was at least available with relatively little effort). . . .

The world I had lost did not seem gone forever—as it would be in 1938. But one day I found myself walled out from that world by a neighing collective laughter. At that time, you see, when I was still in the same class with Cousin Wolfgang, who was only a few months older than I and hesitant in his intellectual development, at the local school of our district (Vienna, Twelfth District, Schönbrunn), I was seduced by the Tempter into believing that I still lived in my lost world. In contrast to Cousin Wolfgang, I was not shy. Miss Fern had taught me a kind of trusting frankness that made me unsuspicious of, albeit reserved toward, strangers. I did not hide the fact that I knew all sorts of things, that I could read and write and even chat in dainty childhood French and fluent nursery English. Vast amazement on all sides; a few of my schoolmates quickly moved away from me, while the teacher (who smelled dreadfully of old clothes), with a self-conscious grin, pressed his scraggly chin into his collar, as an intention warmly fermented beneath the Adam's apple and the diaphragm to mollycoddle me into becoming an instrument of humiliation for my coarse schoolmates.

It was not yet in my nature to see through such political maneuvers—that was to be the first fruit of my education—and I called attention to myself by boldly letting the small, naked worm of my finger push out from the compost that was the mass of pupils: I announced that I could even recite a few stanzas of a rather difficult and very beautiful English poem. Very well! Permission granted. I was planted in front of the blackboard. The teacher stood by his desk with a squashed smile, embarrassed, twisting his brownish-yellow cuff. Hurling out my arm toward him, raising an accusing finger against him, I commenced:

> Has God, thou fool! work'd solely for thy good,
> Thy joy, thy pastime, thy attire, thy food

(now, as Miss Fern taught me, face the audience!)

> Who for thy table feeds the wanton fawn,
> From him has kindly spread the flow'ry lawn:

(arm and finger yanked toward the ceiling)

> Is it for thee the lark ascends and sings?

(shaking my head in ecstasy)

> Joy tunes his voice, joy elevates his wings.

(taking a small step forward; then, somewhat softer, more intimate)

> Is it for thee the linnet pours his throat?
> Loves of his own and raptures swell the note.

(again addressing the teacher, firm)

> The bounding steed you pompously bestride
> Shares with his lord the pleasure and the pride.

(thundering)

> Is thine alone the seed that strews the plain?
> The birds of heaven shall vindicate their grain.

(*again to the audience*)

> Thine the full harvest of the golden year?
> Pars pays, and justly, the deserving steer:

(*proclaiming*)

> The hog that ploughs not, nor obeys thy call
> Lives on the labours of this lord of all.

Well, that was it. As I stood there, highly satisfied—Miss Fern would have praised me for an excellent recitation—there was silence. But then it broke loose. Beginning with one of the little friends with whom I was destined to sail out into the blue ocean of cheerful knowledge, an uncontrollable splutter emerged from his snot-clogged nostrils—and that was the signal for a collective discharge. They erupted. They howled and bawled with laughter. They doubled up, rolled over one another, curled up and through one another, pissed in their pants in fits of vulgar orgasm . . . and here I must try to be very clear in describing what this laughter produced in me.

It will instantly put you on the wrong track if I tell you that my first emotion was erotic pleasure—yes indeed; I made the acquaintance of a feeling I had never known before, something that I now can name: mortification. And this was also (aside, naturally, from my Freudian baby-lascivity, and so on) my first erotic stirring; more precisely: it intimately involved my first conscious erotic stirring . . . but be wise enough to avoid an "Aha!" (uttered with pleasurably closed eyes and leaving an aftertaste)—This delight, I tell you, was ethereal. . . . You can believe me: I have since relived those moments thousands of times: I have had every chance for conscientious analysis. In the foreground—inundating me with a hot wave of blood—was: mortification. Behind it, something else opened up, and there the erotic budded. But needless to say, at the time I did not realize what it was. I merely sensed it. From then on, it was to remain in me as a certain, albeit not effable urge.

The yowling and neighing of my little schoolmates naturally had an immediate and painful effect. I saw the shaking and rolling of the little stubble-skulls, the obscenely gaping mouth-caverns and red ears dissolving into a rainbow-sparkling radiance in a monstrance of tears, heard their roar through a sharp seething in my ears, tickled by a sobbing from my throat. Nevertheless, this was, so to speak, a straightforward matter: it erected the wall that separated me once and for all from any kind of fellowship, barricaded me outside the much-lauded community in which the others lived so well, so self-complacently. I, for my little part, was now assigned my destined place. I felt as lonesome and abandoned as the Ace of Spades in the hollow of a not yet apperceived recognition. Only much later should I understand that from that moment onward I belonged to those who destroy cities, not to those who build them. I only knew that I was mockingly watched by the eyes of that model Florentine girl whom Miss Fern had planted as an anima in my soul . . . and my hatred of her moved into my dear endocrine glands and settled there for all time. Hatred: the "measuring emotion," as Stella so accurately put it. I knew that I would get my revenge.

And that is why, dearest friend, this humiliating early experience regrettably did not have an edifying Dickensian consequence. I did not tarry in majestic isolation, filling the hollow of a not yet apperceived recognition with zealous study, safeguarding the dangerous terrain of the emotional world with solid knowledge. My vital self deserted with flying colors and joined the ruffians. For even though the laughter of my tormentors had irrevocably barred me from their community, I became the leader of their brutality. For twelve long years, I was the conductor of their collective baseness. Whenever anyone more finely textured, helpless, apparently awkward wandered into the common lowlands and stimulated the collective mirth, it was I who sounded the alarm with a first splutter from snot-clogged nostrils.

Only once did I reveal on what side I really stood. I have to beg for your kindly patience about this trial, too, or my early experience will not enjoy the counterpoint that life manages to arrange so well. I'll keep it brief:

A few years later, Cousin Wolfgang's educational path had already separated from mine. Uncle Helmuth's explanation of the principle of the steam engine had not found the same swift grasp in him as in me; he was considered backward in many respects, anyhow, and so they decided to give him a humanistic education and me a more scientific one. My only cultural accomplishments were occasional cartoons (drawn clandestinely under my desk, unnoticed by the teachers). They were accurate, mordant caricatures, and so successful that the fame of my genius reached the upper classes. Where a pupil named Czerwenka (isn't it odd what trivial details stick in the mind?) was having certain difficulties in keeping up with his class and lacked even halfway decent marks in just about every subject. He turned to me with a request initiated with a poke in the ribs: could I prepare a drawing on the theme of "summer," a homework assignment, which he could hand in as his own?

Why not? I even enjoyed the idea. Asking a few questions off the point, I took Czerwenka's intellectual measurements and gazed at his thick face and ink-stained (incidentally, conspicuously small, effeminate) hands in order to fathom his psychology. In the very next class (descriptive geometry), I drew a picture of Summer such as might presumably be reflected in Czerwenka's innermost being: a canal shore with the exposed innards of a gas plant in the background—everything shaped roller-like, a kind of cyclopean cylinderism—and in the foreground, a group of sphere-headed bathers, sinking elephant legs and barrel torsos into the sluggish water. Thick, sure contours—you would have recognized a talented imitation of Léger.

Czerwenka was most satisfied. This was precisely what he wanted and would have put on paper, but, alas, he had no knack for expressing himself with a pencil. The drawing teacher seemed to know this too. He told Czerwenka point-blank that the drawing could not be his. Who had done it for him? Czerwenka, cornered, gave him my name. "I don't believe you!" said the drawing teacher and sent for me.

The drawing teacher was a gangly, jittery, rather young man who, it was rumored, had an artistic private life: he was counted among the talents of the Viennese Secession, was honorably represented with dynamic pen-and-ink drawings in its annual exhibits, and taught at our school only because of artistic destitution. His indifference to our achievements seemed to confirm this gossip about him. As for me, I had always used his classes to do my homework for the next few classes, where, in turn, I pursued my drawing activities. He had noticed this and had shrugged, with that scornful disgust that is the final weapon of a broken-winged teacher against the ring leader of class perfidy.

For the first time, I stood before him face to face. "Did you draw this?" he asked, holding the drawing out to me amid the tense silence of the upperclassmen.

Czerwenka morosely nodded toward me, his eyes downcast. So I said, "Yes."

The drawing teacher pushed a piece of chalk into my hand, pointed at the plaster model of a flayed muscleman bending an imaginary bow in an unrealistic lunge, and said, "Copy that!"

I began at the nape of the skinned bow-bender and with one stroke drew the S of the back line down to the corded nodules of his buttock musculature and along the thigh, the back of the knee, the calf, to the heel—I got no farther. For the drawing teacher ripped the chalk out of my hand, peered at me wildly under the tangled shock of hair on his forehead, sized me up and down, and said, "You bastard!" Stomping back to his desk and tossing the chalk into the dusty cardboard box at the blackboard, he muttered, as though to himself (but so loudly that everyone could hear), "And someone like this is vegetating in this idiotic school!" Before reaching his desk, he turned back to me and shouted, "Tell your parents they're morons—morons and criminals! Tell them that I said so. My name is Weidenreich—Leopold Weidenreich. Go on—get the hell back to your class!"

An artistic temperament. Imagine the difficulties I would have caused him had I actually delivered his message to my foster parents. He seemed, incidentally, to have realized as much himself. Thereafter he never even deigned to glance at me, the striking Herr Weidenreich, and I remained untroubled by any effort on his part to cultivate my gift, the efflorescence of which promised so much that he could go off the deep end at the mere thought of its remaining undeveloped.

The incident might have had no aftermath if I—yes, now look—if I had not been surrounded henceforth by an enigmatic aura—how shall I put it?—as though marked by a mark of Cain that separated me from my classmates far more than my obscure background, my (now rather rusty) knowledge of languages, my hysterical clowning, and my cantankerous way of spoiling for a fight. This aura rather annoyed them and turned them against me, and yet it had definite authority. A short time later, Czerwenka (six foot three and three years my senior, but now only one class away from me) advanced toward me to deliver the punches he had planned for me. I checked him with a single glance that blended grandeur and malice; the mere glance of my eyes drew an opaque veil over his. He took off with his tail between his legs.

Incidentally, it would be appropriate to point out here that this aura of malicious grandeur was certainly not restricted to the milieu of my school in Hietzing. For example, I can recall with clarity the time when Cousin Wolfgang (who knew nothing about this incident with the art teacher) hissed at me in venom-bloated despair, "You and your arrogant ways—UNTO EVERY ONE THAT HATH SHALL BE GIVEN, AND HE SHALL HAVE ABUNDANCE!!!" This could have been a proud moment in my young existence—just like that other moment, when you imparted the same words to me, your mouth aglow with loving envy. . . . It could have been one of my great moments, except that (here as with you, and also as with Weidenreich) the mere glance of the eyes of my anima (which eyes I had meanwhile removed from Miss Fern's fading Florentine charge and inserted in various other heads attached to riper bodies) pulled an opaque veil over mine.

But something else occurred after my being pilloried as a ridiculous bearer of culture and a somber member of the elect: I began wandering around the city. I sought the City as a hunter stalks his game. I played hooky, and rambled. I went on exploratory journeys through the streets of Vienna for days on end. I would come home in the evening, then, next morning, start where I had left off the previous day. My more than measly allowance went for subway tickets. My scholastic performance declined proportionately. Torturous scenes developed with Uncle Helmuth, who, as my legal guardian, felt obliged to interfere, and also with Aunt Selma, who could not bear having "her" child compare so shamefully with Hertha's child. For Cousin Wolfgang was a marvel of scholastic triumph. He was soon wearing thicker and thicker glasses, in which you saw either a gigantically magnified pupil or yourself dwarfed and topsy-turvy. The fuzz of manliness erupted prematurely on his upper lip, pimply chin, and calves. His cowhide school bag, with its bleak barracks aroma from the cheese sandwiches and wet bathing suits, a smell announcing his return when he came up the stairs, weighed a ton because of the books—pure, sheer intellect in old, thick, musty tomes. But I was roaming about Vienna. With drawn flanks and Aunt Selma's bewitched gaze, I was seeking the City in the city. With the drawn flanks of a stray cat and Aunt Selma's spell in my eyes, I sought, in Vienna, the city of humanity: ANTHROPOLIS—

and I knew I wouldn't find it, because I was isolated from the others and I hated them. Always and everywhere, I found only the past, life already lived, striking me as livelier than present-day life. Cultural refuse. Testifying to a history that had become fiction. I sought Paradise and found that I had lost it. Eventually, I gave up running through the city and I went only to museums. Hence the bit of culture that I can display.

Chatting thus with my dead friend, I had soon covered the distance to Kehl and driven across the Rhein—once again Germany's border, not its river, as a couple of disagreeable night-waking policemen and customs inspectors, of the "We're not like that but we've gotta do it" sort, so vividly forced me to realize. I left Strasbourg and its cathedral tower rammed like a thorn in the flesh of the night as it veered to my right in the blackness behind the blue-tinged halos of arc lamps; then I once again slit open the wind-blasted nightland with the beams of my headlights.

By the time I neared Reims, the gaze of the Munich girl had bored so deep into me that I sprang a leak. I yearned for human contact.

I had driven into a rainstorm. The windshield wipers cut two tiny shiny segments out of the night, now interwoven with silver threads of rain that shot through the headlights and scattered on the hood. Watery veils enshrouded me. Beyond the roadside trees, whose branches rattled against the darkness, the landscape tossed and turned in a nightmare. Every clod of earth here was fertilized with the bone meal of two nations. Claustrophobia overwhelmed me in my bathysphere. I turned off toward Reims, toward the halo over the city where the city's heart seemed to glow white as in a crucible.

Obliquely illuminated by spotlights fixed on the surrounding houses, the cathedral stood cadaverously mute in the deserted square, wanly scattering the reflection of its charnel-house yellow into the darkness behind the shivers of rain, which had now become misty and fine. I knew a hotel somewhere close by—the one where I had once spent the night with Schwab—but I also wanted to stretch my legs after several hours of hard driving. So I parked the car, took out the essentials for overnight, locked up, and walked across the square—

and above me floated an angel, smiling blindly into the night.

The city was dead, except for a group of three men and two women about to climb into a car at the end of a line parked along the curb. One of the men was unlocking the car door; one of the women wore a hat like a flapper's; its narrow brim cast a shadow over her eyes; the nose and lips underneath were well shaped.

Walking past, I tried to drill my gaze into her eyes, but they were undiscernible beneath the shadow, which lay upon them like a domino mask. She turned away, saying, "... *et si tu penses qu'ils te font payer trente mille balles pour une nuit, tandis que dans le Midi tu as une très belle chambre pour quinze mille maximum* ..." (Beloved! And we could have flown through the starry spaces together! ...)

In the hotel, which reeked of wine, like an old barrel, from basement to roof (the restaurant was already closed), I took a room, fell into bed, and dropped off instantly.

I awoke from my dream at dawn. As usual when it had taunted me, I lay paralyzed for a while until its images drifted away, one after the other. Having sucked their fill of my marrow, they slipped back into the unsupervised world whence they had crept up. What lay here now was like a negative of myself: it bared black teeth at me from between white lips. I had devoured the ashes of my confidence in life. For a fragment of the instant that shattered on the threshold between dreaming and awakening (when I realized with holy terror that I had dreamed *the truth* and had indeed truly killed someone), I was—without illusion or delusion, without guile or ruse—myself. I was, in an innocent, childlike way, MYSELF. But with the next splinter of this instant, my certainty was already dissolving (and I with it), and what was left of my dream was merely an echo and eventually merely the memory of an echo, like the empty after-feeling of pleasure following a night of love. And I was again what I usually am: an echo of the I that I had been at some time or other (a time untraceably lost in oblivion, and perhaps even then only a blessed instant).

I wasn't awake yet, merely on the verge—that is to say, exchanging the immediate for the mediate, exchanging lived reality for words. The more consciously I awoke, the more verbal I became. Images were replaced by vocables. What I had been waned. The remaining vacuum filled up with the gruel of the effable. Filled up and became the walk-on who, each morning, under my name, tackled the daily existence of a forty-nine-year-old scriptwriter with literary ambitions:

—in the daily betrayal of the genius in us, who is at home in the fable world of dreams: where fish have voices to speak to us, and flowers eyes to look at us, and where we, passionately open like listening children, experience ourselves in inconceivable anxiety and bliss, suffocating because of nameless guilt or fleeing from unnamable threats, rooted in the ground and turned to stone, or lightly floating over smiling lands and domed cities . . . and unamazed, because all wonders are natural here: the immaculate conception is taken for granted, as is the resurrection of the body after death; of all possibilities (which are realities gravid with the miracle of life here), only one never fully comes true: falsehood, *because, encapsulated in itself like a glass vessel, it is always transparent as illusion, always appears as itself, simply as falsehood—*

until, in my awakening, the images are replaced by words, which force us into grammar and thereby back into time: where, in the unceasing decay of the present into the never-again of the past and the not-yet of the future, we become victims of a self-imposed illusion, an abstract reality that we have created and in which we soon yield even with our souls to the necessities enjoined upon our bodies—

and thus, pedestrians instead of flyers, girded about with phrases, hiking boots laced with locutions, and knapsacks full of commonplaces, we march, supposedly rational, to our lightless destiny—

I was awake. The reality of October twelfth was ready to receive me as though it were the first day of Creation. I surprised this day when it was still embryonic. The light still had something of the sap-milk of buds. The night had not entirely defoliated; its colors had not yet fully emerged and its contours were only just becoming firm. But day's capsule was already breaking open. The objects around me celebrated their rebirth into the seeable. Over the small, worn carpet in front of the bed, the lightly flowing sunshine of a French autumn day poured more and more amply, insinuating a shadow into the *sérail* motifs of the pattern, the shadow of an obscenely bent chair leg in Louis Philippe style, the chestnut-brown wood absorbing the rays and letting them blaze up on its embossments.

This, and the tenacious smell of wine, which the sharp air, penetrating through the open window, could not drive out from the discolored crimson rep of the curtain, sufficed to place me immediately in the here and now and to conjure up the things around me: the well-worn plush-cushion luxury of the provincial hotel room, the bright street with the two rows of (now leafless) lindens where the first sounds of car engines would soon come, the cozy old town behind them, laced tighter and tighter in the corset of iron-concrete construction (hence shorter and shorter of breath), the still vast and broadly waving, not autumnally fire-red wine-grape-land in which it snuggled . . . and above all this, the hard dome of a sky that grew more and more spiritual the closer I came to Paris—

Paris, damn it, Schwab! . . .

and instead of putting up with this as if my dream had merely changed its theme and motive (once, ages ago, this was how I had known how to live: effortlessly gliding from the reality of dreams into the unreality of days), I now frantically tried to hold on to the terror of my dream in order to wrest from it the key to the incomprehensibility of my waking existence, and in so doing, I plunged more and more hopelessly into the vortex of the verbal; I transformed image substances into notions, which instantly hijacked those images from their magical realm into logical connections, in which they lost all meaning; I got tangled up in word structures that shredded conscious experience into temporal and spatial processes; I used the polished and prepared surgical kit of concepts (*murder, disgrace, conscience*) to shoo away the reflections of what I had felt and with which it had provoked the echo of meaningfulness.

Thus I lay awhile, immobile, enfeebled, and discouraged, still throbbing from an assault by deep fright against the center of my essence—and I was already mentally wandering again along off-roads and side roads, behind myself—

I thought, for instance, Just what am I? Am I what just now so dreadfully afflicted me in my dreams? This caricature of Raskolnikov: the craven murderer who kills an old crone because she sees through his baseness? Am I what is lying here and thinking about itself? The body, which is self-familiar to me with its needs and urges, its gradually commencing disintegration (which makes me love the body all the more tenderly), the brain—this clown!—whose monkeyshines and escapades, conjuring tricks and acrobatic feats, I know so well, no willing, reliable, systematic worker like Cousin Wolfgang—like you, dear Schwab!—but a skillful climber of smooth walls, a nimble jumper, a good, swift diver, a fearless reconnoiterer and fabulously cunning thief? . . .

naturally, I am both the one and the other and all this at once; and, beyond this, a wealth of other possibilities that could take form in certain situations. . . . But whatever I may be, it can be uttered, it is articulable: it congeals as something shapable—except for an ineffable remnant, which is really I.

And now I ask: how much textual material does it take to select any one of the human possibilities and present it in words, clear-cut and unmistakable?

It is obvious that the tens of thousands of words in a language allow for an infinitude of combinations, enough to revive even the very finest nuance of a human existence. So it is better to ask: *How little does it take?* Three sentences? More? If we focus on the gospels individually, we can see that each is barely the length of a brochure. Hence, for young Werther, an almost luxurious extravagance was deployed. Yet King Lear, for example: he's there in just a few dozen phrases. And besides: who wants to go that high? For a normal case, all we need is a brief excerpt from Lao-tse, and editorials, Art Buchwald, Bambi, and a Biblical verse. . . . What am I saying! All it takes is simply the utterance of a name—Johannes Schwab, for instance—or simply and plainly the little word *I*. . . .

Thus I lay there and was soon recomposed from self-chitchat to what I really am.

Besides, the day was lengthening. I had to go to Paris. So I got out of bed and went over to the wash stand to look at my face in the mirror above it. The more thoroughly I nailed in my stare, the more vacant my face became. I was able to confirm that my eyes are an intense blue (I have been told so repeatedly, and I ought to resign myself to sharing my outstanding physiognomic feature with popular depictions of the Mater Dolorosa and the Hitler Youth). But despite utmost concentration, nothing else about myself came to mind. The scouting trip through clefts and fissures left by life in my epidermis proved as abstract and fruitless as a theoretical promenade along the footpaths shown on a landscape relief map in a spa pavilion. If absolutely necessary, this man could be expected to kill, to murder, but the likelihood was neither revealed by a special sign nor excluded. I soon gave up on myself and began to shave.

The day was as bright as it had promised. The sidewalk glistened metallically with rainwater that had not yet evaporated, and oval drops glittered on the roofs and hoods of parked cars. The cathedral looked like a disabled veteran that a cunning art historian had patched together from several disabled veterans. I went to my car and unlocked it—

and above me floated a great angel, smiling a Mona Lisa smile into the autumnal skyblue.

During the drive to Paris, I tackled my dream systematically. Earlier, whenever that nightmare had ambushed me, such efforts had proved fruitless, and this was the case again. The images could be summoned, but not the terror. I know the sequence by heart. I can run it forward and backward like a film at the editing table and linger on any detail:

It is always the same giant office building, with empty corridors leading to empty hive cells, and elevators whose empty cages counter-rotate up and down like bubbles in slowly boiling test tubes. Somewhere high up under the roof and deep in the basement, they change their minds and directions, rattling and rumbling through cyclopean cogwheel innards. The risen ones now sink downward, the sunken ones rise up again, and so on for all eternity: even in my dreams, I'm a sleazy symbolist. It is night. I have let myself be locked in, unnoticed by the building guards, and I am lying in wait for the cleaning woman. She is gray and worn out with drudgery, an old woman. I can picture her body: worm-eaten flesh hanging in four skin pouches from the leather-covered skeleton; two of the pouches dangle in front, on the monkey bars of her rib cage, two in back under the primeval pelvic bone-butterfly—a beggar costume of a body, as in medieval *danses macabres*. She covers it with slovenly old-crone clothing: coarse, urine-sintered underwear beneath strata of sweat-yellowed smocks and aprons whose color has been leached out by laundry water and caustic detergents. All this fills me with violent disgust. Nausea chokes me. But I wait for her, smiling. It is a murderer's smile, *sharpened like a writer's pencil.* . . . And while I try to lure her to the basement under some flimsy pretext, I realize that she sees through me. She knows what I am planning to do to her. Knows that I want to silence her. Knows that I know that she was the witness to an unspeakable baseness, and that I am going to murder her for that reason.

Thus, she knows what will happen when she steps across the threshold to the cellar into which I force her. By entering, she is the one who lures me to my crime.

She wants to convict me: I still haven't revealed my intention and yet I am already in her hands.

Panic seizes me: only now does my vileness become manifest and grow in enormity. . . .

I grab a coal shovel. It bears dreadful witness against me; I see it in her eyes, see *myself* in her eyes. By showing me myself, like a mirror, she forces me to admit to what I am. *I have to murder her because I am a murderer.*

I lift the shovel. I could put it down again, I could pretend I was indulging in a gross practical joke—but her eyes are relentless, they shriek out my condemnation. If I let her escape now, then I'll be done for.

The first stroke hits her across the skull and smears her gray old-crone hair with brains and teeth, but does not snuff out her eyes. Now no amends can be made. Now she will merely testify the more dreadfully against me. . . . I smash away at her in an impotent chaos of shame and pleasure and disgust. The more surely her bones break and her abominable and atrocious flesh becomes one with the plunder of her clothes, the more irrevocably I become one with myself; the more terrible is the truth that she has recognized in me. . . .

And here my horror blasts the dream. I know that I am just dreaming all this—and when I flee into awakening, I am attacked by *recognition:* I know that this once really happened.

And I have thereby lost it. Only its echo resounds in me.

I DROVE THROUGH one of those blue-and-gold autumn days that make us believe that the world of children's picture books still exists. That we are capable of restoring this world. Somewhere in the countryside, where the high trees are reflected in a small pond at the edge of the fields, beyond which distant mountains stand blue, and where we shall all settle someday when we have had what is called success in life and the condition of our coronary arteries has not yet forced us to live near a hospital: in some village that has remained as true to nature as possible, and that the influx of movie people and songwriters has preserved from violation by modern barbarity and refurbished with rustic authenticity . . . where the world shall once again be as it was in our childhood, though autumnally mellowed, wisely purged, days following one another as full and pure as the vesper bell tolling. Days of the harvest of life, in which the plain and simple things are gathered in, the things we take for granted. In the morning, the rooster on his command hill of dung greets the sun with the saber blade of his crowing, the barnyard dog stretches with a wagging tail, the ducks quack their way to the pond with wiggling arses. Noon light dapples the fieldstone pavement under the lime trees by the barn, the windowpanes reflect the rusty foliage of the walnut tree in the blue of the sky with its cumulus cloudlets, and the silvery threads of Indian summer drift over the fields. Behind the violet of the faraway mountain range, the evening kindles a cold glow, over which the bell of heaven tolls sootily. The lime trees swish, the cows moo in the byre, the farmhand leads Farmer Brown's horse to the blacksmith—

> Whose cock was all rectangular,
> But love showed him a guile.
> He stuck it in a vise to file
> It smooth into a cylinder.

That is the goal of our hard labor. This beckons as a reward for an upright life of crookedness—it already beckons to me; I feel I can grasp it. A movie starring Nadine Carrier could not possibly fail. A movie that has not bombed is bound to pull the next one

after it. So: three solid scripts for Madame Carrier (if possible
with a percentage of the gross), and everything would be hunky-
dory. You can get a small farm in cider country: very easy what
with the rural exodus; they're a dime a dozen. And all my sins
would be forgiven. There'd be a house for my son, and he could
say, "This is *our* house." Maybe Christa would come back to us.
The old woman of my dreams would be killed off and all the dead
would stay dead. I'd finally have peace and quiet to write my
book—

my Book

the book that bears witness to being a human being in this
era—a breathtaking success!!!

the highest-sales-storming, best-seller-list-peak-surpassing sensation!!!

A BOOK WRITTEN BY THE CONSCIENCE OF OUR RACE!!!
FANFARE!!!

and the smashing of cymbals will pulverize ten thousand white
doves like confetti in the air—

and rolling and foaming out of the seething of the boundless
crowd emerges the mighty back of the whale

EXCITEMENT

and sends the swarming of the doves the skyward fountain of

JUBILATION

the upward proliferating atomic mushroom which tears out its
stem together with the root fibers of uptossed

caps	coifs	papakhas
hats	shakos
bonnets	képis
hoods
berets

while the whale EXCITEMENT powerfully rolls over in the ball
bearings of its back, into the deep again so that the whirlpool crater of its suction wreathes into

APPLAUSE

in a swelling surge that sends the phonometer into the high numbers way over the red borderline of decibels audible to the human
ear and the crowd gapes open in the wedge-blare of trumpets

!!!CLEAR THE WAY!!!

for
in the surging of red flags
it comes zooming along,
the troika
of the

ZEITGEIST

drawn by the three stallions

KARL MARX
ALBERT EINSTEIN
SIGMUND FREUD

!!!THREE GERMANS!!!

creators of our world era
who have carried the mind of the West beyond the Gobi Desert
all the way to the Middle Kingdom of China—
The children's choirs sing:

> Lao-tse
> Mao-tse
> sock them in the snout-tse
> smash them in their kissers free
> give it to them one two three!

!!!THREE GERMAN JEWS!!!

so that the Protocols of the Elders of Zion may be realized by the
chosen people within the chosen people

The Kyffhäuser *a cappella* chorus sings:

> Yankee doodle
> Flirty Gerty
> Sighing for a Jewish noodle.
> Gerty is a pastor's daughter,
> Never does the things she oughter.

and over all their silver-haired evangelist heads (Einstein silver above; Freud below; Marx all around), they wield a banner saying

ARISTIDES

—an evening star in the firmament of the waning novel—

!!!   !!!   !!!   !!!   !!!

(in the microphone, the breathless voice of the blurb writer: ". . . with his brilliant style, which reflects reality in a thousand facets, a style oscillating between crystalline hardness and rubbery flexibility, ironical, often even parodistic, then again as simple as Biblical prose, yet utterly precise, always superbly precise, this panchaotic synoptist grasps the panorama of the present day as Bismarck once grabbed his king by the scabbard, virtually clutching, as it were, the reader's sense of human responsibility by the moral balls . . .")

and
SILENCE

so that you can hear a pin drop: the one with which the President of the Republic of VIEILLE FRANCE is about to stick the Grand Cross of the Legion of Honor on the brilliant publisher's breast (the pin has slipped down the hard-currency-filled wallet in the philistine lounge suit: M. Malraux hands Le Général another pin)—

while the honorary members of the Comédie Française playing the roles of the latest Nobel Prize laureates (Ghana, Lapland, Monaco, San Salvador, Central Vietnam, Honduras, German Democratic Republic, Holland, Tibet, Indonesia, Panama, Swit-

zerland) spray a triple salvo of ink with their Parker fountain
pens
in honor of the first

STATELESS MAN

ever to be accepted into the Olympus of the moralistically vita-
min-rich, socially redeeming, full-calorie literature (whispering
in the audience: *"Mais qu'est-ce-que c'est qu'un apatride?"*—
*"Quoi? Tu connais pas ta mythologie? Ce que tu peux être con!
Ce sont eux qui bouffent leurs enfants. Tu n'en as pas entendu
parler?"*)
but then
a bard's mane swings:

SIR JOHN LENNON

of the

BEATLES

and the eardrum-splitting whistling of bats originates with the
sulfur-yellow hell of epoch-making puberty—
and while it is filled with thrills from the first zap of an electric
guitar
the white elephant comes swaying along on pneumatically
pounding rubber soles

his name is
BALLYHOO

and the question mark of his trunk carries a board on which is
written

QUO VADIS WESTERN WORLD?

and he rolls along in the guitar's sweet vibes, which are followed
by the shrill voices of a hundred thousand bats—
and he is fantastically beautiful:
in each of his rubber joints, stamped into his bark-skin like
thumb prints of titan gangsters, ten times a hundred Negro
boxers roll their shoulders;
in each of his steps, shuffling with the sole-pressure of ten times

a thousand atmospheres, ten thousand Puerto Rican boogie-woogie dancers swing their chicks so hard that they petrify into body-halos like the divine whores of Angkor Wat;

in the swaying of his fullness, directed by the Cuban cigars of five times fifty-five Wall Street tycoons, the opulent hips of ten times a thousand batter-battened Aunt Jemimas—

we now all sing:

bigbig is BALLYHOO and beautiful:

his toenails, elegantly clipped like the gateway arches of Kairoan and as red as the flesh of the Persian Revlon Melon, are the shields behind which thousands of wishful fantasies feel safe; his forehead, wisdom-buckling up to the bare skull, like that of Socrates, but flat, narrow, and domineering under it, like a Florentine coat of arms, is, like the southern firmament, strewn with myriads of pearls of the HONDA breed; from the meager wreath of his white eyelashes, TWIGGY's peacock eyes peer, golddust-powdered; of his mighty tusks (their ivory is milky like DAUM glass, they are curved into lunar sickles like the papyrus barks in which the pharaohs had themselves rowed through the indigo velvet of nights in the Valley of the Nile), the left one is encrusted with amaranths and is known as LIBERTY, the right one inlaid with an ivy tangle of green copper and known as TIFFANY: they carry us through the fragrances of NEWMOWNHAY; the gentle palm-frond fanning of his ears blows ten times ten million posters into the pagoda of the sails of the full-rigged ship VOGUE; on his back as tremendous as the snowy flanks of the Himalayas, tassled like a cardinal's hat in the red braid of the fashion fiber COCO CHANEL, sways the all-purpose object

PANDORA

a female torso in segments that can contract telescopically, made of LALIQUE, and may be used as a dresser, a dummy, or an *anima*

and around him the mannequins stand like coral branches, from whose twigs chains hang like spider webs in which the gold beetles of the jewels are caught; dreamy, the veil-fishes of the most delicate lingerie swim back and forth among them; like frost, like mold, elegant furs are draped over them; in the breathing of beauty sleep, their shampooed hair floods in slow-motion rhythm . . .

and BALLYHOO hurls the sign that says:

QUO VADIS WESTERN WORLD?

far behind into the ecstatically yelling mob (whoever catches it can soon wed the giant SUCCESS) and stretches his trunk up to the greeting, blessing, trailblazing erection

and lifts it steep and thrusts it out of the giant exhaust high into the sky where even the lightning rod of the Vampire State Building no longer scrapes them,

the stream of PAPER with which ten thousand breathlessly chaff-chopping rotary presses incessantly feed him:

plunge their roaring torrent all the way up to the cirrus

cloudlets sailing in the icy wind of the stratosphere; so as to fan out featherily with them over the continents and descend like manna over Manhattan

and Adelaide, Athara, and Agrigento

and Bissau, Berne, and Basra

and Chuch'i, Charleroi, and Coventry

and Delhi, Diredawa, and Dar es Salaam

and Elk Point, Etumba, and Elberfeld

and Florence, Fukushima, and Fort Knox

and Gombe, Galveston, and Georgetown

and Hebron, Hoboken, and Hyderabad

and Inverness, Isalmi, and Izmir

and Jawhar, Jiggalong, and Jurf ed Deraswish

and Korsör, Kimberley, and Keflavik

and London, Linz, and Little Rock

and Madras, Montevideo, and Mandalay

and Natal, Nashville, and New Orleans

and Oklahoma, Olasvik, and Oallam

and Penang, Pittsburgh, and Pucallpa

and Quebec and there aren't many more Q's

and Reggane, and Rome, and Riobamba

and Surabaya, Salem, Sfax, St. Pölten, and St. Louis,

Tampico, Tocca, and Tamalameque

Ulm, Udine, and Ullapool,

Vancouver, Västmanland, and Viroflay,
Waipio, Westchester, and Winnipeg
Xanthi, Xique-xique, Xaparais
Ypern, which just about does it,
and Zofingen, Zenit, and Zaragoza—
      —read it today in the *Times Literary Supplement,* the sensa-
tional computer prediction of the unique success of the book!!!!
The machine, data-fed by a committee of market researchers
under the supervision of Mary McCarthy, draws the ascending
curve of the dizzying edition-record-breaker
      seventy-seven times at the top of the Book-of-the-Month Club;
the stage version running on Broadway for two years; eleven
months at London's Aldwych Theatre; seventeen full weeks at
the Comédie Française; Felsenstein is planning a production in
East Berlin; the TV version beamed by satellite *Xenia 29* from all
stations in the Western hemisphere; presumably crowned by a

MAMMOTH MOVIE
A Wohlfahrt Production
of
INTERCOSMIC FILM ART

absolutely superstar cast:
Marlene Dietrich at the soda fountain;
Frank Sinatra as caddie;
Richard Burton and Liz Taylor as Philemon and Baucis;
in all other parts: Peter Sellers
      The net receipts of the world premiere, with the presence of
Princess Margaret, Lord Snowdon, Igor Stravinsky, and Jacqueline Kennedy Onassis, will go to charity (despite the hundred-
and-thirty-six-million-dollar budget of the film);
      a dance performed by the Mongoloid Ballet of the United In-
sane Asylums of New Jersey;
      plus, as already agreed, the publisher has announced a

COMICSTRIP VERSION

for the further diffusion of this monumental intellectual work,
which is not easily accessible to people of all educational back-

grounds (to be syndicated in more than one hundred and seventy-six leading dailies in fifty-eight countries simultaneously)—

!!!ATTENTION!!!

fan clubs, autograph collectors, organizers of culture conventions, cocktail-party hostesses, advertising specialists!!!
As is well known, the author, who lives in extreme isolation on his mountain farm near Gstaad (and is now on safari in East Africa), avoids any kind of publicity; requests for social events, television appearances, round-table discussions, and commercials are to be directed to the publisher. For information on the background and foreground, the physical statistics, skull formation, palm lines, sexual habits and proclivities, horoscope, hobbies, etc., please consult the life story penned by Bill Pepper with the personal cooperation of the author:

The Working Beast

(airtight information on all the links between biography and fiction!! The complete key to the characters, places, episodes!!! Also see the depth-psychological study by Dr. Hertzog!!! As well as the monograph put out by the same publisher: Aristides par lui-même! A Portrait in His Own Words, profusely illustrated with previously unpublished material, including rare photographs of the author with Louis Armstrong, Gina Lollobrigida, Dr. Barnard of the Groote Schur Hospital, Moshe Dayan, and many others. In paperback for only five-ninety-five!!!)—

but until then, we'll live on advances, comrade! Both financially and morally (as if this weren't the same thing for Christa and associates). We are living toward a promise—living as sheer abstractions: anticipating a future that hovers before us like the proverbial carrot in front of the donkey's mouth—

and thus the procession winds up without much ado. *Ferme le pot de confiture*, as Gaia would say; the audience disperses—only you and I, brother Life-Dreamer, jog along undaunted behind ourselves:

always on the same gray mount of a present that will be no different tomorrow from today; always a new day in which we await ourselves the next day; always a new loan of twenty-four hours on a property that may contain only twenty-three—

hours that we let wane by serving the piglets, pouring swill into their troughs and then consuming what they leave over for us; hours of frittering and, of course, also hours of desperate wishful thinking:

fallen angels from imagination's realm—

which make the mark of Cain on our foreheads light up when the urgent pleading appears in our eyes:

You who are entangled in the chaos of our life and fear being throttled in it—be patient for just a bit longer: we are not lying when we say:

I have only to doff my gray coat in order to be king.

And you who think you have seen through our flimflam, you who hate us, despise us, want to shrug us off, ignore us contemptuously—just wait:

The day will come! The day of vengeance will come.

And you who love us—oh, do not torture us. The day will come, it will come for sure, it may come tomorrow—

end of the flagpole.

□   □   □

I DROVE VERY FAST. It was a precarious morning, and my mood was as fragile as the glass-spun light in which autumn lavishly wastes its colors: postdiluvial, a rainbow across gurgling water. I floated above it, kept my sensoria under a steady, gentle pressure like that of my sole on the gas pedal, the quivering of the speedometer needle, and the dials of the tachometer and the oil gauge.

Like these, my sensoria were, of course, ready to drop to zero as soon as I let up. I had to keep them at full speed, even if it became dangerous. Life is just a risky business; I don't cudgel my brain about what could happen if I'm doing a hundred ten and a tire bursts or a piston jams because of some worn-out valve in the bowels of my car. The results wouldn't exactly be edifying, but that's life, things like that happen. . . .

incidentally, that was an amusing notion. It could really happen—and what if it did? What if my car flew from the road at this speed, caroming back and forth like a billiard ball between the boulevard trees, and eventually boring into the plowland beyond? Wouldn't that be a godsend for my son? He could turn me into his myth (which, if I went on living, he could not, presumably, do: "My father died before he could finish his work"—that sounds nice when the father is twenty-four, less nice when he's seventy; forty-nine is the outer limit anyway). . . . In any case, the idea was pleasurable because of its novel-like dramatics. I saw the ruins of my vehicle, a wheel ripped from its axle, springing far into the field, reeling and fluttering around its tire like a decelerating top. The metal casing was squooshed up like a discarded piece of tinfoil, the engine block had been shoved in, blood was oozing underneath into the peacock-blue, iridescent oil. . . .

perhaps my hand was dangling slackly from the half-shredded door, with the frame bent in like an hourglass (a jewel from Gaia's story about the youth of her mother, the alleged Princess Jahovary: the hand she suspended in morbid grace over the balustrade of the box when she was taken to the opera as a girl; her governess whispering to her, "*Gabrielle, n'oubliez pas la main morte!*" and the totally different meaning of *la mano morta* in Italian: a lecherous paw in a crowd, wedging, as though accidentally, between a girl's thighs—fine: it boiled down to the same thing).

At any rate, what I imagined could actually occur a few miles down the road would probably occur someday, if I kept driving through the countryside in my foolish fashion. It was even bound to come; I have known my death for a long time—now I suddenly feel it very close.

I am not timorous, which is why I drove no slower than before—in fact, even faster, more daringly, passing other cars more heedlessly, taking curves more ruthlessly—but my throat did tighten:

if I died (not necessarily today or tomorrow or the day after but perhaps in a couple of weeks, in six months, in a year), then I would be dead *without having written my book*—and that seemed like eternal damnation to me—

All at once, I knew what dying meant. This was no ineluctable biological phenomenon, no final decay of an organism, its dissolution and transformation into other kinds of matter; this was the death of my soul:

my book would never exist; it would be snuffed out with me, as though it had never existed.

And that would be as though I had never existed. My book, the only thing that bore witness that I ever had some reality, would forever be hidden in a dream.

□   □   □

IT WAS IN MY HAMBURG DAYS that I began dreaming the dream of my murder—during the first few years of my marriage to Christa, though it seems to me it started only when I was thinking about my book. Occasionally, the dream varied in structure. Sometimes, I had already killed the old witch, was about to bury her, and was trembling with fear at being caught unawares; drenched with sweat, I was drudging away at forcing her unexpectedly bulky old-crone bones, and the plunder and tangle of pauper's clothing, misbegotten flesh, brains, and blood-smeared hair, into the narrow pit I had dug with the shovel—I know they're on my trail, they're about to look for me here, they're already coming down the steps of the basement, whence I can no longer escape. . . . Or else I had already buried the corpse; I was no longer in the basement but knew they were finding it there; she has moldered upward to bear witness against me, her carcass will expose me as her murderer—that's what she wanted, she wanted me to murder her, she descended to the basement with me wittingly, intentionally, in order to become one with my murder, instantly, at the first stroke (with which I had by no means wanted to kill her). . . .

I learned all this by heart long ago. I knew the consequences: the taste left in my mouth for days, the enjoyment left in my mind for days—

I have grown accustomed to living with it. It has not recurred that often—perhaps four or five times during the past eighteen years (enough for domestic use). A few days later, the hunt (for big game, so to speak) ends, making room for the everyday snares and traps: the bird-catching of lived moments (sometimes there's a particolored goldfinch; sometimes one begins singing; sometimes one even speaks: if I close my eyes, they whir about in my head—but the cage has holes: the ones I want to keep fly out and the others stay, even when they have died: decay with dusty plumage in the corners, piles of fusty rubbish . . .).

for a while, something archetypal lingers marvelously in me: large, silent, indecipherable, like the stone faces on Easter Island—

then, diurnal drudgery carries me off.

□   □   □

NOW AND THEN, I tried to track down the origin of this dream in myself. I visualized the time, the days, that preceded it. For instance, a humdrum day one and a half or two years ago here in Paris (in the constellation of Gaia, whom I loved at that time, Venus ascending, Mercury in the first house): we lived sumptuously and with costly joys, spent our days sybaritically; bought our salmon and caviar (as well as vodka) at Petrossian, venison and fowl at Fouchon, cheeses at Marboeuf; the only arguments were about things like whether we preferred the *vins des Côtes* (Ausone) or the *vins des Graves* (Cheval Blanc) to Saint-Émilion (and which vintage, needless to say); we agreed about Chablis (Blanchots, Les Clots, Grenouilles, and Vendésis); with trout, we particularly esteemed a Pouilly fumé. We drank Burgundy less often (and if so, it was Clos de la Ferrière or Clos de Bèze-Chambertin); our selection of calvados, marc, kirsch, poire, framboise, cassis, as well as cognac and armagnac, was presentable. In short, the days began with sensual joys, sensual feasts, and ended with sensual intoxications. Our wakening in the blond pearwood Second Empire bed was a dove-like billing and cooing (which, to be sure, usually degenerated into a wildcat mating). Then we bathed amply, voluptuously. Floris of London supplied us with bath oils, bath salts, soaps, toilet waters, *pots pourris*;

otherwise, Madame remained true to the products of the House of Guerlain; I for my part held steadfast to Kniže Ten and Kniže Polo; in summer, however, I loved the somewhat vulgar freshness of Tilleul from d'Orsay. Eventually, we harnessed up: *Madame très chic, très simple, assez sportive* in her Balenciaga *tailleur,* a delightful little hat, long gloves of course (in this respect, one can always rely on Hermès), the pocketbook, however, from Germaine Guérin—everything we owned, everything we used, everything we surrounded ourselves with, was exquisite, unique, at least top quality (although we often came across simply enchanting finds at the Prisunic). The Rothschilds served as our model for the soundest, most unimportunately luxurious lifestyle. Madame herself is something unheard of, inimitable, *un vrai objet:* a Creole (to put it delicately), superlifesized in every respect, especially in the physical: chocolate-colored, over six feet, a live weight of one hundred fifty-two pounds. Dame Africa from the Gobelin cycle *The Continents:* tropical, fruit-proliferating, leopard-spitting Louis XIV sumptuousness. Yet Madame had the affectionate tenderness, the lily-of-the-valley-delicate intimacy, the entrancingly alert coquetterie of the *midinette.* At the same time, she was a tremendously capable businesswoman (record industry). A lady with an executive's vitality, the precision brain of a nuclear physicist. Being a Frenchwoman, Madame was naturally a housewife in the best sense of the word, an outstanding *maîtresse de maison* and of course one of the best-dressed women in Paris, which means in the world. (Only the footwear left something to be desired: this was where *le côté noir* revealed itself. The niggers in Madame's family tree expressed themselves more eloquently here than in her radiant corn-golden mulatto skin.) It was sensual bliss to dress this mountain of smoked flesh in *haute couture.* Furs, for instance, came to true life on her: when she donned her sporty lynx, the packs of hounds started to bark in Rambouillet, the huntsmen blasted a view-halloo; when she wore her autumnal chinchilla, the leaves of Fontainebleau turned golden-yellow; in her sable, she dashed about like a troika team. Certainly I helped Madame with her toilette. I loved this tributary rite of dressing, I loved my adoring chambermaid service. I see myself as a perfect *femme de chambre*. With transfigured eyes, I hold out Madame's lingerie (lemon-yellow frothinesses, with umbra darkening behind them.) I gather up hastily scattered brassieres and laddered stockings, tuck them away out of Madame's sight. I help her into her petticoat (taking great care with the lacquered pagoda of her hair); Madame is impatient—you understand, we stayed in bed too long. As usual, Madame has precise appointments to keep; her time is money, on which I live, with the help of which I will complete my book, write a masterpiece. So we do not tarry over breakfast; I'll munch a slice of ham from the icebox later on, drink the tea she has left standing. I quickly fill her handbag—compact, lipstick, checkbook, purse, driver's license, address book, house keys, cigarette case (Fabergé), lighter, a small shopping list (on which I have quickly and secretly scribbled "*Je t'adore!*")—Madame is practically out of the house, I run after her, helping her into the ocelot (it'll bite me any second), I race ahead into the hallway to buzz the elevator, a kiss—"*À tout à l'heure, mon ange!*"—the scissors-gate moves past her Three Magi moor's face, closing across it like a coarse-meshed veil, then she sinks to my feet, sinks to the floor like Rumpelstiltzkin, is swallowed up, I peer into the shaft, which deepens before me, then breathing a sigh of relief I return to the apartment (it looks as though a murderous burglary has taken place, but I'll have it to myself for a full day), I'm still in my bathrobe, still unshaven, from the bathroom window I can see into the courtyard, where the small fiery-red Morris runs back in an arc and then forward again, swings in to the *porte cochère*, and she looks up to me, waves from the car window, *très jeune, très dynamique—ah, ce que je l'aime!* (she'll soon be thirty-four, looks twenty-nine, if not younger). A little dizzy. I don't sleep enough, you understand. I buckle down to work—that is, I get into shape for it.

The important thing is to keep in the mood. If I wish to write a topical book, I must do so with sovereign composure, ironic distance, lucid insight. The dark passion of the professional starveling is antiquated. Nowadays, great literature is a business for sophisticated people, and Gaia's sublime sense of art, her connoisseur's flair, the clarity of her French mind—to which her exotic exterior offers a wonderfully piquant contradiction—

challenge me to peak performance, for which I dress contrapuntally, choosing the attire of Major Thompson: dark-gray, double-breasted flannel suit with discreet chalk stripes, a tough Horse Guard sit to the necktie, the feather-light hat from Lock Britishly balanced on the eyebrows, the cornflower in the lapel, an umbrella rolled needle-sharp (Rumpelstiltzkin in the dandy: oh, how good that no one can tell that I'm carrying a Bibliothèque Nationale card in my pocket!). Thus absolved of the profane zealotry of a working man, I saunter out into a Paris that fits me as snugly as my dogskin-leather gloves (a Paris teeming with *flâneurs* as perhaps the dog that supplied my glove leather once teemed with fleas).

City of idlers, city of strollers, traversed by packs of tourists, window shoppers, suburban scouts, provincial boulevard hedonists—while the streets are boiling, boiling away energy, boiling away action, combustion-engine-driven dynamics, every kind of purposeful efficiency: a need for a higher living standard, a desire to shape the future, an economic commitment, a political commitment, an erotic commitment—every kind of greed, drive, compulsion, madness stepping on the gas, throwing the shift, clutching the wheel, expelled from the exhaust. . . . The weather is delicious; dove-blue Paris has donned lemon-yellow lights, and I stroll along the Avenue Foch as far as the Bois de Boulogne, circle around the pond, twinkling with golden scales, study the ducks, the children, the dogs, the loving couples, wander back to the Place de l'Étoile and then a bit down the Champs-Élysées (briskly, briskly! you're getting to the age when you have to watch your form and figure!). At Faguet, on the rue Washington, I select a jar of apple, sour-cherry, or currant jelly for Gaia's breakfast table (should she ever—perhaps on a Sunday—arrange the leisure to relish it). At Fouquet, I order an apéritif and read the newspaper (there's nothing interesting in it).

At noon, we meet in a substantial, intimate little restaurant known only to very (but very!) knowledgeable Parisians and not imperiled by touristry (a *blanc de veau chez Anna*, a *sôle aux champignons chez les Fils de Charpentier*). If Madame does not have one of her urgent appointments right after, we indulge in a little treat for the eyes (drop in at the Musée Camondot to look at furniture, an exhibit of illusionist designs at the Orangerie) or we run a few errands (a geode of rose quartz at a mineral dealer's on the rue Guénégaud, curtains for my study at Halard's), and then we separate—"*Allons, mon ours—fermé le pot de confiture—chacun à son boulot!*"—for she's discovered a skiffle group that's more interesting than Ken Coyler's, she wants to cut a few demos and sell them to Odéon, perhaps manage the group.

I, for my part, return home to my work. It may not be the ideal hour—I work best at night or very early in the morning—but this mustn't count now, so much depends on this work, Gaia's waiting for my book, she knows it's going to be a big, significant novel, she is my muse and my Maecenas, I'd be a scoundrel to disappoint her, that would be a blow to her, a blow she could never overcome. So I have to force myself to be disciplined, to try to create (difficult as this may be on a full stomach). I rummage about in the notes, sift carefully through the existing material, work on two pages of a chapter I sketched years ago, shift it around, draw a new structural draft, clarify the situation, purify the dialogue, chew amply on the pen, pour a jigger of whiskey to fire the creative (the Dionysian!) element—it's five o'clock anyway, and what am I supposed to do? I'm no robot, a man's got days on which he's in no mood for creative writing, this isn't exactly greased lightning, you know! . . . The whiskey is excellent (Glenmorangie), I pour myself another jigger, realize I'm tired, weary, empty; the incessant enjoyment of every moment wipes me out, saps all my strength; this ought to be depicted—the sweet paralysis of an existence that is lived with all too intense enjoyment—and I lie down on the sofa to figure out if and how this can be integrated into the theme of my novel, wake up at seven, thank goodness—I've still got a good hour (she never comes home before eight or eight-thirty) . . .

I go through my manuscript from the very beginning, cross out a few pages, rewrite a few others, while the hour passes like the blink of an eye and Gaia is already whirling in (vanilla wind of exotic spice shores), freshly lacquered (she dropped in at the coiffeur), her Moor's cheeks glowing ("*Tu sais, mon ours, il fait assez froid ce soir*"). Glancing over my shoulder at the manuscript ("*Voilà! Toujours à la page treize—comme si je ne le savais pas!*" with scarcely a very fine shadow of bitterness in her voice), she must be in a good mood (thank the Lord!) and when she's in a good mood then it's a festival, it's paradise on earth: the lamb and the tiger cat-fighting like brother and sister, laughing, joking, nuzzling ("*Je t'ai eu, salaud: tu n'as pas travaillé cet après-midi, tu as bu, tu as dormi et tu as rien foutu—confesse, canaille!*"), I love her, she is my sister, I don't have to lie to her ("*Je te le jure, mon amour: j'ai récrit au moins dix pages et j'en ai gagné au moins trois toutes nouvelles!*"). She asks over her shoulder how many I crossed out, she's already going to the bathroom, intending to warm up by jumping into hot water (Lord, preserve this house!), I follow her, perch on the edge of the tub, around the twins of her solid little breasts (the designer's name is Maillol), the hot blue water smokes boreally, an adventurously contradictory geography: an Arctic atoll in the copperlight of a desert sunset. In the depths, a sunken continent lies darkly, attempts to rise: Leviathan, from which the waters cascade, telluric birth out of the boiling ocean, growing up into the rain-fecundated Earth Mother, a brown breadtree with honey dripping from its branches, a stream of water runs from her throat, quickly narrowing between her breasts, catching in the pit of the navel, one drop jumps across, races over the smooth curve of her belly and flees into the black bush wedged between her powerful thighs, a rough black chalice. I wrap her in a violet bath towel (from Ernst Jünger's *Paris Diary:* ". . . She invited me to have a cup of chocolate—I brought her a bouquet of violets"). I rub her dry, powder her armpits with a pistachio-colored puff, kiss her solid purple-brown nipple almost accidentally ("*Ah, non—pas maintenant—arrête! Mais tu es un obsédé!*"). We change into our evening attire—lounge dress, of course; we have absolutely no intention of going out, *au diable* with Lasserre and Tour d'Argent; after all, we're not Americans, *on reste chez nous:* what France has to offer us is (beyond the bell-tolling of her great architecture, the lark jubilation of her painters, the radiantly spiritual gravity of her wines, the full artful piety of her cuisine) *la douceur du foyer,* and we enjoy the sweetness of home solemnly, this is what distinguishes us from the barbarians, from the jetting nomads, the civilized steppe-peoples who are assaulting this venerable continent like a scourge of God—we oppose them with the bulwark of an intimate knowledge, a connoisseurship, known only to the most familiar initiates, a sublime culture of specialty shopping, a trained and picky superiority. We celebrate our sensory feasts: Madame—in her moss-green wool skirt (with a red underweave, roughly the Menzie hunting tartan), below which shine the silver buckles of her patent-leather pumps (Lobb of Paris); above she wears a lobster-colored silk blouse, a peacock-blue cashmere shawl around the shoulders (why didn't Renoir ever paint a mulatto?)—sets a low table in front of the fireplace in the salon (the staff are not put upon in the evening; they normally prepare the table in the dining room, but tonight we feel like a *petit dîner intime*): heavy English silver (late eighteenth and early nineteenth century, the bowls by Peter Storr), the Baccarat glasses dug up for us by Baalbeck from the collection of the Duc de Mouchy; because of the evening frost, we use the Russian service, a hard, reflecting, ice-colored porcelain with a blue, delicately bled—all but hoar-furred—Cyrillic pattern, and Madame lights the candles in the Empire girandoles; I (in my bottle-green velvet jacket, white spun-silk turtleneck, velvet pumps with embroidered monograms: Camfora of Capri, 1950) break my fingers on the new plastic ice tray. The choice of wines is taken care of, and since there's not much more than some smoked salmon and half a cold grouse from yesterday's *déjeuner* (with Putzi Lambrino, Nicky Ravanelli, Marie-Christine de Brouilles, the last almost a bit too *yéyé* for her sixty-eight years), the problem isn't great, and we can down our first cuttingly cold vodka ("*à la tienne, ma grosse cocotte!*"). It's a pleasure to watch her toss back her blackamoor's head as she pours the drink down her throat, her full neck tensing, her chubby brown hand putting down the glass and reaching for the fork, and it makes me weak to see with what pleasure she pounces on the food: she skewers a piece on the fork, lifts it to the sumptuous cup-shaped blossom of her carnivorous mouth (the rich, soft flesh of smoked salmon is an especially tempting prey), the purple bulges of her lips, notched like elephant hide, spring open, peeling from the two lecherously glittering rows of teeth, which open like a trap (with the rosy reptile head of the tongue lurking in the cavern behind), the lip-bulges (smooth now when stretched) gape so greedily that the gums become visible (a jagged wreath of sheer, bright flesh over the bone palisades of the teeth: the jousting collar of a cannibal heraldry), the piece of salmon hovers on the fork tines (precarious moment of predator feeding), cautiously approaching the polymorphous beast—the tongue flicks out, glues itself to the crude piece and draws it in, the teeth snap to, the lip-bulges close softly and relentlessly upon the fork, which is pulled out empty. What takes place behind the lips now—they hint at it with a kneading, pressing, and stretching—must be blissfully murderous. At this moment I am all salmon: there, in the darkness, I am will-lessly tossed to and fro by the nimble tongue-reptile, minced, slimed, crushed, releasing my juices and shooting down with them into an even deeper, more abysmal darkness. A small cluck, germ of a sob, in the brown column of her throat seals my fate. Thank goodness I can identify with the next and then the following piece; I am entirely flayed, entirely raw flesh (a true-blue masochist would plunge into paroxysms in my place), but only for the duration of the salmon; the cold grouse already has something cadaverous about it—if the Haut-Brion 1923 didn't provide a flamboyant supply of blood for the pale meat, then the notion of necrophagia could spoil my appetite. A pear compote with a delicate touch of clove and a sharp shot of mango chutney restores purity, *à l'indienne*, as it were, then for coffee we move to the sofa, while in the two superimposed glass spheres of the Kona machine (freely adapted from Jakob Böhme) the mocha substance is gradually created from the first, incorporeal primal grounds. I quickly clear the table, Madame meanwhile inserts the afternoon's tape into her portable deck, the newly discovered skiffle group is dynamite, I'll soon hear how good these guys are, she pours the coffee into our cups (recently brought back from Tunisia, turban-shaped, with delightful apple-green and peach-red stripes), I fill two of our beautiful snifters with honey-hued calvados, we snuggle on the sofa. This is right, I participate physically in her professional experience, as she does (by disappointment) in mine. She presses the start button of the recorder, and the room fills with psychedelic emotion, fills with rhythmic washboard scraping and grooved drops of a vibraharp (first indolently, then alternating faster and faster and swallowed up, but then rain-showering down and drawn out by the beat into swinging wave stripes), in almost breathless syncopes the knitting needle of a flute stabs in and joins them in the ghost of an old, familiar tune—I know that, I've heard it some time or other. . . . Under Madame's dark jungle-gaze (black moon in white sky) I mull over it, strenuously listening—just *what* is that? . . . The melody is as ensnarled as an Irish Bible initial—and then the surface splashing brings me the name: Bach, of course, the D-minor fugue from the *Art* of the same, yes indeed, that's it; undulated with vibrations, rippled up and driven down by rhythms, Madame is proud of me, not everyone would hit on it so soon (*"Bravo, mon ours! Mais tu es malin comme un singe! Ah, ce que j'ai froid aux pieds—prends-les dans tes mains, mon petit!"*), her feet really *are* icy, I puff on them, warm them up, rub them between my palms, bed them on my chest (*et tes pieds s'endormaient dans mes mains fraternelles*), she still isn't completely satisfied with the recording, one reason for her (professional as well as personal) success is her relentless perfectionism (mine is the reason for my failure), it is almost impossible to find a sound engineer with an ear, the good people are all under contract elsewhere, the ones left over push the buttons mechanically, they're deaf, they're stupid robots, and every minute costs a fortune . . . that's right, darling: chat away, unburden yourself in a heart-to-heart in my arms, it's evening and the fire warms us (*nous avons dit souvent d'impérissables choses les soirs illuminés par l'ardeur du charbon*) . . . incidentally the chieftain of the skiffle group is an attractive young Englishman who looks fabulous with his Viking beard and Balkan lambskin jacket . . . I feel a pang of jealousy: I know the quartertones in the range of Madame's voice, the syncopes in her speech rhythm: *"Si tu me cocufies, carogne, je vais te tuer!"* Her laughter is defiantly uterine, it drives me crazy, the colored slut, let's reverse the classical model and put it into its negative, with a white Othello strangling a black Desdemona . . . she's as strong as a beer-wagon horse, but I've got my tricks, she's already panting under me (*"Attention, ours! Le verre—tu casses le verre, imbécile!"*), I give her enough time to drink up, but then . . . the great affection makes me indolent, I sit on her lap, she cradles me gently in her powerful arms (*c'est là que j'ai vécu dans les voluptés calmes / au milieu de l'azur, des vagues, des splendeurs / et des esclaves nus, tout imprégnés d'odeurs*), I love her, I kiss her with ardently closed eyes: baby blisses, primordial home of mucous membranes, wonderworld of warm body fragrances (*et je buvais ton souffle, ô douceur, ô poison* ... how does it go after that? ... *Qui me rafraîchissaient le front avec les palmes*—that's a different part, but it fits: *qui me faisaient languir*) ... the fire in the hearth burns slowly down, I stare into the glow, which starts to blink at me with black eyes, I'm snugly exhausted, the implacable experience of the singular, the extraordinary, the exquisite, fills me with steady, intense sleepiness, Madame leafs through the latest fashion magazines, I slowly sip my calvados, even this is strenuous: every exquisite move made becomes a cultic gesture, I am too sloppy for such priesthood, I cannot celebrate myself in every moment of life, one really needs the energy of a Rastignac to be a full-fledged citizen of Paris, I don't have it, I'm a lazy barbarian brooding about the ephemeralness of things ... in the fireplace, the black eyes splinter off in the fiery glow and turn ashen-gray, a final log is consumed, a lonesome salamander, I place the fire screen before its flame-darting rump (the reptile hisses softly), I yawn so hard my cheeks crack (good heavens: another day is done, and my book? ...), she's reading an endless article in *Vogue*, it must be very interesting, I wish I could read, anything, I haven't been able to read for months, at best my weekly horoscope in *Elle*, why bother with anything else? Now, for instance, we could have been in bed for an hour already, sleeping (*D'accord, mon ours—tu penses à ton travail très tôt le matin, n'est-ce pas?*—naturally, what else?), we go to the bedroom, undress—and then comes the big moment (secretly feared): "*Ours! Tu sais ce que tu dois faire—allez hopp!*" and taking an enormous leap, she jumps on my back, it's the nicest thing in the world for her, there's nothing she enjoys more, nothing more intimate (a childhood dream, she's confessed to me: being carried by a lover—no man has ever been prepared to do so)—so I allow one hundred fifty-two pounds of live weight to heave up onto my shoulders, under her impact my ribs crack from the vertebrae, my ears roar, I see red curlicues, but I bravely trot through the entire apartment with her: bedroom, dining room, salon, her study, my study, the vestibule, the guest rooms, three times all around, then I unload her in the bathroom (*Bravo, ours! Tu as été très fort ce soir—presque aussi fort que le père Bouglion—et Dieu! ce qu'il était fort!*"). I love her, I stand at the bathroom mirror, brushing my disheveled hair, she stands behind me and says, "*Tiens! C'est comme ça que tu te vois....*" What? What does she mean? *Qu'est-ce qu'il y a?* "*Rien. Je t'ai seulement vu comme tu te vois toi-même.*" So what? What's so special about how I see myself? "*Tu ne te vois que dans le miroir, n'est-ce pas?*" Naturally not, where else could I? "*Et je te vois différemment.*" One hopes. So what? "*Rien de spécial. Pour une fois je t'ai vu comme tu te vois?*" "*Viens, ne dis pas de bêtises—allons vite!*" And lights out, shuddering with bliss under the fur cover, snuggling together, flesh entangled with flesh, flesh galore, flesh in masses, in mountains, pulsated blood-warm, spice-scented, coffee-brown female flesh ... I think of the salmon in her mouth and, suicidally, sink the defective teeth of the Caucasian race into her.

Thereafter, my dream....

□ □ □

OR ANOTHER TIME, a year earlier, the period of my martyrdom. The no less bizarre creature whom I loved during that period was named Dawn. An American. Twenty-one years old. Extremely beautiful. A fashion model by profession. A psychopath. A virgin when I met her (soon no longer, but God alone knows with what terrible effort). Drove me crazy with her unpredictable ways.

At the time, she's vanished somewhere in Paris, I'm stuck in Hamburg, Wohlfahrt has promised me a movie, as usual it's taking forever but I can't get away, I'm in hot water, Christa's suing me for her alimony, I've got to scrape up the money for my son's tuition, creditors are storming my door, my patrons here (Rönnekamp, Schwab) are avoiding me like a leper, I've milked all of them for cash, Big-Time Publisher Scherping won't give another penny for the book I've been promising him for years.

Yet daily, nightly, I phone away a fortune. It took me two

weeks to find out that Dawn had landed in the Hôtel Épicure again, heaven only knows in what condition. In any case, I can't get her to the phone: morning noon and night I talk to Madame, to the handsome Pole, I leave messages that are never passed on, directions no one gives a damn about, I act like a total lunatic. Strangely enough, I'm working marvelously despite everything, I've written two presentable chapters of my book, it took me only a few hours to hand Wohlfahrt a treatment based on a theme now popular with distributors and he was jubilant ("Damn it, baby, we're gonna knock those guys on their asses!"), and on the side, I've got three subjects of my own that I'm penning, or rather ball-pointing: the words are simply scurrying across the paper. And I'm getting fatter and fatter. The broad is battening me.

The broad: a chance conquest. Not undeliberate: I've been separated from Dawn for over a month, haven't touched another woman (to put it in cultivated terms); this probably explains a good portion of my hysteria, a symptom of abstinence I'm not used to. Besides, when it comes to monogamous relationships, I have an obnoxious tendency to overcommit myself—and one can see what comes of it, one can tell by the telephone bill. I am at the mercy of the women I love, I become burdensome, like any dependent sooner or later, love is child's play—namely, so cruel, so destructive, so ruthless, so stupid, and woe to him who loses, for in the struggle of the sexual organs there is no mercy, and the colder party has the upper hand. In short, I need distance—from Dawn, myself, the *situation* (*hommage à Monsieur Benn!*). Soon I no longer feel like a man; if a woman were to carry on the way I've been doing these past few weeks, she'd disgust you and you'd tell her to go to hell; with a man, this is really demeaning, humiliating. A matter of convention, I know; I can ask myself ten times a day why it's not manly to love a woman, but it just isn't, at least not like this. Bondage is downright ludicrous, and who wants to be a slaveholder? But the broad is, as it were, an exercise for sedentary muscles. An erotic lightning rod. A spiritual garbage incinerator. A marvelous person.

The broad. I got to know her when registering at the immigration office. As a stateless person, I had to renew my residency permit. As usual, hours were spent waiting in the corridor, wedged in between foreign workers and other ungroomed types, all of them my brethren: circus performers, peddlers, Maghrebinian students, Calabresi, Sicilians, Hungarian refugees, they change their countries but not their shirts, they smell of the shabby clothes they sleep in, hang around government offices, smoke foul-smelling cigarettes, cough up their mucus in the corner spittoon as if they were vomiting. Then who should come walking down the corridor but *she:* a very well groomed petite bourgeoise, bloody fucking middle-class, with the accent on the second adjective, I hope. Her clothes are as flawless as they are tasteless, a bottle-green suit with a nutria collar, a bizarre plant of a hat, the whole creature medium height, a bit plump, which I like (my Viennese formative years), in her late twenties (earlier, they can't screw, too embarrassed or too curious, inhibited; anyway she probably lets go completely), correspondingly sassy— acts as though she didn't see me, yet her nostrils flare like a mare's at the stud station. The strenuous effort to take no notice of me makes her movements jerky, I sit poised on the bench, my legs crossed, I look her over with insolent thoroughness: the hat above all, the breasts (voluptuously snug in Maidenform), the handbag, the arse, the legs (excellent: narrow ankles, full calves; they weaken my heart). My inspection ended, I look away again: neither satisfied nor disappointed, I have merely registered her; I soundlessly whistle a little tune over my lips, peering absently through the window into the pale coastal sky.

I am convinced she's followed every detail of the game; it doesn't matter whether or not she's seen through it; all the same, it sparks the desired reactions. Now she really becomes aware of herself (and her awkwardness) but switches to the offensive, becomes aggressive in a feminine way, stands ostentatiously (with her back to me) at the window, through which I stare into the anemic heavenly void, but then she turns around, cuts my line of sight again and (certain of not leaving my field of vision) goes to the office door. Very attentively reads the letters of name groups on the door as well as the names of the officials processing the respective group: A–E, Handke; F–K, Löschmann; L–R, Janitzki; S–Z, Kühnle. By all means, study the writing on the wall as carefully as you can, my dear lady. There are situations that, at first blush, seem ineluctable, this can be confirmed by Nadine, they become all the more piquant if you delay them, in her circles especially this is probably considered good form (à propos: in art as well as in screwing, delay is most helpful). But she is more discerning than she appeared to be, and comes back quite emphatically, recrossing my line of vision (hung out, like an Elbe fisherman's line with an earthworm on the hook, in the watery distance beyond the windowpane). Before she can make any further decisions, I shift (to offer her room) half an arse on the bench. She promptly sits down; I naturally pay her no heed, absent-mindedly light a Rothman taken from the Fabergé case, exude the fragrance of a victorious power. This must collide with early impressions of hers: budding twelve-year-old girl with half a kilo of black-market butter under her skirt goes through the British check point at Aumühle, the last urban transport station on the way to Lauenburg; will the soldiers look for the concealed booty? . . . Such experiences make this generation accessible. Early humiliation and anxiety always do a fine job of preparing the erotic soil; smells, for instance cigarette smoke, are an excellent device for stirring up this past in the subconscious; phonograph records come later. Now, the sensoria of the left half of my body register that she has taken the bait, it becomes perceptibly warmer between us, from the corner of her eye she gauges my suit, the quality of my linen, and presumably the quantity of the hair on my chest—well, what do you think of me, dear lady? A distinguished foreigner, no doubt (shit, as if he *needed* to go to the immigration office; any Persian nut importer sends someone else to take care of this kind of business for him, even if it's his own brother-in-law). Still and all, I *am* a writer, a film writer, interested in milieu studies; this immigration office is without a doubt a literary gold mine, with all these colorful destinies, wouldn't you agree? Why, these citizens of serf nations could give you the plots for entire novels, there is a folkloristic tendency in Nobel Prize–winning literature, a sort of shtetl coziness, what you have here is even better, nowhere else could you find such a wealth of diverse human situations, at least not in humdrum West Germany, we all know that sociology is invalidated by the society of equality, one need only know the phenotype. Here, however, true life can still be found, although ultimately no one gives a shit. I shoot my hand from the sleeve, look at the now visible (to her as well as me) Cartier watch, then turn to her with no transition, as though continuing an only just interrupted conversation, and say, "I hope you've brought along enough time."

And she very willingly replies, "Oh, this is nothing new for me." She speaks (as expected) a penetrating Hamburg German, in the direction of Harburg.

I ask her disingenuously, "You're not German?" She *is* German, but her husband is Lithuanian, only they're divorced (there you are), but her citizenship still isn't cleared up, "all this endless red tape," and last year she wanted to go to Italy.

One thing leads to another, and three hours later I'm lying in her bed, a Murphy on the wall of a ten-by-twelve-foot room; she lives in a studio flat with a bathroom and kitchenette in a high-rise development somewhere in the wasteland behind the Hagenbeck Zoo, but she does have "a bit of a dooryard" (dropping her *R*'s the way people do in Hamburg), fourteen feet wide, thirty-five feet long, the flanks shielded by two strips of canvas against neighborly in-sight (at least from next door); between these strips, the eye rolls as though down a bowling alley (with a leap over the pathetic asters at the far end) into the yawning void of the central park. The housing development is still young, no lawn has been started as yet, but camomiles, a resistant weed, are stinting out of the mortar-laced soil, a slum-summer breeze that endures through everything seems to have settled in, there is apparently no such thing as different seasons, in any case the playground is as good as finished, it will open next year (the year after at the latest), red and yellow and green and violet paint, the iron pipework of the swings, monkey bars, and slide are already looming from the cement-framed gravel (a Paul Klee execution site: gallows and torture wheel for little stick figures with zero heads). Farther along, at a dramatic standstill, the concrete squadron of the high-rises in triad echelons comes thundering toward the playground: instead of gun turrets, the box balconies emerge from the hatches. At sunrise and at sundown, the shadows of the nine (or twelve) giant phalluses (three are always in reserve) shoot east to west, then west to east, across the bare surface whose border is the skyline, there's nothing beyond it, the world ends there in Ptolemaic fashion, we live right on its edge. Here in the foreground, on the wide (first) step of the three composition-stone steps, under a green sunshade with stitched-on toadstools, there are two chaise longues and a small wheeled table with a bottle holder, ringed by six flower pots with hyacinth bulbs, two with brownishly proliferating asparagus, three geraniums, and one mimosa (donated by myself and now without blossoms). Here, I make myself at home when visiting her. It's already quite cool out, there is supposed to be snow in the Alpine foothills, but I'm a fresh-air fiend, I get claustrophobic in the little apartment, she understands. Our relationship has become quite close in a rather loose way. The incredible has come true: in a city where (as my experiences during my married years with Christa taught me) each and every one of the two and one half million inhabitants (not counting the Perioecians) knows everybody else, knows everything about him, has all sorts of connections with him, can check every step he takes (and usually does), she has no idea who I am, our circles never cross, my present Middle Kingdom (like all earlier ones) is on a different planet from hers. She seems to take me for an occasionally transient businessman (an Austrian? an Argentine German?), she doesn't ask me for details or particulars, not even where I live when I don't spend the night with her (which I seldom do), if and when I'm coming again. I call her up when I feel like it (at my age, anyway, such needs are irresistible at most three times a week), and simply say, "Are you going to be home this afternoon?" It sounds (and is meant to sound) as prosaic as asking when you enter a railroad compartment, "Is this seat taken?" And she's never answered anything but "What time are you coming?" She always speaks in the same monotonous, slightly nasal tone; suburban bleakness then settles into the earpiece, the emptiness of drab, lonesome Sunday afternoons; already spiritually groggy, I show up at her place at the announced time—and then I have to pull off a one-hundred-eighty-degree readjustment act. Adapting to the reality of the 1960s is not easy for me: when, for instance, I reach the building door (I always need at least a panicky half hour to find the right one: one of thirty-six perfectly similar building doors in twelve

perfectly identical concrete blocks), I press the button under a certain (her?) name in the aluminum plate (one of sixty-six bakelite buttons in punched holes under sixty-six perfectly similar cellophane-covered plastic name platelets in twenty-two triple rows like an accordion keyboard—and just what is her name?). At such times, I feel I'm being sucked into a vacuum. I realize these are merely behaviorial problems. With a little more practice (perhaps consultation with a psychologist: Professor Hertzog would doubtless make himself available), I could soon easily get the better of them, above all, rid myself of the neurotic associations that still occur. With the venomous buzzing of a wasp squashed under a shoe, the door lock springs open behind my left renal area. The buzzing has something definitive, irrevocable about it: that's how the automatic lock snaps open and shut on a life prisoner's solitary-confinement cell. Yet I am entering an apartment house in which the community should be burgeoning; why are these buildings so empty? These termite houses should be teeming with people, whole tribes must be living here, but you don't see them, you barely hear them (and if you do, they're abstracted into a hum of plumbing). Nevertheless, I picture them as anthropomorphic, flattened like the trolls in a Dubuffet painting and yet palpitating (the insane Maupassant foresaw them in the *horlà*, who comes after man). I won't run into them, alas. They have been swallowed up by the residential mechanism, incorporated into it without a trace. I cannot expect any more spiritual utterance than a question from a fetal voice emerging from the sieve holes of the mouthpiece under the buzzer-and-name-platelet mountings before the door lock springs open, a question wrapped in a rustling tinsel and pickled in machine oil: "Hello? Who is it?"

What can I answer? Even if I dared to say "I," I wouldn't be taking a safe position. On the contrary, I'd have to give up that assertion. The signal of technological behavior patterns that would allow me into the honeycomb labyrinths, here or there (beyond this, the conversation with the metallic voice ghost would not thrive), would be irrelevant. The residential mechanism overcomes dehumanization by multi-digited repeatability of the same setup: it basically makes no difference whether I go here

or there, I would merely be arriving at an experience that can be repeated at random. Each of these twelve enormous housing machines is threaded with the capillaries of six stairwells (exactly similar to the one I now enter), each of which leads, on each of the twenty-two stories, to three medium-size or studio flats. That makes 4,752 four-to-six-celled lairs for consumers of the goods of life on an elevated self-service level. Theoretically (with just one studio flat per landing), the same experience with one of 1,464 unattached women, not intrinsically different from the broad, could be granted to me 1,464 times: I enter and find my bearings with somnambulistic sureness in the very same topography; to the left of the tiny vestibule are the bedroom and bathroom, to the right the living room and kitchenette; through the half-open (and intersecting) door, I see a female shoulder busy over kitchen matters (the shoulder covered with the synthetic-and-wool of a thinnish sweater lightly fragrant with cologne, soup greens, and femaleness, the odors vie for predominance, the female smell wins by a nose over the soup greens, the cologne evanesces in a field of straggling contenders). I sense the erotic appeal of the eel-round flesh of an upper arm naked from shoulder to elbow, the stays of the brassiere under the armpit, the curving of the back adorned with half the ribbon of an apron string, the plump roundness of the hip in a plaid skirt jersey skirt corduroy skirt who-knows-what skirt, the somewhat crooked seam of the nylon stocking over a full calf. The head is covered for the time being; if it moves and a slice of it becomes visible, then one may assume with a likelihood verging on certainty that the neck hairline, razor-cut too high, would irritate me in all 1,464 cases, that a voice with a monotonously singsong and rather nasally constricted Hamburg tone would say, "Hi there, just make yourself at home till I'm ready, everything's prepared out there—a whole bunch of magazines just came in!"

So I simply go out to the yard; it is not as if I were expected, it is merely inconceivable that I would stay away. The wheeled table already offers what she calls a "little snackypoo": a small basket of black bread ("Just try it, it's whole-grain bread") rye bread caraway-seed bread graham bread aniseed bread crispbread salt sticks cheese sticks, a little board containing ham ("Just dive

right in, that's home-made cottage-cured ham"), her familiarity is quite neutral, impersonal, noncommittal, the act of taking possession occurs by way of the exceptionally rich offering of first-class consumer goods: smoked goose breast ("It's a home recipe, from refugees from Pomerania"), fat liverwurst ("You'll never get that in a normal store, it comes from Holstein, straight from the farm"), a small crock of butter ("genyuwine country butter"), a stone jug of Steinhäger beer ("Drink some right away, it's nicely chilled"), a bottle of Bommerlunder, half a bottle of kümmel, a remnant of cognac, reams of paper napkins, a small dish of salted almonds, another of sweets, a cup containing cigarettes (Copenhagen brand: gull motif), an ashtray (Rosenthal porcelain decorated by Bele Bachem's artistic hand with a cat-faced debauchee in a corset and laced boots plus a Montgolfier floating high in the air), the weekly magazine pile ("Knowledge Is Power")—all she'd have to do is have my slippers ready ("Why don't you take off your tie, it's a lot more comfy"). I promptly stretch out in the chaise longue, hack off thick slices of whole-grain and rye bread, goose breast and home-cured ham, heartily heap up liverwurst on playing-card crispbread, poke the salt sticks in the butter, the cheese sticks in the mayonnaise. I need something to hold on to, something solid in this boneless situation, in this strangely abstract world, the life giving food has to produce the reality of life I lose when I walk into the hallway here and certainly under the sunshade with stitched-on toadstools in this sunless wasteland. I try to find the reality of life in the illustrated magazines, I peruse *Der Spiegel, Stern, Good Housekeeping, Better Living, Modern Woman, Radio and TV Guide;* while doing so I slip more and more deeply, more and more hopelessly, into abstractness, also losing my (already diluted) identity. I am dragged into a no-man's-land of reality. I am most intimately, most personally spoken to (as among gallows birds and pastors' daughters), initiated, involved, drawn into complicity. Editors honor me with letters, fraternally presenting me with their ethical motives (not neglecting to add their passport photos), sibyls whisper their queenly wisdom to me in a uterine tone (with a profound gaze, a Mona Lisa smile around the vulva that appeals directly to my gonads). This is flattering, but it's not meant for *me;* what is meant and addressed is something in me that is no longer Me, no longer I, but probably one of the countless sub- and co-I's of my experiencing I. I don't want to be pedantic—that would promote total dissolution. But anyway it's something embarrassingly general into which the substance of my I (perhaps slashed open by the categorical imperative) runs out—whether the id of the psychologists (according to Sigmund Freud, the pleasure principle rules unrestrictedly there) or the One of the existentialists (according to Jean-Paul Sartre, the world of the *salauds*) makes no difference to me, it's not ME, not I—and yet it is, but not really. . . . There is evidently a collective I in me, into which any other I (together with its idiotic demands) can be projected, a communal multiplicity in which everyone can identify with everyone else, everyone with all the others, all with everyone. Otherwise, I couldn't be expected to let myself be drawn into matters that are not at all my matters, utterly remote from the things that really affect me and certainly remote from the things that I can affect with my *actions.*

Here, no borders of a Middle Kingdom are any longer respected. What in God's name do I care about the Congo? What am I to do, what can I do about the extermination of the giraffes in East Africa or about Konrad Adenauer's stubbornness? . . . Yet here, these issues are urgently presented to me as though my material and spiritual welfare depended on them, my happiness, my moral integrity, my ethical climate. This surprises me somewhat. I am struck by the boldness of the published word. We hadn't had this before in this country. It almost makes me feel there is now no danger in making daring statements. Perhaps this was always the case, but intelligent self-censorship always considered the possibility of consequences. However, consequences no longer seem to occur. Anyway, it is flatteringly assumed here that I have taken part in this agreeable development, that I embody the aggressive new West German journalistic élan. Far from it: I live abroad too much, where events occur much less robustly, with kid gloves on, as it were. I am struck by the aggressiveness with which, for instance, a government minister is publicly accused of corruption here; since his continued stay in office would lead one to conclude that he can effortlessly refute the charges, why doesn't he do so? There's something out of kilter: either the accusations are false, which would have to have consequences, or they are correct, which would certainly also have consequences. But nothing happens; the whole thing seems to take place in a vacuum. Perhaps there are two realities: a pedestrian reality, so to speak, in which I move, in which probably most of the Middle Kingdoms lie—that is, in which what I and everyone else directly experiences takes place—and another reality, superordinate, vaster, and more comprehensive, in which the dramatic public events that I see here take place: a superreality, in which the gods struggle as in the *Iliad*.

But then, these latter events go beyond me, concern me only indirectly, as a consumer of destiny, so to speak. I no longer have the *law of action* in my hand. So why should this superreality be brought home to me in such a bewilderingly direct fashion, as if goodness knows what were contingent on my feeling involved in it? The illustrated newsmagazines leap at me, they almost harass me; like a total stranger grabbing my arm in the street and sputtering his conflict-laden experience-broth at me—from his marital problems to his philosophical ideas, his professional, athletic, and erotic perils, possibilities, prospects, his difficulties in raising his children, his traffic delinquencies, his thoughts on urban planning the fight against cancer food for the world ideas on American Russian Chinese Persian Venezuelan domestic and foreign politics Fidel Castro Onassis Anita Ekberg Karl and Groucho Marx—not because he mistakes me for an old acquaintance with whom he has often discussed such issues and problems (or because he recognizes me as especially open and receptive to them) but simply because he has pulled me out by sheer chance from several tens of thousands, and I could just as easily have been another passerby coming his way—he merely assumes in sovereign schizoid autism that whatever regards concerns occupies excites exasperates him is bound to regard concern occupy excite exasperate someone else, ergo that I must instantly be passionately moved and captivated.

Okay, fine. It is the same violation as the one effected by literature. Dostoevski does the same to me, Henry Miller even employs my libido for this purpose, but with them I at least know that this is fiction, it is meant to pull me out of the reality of the here and now and transpose me into a different one, removed from time and space, a superreality that sovereignly fills its own time and space, so that experiencing it makes me realize all the more keenly what *reality* is, I may grasp it all the more clearly, comprehend it all the more fully.... This is splendid, my eyes ought to brim with tears in sheer gratitude: the writers want my best, they hand me keys that give me access to what lies in (and behind) my Middle Kingdom, beyond the pedestrian reality I can directly experience: its symbolism, its transcendence ...

but that is just what the annoying sleeve-tugger on the glossy pages of the illustrateds does not do. On the contrary: he speculates with robust naïveté on the fascination of existence that is transmitted close to the skin, sour on the stomach, and warm as the breath (and granted: such fascination is huge in this modern world, which sails out into the abstract with bloated sails!). And it is certainly true of the magazines in this bunch—which I peruse, more and more excited, more and more addicted, more and more obsessed—that they present my pedestrian reality and no other, I may not doubt it, it's printed here in black and white and color, the camera, as we know, does not lie. To be sure, it has only a wraith-like similarity to what I actually experience (especially here and now: right at the edge of the world, lying in a yellow-and-white-striped chaise longue surrounded by pathetic flower pots, under a green, toadstool-stitched sunshade, which stands in something that one can describe at best as the negative of a garden, ringed by roaring emptiness, from which 2,336 window-panes, in front of me, over me, and at either side, gaze down blankly, and 540 concrete terraces are reproachfully held out at me like empty boxes, like beggar's bowls of a humanity cheated of itself), but this reality in the illustrated magazines, parsed in still photos and served up like a well-shuffled pack of cards, is not entirely alien. On the contrary, it is even traumatically familiar, intimate; a déjà vu experience afflicts me several times on every page. I've seen all this before (indeed, many, many times), though most likely just in other magazines; still, I can imagine I experienced these things myself, and could re-experience them at any time at any step along the way—

Thus, it is not directly my pedestrian reality but, so to speak, its superreality, meant to be experienced by me in its fullness, as I experience it here and now: from the void of an abstract super-reality I have previously overlooked and failed to heed only for lack of sufficient attention and for want of a sense of the factual.

Okay, fine, I'm ready to accept this. My profane experiences hardly suffice to make me fully cognizant of the reality around me. Nor am I surprised that it is so full, brimming with the un-expected, the astonishing, the wonderful—but why are these unexpected astonishing wonderful matters presented to me as the most humdrum everyday matters (indeed, as *my* everyday expe-rience)? I certainly don't doubt that they have reality, are reality, but I am very far removed from it. The struggle of the gods over us mortals may also decide my destiny, but that does not mean that I can intervene, that I can interfere and say, "Hey, fellows— calm down! This really won't do!" Then why does the superreal-ity of the magazines simulate this possibility for me? Why does it strike me with every picture (of oil sheikhs lunar-rocket passen-gers duchesses poisoners), with every report (of earthquakes jungle warfare atomic explosions floods) as the most up-to-date topicality I can encounter at any step of the way? Things become so grandly colorful and dynamic only in my dreams, at best. There, my hand meets Haroun el Rashid's in the lamb pilaf, I fly to the moon, sleep with duchesses, am poisoned by green-eyed sorceresses, the earth quakes under me, machine-gun muzzles emerge from the thicket of fat tropical plants like the eyes of a *Douanier* Rousseau tiger and aim at me, and ultimately God's wrath blows up the planet. . . . But if I simultaneously experience myself as immobile, trapped in the vacuum of a void from which there is no escape, while a thousand voices whisper to me, shout at me, cry to me, "Do something! Get involved! Intervene! Stop the monstrous thing from happening! Prevent the horrible thing!"—if that happens, then the dream turns into a nightmare, the events pass over me, press down on me, crush me.

And that is exactly what the superreality does in the illustrated magazines on my lap. Their reality is not to be doubted, but it takes place beyond my immediate realm of experience, beyond my Middle Kingdom, it takes place powerfully, sovereignly, beyond any influence of mine; yet its topicality presses under my skin, and no matter how I turn and twist, I can ignore nothing that happens here, it happens to me, happens here and now—though it is a here and now that exists past me, growing beyond its own ephemeral self, of course. The NOW comprises not only the moment, the day, the week, but the entire epoch; the HERE is not limited to the dooryard in the high-rise development where I am lounging, to my present Middle Kingdom, to Hamburg, to West Germany—no, it encompasses all realms, all kingdoms, the globe, the cosmos—

and, needless to say, it overpowers me, does not tolerate me outside itself, I merely belong inside it, belong *to* it, in any case: after all, the superreality is the totality of all current events, the magazines draw a weekly interim balance from it, a rough estimate, as it were, with the praiseworthy goal of telling me about everything as far as possible, letting me participate in the whole. . . . On the whole, however, everything (including me) is one and the same, no matter how one thing or the other may behave (however I may behave); everything exists quite simply by dint of its existence, no matter how active or passive—hence, I too am in it simply by dint of my existence, whether I intervene "actively" in reality or stay lounging here inactively in my chaise longue, experiencing the events at second hand. I realize I must not confuse the *totality of current events* with so-called *current history.* The latter, of course, requires my active participation. I must not be passive with it. I might drop out of reality, be given the go-by, remain forever invisible, eradicated.

I must therefore act merely in order to exist, I must become a member of the German parliament or detonate a bomb that shreds at least three members of parliament (if not a chancellor), I must fly to the moon or poison someone. The more effectively my action interferes with current history, the more defined is my existence. But superreality is simply not current history, it is the *totality of current events* in its fullness, and in this totality, current history dissolves, whereby all my efforts to intervene actively dissolve as well. There are, as one can clearly see, many different kinds of current history at the same time: that of the United States of America looks different from that of the Congo (hence, Frank Sinatra's looks different from Lumumba's, and mine looks different from Wernher von Braun's). And yet all of us, with our various current histories, are contained in the entirety of current events—all present, whether as oil sheikhs or big bankers, lunar-rocket passengers or record-breaking athletes, movie stars or duchesses, popular singers, politicians, or gangsters, poisoners, bomb throwers, or other foul-players—or else as amateur gardeners, animal protectors, good Samaritans, quiet book readers, anchorites, blissful navel contemplators, marijuana smokers. Everything exists in the superreality. Thus, it is not *reality in motion*, like history, but rather the unchanging state of Being per se, of which sometimes this and sometimes that becomes visible. And, visible or invisible, everything exists in it; hence, I too: whether as someone experiencing a collective destiny or someone shaping a collective destiny, whether as a head of state or as a Trappist monk, an anonymous nobody or a wanton seeker after fame and glory. Whatever occurs in the superreality occurs only as something existent, thus entirely without a value stress, the bomb-thrower peacefully next to the navel contemplator, the poisoner fraternally next to the Samaritan. . . .

In this sense, superreality is almost paradisal, its effect is paralyzing, soporific, like an old lullaby that goes "Such is life, my child. . . ." I am challenged to stay in my chaise longue and content myself with what I can experience vicariously (on the weekly balance drawn by the magazines). But on the other hand, what I thus experience is so monstrous and violent, so fills my consciousness to the bursting point with phenomena events occurrences incidents, that it keeps stretching further and further, becomes more and more expansive. Superreality has the explosive character that physicists usually attribute to cosmic events; while I rest here as a silent nucleus of overall events in the chaise longue I simultaneously fly out into the universe at a furious velocity. It is ridiculous to hold fast to the old, out-of-date idea of action, to the obsession with activity or passivity vis-à-vis history—this would mean something only if I were allowed to have a history in the absolute sense, only if *I* still had a history. This history would be the skin, the solidifying envelope, of the person. What once held together my I (at least in my imagination), giving it distinguishable, recognizable form, was the concept of a personal history. But this now proves to be a typically subjectivistic error, showing only my infantile limitation of vision; it is schizothymically autistic, correlating with my leptosomic habitus: superreality enlightens me, makes me understand that my psychoaesthenic proportion is quite beside itself. Hertzog ought to prescribe group sex for me, so that I can finally realize that I have no history. The trivial circumstances of my life are stereotypical, and they integrate me pitilessly into the masses. I am (despite the silly trials and tribulations that I regard as circumscribing my personality) ultimately, unavoidably, quite simply, a contemporary. As such, I experience a banal variant of global destiny as a member of Western Civilization—and as such, in turn, am merely a mote of dust in the cloud configurations of the history of mankind, nay, of the earth—in my present situation, I am nothing more than a phenotype of my historical position and destination, by necessity earning money (at least making a living, however tardily), an unwilling taxpayer, renter, consumer, transportation user, and, especially as the last, inevitably and automatically a *zoon politikon*.

To grasp the notion of the self physically, at least, I must bite heartily into my ham sandwich, chew, swallow, wash it down with a small glass of Bommerlunder or kümmel, smear a blob of liverwurst on crispbread, munch the hard, splintering crumbs well salivated with the soapy liverwurst mass, push in a cheese stick, rinse the greasy mouth cavity with corn whiskey, oppose its sharpness with that of a chocolate-covered peppermint. So I am eating dialectically at least, in boorish theses, antitheses, and syntheses of palatal stimuli. It helps me to feel that I do exist. How? This is given by the situation. Where? This is harder to establish. Hamburg is no longer what surrounds me here; it could just as well be Detroit or Sofia or even Minsk. It is purely and simply suburbia, a geographic superreality with no precise location. That too is an antiquated prejudice, an outmoded experience-cliché of the nineteenth century—Fridtjof Nansen struggling to get to the Pole, Mister Stanley I presume to the sources of the White Nile—but forget that nonsense, one cannot escape suburbia today, it devours the cities exactly the way it does the so-called (here truly) flatland. By tomorrow, I'll be able to take the subway from here all the way to Palermo without leaving the jurisdiction of suburbia, without arriving anywhere but in suburbia, without experiencing anything but the sapping experience of the unreality, suffocating emptiness, abstractness of these death houses larded with a lemur people, the desolation around them, before them, behind them, beyond them. . . . It's to be had everywhere, in Palermo as well as Salonika, in the same consistent quality, the same picture here as there. No matter from what side one views the buildings, they have both a phallic and a sepulchral quality, always looming apocalyptically over the horizon—a horizon without foreland: a bare patch of curving earth. Like arm-amputated grave crosses seen from a frog's-eye view, they bore into the sky, which therefore soon bleeds to death.

But before this happens, I still have a good half hour. I usually come by around five in the afternoon; so on cloudless days, even in late fall (already early winter in the Alpine foothills but still a coolly restrained slum summer here), I've got at least one and a half hours of surrender to the magazines in the sterile light of an eternal Sunday-afternoon emptiness, while the broad, who has been in the kitchenette since four o'clock, prepares something tasty for supper: "No, no, dear, you really can't help me, this is women's work—besides, you've got something to nibble on, anyway. I've got smoked eel too, dear, really fresh, from Kiel."

I can use it, thank you, I need something solid. Otherwise, the superreality will carry me weightlessly out into the void; my collective ego is in a moral clinch, so to speak, with my superego. Like Atlas, I carry the earth on my shoulders—and behold: it is light. Notwithstanding all the problems of determining a fair border for Manchuria, notwithstanding all the difficulties in Nigeria's domestic politics, notwithstanding the mass slaughter of baby seals off the coasts of Newfoundland, even notwithstanding the peril of overpopulation, the globe does not press down on me at all. On the contrary, it is as weightless and iridescent as a soap bubble and carries me, floats with me, into space.

There, incidentally, the day is actually vanishing, rarefying in a way that makes me experience the forlornness of the planet in outer space. The sun is not setting, but has disowned its satellite forever, its light is now a mere echo fleeing after it, the sun steals away, slips behind the diagonally echeloned triple formation of the Western high-rise block, transforming it for brief seconds into the modernistic trinity symbol from the display window of a progressive shop for devotional kitsch, a few final preclusive rays even quickly imitate the monstrance, then the dazzling humbug is snuffed out, three angular, leaden-gray thorns stick bluntly in the flesh of the sky, making it decay, its vital juice decompose, its hemoglobin (horribly filled with pus) congests over the curvature of the earth, running out beyond it, into the universe, only lymph remains, watery so long as a final reflection of solar gold is still trapped in the 396 windows of the southern squadron wing, this final reflection oozes away upward, strangely (as if through a fine-meshed latticework), then comes the moment of tipping over, I have anxiously looked forward to it the whole time.

The instant I press the buzzer into the aluminum plate on one of the seventy-two entrance doors, I know: I have come to experience this dying of the world. The monosyllabic signal exchange by telephone ("Are you going to be home this afternoon?" "What time are you coming?") is already the upbeat for this overture, the leitmotiv for a tormenting poetry, a poetry with exchanged light values, as it were, a negative of poetry. It now drenches the essence of the final moments of a day whose borrowed light nevertheless simulated a possibility of life on the lost planet, a *fata morgana* play of definitive refractions. But now it's past, the sky is a flinty polish, with three triple groups of thorn-shaped lead inclusions sticking in it, I feel its dead weight on me, it presses me into the rock where I lounge on a basalt chaise under the dome of a brazen sunshade with toadstool-shaped iron-oxide spots, it pushes me down with my last shriek of anxiety in my throat—I don't want this, let anything happen, let the world petrify, but this *must* not happen, I must not be discovered in this geological era, this will lead to paleontological errors. I do not belong to this epoch of the world, it is not my epoch, it has swallowed me together with my former world and its various Middle Kingdoms, and it is deceptively using their myths. I protest. It was a *human* myth that designed ANTHROPOLIS, the city of mankind; it was the dreams of *human beings*, not of *horlàs*, that

this nightmare stole for its own monstrosity. This is corpse rob-
bery. Every cubic meter of concrete from which this Stone Age
was formed contains a cynical utilization of rubble. Even its bar-
renness, its heartrending emptiness, was finagled; it has appro-
priated the tormenting poetry of the bomb-crater fields of *my* era;
everything that might hint at the former presence of human life is
stolen from *my* epoch and falsely taken over into this nowness, is
abstracted, is doctored into its own negative. I must warn the
twentieth millennium's explorers of primordial times: if among
my fossils, beneath the stony cigarette butts and petrified ashes,
they find the affected figure of a Montgolfier on a porcelain shard,
that cannot enlighten them about what a balloon in the sky meant
to me in my childhood. The petrified spinning wheel that may be
found in one of the honeycomb cells as a decorative old-fashioned
domestic item (transformed into a flower-pot holder) does not
belong here. The power shovels that dug the foundations of these
gigantic death houses bumped into this spinning wheel, unearthed it with other junk, perhaps from houses that once upon a
time stood in this place, and pushed the archaic (almost African)
ornamentation of their half-timber gables from the blossom balls
of the cherry trees into the melting of airy spring cloudlets in the
blue sky.

But how am I to prove this? I will be dated not according to the
memories under the potsherds of my cranium but according to
the contents of my stomach. Remnants of black bread and cottage
ham, liverwurst and country butter, kümmel and corn whiskey
will corroborate the erroneous assumption that all these things
belong together. No one will stand up to testify that this necropolis employed all kinds of anachronisms to feign life. Even Nature,
long assassinated, still haunts the detergent-blue sunniness of the
ads in the glossy magazines. What can I do to denounce this perfidious abstraction? It is too late, I did not depart from the evolutionary cycle in time, I neglectfully outlived myself and have
been taken over as an anachronism into the new geological era.
And now the chickens are coming home to roost. For three decades of life (misappropriated by the science of prehistory), I
(along with untold other museum pieces) have served this stone
world as a biological alibi, I will be ruthlessly counted as a part of

it in the omnium-gatherum of its archaeological treasures; whether the investigators stumble upon a hand ax or the crank of a funnel gramophone in the stratum a few meters under me, not even a dog will be taken in, I've held both objects in my hands, either one can be my burial offering. Geologically, I belong to the era between the Neanderthal and the *horlà* that comes after man, a tiny span of time in the history of the planet, and whether I would rather be located a minimal fraction of a particle closer to the one than the other in this tiny splinter of infinity is irrelevant; given the spaces of eternity we calculated with, half a dozen zeros more or less makes little difference. . . .

Out here, incidentally, it is becoming bitter cold, the flinty polish of the sky is growing dull, the nine lead-gray monoliths, counter to the laws of atomic disintegration, are transmuting into an even heavier metal, moving one step closer together. In the grid pattern of their 2,336 windowpanes, the first lights are beginning to glow in crossword-puzzle fragments, abstract life signs of the *horlàs;* I flee toward them, for whatever posterity may think of me, I now require feigned life. Nourishing kitchen smells already promise it—good solid food will be served for supper, juicy roasts and steaks and pork loins, lavish gravies poured over mealy potatoes, sauerkraut and red cabbage, cauliflower and brussels sprouts and turnip greens, slippery puddings in vanilla sauce, strawberry sauce, raspberry sauce, soon it'll come rolling up. ("It's ready, dear! Bring along the Bommerlunder if you want to have another quick drink!") We'll wash it down with venomous Riesling, Krötenbrunn, and Liebfraumilch, perhaps beer, which will keep me burping for hours. Our Lucullanism has a Lutheran breadth, I would never have believed that I could eat so much. Through the chewing noise in my ears, I can barely make out her noncommittal admonishments: "Nice, huh? Good eating!" and "Tastes good, doesn't it?" I nod, grunting (one doesn't speak with a full mouth!); nor, after I swallow, do I object to or contradict her chatter ("Well, at the new self-service store—oh, it's fabulous, dear—they have a contract with a fruit-and-vegetable importer who brings the produce direct so there's no middleman, and so on"). What could I say, anyway? When I read an analysis of the Common Market in *Der Spiegel* or an exposé of tax breaks for building contractors in *Stern*, I react at best with a snort. If I put up with the one, then why not the other? Besides, I'm tracking down the poetry of emptiness, I listen for it when the broad talks about her streamlined, well-engineered household appliances ("You've just gotta see it working, dear. A whole new kind of hot-water heater"—the word causes her difficulties, like syncopated gutturals in Arabic: hahht-wawdeh-heeedeh—"it's also a coffee roaster, steam iron, dish dryer, fruit pitter, bottle rinser, garbage disposal, it's brand new, from General Electric"). Her old merchandise knowledge, shopping expertise, price awareness are stupendous, like the specialized learning of a bacteriologist or a Sanskrit scholar. The interpersonal aspect is also included ("Well, you can get the same tie at Münnemann & Möller for only half the price"). She goes no further into personal matters, except in more or less concealed erotic offers ("That blond on the third floor, dear—you've never seen her, she's very chic—well, she's asked me about you twice already, where you come from, and so on, I think she likes you, she's got a boyfriend who's on the river police, he's got a small house on the Elbe, which he inherited, they have group sex there on weekends").

Still and all, this is a curtain raiser before getting down to the real point of the visit: the Murphy bed in the bedroom has already swung down out of the wall ("A real bed takes up more than half the space, it's a lot more economical to fold it into the wall"). But it's not so simple, the structuring of sex uses Bele Bachem's corseted debauchee as a model, her claws dig into my hand as it tries to sneak under the sweater ("You little thief, you!"). After some rather intricate fiddling, the brassiere finally snaps open, her eyes deepen, she painfully bites my earlobe, then I'm promptly sucked into the maelstrom of a four-minute French kiss, no sooner can I draw my breath than the struggle with the girdle begins, but no ("I can't just undress like at the swimming pool and spread my legs, dear, there's no excitement to that"), first stocking after stocking must be detached from the complicated garter-belt mechanism, rolled down individually from each thigh, a kiss in the hollow of the knee (which she has artfully slung around my neck: "Trying to drive me crazy again, are you!"), and in order to get to the girdle again, I require some unwinding (Laocoön); pulling it down is then relatively easy (at least no harder than a rabbit skin), it comes rustling off the already damp buttocks, their notch feels marshy, a peatbog burial ground, one heartens oneself with amorous truisms (*une femme qui ne mouille pas—c'est comme un homme qui ne bande pas*). Ramming my right middle finger in all the way up to the proximal knuckle (my hand trapped between iron thighs: "You'd like that, wouldn't you? Just jerking me off like that!"), I can finally think about unbuttoning myself (while sucking on one of her nipples: "Oh yes, that feels good, dear!"). For the actual act of love, I then have to carry her like a kill into the Murphy bed ("Just feel those springs under the mattress, dear—chrome steel, it doesn't rust so easily"), a frivolously added-on cliché ("If you don't rest, you don't rust") entangles me once again in the breathtaking thoroughness of one of her kisses: what follows is of the highest technical perfection, with something of the glistening enamel industrial-products luxury of the magazine ads, it aims at one's happiness, which is suspended from a safe interest rate and full-coverage insurance ("Make sure that the excitement curves meet harmoniously in the culmination points!"); all the positions shown in sex manuals are tried out, the accompanying moans have an ad-copy character ("Just see if you can find anyone who's better than me!"), any original features that break through aim to stimulate ("Trying to fuck the shit out of me, are you?"), and the depth of the aimed-for fulfillment is set by psychological remote control ("Yeah—now—yeah—baby—give Mama everything!").

But that's it for now. She jumps up, marches into the bathroom, there are alternating gurgles of pipes and faucets while I smoke a cigarette, take a little (cleverly set up) baking soda with a sip of water, slowly begin to dress. She comes back from the bathroom—"Do you have to go so soon?"—the question is asked quite impersonally, a manner of speaking, so to speak, even the finest ear could not detect any implicit protest. While I then lay claim to the bathroom, she telephones for a taxi ("A gentleman would like to be driven downtown"). The leave-taking is (although jestingly intimate) casual ("Well, dear, be good now, but not too good!"). She holds open the apartment door, waiting to say good-bye, and as I pass her going into the hallway, she raises her arm to buzz open the building door, her dressing gown falls open, there is a split second of breast splendor—but before I can even think of returning, she has pulled it out of sight with a quick sleight of her left hand. The building door springs open with a hissing squashed humming of wasps, I don't have to turn my head, I know she's still standing there, intersected by the door and door frame in a narrow rectangle of light that is denser and yellower than the neon lymph in the hallway. When I get to the front door, she sends a last "So long!" after me (it topples from a headvoice C down to the A: "*So* long!"), and I slam the stubborn reluctant door behind me: an air cushion in the cylinder catches the swing, and the door settles with slow dignity and a pejorative hiss into the lock. The final snap is salvation, I hear it as I flee, hunched into the artificial-leather upholstery of the taxi, I give my address to the cloddish male rump in front of me, and a hand (lit by the blue dashboard light) turns a key, the engine, rattling, kicks on, a pull on the lever sets the car in motion, in the rearview mirror the outlines of the first, the second, the third high-rise block (covered with radiant square mildew spots) dance darkly in the cobalt-blue, and then the entire development is visible: Stonehenge, starting to fluoresce in its decay. . . . It swings to the left and out of the mirror's range while we dip rightward into the bright flurry of an arc lamp.

Thereafter, at home, in the blissful solitude of my rented room, my dream. . . .

□   □   □

THERE IS NO BASIS whatsoever for assuming that S. could actually be connected to my dream. It was probably pure coincidence that at the very moment the slip of paper with Schwab's name came into my hand, the fear hit me like a punch in the solar plexus—the fear that my murder was real, was not the projection of some triviality that had slid into my subconscious and been dramatically enlarged there by the residues of old established guilt complexes, was truly what my dream showed me: the gruesome killing of an old crone for no other reason than to prevent some even more shameful ignominy from coming to light. The momentary *recognition* is almost pleasurable: it is a holy terror that strikes me ... but there's no way this sort of thing could be triggered by the thought of S., much less by my projecting him into a fictional character: a ridiculous notion, inspired by an over-wrought brain. A hint of burnout, presumably. Nevertheless ...

I have an astonishing number of jottings about S., an alarming number. Almost every one refers to him in some way or has a later note connecting to him. But the explanation is simple: I must have reworked most of the other jottings during countless revisions of countless versions of my book, with various kinds of structures. Except, of course, for the jottings that were done pe-ripherally, so to speak, and not in terms of a specific plan. Granted, this did not come without some specific idea: I cannot deny that I was tempted to depict the character of a certain Jo-hannes Schwab: a generously constructed figure, an editor in a publishing house, a guru of intellectuals, well read to the point of blindness, well informed about anything worth knowing to the point of despair, hence disoriented, painfully matured by aban-doning his once passionately nurtured ambition to write a book himself (one of the masterpieces of the century, the classic of the era, needless to say, an opus that would inscribe his name death-lessly in the pantheon of literary titans), a great-minded, great-hearted man, inspired by lovely envy to admire lovingly all those he regards capable of accomplishing such a masterly feat in his stead (Nagel, me), hence (I would almost have said) an alco-holic, based faithfully on my friend S. in all other features and characteristics. . . . I won't deny that I was tempted to record such a blockbuster of a featured player. Thus the many slips of paper with his name (or the initials J.S.). In the end, the explana-tion is simple. It can all be like this, or else entirely different.

Still, I likewise cannot deny that I am more and more obsessed with the belief that S. is standing before me, as vivid and physical as in the moment of my *recognition* of my murder. I mean to say, in the same stunning *presentness*, with the same almost blissful terror that hits me like a punch in the solar plexus—no, deeper, below the belt. A holy terror, I called it, and I commit myself to this expression, ludicrous as I find it, however much it may evoke the abstruse formulations of my years in Vienna

(Uncle Helmuth's and Aunt Hertha's transfigured secrecy whenever they came home from one of the séances of their spiritist community: initiates who had penetrated beyond the primitive practices of moving tables and conjuring up spirits, penetrated into the occult and thereby into the transcendent; who now virtually had a direct connection to Creation's switchboard, a through line to the Good Lord, who, as chief mechanic, kept a universe of his own invention and personal patent operating eternally by utilizing, as the motor power, energies released by the tension in the polarities of good and evil, light and dark, up and down, positive and negative, and similar pairs of opposites . . .

no *perpetuum mobile*, alas, when one does not place the promised final victory of good at infinity and bury the hope that the light of the Last Judgment and everlasting transfiguration is nigh: an illuminating metaphor for electricians and grease monkeys, in which they could read their ranks in the universe on all sorts of do-it-yourself power meters . . .

a troglodyte theodicy, which I assimilated in those days with my own mental flights into metaphysics— for example, when gazing from the window of our apartment in Vienna's Twelfth District up into the rectangular chunk of starry sky revealed by the air shaft between the front and back wings:

primal situation of man: overwhelming juxtaposition of his nothingness with infinity:

there I sat in the window niche, gazing up into the immense, silver-dusted firmament beyond the fire walls, staring bewitched, like a nix who knows of a different world in the celestial circle above the well shaft, a world about whose alien life she has an inkling as it fills her with strange yearning: exiled, trapped in the narrowness of my Self and tempted out of it and beyond it by an enigmatic *something*—

and as far and high as my imagination could carry me out of myself, it never brought me to where *something* beckoned.

For beyond myself, I was stretched over and above myself. My Self dissolved, was absorbed in cosmic vastnesses. I flew over the

city of Vienna and beyond, over all the beautiful cities that mankind has built and destroyed in the eternal conflict between good
and evil, up and down, positive and negative, while incessantly
dying within itself and rising again from within itself. I flew over
continents and over the planet and into the universe, into the icy
spaces of Creation, veiled and dimmed by astral whey, where
light had not yet been separated from darkness,

and soon the earth was a mere speck of dust scattering with
myriads of its kind in a tremendous explosion into infinity. I, my
Self, shrank accordingly, of course: so utterly into the microcos-
mic that ultimately I was hurled out again into the macrocosmic,
as it were: I BECAME THE UNIVERSE.

When I, my Self, burst through my human dimensions, the
whole world burst with me in the clattering shatter of categories—and the thing that rose again from it, like the phoenix, was
I. Though poorer by one universe than before. . . .

My dead friend S. did not need to feel such anxieties anymore.
Now, he *knew*. Now, he was freed from the monkey cage of his I,
dissolved in the universe: with the possibility of peering into the
plan of the Creator and Head Mechanic of the Universal Mechanism and understanding its wondrous ultimate meaning [or else
the even more wondrous lack thereof]. . . . It was regrettable,
however, that this knowledge was no longer *his:* he had paid for it
with the loss of his I [in accordance with Miss Fern, dispenser of
wisdom in my childhood: "You can't eat your cake and have it"],
and it was confusing to reflect that a total consciousness is one
that is totally released; that is: totally dissolved in everything,
hence extinguished. Still and all, such a consciousness promises
us a certain state of contentment, and I simply cannot understand
why S. is bothering me so much. [So much that, for instance, I
am now frightened because I have perceived S. as "*something.*"]
Schwab's presentness is a challenge, a demand I cannot evade.
The holy terror that overcame me when I identified my sense of
guilt about a murder with S. is a demand. It comes from where he
is now.)

Among the jottings that his secretary (Fräulein Schmidschelm,
a.k.a. Schelmy) sent me after his decease, there is one in which he
says that once (during a lunch at Laget: he had seen me home;

that is, here, to the Épicure), I inferred that he was planning to write "a book of a religious nature"; i.e., his theodicy. I had to check this: no doubt I made a note of it; after all, our Russian duel as each other's potential biographer was in full swing. Still, I must congratulate myself upon my clairvoyance back then: this intention is now obvious. I feel the need to importune my dead friend with another of the monologues I've made for him. After all, what I have to tell him is in his interest—which he violates whenever he pushes me off into the transcendental. The point, I would like to tell him, is to draw borders: I seek my outline in order to find the outline of my book. Or, if you will, vice versa: I seek the outline of my book in order to outline myself. It comes to the same thing. Micro and macro are interchangeable here too; they are merely symbols of a multidimensional relationship. If, for example, my story is that of a man who carries within himself the picture of a man who carries within himself the picture of an adolescent who carries within himself the picture of a child, and the man and the adolescent and the child are one and the same Self, then, quite logically, the child carries within himself a child who carries within himself an adolescent who carries within himself a man who is carried within himself by a man who carries within himself a man who carries within himself an adolescent who carries within himself a child and *ad infinitum* to and fro and on and on . . . and yet it always remains one and the same Self. . . .

And now inscribe a book in this Self (or around this Self), then you can form a simpler and even more bewitched series: a man who wants to write a book about a man who wants to write a book about a man who wants to write a book . . . and this diabolical circle is our case, dear friend: we dash around in it in a ring like rats in a trap, without ever reaching each other; and when we ask about the meaning and purpose of the whole business and what impels us to ask about a meaning and purpose, then we really get into a maelstrom. But, whatever, *I* am nothing but my story. And this story is my book. So I can say: *I am my book.* A statement that obviously can't hold a candle to the Sun King's proud words *"L'état c'est moi!"* I haven't even established my kingdom. I have been trying to do so, but in vain, for nineteen years now, two more years than Joyce spent completing *Finnegans Wake.* You may at best expect something equally obscure, albeit far less brilliant. I have been a king without a country ever since you installed me as pretender to the literary throne—with, presumably, the respectful trust that I would find my kingdom and define its borders myself. My deepest, deepest thanks, retrospectively! For even while you were alive, you kept an eye on me, you noted snidely any territory I might have overlooked, you noted my annexations with such flattering envy that I kept going out in quest of virgin territory. . . . It's all too understandable: you didn't want me to disgrace you. You had told everyone so much about my brilliance that any disappointment would have embarrassed you. People were eagerly waiting for my book; it had to be worthy of its initiator. . . . Today, at best only Scherping is waiting for it, because money *is* more important to him than the pleasant spiritual agony of thinking that he'll never earn back the advances he's been giving me all these years. Nevertheless, your demise obliges me to show the world that you were not mistaken and that I am not a loser. I would have to be made of stone not to have sensed the meaning of the gazes focusing on me at your funeral. The book that people are expecting of me demonstrates not only who I am, but also who you were.

And I am still ready to write it, at least, this book. After seven agonizing nights and days, I am ready to write *you*, Schwab. For that's what you are asking of me. How else am I to understand your omnipresence in my mental life? You want me to write you: in your intention to write me as I write you.

Fine: that would be relative child's play. Unfortunately, you won't be satisfied with this. You want to *materialize*, in Uncle Helmuth's terms: from the vaporous or gaseous or ethereal state in which you find yourself as a deceased person (the pure soul, if you please), you wish to transform yourself back into the denser human state of flesh and bone and skin. In a word: you want me to bring you back to *life.* This involves great difficulties. You see, the few biographical strokes are enough only for an obituary. Johannes Schwab: the name is a full program equipped with a curriculum vitae, but by no means with blood-throbbing life, especially not a life lived in the melancholy of a Hyperion: heavy with thought and poor in deed. That's what you need me for. Even your full reality has to be achieved in the *Other* ever since our colleague Sartre. You need me as a mirror, Schwab. Just as I need you as a mirror, as the *Other*, whom I must reach in order to be *I*. Please don't keep pestering me with metaphysical digressions. Don't keep making me dash about in my own brain like a rat in a trap, with the cat pushing its face up close. Do not slit my skin in order to let me ooze off into the transcendental: that's where I truly lose myself—and thereby you. That's trying too hard, man. I can write you by writing myself as you would write me; I can be your mirror, your medium, through which you materialize, in Uncle Helmuth's terms: I can make you come to life, for a writer's quill can create life and certainly wake the dead . . . but it will be a different, new book that I must write, a book containing me and you . . . do not try to convince me that this would require a third party: the Good Lord. Do not force him into our overloaded, our bursting plan. With you alone as a mirror image and partner in the rat-dash for form, we destroy the wonderful vision that I had of my book during the drive from Reims to Paris: a glass cathedral, shaped according to organic laws, as clear and beautiful as a crystal . . . this, I say, shattered into fragments, extinguished, *kaputt*, even without the Almighty as the third member of the trio. I cannot manage it with him; it ought to be more honest; for the time being, I am again halting my labor on the masterwork of the era, contrite and modest (*ridimensionato*, as the Italians so profoundly put it). I am resuming my service with the movie piglets and my refuge with Nadine.

She'll welcome me. We're of the same stock, she and I. She too lives a literary life. Of course, not in the counterfeit promise of eternally unrealized potentials. She transforms family-magazine literature into the gold of life. As a film star of the foremost second class, she has long since stopped belonging to the cinema; she now belongs to vast circles of readers

and thus (mindful of her lofty mission) she now lives the vicarious emotional life of millions, a never-ending series of high-frequency pulp novels:

THE LOVE LIFE OF NADINE C.
Installment #39
The Chips Are Down
The episode is terminated
SUSPENSE!!!
Who will be the next man?

I'm the ideal partner here. The more hopeless the liaison from the start, the more suspenseful the course of events promises to be. And the more stylized the variation on the everlastingly identical theme of hopelessness from Beckett to Ionesco.

Nor would I have to burden my conscience: Nadine has as little to fear from me as I from her. Whatever we do together takes place in the dimension of hopelessness. We move weightlessly through the space of the zero point. Thus, we'd both get our money's worth, with neither of us having to pay with himself. The alternation of hopeless literary experience and hopelessly lived literature would take on the grace of a *pas de deux*.

And the, so to speak, chemically pure literature would be set down in the entertainment section of the illustrated weeklies (where it has always been at home):

NEW AND ENDURING HAPPINESS
FOR NADINE CARRIER?

Her relationship with Guitarist X came to a painful end. X could not help her get over her disappointment with Bobsled Champion Y. Nor could he help her forget the cataclysm of her love for Fashion Photographer Z. But now, France's most popular screen star has been regularly seen in the company of Screenwriter A (author of such hits as *Heart's Blood*, *The Royal Eagle Project*, and *The Man in the Plastic Helmet*):

—leaving nightclub "8" in Rome—
—skiing in Courcheval—
—shopping on London's Bond Street—
—on location for her latest movie *The Prodigal Daughter* (scripted by A) in Cannes—
—at the beach in Acapulco—

—at the annual pilgrimage of the Gypsies in Camargue—
—in the diva's country house park on the Oise—

NADINE CARRIER IN SEVENTH HEAVEN AGAIN!
Friends confirm the rumor that France's most popular movie queen is planning a May wedding with the very busy screenwriter . . .

A BABY FOR NADINE CARRIER?
Upon leaving the world-famous hospital, the smile on the face of France's most radiant star seems to confirm the rumor (here accompanied by the successful . . .

NO BABY FOR NADINE CARRIER
The disappointment on her face shows all too clearly that . . .

CLOUDS ON NADINE'S HAPPINESS?
During location shooting of her movie *Take Me!* (scripted by A), the well-known author showed movie starlet B (who debuted in *Fever Curve*) an interest that went beyond professional considerations . . .

NADINE DEFENDS HER LOVE!
Her relationship with her steady beau was endangered by a recent crisis. But now the woosome twosome have reconsmiled and are spending quiet weeks again in . . .

NADINE DISAPPOINTED BY LOVE AGAIN?
Our photo reporter managed to get a shot of the extremely shy . . .

A CAREER OVER THE BROKEN HEART OF CARRIER?
Movie starlet B accompanied by Nadine's previous steady beau:
   —leaving the Zoum Zoum nightclub in Cannes—
   —skiing in Cortina d'Ampezzo—
   —shopping on Zurich's *Bahnhofstrasse*—
   —during the location shooting of her movie *Till the Seventh Member* (scripted by A) in Munich-Geiselgasteig—
   —on the beach at Marbella—
   —by the swimming pool of her villa on Lake Schlier (Lake Tegern, Lake Constance, Lake Wörther, Lake Como)—

STARLET'S ESCORT KNOCKS DOWN PHOTO REPORTER!
Upon leaving, the previous and now steady escort brutally attacked our . . .

IS THIS THE END?
Her tense face since her separation from her previous and now steady shows all too clearly that . . .

NEW LOVE FOR NADINE CARRIER!
We managed to get this unique snapshot—
—upon leaving the—
—while skiing in—
—when shopping at—
—on location at—
—on the beach at—
—during the annual—
—in the verdant countryside of—

IS NADINE CARRIER ABOUT TO WED
—racing-car stable-owner C?
—coiffure creator D?
—breast-stroke champion E?
—sociologist F?
—playboy G?
???
??
?
(Read our next installment, #40)

I, for my part, would merely have shortened the path to current immortality.

For assuming I didn't eat humble pie this time, sparing Nadine and myself a joint pulp romance, remaining here in my hideout, beating down all my weaknesses, difficulties, afflictions, and reservations; feeding on wheat germ and yeast; standing on my head for six minutes every morning to circulate the blood through my brain; and drudging along with Aunt Selma's tenacity in this cell of godforsaken human loneliness until I finished my book (and it would indeed be a book that bore witness, before the conscience of our race, to being a human being in this era)—what would be the happy end of this poignant story?

Let Scherping take the floor:

"Damn it, it's not so important what a man writes. People want to know how he brought it about. What does the guy who fabricated this stuff look like? What makes him different from me, what is there about him that he can pull himself out in this (profitable!) way from the dismal affair of Taedium Vitae? You've got to understand the poor souls who are so bitterly dependent on vicarious experiences. They don't want to hear any more old wives' tales. People aren't interested in stories, people are interested in existence—you understand? Do you seriously believe that anyone today has any interest whatsoever in Ulysses' adventures? As a juvenile book, maybe. But if you can come up with a book that scientifically demonstrates Who Was Homer?, it'll be on the best-seller list months before it even comes out. Take my word for it—after all, I serve experience to people—values have shifted. Anyone who wants stories goes to a flick or sits in front of the tube or scans the funnies. Today's book reader is a literary scholar— above all, a psychologist. He wants an analysis not only of the book but of the author—personal, flesh and blood: shaving early in the morning, creating, having sex (marital and adulterous), and, if possible, folding his hands for his nightly prayers. The reader wants to know: what induced this man to write this book in this way? The educated reader wants to get to the root of literature: the dichotomous, the suspicious, the crack in the author's personality. He wants accurate information: what was Shakespeare's real name? how schizoid was Goethe? how queer was Proust? how good was Hemingway with handguns? And so on and so forth. . . . The masses—the masses are adequately served by a hundred thousand publications. But in literature, they now go very personally into everything: color of eyes, shape of nose, cut of hair, and distinguishing characteristics. The literature they create is, so to speak, their own 'wanted' poster. Only then are they recognizable. Only then does the public retain their physiognomies. That's how the writers achieve prominence and get into the newspapers."

So (posthumously or otherwise), it all ended the same way:

OUR PHOTO REPORTER MANAGES TO SHOOT
THE WORLD-FAMOUS CELEBRITY
(if possible in exotic company)
—while leaving the—
—while vacationing in—
—while attending a—
—on location at—
—at his desk—
—at the annual—
—laid out under—

(under floral tributes, today no more luxurious for Nobel laureates than those under which my friend Schwab finally came to rest)

JACOB G. BRODNY
LITERARY AGENT

Could you please come and have lunch with me at Calvet's tomorrow?

12:30 OK?

B

Est Deus in nobis, agitante calescimus illo.

OVID

Whatever we see could be other than it is.

Whatever we can describe at all could be other than
it is.

LUDWIG WITTGENSTEIN
Tractatus logico-philosophicus

I is no obstruction in dealing
with other people;
I is what they ask for.

From the diary of W<small>ITOLD</small> G<small>OMBROWICZ</small>

□   □   □

A<small>LL KINDS OF THINGS</small> drop down the air shaft outside my window:
garbage—
withered linden leaves wafting down from the roof (God knows from where)—
bones of smoked fish—
spit-out peels of the sunflower seeds that the monkey-eyed Algerians chew—
sometimes in the evening hours: cottony October fog—
and cigarette butts, condoms, sanitary napkins, hairpins—
but no light: no unfiltered flash of sunlight.

Only once have I seen the shaft fill with something that seemed to shine in itself in complete transparency, like pure, ethereal gas; namely yesterday: the morning after the night when I walked here through the fog before my encounters with the literary agent Jacob Brodny and the girl at the Madeleine.

I had slept for a couple of hours and, in effortless renunciation, eluded the magic image-weaving of some dream (to be drawn up by me, smoothly and imperceptibly and without a shredded tangle, the way the surfacing merman pulls the watercress over his fish-mouthed skull)—

(Incidentally, I recall dreaming that I had to lead my foster mother Aunt Selma along the narrow ledge of a building wall—I no longer know where to. Anyway, it was high and dangerous, and suddenly a stone crumbled under her foot; she tried to cling

:: 459 ::

to me, but I wrenched loose, she plunged down, and I grabbed hold of the smooth wall, closing my eyes and waiting to hear the dull thud of her body on the sidewalk below. But nothing came, and when I peered down, I saw her: either her legs had dug into the ground or were totally crushed, for she sat in the billowing skirts of a bright summer frock as though in a flower cup, waving happily up to me. . . .

For the first time in years, I felt myself awakening with no perceptible malaise—and I instantly knew that I was in Paris and under what circumstances and where (in which mangy hotel room) and to what torments with my papers I would have to open my eyes. So I did not open them right away. I lay there, enjoying my precarious peace—

enjoyed *myself*: yes indeed: myself I-brimming I-towered (the vertical Anglo-Saxon I)

I man-animal

and as such, heartrendingly split in two: I physical and I abstract.

What is a woman like when she awakes? Embedded in herself, twin-hilled: a more intimate body, breathing life, renewing itself from life, physically more uniform: skin-I, flesh-I, hair-I, and yet an inner cavern: I *de profundis*, well and source (my foster mother in the flower cup: as if floating on the watery surface: images of flooding)—

I wellspring (I'd like to know what kind of a face I make during an orgasm. I once tried to catch it in a mirror: it didn't work, of course. What I saw was an embarrassingly indiscreet face—embarrassingly convicted of its embarrassment. Yet strangely bloated in shock: like a garden hose when it's stepped on. Like Schwab when he had to see or hear something embarrassing) . . .

Schwab and the scene with Gaia in the car: we in front (very uncomfortable), he supposedly drunk and unconscious in the back. . . . I must have acted quite predatory: guttural sounds squeezed out through grinding teeth and the like—

was that why Schwab thanked me? . . . (Gaia, by the way, came entirely without jungle shrieks, completely interiorized, an inner shudder. Christa sobbed blissfully, albeit only during our engagement. Dawn? I don't remember; I remember almost nothing about Dawn; only her breasts, the way I finally peeled them out of the onion sheaths of her bedtime armature that first time. . . . Few women emit that beautiful shriek, like Stella and sometimes Gisela . . .)

At last (for a long time now) I am sovereignly I myself: undisturbed by remorse that I am as I am. I carry incised within myself the image of the girl I slept with last night: How does it go in the *Arabian Nights?* "As if someone had been pricking my eyelids . . ." Only her body—I no longer remember her face—

the linear curves of a young female body and their punctuation: from the angle of the raised arm propping up the head (the hand drowned in the whirling torrent of hair), drawn in an arc into the sea-shell of the underarm and then lifted to the apple roundings of the breasts, from whose buds a rhythmic slope runs down to the flat declivities and curvatures of the flanks and belly, where the line, to which the now entirely symbolic flesh is confined, swings out again from the violin-like constriction to the voluptuousness of the hip, from which a thigh rises, exposing its inner surface in the steep, indolent vanishing

She sleeps, very happy and relaxed. So I'm still together as a man (Kisa Gotami at the sight of Buddha: Blessed indeed is the mother, blessed indeed is the father, blessed indeed is the wife whose is a lord so glorious). I am even still young enough to imagine beating up someone—the handsome Pole with his awful arms, for instance. Schwab always wanted to do that. He was presumably a lot stronger than I—at least heavier. Cousin Wolfgang also carried a powerful thorax on his somewhat short legs and epicene Germanic hips (from Uncle Helmuth).

In the first of my formative years in Vienna, Wolfgang was tormentingly superior to me (but never took advantage of it), but I soon caught up with him. By fourteen or fifteen (disgusting: the masculine version of pubic hair all the way to the navel, on boyish skin), I beat the hell out of him. I wasn't stronger, but tough as a whip—I had the more beautiful mother (and the bewitchment of my foster mother Aunt Selma in my eyes . . .). By the way, there was nothing nix-like about her in my dream: she was smiling: *ce si joli sourire de toute jeune fille qui était vraiment elle.*

Both are now dead, mother and foster mother, dissolved in the fog. *Sur le chemin de la mort, ma mère rencontra une grande banquise.* . . . Cousin Wolfgang too is dead; and so is Schwab— *elle nous regarda, mon frère et moi, et puis elle pleura.* And in my dream, she had her pretty smile: *un si joli sourire, presque espiègle* (a pretty word: it comes from *Till Eulenspiegel*). *Ensuite elle fut prise dans l'opaque.*

The girl from last night—she too came out of the fog. I recited poetry to her too—songs of life:

> Mon enfant, ma soeur,
> songe à la douceur
> d'aller là-bas vivre ensemble!
> Aimer à loisir
> aimer et mourir
> au pays qui te ressemble—

Gigolo language. Ice-dancer language. Gaia on the telephone: swaying cadences—stop (to listen)—start again—then released: the swing of a wide arc—leap—pirouette—she stands still again: the next arc already tensing in her. . . . I love listening to her: with no one else does French sound so melodious, so artificial. . . . I wait for the glass-bead tricklings of the next few sentences, look at her mouth: scarlet (*gueule*), behind it the predatory teeth of her black father (his lips like stamp pads) . . .

Gaia too is dead. I am surrounded by dead people. Barely forty-nine years old and already in the best society: *Silently over Golgotha, God's golden eyes open.* . . .

I felt it would be a good day. I could not wish for a better day for my protracted vice, my passion for constructing sentences whose rhythmic tensions and solutions release the Eros of language

in the mysterious appeal and attraction that the Word exerts in its wizard-like combination with other words: so that not only does it pass itself along to the next word and the one after that, as in the Archime-

dean whorl, by way of transmitting a specific and intended meaning
(so as to make a series of linked signals produce an image with which
experience is transmitted, as a sign whose transcendent shadow,
shifting like that of a sundial, forces the other signs grouped around it
to yield the secrets enclosed within them) but also (beyond language) a
kind of whispering begins, an echoing in the spaces around the words,
spaces that would have remained closed without the overtones of the
multivalence of each word, spaces that now expand like the expiring
sound waves of a tolling bell, followed and driven on further tolling:
each stroke of the bell is the assault of a primordial signal on the vessel
of our soul. . . .

That's how I should have awoken all those days: in calm surrender to bed-warm sensuality. I am thinking about the girl from
last night: for a few hours I loved her. I still feel her perfume on
my skin. On her inner thighs and under her pubic hair, she is taut
under dried saps. I gratefully experience the feeling of having
done my proper duty as a man—this steels you for defeats in the
future and the past. My mind was as blank as a Gelderland windowpane. Not a particle of ambition, not a speck of guilt: nor do I
care about the insanity of my existence: locked up in a tacky hotel
room, concealed from any kind of creditor, holed up within myself, denying true reality, living crazily in invented realities: a
woeful demiurge, cobbling his world together out of paper and
ink, paper and printer's ink, an onanist of creation pleasure—yes,
a self-satisfier, devoted to the pleasure of words—
    I do not care: I am walking a tightrope. I am ice-skating across
the rope: start—sweeping out of the curve—leap—pirouette—
into the next arc—my Doomsday is remote today:

> Le ciel est, par-dessus le toit,
> si bleu, si calme!
> Un arbre, par-dessus le toit,
> berce sa palme. . . .

(perhaps that tree beyond the roof really exists somewhere—otherwise, where would the linden leaves come from? . . .)
    I am in Paris, I thought. Are you listening, Schwab? I am in
Paris—which you loved so much, "as if it were life itself"

Mon Dieu, mon Dieu, la vie est là,
simple et tranquille.
Cette paisible rumeur là
vient de la ville—

(and you plunge into the *paisible rumeur*—I yank you back—a cabby's head emerges from a taxi and yells: "*Dis donc—le trottoir: c'est seulement pour les putains?*"—do you remember?) It was by the Madeleine, where you picked up that hooker—only it wasn't lights out: *la ville lumière* was drowned in fog—the bright, lovely underworld. . . .

and whatever you have to say: my soul will be forgiven

God spoke a gentle flame to his heart: oh, Man!

I know today will be a good day. I am as God originally meant me to be: a breathing creature that does not regard its existence as a curse: I lie here and feel *myself* in the creature bliss of existence. I am still aglow with the images of my dream, images that are signs for other meanings: Aunt Selma's smile means *woman:*

woman's flesh, woman's fullness, woman's warm skin, in which the spherical triangle of pubic hair is sharply inserted in pure contour: powerfully streaming from the base to the vertex, into the closure of the thighs, insular and mystical like the grove around a grotto temple—

here I am I-towering:

violently a black horse rears: the hyacinth curls of the maid grab at the ardor of his purple nostrils. . . .

I look for the face of a girl and do not find it in me. It is often quite close, but when I think I'm about to recognize it, it dissolves like the dream images of my murder. Nevertheless, I know: My soul will be forgiven.

FOR UNTO EVERY ONE THAT HATH SHALL BE GIVEN, AND HE SHALL HAVE ABUNDANCE, BUT FROM HIM THAT HATH NOT SHALL BE TAKEN EVEN THAT WHICH HE HATH. . . .

All my power (and all my fear) is rooted in this word, and no one is left around me to measure its truth by.... Truly, Brother Schwab: your death was a severe stroke of fate for me. You were the best years of my manhood, such as Cousin Wolfgang was for my adolescence: the lovely echo, the magic mirror on the wall. I know every last feature of your face and his. The nervous pride of the brow. The twitching vulnerability of the mouth. The bright lurking and the despair in the eyes....

He is as dead as you, my cousin Wolfgang. However, he has not afflicted me posthumously anywhere near as much as you have—at least not for a long while. You were kind enough to replace him. Your eyes and his were quite ludicrously the same. Never will I forget his gaze when in August 1939—shortly before I went to Rumania to be a soldier myself—he came to me in plain military gray: wordless, making the effect of an Expressionistic stage entrance. His globular eyes peered through glasses as thick as bottle bottoms (just like yours: all in all, he could have been your twin), and these eyes expressed, in an effably stupid gape, "Well, what do you say now?..." And they almost burst with fear to find out what I might say.

Wasn't this often your fear too, friend Schwab? Otherwise, in order to have a brother, I could have made do with Nagel. He was never afraid of what I might say. He did not seek his defeats in me. He evaded me in a manly way (for, basically, measuring is what it's all about, isn't it?).... Let me reveal one of the secrets that made you blush when you were alive, a medium-size depth-psychological secret (but don't tell Hertzog): *I was never afraid of being beaten up by you.* If by anyone, then Nagel (although that's absurd: the poor man has only one arm, after all). Nagel doesn't want to measure himself by me. You always did. I for my part am sorry: I want to measure myself against the handsome Pole. Remember his arms? Fantastic, damn it!... I sometimes daydream about smashing him in the kisser—and then ... As Scherping knows, what happens when a man imagines *he can be helplessly prey to his defeat?*

(Schwab's confession: the blush in his face when he told me about how he came home and ran into his wife Carlotta's lovers on the stairs, how he confronted her, and she told him straight to his face, "Yes, a man comes every day when you're not here."

(and John's stony expression when I returned with Stella, both of us still glowing. . . .

(or I in front of Dawn in the sleeping-car, in the morning: I had lain awake all night in the next compartment, she sitting on the bed, the mucous stain half concealed on the sheet, and I ask, "What about your friend?" "Oh, he left. He got off the train somewhere last night." Our last—no, next-to-last—meeting. She talking in the phone booth, I outside listening: "But I love you— you can't leave me. . . ." These are male experiences: they lead to measurings.)

Each man sees his defeat in the other: that's the simple solution to the riddle of brotherhood. (Are you really blushing now? What's it like when a soul blushes? Like when the light in the air shaft outside the window filled up with the redness of dawn?)

However, I am speaking the truth:

Everyone seeks his murderer in the other; that makes human beings brothers. It's as simple as a true romance, "and so marvelously symbolic," as Fräulein Ute Seelsorge would say. I was always sympathetic with her attraction to Nagel: it is fascinating to watch him pass from sheer courage to despair; but did you ever take him seriously when it happened? And you don't even know everything about Nagel. What you admired, why you envied him, was relatively easy to endure: his cast-iron character; his boy-scout single-mindedness; the raging ardor with which he wrote book after book; his poignant wrestling with the angel of literature (Hemingway as Gabriel); his touching and unswerving faith in the writer's mission. . . . What if you found out that he has given up all those things—in favor of political action?

He is a man of honor, our good Nagel . . . like you . . . isn't that so? May I ask what you died of? Surely not the combined alcohol, uppers, and downers? I suspect you died because they didn't take it seriously enough that you failed to take yourself as seriously as Nagel.

And now I'd like to know what fascinated you about me, friend Schwab. The evil? . . . That's a fabulous notion. Evil. Admit it. Be honest for once (it can't matter to you anymore): what was the measuring between us? what did my irony challenge in you?

Or rather: *as* what did it challenge you? as evil? That should have occurred to me for my last draft of the book—what a lummox I am! I have the stuff of seven best-sellers in me and stand in front of literature as if it were a barn door—

of course: EVIL was the basis of measurement between Schwab and me. EVIL tempted us in each other. . . . If that's not a find! . . . I'm going to turn it into a movie: *The Tempter* (get the title registered right away!).

BELOVED TEMPTER
An Intercosmic Film
Script: Aristides Subicz.
Lead actress: Nadine Carrier (this time playing a man)

If this doesn't spur some get-up-and-go into the curly tails of my piglets! Done very discreetly, you understand, very delicately: a man, by means of sheer irony—okay?—gets another man—his bosom buddy, of course—to—what?—well, obviously: *to commit a murder* . . .

(call Wohlfahrt immediately: he'll be beside himself; he'll fly to Hitchcock with the idea tomorrow.)

I knew it: this is going to be a creative day; the idea is brilliant. Eventually, it'll lead to the *theodicy*, which was so important to Schwab. EVIL in its sublimest, most perfidious variations: love, friendship, brotherhood. The brotherhood of Cain and Abel. . . . It would have fascinating dramatic high points: Cousin Wolfgang's appearance, for example: "Well, what do you say now? . . ."

Nothing. What should I have said? A man is given the chance to survive the first half of a struggle between maddened nations, survive it calmly and well fed in a brown shirt, but his conscience does not permit him; or rather: *the Tempter* has aroused this conscience in him. . . . So, at the very start, for the Polish campaign, he plants himself before him in a poignantly simple military gray, and his eyes ask with defiant anxiety, "Well, what do you say now? . . ." Plants himself with clumsy significance before the tempter, like the lead actor in an Expressionistic play, his very entrance fulfilling a bit of German destiny, the man in military gray symbolizing Langenmarck, Stalingrad ... and his eyes, mole-blind from reading so much Stefan George, heartbreakingly tragic and defiantly anxious, ask, "Well, what do you say now? ..."

I have nothing to say. Not to you, either, dear Schwab. I lie here and breathe *myself* in the creature bliss of existence. I've got seven days and nights of a Descent into Hell behind me and presumably a few more days and nights ahead of me: I KNOW THAT I AM A MURDERER—like anyone who has a brother.

I know my measure of guilt. Even for certain deaths (including yours) for which I am only very indirectly responsible. Cousin Wolfgang, for example, would not have had to pass away so prematurely but for me ("Well, what do you say now? ..."); likewise Stella; likewise Gaia. But this was, so to speak, my midwifery for death. Everyone practices it occasionally and also finds his own helper when his hour comes. Nor do I want to mention the corpses that still walk about on two feet in broad daylight: Christa in Hamburg or Dawn in her madhouse. And perhaps also my once so deeply beloved son—a growing corpse, a corpse apprentice, so to speak—will soon mature to manhood, find a trade, woo a wife, make babies: all this as someone who died prematurely, killed by his father.... I did it in order *to be close to an Other*. The way Nadine always wants to *be close* to someone. Like Christa, when we first met in the hell of Nuremberg—like Dawn: initially her awakening, her happiness, and then the plunge back into solitary confinement with herself—

Why did you die, Schwab? To reach someone else? ... To show me and Nagel and Carlotta and Hertzog and Scherping and goodness knows whom else that your tormented *existence in contemptuous conditions* was no fiction, no literary as-if, but a dreadful reality? ... I imagine that your dead eyes must have contained the same defiantly anxious question as Cousin Wolfgang's eyes when he stood before me, dressed in military gray for the sacrifice: "Well, what do you say now? ..."

Let me tell what I say: your murder was not properly structured; your sacrifice was in vain; you proved nothing but yourself as a biological backfire; you did not kill yourself because your despair at *existence in contemptuous conditions* did not even let you write about it; the truth is: you lived in despair *because you had to kill yourself.*

You taught me a great deal about life, Schwab: you made me realize in what way I am superior to all of you: I ACCEPT THIS EXISTENCE IN CONTEMPTUOUS CONDITIONS HUMBLY AND GRATEFULLY. This is my HAVING for whose sake I am GIVEN. . . .

I am like that wolf in Bessarabia: I bite around me, slavering, I bite into my flanks, and the bullet that is to release me shoots only my leg off, and I limp away on three legs, grateful TO BE ALIVE. . . .

That is my monstrous power: the power with which I murder even when I don't murder with my hands: FEAR IS MY POWER: wolf hunger and wolf tenacity and wolf fear in my sucked-in belly. . . .

The fear, for instance, THAT I WILL NOT WRITE MY BOOK: this book with no solid ground plan or outline, no foundation-laying idea, no shaping principle. This book, which increases and proliferates like a cancer, nourished by my moods and whims, by my hopes, wishes, dreams, and visions, my ecstasies, illuminations, contritions, despairs, revelations, insights, perceptions, wrong erroneous foregone conclusions, drives, compulsions, likes and dislikes, by my wisdom and by my folly. . . . This book, which grows out of all these things like one of the monstrous houses that fools build somewhere in provincial nooks, remote from the times, like turned-up giant-dwarf grottoes among the gillyflowers and Aaron's rods of their rustic gardens; in a hundred arches, stairways, galleries, oriels, and balconies; gabled, domed, and be-towered; crowned with merlons, steps, ramps, balustrades; adorned with blind niches, vases, rosettes, and lanterns. I want to say *everything* in this book: everything I know, presume, believe, recognize, and sense: everything I have gone through and lived through; the way I have gone through it and lived through it; and, if possible, why and to what end I went through it and lived through it. . . .

And I say it with the ardor of credulous simplicity—with blind faith in God—that a specific form must be ultimately ingrown in something that is so immediately and compulsively produced out of necessity (and against all expectations to the contrary). . . .

And while I was thinking all these things, a memory flashed through me, terrifyingly, a memory of a conversation with S. (in front of Pollock's canvases at the first Documenta? or later? at some trashy Action Painting show here in Paris?). Anyway, a conversation I outlined rather accurately and didn't come across while going through my papers during the past few days. A conversation that must be misplaced or lost, like so many other things . . . and (precisely because it's been lost) seemed to contain something that must finally, as the conceptual essence of my book, contain the key to its form . . .

A conversation with Schwab about snails and the houses they produce out of themselves as the expression of their species: always quite typical and yet individually distinct in pattern, coloring, and ultimate form. . . . Plus a quotation from Valéry, which Schwab, of course, promptly had at hand, and which I will never find again without my notes and books. . . .

And with that, I was at last fully awake into the dear day.

□   □   □

IT WAS YESTERDAY'S DAY. I did not get up or open my eyes. I lay motionless and tried to guess what time of day it was: was it early morning? late afternoon? Subterraneanly, I was seized with the desire to get up quickly and go to the Madeleine, where the hooker I had left last night might still be plying around. But there was time for that tomorrow. I remained supine. What absorbed me was the lost jotting.

It was, of course, nonsense to imagine it could contain any tiding of salvation, a magic word that would be the key to my book. Yet all my thoughts were fixed on that jotting. It seemed to me I should have thought of it when, with the first jotting about Schwab to come into my hand, the terror of my dream and the *recognition* of my murder pounced on me. And this, I felt, signified that the two were mysteriously connected: the dream about my murder and the lost contents of the jotting. I ought to recognize this connection so that it might become clear: the *it* that was about to express itself through me.

As far as I could recall (and it was now enormously important for me to recall), I had slipped the note on the conversation back then (when?) into the folder marked HAMBURG—MISCELLANE-OUS: presumably as the model for one of the fireside chats in Rönnekamp's salon: the cultural chitchat—so cultivated as to be stageworthy—of old pederasts in front of disdainfully bored young homosexuals; boys with breathlessly husky voices and skulls clearly marked in their smooth doll heads, exotically beautiful, like Siamese cats; and ordinary seamen dragged over from the docks (stupidly blue-eyed, sweat-fermented, with laborer's fists like hammers, sexual apparatuses bulging out of snug flies, rosebud-like carbuncles where their Sunday shirt collars sawed into freckled necks) . . . all these things in Folder C.

In those days (happy days of innocence!), I took a schoolboy-like pleasure in describing such *causeries,* and enriching the ghostly self-exposures—the regular Saturday-night stripteases down to the bone of Wilhelminian, Hanseatic humanism, which Carlotta watched with her lazy eyes and sensually puffed cheeks—with small fragments from my occasional exchanges of ideas with Schwab. . . . A malicious act against S., of course, a despicably cheap betrayal and, for that, twice as painful to his virginal mind, a treason against our intimate intellectual rapport. . . . He would surely have understood immediately what I was driving at when he found his remarks (chastely costumed as questions: "Don't you really think that it might possibly be different, namely . . . ?") placed apodictically into Rönnekamp's tart auntie-mouth—

Rönnekamp's pale, sharp private-dick profile (Arsène Lupin, avenger of the disinherited—the main readings of my formative years in Vienna) and the fanatically cold vanity in his tropically lashed eyes when he snapped in his hard Baltic accent: "This, gentlemen, is simply the very antithesis of art!"

Happy days of my youthful callowness, when the sketches for my book were still briskly drawn from human life (and who would ever have dreamed back then that it would not be granted me to present it to Schwab in a finished manuscript and relish my first triumph in his disdainful envy)!

At any rate, and be that as it may. Now the jottings were lost. In the past few days, I had meticulously combed the folder marked HAMBURG—MISCELLANEOUS, and had not come across the jotting. Nor had I missed it when going through the folder, even though an obviously connected list of idiotic questions about the philosophy of art had come into my hands:

Does the supposed distortion of a Romanesque lion have an artistic aim? Or did the Romanesque simply "see things that way"?

Is art a by-product? That is: did Giotto paint his frescoes as an artist or as a pious Christian?

To what extent would the literary value of Samuel Pepys's Diary *be greater had it been fiction?*

[and so on]—

These things could truly have been uttered in Rönnekamp's salon or even in Witte's refined home: as at a round table of *Kultur*-bearers, among whom Christa appeared like a regrettably mute unicorn, quite properly manipulating a knife and fork (what exquisite things she would have yielded had she been granted the power of speech!). Grouped around her: the director of the School of Arts and Crafts with his wife (a former ballet mistress); the publisher of the *Financial Gazette* with his wife (a doctor of philosophy); a cybernetics teacher with his wife (intimidated petite bourgeoise; incidentally, the only one who got Christa to speak, three brief sentences about a pudding recipe). And at the high point of the discussion, somewhere the question "Boots, you feel, are a Freudian symbol?" Which is patriarchally rebuffed by Witte: "Please, not at the table!"

Again, and yet again: happy days! For just imagine if I had published that dance of death back then, that macabre post-war German round: Christa, Rönnekamp, Witte, and Carlotta: the victims of the resistance movement and the sodomy law, the economic-reconstruction miracle, the *Financial Gazette*, arts and crafts and cybernetics, Doktor Oetker's pudding powder and Professor Doktor Jaspers's philosophy hand in hand, and: reach for the violin, Dame Past! *Kultur* starts playing in an Isadora Duncan dress. A bit nibbled at, of course: the ivy is growing out of *Kultur*'s eye sockets. But these are true values, salvaged from the rubble, dusted off and freshly polished:

but, no doubt about it, that list was part of another (fragmentary) jotting that I had found floating loosely in the folder labeled MAGMA and transferred to the new folder labeled SCHWAB (although I can no longer recall my intention—certainly not as a model for a conversation with him? Impossible!):

—in literature too (militant since Dada) the tendency to emulate artificially the immediacy of involuntary production. Naturally, then, a reliable judgment on the aesthetic value of such products presumes a critic outside the species and genus, as remote from such products (and their authors) as the man from the snail's house whose beauty he recognizes: at the very least, it presupposes a person at a reliable distance in time—as, say, we to the art of Romanticism. Hence the question: how many centuries (or decades—the gap is shrinking visibly) must pass for us to be able to appreciate correctly the style of an era? the thing that adheres without exception to each and every one of its artistic creations, so characteristically that one can fairly recognize it at first sight; namely the thing, that is produced along with it, unconsciously and involuntarily, as if the Zeitgeist were guiding the hands (so compellingly that a mediocre contemporary copy is harder to distinguish from the original than a masterful copy done in a subsequent era; and this later copy, in the different penmanship guided by the Zeitgeist, reveals itself to be a copy no matter how brilliant the copyist or counterfeiter)?

Europe transformed into prattle. The topic for a Round Table Discussion. Participants: the art historian Frau Doktor X, the sociologist Professor Y, the sculptor and Ernst Barlach Prize laureate Professor Z, and the successful writer Nagel as moderator. . . . And now for the bubbling, foaming, and fermenting of the cultural twaddle:

We are blind to the peculiarity in the expression of our own era (its so-called style). Today, nothing enables us to discern what will subsequently make a painting by Kandinsky attributable to roughly the same time as one by Augustus John—while we can already see that Corot and Seurat were contemporaries, not to mention David and Delacroix. And the further back we look, the more clearly we see the common features in the character of this epoch's handwriting, and the more modestly the individual distinctions in handwriting recede into the background. We also involuntarily retreat from the style of the immediately preceding era (when we have sufficiently detached ourselves from it to discern it). We regard it as unbearably mannered, dusty, trivial. A breaking of images commences, an iconoclasm—until the gradually increasing distance uncovers that era's charms and lets us read between its lines, as it were. This too proceeds in undulations of presumably measurable frequencies and interfrequencies.

So much for the extant note: a pulverized *feuilleton*, which could be preserved in its dryness, ground into a word-gruel, and stuffed into the mouths of characters in novels. Frail Calder mobiles orbit overhead, and the cybernetics man sits in the corner of the sofa with crossed legs and chats about art: "The phenomenon as such, mind you, is highly interesting—may I have a bit more sugar for my coffee, dear madame. . . ."

And though I knew that the lost jotting could scarcely contain anything more essential, I now missed it with an impatience that drove me to despair.

□   □   □

REMEMBER ONE THING: I had only just awoken. I thought, saw, felt all this in the moment of awakening itself: it was my awakening; it coincided with the signals: vanishing dream—hotel room—Paris—now—here—today—I—

My consciousness was still rubbing its eyes at all this; it was still surprised at, and almost caught unawares by, the things it had to register: it was not fully operative; in pajamas, so to speak, and not yet in pants. Its hair was still disheveled, and it was still chewing its emotive breakfast bread: the foster mother in the flower cup, the fear on the building ledge, the plunge and the salvational gesture of waving from the depth, the erotic tiding. . . .

Behind these things, however, everything else was already seized and stowed, waiting to be processed: a fermenting gruel of images, perceptions, thoughts, associations, emotions, reflexes; the tremendous mass of surging abstractions that a brain must cope with to set a man's daily schedule into motion—a writing man, who feeds it with himself.

The accursed nut-kernel-shaped beast under my scalp was already roaring to be fed again. It was already raging in its shell again, this disgusting, gluttonous heap of soft, pale, skin-covered, inwardly twisted, layered pudding mass marbled with bloody veins and arteries. It plopped down heavily again upon my existential creature comfort, squeezing the bliss of vegetation, a bliss as warm as cow's milk. It was already eating again into my divine sonship, that fat caterpillar, eating me off the Tree of Life. . . .

And I rebelled against it, offered my animalish body against it: my proud morning glory: my I-towered I: the warmth of my limbs under the blanket, which I had pulled up all the way to the tip of my nose, my dear skin smell, the resilience of my sinews, the solidity of my muscles, the sweetness of my saliva, the vital sustenance of my breath. I mobilized my gonads, which were quite active anyhow: I reviewed the gamut of last night's erotic images and sensations, of other nights of love, untold nights of love, real or dreamed—all this to withdraw my brain's food: *me*. To save myself from myself, carry me into a different greedy center of my life and being, abstracted from myself into the throbbing, swelling, tensing, urging of a stiffening member—

but it now throbbed, tensed, urged into emptiness, into nothingness . . . the images remained images, abstractions; the emotions dissolved in their own echo; the produced juices shot back and operated as poisons: the nourishing juices of abstractness—

What remained was an impatience that snorted, stamped, reared like a stallion: a powerless desire to *realize* myself, to redeem myself in some way from this existence in a vacuum; from this life in abstractness, which my brain mass reflected for me before immediate life.

What the devil had happened? I had once again mislaid, lost, destroyed a jotting—in any case, done away with it. Who cares? What was it anyhow? Some hot air about art.

Art. When I hear the word, I first see Gaia before me: Gaia in a flowery hat. Whenever a conversation spirals up into cultural heights, I see Gaia before me with that hat: a giant chocolate doll with a peony cake on its head. Gaia, the powerful, the splendid-bodied: a dark height of six feet, seventy-seven kilograms live weight, one hundred fifty-two pounds of mahogany-brown, vanilla-scented mulatto flesh, shimmering corn-gold at the curve tips and darkening to brownish violet in the shadowy spheres, corseted, ruffled, bowed, and ribboned into a gigantic sofa doll: the chubby little hands raised delicately with crooked pinkies, as though wielding a small, invisible baton to accompany her precocious, amazingly knowledgeable, extraordinarily suave and sophisticated sentences.... The whole thing superdimensional, however; gigantic: Gaia, the chocolate *caryatid*, bearing upon her head the dusty, disheveled, magnificent patchwork array of blossoms, the blossoms of Refined Culture....

And because her skin was earth-brown covered with corn-gold and not anemically colorless; because the mystery of a different race flashed in her enameled eyes, in the glittering rows of her teeth, in the mirroring patent-leather of her hair, denouncing every word of her put-on cultural blabber, giving it a wild, unused naturalness, a red originality of the blood, which still surged under paw strokes and predatory shrieks, close to the earth, which craved to drink it up—because, of all these things, she was barbarously beautiful, cannibalistically ornamental ...

Yes indeed! *She* could afford to chitchat about art. It suited her. It complemented her resplendent exoticism, made it poetic: palm-filled atolls fanning on the blue sea, sugar-cane plantations rustling under aromatic breezes, sails billowing: the word "culture" regained its literary meaning: became colonial.... A Negro in a leopard-skin loincloth is a savage, but a Negro wearing a tuxedo dickey and starched cuffs becomes a poetic picture-book Negro: becomes art—while a lymphatic paleface chitchatting about art, a watery-eyed mealworm-skull, who recited poems in his childhood, making himself heartily ridiculous, who attaches reflections on the philosophy of culture to every fart—why, these are mere fragments in the vomit that this mortally ill white race keeps throwing up—

And I have bathed in this vomit: I took it for dragon's blood that makes the skin invulnerable—alas, a linden leaf dropped between Siegfried's shoulder blades (from the *arbre par-dessus le toit*, perhaps, who knows?) from somewhere out there in the golden blueness that filled the fog yesterday and is now so brightly illuminating the shadows in the air shaft. . . .

A mood-moment. This sort of thing should not be underrated. The weather yesterday was still affecting me. In the weather I recognize myself in my paleontological strata.

We must remember: for me, weather has always been more of a psychological than a meteorological phenomenon. The days of my childhood, for example (which I count as lasting until my mother's death), were never marred by even the smallest cloudlet. Sparkling blue sky everywhere (particularly dense, of course, above the Côte d'Azur). The stolidity of my formative years in Vienna was something I allowed to pass over me with my head drawn in: I no longer remember when it rained or when the sun shone. Unusually clear weather (clear as glass and almost painfully cold) prevailed in Vienna in March 1938, at the so-called *Anschluss*, the annexation (or upheaval), and it remained sunny throughout my summer with Stella in the Salzkammergut.

Distinct changes in the seasons (childlike delight at the ardor of the snow break, for example, at the black crumbly earth thawing free underneath, the starry-eyed primroses sprouting in last year's wet, yellow grass, the first bright, tender green on the birch branches and so on, the leaden sky under which the white balls of cherry blossoms explode, weeks of summer heat thick with flowers when the horizons flicker like fire lanes, apocalyptic downpours whipping the silvery, surging cornfields, lightning flashes and thunderclaps, then abrupt silence, a steaming sigh of relief in Nature—but the end of the world was only play-acted, everything is sparkling again, the red poppy glows again in the yellow of the wheat next to the truehearted blue of the cornflowers, a blinking dripping from the leafy roof of treetops with the clouds rolling apart overhead, the day mistily brooding to a close, a magical mosquito dance as the shadowy webs of evening weave thicker and thicker, then the moon rises big, round, and clarifying, yes, indeed; at last, the blue-and-gold self-immolation of autumn)—these pleasures, long since anachronistic, I could experience after my childhood only upon returning home to Bessarabia. But then, it was almost winter.

And oddly enough, this winter has already skipped across a few years of military events (I spent them under arbitrarily changing climatic conditions, like a mouse zigzagging around inside a cage of predators where the beasts pounce on one another: one had little chance to consider the weather). It was the Ice Age anyhow. But true winter—a crisp snowland, in which the kneeling world turns its back on you in the sweeping storm of ice crystals, the angels are frozen to the earth, they cannot raise their eyelids, frozen stiff over their blind eyes—true winter, I say, resumed for me only when the weapons fell silent.

As we know, not only the weapons fell silent. The cities fell silent too—that is, whatever was left of them. They were nothing but chains of streets leading through rubble fields, acres of brick debris, mortar, cement fragments under bonnets of snow: white, hilly districts where the frost softened and leveled the harsher contours with its pitiless grasp. Here and there a cracked lighting pole showed its dangling wires, here and there a section of wall loomed, with its back to the horizontal sweep of the ice wind. Basement caves that were not filled in were tenanted by people. They too were silent (understandably).

I was granted this winter experience in Hamburg-on-the-Elbe (frozen over) in 1945–46, 1946–47, and 1947–48.

Needless to say, various mild months occurred in between. At times, the rubble landscape even donned a camouflage-green-splotched frock. Perhaps, people even sweated there occasionally, healthfully sweated out the excessive water content of cabbage, potatoes, and fodder beets—ultraviolet sun rays might ease hunger edema—but all in all, the winter withdrew only temporarily and soon returned with an even icier grip on the city ruin.

All this is known. Most of my German contemporaries went through it, too (meanwhile, cinematic artworks have come to us from America, visionizing the day after the world annihilation by hydrogen bombs: the mood is pretty much the same), so I can spare myself the trouble of describing it in detail. The only interesting thing is that this grim wintertide stayed with me rather traumatically—but actually because of its loss.

People don't know (or at least don't generally remember) that it was heartrendingly human. It was certainly no radiant humanity (like, for instance, that of Herr Doktor Albert Schweitzer, R.I.P., who was being held up to everyone as an example) but, rather, the dismal, gray-faced humanity of slums—and, despite all the anguishing nuances, the story is ultimately of Biblical simplicity: the evil were bad, the good good; the lukewarm lukewarm, the fiery fiery; the wise wise, the fools foolish; the smart people smart, the stupid ones stupid.

That's how simple the world was (until the day when the weather changed again as though by magic, marked in my notes as the "day of the currency cut"): almost a picture-book world.

People dealt simply with one another (almost everyone wore rags). If you had nothing to say, then you held your tongue (although the man who held his tongue was not necessarily the one who had nothing to say); but if someone talked, you listened. If he talked nonsense, you promptly told him so: people weren't timorous in those days (they had already learned the meaning of fear). If you asked someone for something and he turned you down, you accepted that as his privilege and didn't hold a grudge. If someone gave you something, you were grateful. If someone robbed someone, you let him go (you would probably have done the same in his place). If you had no bed to sleep in, you pushed a couple of sleeping people closer together and lay down next to them—and if they drove you away, they had bad dreams afterward. Anyone who didn't want to share his piece of bread ate it alone and was ashamed (or else wasn't: that was his privilege). Any man who coveted his neighbor's wife was a wonderboy: just where did he get the calories from?!

Most likely, a very few did live in joy, in the lap of luxury, on the gravy train. But they were marked. Marked not to be condemned but to be marveled at: extraordinarily vital (or miserable) existences. To put it tersely and topically: the middle-class categories were canceled. Values were drawn not from ideologies but from living reality—in nouns, not adjectives: my friend the black-marketeer, that arsehole of a food official. Unsophisticated, plain, and simple.

All in all, it was a wonderful time.

It was the time when Christa had every reason to be jealous of Nagel. I truly loved him. His makeshift home was a garden house that a couple of close bombs had torn askew (our home was the remnants of the adjoining villa on the Elbchaussee: Christa was counted among the relatives of the conspirators of the Twentieth of July, to whom the arseholes at the housing office gave preference). And here, I made up for the boy-scout romanticism I had avoided in wise timidity during my formative years in Vienna (albeit not without envying my cousin Wolfgang, who joined everything). We distilled beet alcohol in an apparatus cobbled together out of two old watering cans. We lay in wait on the Elbe ice to catch starving coots. Once, we even bagged one, and in order to roast it festively, Nagel burned his cello (he couldn't play it now anyway, with one hand). In the evenings, when we snuggled under an old horse blanket like orphaned brothers, field-flower bouquets of delightful stories blossomed from the fiery mouth of the little iron stove (to which we had fed Christa's portable gramophone—I too wanted to give with an open hand). Christa, however, lay abed in the ruined villa and pouted.

No one could tell such marvelous stories as Nagel. He had lived through a lot and was a keen observer. After all, he had made up his mind to write at a very early age—a reader of Jack London and Joseph Conrad, later an enthusiastic adept of Knut Hamsun, and then, of course, Hemingway. He had had all the experiences that I had not had: the hard, deliciously variegated, adventurous "reality" of life. Everything I still have not managed to experience. When scarcely an adolescent, he had run off with a circus. For one and a half months—still and all. When they caught up with him, his parents put him in the dog house, but six weeks later, he was off again: signed up as cabin boy on a tiny freighter that plowed the Baltic Sea. Only one round trip, to be sure, but the wind hit a Force Nine three times. His father was a beer-brewery engineer in Harburg. At sixteen, Nagel could drink like a fish and was kicked out of the Hitler Youth for insubordination. A resistance fighter, obviously. Shortly before he was supposed to graduate from high school, he slapped his teacher, was expelled, and entered the Labor Service. He dug ditches in the hills of the Rhön and learned how to fly a glider; he fell from an altitude of thirteen feet and broke his leg. Wearing a cast, he took a makeup exam; and no sooner could he walk again than he strapped on a rucksack, according to the good old German tradition, and, with the laudable humanistic goal of hiking along the entire route of Goethe's first voyage to Italy, set off. But because he was on the verge of conscription, the arseholes at the passport office refused to give him a passport; embittered, he went to the coal district of Upper Silesia, where he worked underground for eight weeks with a safety lamp on his forehead (I was familiar with his white-toothed smile in the blackened face from his dealings with the iron stove). Then he had an idea. He went to Munich and, by way of old comrades from the Labor Service, contacted a certain Party agency, which, after a brief training period (he already knew about explosives from the mine), sent him across the Alpine border to infiltrate Austria as a provocateur.

There, however, he did not spend much time provoking the Schuschnigg regime, which was decaying anyway (his opinion of Austrians was never high; he found fault with me, too, certain features that he ascribed to my formative years in Vienna: inadequate solidity of character, for instance, hence also careless squandering of a certain talent for linguistic artistry). He gave up political agitation among the *cis*-Leitha arseholes and (a forerunner, a pioneer, of hitchhike tourism) thumbed his way across Switzerland to Italy. There (more dynamic than Goethe), he forged ahead through Terracina, all the way to Palermo, crossed over to Libya, traipsed along the North African coast to Ceuta (a florilegium of small adventures—nowhere near as vividly narrated as on those frost-crackling winter evenings under the horse blanket—has just been put out by Scherping). Next, he crossed the Fretum Herculeum, navigating his own sailboat, and, by way of Spain and France (five fantastic days in Paris: brothel visit and so on!), he came back to Germany. While crossing the border, he was intercepted. He had neglected to obey his draft notice, had not begun his military duty punctually, and was therefore considered a deserter. The outcome could have been painful, but his father (fortunately a World War I veteran, Iron Cross First Class, gold Party pin) ironed the matter out. Of course, the offspring was promptly inducted into the Wehrmacht.

Uniformed, shorn, given hell, thrown in the guardhouse, put on latrine-cleaning detail ("I've gonna make you work your ass off like Augeas, you fucker!"). Then, as a reward for the work accomplished, he was allowed to belly through the Lüneburg Heath in full battle dress and kit. As a revenge, Nagel (familiarized, by the way, with the teachings of Sigmund Freud during his travels abroad) drew the necessary conclusions from the twofold Oedipus situation with his father the beer-brewer and with Father State and became a Communist. However, an active cultivation of this anything but popular ideological direction was obstructed by the war.

But in those days, when the ice wind tattered the angels' frozen feathers, something glowed over the skew garden house of the villa on the Elbchaussee: the star under which our allegedly rationalist and yet ardently myth-believing century has ever sought the start of a new Golden Age.

Nagel had ignited the star. He had, of course, enriched it with evangelical rays (he had met God in the war—a story that has been served up to his readers in several versions), but the model was still recognizable.

From among returnees and stay-at-homes, refugees, stragglers, and drifters, a small circle of like-minded and simply conversation-minded people had formed around him, and this circle now drank our home-brewed beet schnapps, rolled cigarettes out of the tobacco Christa raised on the manure pile (meanwhile, she lay abed and pouted), and overcame the unovercomable past (which back then was the present of yesterday). People discussed Karl Marx, Ortega y Gasset, and Hemingway, the Bible, Hermann Broch, Camus and Sartre, Max Weber, Hegel, Kierkegaard, and, promiscuously and chaotically, just about everything in the wind. Anyone who came emptied out of his pocket not only crumbs of sugar, ersatz coffee, herring paste, or cigarettes but also the tiny hoarding bag of his knowledge, emaciated by twelve Nazi years. He would bring along a book he had smuggled through the Thousand Year Reich—a volume of Karl Kraus, James Joyce, Musil, Kafka—or simply a foreign newspaper, or a report on a radio program he had recently listened to, probably still with the subliminal fear of being caught. Intellectually, too, it was a slum; "but," as Nagel later wrote, "in intellectual matters, hunger is a miracle-spawning virtue. Though the loaves be as meager as at the feeding of the five thousand, not only does one eat one's fill, but one also gathers twelve baskets from the crumbs that are left over."

Karl Nagel would not have had to encounter the most fatherly of all fathers in order to add the four rays of the Evangelists to the pentagram of politically applied historical materialism. This too was due mainly to the weather. The weather was so grim that a small iron stove, heated fairly well with now superfluous cultural instruments (we had already tackled the wooden paneling in the villa library and the shattered grand piano in the drawing room), was a wellspring of upswelling gratitude, which, in light of the prevailing circumstances, was bound to overpour into the metaphysical.

The point is, public transport operated poorly, and private means in those days meant two legs (of normal mortals, surviving tenaciously despite hunger edema), and not everyone had two legs: at least three of our intellectual companions were left with only one—or one and a half, or one and three quarters. But anyone who came wandering out all the way to the Elbchaussee on foot (or even on crutches!) had to cross the icily whistling wastelands of the Reeperbahn and Altona, thus offering up a sacrifice of almost mystical grandeur—that noble self-renunciation that puts a legendary touch on the formations of primal communities. The at first sporadic but then more regular get-togethers, where we talked ourselves into a fever pitch like Dostoevskian students, took on a character of consecrated hours. Even spiritual chariness had a certain crèche-like intimacy.

All kinds of things were talked about, and if we sometimes reached one of those moments of collective reflection that occur when someone comes out with a newish truth that is not yet shopworn, then something like a simple poignancy in the mind occurred. "Our crèche piety," I called it when telling Schwab about it later: "There it lay before us in the straw, naked and helpless, the new itty-bitty truth; the shepherds couldn't take their eyes off it; even when three Technicolor kings came out of the bitter-cold, snowy night with an ox and an ass, it remained in their eyes, the itty-bitty little truthlet. May it now grow and become the All-Inspirer. It is already radiating with starry brightness to all eyes that look up to peer at one another. . . ."

This was soon to change, when we got our first pope in Hertzog.

Hertzog joined us by chance; but Nagel denied the existence of chance: hence, God sent Hertzog to us. This happened in one of the green-camouflaged months, under the meteorological phenomenon of a violent downpour. We—that is, Nagel and I, the identical twins, as Christa called us—were tinkering around with the roof shingles on the garden house. We were about to take refuge under the overhang when we collided with a figure, in the slanted hatching of thick raindrops, who evidently had the same idea. It was an unusually lanky and, of course, given the period, scrawny man—a gentleman, one might say, despite the socially equalizing and also dripping clothes; so at first I assumed that one of Christa's countless relatives was dropping in. He promptly and cordially apologized for trespassing on the rubble property, but, as he explained, he had no umbrella. Oh, well, there were worse lacks in those days.

The rain lasted longer than its vehemence might have suggested it would. So Nagel, who was bored, suggested that we wait inside until it let up. The unknown gentleman accepted gratefully; we all introduced ourselves, shaking hands according to the fine German custom—with the inevitable moment of embarrassment in regard to Nagel when the stranger's hand remained hovering, unseized, until its owner realized that the right hand he had aimed for was missing and the left hand was being offered in its stead. And thus, we were finally in the drawing room, please have a seat, wherever you can, yes, may I over here, wherever you like, there are no reserved seats here, if you like we can hang your jacket on that crate over there to dry out, unfortunately I don't have an umbrella, who has an umbrella nowadays anyhow, there's no such thing anymore, it would really look funny, so you're a psychiatrist? Yes indeed, formerly professor at the University of Greifswald, you know. Paul Hertzog's the name, Hertzog with "tz," please, then, of course, I practiced at the various war theaters. Shocks, yes? Traumatic neuroses, and so on, that's right, I couldn't imagine this kind of research could be done in the Third Reich, and at Greifswald, to boot, right? But weren't the mentally ill simply done away with by euthanasia? A few, of course, regrettably, but still fairly late and depending on the war situation; however, research as such did not stop altogether, by any means— Eventually, Herr Professor Hertzog with "tz" got a beet schnapps and a cigarette made with Christa's home-grown tobacco, many thanks, but I think I have my own somewhere, no, go ahead, it's not Virginia of course, you're much too kind, no, I can't roll them, I'd rather you did it for me, you see, manually I'm awfully clumsy, why you're amazing, with only one hand—here you are, you've got to do your own licking, research you say? Yes indeed—Herr Professor Hertzog spoke very interestingly about the foundations and objectives of psychiatric research during the Third Reich, Nagel threw in Freud, yes, now, of course the man hasn't been credited highly enough for what he did, but—well, everyone knows that Freud isn't everything, C. G. Jung, now that's a little closer to the bone

In short, it ended with Professor Hertzog's unshakable assertion that man has an innate and irrepressible need for religion, no doubt about it, one can demonstrate it scientifically, certain mental disturbances can even be diagnosed indisputably as deficiency syndromes in this respect, mental scurvy, as it were, faith hits it like lemon juice, I'm speaking to laymen here of course, professionally I would put it differently, oh please don't go out of your way, these are issues we're all very interested in, by the way, if you'd like another, we brew it ourselves, you know, yes, thank you very much, it's damn strong, but the effect is all the more Dionysian, you see how you quite unconsciously keep bringing up supernatural things; as I've said, mental needs can be no more impunitively suppressed than physical ones, there's a wide-open field here, especially for social psychology. But this is a nice coincidence. You see, we've been discussing this for several weeks now with a couple of friends, more in political terms, why that goes without saying, it is a highly political problem, indeed, just look: your class-stratified state is conceivable only on the basis of the patriarchal principle, without the notion of God as the most fatherly father there can be no bourgeois social structure, naturally not, but that proves precisely what I'm saying: the need for religion is natural and innate in man, just like, say, the sexual drive, and Freud showed us what happens if you suppress it, well, and rationalism is simply the other repression, just tell our friends that, why it's obvious, we saw it in the Russians with our own eyes, despite a quarter century of Communism those people keep swarming into the churches, well, the war machine functioned there for completely different reasons, you can't do without psychology even here, which is what rigid materialism would like you to do, isn't it, incidentally Stalin is also a father, and *what* a father, and you can't say the Russians have a truly classless society, on the contrary, the Kremlin elite has distinctly aristocratic features, granted, not on the outside, no, there's absolutely no way you can claim that, hahaha, but Moscow's betraying Communism in many ways, and the point is: how does a classless society establish its own notion of God, yes, the process must be reversed, first alter the notion of God, then establish the appropriate state, perhaps matriarchal, why not, I tell you, it's the theologians who are at fault here, so listen, just drop by in the evening, then we can thrash this out with our friends, I'd love to, why not, it would interest me no end, you seldom come into contact with open minds, especially in young people, well, we're not all that young, alas, but that makes no difference, you're as young as you feel, so do come by anyway if you have nothing better to do, I couldn't imagine anything better, certainly not nowadays, well really. . . .

He came. Not right away, to be sure. Cunningly, he waited until winter. But then, the green-camouflaged months soon passed. Nevertheless, Nagel was in a bad mood. He evidently expected Professor Hertzog with "tz" to reconstruct his *Weltanschauung*, which had got considerably out of joint since the encounter with GOD the Father.

Until then, it was solidly founded on Darwin; Marx and Engels were firmly joined on top; and Nagel had even managed to insert the seductive Nietzsche seamlessly and to glue in Freud. But since that encounter with GOD the Father in the steel tempest of the war, his ideological edifice was stretched thin as though by bomb suction, "puffed through," as the rubble-dwellers put it in their jargon; and his gruffness in discussions bore witness to the awful draftiness in his spiritual home. Whenever I felt like teasing him (no one could so easily and ludicrously be made to fly off the handle as Nagel), I would advise him in case of intellectual inclemency to appeal to the man who had a need for religion as ardent as a need for an umbrella. Where was he anyway? Karl Nagel would instantly get mad as a hornet.

However, when winter came, so did Hertzog. A downright epiphany. Since last we'd met, he had joined the resurrected university as a fully tenured professor and senior registrar of its neuropathological hospital, thus appearing among us whipper-snappers with a corresponding authority as a complete human being and scientist. Not only that, but he had succeeded in convincing the military government of the occupation forces that he had heroically resisted the euthanasia of five patients—members of the Nazi Party. And true virtue is rewarded even by victorious armies. Thus, he came as a father: bringing along a bottle of real schnapps and two packs of English cigarettes. Santa Claus in person. In his sack of goodies he even had a "paper" down cold (not written, needless to say, though evil tongues maintained later that he had submitted it as a post-doctoral dissertation at the university). He carried the ideas in his head. He had only to open the mouth-trap lower down and the ideas, marvelously formulated in a gentle baritone, ran out. Every sentence demonstrated how conscientiously he had worked through the subject matter. It had become so air- and water-tight that there was little we could do but listen. The topic was obvious. Subsequently, it appeared in countless versions, variations, combinations, in many, many domestic and foreign journals and reviews and just plain magazines, thereby acquiring worldwide fame. Naturally, of these publications, only the popular-science ones are accessible to me, those where the multi-expert, who communicates with colleagues in a kind of Freemason's secret code, speaks to the layman as though to a feeble-minded illiterate. And if I remember correctly, these articles are crowned with titles like "Faith and Psyche," or "Mental Illness and the Bonds of Religion," or "The Psychiatrist as a Christian Minister," or even "Savior vs. Salvation in the Mental Clinic." But I may be mistaken. For our little group, at any rate, which he seemed to regard, flatteringly but alas wrongly, as the nucleus of the postwar German political elite, the contents of his paper were framed in the title "The Need for God as a Principle for Forming the State."

One must not overestimate the effect of Hertzog's speeches and writings on subsequent German intellectual life. And even less on political life. He merely served as an alibi. Every conjurer knows the term "misdirection": a diversionary tactic that, at the decisive moment, shifts the audience's attention from the fingers about to perform the actual sleight-of-hand. Postwar German development used Professor Hertzog in this way and got along without any actual reference to his ideas. And he was not alone in this respect: the generous occupation-supported interregnum of intellectuals in Germany from 1945 to 1948 (*Kultur, Kultur über Alles*) was a happy but politically disastrous period.

Nevertheless, Hertzog is pretty much the only one of the then princes of the mind whose head (or mental balls) was not sliced off by the currency cut. His academic career remains unflaggingly on the zenith. As does the size of his clientele. He is a shining light at all kinds of national and international congresses—that clever fellow who effortlessly manages to reconcile humanism and technology, Plato and Lenin, Freud and Saint Paul (plus Picasso and Michelangelo, Proust, Joyce, the Bauhaus, Apollinaire, Salvador Dali, Rilke, Alban Berg, Dada, Nijinski, Herbert von Karajan, and, over and over again, Karl Nagel—for, needless to say, he's also keenly interested in the arts). No doubt about it, this is a bravura performance, and indeed one of high symbolic content, if one understands that only a psychiatrist could succeed in pulling it off.

But I digress, and indeed far beyond that wintertide that left so much melancholy yearning in my mind. What I wanted to talk about is the weather: the bitter-cold winter weather during that period, and the hallowed hours in Nagel's garden house. With Hertzog, they openly acquired the character of a divine service.

To be sure, we first had to go through a brief and occasionally stormy process of fermentation.

This was due not just to the topic of the "discussion evenings," as our once disorderly, beet-schnapps-fired palavers were now suddenly known. The chief cause was that we now *had* a topic. Earlier, you see, we had jumped erratically from one subject to another—with the rough directness that set the tone in those days. The vocable "shit," now vivaciously circulating again, was in great favor before the currency reform. But the rough exterior concealed a heart of gold: an almost childlike openness of minds and feelings. We talked about anything "that came up"—and so many things came up, because everything was new as in childhood. From the flat Ptolemaic world, the world had emerged band-box fresh. "The phoenix," said Nagel, who was already tending toward complex metaphors, "naturally knows, like any magician, the most dazzling way to perform his feat: on a *tabula rasa.*" If only he had known then how right he would be at the currency cut!

Anyway, we talked about whatever crossed our minds, and in greatest detail, of course, about the things that were truly new in our lives. Christa, for instance, harped incessantly on the food shortage, Nagel on God, the rest of us on the preparation of beet schnapps and the American short story, nuclear fission and its possible consequences, existential philosophy, the Anglo-Saxons, Russians, and French and their behavior during and after the war, radio programs ("The Cultural Word"), diverse treatments for the clap, the possibility of attaining higher caloric values by inserting rabbits into the consumption process of cabbage. And over and over again, needless to say, Germany's present and future. With Hertzog, however, this higgledy-piggledy hodgepodge was sieved for so-called *cardinal questions.* And these, in turn, had to be systematically analyzed. The key factor derived from the gap that our unslaked need for religion had sucked out of the world of experience. In terms of a working hypothesis, it was initially most suitable to fill that gap with Jesus Christ.

In the presence of an epistemological stopgap with such lofty moral prestige, we soon stopped laughing (our earlier laughter had been grim, but frequent). Now, I do not mean to claim that our conversations (or rather now: debates) therefore became duller. The chief pleasure had always been the thinking itself—however informal, even innocent (childlike, you see): a kind of intellectual game of tag for letting off steam until you got tired; there was no meaning, much less purpose, to it. But now it became a sport, indeed a club sport under rigid leadership, a competitive sport. Sports, too, are pleasurable—a competitive sport, to be sure, is a strenuous pleasure, achieved sometimes at the cost of a good mood. And, in contrast to tag, a bit abstract.

Hence (and also because the son of God had so dominatingly turned into a gymnastics trainer), a few of our buddies left the group—regrettably, not the worst ones. But those who stayed made it a point of honor to show that the missing ones were missing something quite extraordinary.

And indeed: experiencing Hertzog in these discussions *was* something quite extraordinary. He came with better and better schnapps and more and more English cigarettes, and at first he acted very loose, equal among equals, a *primus inter pares* by sheer chance, yet incredibly cheerful, rubbing his hands spiritually, as it were, at the joyous prospect of a good, juicy conversation, a real roast goose of a debate, nicely stuffed with apples and chestnuts and cloves. He cheered the small community (which, for its part, was keen on the intellectual skeleton of the goose) with parish-priest-like jokes. (Some of them were quite daring. For instance, I remember one about a patient who is in the habit of running around with his forefinger up his arse because he imagines he's got a bee inside that might fly out at some embarrassing moment; he's promised he'll be cured; he's anesthetized; a huge cloth bee from a toy store is placed on his bed, and when he awakes, he's told that the bee has been removed from his body and he doesn't have to worry anymore about its slipping out at the opera or at his father-in-law's funeral; the patient thanks the staff exuberantly, but then he promptly rams his finger back up his arse because he's scared the bee will fly in again, haha-haha!).

At this point, however, Herr Professor Hertzog switched over from humor to popular-scientific seriousness; he explained that the anecdote had a kernel worthy of study: you see, the little flimflam of the alleged surgery on the crazy patient (for supposedly removing the bee from his arsehole) was an ancient and utterly wise medical custom, a tried-and-tested therapeutic method of shamans: a casting out of the devil, a feigned exorcism; psychosomatic medicine has established the mental and spiritual origin of many organic illnesses; we still have to clarify whether and to what extent such disturbances cannot sometimes be traced to a genuine state of possession—that is to say, whether the actual psychological nidus did not derive solely from a self-created malfunction of the mental and spiritual mechanism (which until now has been pictured rather too mechanistically), or whether something from *outside*—let us quite undauntedly use the popular term for it, a *demonic power*—takes control of a man's mind and soul. As far as many neuroses and psychoses were concerned, he, Hertzog with "tz," believed, on the basis of his rich practice and with a likelihood verging on certainty, he could maintain that, with a surprising number of cases, which provided ample food for thought, such an assumption could not be brushed aside.

In short: today we make do with the meagerly few notions with which the psychology of the Freudian school operates—you know, "superego" and "ego" and "id" plus "libido" and "death instinct" and so on—but we cannot manage solely with them, in many cases they simply "just don't make it," as you would probably phrase it, unscientifically but accurately, the concept of "physis," for instance, the inherent human drive to develop upward (i.e., our innate striving for sublimity, truth, goodness, nobility, beauty, you know) has always been shrouded in mystical twilight, there is some sort of superhuman, if not supernatural, force obtaining here, hence the superego should not be regarded purely as a product of the milieu, it is not merely the cane of the father and similar authority figures that creates and stamps the ethical elements in our souls, no, no, by no means: quite undeniably, there is something else beyond them, a—I shall come out with it plainly—a spirit poured into us (well, it's Whitsuntide, I ween, when Nature gets so very green), why shouldn't the id, which gains such a destructive upper hand in case of the malfunction or nonfunction of the ego, which deals with the reality principle, and of the superordinate and controlling superego—why should id consist of more or less repressed drives and not quite objectively—*materially!*—also contain something that opposes that very *physis*, that urge for upward development, for both ethical and aesthetic perfection? Yes indeed, why not truly? If one assumes the one as existing and thus as the acknowledged good, then in and of itself it already presumes its correlative opposite, does it not? *How*ever: we are speaking about medical phenomena here, so if I use words like "good" or "evil," then I am applying these concepts much as, say, an electrician employs the terms "positive" and "negative"—I mean, not as value judgments but merely as *termini technici* of a polarity that exists purely and simply, so do not believe, ladies and gentlemen, that we men of science would ever give up our fundamental impartiality, oh no, absolutely not, to a certain degree we even feel compelled to integrate the concept of disease into a universally framed process of life, after all, disturbance, destruction, death, demolition are part of the overall *bios*, one must take into account the constant renewal of Creation, it is, alas, not thinkable without the steady decay of life—however, as far as the above-mentioned neuroses and psychoses are concerned, we can (although the former, the neuroses, have already been recognized as defense mechanisms, febrile conditions of the soul, as it were, issuing in fact from a recovery tendency)—we can thus establish a good number of illnesses that are traceable to conflicts of faith or to an unsatisfied need for faith. All manner of traumatic leftovers, residues of old religious conceptions in the superego, which are now being thwarted by an attempted adjustment to a godless reality, are almost more destructive than a need for religious attachment; like everything else in God's world (inconceivable without the correlative of the devil), faith, too, has two sides: a positive, health-preserving, healing side, and, under certain circumstances, a negative, health-imperiling, destructive side as well—if, for simplicity's sake, we do not just say a *salvational* side and a side *twisting into the demonic.* . . . After all, the *praxis* of therapy has shown that even in cases in which religious motives could not be directly established as morbific agents, a cautious guidance to the experience of faith managed to bring excellent results; and whenever one could speak of a true state of possession, the results were magnificent, and nothing else could help but the correlative antidote, like the homeopathic principle *simili curant similes*. The demonic, you see, can be tackled with neither medicaments nor scalpels, although neurosurgery has made considerable advances thanks to the experiences gathered during the war in an agreeably large number of brain injuries; and modern pharmacology, which originated in alchemy, is now developing specifics that have an amazing and profound effect on the psyche—but here, in particular, extreme caution is advised, we shall have to observe very closely the effects of these on many, many patients. . . . In short, in his discipline—namely in the task of taking patients who tweet like canaries and leading them back to vital harmony—the most proven remedy has turned out on occasion—naturally, on the basis of a diagnosis founded on a psychological analysis attached to the previous thorough examination of the physical state of health of the patient—(my ears itched: I lost three precious minutes yielding to the temptation of checking the grammatical construction of the clause)—I (Hertzog was saying) have, as I have said, determined that careful and skillful guidance to new religious contents has turned out to be a proven method—but I already said that—as I have said: it has turned out that such guidance to new religious content and thus to a new religious experience constitutes an effective therapy in regard to mental-spiritual disorders—

Period. Paragraph. A chance to clear one's throat. Could I possibly interest you in another drop of, no, well please, really, many hearty—the schnapps is excellent, by the way (schnapps, you fool, this is real scotch!)—anyway, as I have said, let us establish that when I utilize the concept of vital harmony—right?—then I do so from my point of view as a physician, after all, I am no lay preacher, I stick mostly to the relationship between body and soul, the good old saying *mens sana in corpore sano* must be understood as a reciprocal relationship: a sound soul also determines the physical well-being of the patient, as you know, we are now speaking of religion as a need of the healthy soul, but nevertheless its ambivalence still exists so far as I am concerned—I mean: the immanent double-poled need, which is termed by the working hypothesis as both "positive" and "negative," right? Thus, we know religion can heal, but it can also lead to critical spiritual crises, states of hysteria, and the like; we must reckon with that, too, and thus we have to deal with the task of manipulating the bivalent notion with utmost caution, we shall thus find it now speaking for our hypothesis, now against it, and this is fully in keeping with the Marxian (originally, of course, Hegelian) dialectical method: analysis, thesis, antithesis, synthesis—right? Incidentally, this is at heart merely the ancient religious view of the polarity of Being—light and darkness, God and devil, good and evil—simply good old dualism, spirit and matter, faith and knowledge, subject and object, this world and the next world, physical necessity and freedom, and so forth, and so on; nothing but conceptual pairs designating the coexistence of two diverse and ununifiable states, principles, modes of thinking, kinds of *Weltanschauung*, tendencies of will, epistemological axioms— and in intellectual history also the polarity of life and death, which is something idealism wants to overcome, you know, although it did not quite succeed, of great interest for psychology in this context are, of course, the teachings of Mach; the history of philosophy, alas, grants German positivism merely a subordinate role, but let us not forge too deeply into philosophy, we'll leave that for later, we'll have very different problems to resolve, the present-day intellectual situation simply demands a new theology, volunteers take a step forward! Germans to the front! We have an enormous mission precisely because of our defeat, but back to vital harmony: the equilibrium between opposites, the resolution of contradictions must be achieved, that is the definition of health: Yin-Yang, Easter tolling of bells, purely materialistic health, that is: conception of life, I mean: exclusively rational thinking excludes the world of emotions, which is rooted deep in the spiritual, and without that world man is inconceivable—or rather, conceivable, yes, but merely as an imperfect human being, a cripple, a mental amputee, our friend Nagel will agree with me here especially since he is an artist; the highest, most valuable expression of the equilibrium of mind and soul, as produced felicitously from tensions of opposites, is art, of course—and art, as a predominantly irrational expression of life (which Karl Marx personally foresaw, after all), is irreconcilable with materialistic thinking; it may be achievable in the gaps of the system but is actually an expression of resistance: metaphysical emigration, so to speak—

a short, nervous clearing of the throat because no one has caught the joke (and how can you tell what is meant to be funny? Extreme caution is advisable: you might laugh at the wrong place, it's better to hold back, an attentive smile always looks good on a listener, nothing can happen to you, at worst your facial muscles freeze). . . .

Hertzog, challenged by failure, now puts his shoulder to the wheel. The notion of health has been clarified, so let's go back to disease, to document what I have said let me give you a few examples—a merry Mardi Gras procession of all kinds of neurosis is drawn up; now it's really hard not to laugh, hilarious all these kinds of lunacy, things get quite wild, and Hertzog realizes it: he soon whistles the neuropathic clowns away and leads us into the real horror chambers of psychiatry, here even the attentive smile is no longer appropriate, so stiffen the corners of your mouth, look at the floor, earnestly but attentively (the ludicrous footwear of the discussion-group members offers diversion), pull yourself together, damn it! Let us concentrate with ethical frowns on the graphically described cases, tut-tut-tut, the things that exist in the world, it's like Hieronymus Bosch, a finger up the arse (Hertzog says "anus," of course) seems like sheer grace in contrast, Botticelli, so to speak—but Hertzog does not wish to be cruel: I feel like Raphael, who, as we know, refused to paint a martyr (even the experts will have a hard time finding the Nietzsche quotation in so much subtlety), so I'll spare you far more dreadful cases (which is too bad: when you read the church fathers of depth psychology, those cases are the most interesting), which cannot be helped by any focus on the experience of faith, alas! Now you will probably say: how can there be such terrible deformations of the human mind? Yes indeed, how? Some most likely have organic roots; schizophrenia, for example, may have something to do with the chemistry of the brain cells, and manic-depressive psychosis may be connected to the glands, this is unfortunately a rather unresearched area, offering science many fascinating problems, psychosurgery, as I have said, is making tempestuous progress, let me just mention in passing the slicing of certain nerve fibers in the brain, which procedure often turns out to be highly beneficial for some patients who have suffered from incurable states of agitation and depression, for the first time in years they now can leave the hospital and lead a more or less normal life, at times, to be sure, they are a bit irresponsible and carefree and must therefore remain under close surveillance to avoid their doing anything disastrous to themselves or others, in some cases the cure seems worse than the illness to their near and dear, but you don't have to worry about that for the moment, thank you ever so much, that's our problem, I mean for us medicine men— the point here and now, today, in our first discussion evening, which I so heartily welcome, is to establish that neuroses and psychoses are increasing at a terrifying speed; the further our civilization moves away from nature and its compelling givens, the more acute the danger grows for everyone—yes indeed, for practically everyone!—just think of America, where the percentage of mentally disturbed people in official statistics is frightening, just think of the high suicide rate in Scandinavia, the higher the level of civilization, the more dubious the whole business becomes, the question naturally arises whether the unspirituality of this civilization, its absolute rationalism, its narrower and narrower restriction on any possibility of providing a valve for our natural drives—whether, as I have said, this mind-and-soul-strangulating world, in which mankind believes it can erect an earthly paradise in materialism, may not be one of the causes for the obvious loss of vital harmony. He, the philosopher Hertzog, believes that he can decisively affirm this and he would take the liberty of maintaining (and demonstrating!) that faith—yes?—the attachment of human existence to a transcendental object, is an inexplicable factor in this vital harmony, which must constantly be striven for— ladies and gentlemen, just listen to language, that treasure trove of human wisdom: "Savior"—this word comes from "save," Latin *salus*, health, as in "salvation" (a new humoristic swerve, surprising here): As a psychiatrist, I construed *"Heil Hitler"* as a chal-

lenge to heal rather than to hail him, unfortunately I was not offered a chance to put this into practice, hahahahaha! This jest finally catches on, and how! After a tour through the hell of
psychiatry and the apocalyptic visions of a world tenanted more
and more densely by psychopaths, the joke has a wonderfully liberating impact, and Nagel's arm stump evinces a reflexive attempt at banging his missing hand on the missing knee of the man
next to him). Joking aside: if we wish to get to the bottom of the
causes (and we must), we won't get any further, as I said initially, with psychoanalysis and so forth, Freud is simply too nineteenth century, this has got around even in professional circles, he
is tainted by the individualism of the era, but even those colleagues who are now finally starting to deal with the relationship
of the individual to society, to the collective, and, beyond that, to
collective life itself, shrink back from the final simple step: admitting that the soul of humanity cannot be separated from the connection with the notion of the Godly—

an instant of effective silence, the voice fading toward a dying
fall:

Western Civilization, my friends, is experiencing itself as a
moribund culture. Observers can actually pinpoint symptoms of
a serious ailment. The question arises whether a transformed, renewed religious experience might lead to a cure even in such a
vast general framework—

(lively once again): But here we have come to the topic of the
evening! . . .

☐   ☐   ☐

> But woe to them that are with child, and to them that
> give suck in those days! And pray ye that their flight be
> not in the winter.
>
> MARK 13:17–18

Christa meanwhile lay abed in the villa and pouted. I must unfortunately say: with good reason.

I did creep regularly to her bed to give her the most precise reports on all our adventures (including the intellectual ones) and to seek solace with her when Nagel surrendered all too ardently to Hertzog's ideology and now generally betrayed the tender poetry of buddyship in many ways. Nor did I hold back with all kinds of tenderness, affectionate teasing, and so forth: after all, I loved her very much, if I remember correctly, very physically; it may be that I am now confusing that with the memory of other and similarly ephemeral happiness brought by erotic possession, but in any case it is one of the good deeds of life that have settled as soothing matter in my consciousness, however dearly they may have cost me—

back then, at any rate, her girlish fragrance, her soft, round flesh, and the warmth of her blond skin made up the capital in my emotional household, and I used the interest to make up for my disappointment with Nagel.

Perhaps I should have told her this at some point; she probably didn't know, though could, of course, have noticed it. Especially when she was expecting a child, I was simply entranced with her, placed my head on her belly, already taking on the milky bloatedness of motherhood, asked her to hold her breath, and I listened, trying to catch my son's heartbeat—the little boy who would trustingly grow up holding my hand and then mirthfully striding toward life, to which I would release him—a sunny life that we upright survivors of the wintertide would have set up for him, perhaps in the city of mankind ANTHROPOLIS. . . .

Naturally, there was nothing to hear but the growling of her empty stomach, but I loved her all the same, and even though all she had to say to my early-paternal ardor was that I had unpleasantly cold ears (she had received the news of her pregnancy not, like me, in a worshipful crèche mood but rather with an annoyed, despairing "That's all I needed!")—she's simply a rather dry person, that Christa, and even her poetry is ultimately her touchiness.

Incidentally, she didn't spend the entire period in bed, of course, merely the bulk of it, including daytime. This bulk was the time I spent with Nagel & Associates. And just what else could I have done in those days, when even the angels were frozen to the earth and the nearest basement movie was a twenty-minute hike away? . . . There wasn't much housekeeping to do. I cooked when there was something to cook, cleaned up the two rooms we lived in, pretty much the only livable ones in the villa on the Elbchaussee. It was bitterly cold, after all, and wood and coal were scarce; Christa saved them for the visits by her countless friends and relatives, the scattered blossoms of East Elbe Junker flora that the polar wind blew our way.

During such visits, Christa had every opportunity to demonstrate how proficient she was in bearing her sorrow in a simple, ladylike fashion. If I was introduced to the droppers-in, they communicated with her by means of a glance. Stateless, eh? What was the father? Unknown. I see. . . . They forwent the shrug with which I was taken as a phenomenon of the times. The conversation then continued in a brittle, piss-elegantly booted and spurred class jargon, as though it had not been interrupted; my offer to have a sip of our beet schnapps was declined with thanks. I took the hint and soon left the like-minded alone. For Christa, however, these were pretty much the only events in our sad life. She had probably had different expectations in her heart when marrying me. She had viewed me as John's protégé, the foreigner and almost ally, the PX-rations recipient and travel-order passenger—

no wonder she retreated and preferred seeing the winter through in her bed.

But when I crept to her, there was closeness again, other skin, flesh warmth, intimacy. We still had things to tell about ourselves; we exchanged the tinsel life treasures of childhood memories. Christa sometimes chatted very sweetly about her childhood in East Prussia: very clear weather again, a very blue sky, a very anacreontic nature, a huge estate household, golden fields of grain and darkly wooded lakes, at night the mighty copper beeches soughing over the gentle fireworks of the glowworms in the park. A rather eccentric mother, who had broken her neck in 1939 while jumping over a ditch (on horseback, of course), an elegant patriarchal portrait of a father, who had been strung up in 1944 as a hero of the resistance, both parents very much alive in her memory. A flock of brothers and sisters with quaint traits of character; neighbors and relatives had saved her from being arrested for guilt by kinship and thrown in a concentration camp: nocturnal cross-country escape on horseback (the roads were watched), two months hidden in the hay of a barn (not without its humorous episodes), soon the all-out chaos began anyway, the refugee trek to Mecklenburg, finally an underground existence in Hamburg, waiting for the end.

A childhood book. I soon knew it by heart. Nagel's stories were a lot more zesty, more anecdotal, blossomed in tropical gaudiness from the *à propos* of conversation. No step-by-step here on girlish feet; these stories leaped about daringly and surprisingly, sovereignly disconnected, held together purely by a keen eye, toppling over into more and more configurations, like the prismatically reflected picture elements in a kaleidoscope.

What Christa told me was the beginning of a novel, with the glassy brittleness of Fontane's idylls, and a tempest of Tolstoyan drama about to discharge over it. Very attractive, no doubt, very gripping, but fragmentary, the opus bogged down in the far too broad beginning, the main character never got beyond the initial stage of development, the sense of events rumbled behind the scenes like stage thunder, many things went up in flames, and stormy sheet lightning flashed over graves and execution sites, but the heroine lay abed and pouted because there were no more county horse shows and no more balls given by the Association of German Aristocracy, gone with the East Prussian wind.

Nagel, in contrast—yes, Nagel!—picked up the splinters and assembled a colorful mosaic of "reality," charged to the farthest point with the mood of a thunderstorm. No thread was needed to string together the higgledy-piggledy characters, settings, themes; the drama behind them set forth the situations, put them in order, arranged them. Any humor only made it more sinister. Any sublimity quickly revealed the dreadful bathos of banality—

But from the barbarism, poetry proliferated like bindweed. Bindweed is not a civilized plant (whatever one may say); it blooms and thrives best in rubble fields and steppes. . . .

For Nagel was writing now. He had always planned to write and was bursting with accumulated material: the things he had seen, gone through, made up. He was working on several projects at once: various short stories, a play, and even the draft of a novel.

Our friendship, which had suffered because of Hertzog and the exuberant growth of the manger-shepherd circle into a discussion group, did not continue to cool, but we saw less and less of each other. He worked fiercely day and night, wrote tirelessly, using his left hand with childlike awkwardness. He did not allow us even a peep at his output. During the discussion evenings with Hertzog, he had come to know one aspect of me better than he had before. "You're too Austrian for me, damn it." I was orphaned.

During this period, the thrifty bitterness began to appear in Christa's mouth, ultimately transforming the artless cupid's bow of her lips into the clasp of a mostly closed purse. I then had to guess what she was thinking. ("Nagel is at least doing something sensible with your endless chitchat.") Once, she had regarded Hertzog as a crafty and villainous customer ("He's just using you people as guinea pigs; he's just observing you and then doing something completely different with it"), but now she began to see him in a new light ("There has to be something to it if it gets Nagel to do some proper work").

Naturally, she didn't put these feelings into words, either. (In general, she was visibly less communicative; even the memories of childhood and adolescence, memories of large cakes on the coffee table under the copper beeches, and buggy rides to neighboring estates, faltered and oozed out into chilly, ladylike silence. Only later, when our little boy could listen, did those memories surge up again, and, much to my sorrow, he absorbed them more ardently than the myths I handed down to him from my various uncles on the Côte d'Azur.)

But I could tell by other signs that Christa did not view the evening get-togethers in Nagel's garden house merely as an intellectually camouflaged collective waste of time by a handful of bums, alkies, and moochers. She now barely protested when the remnants of the pool table from the half-buried den, then the cue board and the window frames vanished into Nagel's stove, followed by all the stationery with the engraved patrician address from the table where he wrote (with his left hand). Furthermore, her transient relatives and acquaintances now evinced a certain interest in my doings. ("I understand you've founded a cenacle with friends, for discussion evenings and so on. One of them even writes, I hear? I'd love to meet the man. Who publishes this kind of stuff? I mean: if ever I were to think of writing about my experiences during the escape . . .") In short, we were becoming respectable.

This was then gloriously confirmed one evening by the appearance of a gentleman whom I stubbornly called Major General Baron Waldemar von Neunteuffel, which was not his real name—I forget what it was—but in any case, he *had* been a lieutenant general or something like that, and the victorious powers had soon set him free because of his various brilliant qualities. Neunteuffel happened not to be one of Christa's relatives, or one of the many acquaintances who had been closely allied with the family for generations. But before entering the garden house, he naturally did not fail to pay his respects to her, as a man who had almost joined the resistance movement and was an admirer of her unfortunate father—"he's laying a wreath," I said, reaping Hertzog's explanation that my cynical proclivities were a symptom of a prematurely repressed infantile sexuality with subsequent masochistic tendencies.

It was Hertzog who had invited Neunteuffel. But the major general did not come alone. He brought along (presumably as a political alibi) a distinguished-looking man with a head that was full of character, whom he introduced as a "victim of Fascism." This man, a Baltic German whose name was von Rönnekamp, had, as an incorrigible homosexual, been placed in a concentration camp during the war. Incidentally, he was later to surprise me and everyone else present by saying he had discerned in me a "truly religious man in the Dostoevskian sense." Major General Baron von Neunteuffel proved to be a versatile, proficient, and—as it turned out—clear-sighted man. With his dependable, alert, and sociable character, he succeeded in loosening the awkward restraint shown toward him by several participants in the group.

Understandably enough, even though we were supposed to be establishing a truly Christian classless society, the shot-off heels under the dyed coats and battle-dress tunics of most of the men there involuntarily clicked together when confronted by the spruce civilian appearance of the major general, who had by no means lost his military air. But the women, of course, were instantly on his side. In the shattered Wehrmacht, he had been one of the youngest officers of his rank, he had garnered the Iron Cross with Oakleaf, and swords, diamonds, WACs, and crab lice, and his blue eyes radiated a zest to share in the German reconstruction, a zest with the same spunk and dash that had brought him high military distinction. So overcoming our resistance was only a matter of minutes. "A good troop leader," as Nagel said appreciatively; he did not dislike the major general but actually found him quite agreeable. Even though Nagel had got no further than the German Cross in Gold, he was treated by Baron von Neunteuffel with a certain officers'-club camaraderie; from now on, it was really a dialogue among initiates, which Hertzog as the consulting egghead could gently steer.

So, anyway, Hertzog delivered his paper: a summary of the jointly worked-out ideological principles ("I would especially like to thank—next to our friend Nagel, of course—Fräulein Ute Seelsorge for her tireless . . ."). The possibilities of practical realization under the given circumstances. Serious doubts, objections, corrections ("I do not wish to fail to express my thanks to a certain friend for his caustically humorous but often for that very reason animating insertions; in our new society, we must also make a place for an Eulenspiegel"). And many thanks for everyone's sincerely comradely cooperation, especially the ever-improving distillers of the helpful beet schnapps (hahahahaha!). Also many thanks to the detergent industrialist Witte, the true host and owner of the rubble property, who has so far been absent from our circle of friends because the all too slow denazification commission has unfortunately not yet enabled him to add the no doubt valuable intellectual contributions of an experienced industrial leader. And in general, many thanks to a kindly providence, which has preserved us from annihilation and allowed us to find one another here in these makeshift quarters, as the primal cell of a new society that far from neglecting tried-and-true human wisdom actually wishes to continue it. *Per aspera ad astra!* Let that be our motto evermore!

Bravo! Be seated! The women have already begun, at their own initiative, to embroider a club banner (unfortunately, silver yarn

is still scarce, but sperm threads will do nicely for the moment).
We thank Herr Speaker for his warm, lucid words. The new-
comer, Herr von Rönnekamp, in particular, can probably not
help being moved at the mention of so many warm, gay feelings.
With special joy, gaiety, and expectation, we now greet our guest,
Major General Baron Waldemar von Neunteuffel (stop scratching your flea bites, Fritz!)—

Major General Baron Waldemar von Neunteuffel took the floor
(took it swiftly, virtually vaulting onto it: Münchhausen on the
cannonball could not have been a defter equestrian). He said it
was hard for him to say how happy he was to be here and see one
of his oldest dreams come true: namely, to see the spirit of the future a-birthing from the rank and file (that is to say, from the
community of all, with no distinction of merit or rank). Especially you, my dear Nagel, must understand how deeply moved I
am. Congratulations with all my heart and soul for the excellent
work you have done! What particularly impresses me is the unadulterated Hegelian spirit of this enterprise; after all, without
this great Prussian philosopher, any future political formation
will be built on sand.

So, many thanks to Professor Hertzog (and of course to you,
my dear Nagel) for so to speak replanting the cross of the
knightly order in the scorched earth and for gathering the liege-
men around you in a truly chivalresque democratic way, inspir-
ing them to lay the cornerstone of the new *polis*. Equality,
fraternity, and liberty (in obeisance!) are, after all, ideals that
have both led to the triumphs of the spirit of Western Civilization
and endangered them when distorted; the most daring things are
tied to the greatest perils; anyone who truly wishes to dance must
dance on volcanoes; we are all forced to do so in the atomic age;
anyone who is not a utopian today is not a realist but a defeatist.
However, being a utopian does not mean seizing impracticable
things from the clouds and designing them into a world of
dreams; it means creating the ideal model for shaping and fash-
ioning reality. This reality is at the door; needless to say, it is
related to all tried-and-true ideals of Western Civilization.
Christianity goes without saying, socialization, too, in the widest
sense, of course; the new political formation will presumably

crystallize on a federal basis; the most important thing now is the economic reconstruction; I can tell you from a reliable source that the Allies have very specific ideas in this respect; in the long run, no one can afford a slum in the heart of Europe; there is still some resistance, but people will soon have to accept the fact that we live in the era of large-scale organisms. Germany cannot be excluded from the European orchestra; we can thus look forward to the future in this point with hope and confidence; it would, to be sure, be dreadfully optimistic to assume that this means the launching of a long era of peace; we must realize, ladies and gentlemen, that the real conflict has not yet been fought to the end; Churchill's far-reaching world-political view was not to allow the Russians to scize half of Europe, but his view was, alas, not shared by all powers; the American now confronts a *fait accompli;* the ultimate struggle will not keep us waiting for long; we Germans find ourselves in the both embarrassing and yet—for negotiations—advantageous position of being a buffer state with, one may say, the power to tip the scales; it is highly desirable that German politicians of the future remember this; I am, of course, not advocating a new German power politics; that would be lunacy, suicide; Europe must henceforth march together and strike together when it is time to strike again, God damn it. But let us very clearly visualize how this will take place: the first phase, of course, will be an atomic attack on both sides of the Iron Curtain. Here in Germany, it will presumably strike at our newly and better-built-up industrial center, the Rheinland, the Ruhr, and so on. You know, of course, that within twenty-four hours of the eruption of hostilities, by the latest, that area will be a radioactive wasteland. Now add a few more unimportant zones, for instance our beautiful Hamburg here with its hinterland, Hanover, et cetera: within the shortest possible time, the result will be total chaos and of course starvation; a situation that cannot possibly be dealt with by mere organization—different from the famine now, where the supply authorities do guarantee a certain survival minimum by means of food rationing. Well, plundering gangs and hordes will throng into the still-untouched areas, and naturally the local population will defend itself; refugees and survivors from nuclear-struck areas will be clubbed to death like stray dogs because of the feared danger of contagion and contamination: a situation worse than the Thirty Years' War. To prevent this from coming about, dear friends, we desperately require the establishment of an effectively powerful German force for maintaining order. It will naturally require utmost tact to wait for the psychologically proper moment when one can make such an institution palatable to the Germans, who have been disillusioned by any sort of military structure. But bear in mind, ladies and gentlemen, that this step will be necessary and unavoidable—

And here, the unexpected occurred; here, Nagel's crowning glory occurred. Twitching his arm stump in the empty sleeve as though trying to pound on the table with his missing fist, he suddenly blustered and shouted that he had had enough of this shit; if things developed as Herr Neunteuffel prophesied, then he hoped that he, Karl Nagel, would have found a way of emigrating to a place where it wasn't worth the trouble to use nuclear weapons, Korea or Siam or God knows where, and if he hadn't succeeded, then he would prefer plundering hordes of radium-contaminated Rheinlanders or Lower Bavarians defending their forest homeland with clubs to any powerful German force for maintaining order. He was fed up to here with all the stupid claptrap; he had more important things to do than waste his time with this chitchat, goddammit; after all, this garden house was not the bookstore at the Cologne railroad station, it was a private home, damn makeshift to be sure, but all the same— So get out, all of you! The whole goddamn bunch of you, get out!

It was fabulous. Hertzog was the only one who made an attempt, at the threshold, to remain. All he got for his trouble was the knob of the slammed door in his back. Hurrying to catch up with Major General Baron von Neunteuffel, who was hurrying toward his car, which had been approved for him by the occupation authorities, he tried to explain that poor Nagel was in the throes of a subliminal religious crisis that made him extremely irritable and also, because of an unresolved father-son attachment, tended to produce an unequilibriated gall-bladder functioning.

The rest of us stood in the starry, frost-smoky night. Herr von Rönnekamp, who seemed uncommonly stimulated by the incident, ecstatically shook hands with every last one of us, holding our hands awhile in order properly to relish each friendly gaze. Despite everything, he said, he hoped to see us again soon, talk to us, get to know us better (the hope was to come true in my case). Then, with a bulbously Baltic "One second! I'm coming!" (which foamed out of his mouth as a small gray cloudlet in the frosty night), he likewise went to the car. Fräulein Ute Seelsorge quickly joined him to see whether there wasn't room for her too. Some of us laughed. Some felt that Nagel had been quite right. One man said, "Okay, but that won't do either!" One girl was weeping silently to herself, and all of us opined that it was as cold as a witch's tit. The little group dissolved and trickled apart.

And I was proud! My shirt buttons almost popped off, I was so proud. Nagel, my friend Karl Nagel, had shown what a grand fellow he was. He had driven the moneylenders out of the temple. He had spurned the tempter. In the teeth of temptation, he had remained steadfast. He had finally, with his own hands (or rather one hand), set sail to steer his life's dream through the winter night.

Yes indeed. That's what he was like. My friend Nagel. A gruff old stick, but he had balls. I still remember his white-toothed smile in his sooty face (darkened with smoke from the stove) when he told me how he had lost his arm. Somewhere in Russia, he and a group of similar daredevils—wild fellows from a penal column who knew they were done for anyway—blasted through an encircled area. In the middle of the night, they had put on snow coats and crawled all the way to a particularly vicious nest of heavy machine guns and anti-tank guns. Nagel led the way as platoon leader. Now, the morning was coming up (he described its rosebuds on the ice with an ardor that did credit to his later full-bosomed spiritual kinship with the painter Philipp Otto Runge). The moment for attack had come. Nagel raised his arm to signal to his buddies: "Storm the nest! Get going!" But nothing happened. No one got up to storm. Only the Russians began shooting wildly, lashing the terrain with sheaves of machine-gun fire. Nagel looked around furiously for the arseholes, who were lying with their mugs in the snow. Why the hell hadn't they started running at his signal? After all, he had raised his arm—
  at this point, he glanced at his arm and didn't see it. The arm

was gone. There was no arm to give a visible signal. It had been shot clean off when he had raised it.

And so all his buddies were likewise cleanly picked off where they lay, one after another, their faces in the snow. They hadn't seen the arm that was supposed to signal the attack.

At the time, Nagel, grimly laughing, called it "a really stupid story." But I'm not sure. Today, when it comes to mind, it strikes me as dismally symbolic.

□   □   □

HOW FAR BACK, how remote this lay in time, and how present it was in my memory! . . . I could reel it off like Nagel himself: all I have to do is apply the pen and it races across the paper. Sheer delight. I write even more fluently than when I concoct delicacies for my piglets. Wohlfahrt & Associates, their snouts zealously snuffling, badger me for something they can smack their lips over: some gaudy, juicily snot-oozing subject to lure yet again some distributor threatened with bankruptcy.

("... *Well, just listen—listening?—this idea is worth its weight in gold: after all, Gloria made* Till the Last Man, *didn't it? — Did you see it? No? Well, this is the theme: a political demagogue convinces the masses of his ideas, which are actually criminal; he starts a war, and the very people who were his most enthusiastic followers, who believed that the man only wanted the best, now have to hold out until the bitter end—*Till the Last Man. . . . *It's sure to be the box-office sensation of the season. And now Victoria's keen on a topic like that, but with a more optimistic ending. The distributors say that the audiences are excited when they arrive but they're down when they leave. Victoria can't afford that—look what happened with* Till the Last Child—*you know: last phase of the war, a crazy old sergeant wants to defend a village even though it's totally useless; since all the men are away at the front, he arms the kids with bazookas, and all of them are wiped out, of course—right? Well, it turned out that audiences were expecting a silver lining of hope on the*

:: 508 ::

horizon. So after a good start in the big cities, the flick's been collapsing in the sticks after just a week. Why don't you mull it over a bit? Find the right solution for Till the Last Woman— *okay? The title itself is sexy; that'll get them to the box office. Besides, with luck even the biggest dummies will notice that it's not meant seriously—but it's supposed to be, you understand, a hard war theme, but not so hopeless; if a couple of broads get bumped off, it doesn't matter, most moviegoers are women anyway; they like it when something happens to another woman. So think it over; maybe you'll hit on something bubbly. That's up your alley, isn't it: harsh reality behind the humor—right?—I've already registered the title, you can't expect any payment for the material itself, but you'll get a nice tidy sum for the treatment, money up front is more important for you than a lot of money later on, I'm counting on a script contract for you, but let me just say this much: it's a unique opportunity, you'll be doing business with Victoria, so show us that I didn't pick the wrong man when I chose you as the writer. . . .")*

Then I'm in my element. Then I do without the handwritten stuff (what symbolism in Nagel's scribbling left hand!)—

Then I fantasize "the thing" right into the typewriter: attack the keys with nimble, forceful fingers, as if I were sitting at a Bechstein in a concert hall—and what should inhibit me here, anyway? The question of quality?

(". . . *Our industry cannot afford an artistic cinema if it is to stand on a sound financial foundation—which comes only from the box-office receipts of entertainment movies. I, as the producer, am obliged to take account of that. . . .*")—

I don't even have to ask what sense the whole thing makes. The answer is obvious: my piglets want to tap money, and some of it will be siphoned off to me—

what, then, should hold me back? my self-respect? the lamentable shred of dignity that we of the sad countenances reserve for ourselves in our work?

(to Schwab: "You needn't look up with such dichotomous embarrassment from your laundry—I know perfectly well what you're thinking: that it's despicable of me to do this sort of thing, yet that you can't ignore *the fact I can do it,* can bring myself to do it and not give a damn. Isn't that what you're thinking? . . . Irrefutable proof of the cynic's energy: I can get away with it. . . .")

what in the name of all that's holy would get in my way? my intellectual honesty? the certainty that I am deceiving?

whom?—and of what? . . .

Just reach into the throes of human life! The teeming of maggots all around. Into Hertzog's Divine World and Neunteuffel's New Reality, into the roaring torrent of traffic participants and roadside-café people—what does reality look like in their brains?

A vortex of images, no doubt. A boiling noise-gruel. A flickering chaos of momentary impressions, diaphragm sensations:

Incident-fragments happening-tatters event-slivers occurrence-splinters—bubbling up and away in the effervescence of ceaseless and ubiquitous occurrence, the total superreality of illustrated magazines—involuntarily captured dissipated perceived interrupted chopped-up ripped-up spliced-up throttled voluntarily jumbled-up incoherently superimposed like the trailer to a film that is never screened in its correct and meaningful sequence.

A day of the white maggot—how does it wear by? what is it like?—a torturous everyday spawn each morning:

Alarmclock-buzzing-terror-second, everlasting and as explosive as an atomic bomb:

Dream-world demolition, dream-reality annihilation. Collapse of the logic of the multidimensional. Solutionless abruption of all events, identity-loss, guilt-feeling for things not taken care of, frustration of non-coping—

Existential panic: tightening dimension-narrowing, powerlessness, primal sense of forlornness, angst, anguish, menace

Irruption of the outer world into the shredded inner world irruption of time into the timelessness of physicality into the world of gravity-defying nonphysicality space-confinement irruption of what is rigidly established into what is arbitrarily alterable exchangeable penetrable irruption of banal design of multiple experience into sovereignly unprecedented unique unheard-of

Reluctant renunciation of the freedom of unreality the uncommittedness of ungrammaticalness helpless striving against being moved by the merciless causality of factualness fragile clutching at melting dream-formations a sense of being swindled humiliation of vulnerability degradation of coarsening

Fettering to the physical: mass load inertia bulk: hard things sharp-edged things hostile things—

Resistance to pain as a mediator of reality, defense, arousal of aggressiveness

Rediscovery of the physical sense of self: self-member-stiffness self-urinary-urgency self-arrogant-morning-erection self-bad-taste-in-mouth self-breath self-warmth self-smell

Gathering, finding one's bearings, getting it all together: mosaic-like reconstruction of the human being who dissolves in sleep every night, mosaic-like reconstruction of the world of facts which is demolished nightly, blurry and bleary, partially snuffed—

Arduous pulling-oneself-together to cope with existence

Everyday treadmill of propitiating the trivial physicality pissing, shitting, hawking, coughing, throat-clearing—spitting, swallowing—

Reluctant civilization-ceremony: teeth-brushing, gargling, washing, shaving, combing—

Meanwhile: recapitulation of existential provisos, necessities, duties

Recourse to history: the hardships successes triumphs defeats humiliations satisfactions of yesterday the day before yesterday and the day before that; transmission of expectations hopes disappointments prospects anxieties coercions into today—

And thus: ordering of reality into the effable, the articulable, the verbally expressible, the grammatical, the chronological. Anything that cannot be said can no longer be part of reality, is pushed under the threshold of consciousness, pads existence with congestions of malaise, defense, anxiety, pleasure, pleasure-quests, pleasure-defense-impulses

From now on this reality seems to take place linearly, in the movement of time, steered by more or less conditioned reflexes and in tension and tension-release, kept vibrating by more or less unchecked affects: as a glimmering, glittering chaos crisscrossed by the meteorites of chance, a uniform three-hundred-sixty-five-day reiteration, constantly changing

Irruption of everyday life with the urgency of necessity, of duty, of time: racing with the clock, with the quota, with the demands of the drives, of forced goals. Cowering under the volley of requests, requirements, requisitions from the other—wife child parent sibling friend

neighbor colleague superior subaltern contemporary compatriot coreli-
gionist party-comrade fellow-man hated loved feared honored des-
pised—flight into the chaos of teeming masses, anonymity as the ulti-
mate refuge of self-awareness, isolation in protective shells—the suit
the car the office the company the union the after-work pub
the club the party the creed the nation. Personality shells. Cell exis-
tence. Monad in the aggregate of monads. Maggot in the maggot-
teeming of a continuous disintegration process—then suddenly unex-
pectedly: the randomness of event

. . . this jerk runs across the street and the light's still yellow—
crash! he's flopped over a car hood: screeching brakes delayed reac-
tion thud (Jesus! Did I pay my last insurance premium? . . .) Hey,
watch it! Watch it yourself, you're behind me, don't tailgate me, I'm
not, give me your insurance number, it's only a slight dent, yeah but
my car's in the garage for the weekend my wife's gone off to visit her
brother-in-law, what's wrong up front there anyway? windshield debris
on the asphalt, an indolently winding trail of blood—goddamnit, the
poor bastard really got it, why that's illegal, crossing when the light's
still yellow—and the way the pedestrians mob the scene, like flies
around shit . . . well, we're in for it now, the road'll be backed up for at
least a quarter of a mile: cops signals whistles yellow-lights siren
squad-car ambulance: they're shoving him in like a loaf of dough into
an oven—is he dead already? And I'm going to be late to work, that's
life. . . .

(And these are the brothers I'm writing for.)

And yet how do they feel that they've lived through this life?
How does it present itself to them in that other dimension, which,
so to speak, races alongside reality in parallel vibrations and
against reality in the amplitudes: always one step ahead of reality,
a step of hope, of expectation, of preconception? Always one step
behind, a step of transfiguration, of dramatization, of twisting
things aright?

How do they experience this fleeting, flickering, monotonous
chaos in their wishful notions, their daydreams, their deceptions,
their obsessions? How do they rationalize it in their figments,
lies, solaces, euphemisms, distortions?

Ultimately as a meaningful order? As a dramatic, dynamic
course of events that always correspond to some idea, always

pursue, or at least bring about, a specific purpose. Thus are always identifiable as a series of causes and effects?

—as if the events that charged down upon us chaotically could be broken down into individual components from amongst which we need only select those that can be threaded in a narratable chronicle and strung on the guideline of a learned notion of life—threaded and strung according to a completely arbitrary event-value that we have established—

whereby we would experience our lives as (hi)story: a florilegium of episodes that, containing literary elements, are culled from the wealth of occurrences and carefully cleaned of all the weeds of anything casual, undramatic, or dramatically inconsistent or superfluous:

so that the episodes are ultimately threaded into a novellike garland of anecdotes, stories, epics, rhapsodies, comedies, tragedies, woven into compellingly thickened peripeteias and rhythmical arses and theses, to be boaed around the person of the I and form his myth—

Even the maggots use the literary in order to overcome the chaos. Even they live literarily—

and I'm supposed to make the devising of tales a matter of conscience?!

So, carefree, I attack the keys of my typewriter: my piglets want a story that reads both simply and grippingly, an adventurous, entertaining, and yet meaningful reality, so that even the distributors will be carried away and actually understand what it's all about

(a story that can be told in three sentences)

at your service:

Till the Last Woman

Berlin, April 1945:

The roomers in a boardinghouse, which is actually a front for a whorehouse under the experienced direction of the owner (Kitty Schmidt), look forward to the arrival of the Russians and the expected surplus of vodka, cigarettes, money, and food period end of the first sentence

In the basement, honorable people have hidden, and the girls, seeking protection from the shelling, witness the rape of a mother-to-be by drunken soldiers, whereby the mother-to-be kicks the bucket period end of the second sentence

This affects them so profoundly that they resolve to give themselves freely wherever a decent woman is threatened semicolon they thus sacrifice themselves each in turn M-dash *till the last woman* colon Kitty Schmidt herself, who at first opposed this sacrificial effort by her girls third and last period end of story

This I can write. With virtuoso life-interpreting fingers, I hammer away at the keyboard of the little Olivetti Lettera. Nothing inhibits me.

this stuff won't get in front of the camera anyway. It is merely spirited out of thin air and laid into thinner air—as a cornerstone for the cloud-cuckoo-home that is known in the piglets' lingo as a "project" or even "our next film project"—

a little fiction, that's all. If it's so much as realized (i.e., filmed), then it will be something entirely different.

Then, real money will be involved. Then, fiction and "reality" will mate. Then, my piglets will become anxious and will therefore work doubly hard. Then, to play it safe ("Damn it, in a movie, every image, every line of dialogue, every scene, must be foolproof; it can't be left up to *one* person"), we'll start the teamwork.

Then, the startled swarm of producer-boarlets will be joined by the pompous drivel of the distributors. Then, the reluctant cinematic legal advisers in the money-lending banks will bring along vest-pocket literati, with flat heads barbered à la Bertolt Brecht, as literary advisers ("... *Herr Jorguleit was very successful doing this for the radio and he will henceforth be available to Victoria ...*").

Then, amid cigar smoke, cigar corrosives, and expense-account brandy, the "project" is subjected to a collective process of intellectual predigestion:

every scene, every image, and every line of dialogue is multiply analyzed to shreds, crushed, insalivated with the psychology of the trade, belabored.

Everybody adds his bit. Everybody draws on his own knowledge of "reality" and "reality"-creating fantasy to inject juices that will make the soon boneless subject ferment into a mash for consumers—so that, finally kneaded and streamlined for the public taste, it may slip through the sphincters of the take artists and lens pullers.

Fine! All I'm after is the check (even if they've clipped three quarters of the amount originally agreed upon).

My name will then stand as the person responsible for a work of cinematic art entitled *Kitty's Girls and the Russians*—

the plot's been changed, in that Kitty's girls are no longer employed in a Berlin cathouse, but are now the wards in a boarding school for aristocratic young ladies in Potsdam ("After all, highborn girls interest moviegoers more than hookers, you have to admit that yourself—something like the Empress Augusta School—right? . . .")—

So Kitty (von?) Schmidt is no longer *madame la patronne* but now teaches local history in the aforesaid institute. ("Just think of *Girls in Uniform*—a worldwide success, American remake, et cetera. . . .")

"Well, and then when the Russkies come, the whole thing can run along as it did before— But wait a minute, we don't want to remind the audience of unpleasant historical events like the rape wave; my wife, for instance, she doesn't like to think about it. Besides, we don't want to screw up the market in the Russian zone. . . ."

So: the girls merely fear being raped, but a lieutenant of the advancing Russian company, Ivan So-and-so-vitch or what should we call him? Gimme a real Russian name—huh? Karamazov? No, Karamazov sounds too much like a battlefield; that's what it's good for, a battlefield—The Battle of Karamazov. But not for us. What? Raskolnikov? I like that, Raskolnikov—you too, Herr Müller-Kapetown? You've heard the name already? So what. In the new version, the character's completely positive; you don't have to worry about copyright problems. . . . Well, anyway: Lieutenant Ivan Raskolnikov has expressly told his men not to rape any woman, but the guys ignore his orders, the delirium of victory and the booze unleash their passions—

"Well, and now Fräulein Schmidt—von Schmidt? Uh-uh! What for? We have to emphasize the social contrast. Previously, Kitty wasn't very popular among the girls because she isn't high-born, you understand? That's what makes the story so up to date; otherwise there's no topical message—well, now Fräulein Schmidt throws herself in front—what? Winkelried? That's what you wanna call her? I don't like Winkelried, too preten-tious. Besides, Schmidt sounds better for bringing out the social contrast—and she kicks the bucket—just like in the song: 'Oh, she suffered, poor Miss Schmidty, 'cause the soldiers sliced off her titty. . . .' Well, and the girls? The girls are saved by Lieutenant Raskolnikov; that makes it a lot more ecumenical, bringing na-tions together and so on; why should we keep fighting with the Russians after so many umpteen years? Doesn't make any sense in the long run. . . ."

Certainly not. My supreme piglet Wohlfahrt (not for nothing is he the business manager and sole owner of Intercosmic Film Art) is once again talking pure gold.

So: in the end, Ivan Raskolnikov marries the girl in Fräulein Schmidty's institute who hated her most because she wasn't highborn—what should we call her? Effie? Effie sounds good, I like it—and now for a real Junker name—what? von Briest? Von Briest is great. So: in the end, amid the ruins of the garrison chapel of Potsdam—pretty good, right? symbolic and so on—in the end, Lieutenant Ivan Raskolnikov marries Fräulein Effie von Briest

". . . And when you see the two of them in the last take placing a simple bouquet of wild flowers on Fräulein Schmidty's grave—and the Iron Cross First Class—no, wait a moment, why the Iron Cross First Class? The war's over, damn it! It doesn't exist any-more. A simple bouquet of wild flowers, a lot more poignant—I tell you: with the final take, there'll be snot and tears, that's the alpha and omega of cinematic art, as old Erich Pommer used to say. . . ."

Fine! Good luck! And tally ho! I was merely doing my duty as a man: showing my brood of piglets that they can always count on more pearls from me (*"the guy is difficult, granted, simply be-cause he gets too many ideas at once—his imagination runs away with him, you just have to rein in his thoughts, then he functions right")—*

I wrote the pile of bothersome obligations off my back: the alimony for Christa (*"I have nothing but sympathy with your situation, but my lawyer won't hear of it: after all, he's in the film business himself, he knows what your income is"*), the tuition for our son in his plutocratic prep school in Holland, the rent, the auto insurance—

I can even think of paying off some of the most embarrassing of my debts—

all this with the labor of a few filthy weeks . . .

I've finally written myself free for a few more weeks and I can tackle my book again . . .

which is what happened in these past seven days and nights—with a more stunning debacle than before, to be sure, although the conditions weren't necessarily success-oriented . . .

but this time the debacle was more thorough, the failure far more spectacular than ever. . . .

□   □   □

THIS IS WHAT HAPPENED:

A Schwab released from the body of cells and floating in air as a pure metaorganism had been annoying me since my return here like a fly stubbornly buzzing around my nose—and I didn't want it to alight on my nose. It came from some carrion. My dream had hatched it—not the dream I had only just slipped away from, being absolved by the shy smile of my foster mother from the flower cup and redeemed. It was actually the other dream, the cellar dream, where an old bag of a cleaning woman lay murdered, her face blurred by a shovel into a Rorschach splotch. . . . And whether it was a dream or a repressed reality—whether (and if so, in what way) Schwab was connected—I did not wish to be bothered by it now.

I lay in bed, keeping my eyes shut. For the time being (at last! after all the tortured days and nights), I was not tuned in to ghosts—to any transcendental individual, no matter how interestingly he manifested himself. At least for the brief time of setting out into a richly creative day (and all its failure and frustration), I wanted to be untroubled by any sort of basement reminiscences: wartime air-raid basement experiences, Viennese occult basement existence, the topography and atmosphere of the basement in which I killed that dreadful crone in my dream (and *where* in reality?). My foster mother's smile from the calyx (*un sourire presque espiègle*) had exonerated me for the moment: I could take a breather without lifting the weight of a sin with each breath. I wanted to think quite soberly about the contents of my notes, and try to restore what I had lost, for I missed it as if it were the key to my book.

It was easy to recall the train of thought. Snails produce their houses at the command of the species; they have no biological choice, as it were; but still, their houses have individual peculiarities. One can tell by the changing styles of art-historical eras that human beings obey such biological orders in the way they express themselves collectively. And one can see that these orders are cyclical in the way they change; that they repeat certain elements of expression in the changing of the expression, reiterate them in terms of time symmetry, as it were. . . . That was roughly the gist. And oddly enough, it completely calmed me down. I enjoyed the notion of a tide-like now-and-again, of something breathing, pulsing through the world, making mankind lean alternately in one direction, then the other, like a wheat field in the wind (and the winds, as if sparked by Aiolos' divinely musical sentiment, truly blow first from here, then from there into the various cultures). This notion virtually carried me away from the planet, putting me far beyond it, in a demiurgical contemplation.

It showed me this mankind *en bloc* in space and time: billions of tiny particles, coagulated into a gray mass that is moved by an invisible power and forced into the strangest ornaments. And this did not frighten me. Quite the opposite: it was an old, familiar thing, like a lullaby. I had hopped into the lap of the world spirit, as it were, and now, relieved (because I was released, for now, from personal responsibility), I curled up in metaphysical relish—

and I watched the grand spectacle purely through indolently blinking eye slits:

It proceeded from the primal beginning and encompassed the entire universe.

I observed the force that leads the teeming of mankind to and fro and occasionally pulls it together and drives it apart like iron filings on a piece of paper under which one moves a magnet. This force, operating on an inexhaustible play instinct of forms, was presumably the same one that formed the first cell from the primal slime and then went on to develop Brehm's fauna and Linné's flora, ultimately crowning the astonishing variety of such creation with man. The planet was infested with mites, which first appeared in dots and specks, then spots and splotches, growing out, soon proliferating hypertrophically, covering the entire surface of the globular shape (slightly flattened at the poles) with mange, which, if possible, was to be transmitted to other stars in the cosmos. . . . And it must have been the same unnamable power that had hurled this planet out into the universe among myriad others with their moons and satellites, making this powdering of the stars dance chaotically in a tremendous juggling feat. . . . Nor did it make any difference whether one of them or a million, with or without mites, died or burst like soap bubbles.

This potency toyed with such riches that if galactic systems emerged or perished in the cosmos, they did not need to be given even a fraction of the significance attached here on earth to the hatching or crushing of a louse. In light of this, it would have been childish to speak of free will, decision, the importance of any action or inaction—of ethical purpose and commencement, of moral action, of the causal relationship between guilt and atonement. . . . And it would have been absolutely hilarious to imagine that one could, as an individual, produce something that was not already prepared for in the collective expression; for instance: write a book that was not being tackled, indeed had not already been written, by a hundred, a thousand others with an urge to express. . . . It was simply a joke of the world spirit that someone lay there, cudgeling his brain about a lost jotting—

It didn't help. There was no way out anywhere. Man is free,

but his will is not: anything he does takes place in terms of the all-creating, all-destroying divine game—and thus I am, thus you are, not only God's most obedient servant and dearest menial but also His partner: we put our noses to the same grindstone. . . . And I for my part lay satisfied in the bosom of the Lord and could hope that sooner or later, as his most obedient servant and dearest menial, I would do my biological duty by throwing Madame on her back in some corner of the Épicure and sticking a nice bun into her oven—a little French bastard who would soon be practicing with a plastic machine gun so as to take part in the game of the great world spirit . . . and if I writhed like a fly on flypaper because my conscience wouldn't let go, whether because of a murder that I could not entirely forget, because of my dead friend whom I had cheated, or even because of my book that I would never write—

it was utterly hilarious of HIM who fed on worlds like a whale on plankton. . . .

"This," I said to Schwab, "is the result of my seeking God. If He does exist, then He's indulged in a bad joke at my expense. I find that He's gone a bit too far."

I sensed something quite unusual piercing my lids, which I kept shut: some light narrowed to the sharpness of a knife. So I opened my eyes.

□   □   □

THE LIGHT (like the wan city light in the murky apartment of my Viennese relatives) came through a crack in the shutters (I usually keep them closed even in the daytime: I live by lamplight: that is how I elude time).

I could not tell whether it was the ethereal and as yet unthickened light of the first hour of morning or the self-transfigured, renunciatory light of a gloriously waning day of sunshine shortly before evening. It seemed to be neither, and yet it was so fluid and bright, such as even the most glorious day of sunshine does not become. Like a sword blade, it sliced through the twilit darkness of the room and cut into my eyes. I had to close my eyes again, and I sniffed and listened (one can hear the quality of time in silence).

It was silent. (It is always almost uncannily silent in this filthy hotel—its sole advantage, by the way. It is so silent that at night I can hear the humming of the telephone on the switchboard in the handsome Pole's desk two floors below me.)

I compared this silence with the memory of other silences into which I had occasionally listened (the dull, heavy ones at night, when everyone was asleep; the brooding, ruminating ones of afternoons when the always cold Algerians, in coats with turned-up collars and army-surplus scarves to the tips of their noses, crept into their beds in large family groups, and traveling salesmen entered their daily balances in their notebooks or, with intricate knowledge of amorous positions, were inside the women they had picked up; and especially a silence in which I had endured sublime misery three years ago in this very room, when I had waited in vain for Dawn to summon me). . . .

an unbelievably eloquent silence, which contained Paris like a dissolved pigment

—the essence of the city in its silence, as if it were not merely that certain forms, colors, images, sounds, noises, and smells worked together to produce its specific, unmistakable impression (the Parisian quality of Paris) but that the myriads of continual, conscious, half-conscious, and unconscious perceptions of a here and now with which the teeming human swarm out there, in the streets and buildings, experiencing themselves as "à Paris," were weaving themselves into something objective, empirically ascertainable, positively material, which entered the people as it did the breathed air, the squares, the trees on the boulevards, and every single stone of this city; and as if this aura of the Paris that is unmistakably to be perceived as Paris first became truly free and perceptible in the silence, so that if one brought a deaf and blind person here without telling him where he was, he would instantly have to sense it as specifically Parisian

The silence this morning was exactly the opposite. True, it also contained the city, but not that aura. You could hear Paris in it, but it was an abstract, panoramic, tourist-picture-book Paris. It contained no people experiencing it. Streets, squares, monu-

ments, gardens, gables, and ledges had a Sunday glow to them—
and were accordingly empty. Each house was freshly painted, so
to speak, with sparkling windowpanes. Each street corner was
meticulously swept. Each leaf on the trees in the boulevards was
varnished. It was a toy Paris: beautiful, perfect—and, as I have
said, abstract. The silence emanating from it was sterilized. It lay
there, scoured clean, like a lovely shell on the beach.

Curiosity seized me, and I got out of bed and went to the window, pushed open the shutters, and stuck my head into the air
shaft.

It was filled with bright nothingness.

This bright nothingness almost made the air shaft burst. The
walls seemed able to stand the tension no longer. They had narrowed, losing their gravity and density. The bright nothingness
scattered their molecules.

I looked up. Very high above the rectangular cutout of the
peep-show box to which the air shaft had shrunk, the sky was
stretching in a deep polar blue. I looked down. Below, on the
dirt-encrusted glass roof of the first floor, frost lay along the iron
beams. Razor-sharp coldness cut into my skin. I looked up
again—and was yanked aloft like a balloon cut free.

For what happened next, the experienced novelist has a few
idiot-proof, well-cemented phrases at his disposal, but he cannot
use them unless he wishes to be regarded as fatuous:

his heart contracted when he realized—

with a stroke that roiled his innermost being he perceived—

an insight punched him like a fist—

as though an inner turmoil had shaken the scales from my
eyes—

thus, I recognized the light and the silence.

They were the silence and the light of the days when the German troops marched into Vienna (in March 1938: it was known
then as "Hitler weather": an icy cold blue sky and a Sunday glow
over the empty, silent world).

Those days were still sharp in my memory (and kept fresh by
repeated and highly detailed reports to Schwab). There was no

reason why their recollection (even, so to speak, from an ambush: on the morning after a good night with a well-paid hooker, pregnant of a creative day here in Paris in the year 1968) should rattle me. (After all, it was not unusual to have frost in October. The political situation—according to hearsay; I read no newspaper—was as precarious as ever, but not immediately alarming; and sudden clear weather was no excuse for drawing the parallel to historic dates marked by extraordinary climatic conditions.)

March 1938 was altogether different—I mean more unusual, more surprising. I knew it by heart, like certain jottings for my book. Dozens of times—if not more often—I had told all kinds of people (not just Schwab) about those days, finding attentive and then soon reflective listeners, whose emotions had lifted my description to artistic heights. During the thirty years that had passed since these memorable days, I had turned them into a showpiece whenever the conversation turned to politics and recent history (for I understand nothing of the former and I live past the latter; in order to join in, I tell about the peculiar weather back then):

How overnight (that is, toward morning of the day of the *Upheaval* or *Annexation*), Arctic cold had fallen upon Vienna despite the clear blue sky; and yet I stubbornly maintain that the lilac shrubs were already blooming in the Heldenplatz and in the Volksgarten. They were trampled down a few days later when one or two million enraptured people the exact figure doesn't matter (I still believe with the great Erich Kästner that one can pack all mankind in a one-cubic-kilometer crate and throw it into the Grand Canyon so that mankind may collectively bite the dust)—as I was saying, the shrubs were trampled down when an entire big-city populace boiled together into a seething gruel of spastically dislocated limbs, twitching arms, hands, and swastika armbands hurled high and thrashing about as if drowning, with undulating banners and roaring mouths. They were welcoming Adolf Hitler, leader, unifier, and expander of the Greater German Reich in ex-Mayor Lueger's imperial city.... But more of this anon.

The bizarre thing about the weather was not just the coldness but, above all, the dematerialized light. With such a brilliant blue sky, one naturally expected the sun to come out at some point during the day—

as a freshly polished brass disk, simply for the sake of the picture-perfect order of the world, which had suddenly gone crazy. But the sun did not come out. The events took place in a light that did not emanate from the sun's rays. It was the illumination of total emptiness. It was the light of abstraction. The coldness, cutting razor sharp into the marrow of bones, peeled out the objects, which were more or less logically lumped together, peeled them so very subtly along the contours of their isolation. It penetratingly clarified them as things. It drove connections apart and turned them into adjacencies. All at once, everything was displayed openly and lucidly. Not, of course, in the interflowing tonal values of a brilliant painting. Everything was separated thing by thing, like a pasted silhouette of colored paper. Despite all the particolored variety in the world, an unbelievable simplification had come about. . . . I repeat—and I am ready to swear an oath—the sun did not come out for three days. It had stopped in the heavens, as on the occasion of Biblical military actions at Gibeon or Jericho, but it had not stopped over Vienna.

Nevertheless, it was light outside. So light that your eyes hurt—for three days. Until the Führer and Reich Chancellor entered the city.

Naturally, I make bold to squeeze historical events together a bit for the sake of poetic truth. It could just as easily have been the fourth or fifth day when the Führer and Reich Chancellor entered the city. But that doesn't matter. For when the sun remained suspended somewhere else in the sky (only not over Vienna; perhaps over Berlin?), time stopped too. I tell you, for three whole days.

That was the bizarre thing about that light: it was not only beyond matter but also beyond time. An everlasting Sunday had commenced and was shining over the world. Had my friend Scherping been present, he would have said, "What a sky! You can fry eggs on it." (He would have been wrong: the sky was more likely to freeze those who were sickened by the times and wanted to survive past the next few centuries, in order to thaw out again when medicine could guarantee eternal life: the SS then performed interesting experiments in this connection at Dachau.) And Vienna was lovelier and more Sunday-like than ever before. It looked as neat as a pin, fresh, with a new coat of paint, as if straight from a toy chest. And empty.

An especially effective vignette in my story was the one about the flower woman. She appears on the first of the three days. All through the night, the soul of the people had boiled. Describing something like this is a choice morsel for a novelist, and I didn't miss my chance. For instance, the encounter with my cousin Wolfgang in a battery of the marching columns (they had massed as unexpectedly as the hosts of iron men that King Laurin stamped out of the soil; and they had marched through the streets to the Rathausplatz, crowding more and more ominously), an encounter that was not without the macabre humor that properly highlights something horrible. (For the postwar German cinema, to which I offered the story on many occasions, the scenery was too costly, although they probably could have found a lot of useful newsreel material; at any rate, my manuscript requires only a bit of tightening and revising to be considered masterful; if I remember correctly, it is filed in the folder marked PREVIOUS EVENTS: VIENNA IV, with the description of Wolfgang's funeral.)

The coagulated flood of iron men smashed the groves on the Rathausplatz and soiled the monument to Ritter von Sonnenthal, presumably because King Laurin's warriors smelled a Jew in the name. However, they did not sing (as they usually did on such occasions). The columns mutely set out again, threading their way in murky order toward the Ringstrasse. At their head, in accordance with tradition, marched a division of uniformed employees of the Municipal Streetcar Company (the trolley conductor of my childhood was not among them). They pulled the monstrous thing along behind them: a worm as black as nightshade, crawling along on thousands of legs, aglint with the will-o'-the-wisps of thousands of eyes in which the pale fire of an hour of decision was glowing.

It now crept out of the trampled-flower-bed earth and grew longer and longer and had no end in sight ... crept past Parliament and past the Opera and past the City Park and, at Aspern Bridge, into the curve toward the Danube Canal and up the canal to Schottentor and then into its own tail. It thus placed a ring around the inner city.

And thus Walpurgisnacht began, lasting until dawn.

At ten-thirty on the day that had thus begun, I strode through a completely deserted Vienna.

It unfolded very agreeably before my tearing eyes (tearing from cold, you see, and because I hadn't slept and had seen all kinds of things through the night, things one sees in oppressive dreams; also, the light hurt my eyes).

Vienna flapped open before me in piercingly lucid, brightly colored individual pictures (the colors of Emperor Joseph's time: yellow and copper-green and sky-blue and glacier-white and streetcar-red/white/red). The city flapped open like one of those panoramic folders sold at railroad kiosks to passing strangers, so that they know where they have been:

—a townscape in its own notation, so to speak: in which the extreme simplification limits itself to indicating tonal values, and in which, even with the most banal and most arbitrary chaos of heterogeneous and contrasting motifs and styles (cathedral and railroad station, soccer stadium and stock exchange, hero's monument and zoo), a certain rhythm is inscribed, a rhythm that takes up the melodic moods of the individual views, combining with them into a musical theme that is ultimately the same as the one you hear in the complicated orchestration of the city after a lifetime of intimate acquaintance

This Vienna was painted by a highly conscientious Sunday painter with frozen feelings (a Danubian Vivin) and patched together into a booklet of picture postcards. And I wended my way through it and took it in one last time in its brilliance and empty glory.

Vienna: capital of Austria and old Europe, now scoured by passing time and washed up on its strand.

I took it in and filed it away with the things that had become a part of my being and had become abstract along with it:

its tenacious, chamois-leather Middle Ages and its buckhorn-button Baroque; its edelweiss-starred Rococo and postmasterly Biedermeier; its grand bourgeois Greater German kitsch and its whining petit bourgeois knavery:

fanfare-loud, panache-sporting self-assurance petrified into state-chancelry emblematics; the ore of imperial sobriety forged into playful latticework; Spanish draconic severity wine-drunkenly dissolved in Perioecian placidity . . . and proliferating from all these the amalgams of engineering and Promoterism: klutzy monumentality and frivolous intimacy, opera and operetta in cast iron and mortar: the Lay of the Nibelungen on apartment houses, and the imperial double eagle hanging at trolley stops as a sign of the Heuriger wine: in bridge arches, middle-class pride bloated into the swank of paunches bearing watch chains, and, in administration buildings, the grace of courtiers demeaned into the humility of pensioners . . . and, over the Virginia cigar, an insidious wink

The Sunday glow of the city was piercing. Naturally, I had known since the previous night what it meant: Vienna had surrendered and stood ready as a bride to receive the groom. A noisy stag party had taken place, a boisterous bridal shower, and this was an hour of the most delicate reflection. Vienna took one last look at itself in the mirror.

And it was frozen. A completely transparent block of ice encompassed Vienna and its spring air.

The Old German neo-Gothic town hall with the cast-iron knight on its spire, from which a long red flag with a black swastika in a white circle was now licking down like a devil's tongue with a pill marked "poison." The slender octagonal tower of the Minorite Church over the lilac clusters of the Volksgarten. (I am not mistaken: the question is not whether it is botanically possible for lilacs to bloom in Vienna during March; the problem is heraldry. Thus, the papal tiaras of the blossom candles most certainly stood white and yellow in the green balls of the chestnut trees on the Ring: the Vienna of hand kisses and fiacres bade a proper farewell to Straus, Strauss, and Hofmannsthal.) The grille-toothed titanic maw of the Castle Gate, which only yesterday had gargled with rickety taxis, grief-wrinkled fiacre nags, and bicyclists with chamois "shaving brushes" on their hats, was now caught in a gaping yawn, as if it were trying to swallow all the stony lion-clubbing and angel-cloud-billowing drama of the castle and the Michaeler Church into the void of the Heldenplatz behind it. The Graben with the kidney-shashlik skewer of the Plague Column and the tower of St. Stephen's cathedral looming so spectacularly over prosperity façades . . .

Heading down the Spiegelgasse, I turned off to the New Market, and there was the flower woman.

She was the exemplar of the Viennese flower woman, as round as a barrel and (not just because of the cold) wreathed and wrapped in untold layers of petticoats, vests, jackets, coats, shawls, as well as scarves crisscrossing her bosom and back; bluish red like a tulip bulb and with fingers sprouting like fat root ends from her knitted wristlets.

She had left her baskets of primrose, violet, and narcissus posies, and they stood there tempting any dog's leg, while she ran—no, rolled—in a drunken zigzag across the empty square. Only Raphael Donner's smooth fountain nymphs, so beautiful and motionless in their slender grace, were watching her twirl and whirl and swirl, while she flung up her sleeve stumps with the root ends, as though trying futilely to take wing—and she shrieked, croaked, panted, *"Heil! Siegheil! Siegheil!"* And although Viennese flower women have voices like Anatolian muledrivers, she sounded very woeful, indeed stifled in the resonance of the huge void, like the lament of a hare drowning in a rain barrel.

Only then did it dawn on me that something extraordinary had occurred: an era had come to an end.

I once saw a city in flames (Emperor Nero would have kissed his perfumed fingertips):

There were so many flames that they looked almost dainty, even loving. Quick as a cat's tongue, they licked out of the blackened window caverns of the houses and up the walls. They flared up wildly in dark smoke and crackling flurries of sparks only when a building collapsed. Then they whooshed and flickered over the glimmering pile of rubble. But overhead, the sky was a dark glow: the incubator of the Apocalypse—

And I stared till my eyes were red, in order to have the image sear into me. You don't see that kind of thing every day.

I told myself, "Hey! People are burning in these houses. The basements they've crept into are buried. The heat is seething the juice out of their bones, they're shrinking into little black monkeys. But if they manage to break out of their cellar holes, then the burning wind will raise them aloft like dry leaves and whirl them into the flames."

But I was only telling myself those things. The wall of fire was impenetrable and was reflected in me just as impenetrably. No shrick pierced it on either side. Then, the young man came toward me.

The young man was imperturbably gazing straight ahead, striding through the heaps of broken glass, the smoldering ruins of furniture, and the tattered snarls of fire hose. He was walking along the more or less intact right side of Kurfürstendamm (for this took place in the Berlin of 1944, on the morning after a turbulent night: one of the solid bombing nights in which the Promoterist splendor of Berlin's Old West Side lost its plaster of Paris amid all sorts of illumination effects that flouted the blackout regulations: the loss being so complete that only the sooty walls remained, and even they were mostly joined and entangled like the fingers of a praying pastor—very few of them were still upright, as a warning). . . .

He was obviously a young man of good breeding, and he wore civilian clothes. This too was not something one saw every day. For it was precisely the young men of the best families who deemed it an honor to do their accursed duty and carrry out their obligation to *Führer, Volk, und Vaterland*, on land, in the air, and at sea, by Minsk and Omsk and Andalsnes and high over the windrowed dunes of drifting sand in the Libyan desert and deep down with the fish by Ullapool. His raincoat with a sloppily dangling belt was unbuttoned, and his hands were in his pockets. He was heedless of his good shoes, which trod over upholstery springs and into the twisted spokes of baby-carriage wheels. And when he had to cross one of the side streets, he stepped rather inattentively down from the sidewalk to the road and tripped. . . . However, he caught himself with the inexplicable, clownish skill of a drunk or other deviate and, after briefly reeling, as if drawn on an invisible string, he strode on: without removing his hands from his pockets or his gaze from the nothingness he was staring straight into.

And I realized, something extraordinary had happened to the young man! And only then did it dawn on me:

Something extraordinary had happened.

I almost always append this episode to the tale of the flower woman: as a paraphrase to clarify the theme to the slow-witted, and have it gratefully taken as a gratis addendum for the quick-witted, who understand it immediately. And I quite regularly reap, with a sigh of metaphysical anxiety, the exclamation "Good God! You ought to *write that down!*"

Yes indeed, I know I ought to write that down (and a lot of other things too). But it's not so urgent as other things I ought to write down. It may be an extremely effective bit of narrative art (at least it's seldom disappointed my listeners). But it concerns me only peripherally (although the end of an era back then—in March 1938—put an end to *my* era: so completely that my previous life seemed to have been lived by a different person from him of the later life: for instance, my childhood before my mother's death was lived by a different child from the one who then grew up in Vienna, ultimately experiencing that March in the year 1938).

I would venture to maintain that the issue is purely an external one. It was (by happening) to have extremely *far-reaching* consequences—certainly not just for myself but, strangely, even enigmatically, for me in particular (although, for the time being, it altered nothing in the externals of my existence).

In any case, it sliced my existence in two again, pushing the earlier portion behind a glass pane, as it were. What now lay behind it was, no doubt, something I had gone through, lived through, at times even suffered through—yet it really had nothing to do with me now. I continued living with it as if I were keeping one portion of me like a tench in an aquarium: more as a hobby then as a necessity.

One portion of myself was entirely abstracted from me, existing in a different element. In a reality that had become unreal. I could observe it with scientific detachment. It no longer aroused my passion, only my occasional interest.

Like Nagel's amputated arm, which lay buried somewhere in Russia while its owner industriously wrote with his left arm in Fuhlsbüttel-on-the-Elbe, that era of my life was separated from me. And even though it sometimes seemed that I could identify with it in some way or other, this was not actually the case. I was prey to the same illusion as Nagel when some sort of nervous reflexes in his arm stump led him to believe that he could move the fingers of his right hand.

In a word: I still experienced myself in that portion—but simply as history.

Even later (years and decades after March 1938), I was forced to carry out such amputations of previous sections of my life; for instance, after my divorce from Christa, in a certain way after Schwab's funeral, and certainly after Gaia's death. So that ultimately my story became that of a man who experiences himself in the story of an adolescent who experiences himself in the story of a boy who experiences himself in the story of a child. Or if you prefer a metaphor: the surrealistic portrait of a man who carries within himself an aquarium in which he swims like a tench. . . . And even though he keeps getting progressively smaller and younger and changing his suit so that ultimately, as a dear little golden-curled sailor, he carries nothing more within himself than the nostalgia for the seed water from which the stork unexpectedly brought him and placed him somewhere on land, he was nevertheless—albeit hazily and mysteriously and tench-like—the very same man! All those cuts separated me from myself like a tapeworm head, from which the same tapeworm keeps growing back (because, in accordance with a biological command, it contains an established design of itself and hence its style, as it were). But none of those cuts supported its effectiveness by using the spectacular circumstances of an historic event. Only the cut in March 1938.

From which one may conclude that my personal history is connected only rather loosely and randomly with World History. *The latter really does not concern me.*

□ □ □

HENCE, NOW, here in Paris, in 1968, it was not memory that stunned me but simply my small interest in it. My gaze up into the peepshow box of the air shaft, through which nothing was to be seen but a rectangular section of the ice-blue sky, sucked me out of time into a sort of removal from time—into a no-man's-land between the here and now and today and the there and then and yesterday long since and frequently separated from me.

I belonged to neither one now. I saw both as equally remote and abstract from me: each a wholly different story. I could tell either—but neither released me.

I peered simultaneously into my two aquariums, each of which contained the other and me in the wake of a tale to be told—as a literary fetus, so to speak. One was a Paris hotel room reeking of bedbug-killer and couscous spices; the other, the Vienna of the annexation by the Third and Greater German Reich.

In both, something swam in slow-motion weightlessness: I—or at least a human being with an unbearable resemblance to me. In one, standing at the window and gazing up the narrow airshaft to the sky, a man of forty-nine, modeled trait for trait on my wanted poster, and with the same personal data, the same name, the same place and date of birth (and its disreputable circumstances), the same color of hair and eyes, the same nose-shape, ear-shape, fingerprints, and distribution of liverspots—hence, in terms of all criminological leads, quite unmistakably I. In the other, the same man, thirty years younger—a callow nineteen-year-old, in whom all these traits were just budding, so to speak, not yet settled in creases, leathery weather-beaten and masculinely marked—yet nevertheless I. Indeed, beyond the shadow of a doubt, I—

and neither concerned me directly. Each was I—but simply as his-story, history: as my abstraction.

Still, a secret rapport existed between the two of them (the realization they were I), in which I was not included. They existed through me and beyond me, in a higher form of existence than I had yet attained. They looked as if they were winking and waving—indeed, even calling to one another, shouting something I could not (or was not supposed to) make out. It sounded like something I knew, indeed knew very well. It sounded like my own echo, but I had forgotten the words of the original call, and the echo had died away no sooner than I thought I had caught it.

They knew the words and had decided to keep them from me. And thus, they (these stories of mine, twice times two times two times two times two stories) aroused my curiosity, forcing me to deal with them and cope with them incessantly, to tell them to myself, over and over again, unceasingly—yet without ever managing to become fully a part of their equation, all their numerators and common denominators, their common multiples as well as, ultimately, the solution to their algebra.

My gaze through the tetragonal funnel of the light shaft yanked me up and out into the cold void, in which I floated away from myself like a balloon cut loose. And, like the hazy strips of soft, perforated cloud covers, the rags of other memories, other histories of my many detached and abstracted selves, soared past me:

a pond in a now entirely mythical land (known as Bessarabia, a name that is speckled like a guinea hen): a small pond in a park, where a delicately old-fashioned boat was decaying

a bridge arching over the Danube Canal in Vienna, under whose slanting shadow, cast transparently into the mealy lit fog, I, a boy of eleven, was placing a toy boat in the black water: in it a candle that was to drift to my dead mother

a classroom at the Realschule in Vienna's Thirteenth District, in whose mountain sorrel a wheat field of youth was rotting on the stalk, year by year

the mermaid eyes of my foster mother, bewitched and strangely hungry for salvation, her gaze with drawn-in flanks, as it were, arousing the same hunger in me

Stella or liberation, sinful lovemaking in the veil-weaving of the frog-croaking one moonlit night over Baneasa, furious mat-

ing behind a boundary ridge on the highway where the car stands with its motor running, predatory pouncing on each other in hotel rooms rented for hours at a time

and John, whom we—still glowing and breathless and with hands trembling—sit facing, with his perfectly immobile face

the war: a pulp event

Cousin Wolfgang, appearing before me in military gray

Berlin in flames, and the gray human faces which the soot of conflagrations has seared so deeply that they reflect

the canteen with German attorneys and witnesses at the Fürth law court, and the purely physiological gratitude in the otherwise perfectly expressionless face of a young girl who is eating, taking in food with all the senses, all the organs, all the cells of her body

the Yuletide Ice Age in Hamburg: Christa and I holding hands and gazing down at our newborn son

Dawn, undressing an Indian doll here in this hotel room while Schwab and I watch in delight—and her stunned look, her sudden blush, when a giant vermilion penis appears on the undressed doll

Gaia dying and Professor Leblanc chatting away at her bedside

And none of these things really concerns me anymore. They could just as easily be made up and have never actually happened. It is a tellable story, composed of many stories—nothing more.

The ice-blue bit of sky over the air shaft was, in any case, wholly undimmed by any of this. It had swallowed it all up into its cold blueness: all of Nuremberg with all its spiritual dousing and crawling grave worms as well as the entire month of March 1938 in Vienna and everything I had been through, gone through, lived through, in between or before or after. True, I could wrest some of these things from that bit of sky, I could resurrect them and bring them back to life—with interest, raised to the level of narrative, an object of reflective contemplation, provoking our thoughts. The sky challenged me with a smile to do so, but this was sheer derision. . . . It had swallowed up so many other things that I had not taken part in: the atomic mushroom of Hiroshima, for instance, and the smoke of the crematory ovens of Treblinka;

the kiln glow of the bombing nights of Berlin and Dresden, of Hamburg, Würzburg, Rotterdam, and Coventry and Warsaw, plus the sweetly burgeoning stench of decay from the fields of corpses at the Bulge and in the Donets basin, at Monte Cassino and El Alamein and Singapore and Waikiki and goodness knows where else. . . . Certainly, others were, fortunately, present in those places: they saw, witnessed, experienced, and are capable of wresting it away, resurrecting it as a narrative: on the level of an object of reflective contemplation or sheer pulp. But this did not concern me, it did not concern me at all.

The bit of ice-blue sky over the air shaft (sixteen feet square): it had swallowed up all Babylon and was completely undimmed by this, without the slightest frizzle of a bellyache, silky smooth, crystal clear, and as deep as a well. And what if mankind were now preparing to hurl the entire planet after it, including itself? What concern is it of mine, what concern of mine? I have nothing to oppose it with but words.

Up there, in the blue, the man who experienced himself as the story of a man who experiences himself as the story of an adolescent who experiences himself as the story of a boy who experiences himself as the story of a child—I, ME, up there in the Arctic blue (still unborn as a story, still not wrested from the blue maws of oblivion, but about to be: always, destined to be so from early on, misborn to mislive my life as a story), with my picture I also carried about a piece of human history—

March 1938, for example:

The Arctic-blue emptiness of those days—and Vienna washed up on their shore like a lovely dead seashell . . .

Certainly: as a story, it was smashing. Blissfully, I stuffed it into the light-blue of Schwab's eyes, how many times—and these eyes were never fed up, they kept gaping, round as tennis balls, gawking through the thick glasses. And thus I never got fed up with telling stories—that is, wreaking vengeance. For that's what it really was, an act of revenge each time. Revenge for the betrayal of our life's dream, for our wasted youth, our now empty and abstract life. . . . Blissful revenge, turning into gall, until even its bitterness was no longer palatable—until I was only chewing ashes:

Yakkety-yak—why am I blabbering to you about the magic and the death of cities—you who saw, who breathed Berlin: *a son, a legitimate offspring of the splendid, legendary Berlin of the 1920s, of the first decade after Doubleyou Doubleyou One—until 1933, until the oriflamme of the Reichstag Fire. That was a different radiant star, a sister star of the city of Paris in the diadem of Europe. I mean, before the hopelessly aged, bull-borne girl donned cowboy pants and New Mexico boots, became the hit of the county fair, despite her crone face and multiply unsuccessful facelifts, the bronco-busting rodeo star Miss Yurop with neon tubes around her Texas hat. . . . Back in that faraway morning hour of the world, when we were all boys, you, friend Schwab, and Nagel and Cousin Wolfgang and I—you, as the firstborn, could spend a few blissful holiday weeks there, in that legendary Berlin, presumably in furuncular late adolescence, but blind from too much reading, and mature enough to note the quickening of your pulse when reading Gottfried Benn and ascribing it to increased distrust, and yet happily enjoying the arts-and-craftsy wordsmithery of Else Lasker-Schüler, and associating jazz with Otto Dix's paintings of the world war or the brown shirts and red-white-and-black armbands of the SA with the songs of Brecht & Weill, Inc.—devouring all this like a whale gulping down plankton: to drink the world, to be drunk on the Zeitgeist—you lucky man! Born with a silver spoon in your mouth! . . . And where is it now, your delicious Berlin? Does it exist in reality and not just on political maps and in the yellow press as the scene of the German Wailing Wall? . . . Cross your heart and own up to it: that city never really existed, it was a legend, wasn't it? A dream that a city dreamed about itself? . . . How can I believe anything else? I was shown a settled spot in Brandenburg and told it was Berlin, and I wandered through it, up and down, in every nook and cranny, before it was destroyed by fire. And I can assure you: nothing there, absolutely nothing evoked even the slightest echo of that legend, of that dream of a city. . . . I am ready to believe in Atlantis and, if you like, in Vineta and, of course, the Baghdad of Haroun ar' Rashid. But the model arch for tinker-toy tinkering (the big Wilhelminian Me-*

morial Church edition in the Kaiser's birthday package for higher social classes, free delivery) this giant burgher toy left to Zille's little people in the back court, this couldn't possibly have been the Berlin that an entire generation dreamed about, even I in the brooding dullness of my formative years in Vienna dreamed about, like a modern Babylon. . . .

I had pictured it altogether differently—not architecturally, of course, but in its atmosphere, as they say: in its mood substance. The legendary Berlin of the so-called System Age must have been magical, like a jungle painting by the Douanier Rousseau: a flimmery-spotted adventure like the face of a predatory feline suddenly emerging out of the sickle-moon-sliced blueness of the tropical night. . . . At least, that was how I had pictured it when I yearningly dreamed about it in the stale air of a puberty-fermenting classroom in Vienna's Twelfth District. A tropical voluptuousness, especially at night, when the entangled lianas of light were reflected in the black asphalt currents and vice waxed in the moor-ponds of darkness, making the overexcited mind fluoresce. So that, from the miasmas of lust-for-life and misery, luxury and crime, the orchids of the intellectual events of art, of strange, bizarrre, baroque existences, of anecdotes, blossomed forth. . . . You used to say you envied me for my formative years in Vienna: Klimt and Schiele, Wittgenstein and Berg, Schönberg and so on. . . . But permit me: in my time, all that was in a different paleontological stratum. It was past and past perfect, not present. It was history, myth, legend: literature, not life. Your Berlin, on the other hand, was, for at least a decade (until 1933), the most vivid present in our existence—granted, not one hundred percent the ANTHROPOLIS of the Utopians, not exactly the New Jerusalem of the pilgrim fathers, but a Babylon: cesspool, chaos, yet all the more beautiful for that, all the more seductive. . . .

But believe me, dearest friend, that was not what I saw burning down in the year of Our Lord 1944, aside from a few remnants not worth mentioning. What I saw was a dried-up, parched-up, silted-up training ground for the populace. A barren metropolis of Perioecians, a steppe city that was already, in essence, half Russian and half American long before its division.

Hence, the other, legendary Berlin must have died quite a bit earlier, silently. And not in slow, rattling final breaths but from one day to the next, like my Vienna in March 1938. . . . When a city dies, it does so from moment to moment, while the people keep treading in their tiny ruts of destiny, life in the streets goes on teeming, the traffic keeps moving with no visible break or jam, the buildings still stand with windowpanes glittering in the sun—and all at once, it's happened: an incomprehensible alteration in the feeling of the world, the quality of life, an indefinable but all the more decisive change of the hour, the beginning of a new phase of life for everyone. . . . It is a planetary if not a cosmic event. There is nothing more anguishing than the death of a city before it vanishes from the face of the earth. This perishing of its spiritus loci *is a metaphysical process, and not even a Hitler can take credit for being its initiator. For all the undeniable merits that this minion of nature acquired in nature's game, I do not truly regard him as directly responsible for the death of Berlin. But rather as an executive organ: the leader of the swarms of maggots that afflict a corpse. Supreme functionary of the decomposition, if you will, the most furious enzyme of disintegration, but not the murderer. After all, he marched into Vienna only after the city breathed out its soul in the ecstatic "Siegheil!" of the flower woman (one of the city's root spirits, no doubt). . . .*

But let's stay awhile in a perished Berlin. Just look: the young man I encountered there in 1944 on a smoldering and sizzling Kurfürstendamm—his stumbling and reeling, the way he kept walking, mechanically drunk, and yet that unswerving gaze into nothingness, that blind seer's gaze that made me realize something extraordinary had happened—that young man was already a citizen of a city of the dead. A walking corpse. He had no living reflexes left. What kept him upright on two legs, and even caught him when he almost fell, was, so to speak, life in a different environment; that was, at best, the reflexes of the teeming maggots inside him—movement, true, but no longer his: a certain sense of balance still, but no longer his. A condition that we perhaps do not sufficiently take into account, we who intend to tell tales about the living. And this, you see, was the extraordinary thing I realized through him. An enormously simple truth: it is not enough to march upright on two legs to live. . . . As a biological process, life is eternal, right? It merely changes form. The maggots that will teem in our cadavers after we die are even, biologically speaking, life to a higher degree—though not our life, alas. In order to preserve what we call our life, the mind must, they say, be preserved. But our mind—is this not our life dream? . . . I know I am telling you very trite things—do forgive me!—the world consists of such trite things, and their phenomenal wealth often confuses us so thoroughly that we lose sight of it—and that is the very point I am trying to express in my awkward fashion. It took a walking corpse to show me that in 1944 I was not witnessing the death of a city, I was attending the cremation of its cadaver: and that the city had died because it no longer dreamed itself. . . . The very genus of city died out because its mind, its dream, its myth, died out: because ANTHROPOLIS, the City of Mankind, had died. . . .

If a city goes up in flames, this does not mean very much. Very many cities have gone to blazes—ancient Rome, for example, a good dozen times before Emperor Nero had it go up in flames again. However, its mind, its dream, its myth, have remained alive for one and a half millennia. And especially in regard to the year of Our Lord 1944, dozens of cities were going to blazes; there was an epidemic of burning cities. The burning of a city was nothing out of the ordinary; the apocalyptic heaven of fire threatened to burst open over Germany at any moment so that a powerful angel might appear and blow his trumpet, announcing the end of a city. . . .

However, the end had long since come to many cities. In Vienna, the angel had already appeared in 1938 in the guise of a Viennese flower woman, and his trumpet had blared out a brassy "Siegheil!" Admittedly, in a burning city, it is hard to distinguish between true events and mere spectacles. But in the Berlin of 1944 it took no Brahman's eye to realize that the incineration of this city was merely the completion of an enormous but compelling causality that had begun a great deal earlier. This was being shouted from the rooftops—insofar as any rooftops still existed and anyone was left to shout from them. However, in March 1938, it took an especially fine nose to sense that time had taken a leap—a spinning leap, so that it was now facing away from its normal direction and would henceforth be zooming backward faster and faster to where it had come from. The Twelfth of March 1938 was the cusp in the swing of time's pendulum—or, if this is more up your alley: the instant of turning between two breaths of God. For the Lord breathes while He dreams Himself in an enormous game of creating and annihilating myriad worlds. And whenever He inhales in order to exhale again or exhales in order to inhale again, time changes, the dreams of human beings change—and somewhere, I don't know where, the Zeitgeist, the style, the epoch, changes—I'm ranting and raving, I know. I know that any newspaper reader can refute me. There are solid causes and reasons for everything and anything; they are delivered to you with the daily paper. Had I read my newspaper carefully, I would not dare say such flimsy things.

One could just as arbitrarily assume that time changed in 1933, illuminated by the oriflamme of the Reichstag Fire, which, so to speak, was the match struck for many subsequent conflagrations—an incident, by the way, that I learned about quite by chance and only many months later—please excuse me, but Vienna was so far away from all "reality." . . . At any rate, I arrived one evening at the location of what I had been taught to view as home *back then: the apartment of my Viennese relatives, stuffed with horrible furniture: crocheted doilies, Colonel Subicz's swords of honor—you've probably found analogous things in Potsdam: sword-knot proletariat; have-nots entitled to starvation pensions and with the most slavishly obedient class arrogance. . . . There they sat in a family grouplet around the radio, my uncle Helmuth as usual, mental substance in his steeple head:* A Manual for Engineers (*a small three-volume edition for domestic use*), the Veda *and the* Upanishads, *Sir Arthur Conan Doyle, Madame Helena Blavatsky (née Halm von Rottenstein-Hahn) and Fräulein Fränzel's* Prophecies. *His spouse, Hertha: a gruel of stupidity and misunderstood femininity. My cousin Wolfgang (whom you often resemble: very intelligent, precariously accomplished, having physically outgrown his boyhood clothes—now staring with his bespectacled eyes and bending slightly, like someone who's got constipation—the better to hear, of course*) . . .

And my aunt Selma: the old broken-down cart nag, her bony hands in her barren lap, the bewitched mermaid-gaze into emptiness (need I tell you I loved her? She taught me how to live tenaciously with despair). . . . And from the radio the broadcast of a recording of the Reichstag Fire trial welled brassily. An historic event, if you please. When I entered unsuspectingly, hence loud and unabashed, they glared at me indignantly, barked at me with dirty looks and shhh's. You could hear Göring's voice, and then that of the presiding magistrate (do you recall the guy's name?). He was very solemnly saying "Defendant van der Lubbe—" Now, at that time, there were no electronic tape recordings, just Stone Age resin disks into which sound waves were scratched in order to be scraped out by a needle. And because that record evidently had a crack or a notch, which made the needle keep jumping into the same groove, the presiding magistrate of the historic court of law kept saying "Defendant van der Lubbe—van der Lubbe—van der Lubbe vanderLubbevanderLubbevanderLubbe. . . ." It sounded funny, like a fart in the bathtub. . . . And that is the only reason that the event lodged in my memory—if you would be so kind as to forgive me, an exceedingly ridiculous matter even today, your Reichstag Fire, an extremely silly oriflamme, and I could never believe that this was the torch that ignited ANTHROPOLIS. . . .

Since then, I have been insisting on my mythology. It is founded on my being an eyewitness. In March 1938, I was there. I directly witnessed an historic event—that is, of course, as close as people like us can get. In any case, fully conscious that it was an historic event. That alone was peculiar. Even back then, I did not read newspapers. I was nineteen years old. I had enjoyed a Realschule *education in the Federal Republic of Austria—that is, historically, not to mention politically, I was about as informed as a carp in a pond. And even though I had grabbed some of the crumbs falling from the richly laden humanist table of my cousin Wolfgang, my horizon of civic knowledge blurred away just behind the* Lay of the Nibelungen, *Emperor Max in the wall of St. Martin's, and a few operetta stanzas rehashed in terms of current events. It would simply have been going too far to expect me to read the final end of Austria in the flower woman's ecstatically bouncing arse—namely, an end of that amortization fund that had ridiculously posed as a sovereign state, a sinking fund of the Habsburg legacy of petit bourgeois staleness, Alpine folklore, and parliamentary fussbudgeting that was the Federal Republic of Austria at that time. And hence also the end of a geographic myth, by which the Ortler was still mirrored in the Adriatic, and behind Fischamend the world was still open far beyond the Carpathian forests, all the way to the mule paths of Macedonia and Bohemia and Moravia with their dark forests and sheaf-laden grain fields together with the hazy croaking of frogs over the ponds of Polish Galicia, still fenced in by the same black-and-yellow toll gates—it would, I tell you, have been asking too much of me to see the end of that notion of the Austrian Middle Kingdom as also the end of Europe, that multishaped, tensely dialectic Europe, which bade farewell to the Guermantes in the west while it wreaked bloody vengeance for a stolen sheep in the southeast, with the same Kalman tunes being fiddled in its ears from Brest to Braila and from Königsberg to Capua; despite the motley of costumes and patchwork of manners and mores, it was nevertheless a formation of the same culture, a world of the same life-dream, the same ideals, the same shalts and shalt-nots, the home landscape of a humanity that, for all the variety of creeds and cults, worshiped the same God, deceived Him here there and everywhere in pretty much the same way.*

Please try to picture the background that the Vienna of the 1930s provided for this imperial myth. You see, the Kalman tunes were not only fiddled into your ears there by café musicians but also, and more frequently, cranked out of hurdy-gurdies by medal-showered, stiffly saluting torsos of wounded Doubleyou Doubleyou One veterans with the black glasses of blind men under regimental caps, and they did not use hands, they cranked with hooks. . . . That was more or less what anything looked like if it was left over from the glory that was Old Austria and old Europe. Vienna may still have been dispatching the Orient Express in three-quarter time, accompanied by the sobbing

Gypsy violins and bedbugs of the puszta czardases and the mar-
row-devouring nostalgia of shepherds' flutes and lice along the
Ialomiţa, all the way to the Golden Horn. But nonetheless
Vienna had long since become part of a different myth. The city
of the Nibelungen. It had long since been spiritually incor-
porated into the longed-for Greater German Reich. Even the
Vienna of 1933, when the VanderLubbevanderLubbevander-
Lubbe *of the Reichstag Fire trial resounded through its philis-*
tine homes, had long since been placed as a bride next to your
true-blue Prussian Berlin (alas, oh, alas, not the legendary Baby-
lon of the 1920s, but rather its people-teeming corpse).

I had dozed away my youth in a classroom, like an unhappy
chained dog dozing away a summer afternoon laced with the
buzzing of flies. And in that classroom, beneath the pictures of
Old Austrian President Hainisch's prize cow Bella and the pro-
tected Alpine flora, hung an oleograph of the German School
Association, very active with its political propaganda. Encircled
by oakleaves and surrounded by black-red-and-gold flags, the
oleograph showed a German-Austrian mountaineer, yodleeolay,
in an Alpine jacket and with a blackcock feather on his toadstool
hat: with his hobnailed shoe and vigorously bent goalkeeper knee,
he was trampling down a border fence-pole and stretching his
hand out to Germania, waiting on the other side in an imperial
crown, blond hair, coat of mail, shield, and sword. . . . For many,
many, countlessly many hours of dull boyhood misery, while
some teacher with a chain-smoker voice, using the Mocznik-
Zaharadniczek method, derived the sine and cosine functions
of a unit circle, my mind seized the allegorical union between the
Alpine country and the Brandenburgian sand box under the im-
perial crown of Charlemagne. And my imagination thrust the
border pole into the lederhosen fly of the costume-party moun-
taineer and wove the protected Alpine flora and oakleaves
around it, the way Lady Chatterley plaited anemones in her
lover's pubic hair. And my fantasy inserted the pole into Ger-
mania, by way of unification, slitting through her exuberant coat
of mail, while she forcefully farted out the entire German School
Association with its gym squads and black-red-and-gold flags and
Mocznik and Zaharadniczek as first and second officers of a stu-

dent corps, riding on Bella the prize cow and alternately singing "Watch on the Rhine" and "Oh thou, my Austria." Sometimes I even did a detailed drawing of the scene on soft-blue graph paper in my mathematics notebook (I was regarded as artistically gifted), thus allowing my neighbors to partake of my nationalistic conviction. And, although they enjoyed my vulgarities in the boyish taste for trivia, they never left me in doubt that they despised me for this lack of a sense of belonging to the German Nation: I was a man without a father, a man without a country, and I did not share the intense feeling of the era, the collective urge to eliminate violently the particularistic old and strive toward some universalizing new, whatever it might be, so long as it promised the happy absorption of the individual in the community of the many, the most, the very most, everyone. At that time, dear friend, when a brotherly—permit me to say, a Brother-Cain-like—Germany lit the torches that blazed over the twelve-year Third Reich of our Austrian compatriot Adolf Hitler and were even supposed to light the way home for us—at that time, in the world-historic, highly significant year 1933, when you were dwelling in that legendary Berlin, which I yearned for because of George Grosz's drawings and Cousin Wolfgang because the Nietzschean superman was allegedly coming into being there—at that time, I say, the younger generation in Austria was afflicted by the collective urge to unite, to unify, to become one, all for one and one for all, above all with our brethren in the not yet coalesced Reich; and it was indeed a beautiful, noble urge, based on an ancient dream of humanity: the dream of the New Jerusalem, the dream of building the city of mankind, ANTHROPOLIS. . . . Nothing could have been further from the minds of the credulous youth than the realization that the cities would die precisely because, with all the striving toward one another, the uniting and the unifying of one and all, they had regrettably lost the individual. While spiritually building the city of mankind, ANTHROPOLIS, they had unfortunately lost Anthropos . . . and although a few know-it-all individuals had long seen this coming and feared it, their warning cries died with a dying fall: the roar of the wind of time drowned them out: the spirit of the time was more powerful than the minds of the time. In any case, my memory of those days is transfigured by an unnamable promise that was held in the breathable air: even gray Vienna was filled with it, the way a foggy day is filled with the gold of the sunshine in the blue sky above. You, with all your knowledge of cultural history, surely know what I mean: after all, even the short-lived style of the era contains the optimism of a human being who is about to shape a new world: the futuristic elements in Art Déco, right? . . . Well, I don't have to tell you, do I; you always knew it, and you certainly know it now: at that time, a new era was looming, everyone sensed it in the year of Our Lord 1933. And in March of the year 1938, my schooldays were practically yesterday. I owe it to Stella's generous hand that my clothing no longer had the bleak, fermenting stench of breakfast sandwiches and pubic urine and blackboard erasers—a stench I had only just recently escaped with a high-school diploma that bore the misleading title of "maturity certificate." And hence, it would be quite wrong to assume that I could have discerned a sign of Satan in the devil's tongue with the swastika poison-pill in the white circle (which, in those March days, would soon be dangling, fiery red, not only from the City Hall but also from the tower of St. Stephen's cathedral, from the Stick-in-Iron House, from Sickartburg's and van der Nuell's botched-up opera house, from the hotels on the Ring, from the Head of Cabbage Building of the Vienna Secession, from the Diana Bath and Main Post Office, and generally from every flagpole and lightning rod and every broomstick thrust out of a skylight and every window bolt and shutter hook of the city of Vienna. . . . If there was anything devilish about it, then it was some gemütlich Viennese diabolatry. The dangling red rag looked like the red tongue lolling out of the raisin-eyed, almond-croissant fig-skull of the prune "Krampus," Santa's hellish little helper, whom the Viennese give to one another as pre-Christmas presents on St. Nicholas' day. And this was familiar and festive. Vienna was as festive as at St. Nicholas' Feast, celebrating a pre-Christmas festival going way back to pagan times. . . .

For you are not going to try and tell me that what made my flower woman dance across New Market like a whipped top was

the thought of incorporating a few goitered peasants of Ötztal
and a few Styrian cider-heads into a Germany already free of
hoarders and Jews, waving its wheat and building its Autobahn,
a Germany that could at last drink Alpine milk.... No, no.
Something far more mystical, more atavistic, had transported
this troll in tulip-bulb guise, making it whirl like a fat fly whose
wings have been ripped out. Vienna was celebrating the empty
festival of a new era.... I've already told you: the sun had halted
invisibly in the universe during those days. God took a new
breath, and that which was happening happened.

It happened on the second of the three days on which the sun
did not appear in the sky (although it exerted all its lights, all its
bright radiance—but not itself or its warmth. It came to pass
that the emptied city filled up with human beings again—pig
swill, I can tell you: a suffocating excess of people. Never before
had Vienna choked so much humankind out of itself. It rolled
out of all the streets, foamed across all the squares, filled every
cubic yard of free space from Hütteldorf to Mariahilf to
Schwarzenberg Square. It hung in clusters from the cast-iron
poles of street candelabra, was baked into druses on the wall cor-
nices, proliferated in umbels out of every window frame, tasseled
over the railing of every balcony, and it seethed and simmered. A
human gruel so thick that the spoon stood up in it (as in fairy
tales about poor people living it up for once).... What had
driven them out into the streets? The Reich Chancellor and
Führer was coming home as the greatest son of the Austrian
homeland.
Okay, Austria had been annexed. Vienna was coming home
into the Reich. All well and good. This was—I can only repeat
it—not so surprising or overwhelming. People had known that
this would happen. It had always been the most ardent desire of
the nation of the Alpine lands. The cowherd in the picture in my
classroom depicted it very graphically. It had always been inside
every second town councilman, to the Aryan core of his being, all
the way to the pole in Germania.... Of course, the national
guard had fired cannon at workers' bastions and policemen had
beaten their rubber clubs with equal violence on Communists,

Jews, and illegal Nazis. But these had been carnival free-for-alls, in which nothing of importance was carried out that had not been carried out in reality long ago. In its mind, its soul, its Eros, Austria, or rather Ostmark, had long been part of Hitler's Third Reich.

Well, then, what was happening now? Why had the people of Vienna and the Austrian federal states gone crazy overnight, sizzling in ecstasy, in delirium, foaming over like freshly tapped beer? Certainly not because something long expected had arrived, something long consummated had now finally become evident! . . . No, no. Something more important was happening. It had something to do with God's breath, or, if you prefer, with the mysterious whirlwinds that your ancient Greeks talk about in certain speculations on nature. . . . In any case: it was happening. . . .

It was happening in a strangely inhuman way. Over the seething human gruel hung its noise, veiling, weaving, echoing—like the croaking of myriad frogs in the ponds around Băneasa during a moon-rapt July night—surging across the dappled surface of thousands and thousands of heads, pulling up the faces. Every cry that mounted, every voice that rose, every word that emerged from a gaping jaw, was caught up and carried further, like a stone hurled flat across a watery surface. These were no human sounds; this was a telluric din, whole gravel slopes were ricocheting and being covered by ones that were caroming back—and others were covering these. . . . And then the spring tide roared up from Mariahilf, coming closer in an eardrum-shredding gush—raging, roaring, thundering ahead of a motorcade that zoomed through the chasm in the wild boiling human gruel, a chasm that opened before it like the Red Sea for the Jews. Long ago, Pharaoh's plumed chariots shattered and perished when the walls of water collapsed upon them, sank with broken wheels in the tumult of helplessly struggling horse legs. . . . But this time the water opened before them, they passed through with dry feet—and speedily: they flew by like ghosts: three, four, five large black open bullet-proof Mercedes escorted by rattling motorcyclists, a couple of plainclothesmen clinging like monkeys on the back of each car; inside the cars, wasp-gold on brown Party-

*bigwig uniforms, blood-red trickle-stripes on generals' uniforms. . . . And in the middle, standing upright, his skull weighed down by an oversize doorman's cap, automatically throwing up an arm like a jumping jack whose other arm has been ripped off—*HE: *doughy face, snuffling morosely on the small black stench of his mini-mustache. . . . It all whooshes by, and the flood closes in on you, you sink with pharaoh's Egyptians, are torn into the depth, struggle, are struck, punched, kicked, and poked, squashed, you gasp for air and your throat is full of your shriek, you choke it up, throw it up with stars before your eyes. The spring tide has rolled over you, and around you everything is swimming, houses, towers, treetops, streetlights, the human gruel in the writhings (afterwrithings) of a collective orgasm. The men have dark circles under their eyes, their mouths quiver slackly, the women have wet spots in their panties, their hair hangs over their faces. Please explain that to me! Something isn't right here. This isn't the way of an explicable world, the kind that's in the news every morning. . . . Even back then, the newspapers were incapable of describing what had happened, words failed them, reason failed them, common sense—at least mine. All I knew was that I had witnessed a natural event—had known it in the Biblical double meaning. Together with Viennese humankind, the Alpine German humankind, I had known Nature: in a tremendous mass coitus—my ears were still buzzing, my knees still buckling, red circles were still dancing in front of my eyes. . . . But what do you want: we had known Mother Nature:* BIG, STRONG, HIGH-HANDED *Mother Nature. . . .*

She had enjoyed giving us all a brief thrashing so that we finally knew what "procreation" meant—namely, not a private pleasure, or even a biological duty in the termite's contribution to the universal process of procreation. No indeed. It was a metaphysical event: a cosmic incident, against which even a protuberance is nothing more than a fart in a bathtub. . . . Certainly, the GREAT MOTHER *allows us our little pleasure—I imagine that the second-long myriads of ejaculations in the big, beautiful world trickle and prickle agreeably through her sense of life. But occasionally, she lets out a big, full, whole fuck: simply to make us see*

:: 548 ::

how serious the matter is: to show us what our real mission is here on earth—just why we were created in the first place. . . .

Oh, I tell you, she made her presence felt very strongly in those days, this powerful lady: she had the upper hand, she conducted the orchestra and was also the great theme and leitmotiv of the festival performance. She was mirrored in the bright Viennese windowpanes, she leaped at you from the adolescents' red cheeks and powerful leg hair—the young people who suddenly walked with such extraordinary self-confidence—right into your line of vision; she resounded toward you from the whir of voices—in words like "renewal of life," "growth," "Nation"—and she created the backdrops in a weather that made your pupils crack: ten below zero Celsius and a bright spring splendor in the air. . . . And she acted hearty and homey and housewifely: she tied on the blue sky as an apron and rolled up her sleeves for a big spring cleaning. It was as if all the Alpine glaciers had come to Vienna, mountain wind was sweeping out its nooks and crannies, every smashed Jewish skull burst open into an edelweiss. . . . Ah, you would feel differently about former fellow travelers (more kindly; less scornfully) if you could have witnessed this festive mood of cosmic spring cleaning. You would be more sympathetic, empathetic, you would understand the subliminal homesickness of an upright North German detergent manufacturer like Witte for such an Eastertide whisk of a scouring cloth by Nature (I repeat: Nature!). *For everyone was seized by it, by this sudden need for fresh air, order, cleanliness, purity. . . . Even Stella, who was Jewish, after all—even she inadvertently said, "I'm not surprised that the sky doesn't darken and split into flashes of lightning. We're not so childlike in our faith in God that we could believe He would do that for our sake. . . . But this freshness, this fragrance of a house that has finally been aired out and put in order—it makes you almost reel. . . ."*

Stella: the intellectual, who had spent her girlhood in the fabled city of Berlin; Stella, who as a child had sat on Flechtheim's lap, and Reinhardt's; Stella, who had corresponded with Kandinsky and Else Lasker-Schüler and received a love letter from

*Archipenko every year: "My beautiful pageboy ..." Stella, who
kept coming in and out of Berlin with her diplomatic passport
(in the piquantly mysterious aura of John's obscure missions)
and who ought to have known what a very different play was
being performed in the wings. Stella, the standard-bearer of
ANTHROPOLIS, spoke these words.... And you still find it incomprehensible that Nagel (that ship's hobgoblin of the categorical imperative) whipped his arm up for four years as an example
to his fellow soldiers in an enthusiastic up-and-at-'em march-
march—until one fine morning when his arm was shot off?...
And you still brood about the fact that Professor Hertzog was a
brigadier general in the medical corps (like Gottfried Benn, incidentally, whom Stella knew so well)?... Or that Rönnekamp,
the Zarathustra Nietzschean, spent the year 1948 with genitally
attached comrades, carrying out the agapes, the communal military banquets, that he had, unhappily, been forced to miss in the
concentration camp from 1939 to 1945?... Yes indeed, where
were you in those intoxicating weeks and months that followed
March of the year 1938? Not in Vienna, I know. But presumably
in your student pad: German literature and journalism, eh? The
proper discipline for bluestockinged upper-class daughters....
At any rate, you were not in Ostmark when it was finally attached to the Reich. Ostmark, which was suddenly much more
robustly Alpine, much more costume-happy and indigenous,
much more imperial in its cultural mission than Old Austria had
ever been since the days of Archduke John of yore.... For if you
had been there, you would have learned straight from the
(mountain-fresh) source what extraordinary resistance it took
to keep from giving in to a certain itchy restlessness—how shall I
put it? The epidermal stimulus of a universally powerful mood
that included not only the urge for peaks, for pure, thin air and a
clear view of distances, but also risk and the pleasurable bewitchment of vertigo—and then into the Alpine hut and into the Alpine dairy maid—goddammit! Into any old black hole, into the
big black mother hole of blindly breeding, blindly eating Nature.
    In the summer following March 1938, I sojourned in the Salz-
burg region with Stella. John now had a lot to do in Prague, and
he had rented a house for her on the Mondsee, where he occa-*

:: 550 ::

*sionally spent the weekend: a wooden house like a cuckoo clock.
We lived a rather earthbound Alpine life there from April to
September. . . .*

*One might have thought that we had screwed enough a year
earlier (the summer of 1937 in Bucharest and its immediate surroundings)—but no: we mated like rutting wildcats, spitting and
howling, in the detritus and under the firs and dwarf pines,
clawed and clamped into each other, rolling down the forest
slopes, panting and climbing up to the peaks to survey the heights
and pouncing on each other there like vindictive demons—in
mountaineering costumes, if you please: I was the cowherd up
there on the slope, wearing lederhosen (very practical because of
the fly) and a quaintly green, stitched jacket with staghorn buttons (whose imprint we then found on her breasts—her behind
bore the imprint of the pine needles.). I rocked my mountain-
lion manliness on naked suntanned knees—and she, she was the
sheer Puster Valley with her narrow, dark head (I chewed up
her neck when I discovered the first white threads in her raven
hair: Ô vraiment marâtre Nature, puisqu'une telle fleur ne dure
que du matin jusqu'au soir!). Her almond-eyed Bedouin head
rose out of decrepit fringed shawls (great-grandmother's trous-
seau: we were supplied by every antique dealer on either side of
the Inn and over and under the Enns). Tiny wood anemones
were embroidered into her silver-buttoned velvet bodice; she
laced them in with belts plated with copper and silver like the
harnesses of brewery horses. And out of them, the heavy linen
skirts (printed on wooden forms) and silk aprons (interwoven
with golden threads) billowed into a brood-hen basket. Your
highly honored compatriots from Neustrelitz, Brera, and Winsen-on-the-Luhe, who were swarming into Salzkammergut after
years of painful separation from their Ostmark brethren and
their dairy products, gaped and gawked when they saw us at the
tavern garden in the evening. . . . And if we then exchanged a few
Rumanian words, their spoons fell into the mounds of whipped
cream they had dished up (in the Old Reich, you see, whole milk
had already become scarce). There was agitated murmuring
(". . . a certain Latin touch in specific isolated valleys here—that
probably explains the aquiline nose . . ."), and this amused us no*

end. I couldn't reach fast enough under all that peasant textile wealth; I yanked my almond-eyed, black-haired, milking-stool princess behind the nearest bush, shoved her behind the closest rock protuberance, and with my wild farmhand-paws peeled her bare Jewess body out of everything that was homespun, hand-woven, embroidered with church-going swank, worn out by wedding-night work. I shredded out her alien-race nakedness, spliced out her cable-stitch-stockinged legs. . . . We committed a miscegenation that was not provided for in the Nuremberg Laws: we rutted blasphemously with all of Alpine nature. . . . And when I was gasping my last breath and only my chamois-leather suspenders were holding me together, and she was lying in the moss among the crushed fern as though she had toppled from high up on the mountain wall and crashed down here, her arms and legs bent in a swastika, her head dangling to the side, only the not quite closed lids still trembling (she's been really dead for twenty-five years now, and that trembling of her lids still reaches me—Stella in Alpine moss: overhead, in the star-seething heavens, glittering fist-size fragments: URSA MAJOR, *ursa minor, Cassiopeia, Betelgeuse, hazy galactic whey—who knows what was already dead while its trembling light still reached us? . . . And cold, white, sawtoothed peaks, towering dark masses shoved right up close to us, megatons of primordial rock squeezing upon our chests . . . and, in the tattered black of the firs, a sublime soughing . . .), when we gradully began to gather our shattered limbs and torn-off antique costume buttons, when we, so weary with wandering, began to drag ourselves back to our cuckoo-clock cottage to sink into the checkered featherbeds (only to be riveted into each other again)—then we knew why we were doing all this: out of fear. . . . Not out of fear of Adolf Hitler and his brown squads and gray iron men and knackwurst-shaped civilian officials with huge killer hands (what did we care about them? we were both foreigners: Stella had a British diplomatic passport and I a conscription order to join the Royal Rumanian Army as a one-year volunteer). What we feared was:* the big cat.

We probably didn't realize how correct our feelings were. And we weren't the only ones. Something had come into our minds, something that left everyone around us in a state of panicky rap-

ture, a furious midsummer-light fear.... And that something, lurking in everything, in all people, all things, all events—like a picture-puzzle face inscribed in them, inhumanly huge and yet terrifyingly human—its name was NATURE.

We were overwhelmed by it. We served this big, strong Alpine nature, served it with our bodies from dawn to dusk. We never let go of each other. If we occasionally needed to recover a little, we walked hand in hand to the decaying boathouse in the reeds along the lake. There, we had discovered gigantic cobwebs in the timberwork under the planks of the pier. We lay down by the webs, caught flies, and tossed them in—and, hand in hand, like Hansel and Gretel, watched them as their struggles in the net of the web signaled the spider in its funnel-shaped hideout, we watched it stick out its nasty head and then jerk out its thick, furry body ... watched it shoot out and, with a cruel technical perfection (which raised goose bumps on the backs of our necks), secure the torn rib threads of the web, then scurry toward the trapped fly, paralyze it with a cunning sting, and start to wrap it up in spinning whirls. Our hands stuck together, sweating, while we watched the powerlessness of the fly in this tighter and tighter hammock ...

and when the fly was finally spun solid, looking like a caterpillar in its cocoon, we killed the spider and destroyed the net. There were so many, after all; they kept us entertained all summer.

> *Said Solomon to Sheba*
> *And kissed her Arab eyes*
> *"There's not a man or woman*
> *Born under the skies*
> *Dare match in learning with us two.*
> *And all day long we have found*
> *There's not a thing but love can make*
> *The world a narrow pond."* ...

Yes indeed, my friend: that's the sort of thing Stella was doing in those days. Stella: it's not surprising that I was capable of that—I am and always have been an avowed nature lover. But Stella! ... However, we must bear in mind that our actions were in keeping with the collective behavior. Something had happened to Stella that happened to pretty much all the people on our old continent: she no longer dreamed about ANTHROPOLIS, the City of Man. The Zeitgeist had turned. The cities were dying. Humanity was building its New Jerusalem outdoors. In the middle of nature. People were striving to return to the Great Mother. She was the new model in their souls—designed by our confrère D. H. Lawrence for the era: a magnificent female with fat clusters of piglets on all teats. A perfect specimen of fertility; the goldfish jumped wherever she pissed. A housewife, I tell you, never emitting a fart without instantly transforming it into chlorophyll. . . . THE GREAT MOTHER—it was actually she who was being celebrated in the Alpine land of Ostmark. The purpose of the radiant Yule night of March 12 in Vienna had been to conjure her up. The millions of termites, drunk with light, ecstatic with fresh air, had danced their termite dance for her alone. She had sent out her favorite son, from Braunau-on-the-Inn, so that mankind might celebrate her and so that she might soon show her true face: her dreadful carrion face. That blood-and-lymph-dripping maggot-sack of her body. The sky-high pyramid of skulls on which she thrones. . . . That was she, our dear Mama. The Führer guaranteed that she did not stir only in the wombs of German maidens, in the hopping of little goats on the flowery meadow, in the blissful sour-milk vomiting of babies, in the testicle-shaking rigid marching step of our boys; she also had to show herself in the full majesty of the Omnivore, who needed only to growl briefly like a predator to have a couple of Jews tossed into her mouth—a couple of thousand, a couple of million—and then, if need be, if that wasn't enough, then a couple of million Aryans in the bargain: one's own sons, one's father, one's mother, the grandchild in the cradle. . . .

Uncle Helmuth had good reason to listen to the voices from the beyond that announced a potentizing of our planet by Adolf Hitler. Austria's greatest son, the former suburban asphalt-walker, whom we had seen as a savior and redeemer, grouchily snuffling into his butcher's mustache under his oversize doorman's cap, as he entered Vienna through the divided sea of the

*people—he truly seemed to be chosen for that mission. Nature
had been alienated from mankind, violated by technology and
art, and he was restoring her to her full rights—and this took
place in the spring wind of the* Zeitgeist; *even a genetic alien like
Stella could not resist.*

*No arguments could refute this. Reason—if it was worth its
salt—had to declare itself off limits. The force that drew and
steered was the collective feeling. Everything that occurred in the
thin air of an incomprehensible, but undeniable, irrefutably
powerful enthusiasm came out of the collective feeling. It was so
primeval, so earthy, so full of life, and yet so pure! It came virtually from the Alpine glaciers and tasted as clean as mountain
air and as fresh as a mountain spring, even over slit bellies. It
foamed with the trout streams through the valleys into the lowlands, tearing along the souls. Anyone who was not destined by
Nature to be a victim or was totally dull and without functioning
sensoria was torn along. His tie was torn from his throat and his
shirt collar was torn aloft and he was offered up—to the* GREAT
MOTHER. *What is man, Czerwenka? Chaff in the wind of time,
Herr Professor. And the wind was blowing out again into the
open countryside. The Garden of Eden had recently become a
natural refuge. Human beings were ensuring its care and protection with rifles. Shielding the Alpine flora and gassing vermin
and Jews. The fictions were pine-needle green and rich in vitamins. And the* GREAT MOTHER *laughed so hard that her sides
ached—as she looked forward to the next big feeding . . .*

□   □   □

IT WAS LIKE A VICIOUS REVENGE when I spoke to my dead
friend:

Revenge on the insatiably alert, bright eyes, clear as water,
gaping from the thick glasses—behind them someone busily
copying everything down, recording every word in the fine-
limbed script of intellectuals, inscribing everything with a sharp
quill in the greasy gray matter of the brain "as if it had been cut

into his eyelid with an engraver's cutter." . . . Why is he storing it up? What does he plan to do with it? How is he going to render it? . . .

"All these things that I'm so recklessly chattering about seem to fascinate you—or am I mistaken?"

His face is nicely reddened: a blond's thin skin, boy-scout lock combed back over the high, narrow forehead (start of a steeple head: underneath, it's more massive, more Lutheran). A few beads of sweat on it. Restrained excitement. He's controlling himself nicely, but the face is not dominated by the eyes, which, grotesquely magnified, gape out of the round steel frames of the glasses; no, the face is dominated by the mouth: mollusk flesh, quivering with sensitivity.

He nods by way of confirmation: *"You are not mistaken. I am fascinated!"*

Hence, revenge for every sentence pulled out. For the sanctimonious simplicity in the sharp alertness. For the quick weighing, for the swift connection of anything he hears. For the spinning of threads, the lying in wait, the shooting at the prey, for the paralyzing sting, the meticulous wrapping and preserving. . . . Revenge for the smile flying up involuntarily amid light breaths—the cruel smile on the nervous lips. For the occasional light sniff from the nostrils. . . .

"I seem to be giving you a great deal of pleasure with my stories? . . ."

"Indeed you are. Extraordinary pleasure. . . ." The irony he manipulates so much more skillfully than I. His superiority. The gentle interspersed questions. The razor-sharp precise comments: the greater suffering, the more cutting experience, the more tested, more knowing patience. And he keeps measuring himself by me. Forces me to measure myself by him. *"If you only knew how much you resemble my cousin Wolfgang. . . ."*

Hackling fraternal hatred in my voice, the voice of Cain:

Too bad you died, Schwab: you could have seen a new, more thorough era. The last time you were in Paris, I gave you a hint about this.

Let's not fool ourselves, dear boy! You've got ants in your pants here, you can't even keep your bottom on your chair for three minutes. And the cause? Sheer panic. You're scared of discovering that this lovely Paris, which is nevertheless and still beautiful, nevertheless and still poignantly Parisian, is no longer itself; you're scared that it died long ago. Just a blank shell: the paling home of a dead creature, still inhabited, but not by those who built it up around themselves out of a compulsion to express something. If so many cities have died, if THE CITY, the myth of ANTHROPOLIS, has died—why should Paris still be alive? True, it's teeming before our eyes—or rather hustling and bustling—as we know: the maggots teeming in a corpse are biologically potentized life. . . . I mean to say: without our noticing it, perhaps during one of our absences, a quiet, bright dying may have taken place—like one of those instantaneous life-changes that amputate our past away from us, so that we undeniably go on living and remain the same persons, and yet no longer live the same lives, even if they are the same on the outside. . . . After all, we know that normally, a real event occurs discreetly. Dramaturgically, it is not proportionate to what it marks. It may be a stroll during which it occurs to you that you no longer love Miss McDonahue, whom so far you have regarded as the nuclear core of your existence. Or a ride on a bus during which it dawns on you that Karl Marx is not the be-all-and-end-all of the world. Such things happen entirely without our interference. A relatively nugatory cause for a sudden, thorough revision of previous thoughts and feelings brings about a sudden, thorough alteration of our entire existence. A private turn of the century, so to speak, which transforms the previous future into something outmoded and the past into a conjecture about any number of possibilities. But you believe that this is your personal, private turn of the century. In reality, the change lies in the times, and everyone is affected by it one way or another. For you, however, it was a turn of essence. And naturally, you go on living, and so does the world, to be sure. The world, as we know, is divided into facts. One thing may be true or not true, and everything else will stay the same. And the truth, the fact, is the persistence of circumstances. The latter, however, change all at once, so essentially that we no longer know for sure what was true and what wasn't—and nevertheless, *all factuality remains as it was. But no longer—how shall I put it?—no longer in the same* innocence. . . . *I am expressing myself quite clumsily again. What I want to say is simple, you know. For people like us, the experience of time is a* gradual increase of guilt. *Perhaps not even a personal guilt so much as a collective guilt. Original sin. The guilt of belonging to the human race. Especially to a dying civilization. Why else would you have the jitters? Why can't you stay seated? Why do you roam the streets of Paris like a hungry wolf? Like a murderer drawn to the scene of his crime?*

Admit it: You feel that you share the guilt for the death of the city. You too have betrayed ANTHROPOLIS. *So you skulk around here to find its corpse—and yet you're too scared to look at it and see your own cadaver. Let me make a suggestion: let us regard the turns of our essence as something positive. Simply as new steps. Metamorphosis existence. Butterfly existence. You've got to pass through the maggot stage. Who knows what's coming afterward? Uncle Helmuth spoke of dematerialization. Let's take the chance! It's totally painless. Without the shock of physical death. First, it happens to our environment. A city dies away under our very noses, as it were. You wake up one fine day, stick your head out the window, peer into the air, sniff at the patch of heaven that you can see over the air shaft, and you ascertain that out there the weather is extraordinarily fine, golden-blue—the fine weather that can have a sedate and superior smile on a foggy day when it lies in ambush for you—time has time, of course. The air is a bit fresh perhaps, but that's good for your smoker's bronchia. So you brush your teeth, shave, put on a particularly attractive necktie, and stroll out into the street—and all at once you notice that the city has died, and you with it, of course. True, everything looks exactly as it did the day before. The houses are standing in their places, the streets are teeming, the cars are rolling shinily along the boulevards, the street of man-in-the-street faces under hats, caps, all kinds of hair, unkempt or combed, meticulously curled or wind-tousled, flows, dances, whirls, halts, dams up, breaks out, ebbs, swells again—and they are all deceased in the* LORD, *and you are too. . . . Fine and dandy! How interesting! How very literary! You have just sloughed off an essence form*

that was previously your self, from now on you are a new self,
forging ahead with new possibilities of experience. The old self
sinks back like the dry husk of a larva from which a butterfly has
hatched. The burned-out capsule of a rocket stage. You yourself
plunge into a new trail with new bright eruptions of fire out of
your behind. . . .

Are you disturbed by the abstractness of the new form of exis-
tence? It is consistent with our loss of gravity. Do we mourn it?
Is it really true that we lost paradise yesterday? Is it true that we
were more innocent yesterday? Just what is that anyway—YES-
TERDAY? A myth. A legend. A fairy tale about ourselves.
Dreamed by those who cannot dream about themselves in a to-
morrow. Is that not the reason for our feeling of guilt? We know
that we are a breed without a future. Yesterday, we could still
dream ourselves ahead. Today, we dream ourselves back into our
dream of yesterday. But keep your spirits up! How does Novalis
put it? We are on the verge of awakening when we dream that
we are dreaming. Why not as maggots? Without a past, if you
please. Without a history. Likewise without a future. Creatures
of the present. Roadside-café people. Limited to a pure here-and-
now. If that doesn't appeal to you—then, dear friend, all you can
do is escape by forging ahead: into perfect abstraction. The pure
butterfly. Dissolve in absolute abstractness—like you up there in
the icy sky-blue. Or like me in my literary existence: as a literary
object. Whether my own or yours. . . .

□   □   □

I STOOD NAKED at the window and peered up through the air
shaft to the sky. Coldness bit into my skin and made my scrotum
contract. I thought of the day when I had looked out of the same
window at an angle, down to the opposite window (whose shutters were now closed), and Schwab and I had surprised Madame
in her nakedness. I thought of her big, maternal breasts, whose
fullness had charged into my gonads. In those days, I was not exactly overfed by the tender virginality of Dawn's breasts (which,
moreover, I had not yet relished). At Dawn's age, Madame's tre-

mendous appendages must have been magnificently bursting, with pale, bud-like nipples.

Rarely does one set eyes on such perfection (much less set hands or kisses or bites). I did once, however, when I was frozen stiff in the collapsed air shaft of a bombed-out house in Hamburg, shortly after my arrival from Nuremberg. She was a victim of the widely feared "rubble killer," a deliciously beautiful woman: stark naked and silkily glittering in her frozen matte nymph-skin gently strewn with feathery snow crystals; only her face was bluish violet, like an eggplant. You see, the rubble killer strangled his victims with a wire noose on a wooden throttle valve. All he had to do was twist it behind the victim's neck to tighten the wire with a horrible lever effect. The eyes of the corpse very sharply revealed the power of this tightening twist: one eye had rolled up at a leftward slant under the caved-in lid, the other gaped dully at a rightward slant toward the stiff nipple. And her tongue had burst out of the cracked lips as though she wanted to lick the nipple (a hanged man supposedly has an ejaculation at the very last moment—what happens to women?)—

Anyway, it was during my breeding season with Christa that they discovered that woman, yet another victim of the rubble killer, and I believe Christa had a good night after that. I was at my peak, as now.

I stood at the open window and wished to be seen in my morning glory. By Madame, preferably, or even one of the fat-arsed Algerian women, Or, for all I cared, by one of the traveling salesmen or the chambermaid who was probably cleaning a room across the way. Or the handsome Pole, who must have been copulating with Madame one floor below, after finishing his night shift. . . .

I wished for a scandal. A voice furiously shouting *"Tu te fous du monde, salaud?"* A window being slammed shut. The telephone: *"Vous n'avez pas honte, monsieur?"* Someone banging at my door: *"Dites donc: ça vous amuse?"*

I wished for *myself as an event.*

It occurred to me that this too was connected with my constant thoughts about Schwab, with what had appeared to me in our

precarious friendship as the *quest for defeat:* Eros, which had let
me pleasurably feel the first conscious humiliation of my life,
when I had been cruelly laughed to scorn by classmates for an
artfully recited English poem. But this was lay psychology. I was
hunting for a different prey. For example: the connection between all this and the *something* that drove me to write.

□   □   □

FUNNY THAT IT WAS really by way of my friend Nagel that I
got to meet the piglets and thus came to write at all (not Wohlfahrt & Associates, of course—that rosy little race didn't exist
back then—just their biological ancestors, the primeval pigs of
the postwar German movie industry; I would almost be tempted
to say—but I would then have to beg forgiveness from Stoffel &
Associates—R.I.P. for this locution; it would by no means be
meant pejoratively; its function would be purely evolutionary—
those species of *Sus scrofa* already domesticated in the Stone
Age, in the order of mammals of the setiferous artiodactyla, who
are at the origin of the noble families of the European domestic
swine).

Decent Nagel, in his above-board literary (and human) uprightness, has nothing to do with the nimble little race, of course,
although every one of his best-selling novels could have been
made into box-office smashes for housewives. But the rise of his
stellar course took place in the constellation of Stoffel & Associates, the ubiquitously long-forgotten heroes and forebears of the
postwar German cinema.

They too, you see, are part of those legendary wintertides of
the years 1945–48, which I (perhaps with a few rare members of
my age group) must recall with persistent nostalgia, though they
have otherwise slipped away from the memory of the German
collective as thoroughly as the glacial periods of the Tertiary.

In those days, in the bronze heavens over Hamburg (rusting
soon after midday, toward the evening), near the Bronze Age
community around Professor Hertzog in the garden house on the
Elbchaussee, another star arose, a star that would soon outshine

Nagel's meteorites before its extinction: the Astra Film Company—boldly wrested from the hesitant occupation authorities, mainly thanks to the vital energy of a man named Horst Jürgen Stoffel.

Stoffel had succeeded in saving a wood-processing plant (which had quite profitably supplied carbine shafts to the Wehrmacht) and had seen to it that it survived the war's end with rather large stocks of timber. Seamlessly adjusting to the new historical conditions, he took the enterprise (which had been evacuated to Winsen-on-the-Luhe) in hand and converted it to the production of Christmas toys—

a highly popular item, for instance, was the so-called Eckermann doll: a droll little troll made of branch knots and sporting a flattened back that could be used as a bookend. Scherping was so delighted that he planned to add it (unrationed) to his edition of Goethe's *Faust* (copyright 1947, all rights reserved), which had been licensed by the military government.

I must not forget to mention that the publishing industry was already beginning to stir. Just as all manner of life was still quivering in the ruins. The red-light alleys at Gänsemarkt and on the Reeperbahn had also remained intact (like the Davidswache and the City Hall).

Horst Jürgen Stoffel was not a man whose enterprising spirit could be restricted to the manufacture of cultural goods. After the Eckermann doll, he started producing wooden soles for ersatz shoes (which soles, to be sure, could be purchased only with rationing stamps). However, his lumber supplies were now categorized as "controlled goods" and subject to a quota.

And it came to pass that from one of the allocations, eight hundred seventy more pairs of soles were carved than could normally be carved by the most efficient utilization of raw material. Horst Jürgen Stoffel thus found himself in a ticklish dilemma: as an upstanding entrepreneur, he was obliged to register the increased output; but if he reported the overproduction, then inevitably the arseholes at the Industry Office would cut the allocations by enough raw material for eight hundred seventy pairs of soles (or else expect the same overproduction for the same allocation from that day forward), and, moreover, they would demand an accounting for the missing eight hundred seventy pairs of soles from all previous allocations. Stoffel got out of this predicament by simply "remaindering" the extra eight hundred seventy soles on the black market.

I don't remember what price was fetched by a pair of black-market wooden soles in 1947—Stoffel, at any rate, got a hundred fifty marks a pair from the middleman, a paltry sum when one recalls that fifteen Wild Woodbine cigarettes cost the same at that time. Still and all, Stoffel had one hundred thirty thousand five hundred marks in his hands. To be sure, that was worth no more than thirteen thousand fifty cigarettes, roughly what a medium smoker puffs into the atmosphere, after a brief incorporation into his pleural cavity, over the course of, say, fifteen months—

what could be more obvious than taking the money, which could so easily dissolve into thin air, and investing it in an industry that creates ephemeral shadow plays? Horst Jürgen Stoffel applied to the military government for a license to produce movies.

Of course, there were other reasons, linked to the times. Hamburg, as we know, is called the Gateway to the World, and during those winter days it was worthy of the name. Never before or since has it been the scene of such animate transience as in the first phases of the mass migrations (not yet arranged by travel agencies but triggered by the advancing Russians), when the natives of Brandenburg (pushed by the Upper and Lower Silesians, who passed through Lausitz and the Magdeburg plains into the Hanover region, and from there northward to Schleswig-Holstein, only to be shoved toward Hesse by the Pomeranians and East Prussians, who were driving the Mecklenburgers before them) advanced into Bavarian territory in order to avoid the Thuringians, who had likewise started moving, while the Rheinlanders, who had been evacuated into the Warthegau, tried to trade positions with the Poles who had been hauled to the mines in the Ruhr; however, the Rheinlanders were severely hindered by the Sudeten Germans, who had been thrown westward (and whose flanks were attacked by Transylvanian Saxons and Bukovinan Germans (Gaia used to say: *What do you need to make a*

*good salad? A spendthrift for the oil, a miser for the vinegar—
and a madman to shovel it over and over*).

Anyway, back then things were extraordinarily animated. Although the means and routes of transportation were demolished
and also inhibited by countless ID checks, incessant swarms of
people trickled along the provisionally patched-up nervous system of the Western Zone road network. Trains were so thickly
breaded with people that they looked like rainworms after rolling
in sand. Railroad stations were military camps. The waiting
rooms were like the dormitory of Sainte-Brigitte . . .

And thus, of course, there were all kinds of unexpected meetings. Human destinies interpleated unpredictably, and attach-
ments formed; Christa (whose meager hoard of language was
enriched with the lovely images of a farmyard childhood) said,
"Cow and donkey harnessed to the plow."

As far as Stoffel's application for a license is concerned, it was
assisted by just such an—at first blush—heterogeneous attachment. You see, the originally involuntary migratory instinct had
also seized hold of the moviemakers. But not necessarily every
survivor of Ufa Films was incited to move from Berlin-
Babelsberg to Munich-Geiselgasteig. A few flocks wound up in
Hamburg. There, in the subterranean makeshift waiting room of
an eye doctor, Horst Jürgen Stoffel had his fateful (fateful for
me) encounter with Astrid von Bürger, the emancipated daughter of a professor of metallurgy at the Technical University of
Berlin. In *Blitzkrieg* times, by way of the School of Physical
Culture, she had become a movie extra at Babelsberg, where a
friendly cameraman had got her a tiny part, in which she had
caught Reich Minister Goebbels' eye and then quickly risen to
Greater German film fame.

Astrid was a caustic girl. In later years, long after divorcing
Horst Jürgen, ruefully renouncing the cinematic art and remar-
rying, this time a solid electronic industrialist named Häberle,
bearing him flocks of children, and moving to an attractive mountain farm in the Alpine lime countryside south of Bad Tölz (and
if she hasn't died, then she's still living there today!), she would
tell about this meeting in an unadulterated Berlin-Charlottenburg
accent:

"Hell, if that wasn't love at first dim sight! . . . I'm sitting on that bench of repentance in the basement office, waiting to be ushered in to ol' Doc Four Eyes because my specs had dropped and the last Russian in Berlin had tramped on them with his Siberian boots, and without one and a half diopters I can't tell the difference between the 'ladies' sign and the 'gentlemen,' and the guy's dragged down the stairs by two other guys like a plaster war casualty on the Pergamon frieze, and they drop him very carefully in an armchair, and he keeps holding that neatly folded handkerchief over his eye, because while he was inspecting his factory in Dumpsville on Shit's Creek, a splinter from one of his dolls flew into his eye, and then he takes the handkerchief off his bloodshot li'l piggy eye and gives me such a heartrending look through his veil of tears, that I feel a li'l sorry for him on account of his pain—and all that plus the blond lock over the thinker's brow, ya know, and him taller than a centurion and stuffed to the hilt, his flesh white as boiled cod—well, I say to myself, Astrid my girl, I say, you're gonna buy that rubber lion, he's one of the blow-up kind, you can let off the overpressure, it's as easy as pie. That's my type of virility—which is why I also like my Häberle. . . ."

But I too (in contrast to Christa and, incidentally, Nagel) did not find the combination of Astrid von Bürger and Horst Jürgen Stoffel to be all that bad. For semantic reasons, to be sure: in my opinion, the two names dovetailed marvelously, and it was with their names that they first entered my life: through Nagel, who came to me one day and spoke so glowingly of the founding of Astra Films and of the sublime couple.

However, Horst Jürgen's temporarily and unilaterally dimmed vision had likewise instantly recognized Astrid as his ideal love object.

Very well! Because of the above-indicated mutual readiness, it didn't take much courtship; besides, Stoffel had only to give a little free play to his organizational talent, and any female would melt. Winsen-on-the-Luhe was surrounded by farms, in which cows, pigs, and all kinds of domestic fowl were still thriving. A wood-processing plant had something to offer, a fair exchange with mutual profit. A good country ham could get a nice number of bottles of whiskey, the whiskey in turn brought willing ears at the traffic office—i.e., a license for a car and a gasoline allocation; with the car one could go in for large-scale butter hoarding; the butter could be exchanged for nylon stockings and plenty of toiletries; for a bottle of Chanel No. 5 any farmer's wife in the Lüneburg Heath would give up her resistance and hand over any home-cured ham. In short, a smoothly running *perpetuum mobile*. No sooner were his eyes fixed than Horst Jürgen read all of his Astrid's wishes in *her* eyes—and behold: her wishes coincided with his—

for what, after all, can be the foremost wish of a movie actress who has only just reached the zenith of her career and suddenly cannot make movies because there is no such thing as a movie company? Don't worry about it, darling, we'll start our own. Here's a ham, you can get so and so much scotch for it, for scotch there's Chanel No. 5, for Chanel No. 5 the good will of the German secretary (and bedmate) of the military government's cultural officer, he'll give you not only a license but also, of course, film, and several automobile permits with the necessary gasoline allocations, which means butter again (and more of it); for butter, cigarettes again; for cigarettes, ham again; after all, we've got to crank up the economy in this pigsty, and first and foremost the movie business.

And in the movie business, Astrid knew every man and every man knew her. After all, the episode with Reich Minister Goebbels had been maliciously inflated by envious and competitive witnesses; everyone in the movie business had been invited there sooner or later, anyone who didn't go was risking his life for nothing—in any case: "Stop carrying on, Karl. When they wanted to stick you in the propaganda company, you preferred to take part in *Jew Süss*—right? Just keep quiet, my lad; they strung up your Lisa for other reasons, not for resisting but because of the Bulgarian she kept running around with, they couldn't find him then because he'd taken French leave—right? Don't imagine you can go to town on that. . . . So, mud in your eye, friends! To Astra! And to the great future of the reborn German screen!"

We received tidings of the rise of the Astra Film Art Company before this star had ascended in full radiance over the horizon. Horst Jürgen Stoffel's entrepreneurial dynamics and organizational talent (supported by Astrid's inside knowledge) kept him, of course, from overlooking the fact that in order to build up a proper movie-production company (and also to get the license), he needed a so-called project—that is to say, a subject to grind through the lens—and for that, in turn, he required the work of intellectually creative people.

But this, too, was no problem. Intellectuals, too, had washed ashore in Hamburg. The radio, run by the occupation forces, had a nest of them. And these people had got through the political filters; you didn't have to worry that their intellectual products might be tainted by the past—

but alas, they *were* intellectuals. The ideas they suggested were miles from what Horst Jürgen Stoffel's healthy folk sensibility expected to see on the screen, especially at an historic moment when the masses, oppressed by collective guilt feelings, were to be granted messianic promise from that very screen.

(*"Well, if it were up to me, the movie would simply have to be called* A Silver Lining to the Cloud—*you don't have to laugh, Astrid, that much I understand about movies, I know they're a mass-market article, I know the public alone decides what it does or doesn't want to see—and believe me, darling, I'm not living in an ivory tower, I have contact with people every day, not old coffeehouse hangers-on but farmers, workers, factory managers, railroad employees, businessmen: these people expect us to give them a guidepost for the future, and a future that they understand, that they can tackle with their own hands, that they can see emerging from the labor of their own hands—believe me, gentlemen, and you too, darling: political philosophy is of no interest to people now, they've had it up to here, it'll come automatically anyway, what they really care about is things that are strictly human, that are close to them: Give us this day our daily bread—right? And then a long pause—and then maybe: And forgive us our debts . . ."*)

Little in this connection could be expected from the intellectuals who were creating "The Cultural Word" at the North West German Radio Network.

(*"Just listen to just one of those programs—why, that's coffeehouse chitchat—and it doesn't even have the pep the Jews developed way back when at the* Romanisches Café.*"*)

Still, that's where the solution came from. One of the secretaries of the church radio program was friends with Ute Seelsorge, who had told her a great deal about the fascinating discussion evenings at the home of a young writer named Karl Nagel—in a word: the cinema bigwig Stoffel came and (to put it in the graphic lingo of the executive world, which, thank heaven, has taken over the cultural business) "made a pitch to Nagel."

From the first few discussions with Horst Jürgen Stoffel and Astrid von Bürger, Nagel returned home with the euphoria of a lover freshly struck by his gracious madness—and thus also duly and ardently communicative. I couldn't help basically agreeing:

"To judge by the name, it seems to be a promising connection: George the Dragon Slayer with the defiant eagle-height in *Horst* [eyrie] and the earthbound rooting in *Stoffel* [material as well as yokel]—plus the North Star, *Astrid*, over the delicate sociological synthesis of *von* and *Bürger* [commoner]—the nobility of the mind, no doubt?"

Nagel bared a fang.

"Is she blond?" I asked.

No. *He* was blond: Stoffel. Straw-blond. She was dark. A queen of Iceland. I was shown a photo (charming dedication, primitively printed: "To my coffin-Nagel [nail]! Astrid")—

Aha, so she was the one. . . .

I should have known, of course. Even after carpet bombs had flattened whole city districts, the unshakable effigy of the beautiful Astrid had kept smiling down from poster tatters at the population (who, according to Reich Minister Goebbels, were not even intimidated by such acts of terrorism) or was wafted along on the singed front page of some Berlin magazine, fluttering in the warm-air currents over the glowing remains of conflagrations.

The face was beautiful, alert, bold, and base—the human epitome of the invincible baseness à la capital of the German Reich. . . .

But good old Nagel couldn't know anything of this. For all his sophistication ("The Bulgarian is the Prussian of the Balkans"), Berlin remained a blank spot on his intellectual map. Berlin in general, and certainly the Berlin shortly before and shortly after Stalingrad. At that time, he had been in the war, good old Nagel, risking his neck, while I . . .

I, in any case, associated this picture with a sassy female face surrounded by Brunhilde hair, redolent of visions of the Berlin slums—

I was afflicted by an entire era: three years of draft-dodging in a virtually manless city crashed in on me; their cynicism melded with a cheeky *spiritus loci*, the bad spirit of a city that has given up its mind. . . . I could hear its dreadful jargon, the pulp-novel name Astrid von Bürger evoked a whole Berlin ballad, churned out of a hurdy-gurdy like a lyrical toilet-paper roll, collapsing at the end of each stanza in a rooty-toot-toot as if under a cascade of shards, and then unabashedly straightening up again like a bounce-back doll. I had to write it all down, at least as revenge for Nagel's betrayal.

I was irresistibly tempted to do something malicious: hadn't Nagel betrayed me, his bosom buddy, in the beautiful crèche period, to Hertzog? Hadn't he betrayed our sacred buddyship even further by retreating into his garden house and assiduously writing without letting me in on his plans, his ordeals and triumphs? . . . Very well! I could write too. It was mainly valuable for myself; an act of overcoming the past—but, of course, it was primarily meant to be funny: I wanted to make Nagel laugh. And if the verses of the poem that I dedicated to the "poet" Nagel evinced all my hatred of the recent historical events, then it was, as Stoffel would have said, "on account of the times." I, for my part, wanted to amuse the good Nagel, not shock, much less offend him. Not even with the title of the poem: "Per aspera ad astra" (subtitle: "The Rise of a Film Star in the Third Reich").

Admittedly, it wasn't a very nice poem. But it depicted the cultural background, the foil against which Astrid von Bürger had to be seen in order to be fully understood and appreciated. And that background could not be depicted in anything but our so-called stave rhyme, following the literary recipes of the greatest German: for a prose description, said Goethe, the background was not important enough.

As for Nagel, it was not only his lack of necessary familiarity with the milieu that kept him from a sociological understanding of the beautiful Astrid. He was in love. Had he known the obvious, he would no longer have believed in the survival of the formal energy of that milieu; he would have regarded the memory evoked thereof as arbitrarily and improperly quoted, and he would have labeled it a rather shabby *ad hominem* argument. But because he was in love, he took my poem without further ado as sheer perfidy on my part. There was a rupture in our friendship, and it could never again be glued together.

Fine. I had no other choice but to feel ashamed. I had not only hurt a friend's tender feelings but, far worse, transgressed against a tendency of the *Zeitgeist*, against the collective desire to forget.

□   □   □

FOR SUCH WAS THE SITUATION in that legendary wintertide. Germans were willing to forget. The world was gray, but was to be reborn. Yesterday was only a rumor now. It had nothing to do with today.

There was, of course, a terrible myth about it. Everyone knew the myth and was burdened with it, as if haunted by the memory of a bad dream. A deeply gnawing malaise, a dull, irrefutable sense of guilt, a constant reminder of an incomprehensible fall of man—this lay at the bottom of reality, padding it darkly and also casting its shadow into the future.

Everyone knew: never again—even if the miraculous should happen, and the houses rose again from the rubble cities, the streets became filled again with the hustle and bustle of people, there were all kinds of comforts again, some kinds of fullness and all kinds of change and variety, as well as summer skies, warmth, sunshine, and not only frost and worry and gray wretchedness under hills of debris—never again would the world be the same as it had been in time out of mind (only yesterday, before its last great decline).

That much was certain. The world had been reborn—but grayer and bleaker by a shadow. There would be no more carefree atmosphere, no cheery optimism, no happiness that did not taste slightly ashen. . . .

But even though everyone knew that happy-go-lucky joy and optimism were lost for all time, no one knew for sure why and how they had been lost.

The dead—it wasn't the dead. We sow our grain in the dust of the dead. It was not the huge murdering. People have murdered since the world began. People will be murdering tomorrow.

So, then, what was it?

In those days, snow fell from the iron sky in nastily beautiful crystals, and it bit painfully into the anemic eyelids of the lost, who trudged through the rubble fields with ashen faces and with sharp shoulders pulled up to their ears because of the cold and grief and misery, and the snow pitted and patted the frost-chewed ruin of a city into a glittering white-furred Arctic, over which the charnel-house reality of yesterday hung like a northern light.

Nothing was forgotten as yet (though everything was rapt in the mystical). Death still followed one step behind everyone like an aide-de-camp. Hamburg was stalked by the so-called rubble killer, who strangled his victims with a wire noose. They were found in collapsed rear buildings, stark naked and frozen stiff, with laced in throats and bluish-red faces, from which tongues and eyes dangled as in medieval gargoyles. No one knew the victims, no one knew where they'd come from, where they belonged, or where they'd been going. Hamburg, the Gateway to the World, a world that had become so suffocatingly confined, was a crossroads now for countless uprooted beings, who, with their lost papers, had also forfeited their names, their backgrounds, their "reality." Their murderer too lived among us, together with the many others. And now, twenty years later, gazing up at the rectangle of blue sky over the air shaft of a lousy one-night cheap hotel on the Place des Ternes in Paris, I felt as if I could have been that murderer—not necessarily the murderer of the nameless victims during the Hamburg rubble period but the murderer of my life-dream, the assassin of the promise into which I was born, into which every human being is born. . . .

But what did all that mean now? Around me everything was dead. Stella was dead and Uncle Ferdinand's Middle Kingdom; Cousin Wolfgang was dead, and the Berlin of the gracious beginning of our life-dream. Schwab was dead and Gaia and the beautiful city of Paris. Dead was the old culture of the Occident with all its Middle Kingdoms, and dead was I, made up of stories of the past, a literary invention, a revenant like my dead friend Schwab. Nothing concerned me anymore.

□   □   □

THE CREMATION OF MY FRIEND Schwab took place three days after his demise on October 18, 1965 (exactly three years ago the day before yesterday). In the commiserating presence of all who were near and dear to him. They turned out to be an amazingly presentable grouplet. It filled out the cremation pavilion at the Ohlsdorf Cemetery down to the last seat; in fact, a few people were even standing in back, craning their necks to catch a glimpse of what was happening. Very little was happening, but all sorts of things were going on. First during a worshipful silence, then during the scrambling clamber of organ-pipe sounds in a fugue by Pachelbel (masterfully performed by a radio organist who used to frequent Lücke's Bar and—as it once turned out—was Schwab's downtrodden first cousin twice removed. He was now rendering him his final family love service as a reward for lifelong scorn).

Honey-golden smoke rose steeply from tall white tapers (pre-Raphaelitely inspirited by clusters of lilies at their bases) into the vault of the fire temple, which curved through parabolic ribs into a kind of Expressionistic Oriental gugelhupf Gothic (an architectural achievement of the 1920s that has already become an historic document in our generation).

I don't know who paid for the funeral expenses. Perhaps S.

himself had taken care of them with regular payments to a burial
society (I began to feel he might have been capable of doing so).

Be that as it may: the wealth of flowers was overpowering.

The lily-mellowed candles in the apse were foamingly encircled by sprays of white lilac like ostrich feathers on helmet
adornments. And in the very midst, where an altar normally
looms in a house of God, a blossoming mound of white roses and
camellias ascended out of a declivity one step down. He was presumably resting under the flowers, having finally passed on into
the lighthearted self-lavishing that had been so difficult for his
prim and prudent character.

A dead man's generosity enabled anyone who liked to worship
this prize piece of a flower growers' contest (Dawn's longing for
the Mardi Gras in Nice!) to do so. Needless to say, Scherping
was present: as a bearer of culture, employer, and erotic rival. He
expressed the first function by means of a silk-lined black hat
(which he held in his lap like a pot-au-feu) and the latter two
functions with a cunning gusto in his apple cheeks. At times,
however, his soft mouth twitched painfully—with the corresponding emphasis of pleasure. The drapery of his face was tied
back for the solemn occasion, but with a frivolous touch, like the
hem of a Belle Époque cocotte, who sees a puddle on the pavement as an excuse to reveal her calves.

And Carlotta at his side was a widow transcending all conventions in so comradely a fashion that no one would have dreamed
of asking how many years ago she had left the deceased because
there wasn't even the smallest spot left on his head for another
horn.

And Witte too sat near her; in his lap, the same civic-
association-representative black hat that is always sported in
Hamburg to show economic prosperity in a dignified way despite
a never denied (and certainly never doubted) lower-class background. Whereas Scherping's hat would, when donned, slide
down over both ears, Witte usually pushed his own smartly off
his forehead: city air makes you feel free.

Witte sat next to the legendary aunt who, in far-off days of youth, when bearing the name Wiebke, like the evening song of a plover, had been temporarily engaged to him; ever since, he had nurtured tender feelings for her. He sat pithily at her side as if ever ready to support her should the need arise—

not only out of devotion but also in the full weather-proof awareness that it befitted him to bear the club banner here—and here more than anywhere else. His apoplectic skull shone like the cocarde of a champion sharpshooter: blue in the red-framed core, surrounded by the blazing white of the silvery lion's mane.

The aunt had slipped her nicotine-tanned paw into the arm of Schwab's niece Uschi (whom so far every man had been permitted to screw); and next to Uschi, his thick eyebrows somberly spiraling into the bridge of the nose, sat her new fiancé, Klaus, in stiff, sap-fermenting young manhood, which, in turn, was jealously guarded by Herr von Rönnekamp, raising his master-detective profile with derisive pride. In short: the more or less immediately affected mourners in this Middle Kingdom were also intertwined by a busily spun sperm thread, which also pulled in more remote people.

In the second row, wedged between the production managers of Scherping Publishers (black hats) and the sales directors (black hats), sat the loyal secretary Elisabeth Schmidschelm (a.k.a. Schelmchen or Schelmy or even Ellie the Alkie), who had once seen better days before being gently nudged into retirement at Lücke's Bar after Schwab's departure.

And over her shoulder (heightened hump-like by the brand-new Persian lamb coat collar—Scherping had been forced to pay her off too with his usual generosity) peered—oh, graceful folly!—the enchanted eyes of Lovely Heli (like Christa's lovely spiritual virginity in Nuremberg):

it is with such timid curiosity that the unicorn's young sticks its head out between the oak trunks in the forest to see if its knight is coming. . . .

I looked out to see if Gisela was coming. There was no reason why she too should not make an appearance and say farewell to someone who had offered up his soul to her like a youth his manhood on the altar of Astarte. But I couldn't find her. Presumably, she took her profession too seriously. It was a Saturday afternoon, a time when the regular clients (as she had reported) turn up at the brothel (Scherping's bad reputation in respectable Hamburg circles was largely due to his occasional mid-week outings there, to devote himself to his dark quest for salvation).

Hertzog too was missing, by the way. True, it's not customary for physicians to come to the bier of patients whose passage to the beyond they have conscientiously made more difficult—and thus all the more desirable (after all, Professor Leblanc did not attend Gaia's funeral either). However, this very special case was more than just a medical relationship, and one might have been justified in expecting that the Great Psychopompous would describe, in his full-weighted presence, the ticklish cases to which he had been summoned to help out not merely *qua* scientist but also *qua* philosopher. But as luck would have it (and luck occasionally has a fatality that goes against the rules), a congress of psychologists and psychiatrists had been convened in Münster on that very day. And a dillar-a-dollar scholar of Professor Hertzog's rank could not fail to attend.

However, the ranks of mourners were serried seamlessly even without these two figures (so important in the history of the deceased): from the grieving to the sympathetic; from the mutely moved to the deeply affected; from the long-time supplier (of alcohol) to the relative by marriage; from the dutifully attending representative of the Municipal Agency for Culture (black hat) to the stigmatized newspaper-reader who had once felt profoundly touched by a *feuilleton* by the deceased and had responded with a letter to the editor, presenting his own intricate thoughts, which had eventually degenerated into a correspondence and finally a personal meeting—

(after all, even when house-moving, everyone learns how much unexpected property has gathered in the nooks and crannies of his home: because you acquired it sometime or other for a temporary necessity or even quite spontaneously and with no special purpose in mind, and you were too easy-going to get rid of it in time. . . . Now just imagine what has been collected in the spaciousness of a lifetime exposed to so many random events, even if one leaves it in the prime of manhood! . . .)

Here, a man had passed on who, whether or not he liked it (and whether or not he might have wished for other cities as his adopted home), had been rooted in the solid, land-cultivating citizenry of a Hanseatic Gotham, which, only yesterday, had been planted in the green countryside with gabled gingerbread houses:

—one of the still well-housed comfort-lovers whose childhoods are gaily illustrated with anecdotes of the clan, from which a whole full chest of the German world of toys comes into being: Grandfather's shop close to the free harbor (which shop proliferated into a supermarket chain) and Mother's farm in the marshlands, which farm his uncle had run into the ground, alas, because he had been rather easy-going and a bit boastful during his stint in the cuirassiers (nevertheless, the moor meadows had brought in some twenty million marks as the building site for a squadron of high-rises); Cousin Apothecary in Ochsenzoll with his jars of poison and his officinal bottles from days of yore (monthly turnover: forty thousand marks); and the aunt who had displayed such a great gift for the piano that she had been sent to the conservatory (where she began her rather shady life, which she ended, prosperously, as the owner of a guesthouse on Schwanenteich): all these Buddenbrooks in miniature and mini-miniature had leaped into the new era so successfully that they became its masters; the wind of freedom had swept them out of their upright nook-and-cranny existences into mass administration, and they now carefully throttled that wind in order to steer it, housefatherly, to their mills—and these upcoming burghers were so archetypal in their tough, sly, prudent economics and attachment to objects that any world-beatifying zeal will be wasted on them and must ultimately admit defeat because of the welfare brilliance of their thick, fat necks—

In front of the flower-laden coffin, their heads were thick and dense as cobblestones. God-fearingly bared or else bonneted with reasonably priced millinery creations, their hair curled mildly, maternally, by permanent waves, or charily parted, thinning, or bald—and from the shoulders down, they were welded into a black-matted block. If, overhead, the organ-pipe sounds had not been clambering through and over one another like puppies in a basket, I would have expected a thundering hymn, as if from one mouth, from the many mouths of these many heads: *a mighty fortress was their God*, and they acted as if this were true for my friend Schwab as well.

My dead friend's irony allowed the survivors elbow room for their life-lie: it sovereignly let them falsify his sloughed-off life to bear witness to the upright character of their own, and to declare as humus and topsoil of his mind what actually had merely given birth to his hatred and nurtured his questionable majesty:

the ridiculous potentate gesture of the Intellectual, who, imperious as Tamberlaine, subjugates the endless terrains of intellect and rules, unrestrained, in the realm of possibility: out of hatred for a "reality" in which he never succeeds in tearing himself from the tangle of narrowminded middle-class interests in which his existence is inextricably interwoven with thousands of fibers

He had succeeded in doing so (albeit in a different manner). Hence, he could afford to be magnanimous.

He left the field to those whom he had once so deeply despised. He lay there, so well concealed under his hill of flowers that one couldn't even tell whether it was really he whom all the snowy wealth of blossoms had buried there, and whether he was actually viewing the spectacle, mildly amused, from some spherical corner of the crematorium's pavilion vault or even from outside (blissfully enraptured, at any rate): the solemn laying of the cornerstone for the show-off building of his edifyingly falsified history. A highly gifted son (and hence afflicted by susceptibilities to the extraordinary) of the most solid bourgeoisie, rooted in the strongest national soil and shaped by the landscape; and his sense of duty toward the collective had ordered him modestly to exert a broad effect as an editor in a publishing house instead of focusing his unusual energy on creating an outstanding work of his own.

Thus he hung on the finally drawn noose of his entanglement in destiny like a home-cured ham from which each of the worshipfully gathered could hack off a slice (washed down with the schnapps of self-poignancy). They were delivering unto the purging fire a lucid, educated intellect that had frequently hinted at genius. A man who had raised his brow over the short-lived squalls of the culture business and held it aloft in the grand wind of the true act of creation. And who, although never personally soaring to creativity, had stalked creativity and recognized it and cleared the way for it, and frequently and happily fecundated it, thus attaining an undisputed rank in the cultural reconstruction of postwar Germany. He was flesh of the flesh and bone of the bone of the mourners around him here and blood of their blood (if not spirit of their spirit).

With all the distance that they, respectful toward his "genuine values," recognized as existing between him and their more modest altitude, he had nonetheless emerged from their midst. They had produced him. And even though he had sometimes made them feel his scorn, he had never repudiated them. On the contrary, he had testified to his fateful attachment to them in many a painful utterance.

And it was to be that way for all eternity. He allowed it. It seemed to amuse him mildly. He was free now, hence without hatred.

And I realized that I had been taken in by his final crafty wickedness.

I was attending an ill-timed festival of reconciliation. Not, as I had secretly expected, an apotheotic demonstration of his passionately lived fundamental otherness (whose dark majesty I, his only friend, would have shared). He let me down. He too now made me feel that *I* was the one who was alone and, hopelessly isolated, truly what the burghers here considered me and my kind: chaff in the wind.

Furthermore, I had arrived a moment late, and I sneaked into the devotional temple when the mutely moved hellos and the mutual displays of presence were largely done with and everyone was primed for the actual act of devotion. And once again, I was embarrassed to realize that here, too, I had joined a group more or less randomly, anyway peripherally, and that I had never been properly involved in the social biotope of the man whose intimate confidant, only friend, and spiritual brother I had considered myself to be. So as not to hug the temple door as an obvious straggler, I squeezed forward along the wall, running a gauntlet of water-clear gazes, and in so doing I began, as the phrase goes, to see the light. Indeed, my eyes encountered another pair of eyes and were entirely lost in them: I henceforth gazed with them—gazed at myself. Saw myself not as in a mirror (Gaia: "*Tiens—c'est comme ça que tu te vois!*"), but with the eyes of the eternally unattained other.

And thus I finally recognized myself as different from the way I had imagined I knew myself. The astonished "*So that's you!*" in those other eyes signified a lightning-like illumination for me: "*So that's me!*"

In the drab of German heads—in which, between hairline and coat collar, the physiognomic characteristics of Frau Professor Else Schumann (bosom friend of the aunt and culture vulture), chauffeur Jochen Zoelke (African battle cap), housekeeper Frieda Harms (curlers under her turban), and auditor Horst Herbert Siemers (black hat) had coagulated into the lymphatic glyphs for *female contemporary* and *male contemporary*—I spied Christa's doll-face standing out sharply: the Gothic globoid forehead ringed by scattered blond curls and crowned by a small, brimless mourning hat, a so-called *toque*, its flat, unadorned cake-form giving chic and fashionable expression, if not to a nun's renunciation of the world, then at least to her unconditional submission to the rules of her order.

This most appropriate headgear had often proved to be sensationally well chosen at memorial evenings for the victims of the Twentieth of July 1944, and thus it was most likely suitable here too. And, under its, as it were, narrow-lipped horizontality, Christa's eternally young sapphire gaze struck me all the harder, saw *me*: me, sneaking on tiptoe along the wall, without a hat, of course (much less a black one), and in an old raincoat (it hadn't been cold in Paris, whereas here, an anticipated November fog cut icily into your bones), hair disheveled (due to the headwind of my "irresponsible speeding"),

just barely making it on time to a bizarre, anything but private, and yet very intimate ceremony, in which they had, for better or worse, been forced to ask me to participate (since I belonged to the unavoidable flotsam of a life that along with many ups had inevitably gone through many downs, inevitably coming into contact with all manner of undesirables)—just barely making it on time to a ceremony that no sure instinct for proper and suitable behavior would have advised me to stay away from.

Was I mistaken? Did Christa give me an encouraging nod anyway? Conciliatory? heartening? Had her small, arrogant mouth softened into a smile?

—the mouth that, after each of her spare utterances, retreated and closed as definitively as the purse of a miser who has yielded a penny's worth of alms; the mouth that—softer, purer, and poetic because of a precocious grief—was repeated in the face of our boy, who carried it into the painful ordeal of innate taciturnity:

in the vise of two fine creases as in the grip of tweezers, inserted in the innocence of the round cheeks: a coyly bent Cupid's bow, destined for tenderness, but despicably scrawled by a never-begun love story in the Latin majuscule M, whose right-hand vertical stroke drops in a priori resignation (Gaia: "Sa bouche traîne la patte, pauvre petite")—

yet without the wry adamancy of the mother who had exasperated me, arousing one of those unjustifiably cruel impulses (with which we take revenge for an eternal—because primordial—misunderstanding; letting myself go, I had told her that her mouth expressed the most recent German tragedy: in the pathological drop of its arrogant curve, it resembled, I said, the signature of Adolf Hitler—

which was why she could not believe that I still loved her, all the same and despite many other things, even though our love had long since become the most efficient instrument in our conjugal torture chamber, because of that primordial lack of understanding, which perpetuated and increased the lack of understanding forever)—

No. She did not smile, nor did she nod. It was an illusion—like the illusion that her head was looming wondrously above all other heads and out from among them—

a nix, suddenly in the still smooth surface of the well, up to her shoulders in the hasty game of tag played by the rings of water, her hair flowing out and splotched with flashes of green light from the depths she rose out of, her eyes astonished by the alien human world she is gazing at.

It was an illusion, but it made me realize what the lack of understanding was all about that had existed between Christa and me from the start.

□   □   □

AMONG THE JOTTINGS of 1965, I can't find anything referring directly to Schwab's funeral (the occasion of my final stay in Hamburg, which lasted for just three days). The date books for 1965 and 1966 are still somewhere with Gaia's posthumous papers—presumably with other personal effects at the Flea Market (whence had come so many of the objects affording the bliss of discovery for browsers and collectors). But I know for sure that while returning from Hamburg to Paris (this time via Saarbrücken), I sketched out a treatise on love. And I think I remember setting down an outline of it during the next few days.

Splendid days, incidentally. The city of Paris was still alive. I was still alive. I had just loved Dawn and I now loved Gaia. Our wanderings through an autumnal Versailles: the brown-blue-golden backdrop to Gaia's exoticism. Her large, brown hand in my coat pocket. The rhythm of our steps in the wet leaves (two of my steps for every one of hers, my caryatid; I, holding Miss Fern's hand as I toddle along the Promenade des Anglais, Dawn at Lake Zurich, toddling along beside me, holding my hand, two doll-like steps on high-heeled shoes for every step I take). Our silence of sympathetic vibrations. A word or two exchanged now and then. The calm question whether I'm writing anything else besides my work for the piglets. Yes, a book. (Shame-faced confession.)

"A novel?"

"I'm not quite sure. There's so much chatter about what a novel is and what it isn't that I don't know anymore. In any case, it's a story that begins with the childhood of its main character and ends with his death."

"Is it very important for you to write it?"

"My friend—you know who I mean—"

"I know. . . ."

"Well, he died because he couldn't write it."

"Is it his story?"

"Mine, of course. Who would dare write anything but his own story? Yes—stories. The kind of stuff I write for the movies. Pulp romances—galore. I have another friend, a man named Nagel. He churns out three a year. He's a candidate for the Nobel Prize."

"How much do you already have of your story?"

"Nothing is finished. I've begun a few chapters. Several hundred pages. Several thousand notes."

"So no outline."

"A sort of notion of the form, all the same. But it's assuming a form all on its own. Or rather, an anti-form. An explosion, consistent with the *Zeitgeist*. A hybrid cell growth. After all, cancer too is just an explosion in slow motion."

"And this prevents you from completing it?"

"Sooner or later it'll complete itself—somehow or other."

"Why don't you make it happen right away?"

"Because I love you. Because I can't write and I don't want to write if I love you. Because I want to live. Make love, not literature."

"But I'll soon stop loving you if you don't do what you have to do."

"I know. But if I do it, my piglets will get very mad at me and not give me any more money. Then I'll have to live on your money, and then you certainly won't love me."

"Don't forget that I'm a professional promoter. I earn a nice income financing talent."

"Musicians. Do you know what a writer earns on a book?"

"A lot of prestige, with which he can squeeze a lot more money out of his piglets than before. I know. I'm the pig of my musicians."

And naturally this ended in a paroxysm of amorous blisses and the solemn promise that I would start working first thing in the morning.

Everything that begins with a lie, says Dostoevski, has to end with a lie. In this case, the lie was that I would paginate every abortive draft, every commenced and abrupted, recommenced and reabrupted chapter, every lengthy jotting, and finally every bit of even slightly bedoodled paper. I could no longer bear the disappointment in Gaia's voice when she looked over my shoulder and said, *"Toujours à la page treize, mon ours!"* I had to make her believe I was forging ahead. After all, I was writing for her and our love. Hence, unassailed by everyday cares thanks to her, I had to write fluently and toward a foreseeable end. . . .

And meanwhile, the hybrid cell growth was running riot not only in my papers, but in her too—in Gaia's gigantic chocolate-brown body.

But this did not come out until later. It was still in the future. Only Schwab was dead and already part of the past. As was the day on which he had lain under his hill of blossoms, waiting to be delivered to the fire in the belly of Ohlsdorf Crematorium in order to rise through the chimney in a different, airier state and merge into the clouds of Hamburg, like Stella at Theresienstadt.

□   □   □

THUS, I HAD COME FROM PARIS to bid him farewell and witness the Hanseatic chivalry of paying last respects to an opponent when his mislived life is to be transformed into the history that serves the life-lie of the general public. I squeezed along the wall of the cremation temple and saw myself through Christa's eyes. Still and all, it would have been nice if she'd really nodded at me and smiled:

Christa, the relentless woman on whom I had suffered such a miserable shipwreck—without ever reaching her, like seafarers in the fairy tale about the magnetic mountain, which, before they can land, draws the nails from their ships, so that they fall apart in the open sea;
Christa, who always remained stand-offish, alien, and who, no matter how hard I tired to get her to forgive me (after our love was lost) had

proved so unyielding that my despair made me do all the mortifying things that make any helplessly demanding lover despicable,

the ultima ratio of the no-longer-beloved, whose lamentable inconsistency draws sympathy to the side of the stand-offish,

the begging tenderness, which prepares the field for revenge, and the feigned coldness that yearns for its own thaw,

the false magnanimity with the schoolmaster's hickory stick held ready,

the sanctimonious understanding geared to recognition and the rage with an eye out for reconciliation,

the tears, torment, and torture, and—worst disgrace—always putting the other in the wrong

(as though a stubborn demonstration that the other is full of failings could ultimately arouse his self-knowledge, which reaches into the depths of his awareness, from which, with all other virtues, mercy too is bound to spring),

in any case, always too much talking,

the monologues flowing along, as wide as the Volga,

the cascades of chatter, released by the most trivial things and never coming to a standstill until every possibility of bypassing them is washed away by a flood of words, of which—when the verbal torrent has finally ebbed—the vicious words remain, decaying, and poisoning the ground; and all this constant instructing, moral reproving and edifying, preaching of salvation and disaster in the breathless urgency of the indignant man who asks for justice (while sentences bubble out of him like blood shrieking "Staunch me!"—and all the shamelessly flaunted misery that makes those who are appealed to— and hard of hearing—even more hard of hearing: because silence is the ultimate haven for dignity).

That's what had become of what had started as love, and that was how I acted in Christa's eyes, and her smile could have exonerated me. *Mais hélas!* I had only imagined it. I saw myself through the eyes of all the others, saw myself squeezing along the edge of the black block of mourners, along the milk-and-lily-whitewashed wall, on which my wet raincoat was probably leaving an ugly streak. All the eyes were as clear as water, and it wasn't hard to guess what those who had known me for years were seeing: hair that had grayed and thinned, a slight corpulence, even a certain casualness in the clothes that had once (as Schwab had phrased it) been disreputably elegant. They were also, I assume, paradoxically familiar with the alien streak in a man who is a stranger not only here but abroad as well—an alien streak intensified by this alien quality, even though he had returned home. They saw runes of life, which may have given them insight into themselves.

Scherping, seeing me, was cut to the quick, I could tell, at the thought of advances running to tens of thousands of marks for a book that would never be published. But, experienced as he was in many kinds of wile, he most likely could not fail to applaud my frequent success in unbuttoning his pocket. Such relationships, he knew, also lead to a friendship of sorts. So he saw me as embodying something of the obstinacy of money: if you surrender to it on a large scale, then it will always demand some irrational interest from you on a small scale. Perhaps he was even grateful to me. He knew this femininely stubborn pettiness of money, accepting it like a good husband who overlooks minor defects in a wife with a number of merits and pleasant traits. I thus made him feel generous. So he took on the gesture of generosity. He looked upon me not without a certain delight. A warm feeling in his chest made the checkbook rise, as it were, from that pleasure.

And Carlotta was at his side, barely aging, the hint of the future matron barely in her face, in the slightly puffy cheeks and tear sacs, under the cowish gaze of a nymphomaniac. She might have been thinking about our first meeting, eighteen years ago, in Witte's office: she was Witte's secretary at that time and his *dame de compagnie*, although still married to Schwab, while I was married to Christa, who had persuaded me, as a young man with ideas, to take Witte up on his suggestion and enter the advertising department of the Wittewash Company.

My visit to Witte's office had not led to this job. But it did lead to meeting Carlotta face to face (and, at a certain point in the "conference," to our launching into a fit of laughter that nothing could suppress or arrest). It led to one of those light-as-a-feather relationships never dramatized by either partner, whose basis is for many years the nearest bed or sofa, and which, unmarred by any other demand, prove to be the most durable and most useful friendships.

Presumably, then, Carlotta (her real name was Hannelore, but she had sloughed off this prosaic name as an adolescent during a three-week sojourn in Florence, where she had assumed the more rigorously formed name)—presumably, Carlotta was not emotionally overwhelmed on seeing me again. She merely sized me up and down with a sober eye to check the extent to which my physical decay, undeniably commencing, could spoil the tastiness of the morsel that she had sporadically inserted into her erotic diet over a long period of time, a quite variegated diet at that. She liked me; that was certain. And she never had any illusions about me.

In those days, I had greatly disappointed Witte; furthermore, my separation from Christa, his protégée, had convinced him how fatefully correct he had been to feel qualms about "part-time artists" (he meant, oddly enough, artistically gifted men who debauched their talents; who lacked the ethical strength to devote themselves totally to art, commit their entire being to it). Witte, of course, had completely excluded me from the precincts of his role as God the Father, promoter, and protector. I figured at the periphery of his Middle Kingdom as a troublemaker; but ever since he had filled his flock almost entirely with women who were full-time artists—ceramicists and expressive dancers—I did not get all too close to his cock-of-the-walk feelings. He had (like most other people) viewed Schwab's friendship with me as the utterance of the non-middle-class leanings that one must accept in a full-time artist (for Schwab's assignment to this category was due to his death, which had proved once again to Witte that a genuine artistic temperament will brook no compromises).

Here, too, Witte could, quite appropriately, play the generous man. And this, as usual, moved him to feel sentimental about himself. Only the strict obligation of a Hanseatic man to act reserved (and perhaps also the suspicion that a news photographer might be present and could possibly publish the photograph) prevented him from waving me over to shake my hand with deep concern.

In private, he would most likely have been rather glad to own such a photograph. One of his favorite words was "tolerance." Even in his early days as a convinced National Socialist (of the Strasser type, to be sure; i.e., a decided opponent of Hitler), he had never gone so far as to demand explicitly that the world be cleansed of my sort. In his heart of hearts, he may have counted me among the things and people against which and whom the Wittewash Company was pursuing its campaign of whiter and whiter washing, more and more thorough detergents Yet his profound feeling was dominated by the generous forbearance of the royal merchant who, when I married Christa, had said to her, "You've danced a bit out of line, dear child. But still, you've got an interesting partner." He sighed, involuntarily resigned to destiny, when he saw me.

So much good will on all sides began to make me feel ill at ease. It bolstered them against the past the way their padded coats bolstered them against the autumnal fog outside. Miss Wiebke, Schwab's wonderful old-maid aunt, the one who had once been engaged to Witte in mythical prehistory, looked at me with loving melancholy, in which nothing recalled that during the lifetime of her adored nephew Johannes she had regarded me as a fiend of the lowest cynicism. Had her life's dream come true and had she become a theatrical producer, she would have cast me in the role of Mephisto in a modern-dress staging of *Faust*, daringly based on Berlin Expressionism of the 1920s (and she would then have screwed me out of my salary with the clearest of consciences). Now, she seemed ready to view me as foster brother to her protégé, who, because of me, had sometimes treated her even worse than usual. And oddly enough, her indulgence was now sincere. Not just because of her grief, which was no doubt profound. There was also a sense of salvation in her. It was as if her nephew's death had released her from something that had prevented her from being herself—had released her from a life-lie.

Fräulein Schmidschelm behind her, Schwab's secretary Schelmy, could relish her own triumph. Now, *she* would be the leading lady at Lücke's. The field was hers. Earlier, Schwab had dragged his aunt along on his boozing tours (against her will, it turned out), finally landing at Lücke's, where unspeakably ludicrous scenes of rivalry had taken place between Schelmy and the poor aunt. The latter would wear housekeeper blouses buttoned up to her chin, with a brooch and a corseted waist, as though she were still an actress and had gone out right after the performance (say, *Mrs. Warren's Profession*) without bothering to change, in order to pop into her regular pub and gulp down a jigger of something or other. For all the popularity that the aunt thus attained (and that was far greater than the popularity she had enjoyed in her theatrical days), she must have felt that this role was forced upon her and that Schelmy more authentically played the part the aunt was trying to play in her old-hag love for the nephew, who had left the nest prematurely: the part of a drinking companion and (in the fog of intoxication, in which everything blurred together) occasional bedmate (also dimmed by the subsequent hangover, like the memory of vomiting and similar embarrassments).

Now, the aunt sat between Schwab's niece Uschi and her brand-new fiancé, Klaus (with Herr von Rönnekamp standing at his side as an auntie-father). The old lady had finally become something she may never have wanted to become, but that she had to be and was actually meant to be in accordance with her true essence and true vocation: the upper-class daughter who had grown into an old maid and developed into the pillar of the family. The tavern original of the past twenty years (the former *grande dame*, known to everyone and always trailing after her boozy nephew) was merely the hybrid cross between this actual life-reality and the life-dream of a career on the stage. And even though (or because) it had been a life-lie, it would now give her a certain glory in a life-reality that had finally come true. *She* was the one predestined to become a myth for the family, and not the star-crossed nephew for whose sake she had lived past herself and then in the end toward herself.

□   □   □

THEY WOULD ALWAYS BE VICTORIOUS in their way—these honorable tavern denizens and sedate brothel regulars, from whose angular shopkeeper-skulls their grandfathers' eyes peered, clear as water (grandfathers who had tilled the marshland between Pöseldorf and Ohlsdorf). The god who was their mighty fortress of burghers never allowed them beyond the pale. Even their most daring fictions rooted them all the more deeply within the pale. As a result, their major and minor fictions—from world improvement to persecution complex, from artistic intention to manic conformism—all these life-dreams and life-lies, all this constant as-if, were somehow repulsively perverse, a gamble of the imagination with only a seeming risk, an *art pour l'art* of spiritual gesture that turned their lives into the caricature of authentic drama. I now understood the core of John's dislike for what he called the "bloody fucking middle classes," and I understood how fundamentally different they were from the Middle Kingdom of Uncle Ferdinand, Sir Agop Garabetian, and Bully Olivera. "*Psychology begins with the bourgeoisie,*" Stella used to say.

I now also understood what Schwab had meant when he said that the novel, as *the* bourgeois art form, has to have something of the ornamentation of medieval Bible initials: something of Richard Wagner's kaleidoscope technique, in which leitmotivs, within an extraordinarily complicated structure, produce order, clarity, and recognizability out of heterogeneity. All these people lived in a nonuniformity and noncompatibility of wishes and desires and, consequently, in a steady spiritual volvulus; this twisting of their bowels could not be depicted more lucidly than in an arabesque from which they themselves regularly kept peering out as their own actual leitmotivs.

Here, too, by trying to see through me, my confusions and possible entanglements, they looked at me through themselves. Herr von Rönnekamp (black hat, but cream-colored gabardine coat with mink collar) let his private-detective gaze, rising darkly from his own private sphere and diving deep into mine, play over me with an ironic smile of sweetly puckered lips, in order to catch me slipping up and thus giving the lie to my claim that I was not occasionally afflicted by homoerotic stirrings. His protégé Klaus, fermenting in more and more densely, more and more darkly hirsute young manhood (which was about to expand to bouncer dimensions), dreamed of himself in movies through me. And his fiancée, Uschi, Schwab's niece—who could never say no, thus suffering spiritual torments that emanated from her like a piquant body smell, so that any man, from the milkman to her doctoral adviser (her major was German), felt challenged to throw her into bed—Uschi hated me for being one of the many men who had done so. Then, behind these people, I saw a tear-stained face—and there she was at last, my nix, my mermaid who had announced herself with Christa: Lovely Heli.

Lovely Heli, bravely defying her timidity toward burghers, had emerged from the whorehouse to accompany to the grave the man she had loved and would love to the end of her days. Her standing behind Uschi was a subtle irony of fate. For she, Heli, had given herself to any man who wanted her, from the milkman to the professor, because she was trying to make up for the ignominy of normally being paid as a professional joy girl ("A person shouldn't have to pay for joy," she had said to Schwab in commercial naïveté; and if it hadn't been for Gisela, who brought her to her senses, Heli would have destroyed herself).

She was very beautiful in her powerful, common way, with her fresh complexion and auburn Hamburg hair, which was now demurely upswept rather than loosely tied into a working-girl's ponytail. And I envied Schwab for her love, which was pristine, like a folksong, and which he had squandered with the recklessness of the untrue beloved in folksongs. All sorts of memories whirred through my head—

for instance, Schwab and I sitting in Heli's room at Gisela's whorehouse, delighted by our view of the narrow hooker alley, whose serried gabled houses preserved a final bit of pre–Kaiser Wilhelm Hamburg; our enjoying the soft, yellow light in the small windows and mellow shadows down in the street and talking about women as being the natural proprietors of reality, each of them able to give birth to a human being, no matter whether a man or another woman; we said that they carried humanity inside themselves and were capable of renewing it out of themselves— while we men bore the curse of unreality because our contribution to this renewal was so abstract and implausible, an ejaculation and nothing more, so that we could not justly believe that we really existed and, in order to have reality, had to realize ourselves in some sort of activity, in a work aimed at re-creating the world, at creating a new reality—in short: some kind of fiction; and therefore, we kept looking for ourselves, always and everywhere, and could not really love anything but what keeps reflecting only us: always only us. . . .

It was probably Lovely Heli's loveliest hour, an arts-and-craftsy intimate experience. She could sit at Schwab's feet, her head in his lap, his hand in her hair, and she could listen to him talking to me—

and he had spoken about the nix, whom he knew from my tales about Aunt Selma, and he had said that the bewitched creature that gazed with listening eyes into an alien world (although something there is calling to it that this was once its world too)—the nix was to float ahead of the story I wanted to tell in my book, precede it like the figurehead of a ship, her hair flowing in the great headwind and her countenance stretching forward, blindly clairvoyant with listening eyes. . . .

and I had to think of how enthusiastically I had gone home, straight from the brothel to Christa and our little boy in Witte's halved villa on the Elbchaussee, in order to renounce all the deceptive promise of the movie piglets Stoffel, Spouse & Associates and to become Nagel's good buddy again, and start on the story right away (for all this had taken place in the mythical past, in the very last days of the Ice Age. Lovely Heli was still practically a child). And Christa and our little boy had been so dreadfully poor that I had gone back to Stoffel, Spouse & Associates, after all. And later, I never mustered the ethical strength to emulate our good Nagel and devote myself to pure, literary writing—I was simply a part-time artist. And as for the story that Schwab had liked so much, I could never really launch it, I kept bringing it back to the dock and rigging it up again, until it had become its own wild and gigantic construction site and never sailed out on its blue adventure. . . .

The nix, at any rate, was still waiting to be nailed to her bowsprit. I kept encountering her blindly clairvoyant gaze, now wept empty in Lovely Heli's eyes. At last I knew why she had been a symbol for me through the many years, a symbol of the never-fulfillable, of the aiming-beyond-all-reality, everlastingly listening ahead into the nothingness of male love. I realize this shame-facedly. For here, in Lovely Heli's eyes, the female force that ma-ternally says yes to anything, the love that holds reality in its hands—here, it wept itself out.

All this, roiled up by the unforeseen presence of much too much of my own past in these indestructible people, began to wear gently on my nerves. It bewildered me to perceive that the whispering stopped when I slipped into an angle of the visual field of mourners who had not reckoned with my approach from behind—a whispering that signified an exchange of experiences and that suddenly broke off when I entered their optical jurisdic-tion:

"... *fall coming so early again—why, I could lie in the sun three hours a day—day in day out....*"

"*... it used to be the* club *in Hamburg, and we're hoping that it'll be the* club *again....*"

"*... what it offers? It offers a delightful atmosphere, it offers chic people, it offers a fabulous band—the great advantage is that when you feel like a bit of chic dancing in the evening, then you can ...*"

"*... well, I'm Protestant, but I've got a certain weak spot for the Virgin Mary....*"

I had thought I knew what it was that made them hush upon seeing me. And evidently, nothing had changed in this respect. I was still fundamentally alien to them, hence suspect, even sinis-ter: a member of an altogether different species, whom you couldn't trust any farther than you could throw him. Thus, I was all the more bewildered by the shameless good will that now ap-peared in their gazes. It could not be due to their having grown accustomed to foreign workers in Germany or vacations on the Costa Brava. The more probable cause was that they knew I did not want to contest their rights. I did not want to arrogate any share of the myth to which they had elevated my brother Schwab in order to honor themselves. Why, I did not even desire any pro-prietary portion of his grave.

TRULY, I HAVE NEVER BEEN CONCERNED with such possessions, nor do I care about them today. I don't even know the location of my mother's grave. (Presumably, she was fished out of the
pond in Bessarabia and then buried somewhere in the small village cemetery, close to the blackthorn hedge; Uncle Ferdinand
had been too tactful to touch on it, and I too cowardly to ask. Nor
would I lift a finger to find out whether any sort of paternal legacy has devolved upon me, assuming I could determine which of
my mother's countless lovers can claim the questionable honor of
having sired me.) My cousin Wolfgang, as I have said, lies in
Vienna's Central Graveyard, to which nothing draws me; and I
was not informed whether the corpses of Aunt Selma and Uncle
Helmuth and Aunt Hertha were salvaged from the basement air-
raid shelter of the building in Vienna's Twelfth District where,
in the summer of 1944, a bomb forever ripped my rather worn tie
to my foster parents. And that was that!

Thus, facing the hill of flowers into which my brother Schwab
had been transformed, I could not understand why his further
transformation into the contents of an urn, and eventually into
humus under a grave slab, should bind me to the Hamburg soil,
which had not succeeded in binding me to itself, even though I
had spent years wearing out my shoes upon it—usually during
long walks when I brooded about the enigmatic fate that had cast
me ashore here in the first place.

True, my dead friend, while alive, had left no stone unturned
in his efforts to convince me I had come here in order to tell
stories, to narrate—but what? A glance at the faces of the philistines here informed me that it was bound to lead to a misunderstanding—whatever it was. For they would again be the victors
and somehow turn it into grist for their mills, whether I told them
edifying tales as Nagel did or tried to play the chaperon for their
consciences, even though they already kept whole packs of chap-
erons for titillation:

—the a capella *choir of Jeremiahs, to whom everyday German life
assigns the cultural business as a sort of natural preserve so that Ger-*

man Cassandra cries will not be missing from the swan song of the West: in the tenor of the eternal (and, alas, ubiquitously betrayed) values of beauty, goodness, and truth; in the baritone of old, traditional humanitarian principles (that not even a dog observes); in the bass of generally (albeit rhetorically) accepted categorical imperatives—

and yet so very dramatic in the gesture of the decent man who has taken the globe upon his shoulders and now summons the whole world to help bear responsibility when it rolls off; so intimately moved by himself in the role of powerless knight whom no one heeds, so that no eye in the public refrains from gaping in fear and pity, and no lips refrain from agreeing: "How true! What a daring and global vision! How terribly ineluctable!"—

while, in the meantime, everyone is making a leisurely effort to get his share of the pie baking in the fire of the Apocalypse, and all people have tranquilly resigned themselves to the fact that everyone's actions are different from what he says and certainly different from what he thinks—

and thus the call of the angel to the Last Judgment is merely one more noise in the tremendous din of universal chatter, a tiny fiber in the overwhelming sound strand that is caught by a few powerful, opinion-shaping institutions and twisted into the donkey-line of the Zeitgeist, which irresistibly draws us toward our collective fate—

These people had more than enough of both storytellers and doomsaying journalists. Their verbal gruel burst through the windows of bookstores and came to them every evening on the more uplifting radio and television programs; it fed the cultural sections in the weekend editions of their family papers (illustrated and unillustrated); it occupied the minds at congresses of their leading scientists and philosophers; it was the major discussion topic in their adult-education courses; it echoed through the utterances of their statesmen and began to break through even in movies (after America had courageously taken the lead, here, too)—

and went as smoothly in one ear as it did out the other. It was part of the sound track of their "reality," an "integrating component" of the sound effects that the present era used as a background in its drive for self-perfection. And had I joined the concert, then, at my demise, they might have treated even me to a hill of flowers, like that man up front there, and, during my lifetime, they might have paid me all sorts of gratis tributes, but never this eerie good will, which seemed to have a smarmy familiarity at its heart. What the hell did they expect of me?

☐   ☐   .☐

IN BIDDING SOLEMN FAREWELL to a man who had been a conscience chaperon not in the cultural division but in self-destructive reality, the congregation of mourners had, of course, hired a shepherd of the soul, a pastor (presumably a Protestant of the Augsburg Confession).

In order to greet the grief-stricken near and dear and take them into his care, the pastor stood facing his flock, with his back to the hill of flowers (where the deceased, quite shy and unsociable, had finally found a refuge where no one could get to him); and the pastor, with an ardent assurance, emanated waves of solace as if to say, Do not despair, your beloved relative is really lying here.

By way of demonstrating that he truly believed in the faith with which he wanted to fortify the faith of all the others, he had disguised himself as a mountebank at a medieval fair. His robe (raven-black and creased: the domino of a macabre heavenly carnival) flowed all the way down to his fashionable department-store shoes and was tied over the shoulders like a sack; over it, the buzz saw of a gigantic, chalk-white furbelow ruff decapitated him, so that he presented his head as though on a plate—virtually his own executioner. The head was anointed with the grease of the edifying word and was slightly askew for a posture of humility. The skeleton of a Gioconda smile hovered around his mouth.

He stood there, looking toward me—and I understood: he waited in loving Christian patience for me, the belated straggler. The assurances of solace, which his thriftily smiling mouth had excreted in small, murmuring rations of verbal gruel, had vanished without a trace into the furbelow rills of his ruff. He was now gathering a new little portion for me. His hands were concealed on his stomach, inside the folds of his sleeves, as though doing something indecent (the right hand didn't know what the left hand was doing). Now, they hastily slipped out to gain hold of my hand—

first, slightly arched in the prayer position of Dürer's mother's hands, lurking as a trap to snatch the timidly offered hand like a broken-winged bird: with two simultaneous lunges, one reaching under the prey, the other quickly covering it. At the same time, he closed his eyes—presumably to roll them toward Jesus behind his lids. And, with his fingers contracting into a meaningful suction grip, his listing shepherd's head tilted back, while his eyes reopened, offering their watery void—sea-blue—to the wafting sighs

It was as if he had spiritually grabbed my balls. I wanted to yank back my hand, but he held tight. And while his mouth over the ruff drawled at me, "You were his best friend—I know!" (How did he know? The church and the funeral parlor were obviously in cahoots, like Interpol), he pulled, or rather pushed, me to a chair standing somewhat away from the first row and directly in front of the heraldic foam of lilac. I compliantly seated myself, thankful that his Lutheranly licensed freebooter grab at my emotional world had not incorporated me, but instead had separated me from his flock—depositing me on the edge of the plate, like a fly that has dropped into the soup.

But I was mistaken. While sneaking along the wall, I had drawn gazes like rubber threads; but since little more than my shoulders and the back of my head was offered to their delectation, those gazes had gradually turned from me and were worshipfully fixed straight ahead, until the downtrodden cousin twice removed had surmounted his Pachelbel on the organ. The galvanized pipe clusters, quivering in their steep flanks, were exuding their final, rigorously structured shrieks into the paraboloid vault of the cremation temple. Then, devotional silence, astir with stifled coughs and handkerchief snorts, fanned out through space.

As usual, I vividly pictured what had to happen:

To my right, there would be a whispering, like reeds swishing the secret that King Midas had donkey's ears ... and Witte's giant figure would rise up out of the whispers, hand his black burgher-hat to his aunt, and ponderously stride toward the hill of flowers in order to turn on his heels at the head of the coffin and show us his countenance: the sea-blue eyes shining in the apoplectic red and surrounded by the flickering white blaze of his silvery lion's mane. He would roll his padded shoulders as though priming himself to lift the flowery slope at his feet—but no: he merely raised his fist to his mouth and cleared his throat resoundingly into his hand, cleared the mucus-lined spaciousness of his cigarsmoker's bronchia into the echoing vault of the cremation temple. Then he dropped his head. Remained in mute concentration. Jerked his white-blazing skull up again in order to hurl out a gaze and enclose us, all of us, and with us Hamburg—and Germany—and the vast ocean—the globe—the starry cosmos—and in it, GOD—enclose us all with a single gaze hurled out into eternity.

Then Witte would speak. Would inform us that we were standing here at the bier of a friend. And, in accordance with his principle in all situations of life, he would be the exemplary, living proof of this fact: he would stand there, dynamic, at the flowery bier of the vanished friend as though on a conquered peak on which he had just planted the flag.

His word was bronze. It gave eternal value to the personality of the deceased. But it also raised an admonishing finger at the human foibles that the dear departed had sloughed off with his corporeal envelope (and as whose dismal witness I sat here, to the side, on the condemned criminal's bench). In this sense, you see, this man (wide sweep of the hand across the flower hill) died vicariously for all of us: filled with the most splendid promise and endowed with all the gifts to make all the expectations about him come true, but foundering on the all-too-human: this gave his premature decease the character of a sacrificial death. Here he lay as a symbol of the fine possibilities inherent in every human being and, alas, not always reaching development because of the all-too-human, a martyr to earthly imperfection (three powerful coughs into the fist, thorax pumped up for the grand finale): here he lies, cleansed of all the slag that marred his earthly travels (involuntary glance at me) and obfuscated his rich talents, so that his road of life was not, alas, a trajectory that hit the bull's-eye of self-realization. But this very failure lends redemptive value to his demise: he died for the average man. His fate is that of most people: much promise and even more expectation sinfully lost to time—Ecce homo!

(*involuntary scraping of Herr von Rönnekamp's feet*)

Witte lapses into silence. His head sinks upon his chest. Then his giant figure detaches itself from the flower hill and, with a sunken head, strides past the pastoral nightshade plant (two nuns humbly bowing to one another as they pass in the cloister), returns to his seat, devoutly lifts the black hat (which the aunt, after holding it in her lap like a soup tureen, eventually placed on his chair), and once again covers the now unoccupied surface with the seat of his pants.

And again, a whispering moves through the rows of leavetakers, like evening wind soughing in the foliage of a weeping willow. And (spurred by Carlotta's poke in his ribs), Scherping rises most ceremoniously and curls in front of his chair like a puppy about to crouch and make a mess; and, with a slight bow that tenses the seat of his trousers, he places his black Sunday hat on the chair as gingerly as if he were inserting a brick into a basket of eggs; and he turns toward the flower hill and stares at it with such a painfully pleasurable look, as if extracting a dagger from deep within his heart while feeling a crafty delight. And then he resolutely heads for the place where Witte was standing; and, while walking, he sends a quick, ironic snort through his nostrils, pulls his head in between his shoulders, like Rumpelstiltzkin, and begins to speak. And he says, if need be, then he too does not wish to refrain from casting a few phrases into the grave of the deceased, his dear editor and difficult friend. And now he stands in front of the flower hill like a Sunday safari hunter who wants to be photographed in front of a bagged elephant and doesn't know whether to put his right foot or left foot upon it. . . .

But of course, I was merely imagining all this. Nothing of the sort happened in reality. Absolutely nothing happened in reality. Except that the silence, astir with clearings of throats and snufflings in handkerchiefs, began to show signs of overextension. Also, a contraction in the skin on the back of my neck indicated that once again many eyes were glued to my nape. Someone in the front row even bent forward to look into my face.

I felt extremely ill at ease. In front of me, rooted near the lilac bushes, stood the pastor, he too a flower: a white disk of petals on a black stalk, with a human head as a syncarp. His eyes too soaked into me. His throat, wreathed by the furbelow ruff, was then cleared—an unmistakable admonition. Finally, a jolt passed through the robe. With flowing folds, the robe began to move and carried the wondrous blossom of the head close to me, lowering the blossom to my nose as though inviting me to take a sniff.

"Would you like to speak a few words," it murmured—without a sympathetically vibrating question mark—from the furbelow ruff.

I shook my head, frightened and bewildered, aware of my incapacity.

"They expect it of you."

This was not the time to negotiate who "they" were and what right "they" had to expect anything of me. So I simply murmured, "I can't!" And feeling that this did not suffice, I stretched my neck and whispered toward the mountebank skull on the furbelow ruff, "I'm too moved."

"The more ardent your words shall be."

It was no use. I had known it from the very start, when sneaking in here and hoping to remain unnoticed. Nothing could be done. I had to go along with it.

So I got to my feet and walked to the flower hill (seeing myself just as I had seen Witte and Scherping in my mind's eye) and stationed myself in Witte's place (hoping that no one would see me there as ridiculously as I saw myself). And I gazed down at the conquered acclivity of white blossoms—

and there was nothing. Nothing. No Schwab. No dead friend for me to mourn. No corpse with a waxen face. No deceased after whom I could send a few ardent words into the great void. A heap of tightly wired flowers on a socle, which loomed out of a pit in the floor. That was all.

A rat hunt began in my brain. Schwab had sneaked away and

left me in the shit. Typical. But just who was he anyway—
Schwab? Did I even know who was meant when people talked
about a man named Johannes Schwab? Wasn't he someone else,
and wasn't the one I meant merely a figment, a fiction of mine?
When had I last seen him? In Paris. At Orly Airport. He had
wept and stuffed my pockets with money. Then he had vanished
faster than that money. Had dissolved more swiftly in nothingness. A memory during his lifetime. And certainly a memory
when the news of his death had arrived. My brother Schwab.

□   □   □

WHEN HAD HE BECOME THAT? During the Ice Age. Mythical
prehistory. Had that period ever really existed? Wasn't it a pipe
dream of mine? Did the people sitting here know anything about
it? Had they experienced those years as I had? Had I really experienced them as I imagined? Now, in this reality of 1965, in a
world cemented to the sky and inundated with numberless kinds
of plastic toys—was it possible to believe in the crèche Christmas
of 1947? Could I give a high-rise *horlà* any notion of the neo-
Gothic clinker-brick villa looming like a citadel from the surrounding landscape of ruins in 1948—the villa in which the
British had installed Hans Jürgen Stoffel as the first postwar
German film producer? A nocturnal script conference there: with
the company scenario editor (former go-fer of the last System
Era intellectuals to find refuge at the Nazi Ufa movie studio), the
head of production (former chief of lighting at Ufa), the head of
distribution (former textile dealer, then war-economy adviser),
the cinema consultant of the foolhardy daredevil bank that intended to finance the "project" (a man with a hitherto immaculate past as a teller), the film officer of the occupation authorities
(child of Auschwitz victims; he had emigrated in time), a representative of Hamburg's cultural senate, which had risen from the
ashes of buildings like the phoenix. All these emaciated executive
faces, colorlessly inserted into lamentable civvies and marked
with the indelible traces of various winter campaigns, were now

notched by something almost more terrible: an urge to overcome the past (by way of the movie business) and to find personal fulfillment in artistic activity ("Creativity, ya know—that's where all these guys in our business get so possessed!").... They squat there, half asleep, as though they had been shit into the titanic club chairs provided by the megalomania of Hanseatic founding fathers: they are exhausted, exasperated after seven hours of grating against one another's narrow minds, ignorance, resentment ("I tell you, gentlemen, if we're to form this brain trust of ours to make our project foolproof, then we've got to make sure that the image of the German woman in wartime is done properly!")—

Yes indeed! But how can this idea be carried out with the actress slated to play the lead in the "project," Primordial Piglet Stoffel's wife Astrid von Bürger, the darling of the public during the last years of the war and now emerging purged from the final collapse, tested by raping Russians in 1945 as well as by nonfraternizing GIs thereafter, a blend of Brunhilde and a flapper.

Poor Nagel! How he had loved her!... And how he had hated me because of her! And yet he should have known that my betrayal was only a parody.... How often had I wanted to explain it to him: "Damn it! Can't you understand that I was trying for a joke!"

It wouldn't have mattered. He was a thoroughly humorless fellow, our friend Nagel. There was no teaching him that betrayal by a friend could be a joke. A man who has just returned from the war minus an arm, arriving in a shattered Fatherland where everything has to be rebuilt, at last, at last discovers what he was fated for, and writes, damn it, writes, arduously and sedulously with his awkward left hand, penning short stories and the beginning of a play and the outline of a novel and another and another....

and his head whirrs with ideas and images, and his heart leaps blissfully in his body because of the wonderful, wonderful life next to the small stove in Witte's garden house in the park of the halved villa on the Elbchaussee—and he's already sold two stories to the radio network, and one is printed in *Die Welt*, which is publishing again, and now he's been offered a movie

(*"We have a specific project in mind for you, dear Herr Nagel: would you like to write a screenplay for us? If so, then we'll come to you."*)

—and he instantly has an idea for a screenplay, a lovely idea, after all it's to be the first postwar German film and it should have something symbolic too. So, somewhere in South or Central America—at least, the guys are wearing sombreros—a man is wandering, a scientist, ethnologist, anthropologist—right?—he's traveling to a remote Indian tribe to study a bizarre custom: you see, the Indians believe that every fifty-three years, corresponding to a cyclical eclipse of the moon (which can be observed from their territory), the world comes to an end, only to be re-created and resurrected the next day. En route, this scholar meets another man with the same destination, and he introduces himself as a government-licensed executioner. He explains that during a famine, a woman of this Indian tribe went to the communal store of grain and stole a handful for her child. According to the natives' law, which is respected by the government, she has to die for her crime, except that the government reserves the right to perform the execution—typical, eh? Hahahahaha! Well, the two men, the scholar and the executioner, reach the Indians at the very moment when they are preparing for the end of the world. Tomorrow night, at one A.M. on the dot, the world will end. Ten after one, it'll be re-created. This is shown very graphically—it's a movie, you know: all fires are put out, everyone strews ashes on his head and lies down to die. Voices howl and teeth chatter when the eclipse begins, and then, when the moon lights up again, the past is past, the world is as neat as a new pin, they rekindle the fires and start baking tortillas with purged souls. Question: does the woman still have to be executed or not? . . .

A nice story, a profound story, as simple as a legend, you can almost tell the plot in three sentences, and Piglet King Stoffel is mad about it and even more so his wife, Astrid von Bürger, the Beautiful the Marvelous, whom Nagel, during the final years at the front, secretly carried in his heart like a schoolboy in love ("Damn it, if you ever get out of this shit alive—you're gonna marry a girl like her!").

Astrid von Bürger, now making movies with her husband,

Stoffel, finds the story fabulous, simply heavenly. But there's that moron of a scenario editor they've picked up, plus a head of production, an absolute prick, who thinks he knows something about moviemaking because he used to push lights around at the old Ufa studio, and then, of course, that phenomenal arsehole of a banker who's supposed to finance the project—and those guys check every single scene to make sure it's understandable and probable and psychologically and anthropologically and astronomically correct, and they want the symbolism to be as clear as if it were banged into you with a club, and Stoffel himself begins fucking around with the story because he figures on difficulties in casting and in finding expensive locations . . . well, to make a long story short:

"Why don't you come along to a meeting, they call it a 'conference,' I'll tell them you're a Young Writer too, then you can see the endless dimensions of human stupidity. . . ."

And I went along and was introduced to Stoffel and his primordial piglets as a Young Writer and was permitted to lean over the hand of Astrid von Bürger and kiss it and peep into her blouse décolletage, deep into the cleavage, and I was forced to watch my friend Nagel being tormented and tortured, to watch a pen-knife vivisection of a fellow Young Writer and to witness a systematic slaughter triggered by an instinctive hatred of one kind of human for another, the murder of the seedling of a work of art—and my eyes bored into the smugly ironical eyes of Astrid von Bürger in order to learn what she was feeling and thinking during this slaughter, she couldn't have overlooked the way poor Nagel loved her, with boyish chivalry and willingness to suffer. And because her eyes endured my gaze so long and amply that they swam, my gaze was lost in them and I suddenly heard her say, "Look, before you kick each other's heads in, let the other Young Writer tell us what he thinks about this whole business. I have the feeling he has some ideas about it."

Was this the right time to say that I found Nagel's story simply fabulous? They kept saying they did—only to pounce on it all the more furiously and tear it to shreds. I figured it was better to point out what they might object to in it; the von Bürger bitch was right, I *had* thought about it while they kept yakking and yakking, and I believed I had found what was wrong. They were using troglodyte arguments about the ending: should the woman be executed (problem film, it'll attract only an elite, but a happy ending'll water down the problem). So I thought to myself, I think the difficult thing about all stories with an open ending is that they sound wonderful in three sentences because they contain an insoluble problem in a single situation, but if you tell them in detail for an hour and a half, breaking them down into a series of situations, then you can't intensify the problem or present it any more clearly, much less resolve it. The story always remains a "what if?"—

I wanted to add that they have to get beyond this; that the ending, which they had been arguing about for hours with their narrow, stubborn minds, was quite harshly and plainly obvious: the movie had to end with the young woman's execution. The audience could then argue on the way home about whether it was just or unnecessarily cruel. But they all pounced on me as if I had tried to grab their favorite toy. Even Nagel yelled, "Goddammit, don't you understand that *we*'re in that what-if situation? Are we supposed to pronounce sentence upon ourselves?"

I was stuck with six men all screaming at the same time, and it was impossible to make them realize, individually or collectively, that they were idiots who had misunderstood me in the stupidest way. So I asked if I could offer them an example of what I meant: "Let's assume that a man shows up at a radio station and claims that God is calling him. His name is Niels Otto Alsen, and he usually introduces himself by his initials: N.O.A. God's voice is calling him, N.O.A., because a new Flood is imminent. He says it's high time to warn mankind. The radio station has to broadcast the news that the Deluge is about to come and that people have to prepare for it. Needless to say, they think he's a fool and kick him out. But an intellectual who's hanging around the editorial office goes after him and maliciously points out the problem: if God has elected him, N.O.A., to tell him about his intentions, it is because he is the only righteous man among millions of doomed sinners. He must not act more humane than God Himself. God won't stand for it. Assuming the radio station really did broadcast a warning, the resulting panic would have consequences more catastrophic than the worst Deluge. So: if the Lord intends to destroy humanity but for one righteous man, then he, this one righteous man, should not interfere with His workings. It is his duty to build an ark, fill it with two of every living creature, and wait until God has done His destructive work in order to begin the world anew on His behalf. Period. That is the 'what if.' The problem confronting a modern-day Noah becomes dramatic now. Where and how will he start his rescue action? How should he populate his boat? He can grab his neighbor's cat from the window sill, but things get tougher with the other fauna. There are several hundred species of finch; where's he going to get a pair of each? Where's he going to find lions, rhinoceroses, elephants? What kind of tools should he take for a new mankind? A knife, a cigarette lighter, an encyclopedia? But each of these contains the seed of new sins? Besides, this is 1947, and where and how is he going to get rationing stamps for the wood and nails for his boat? Wouldn't he, the only righteous man in God's eyes, have to commit all sorts of legal offenses in order to carry out God's mission? And so forth. . . ."

But I couldn't get any further. I couldn't demonstrate that this story too could not be told beyond this point because it has no end, it expands like a fan yet without moving, without coming to a dramatic point, without making the conflict clearer than it already is—

I couldn't do it, because they all leaped on me as one man and shouted at the top of their lungs: a solution at last, the idea was wonderful, much more plausible, much more symbolic than Nagel's story. Stoffel jumped to his feet and gave one of his conference speeches: "Well, gentlemen, dear Astrid, I believe the solution has come to us from an unexpected source. Here we finally have the film we want, which will liberate the problem of our times from the eternal German guilt complex and raise it beyond the actual German situation to a universal level. . . ." And he opened a bottle of champagne, which was a great rarity on the black market.

Nagel, however, had got up and quit the premises without a word of good-bye. When I tried to dash after him, the idiot, to get it into his thick head that I had wanted to help him with my parody, Astrid von Bürger held me back: "Leave him alone until he's over his anger. He'll realize how childish he's acting." But he never did realize it, my friend Nagel. He never spoke to me again.

□   □   □

AH, AT THAT TIME, pretty much everything in my life began to go awry. We had our little son, whom I could love above anything else, and he too loved his daddy above anything else, but things just wouldn't work with Christa and me; she kept getting more and more bitter, more and more uncommunicative; I had disappointed her, I had not brought prosperity and conviviality into her life, only want and shame; I, the husband, had lost the war, Hamburg was a flattened city, you could see all the way across town, only the red-light street near the Goose Market and the other one behind David's Watch had been spared, symbolically, by the bombs (incidentally, the theater, tax office, and police station too). I was doing my best for the reconstruction of conjugal tenderness, but it was not easy, nor was it successful: Christa's perfidious way, the instant she got to bed, of placing her arm across her face so that her elbow lay on her mouth like a bulwark—the mean little mouth that I liked to kiss so much—frustrated my feeble attempts. To be sure, she was very frightened, the poor thing, there was a shortage of everything, you really didn't know how you were going to survive from day to day. At night, the rubble killer roamed the streets. I myself often had horrible dreams, I murdered a cleaning woman with a coal scoop in a cellar, ran around during the day in Witte's shattered library and made up Gothic stories for Stoffel, Spouse & Associates—after all, I had become the house author at Astra Film Art; every other week, either a new project was tackled or an old script reworked and revised, they were busy for the sake of the busyness, and I had to lubricate it with brain grease; but I didn't have the moral grit to toss the whole garbage aside, there was always that prospect of an incredible amount of money, and it remained a prospect, it soon had something religious about it, this constant promise of pecuniary grace, salvation, and bliss; Christa believed

∷ 606 ∷

in it with as much ardor and unfulfillment as Witte (a Protestant) believed in the Virgin Mary.

But I also felt a certain defiance toward Nagel. He wouldn't greet me even when we ran into one another in the ever wilder, ever ranker garden of the villa on the Elbchaussee, he wouldn't respond when I called out to him, telling him not to be such an arsehole, he turned his back on me and slammed the door of the garden house behind him. The light burned in his little window late into the night; he was nearly done—Witte told Christa—with his first novel and was already working on a second one; his play, said Witte, wasn't going so well, but there were very interesting things in it; as for movies, he (like Witte himself and most likely Christa too) did not consider them real art. In short, a genuine artist, not a part-time one like me.

Well, I didn't want to be outdone, and so I thought up a number of truly lovely films, all based on the "what if?" principle. For instance, a New Guinea movie: a missionary has spent twenty years trying to get a Dajak tribe to give up head-hunting; and when the solemn renunciation is celebrated with a great feast, a government commissioner shows up and offers five pounds sterling for every Japanese head; war has broken out, you see, and the Japanese might invade at any moment. . . . But of course, at that time it was impossible to make a movie in New Guinea, and the other projects likewise came to nought for some reason or other. I kept writing countless and largely unremunerated scripts for Astra Film Art; some of them were even filmed during the next few years, although in completely revised versions. But for Witte, I was and remained a "part-time artist"; and, I'm afraid, for Christa, too.

□   □   □

MEANWHILE, I've got used to being one. But back then, script conferences with Stoffel, Spouse, & Associates lay on my mind like millstones. The filmmakers were shit into the Aesir sofas in front of the Valhalla fireplace, and turd columns of thick cigars rose from their mouths, pursed into buds. Such scenes aroused the most dreadful notions in my head. I was unable to interpret this potpourri of a living room in the Hanseatic villa—an omnium gatherum of clinker-bricks, cast iron, and stained glass—as anything but a cabaret parody of a Wagnerian opera. The gray manager-mugs on the giants exhausted by conferences fitted in nicely à la *Götterdämmerung*, and Astrid von Bürger was beautifully typecast in the domestic garment of an Ufa star, a sort of Nibelung dressing gown in royal blue with scarlet lining, which she always forgot to button from the mons veneris down, so that each of her calculatedly negligent movements revealed kilograms of German female ham. The memory is lodged traumatically in my soul: her arms are flung far apart on the ox-leather bulges of the sofa upholstery; her torso is bent back, the twin breasts, howitzer shells, practically bursting through the (here decently buttoned) silk; and over them hovers her—alas—really beautiful Brunhilde head (the head that seduced Nagel at the front, his dream of the "best friend's sister"). A powerful flood of short dark hair, virtually a banner of Berlin freshness, dangles over her eyebrows, and her big-cat eyes are observing the effect of her erotic presence: a drumbeat into the diaphragm of every man in the room. At the center of the room, her husband, Stoffel, is roaring, with a snifter (black-market cognac) in his left hand and a (black-market) Havana in his right hand. Primordial piglet Stoffel, his own totem pole, as it were; six feet six inches of bombastic tremendous stupidity whetted (witted?) by a certain shrewdness; a double hundredweight of crooked cunning combined with the upright joviality of a suburban *bon vivant*; a gigantic manchild, still emanating the sweet-and-sour odor of mother's milk; blond, fat, rosy, moody, ridiculous, and dangerous: the horrifying epitome of German vitality bulldozing everything in its path. . . .

There he stands, on solid seafarer legs, inspired by the model of the Hanseatic cog on the window sill, bucking the weather, towering in the pea soup of cigar smoke and Hennessy vapors, swaying in the waves of logorrhoea that have been pouring out of him for hours; with arm stumps and flapping elbows, snifter and cigar in his sausage fingers, he beats time to his rhetoric, and, with hypnotic gazes from his small, light-colored pig eyes and a spooky play of his features, he tries to make his spouse, Astrid (who pretends not to notice), aware that the skirt of her slit Blessed Virgin frock has slipped off her lap so that over the silver-slimy snail-paths of her nylon stockings (from the American PX) two succulent, quartz-lamp-browned thighs are visible all the way up to the groin. . . .

It is heartrending to see how greatly this irritates him, even though he wouldn't dare say a word about it or walk over and shift a corner of the old-fashioned dressing gown to cover the splendidly conjugal boundaries that his spouse so hospitably presents. His face twitches like the face of a sleeping man when the legs of a fly stroll across it, his eyes blink, his breathing is audibly heavy, his intonation more and more menacing:

". . . and so, gentlemen, and dear Astrid, once again, I can sum up the results of this conference as quite positive in the following terms: for me personally, the project seems to have made great strides thanks to the night's discussion and especially thanks to the objections—approved by all of us—the objections raised by our friend from the bank, Herr Jansen. Reason is where the money is. Certain details in the treatment aroused in each of us—and I am expressing myself with some amount of restraint—an impression of superfluous, highfalutin intellectuality. But now, thank goodness, all those aspects have been omitted, and the author will be so kind as to replace them with new and—hopefully!—better things. However, beyond that, we are all—and I believe I am speaking on behalf of everyone here—we are all as convinced as ever about the project—one hundred percent. And if this isn't a film that can bring us back to the peak of the good, old—I mean: the *pre*-Nazi Ufa—yes indeed, dear Astrid, we all know and appreciate your merits, but you can't possibly claim that the German cinema during your Doktor Goebbels days could be compared to what it used to be—huh? Well, then! If we can work our way back up to the top with this project—incidentally, I think you've lost a few buttons, darling— What? No, it doesn't bother me, I'm only pointing it out for the sake of order—anyway, as I was saying: if the postwar German film doesn't reveal a desire to regain its supreme position, then my name's not Stoffel, and I will never speak another syllable to you, dear friend!" (meaning me).

When my experiences ran along those lines, making me realize the net I was caught in and getting irredeemably tangled in chasing the chimera of money, which in the movie business, as we know, can never be chased but favors only those of movie-erotic means, inveigling the needy into leaping at it the way fools leap at confetti during the Mardi Gras in Nice—

when I found myself before the mountain of shit that has to be chomped through in order to be allowed brief sojourns in Neverneverland (where I was quickly permitted to play the rich daddy for my little boy and bring Christa some pathetic bit of blackmarket luxury, which she didn't even want), when I perhaps achieved, temporarily, an even more pathetic bit of respectability, which Christa truly and very sorely missed in her marriage to me: a threshold swept clean of embarrassing creditors and scandalous rumors, a threshold her Junker relatives could cross, willingly and honorably—

when I was walking home from Pöseldorf, the site of the clinker-brick Valhalla that the occupation authorities had requisitioned for Stoffel, Spouse & Associates, and when I headed toward the Elbchaussee, where my darling little boy was waiting for me, as was Christa with her elbow over her mean little mouth in Witte's sliced-in-half Swiss villa, and when I had brooded enough about what it was that always kept bringing me to strange worlds and alien people and dream-like and traumatic experiences, I would then turn off on the Reeperbahn, right behind Davidswache, make a left on the Herbertstrasse, and seek refuge with Gisela in the whorehouse.

The day was usually dawning, even though all kinds of lights were still burning on the empty Reeperbahn: the stars of the streetlamps piercing the stone sky like needles; and the bulbs in the grottoes of pinball arcades giving off a gaudy, theatrical glimmer; and the garlands of lamps hanging over the war-damaged façades of the dance halls; and, across the street, a wretched kerosene lamp smoldering sootily on the counter of a sausage-stand, where a couple of bleary-eyed loafers and gadabouts hung around. In the empty vastness beyond, there was something of the forlornness of Bessarabian cities left all to themselves in the tension between a yearning for the evening west and the agonizing promise from the east. And I entered the red-light alley as if I were coming home.

I don't know for sure now whether this took place in the midst of the Ice Age or after the grand, world-changing flimflam of the currency cut—the criminal conjuring trick in which Stoffel, Spouse & Associates took part as fascinating shamans. It probably occurred on the threshold between the two; the crèche period, at any rate, was past, and one of the few clean places in the world was the brothel.

At some point, I forgot a few pages there, the draft to a screenplay presumably, it couldn't have been anything else back then. Scherping, who was a regular customer of Gisela's, found these pages, read them, and took them along—a publisher for all seasons. He showed them to Carlotta, who had meanwhile left Witte and had become Scherping's secretary and *dame de compagnie*. And Carlotta showed them to Schwab, with whom she was living in conjugal union, and said she thought she knew who the author was—we were seeing each other from time to time.

Thus it was that Schwab, an editor at Scherping Publishers, set out to find me and talk me into writing books. After all, it was reconstruction time, and literature too had to be created *ex nihilo*. But why, exactly? . . .

I also don't know whether to interpret it as symbolic that my road to writing began in the whorehouse. But I can see Schwab when we met for the first time. He was taut and lanky, like all of us at that time; the scant wartime and postwar diet suited us. His hair was cropped short, and his thick glasses made him seem as if he were sorry he hadn't died in action on the first day in Poland, like my cousin Wolfgang. *He* appeared to interpret the origin of our acquaintanceship as symbolic. He handed me the pages Scherping had found in the whorehouse and said that he, Schwab, had read them with the greatest pleasure. He then made it clear to me with some embarrassment that he knew where

Scherping had got hold of them, and added with a heart-winning smile, "I envy you for your right of domicile there." My brother Schwab.

□   □   □

I KNEW WHY the burghers had piled up such a lovely flower hill for him here. They were tied to him in the same way they were tied to me. Their act of taking possession of him as one of their own and the dreadful benevolence that crept into their eyes whenever they looked at me were one and the same. They saw us as losers—and that was why they identified with us.

I could now look up and peer into their eyes and see myself in their eyes as a lotus eater among lotus eaters. We had all forgotten where we came from and where we were going. We were all whirling in the whirlwind of our delusion, our epoch's delusion, floating, sailing, reeling, plunging, and soaring up again on the pinions of our fictions and illusions, whirling chaotically in an unreal carnival of realities, while around us the squadrons of *horlà* fortresses grew into the sky and the all-covering cement would soon wipe out our very last traces. And with us, our finest dream visions would come to an end: the gardens and the cities, the Eden of regulated nature and Babylon within it, and the New Jerusalem to be built, the city of ANTHROPOLIS.

"Peace be with us, Brother Schwab," I said to the flower hill at my feet, "we've got thousands of reasons, but no right and no occasion anymore to despise the burghers here, because all of us have died with our world—you may be a little more dead here in your blossoming grove than we are; but these are differences of degree; in essence, it's the same. We—you and I and our true blood relatives, the *Zeitgeist* contemporaries in the roadside cafés—we can now make peace with one another. Granted, they muddled up our lives with their shaman guiles, with their currency cuts, they screwed up our worship of the Baby Spirit in Nagel's garden house, and in the insanity of their fictions they destroyed beautiful Babylon and all the even more beautiful plans for the New Jerusalem. But in all fairness, we have to admit that we and those like us, the so-called intellectuals, eagerly beat our drums in accompaniment. The drumbeat was mostly confusing, and that only helped them. Yet it was never clear whether we weren't just beating *their* rhythm, and indeed beating it most effectively whenever we thought we were drumming our sheer hatred of them out of ourselves.

"We can hedge all we like, but we are their brethren in this perishing world, and the more violently we rebel against them, the more firmly we follow the logic of our decline. We follow this logic in any case, whether as revolutionaries or as conformists. For just as there is no escape from the cage of our Self, so too there is no escape from the pens and prisons of our diverse Middle Kingdoms. No matter how isolated we may feel inside them, in the defiant pride of the individualist or in the misery of the lonesome man among too many, as a stigmatized reformer or as a cynical exploiter of the system—we merely express the prevailing trends and moods, we are merely witnesses to the state of affairs, symptoms, scale points on the fever curve, points on the life stages of our world within the world. As redeemers or wanton strivers, as geniuses or run-of-the-mill morons, we are tiny particles of some collective whole whose will we carry out—thereby fulfilling its destiny. None of our gestures can be dissociated from these states and currents, which furrow us like a wheat field in the wind—in the wind of the *Zeitgeist*, which, in any Middle Kingdom, sets its own time.

"We should never have forgotten these things—we who sought our salvation in writing. We would have become more tolerant, at least more reticent. We would not have transformed other people's dreams into nightmares, because we thought we were the only ones awake. Wasn't the thing that made us believe we were awake a far more terrible nightmare? . . .

"We are about to awake when we dream we are dreaming—isn't that so? That was the utterance that made us blood witnesses, martyrs—do you remember? All right! Instead of resorting to anything (even the destruction of our artistic devices) to prolong our ever frailer, ever more transparent trance, to keep dancing the shaman's dance of artists, we late-born senile Young Writers, we sorcerer's apprentices of the anthracite-gray magic of the Word should have awoken, *ni plus, ni moins.*

"Our suffering! The way we feel the wind of the *Zeitgeist* when it barely comes up as a breeze, and the arms of our mills move with it instantly, rather than waiting till the storm shakes the trees and makes the fields bow down to the earth—how proud we were of this ability of ours! How we fancied knowing, before others knew, that the time was past when one could speak about the individual and his plights in the collective of others; or that one feels as stir-crazy in the solitary confinement of any Middle Kingdom as in the terrifying capsule of the Self; and that the knock signals sent from one to the other merely knock them apart all the more thoroughly, these individual worlds within the world; that here too, the cells began to proliferate, and the entangled circles of the individual worlds, Middle Kingdoms, and Fatherlands fell apart, while the totality proliferated exuberantly into a tremendous cancerous tumor—so that one could no longer speak about Man in General and certainly not about the torments of the isolated, unrelated Self; in fact, one could speak about nothing now, because nothing could now be articulated to the Self in the cry for help uttered by the human cancer tumor. . . . Our sorrow! The sorrows of young Werther when he reached for a quill instead of a pistol—for instance, his despair about the things that tried to express themselves out of him and the things that he succeeded in expressing

as if the gods wanted to make us realize that it is not up to us to say what ought to be said, but as if it were up to their arbitrary will to time such utterance, as if the gods wanted to force us to realize that this arbitrary will is divine in its enormous dissipation—

for even the stupidest man, saying something that no one heeds, will sooner or later utter a basic truth, for which a Thales would envy him; something occurs at some point to even the dullest head (and then drops out again), something capable of expanding the spiritual and intellectual horizon of mankind by a good big step; in beer-garden chitchat, one may hear an insight that, if uttered before attentive lis-

teners, might stamp its utterer as a genius; and in his dreams, every child surpasses Homer and Dante—

while the poor fools who feel destined to speak must earn every word in harrowings of hell until they finally reach the humble awareness that it is a matter of luck whether a crumb falls to them too from the steadily wasted and squandered opulence—

"Weren't these childish things? Puberty problems? Of course. But we took them damn seriously. Yet we lived on as if they did not exist. In spite of our task to fulfill a promise. A gift means having a substance, so they say morality gives expression to this substance; talent means finding this expression in an interesting way, with the insight that the word spoken for communication separates more than it connects, that little else is possible but the flight into absurdity, into humor, satire, parody. Then, you see, we were finally—and admittedly what we had always been before, unconsciously, with the ludicrous arrogance of various kinds of grandeur—the clowns and court jesters of the middle classes. Albeit with the fool's privilege to say what's on our minds. Now, we believed we could finally have fun doing the things we had once done in beery earnestness: celebrate a funeral. We antiburghers carried ourselves to the grave in the universal carnival of 'realities.' As the clowns of the burghers, we were burghers in the final phase of a logical development. Just as parody is the final phase of an art, so too the burgher has to become his own parody as an artist and bohemian. Indeed, if possible, as a celebrated artist and bohemian. To recognize the burgher in his apotheosis, one must see the procession of the BIG ELEPHANT BALLYHOO as *pompes funèbres*. This is the only way to show how awfully futile it was, the only thing we really wanted to do: take revenge."

He who writes takes revenge—wasn't this too a discovery that mellowed our suffering, that gave us a feeling of majestic superiority? Now, we had the choice: either nobly to forgo revenge and hence final salvation and enter the icy void without further ado— like you, my dead friend—or else clamp our teeth into our neighbor and proliferate with him in the slow-motion explosion of metastases, and, according to that old German proverb, one's neighbor is really oneself; charity, we all know, begins at home, right?

This is the final, macabre joke of the middle-class jokesters: the hara kiri of the brains. The voiding of the contents of brains for a trichinosis inspection before blue eyes. The presentation of the no longer expressible Self in its timeless presence, in which the past and the future are shuffled together, memories and wishes, traumas, anxieties, and fears, like a well-shuffled pack of cards, and formless, proliferating with millions of its kind in a fermenting dough—I—SELF—I—SELF—I—SELF

It was on a day in Vienna—the last of the three days on which, as I stubbornly maintain, the sun stood still in the heavens. The Führer and Reich Chancellor of the now truly big Greater German Reich was staying at the Hotel Imperial—the world comes to an end nobly and symbolically!—and now he wanted to show himself to the ecstatic nation of Ostmark people. Not just whooshing by, as on the second day—through the dividing sea of the people, hurrying as though fleeing—but static at last, lapidary, and entire: that is, as a torso. If we do not naturally tend to place a great personality on four legs by inserting a horse underneath him, then he is most effective as a bust—there must be something wrong with our extremities, they seem humanly convincing only on crucified bodies.

The Führer and Reich Chancellor knew this, of course. He wanted to show himself to his Ostmark people as monumental, as red-blooded and rut-breasted, so to speak: I embrace you, all you millions. Let me kiss the whole, wide world! (In the enveloping battles later on, the text was varied: let me kill the whole, wide world!) And the ecstatic people of Vienna came swarming out in oppressively full attendance to throw themselves at this bust. Vienna was empty again. As shiny as a shell washed ashore. It became clear what a city really is: this enormous hive, this once so beautifully formed and now stone honeycomb, proliferating hybridly and pumping millions of human beings through itself in a pulsating osmosis. . . .

(You see, friend S.: the difference between our current states of being—mine here at your flower mound, and yours under-

neath it or perhaps dissolved in the air we breathe, in the heavenly blue with which even this rainy-gray day may be lined —this difference only in degree between two varieties of dead men boils down to the fact that I have to keep asking the same old questions, while you—unlike the pastor, who believes he has an answer to these questions—no longer have to ask them. Witness to your satisfaction that this time it is I who envy you).

Very well! Back then, in Vienna (and we must not forget: it was always the same weather, beribboned with springtime blue but arctically cold, and the sun stood still in the heavens), back then this honeycomb was pumped empty, down to the last rathole. Anyone with legs or even without, anyone who could at least manage to creep or crawl or drag himself along on crutches or on the leather seat of his pants, or roll himself along on a rolling board, or be supported, carried, or pulled along by a nurse, a son-in-law, a daughter, a grandchild, on litters or in a mackintosh sack; everyone, down to the last man, the last woman, the last child, the last old man, was sucked out of his home and had flooded to Heldenplatz, Heroes' Square, and was damming up into an enormous gruel of human flesh, thickening into a human dough stream with particolored sugar and proliferating and fermenting and rising higher and higher: the horses of the rescuer from the Turks and of the victor of Aspern reared in vain to escape this human dough, which welled and swelled up to them and eventually covered them, a dreadful cake of millions of individual creatures—and it roared.

The human dough palpitated and roared in short, gasping breaths at the icy blue sky stretching overhead: Heh-hi, heh-hi, heh-hi, heh-hi, heh-hi. . . .

The individual voice might have been articulating the flower woman's hysterical Siegheil! on the first day; but in millionfold accumulation, it was a fluttering, shallow-breathed roar. And it rose all the way to the celestial vault, which sent back a ruthlessly icy smile, and the roar reverberated back, echoed hauntingly through the empty city, which had now become its own charnel house: Heh-hi, heh-hi, heh-hi, heh-hi. . . .

And then it choked, whirling and retching, bellowing in a vomitatio *that turned the innards inside out and burst into the cosmos . . .*

for far, far beyond the vast square, over there on the sandstone-colored façade of the imperial castle, where the thick black-and-white swastika spiders of the national insignia billowed restlessly in a tangle amid the bloody surge of flags, a microscopically tiny, mustard-brown manikin had stepped out on a tiny balcony and shoved his chest against the balustrade and raised a tiny arm for the German salute and turned his minimal tiny head (now, without the oversize doorman's cap but merely smeared by the skewed ink-wiper of a strand of hair), turned it to and fro, slowly—a tiny mustard-brown particle, a single part in the proliferating human dough (think how infinitely tiny his mustache must have been!) . . .

You must forgive me, but I was really standing very far away—or rather, hanging very far away from the manikin, hanging in a cluster of people, with Uncle Helmuth and Aunt Hertha and Aunt Selma, on the shaft of a candelabrum beyond the vast square at the gates of the People's Park. We had not been able, alas, to conquer any better places in the human dough; Cousin Wolfgang, however, had been rewarded for hush-hush underground loyalty and, freezing in the white shirt and black-booted trousers of the national warrior, he was permitted to stand in the middle of his marching column block barely a hundred and fifty yards away from the Führer and palpitate in the rhythmic Siegheil! *of the mass beast—again in rhythm, I say. For after the mustard-brown manikin on the far, far balcony let the booming incense of the shouts to the heavens for a while, he lifted his hand, and the roar was now scanned as a stamping hi-ha, hi-ha, hi-ha. . . .*

And the manikin (he was now surrounded by a bronze-brown and blood-rippled general-gray retinue—and Cousin Wolfgang told us afterward he had even seen his blue eyes), the manikin let the hi-ha boom into the heavens for a while and reverberate from the emptied Nibelung city (and Uncle Helmuth bellowed into my ear that such a concentrated, rhythmically organized discharge of sound from such a tremendous human aggregate had to transform itself into energy waves, which charged the willpower accumulator of the manikin up there on the balcony with unbelievable tension). And then the manikin lifted his hand again, and silence reigned—what am I saying: a column of silence descended from the heavens and pressed down upon the human cake and choked every sound . . .

and the manikin began to speak (and his voice thundered through the aggregate of the many hundreds of loudspeakers suspended among the chestnut candles, and his voice was almost as tremendous as the roar of the mass monster),

the manikin began to speak and he said, "I . . ."

and whether it was the fault of the metallic tone of the loudspeakers or the rapscallion baritone of the manikin or his understandably profound emotion (for, after long years of struggle, he was back in his homeland for the first time, returning triumphally as her greatest son—recognized at last in his greatness and at last victorious)—

in any event, this "I" came out as an "Oy"—and was instantly reattacked by the chevy-chase of the heh-hi, heh-hi, heh-hi of the beast, a human cancer tumor—

and it was repeated lamentably: "Oy . . ." And once again, the roaring predator's breath of the monster, a human metastasis, pounced upon this yearning diphthong and yanked it down and into its panting heh-hi, heh-hi, heh-hi. . . .

and the manikin courageously reiterated his lamentable "Oy . . ."

the tension of the willpower accumulator did not yield, but the record evidently was scratched or cracked: the needle kept hopping in the same groove: "Oy . . ." Heh-hi, heh-hi, heh-hi. . . . "Oy . . ." Heh-hi, heh-hi, heh-hi. "Oy . . ." Heh-hi, heh-hi, heh-hi. . . . "Oy." Heh-hi, heh-hi, heh-hi . . .

and finally the manikin managed to blurt out, "Oy am sooo happppy. . . ."

But this was merely a putt-putt-putt: it sounded squashed and washed out and bangy, like a fart in the bathtub: vanderLubbe-vanderLubbevanderLubbe. . . .

Yet the thing that rose grandly to the heavens, where it was eerily registered for the rest of my life, was that eerie dialogue *between the I and the masses, and that pathetic sound, that heart-burstingly lonesome call of a toad, rising beyond all ear-splitting croaks of frogs: "Oy . . ."*

The manikin had vanished from the balcony. And the human dough kept palpitating in its resonant, million-throated heh-hi, heh-hi, heh-hi . . .
and flattened it again into a shallowly surging roar, for now the manikin was suddenly in the midst of the human dough and cutting through it.
This time, he sliced through it like a shark's fin, slowly and calmly—after all, he was entirely in his element. He stood upright and exposed in his bullet-proof but open Mercedes, but neither the car nor the cops encrusting it were visible, they were kneaded into the fermenting dough. Only the manikin loomed above it and sliced closer, ringed by the roaring madness of ecstasy all around him. And he kept slicing closer through the human dough, closer and closer, toward me, until I could look into his eyes.
He had put his oversize doorman's cap on again and snuffled morosely on his minimal mustache. Very slowly, like one of the automatons in the Prater that begin to move when you hit the bull's eye on their bellies, he lifted and lowered his right arm, displaying his slightly curved palm. His left hand held tight to his belt buckle, as though he were afraid that his pants might fall down. He seemed withdrawn, pensive, and very solitary. And his eyes radiated, sky-blue and foolish.

□   □   □

EIGHT YEARS LATER I managed to witness another historic event, in which, so to speak, the balance was drawn after this and several subsequent ones:
At the defendants' bench in the Nuremberg Court, one defendant gets to his feet, eerily lizard-like, a saurian emerging from the primal ooze: Rudolf Hess, the Führer's deputy. He lets his arm move up in order to be sworn in as a witness with a la-

mentably raised forefinger. It is impossible to say whether he is merely pretending to be crazy or really is crazy. If he's just pretending, his act is brilliant, with a highly effective dramatic climax at just the right moment.

It is the tormenting hour when the defendants make concluding statements before judgment. For nine months, this hour has been marked in all minds as a coming event. For nine months, they have looked forward to it impatiently. More and more hope has adhered to this hour. The hope that these final words of the defendants would make it clear what monsters and monstrosities have been on trial here. The hope that this leadership elite of the Third Reich would finally own up to being the true perpetrators of the crimes they are being tried for here: the destruction and conflagration of a continent; the rape of a civilization professing Christian principles; the bloody besmirching of the name of a once great nation until the end of history; the final annihilation of faith in the moral reliability of mankind.

For nine months in Nuremberg, people have been waiting, in greater and greater despair, for one of the twenty-two prisoners at the bar to step forth from behind the mask of a banal average man, a mask that has made it impossible to comprehend that he—an irreproachable officer, an excellent office manager, a solicitous paterfamilias—allowed what happened to happen, a mask that made it hard to believe it really did happen and was not just dreamed or invented by sick minds. Nine months, prolonged more and more unbearably, with weeks of tedious readings of documents and interrogations of witnesses, days in which horror has become an everyday routine and finally a matter of the bleakest boredom. And throughout these nine months, one has looked forward to the moment when some dark confession, some satanic word, some perverse thought—expressed defiantly or involuntarily—might reveal that a drive, a desire for evil had been operating, and that the dreadful things exposed and testified to every day did not take place only because they were not prevented.

Such a revelation would give the prosecutors and judges the security that righteous men feel toward evildoers. This trial has been put on too hastily, with too much governessy indignation and idealism and on a very flimsy legal basis, and the hoped-for revelations will make it look more like an act of justice and not just a superfluous humiliation, a process of revenge wreathed in embarrassing claptrap and carried out against inferior losers by men who just barely won, and who might be accused of the same crime tomorrow, since they too failed to prevent what happened from happening.

However, the expectations are not realized. The evil does not care to be seized hold of. The defendants of Nuremberg cannot be reduced to the proper dimension and proportion in regard to the crimes they are being tried for. No dolus can be demonstrated. Their crime is that of mediocrity.

They are a representative average. Their demonic quality is that of utter lack of imagination. Their perversity is the fundamentalist attitude toward rules and regulations. They merely did their duty. They remained true and loyal to their Führer through thick and thin and night and fog, that's all. It never occurred to them that they were dangerously behind the times, and that in the world of relativity, they were practicing the unconditionality of the virtues of medieval vassals. As average Europeans, they drew their models from the dumping grounds of history. They learned how to obey in silence. They signed thousands of death warrants in their bureaucracy and were responsible for running it smoothly. That was their job, and that was what they got paid for. They can cite this fact. This too is law. It was valid for their accusers and judges too. They have nothing to reproach themselves for.

They have insisted on this for nine months. Was it not naïve to expect that now, at the last moment, they might admit to being artful scoundrels, and that, in their last words to the public, before a noose around their necks cuts off any possibility of further utterance, they might reveal something of the secret of how the evil nesting in souls erupts suddenly and leads to the annihilation of the world?

One of the concluding speeches has already been given. Amid an embarrassed silence in the courtroom, Göring, the first to speak, has cast down a few nasty, bumptious phrases. He was plainly nervous, annoyed and muddled. Even he, who, with his occasional vestiges of personality and authority, had maintained something like the dignity of a gang boss and something like gallows humor, now seems pathetically second-rate and humanly shabby. His words are cheap rhetoric. Whatever the court decides, he sullenly barks, he leaves the actual and final judgment to history: a future German youth will pass the just verdict on him and his comrades. Period. He sits down again, fat, pale, disreputable.

If everything else had not been in this style, then his words would sound horrifying. The future German youth is growing up out there, in the rubble fields beyond the walls of this courthouse, guarded like a fortress, beyond its barriers, beyond the heated rooms, all the food in the cafeteria, the fragrant cigarettes and manicured fingernails of the secretaries and all the grandiose fictions and abstract rules of the court proceedings. There, beyond this Middle Kingdom here, an entirely different reality prevails. The youth growing up out there was conceived in Quonset huts by more or less maimed fathers and edemic mothers; no sooner could this youth crawl than it learned how to pilfer potatoes and risk its life gleaning coal chips on railroad embankments and filching cigarette butts from the fingers of Allied soldiers. In all likelihood, this new generation will create its myths independently of moralistic reflections on history. Yet here, in here, those words sound like dreadful claptrap. Embarrassing claptrap: they remind everyone that here, everything is claptrap and must remain claptrap. That the more and more threadbare, more and more brittle as-if of this trial—which was meant to apply the legal conception of the civil code in punishing the deliberate and generally perpetrated annihilation of entire human races—cannot have anything but a claptrap ending.
The dreadful thing, the ridiculous thing, the poignant thing about the Nuremberg Trial is that it is built upon claptrap and thus has nothing else to put forward but simply claptrap. It is the desperate attempt at inflating the claptrap on which our civilization rests, the noble, sad, quixotic tilting of Western fictions at the windmills of the reality of human nature. Of course, the

magic of these fictions is still powerful enough to keep the trial going. Their magic has sufficed not only to make the prosecutors act shocked, indignant, and full of holy zeal, and the judges dignified and aware of their high office (albeit with an occasional skeptical shake of their heads), but (more astonishingly) to make the accused perform their parts as lawful defendants. Yet that is precisely what makes the events here so spectral. It turns them into a ghostly spectacle. Nothing has any reality.

The Weltanschauung of these men allowed them to, actually demanded that they, kill millions of people in order to guarantee the purity of their nation. And it is not possible to accept that the defendants will now try to wriggle out of these charges like crooks in a cheap bar. It is a ghostly experience to see with what servile eagerness these cynics of the will to power, these fumigator executives of racism outdid themselves in lending a helping hand to the judicial process when they had to assign responsibility to a former brother-in-arms and present themselves as victims of misunderstandings. It was absurd and repulsive to watch these ever faithful, upright citizens with their miens of injured innocence and gestures of insidious hostility, with their attempts at self-justification by citing orders they had received and official duties they had had to perform as a matter of course. So that Jewish prosecutors, beside themselves with fury, despair, and mortification, suddenly played the devil's advocate, using arguments of Nazi ideology merely to give their defendants a fiction of free choice in the commission of crimes—and thus give them a very last shred of human, if devilish, dignity, thereby rescuing the dignity of the court, which dignity threatened to dissolve in the miasmas of cadavers and the stale, stuffy smell of petit bourgeois receivers of orders and executors of programs.

True, when Ribbentrop, as third speaker of the concluding statement, was talking, he said something about the incompetence of the court, arrogantly grumbling that if he were to be hanged, he would not formally recognize it. But it's a bit too late for such protests, and his words go unheeded. They too remain claptrap. Besides, they sound like everything else coming from him: insolent, presumptuous, and stupid. And anyway, the real sensation has fizzled out: Rudolf Hess's concluding statement.

Now, it's his turn. He was Adolf Hitler's deputy. His most loyal vassal. The John among his disciples. Here, he no longer seems to be of this world. He sits there, mentally departed, with a blanket over his legs, like a resident of an old-age home. A military policeman—his face contracted like a bulldog's by the polished chrome-steel helmet with its tight chin strap—sticks out his junior-officer paws in their full-dress white-cotton gloves and shoves the microphone under Hess's nose. But, with the motion of brushing away a cobweb, Hess pushes it aside and raises his forefinger like a schoolboy who wants to leave the room.

It is a pathetic little white worm of a forefinger. It rises, timorous and crooked, as if crawling out of a hole in the ground and peering into the hazardous world with a nauplius eye on the fingertip—a dwarf-like harbinger sent out for reconnoitering by its lord and master.

His head also seems to be emerging from the primal ooze, it too squints perplexed into unknown creation. A saurian head: the weight of the upper skull has squashed the mouth into the flat lower jaw and distorted it into its breadth, hopelessly unsated. Yet this is a tame, a humble saurian. Its eyes are so gloomy with despair as they ogle out of the shadow of the Nietzsche brows, which hang bushily from the socket arches and grow together at the top of the nose as in a criminal's face; indeed, the eyes exert an almost suction-like effect. One looks into them as into the orifices of two periscopes that are camouflaged for maneuver purposes and that are slowly screwed upward as they turn to and fro, scanning around.

They turn on the pale stalk of a withered neck, which grows out of the now oversized shirt collar; with a male choir singer's Adam's apple whipping up and down between baggy skin and sinews, the throat emits a sullenly lamenting little voice. Extremely submissive, this little voice asks the High Court for permission to remain seated during the reading of the concluding statement.

The black-smocked Punch-and-Judy torso of LORD JUSTICE *Lawrence at the judges' table opposite the defendants' bar nods paternally as in a puppet theater, his iron-framed spectacles slid-*

ing down his nose; with the old-man vibrato/tremolo of digni-
fied Anglo-Saxon bombast in his voice, he proclaims that the re-
quest is granted in light of the defendant's poor state of health.

The defendant utters his thanks, audibly touched by such pa-
triarchally strained humanity and, while his periscopes scan an
imaginary horizon, he pulls a few sheets of paper from the folds
of the blanket slung around his knees, the blanket of a Baltic Sea
vacationer. The room is deathly still, the defendant's fumbling
very ponderous. Finally, he's ready. In a droning voice, Hess
begins to read off a text that was obviously prepared by his attor-
ney.

This too is merely claptrap. The protestations of a completely
honest man who must deal with charges that are not quite
groundless yet unjustly harsh, and who must now make a manly
upright effort to kiss a few arses rhetorically, to creep into any
available hole inside or outside the court, and to do so quickly,
making the best possible impression before a general closing of
sphincters.

There's a hollow feeling at the pit of the stomach, even, ap-
parently, the defendant's. He lowers the sheets of paper and
shakes his head indignantly. No, he says resolutely, he won't go
on. They have forced him to read his text in order to hinder him
from communicating something of extreme importance. He is
visibly agitated and gets to his feet after all, but so shakily that the
papers and the blanket slide from his lap. Göring, who sits next
to him, tries to pull him back on the bench by the tail of his
jacket. But Hess shoves Göring's hand aside and hisses to him
that he has to let him do his duty. He stands there, large. Stands
there and moves the periscopes of his eyes about as though seek-
ing something.

He seeks it far, far beyond the table with the Last Supper fig-
ures of the eight judges facing him on the long wall, far behind
the now empty witness stand on the short wall to his left and the
glass lock-up booth next to it; behind it, the simultaneous trans-
lators are waiting for his next words in order to turn them, in-
stantly and uncolored, into French and English and Russian and
let them whir up like a small swarm of birds.

As a rule, one scarcely hears it, this gaudy swarm of words. It whirs up and scatters, slipping into the rusty and encrusted headphones made of former Wehrmacht supplies and hanging from every seat in the courtroom, albeit seldom used. And even though the words trickle out as dwarves from the uselessly dangling earphones, it is so still in this room that you can hear every one of them. The periscopes of the defendant Rudolf Hess sweep through the space.

They scan an imaginary horizon. He turns them to the right, they sweep across the stunned heads of the attorneys, who are looking at him, and across the tables of the prosecutors and their astonished miens to his right, across the barrier separating the public, from which hundreds of pairs of eyes are staring at him—but what they seek lies far beyond, outside this room, far outside this building, guarded like a military camp, and beyond Nuremberg, shamefully bombed and flattened, and beyond Germany, covered with silent lunar craters, and beyond Europe, smashed and shattered, and perhaps even beyond this planet, which the mange of mankind has so dreadfully attacked and violated. And while they search, his saurian head speaks, and his sullen and exhausted little voice says that the important information which he has to communicate and which they have been trying to hinder him from communicating concerns matters that the initiated have long been aware of, but that have not been made sufficiently accessible to the general public. During the great show trials in Russia, the press pointed out the incomprehensible self-accusations of the defendants and expressed the suspicion that these self-accusations could have been obtained only with the aid of drugs. Nevertheless, it still has not gotten around urbi et orbi that certain pharmaceutical preparations, in the form of injections or tablets, are able to transform the most solid character into a toy with no will of its own, a malleable tool for any intention whatsoever.

Now, all at once, the suspense of sensation crackles in the room. All past events suddenly become more present. The light of the neon tubes becomes harsher. The nightmare mood becomes more intense in the small courtroom, which is almost boudoir-like, intimate, after nine months of horror-filled proceedings. Reality becomes more real.

This is now transmitted telepathically throughout the gigantic honeycomb of the Fürth Palace of Justice. Outside, the corridors and the other cells are alive. All at once, the termite hill teems. Even the most out-of-the-way nooks and crannies have been alerted that something is happening in the magically charged core cell, where, throughout these months of tenacious exposure of atrocities, horror has gradually become boring and indignant gestures have become bleak. At the same time, a sense of frustration has developed, arousing a universal wish for something extraordinary to happen, no matter what, no matter how, no matter to whom—merely to end the awful stagnation of horror, to stir it up, to bring the salvation of movement. No matter what might happen—the personal appearance of Hitler, still alive and remorsefully declaring his readiness to turn himself over to the Nuremberg judges; or the entrance of a host of angels, opening the prison cells with flaming swords, because the prisoners are innocent—even something fantastic could happen so long as it occurred as an occurrence *and released the events here from their* state of static being.

For this is the torment that everyone here feels, even a rubber-neck sticking his nose into the Nuremberg Trial: the ineluctability of a state that cannot be changed. The static, immobile presence of horror (so oppressively depicted in the best present-day writing—isn't it?). The omnipresence of hopelessness. The anonymity and ubiquity of evil. The continuous existence of murderousness in the human condition. The impossibility of eliminating that existence. . . .
The habituation to horror has paralyzed every person in the Nuremberg court. Its omnipresence has allowed no movement. One murder is dreadful and reprehensible. The murder of ten people is an abomination. The murder of one hundred people goes to the limits of the imagination. The murder of several million people is an abstraction, to be grasped only with statistics. Crime becomes a matter of quanta. The murderer cannot be placed in any conceivable relationship to his deed. One cannot imagine a just punishment for him. He is no longer a murderer by means of a direct deed. He is an executive particle of an over-

all executive action. He no longer acts. He performs his part in organic events. The causality of guilt and atonement, crime and punishment is canceled. Indeed, all causality is thereby canceled. Time stands still. . . . I don't know who said that limbo must be worse than hell. So it doesn't matter what the event may bring, it will bring temporary salvation. Even if it spelled an end to any further attempts at distinguishing good and evil, it would still be the final fulfillment of an increasingly vital wish.

And this great moment seems to have come. The room fills up with people. No one hears them or sees them coming. They jam in. The room fills up like a pond with an underground source. Where one person was standing there are now three. Three heads stick together to hear the translations out of earpieces of antediluvian headphones from shot-up tanks or crashed airplanes or sunken U-boats. What will he say now, the defendant Rudolf Hess, the deputy of that "Oy" of March 1938 in Vienna? Will he reveal that the accused of Nuremberg are drugged? Or that they were drugged in the days of the Third Reich? Or the judges? People wait in utter suspense.

The defendant Rudolf Hess once again raises his small, white worm of a forefinger. This time for the oath. He pronounces the formula. He swears to tell the truth, the whole truth and nothing but the truth, so help him God.

And even though the black-robed torso of LORD JUSTICE Lawrence at the judges' table opposite him clears its throat, admonishing him paternally that the defendant need not be sworn in again, since all his statements here in the courtroom are under oath anyway, the defendant declares that he nevertheless wants to tell the truth this time and nothing but the truth.

Then, he starts talking. He tells about his flight to England and the way he was received there after landing; his reception was at first formal and reserved, and then he was interrogated and taken to a camp, where he was treated with utter courtesy and solicitude. In particular, his physician, a man named Dr. Johnson, soon grew so close to him and was so unreservedly friendly that he, the not yet accused, the as yet still interned Rudolf Hess, finally told him, Dr. Johnson, something that had been on his mind for some time: all the people he had come into contact with, *all the officers and functionaries who had interrogated him, as well as all the guards in the camp, had strangely radiant blue eyes, as clear as water. . . .*

Now, they all feel shudders up and down their spines: Everyone knows who had such strangely radiant blue eyes, as clear as water, Aryan eyes, the eyes of pretty much everyone in the Greater German Reich, and they know that those eyes supposedly exerted an irresistible fascination on everyone who encountered their gaze. Is this what the defendant Rudolf Hess is aiming at?

Even though it's not altogether clear, is he ultimately trying to say that when he was in England, he realized that Adolf Hitler, the man who led Germany to destruction, had been under the influence of drugs? Or was he the will-less tool of the Secret Service or some far more obscure and anonymous power in the background? The Freemasons perhaps? Or the Elders of Zion? . . .

But this is too literary to be probable. Too parodistic. Too artistically dramatic for the pulp fiction of life's "reality." Such spectacular devices are used only by the guild of adventure novelists and comic-strip authors. For the most intricate plots, reality has far less demanding dramaturgical devices. Usually, the crudest motivations and stupidest solutions. The suspense gets unbearable.

Yet the defendant Rudolf Hess won't let the cat out of the bag. He increases the suspense to the limits of patience. He goes into detail about which people at the camp in England had these strangely radiant blue eyes, as clear as water. And he tells of how Dr. Johnson now observed the very same thing, coming to him every day with a newly discovered pair of blue eyes as clear as water. Until—yes, until he, the defendant Rudolf Hess, was forced to perceive that he too, Dr. Johnson himself, had these strangely blue eyes as clear as water. . . .

It was still deathly silent in the Nuremberg courtroom. No sound, no motion. Nothing stirred. The dammed-up human pond stood still. But all at once, the suspense was gone. It was *gone in a bizarre way. It had not let up. It had not eased up little by little to tear off like a hanging thread. It had, so to speak, run out of this world. It had crossed some mysterious threshold and had run out into a different dimension. The pond was dead. It was no longer dammed up and it did not flow out. It stagnated, it began to decompose.*

And this was how it was after LORD JUSTICE *Lawrence cleared his throat with literary thoroughness, à la Dickens, as it were, and rapped his pencil on the table top and spoke in a paternally strict voice to tell the defendant Rudolf Hess that he should finally get to the point, he had already been speaking for twenty minutes, and he must bear in mind that twenty more defendants were waiting to make their concluding statements. And it remained as it was when the defendant Rudolf Hess responded by shrugging his shoulders and sullenly said that if they didn't want to hear what he had to say, he would simply stop; and even when he very ponderously rolled back into his wheelchair-invalid blanket and sat down to stare into the void with empty periscope shafts.*

It was meaningless, both for the defendant Rudolf Hess and the Nuremberg Court of Law, and for us who were permitted to witness this historic moment. And it was meaningless for the world outside, beyond the guarded walls. And certainly for the new German youth which was growing up out there in the rubble dumps. All of us had long since passed into a different state, into a dimension that had not been human for a long time.

Nothing more was happening to us. There were no murderers anymore and no victims, because there was no more human reason able to distinguish between good and evil. Madness was growing hybridly, welling and swelling and forming metastases like everything else around us. There was no more guilt and hence certainly no more atonement, hence no destiny and thus nothing more to narrate. We should have known this, my brother Schwab. We shouldn't have pushed one another to write. Why? For whom? To what end? Peace could have been with us long ago, my brother Cain.

Naturally, I said none of these things at Schwab's flower hill. They merely passed through my mind while I said something totally different. What? I don't even know anymore. And it made no difference at all, whatever it was. For I hadn't noticed that a microphone was hidden at Schwab's presumable head in his new condition as a flowery hedge. Without realizing it, I spoke right into the microphone, and even though I spoke softly, my voice boomed a hundred, a thousand times louder through the cremation temple, bellowing into the paraboloid vaults and thundering and crashing back upon itself—an acoustic pandemonium, deafening every eardrum in the place. Afterward, Carlotta told me that her ears had buzzed for hours. It was as if you had expected a line of poetry and were given *Mein Kampf* to read instead, she said.

I kept my concluding statement short and then quickly returned to my penitent's stool.

Meanwhile, however, the black-and-white pastor-blossom had ambulated over to Schwab in his new condition; perceptively, he stationed himself at the putative feet, far away from the microphone, and now he chewed a small portion of consecrating verbal gruel. At almost the same time, the downtrodden cousin twice removed began to play the organ; and while he made a steep fugue of pipe tones rise into the vault, I saw—first with terror, then with mounting delight—that Schwab was sinking into the pit from which he had been looming, and I saw two curving walls at his flanks, and they closed over him, forming a small barrel.

He had passed into his element.

END OF BOOK ONE